Praise for *New York Times* bestselling author

# NORA ROBERTS

"Move over, Sidney Sheldon:
the world has a new master of romantic suspense,
and her name is Nora Roberts."
—Rex Reed

"Nora Roberts just keeps getting better and better."
—*Milwaukee Journal Sentinel*

"When Roberts puts her expert fingers on the pulse
of romance, legions of fans feel the heartbeat."
—*Publishers Weekly*

"John Grisham, watch your back!"
—*Entertainment Weekly*

"A consistently entertaining writer."
—*USA Today*

"Roberts has a warm feel for her characters
and an eye for the evocative detail."
—*Chicago Tribune*

"…an author of extraordinary power."
—*Rave Reviews*

"Compelling and dimensional characters, intriguing
plots, passionate love stories—Nora Roberts…
romance at its finest."
—*Rendezvous*

"Nora Roberts is the very best there is—
she's superb in everything she does."
—*Romantic Times Magazine*

# NORA ROBERTS

# NIGHT TALES

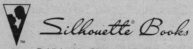
Silhouette Books

Published by Silhouette Books

America's Publisher of Contemporary Romance

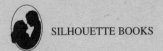 SILHOUETTE BOOKS

NIGHT TALES

Copyright © 2000 by Harlequin Books S.A.

ISBN 0-373-48410-0

The publisher acknowledges the copyright holder of the individual works as follows:

NIGHT SHIFT
Copyright © 1991 by Nora Roberts

NIGHT SHADOW
Copyright © 1991 by Nora Roberts

NIGHTSHADE
Copyright © 1993 by Nora Roberts

NIGHT SMOKE
Copyright © 1994 by Nora Roberts

Dear Reader,

The night is a time for danger, mystery—and romance. And *Night Tales* is a special collection that brings together four connected books for the first time in one volume. These books feature characters who are creatures of the night, whether for work or play—or love.

There's something intriguing about night people. The way they think, the way they live. In *Night Shift*, Cilla O'Roarke loves being the voice of the night hours during her deejay shift—until a dangerous stalker forces her to share her evenings with devastatingly handsome police detective Boyd Fletcher.

Sometimes night is the only place for a hero who lives for the kind of justice that is often found outside the law. Gage Guthrie in *Night Shadow* is just this kind of man—and the perfect hero to rile Deborah O'Roarke, a beautiful assistant district attorney who only plays by the rules.

Night can also provide the perfect cover, especially for Colt *Nightshade*, a maverick investigator who finds the darkness especially suited to his work when he joins forces with sultry Lieutenant Althea Grayson.

And in *Night Smoke*, Boyd's sister Natalie watches her dreams go up in flames against the night sky. When she turns to arson investigator Ryan Piasecki for help, another kind of heat is generated.

I hope you enjoy these stories. Look for *Night Shield*, a brand-new *Night Tales* story, and watch what happens when Boyd's by-the-book detective daughter has to work side by side, night after night, with a dangerously sexy stranger she isn't sure she should trust. *Night Shield* is available this month from Silhouette Intimate Moments.

All the best,

*Nora Roberts*

# CONTENTS

# Night Shift

To Kay in Denver
And with appreciation to the staff of WQCM

# Chapter 1

"All right, night owls, it's coming up on midnight, and you're listening to KHIP. Get ready for five hits in a row. This is Cilla O'Roarke, and darling, I'm sending this one straight out to you."

Her voice was like hot whiskey, smooth and potent. Rich, throaty, touched with the barest whisper of the South, it might have been fashioned for the airwaves. Any man in Denver who was tuned in to her frequency would believe she was speaking only to him.

Cilla eased up on the pot on the mixer, sending the first of the five promised hits out to her listeners. Music slid into the booth. She could have pulled off her headphones and given herself three minutes and twenty-two seconds of silence. She preferred the sound. Her affection for music was only one of the reasons for her success in radio.

Her voice was a natural attribute. She'd talked herself into her first job—at a low-frequency, low-budget station in rural Georgia—with no experience, no résumé and a brand-new high school diploma. And she was perfectly aware that it was her voice that had landed her that position. That and her willingness to work for next to nothing, make coffee and double as the station's receptionist. Ten years later, her voice was hardly her only qualification. But it still often turned the tide.

She'd never found the time to pursue the degree in communications she still coveted. But she could double—and had—as engineer, newscaster, interviewer and program director. She had an encyclopedic memory for songs and recording artists, and a respect for both. Radio had been her home for a decade, and she loved it.

Her easygoing, flirtatious on-air personality was often at odds with the intense, organized and ambitious woman who rarely slept more than six hours and usually ate on the run. The public Cilla O'Roarke was a sexy radio princess who mingled with celebrities and had a job loaded with glamour and excitement. The private woman spent an average of ten hours a day at the station or on station business, was fiercely determined to put her younger sister through college and hadn't had a date in two years of Saturday nights.

And didn't want one.

Setting the headphones aside, she rechecked her daily log for her next fifteen-minute block. For the space of time it took to play a top 10 hit, the booth was silent. There was only Cilla and the lights and gauges on the control board. That was how she liked it best.

When she'd accepted the position with KHIP in Denver six months before, she'd wrangled for the 10:00-p.m.-to-2-a.m. slot, one usually reserved for the novice deejay. A rising success with ten years experience behind her, she could have had one of the plum day spots when the listening audience was at its peak. She preferred the night, and for the past five years she'd carved out a name for herself in those lonely hours.

She liked being alone, and she liked sending her voice and music out to others who lived at night.

With an eye on the clock, Cilla adjusted her headphones. Between the fade-out of hit number four and the intro to hit number five, she crooned out the station's number four and the intro to hit number five, she crooned out the station's call letters and frequency. After a quick break when she popped in a cassette of recorded news, she would begin her favorite part of her show. The request line.

She enjoyed watching the phones light up, enjoyed hearing the voices. It took her out of her booth for fifty minutes every night and proved to her that there were people, real people with real lives, who were listening to her.

She lit a cigarette and leaned back in her swivel chair. This would be her last quiet moment for the next hour.

She didn't appear to be a restful woman. Nor, despite the voice, did she look like a smoldering femme fatale. There was too much energy in her face and in her long, nervous body for either. Her nails were unpainted, as was her mouth. She rarely found time in her schedule to bother with polish and paint. Her dark brandy-brown eyes were nearly closed as she allowed her body to charge up. Her lashes were long, an inheritance from her dreamy father. In contrast to the silky lashes and the pale, creamy complexion, her features were strong and angular. She had been blessed with a cloud of rich, wavy black hair that she ruthlessly pulled back, clipped back or twisted up in deference to the headphones.

With an eye on the elapsed-time clock, Cilla crushed out the cigarette and took a sip of water, then opened her mike. The On Air sign glowed green.

"That was for all the lovers out there, whether you've got someone to cuddle up with tonight or you wish you did. Stay tuned. This is Cilla O'Roarke, Denver. You're listening to KHIP. We're coming back with our request line."

As she switched on the tape for a commercial run, she glanced up. "Hey, Nick. How's it going?"

Nick Peters, the college student who served as an intern at the station, pushed up his dark-framed glasses and grinned. "I aced the Lit test."

"Way to go." She gratefully accepted the mug of steaming coffee he offered. "Is it still snowing?"

"Stopped about an hour ago."

She nodded and relaxed a little. She'd been worrying about Deborah, her younger sister. "I guess the roads are a mess."

"Not too bad. You want something to go with that coffee?"

She flicked him a smile, her mind too busy with other things to note the adoration in his eyes. "No, thanks. Help yourself to some stale doughnuts before you sign out." She hit a switch and spoke into the mike again.

As she read the station promos, he watched her. He knew it was hopeless, even stupid, but he was wildly in love with her. She was the most beautiful woman in the world to him, making the women at college look like awkward, gangling shadows of what a real woman should be. She was strong, successful, sexy. And she barely knew he was alive. When she noticed him at all, it was with a distractedly friendly smile or gesture.

For over three months he'd been screwing up his courage to ask her for a date. And fantasizing about what it would be like to have her attention focused on him, only him, for an entire evening.

She was completely unaware. Had she known where his mind had led him, Cilla would have been more amused than flattered. Nick was barely twenty-one, seven years her junior chronologically. And decades younger in every other way. She liked him. He was unobtrusive and efficient, and he wasn't afraid of long hours or hard work.

Over the past few months she'd come to depend on the coffee he brought her before he left the station. And to enjoy knowing she would be completely alone as she drank it.

Nick glanced at the clock. "I'll, ah, see you tomorrow."

"Hmm? Oh, sure. Good night, Nick." The moment he was through the door, she forgot about him. She punched one of the illuminated buttons on the phone. "KHIP. You're on the air."

"Cilla?"

"That's right. Who's this?"

"I'm Kate."

"Where are you calling from, Kate?"

"From home—over in Lakewood. My husband's a cab driver. He's working the late shift. We both listen to your show every night. Could you play 'Peaceful, Easy Feeling' for Kate and Ray?"

"You got it, Kate. Keep those home fires burning." She punched the next button. "KHIP. You're on the air."

The routine ran smoothly. Cilla would take calls, scribbling down the titles and the dedications. The small studio was lined with shelves crammed with albums, 45s, CDs, all labeled for easy access. After a handful of calls she would break to commercials and station promos to give herself time to set up for the first block of songs.

Some of the callers were repeaters, so she would chat a moment or two. Some were the lonely, calling just to hear the sound of another voice. Mixed in with them was the occasional loony that she would joke off the line or simply disconnect. In all her years of handling live phones, she couldn't remember a moment's boredom.

She enjoyed it tremendously, chatting with callers, joking. In the safety of the control booth she was able, as she had never been able face-to-face, to relax and develop an easy relationship with strangers. No one hearing her voice would suspect that she was shy or insecure.

"KHIP. You're on the air."

"Cilla."

"Yes. You'll have to speak up, partner. What's your name?"

"That doesn't matter."

"Okay, Mr. X." She rubbed suddenly damp palms on the thighs of her jeans. Instinct told her she would have trouble with this one, so she kept her finger hovering over the seven-second-delay button. "You got a request?"

"I want you to pay, slut. I'm going to make you pay. When I'm finished, you're going to thank me for killing you. You're never going to forget."

Cilla froze, cursed herself for it, then cut him off in the midst of a rage of obscenities. Through strict control she kept her voice from shaking. "Wow. Sounds like somebody's a little cranky tonight. Listen, if that was Officer Marks, I'm going to pay those parking tickets. I swear. This one goes out to Joyce and Larry."

She shot in Springsteen's latest hit single, then sat back to remove the headphones with trembling hands.

Stupid. She rose to pluck out the next selection. After all these years she should have known better than to freak over a crank call. It was rare to get through a shift without at least one. She had learned to handle the odd, the angry, the propositions and the threats as skillfully as she had learned to handle the control board.

It was all part of the job, she reminded herself. Part of being a public personality, especially on the night shift, where the weird always got weirder.

But she caught herself glancing over her shoulder, through the dark glass of the studio to the dim corridor beyond. There were only shadows, and silence. Beneath her heavy sweater, her skin was shivering in a cold sweat. She was alone. Completely.

And the station's locked, she reminded herself as she cued up the next selection. The alarm was set. If it went off, Denver's finest would scream up to the station within minutes. She was as safe here as she would be in a bank vault.

But she stared down at the blinking lights on the phone, and she was afraid.

The snow had stopped, but its scent lingered in the chill March air. As she drove, Cilla kept the window down an inch and the radio up to the maximum. The combination of wind and music steadied her.

Cilla wasn't surprised to find that Deborah was waiting up for her. She pulled into the driveway of the house she'd bought only six months before and noted with both annoyance and relief that all the lights were blazing.

It was annoying because it meant Deborah was awake and worrying. And it was a relief, because the quiet suburban street seemed so deserted and she felt so vulnerable. She switched off the ignition, cutting the engine and the sounds of Jim Jackson's mellow all-night show. The instant of total silence had her heart leaping into her throat.

Swearing at herself, she slammed the car door and, hunched in her coat against the wind, dashed up the stairs. Deborah met her at the door.

"Hey, don't you have a nine-o'clock class tomorrow?" Stalling, Cilla peeled off her coat and hung it in the closet. She caught the scent of hot chocolate and furniture polish. It made her sigh. Deborah always resorted to housecleaning when she was tense. "What are you doing up at this hour?"

"I heard. Cilla, that man—"

"Oh, come on, baby." Turning, Cilla wrapped her arms around her sister. In her plain white terry-cloth robe, Deborah still seemed twelve years old to her. There was no one Cilla loved more. "Just one more harmless nut in a fruitcake world."

"He didn't sound harmless, Cilla." Though several inches shorter, Deborah held Cilla still. There was a resemblance between them— around the mouth. Both their mouths were full, passionate and stubborn. But Deborah's features were softer, curved rather than angular. Her eyes, thickly lashed, were a brilliant blue. They were drenched now with concern. "I think you should call the police."

"The police?" Because this option had simply not occurred to her,

Cilla was able to laugh. "One obscene call and you have me dashing to the cops. What kind of nineties woman do you take me for?"

Deborah jammed her hands in her pockets. "This isn't a joke."

"Okay, it's not a joke. But Deb, we both know how little the police could do about one nasty call to a public radio station in the middle of the night."

With an impatient sigh, Deborah turned away. "He really sounded vicious. It scared me."

"Me too."

Deborah's laugh was quick, and only a little strained. "You're never scared."

I'm always scared, Cilla thought, but she smiled. "I was this time. It shook me enough that I fumbled the delay button and let it broadcast." Fleetingly she wondered how much flak she'd get for that little lapse the next day. "But he didn't call back, which proves it was a one-shot deal. Go to bed," she said, passing a hand over her sister's dark, fluffy hair. "You're never going to be the best lawyer in Colorado if you stay up pacing all night."

"I'll go if you go."

Knowing it would be hours before her mind and body settled down, Cilla draped an arm over her sister's shoulders. "It's a deal."

He kept the room dark, but for the light of a few sputtering candles. He liked the mystic, spiritual glow of them, and their dreamy religious scent. The room was small, but it was crammed with mementos—trophies from his past. Letters, snapshots, a scattering of small china animals, ribbons faded by time. A long-bladed hunting knife rested across his knees, gleaming dully in the shifting light. A well-oiled .45 automatic rested by his elbow on a starched crocheted doily.

In his hand he held a picture framed in rosewood. He stared at it, spoke to it, wept bitter tears over it. This was the only person he had ever loved, and all he had left was the picture to press to his breast.

John. Innocent, trusting John. Deceived by a woman. Used by a woman. Betrayed by a woman.

Love and hate entwined as he rocked. She would pay. She would pay the ultimate price. But first she would suffer.

The call—one single ugly call—came every night. By the end of a week, Cilla's nerves were frazzled. She wasn't able to make a joke of it, on or off the air. She was just grateful that now she had learned to recognize the voice, that harsh, wire-taut voice with that under-current of fury, and she would cut him off after the first few words.

Then she would sit there in terror at the knowledge that he would call back, that he was there, just on the other side of one of those blinking lights, waiting to torment her.

What had she done?

After she dropped in the canned news and commercial spots at 2:00 a.m., Cilla rested her elbows on the table and dropped her head into her hands. She rarely slept well or deeply, and in the past week she had managed only a few snatches of real sleep. It was beginning to tell, she knew, on her nerves, her concentration.

What had she done?

That question haunted her. What could she possibly have done to make someone hate her? She had recognized the hate in the voice, the deep-seated hate. She knew she could sometimes be abrupt and impatient with people. There were times when she was insensitive. But she had never deliberately hurt anyone. What was it she would have to pay for? What crime, real or imagined, had she committed that caused this person to focus in on her for revenge?

Out of the corner of her eye she saw a movement. A shadow amid the shadows in the corridor. Panic arrowed into her, and she sprang up, jarring her hip against the console. The voice she had discon-nected barely ten minutes before echoed in her head. She watched, rigid with fright, as the knob on the studio door turned.

There was no escape. Dry-mouthed, she braced for a fight.

"Cilla?"

Heart thudding, she lowered slowly into her chair, cursing her own nerves. "Mark."

"Sorry, I must have scared you."

"Only to death." Making an effort, she smiled at the station man-ager. He was in his middle thirties, and he was drop-dead gorgeous. His dark hair was carefully styled and on the long side, adding more youth to his smooth and tanned face. As always, his attire was care-fully hip. "What are you doing here at this hour?"

"It's time we did more than talk about these calls."

"We had a meeting just a couple of days ago. I told you—"

"You told me," he agreed. "You have a habit of telling me, and everybody else."

"I'm not taking a vacation." She spun around in her chair to face him. "I've got nowhere to go."

"Everybody's got somewhere to go." He held up a hand before she could speak. "I'm not going to argue about this anymore. I know it's a difficult concept for you, but I am the boss."

She tugged at the hem of her sweatshirt. "What are you going to do? Fire me?"

He didn't know that she held her breath on the challenge. Though he'd worked with her for months, he hadn't scratched deep enough beneath the surface to understand how precarious was her self-esteem. If he had threatened her then, she would have folded. But all he knew was that her show had pumped new life into the station. The ratings were soaring.

"That wouldn't do either of us any good." Even as she let out the pent-up breath, he laid a hand on her shoulder. "Look, I'm worried about you, Cilla. All of us are."

It touched her, and, as always, it surprised her. "All he does is talk." For now. Scooting her chair toward the turntables, she prepared for the next music sweep.

"I'm not going to stand by while one of my people is harassed. I've called the police."

She sprang up out of her chair. "Damn it, Mark. I told you—"

"You told me." He smiled. "Let's not go down that road again. You're an asset to the station. And I'd like to think we were friends."

She sat down again, kicking out her booted feet. "Sure. Hold on." Struggling to concentrate, she went on-air with a station plug and the intro for the upcoming song. She gestured toward the clock. "You've got three minutes and fifteen seconds to convince me."

"Very simply, Cilla, what this guy's doing is against the law. I should never have let you talk me into letting it go this long."

"If we ignore him, he'll go away."

"Your way isn't working." He dropped his hand onto her shoulder again, patiently kneading the tensed muscles there. "So we're going to try mine. You talk to the cops or you take an unscheduled vacation.''

Defeated, she looked up and managed a smile. ''Do you push your wife around this way?''

''All the time.'' He grinned, then leaned down to press a kiss on her brow. ''She loves it.''

''Excuse me.''

Cilla jerked back in what she knew could easily be mistaken for guilt. The two people in the doorway of the booth studied her with what she recognized as professional detachment.

The woman looked like a fashion plate, with a flow of dark red hair cascading to her shoulders and small, elegant sapphires at her ears. Her complexion was the delicate porcelain of a true redhead. She had a small, compact body and wore a neatly tailored suit in wild shades of blue and green.

The man beside her looked as if he'd just spent a month on the range driving cattle. His shaggy blond hair was sun-streaked and fell over the collar of a denim work shirt. His jeans were worn and low at the hips, snug over what looked to Cilla to be about three feet of leg. The hems were frayed. Lanky, he slouched in the doorway, while the woman stood at attention. His boots were scuffed, but he wore a classically cut tweed jacket over his scruffy shirt.

He didn't smile. Cilla found herself staring, studying his face longer than she should have. There were hollows beneath his cheekbones, and there was the faintest of clefts in his chin. His tanned skin was taut over his facial bones, and his mouth, still unsmiling, was wide and firm. His eyes, intent enough on her face to make her want to squirm, were a clear bottle green.

''Mr. Harrison.'' The woman spoke first. Cilla thought there was a flicker of amusement in her eyes as she stepped forward. ''I hope we gave you enough time.''

Cilla sent Mark a killing look. ''You told me you'd called them. You didn't tell me they were waiting outside.''

''Now you know.'' He kept a hand on her shoulder, but this time it was more restraining than comforting. ''This is Ms. O'Roarke.''

''I'm Detective Grayson. This is my partner, Detective Fletcher.''

"Thank you again for waiting." Mark gestured her, then her partner, in. The man lazily unfolded himself from the doorjamb.

"Detective Fletcher and I are both used to it. We could use a bit more information."

"As you know, Ms. O'Roarke has been getting some disturbing calls here at the station."

"Cranks." Cilla spoke up, annoyed at being talked around. "Mark shouldn't have bothered you with it."

"We're paid to be bothered." Boyd Fletcher eased a lean hip down on the table. "So, this where you work?"

There was just enough insolence in his eyes to raise her hackles. "I bet you're a hell of a detective."

"Cilla." Tired and wishing he was home with his wife, Mark scowled at her. "Let's cooperate." Ignoring her, he turned to the detectives again. "The calls started during last Tuesday's show. None of us paid much attention, but they continued. The last one came in tonight, at 12:35."

"Do you have tapes?" Althea Grayson had already pulled out her notebook.

"I started making copies of them after the third call." At Cilla's startled look, Mark merely shrugged. "A precaution. I have them in my office."

Boyd nodded to Althea. "Go ahead. I'll take Ms. O'Roarke's statement."

"Cooperate," Mark said to Cilla, and led Althea out.

In the ensuing silence, Cilla tapped a cigarette out of her dwindling pack and lit it with quick, jerky movements. Boyd drew in the scent longingly. He'd quit only six weeks, three days and twelve hours ago.

"Slow death," he commented.

Cilla studied him through the haze of smoke. "You wanted a statement."

"Yeah." Curious, he reached over to toy with a switch. Automatically she batted his fingers aside.

"Hands off."

Boyd grinned. He had the distinct feeling that she was speaking of herself, as well as her equipment.

She cued up an established hit. After opening her mike, she did a backsell on the song just fading—the title, the artist, the station's call letters and her name. In an easy rhythm, she segued into the next selection. "Let's make it quick," she told him. "I don't like company during my shift."

"You're not exactly what I expected."

"I beg your pardon?"

No, indeed, he thought. She was a hell of a lot more than he'd expected. "I've caught your show," he said easily. "A few times." More than a few. He'd lost more than a few hours' sleep listening to that voice. Liquid sex. "I got this image, you know. Five-seven." He took a casual glance from the top of her head, down her body, to the toe of her boots. "I guess I was close there. But I took you for a blonde, hair down to your waist, blue eyes, lots of... personality." He grinned again, enjoying the annoyance in her eyes. Big brown eyes, he noted. Definitely different, and more appealing than his fantasy.

"Sorry to disappoint you."

"Didn't say I was disappointed."

She took a long, careful drag, then deliberately blew the smoke in his direction. If there was one thing she knew how to do, it was how to discourage an obnoxious male.

"Do you want a statement or not, Slick?"

"That's what I'm here for." He took a pad and the stub of a pencil out of his jacket pocket. "Shoot."

In clipped, dispassionate terms, she ran through every call, the times, the phrasing. She continued to work as she spoke, pushing in recorded tapes of commercials, cuing up a CD, replacing and selecting albums.

Boyd's brow rose as he wrote. He would check the tapes, of course, but he had the feeling that she was giving him word-for-word. In his job he respected a good memory.

"You've been in town, what? Six months?"

"More or less."

"Make any enemies?"

"A salesman trying to hawk encyclopedias. I slammed the door on his foot."

Boyd spared her a glance. She was trying to make light of it, but she had crushed out her cigarette and was now gnawing on her thumbnail. "Dump any lovers?"

"No."

"Have any?"

Temper flashed in her eyes again. "You're the detective. You find out."

"I would—if it was personal." His eyes lifted again in a look that was so direct, so completely personal, that her palms began to sweat. "Right now I'm just doing my job. Jealousy and rejection are powerful motivators. According to your statements, most of the comments he made to you had to do with your sexual habits."

Bluntness might be her strong suit, but she wasn't about to tell him that her only sexual habit was abstinence. "I'm not involved with anyone at the moment," she said evenly.

"Good." Without glancing up, he made another note. "That was a personal observation."

"Look, Detective—"

"Cool your jets, O'Roarke," he said mildly. "It was an observation, not a proposition." His dark, patient eyes took her measure. "I'm on duty. I need a list of the men you've had contact with on a personal level. We'll keep it to the past six months for now. You can leave out the door-to-door salesman."

"I'm not involved." Her hands clenched as she rose. "I haven't been involved. I've had no desire to be involved."

"No one ever said desire couldn't be one-sided." At the moment he was damn sure his was.

She was suddenly excruciatingly tired. Dragging a hand through her hair, she struggled for patience. "Anyone should be able to see that this guy is hung up on a voice over the radio. He doesn't even know me. He's probably never seen me. An image," she said, tossing his own words back at him. "That's all I am to him. In this business it happens all the time. I haven't done anything."

"I didn't say you had."

There was no teasing note in his voice now. The sudden gentleness in it had her spinning around, blinking furiously at threatening tears.

Overworked, she told herself. Overstressed. Overeverything. With her back to him, she fought for control.

Tough, he thought. She was a tough lady. The way her hands balled at her sides as she fought with her emotions was much more appealing, much sexier, than broken sighs or helpless gestures could ever be.

He would have liked to go to her, to speak some word of comfort or reassurance, to stroke a hand down her hair. She'd probably bite it off at the wrist.

"I want you to think about the past few months, see if you can come up with anything, however small and unimportant, that might have led to this." His tone had changed again. It was brisk now, brisk and dispassionate. "We can't bring every man in the greater Denver area in for questioning. It doesn't work that way."

"I know how cops work."

The bitterness in her voice had his brows drawing together. There was something else here, but this wasn't the time to dig into it.

"You'd recognize the voice if you heard it again."

"Yes."

"Anything familiar about it?"

"Nothing."

"Do you think it was disguised?"

She moved her shoulders restlessly, but when she turned back to him she had herself under control. "He keeps it muffled and low. It's, ah…like a hiss."

"Any objections to me sitting in on tomorrow night's show?"

Cilla took another long look at him. "Barrels of them."

He inclined his head. "I'll just go to your boss."

Disgusted, she reached for her cigarettes. He closed his firm hard-palmed hand over hers. She stared down at the tangled fingers, shocked to realize that her pulse had doubled at the contact.

"Let me do my job, Cilla. It'll be easier all around if you let Detective Grayson and me take over."

"Nobody takes over my life." She jerked her hand away, then jammed it into her pocket.

"Just this small part of it, then." Before she could stop him, he reached out and tucked her hair behind her ear. "Go home and get some sleep. You look beat."

She stepped back, made herself smile. "Thanks, Slick. I feel a lot better now."

Though she grumbled, she couldn't prevent him waiting until she signed off and turned the studio over to the all-night man. Nor did her lack of enthusiasm discourage him from walking her out to her car, reminding her to lock her door and waiting until she'd driven away. Disturbed by the way he'd looked at her—and the way she'd reacted—she watched him in the rearview mirror until he was out of sight.

"Just what I needed," she muttered to herself. "A cowboy cop."

Moments later, Althea joined Boyd in the parking lot. She had the tapes in her bag, along with Mark's statement. "Well, Fletcher—" she dropped a friendly hand on his shoulder "—what's the verdict?"

"She's tough as nails, hardheaded, prickly as a briar patch." With his hands in his pockets, he rocked back on his heels. "I guess it must be love."

# Chapter 2

She was good, Boyd thought as he downed his bitter coffee and watched Cilla work. She handled the control board with an automatic ease that spoke of long experience—switching to music, to recorded announcements, to her own mike. Her timing was perfect, her delivery smooth. And her fingernails were bitten to the quick.

She was a package full of nerves and hostility. The nerves she tried to hide. She didn't bother with the hostility. In the two hours they'd been in the booth together, she had barely spoken a word to him. A neat trick, since the room was barely ten by ten.

That was fine. As a cop, he was used to being where he wasn't wanted. And he was just contrary enough to enjoy it.

He liked his job. Things like annoyance, animosity and belligerence didn't concern him. The simple fact was that negative emotions were a whole lot easier to deal with than a .45 slug. He'd had the opportunity to be hit with both.

Though he would have been uncomfortable with the term philosopher, he had a habit of analyzing everything down to its most basic terms. At the root of this was an elemental belief in right and wrong. Or—though he would have hesitated to use the phrase—good and evil.

He was savvy enough to know that crime often did pay, and pay well. Satisfaction came from playing a part in seeing that it didn't pay for long. He was a patient man. If a perpetrator took six hours or six months to bring down, the results were exactly the same. The good guys won.

Stretching out his long legs, he continued to page through his book while Cilla's voice washed over him. Her voice made him think of porch swings, hot summer nights and the sound of a slow-moving river. In direct contrast was the tension and restless energy that vibrated from her. He was content to enjoy the first and wonder about the second.

He was driving her crazy. Just being there. Cilla switched to a commercial, checked her playlist and deliberately ignored him. Or tried to. She didn't like company in the booth. It didn't matter that when she had coolly discouraged conversation he had settled back with his book—not the Western or men's adventure she had expected, but a dog-eared copy of Steinbeck's *East of Eden*. It didn't matter that he had been patiently quiet for nearly two hours.

He was there. And that was enough.

She couldn't pretend that the calls had stopped, that they meant nothing, that her life was back on its normal track. Not with this lanky cowboy reading the great American novel in the corner of the booth, so that she had to all but climb over him to get to the albums stored on the back wall. He brought all her nerves swimming to the surface.

She resented him for that, for his intrusion, and for the simple fact that he was a cop.

But that was personal, she reminded herself. She had a job to do.

"That was INXS taking you to midnight. It's a new day, Denver. March 28, but we're not going out like a lamb. It's eighteen degrees out there at 12:02, so tune in and heat up. You're listening to KHIP, where you get more hits per hour. We've got the news coming up, then the request line. Light up those phones and we'll rock and roll."

Boyd waited until she'd run through the news and moved to a commercial before he marked his place in his book and rose. He could feel the tension thicken as he sat in the chair next to Cilla.

"I don't want you to cut him off."

She stiffened and struggled to keep her voice carelessly sarcastic. "My listeners don't tune in for that kind of show, Slick."

"You can keep him on the line, on the studio speakers, without sending it on air, right?"

"Yes, but I don't want to—"

"Cut to a commercial or some music," Boyd said mildly, "but keep him on the line. We might get lucky and trace the call. And if you can, keep the request line open until the end of shift, to give him enough time to make his move."

Her hands were balled into fists in her lap as she stared at the lights that were already blinking on the phone. He was right. She knew he was right. And she hated it.

"This is an awful lot of trouble for one loose screw."

"Don't worry." He smiled a little. "I get paid the same whether the screws are loose or tight."

She glanced down at the clock, cleared her throat, then switched on her mike. "Hello, Denver, this is Cilla O'Roarke for KHIP. You're listening to the hottest station in the Rockies. This is your chance to make it even hotter. Our request lines are open. I'll be playing what you want to hear, so give me a call at 555-KHIP. That's 555-5447."

Her finger trembled slightly as she punched the first lit button.

"This is Cilla O'Roarke. You're on the air."

"Hi, Cilla, this is Bob down in Englewood."

She closed her eyes on a shudder of relief. He was a regular. "Hey, Bob. How's it going?"

"Going great. My wife and I are celebrating our fifteenth anniversary tonight."

"And they said it wouldn't last. What can I play for you, Bob?"

"How about 'Cherish' for Nancy from Bob."

"Nice choice. Here's to fifteen more, Bob."

With her pen in one hand, she took the second call, then the third. Boyd watched her tighten up after each one. She chatted and joked. And grew paler. At the first break, she pulled a cigarette out of the pack, then fumbled with a match. Silently Boyd took the matches from her and lit one for her.

"You're doing fine."

She took a quick, jerky puff. Patient, he waited in silence for her to respond. "Do you have to watch me?"

"No." Then he smiled. It was a long, lazy smile that had her responding in spite of herself. "A man's entitled to some fringe benefits."

"If this is the best you can do, Slick, you ought to look for another line of work."

"I like this one." He rested the ankle of his boot on his knee. "I like it fine."

It was easier, Cilla decided, to talk to him than to stare at the blinking lights on the phone and worry. "Have you been a cop long?"

"Going on ten years."

She looked at him then, struggling to relax by concentrating on his face. He had calm eyes, she thought. Dark and calm. Eyes that had seen a lot and learned to live with it. There was a quiet kind of strength there, the kind women—some women—were drawn to. He would protect and defend. He wouldn't start a fight. But he would finish one.

Annoyed with herself, she looked away again, busying herself with her notes. She didn't need to be protected or defended. She certainly didn't need anyone to fight for her. She had always taken care of herself. And she always would.

"It's a lousy job," she said. "Being a cop."

He shifted. His knee brushed her thigh. "Mostly."

Instinctively she jiggled her chair for another inch of distance. "It's hard to figure why anyone would stick with a lousy job for ten years."

He just grinned. "I guess I'm in a rut."

She shrugged, then turned to her mike. "That was for Bill and Maxine. Our request lines are still open. That's 555-5447." After one quick breath, she punched a button. "KHIP. You're on the air."

It went smoothly, so smoothly that she began to relax. She took call after call, falling into her old, established rhythm. Gradually she began to enjoy the music again, the flow of it. The pulsing lights on the phone no longer seemed threatening. By 1:45 she was sure she was going to make it through.

Just one night, she told herself. If he didn't call tonight, it would be over. She looked at the clock, watched the seconds tick by. Eight more minutes to go and she would turn the airwaves over to Jackson. She would go home, take a long, hot bath and sleep like a baby.

"KHIP, you're on the air."

"Cilla."

The hissing whisper shot ice through her veins. She reached over reflexively to disconnect, but Boyd clamped a hand over her wrist and shook his head. For a moment she struggled, biting back panic. His hand remained firm on hers, his eyes calm and steady.

Boyd watched as she fought for control, until she jammed in a cassette of commercials. The bright, bouncy jingles transmitted as she put the call on the studio speaker.

"Yes." Pride made her keep her eyes on Boyd's. "This is Cilla. What do you want?"

"Justice. I only want justice."

"For what?"

"I want you to think about that. I want you to think and wonder and sweat until I come for you."

"Why?" Her hand flexed under Boyd's. In an instinctive gesture of reassurance, he linked his fingers with hers. "Who are you?"

"Who am I?" There was a laugh that skidded along her skin. "I'm your shadow, your conscience. Your executioner. You have to die. When you understand, only when you understand, I'll end it. But it won't be quick. It won't be easy. You're going to pay for what you've done."

"What have I done?" she shouted. "For God's sake, what have I done?"

He spit out a stream of obscenities that left her dazed and nauseated before he broke the connection. With one hand still covering hers, Boyd punched out a number on the phone.

"You get the trace?" he demanded, then bit off an oath. "Yeah. Right." Disgusted, he replaced the receiver. "Not long enough." He reached up to touch Cilla's pale cheek. "You okay?"

She could hardly hear him for the buzzing in her ears, but she nodded. Mechanically she turned to her mike, waiting until the commercial jingle faded.

"That about wraps it up for this morning. It's 1:57. Tina Turner's going to rock you through until two. My man Jackson's coming in to keep all you insomniacs company until 6:00 a.m. This is Cilla O'Roarke for KHIP. Remember, darling, when you dream of me, dream good.''

Light-headed, she pushed away from the console. She only had to stand up, she told herself. Walk to her car, drive home. It was simple enough. She did it every morning of her life. But she sat where she was, afraid her legs would buckle.

Jackson pushed through the door and stood there, hesitating. He was wearing a baseball cap to cover his healing hair transplant. ''Hey, Cilla.'' He glanced from her to Boyd and back again. ''Rough night, huh?''

Cilla braced herself, pasted on a careless smile. ''I've had better.'' With every muscle tensed, she shoved herself to her feet. ''I've got them warmed up for you, Jackson.''

''Take it easy, kid.''

''Sure.'' The buzzing in her ears was louder as she walked from the booth to snatch her coat from the rack. The corridors were dark, catching only a faint glow from the lobby, where the security lights burned. Disoriented, she blinked. She didn't even notice when Boyd took her arm and led her outside.

The cold air helped. She took big, thirsty gulps of it, releasing it again in thin plumes of white smoke. ''My car's over there,'' she said when Boyd began to pull her toward the opposite end of the lot.

''You're in no shape to drive.''

''I'm fine.''

''Great. Then we'll go dancing.''

''Look—''

''No, you look.'' He was angry, furious. He hadn't realized it himself until that moment. She was shaking, and despite the chill wind, her cheeks were deathly pale. Listening to the tapes hadn't been the same as being there when the call came through, seeing the blood drain out of her face and her eyes glaze with terror. And not being able to do a damn thing to stop it. ''You're a mess, O'Roarke, and I'm not letting you get behind the wheel of a car.'' He stopped next to his car and yanked open the door. ''Get in. I'll take you home.''

She tossed the hair out of her eyes. ''Serve and protect, right?''

''You got it. Now get in before I arrest you for loitering.''

Because her knees felt like jelly, she gave in. She wanted to be asleep, alone in some small, quiet room. She wanted to scream. Worse, she wanted to cry. Instead, she rounded on Boyd the second he settled in the driver's seat.

"You know what I hate even more than cops?"

He turned the key in the ignition. "I figure you're going to tell me."

"Men who order women around just because they're men. I don't figure that as a cultural hang-up, just stupidity. The way I look at it, that's two counts against you, Detective."

He leaned over, deliberately crowding her back in her seat. He got a moment's intense satisfaction out of seeing her eyes widen in surprise, her lips part on a strangled protest. The satisfaction would have been greater, he knew, if he had gone on impulse and covered that stubborn, sassy mouth with his own. He was certain she would taste exactly as she sounded—hot, sexy and dangerous.

Instead, he yanked her seat belt around her and fastened it.

Her breath came out in a whoosh when he took the wheel again. It had been a rough night, Cilla reminded herself. A tense, disturbing and unsettling night. Otherwise she would never have sat like a fool and allowed herself to be intimidated by some modern-day cowboy.

Her hands were shaking again. The reason didn't seem to matter, only the weakness.

"I don't think I like your style, Slick."

"You don't have to." She was getting under his skin, Boyd realized as he turned out of the lot. That was always a mistake. "Do what you're told and we'll get along fine."

"I don't do what I'm told," she snapped. "And I don't need a second-rate cop with a John Wayne complex to give me orders. Mark's the one who called you in, not me. I don't need you and I don't want you."

He braked at a light. "Tough."

"If you think I'm going to fall apart because some creep calls me names and makes threats, you're wrong."

"I don't think you're going to fall apart, O'Roarke, any more than you think I'm going to pick up the pieces if you do."

"Good. Great. I can handle him all by myself, and if you get your kicks out of listening to that kind of garbage—'' She broke off, appalled with herself. Lifting her hands, she pressed them to her face and took three deep breaths.

"I'm sorry."

"For?"

"For taking it out on you." She dropped her hands into her lap and stared at them. "Could you pull over for a minute?"

Without a word, he guided the car to the curb and stopped.

"I want to calm down before I get home." In a deliberate effort to relax, she let her head fall back and her eyes close. "I don't want to upset my sister."

It was hard to hold on to rage and resentment when the woman sitting next to him had turned from barbed wire to fragile glass. But if his instincts about Cilla were on target, too much sympathy would set her off again.

"Want some coffee?"

"No thanks." The corners of her mouth turned up for the briefest instant. "I've poured in enough to fuel an SST." She let out a long, cleansing breath. The giddiness was gone, and with it that floating sense of unreality. "I am sorry, Slick. You're only doing your job."

"You got that right. Why do you call me Slick?"

She opened her eyes, made a brief but comprehensive study of his face. "Because you are." Turning away, she dug in her bag for a cigarette. "I'm scared." She hated the fact that the admission was shaky, that her hand was unsteady as she struck a match.

"You're entitled."

"No, I'm really scared." She let out smoke slowly, watching a late-model sedan breeze down the road and into the night. "He wants to kill me. I didn't really believe that until tonight." She shuddered. "Is there any heat in this thing?"

He turned the fan on full. "It's better if you're scared."

"Why?"

"You'll cooperate."

She smiled. It was a full flash of a smile that almost stopped his heart. "No, I won't. This is only a momentary respite. I'll be giving you a hard time as soon as I recover."

"I'll try not to get used to this." But it would be easy, he realized, to get used to the way her eyes warmed when she smiled. The way her voice eased over a man and made him wonder. "Feeling better?"

"Lots. Thanks." She tapped out her cigarette as he guided the car back on the road. "I take it you know where I live."

"That's why I'm a detective."

"It's a thankless job." She pushed her hair back from her forehead. They would talk, she decided. Just talk. Then she wouldn't have to think. "Why aren't you out roping cattle or branding bulls? You've got the looks for it."

He considered a moment. "I'm not sure that's a compliment, either."

"You're fast on the draw, Slick."

"Boyd," he said. "It wouldn't hurt you to use my name." When she only shrugged, he slanted her a curious look. "Cilla. That'd be from Priscilla, right?"

"No one calls me Priscilla more than once."

"Why?"

She sent him her sweetest smile. "Because I cut out their tongues."

"Right. You want to tell me why you don't like cops?"

"No." She turned away to stare out the side window. "I like the nighttime," she said, almost to herself. "You can do things, say things, at three o'clock in the morning that it's just not possible to do or say at three o'clock in the afternoon. I can't even imagine what it's like to work in the daylight anymore, when people are crowding the air."

"You don't like people much, do you?"

"Some people." She didn't want to talk about herself, her likes and dislikes, her successes, her failures. She wanted to talk about him—to satisfy her curiosity, and to ease her jangled nerves. "So, how long have you had the night shift, Fletcher?"

"About nine months." He glanced at her. "You meet an... interesting class of people."

She laughed, surprised that she was able to. "Don't you just? Are you from Denver?"

"Born and bred."

"I like it," she said, surprising herself again. She hadn't given it a great deal of thought. It had simply been a place that offered a good college for Deborah and a good opportunity for her. Yet in six months, she realized, she had come close to sinking roots. Shallow ones, but roots nonetheless.

"Does that mean you're going to stick around?" He turned down a quiet side street. "I did some research. It seems two years in one spot's about your limit."

"I like change," she said flatly, closing down the lines of communication. She didn't care for the idea of anyone poking into her past and her private life. When he pulled up in her driveway, she was already unsnapping her seat belt. "Thanks for the ride, Slick."

Before she could dash to her door, he was beside her. "I'm going to need your keys."

They were already in her hand. She clutched them possessively. "Why?"

"So I can have your car dropped off in the morning."

She jingled them, frowning, as she stood under the front porch light. Boyd wondered what it would be like to walk her to her door after an ordinary date. He wouldn't keep his hands in his pockets, he thought ruefully. And he certainly would scratch this itch by kissing her outside the door.

Outside, hell, he admitted. He would have been through the door with her. And there would have been more to the end of the evening than a good-night kiss.

But it wasn't a date. And any fool could see that there wasn't going to be anything remotely ordinary between them. Something. That he promised himself. But nothing remotely resembling the ordinary.

"Keys?" he repeated.

After going over her options, Cilla had decided his was best. Carefully she removed a single key from the chain, which was shaped like a huge musical note. "Thanks."

"Hold it." He placed the palm of his hand on the door as she unlocked it. "You're not going to ask me in for a cup of coffee?"

She didn't turn, only twisted her head. "No."

She smelled like the night, he thought. Dark, deep, dangerous. "That's downright unfriendly."

The flash of humor came again. "I know. See you around, Slick."

His hand dropped onto hers on the knob, took a firm hold. "Do you eat?"

The humor vanished. That didn't surprise him. What did was what replaced it. Confusion. And—he could have sworn—shyness. She recovered so quickly that he was certain he'd imagined it.

"Once or twice a week."

"Tomorrow." His hand remained over hers. He couldn't be sure about what he'd thought he saw in her eyes, but he knew her pulse had quickened under his fingers.

"I may eat tomorrow."

"With me."

It amazed her that she fumbled. It had been years since she'd experienced this baffling reaction to a man. And those years had been quiet and smooth. Refusing a date was as simple as saying no. At least it always had been for her. Now she found herself wanting to smile and ask him what time she should be ready. The words were nearly out of her mouth before she caught herself.

"That's an incredibly smooth offer, Detective, but I'll have to pass."

"Why?"

"I don't date cops."

Before she could weaken, she slipped inside and closed the door in his face.

Boyd shuffled the papers on his desk and scowled. The O'Roarke case was hardly his only assignment, but he couldn't get his mind off it. Couldn't get his mind off O'Roarke, he thought, wishing briefly but intensely for a cigarette.

The veteran cop sitting two feet away from him was puffing away like a chimney as he talked to a snitch. Boyd breathed in deep, wishing he could learn to hate the smell like other nonsmokers.

Instead, he continued to torture himself by drawing in the seductive scent—that, and the other, less appealing aromas of a precinct station. Overheated coffee, overheated flesh, the cheap perfume hovering around a pair of working girls who lounged resignedly on a nearby bench.

Intrusions, he thought, that he rarely noticed in the day-to-day scheme of things. Tonight they warred with his concentration. The smells, the sound of keyboards clicking, phones ringing, shoes scuffing along the linoleum, the way one of the overhead lights winked sporadically.

It didn't help his disposition that for the past three days Priscilla Alice O'Roarke had stuck fast to his mind like a thick, thorny spike. No amount of effort could shake her loose. It might be because both he and his partner had spent hours at a time with her in the booth during her show. It might be because he'd seen her with her defenses down. It might be because he'd felt, fleetingly, her surge of response to him.

It might be, Boyd thought in disgust. Then again, it might not.

He wasn't a man whose ego was easily bruised by the refusal of a date. He liked to think that he had enough confidence in himself to understand he didn't appeal to every woman. The fact that he'd appealed to what he considered a healthy number of them in his thirty-three years was enough to satisfy him.

The trouble was, he was hung up on one woman. And she wasn't having any of it.

He could live with it.

The simple fact was that he had a job to do now. He wasn't convinced that Cilla was in any immediate danger. But she was being harassed, systematically and thoroughly. Both he and Althea had started the ball rolling, questioning men with priors that fit the M.O., poking their fingers into Cilla's personal and professional life since she had come to Denver, quietly investigating her co-workers.

So far the score was zip.

Time to dig deeper, Boyd decided. He had Cilla's résumé in his hand. It was an interesting piece of work in itself. Just like the woman it belonged to. It showed her bouncing from a one-horse station in Georgia—which accounted for that faint and fascinating Southern drawl—to a major player in Atlanta, then on to Richmond, St. Louis, Chicago, Dallas, before landing—feet first, obviously—in Denver at KHIP.

The lady likes to move, he mused. Or was it that she needed to run? That was a question of semantics, and he intended to get the answer straight from the horse's mouth.

The one thing he could be sure of from the bald facts typed out in front of him was that Cilla had pulled herself along the road to success with a high school diploma and a lot of guts. It couldn't have been easy for a woman—a girl, really, at eighteen—to break into what was still a largely male-dominated business.

"Interesting reading?" Althea settled a hip on the corner of his desk. No one in the station house would have dared whistle at her legs. But plenty of them looked.

"Cilla O'Roarke." He tossed the résumé down. "Impressions?"

"Tough lady." She grinned as she said it. She'd spent a lot of time razzing Boyd about his fascination with the sultry voice on the radio. "Likes to do things her own way. Smart and professional."

He picked up a box of candy-coated almonds and shook some into his hand. "I think I figured all that out myself."

"Well, figure this." Althea took the box and carefully selected one glossy nut. "She's scared down to the bone. And she's got an inferiority complex a mile wide."

"Inferiority complex." Boyd gave a quick snort and kicked back in his chair. "Not a chance."

With the same careful deliberation, Althea chose another candied almond. "She hides it behind three feet of steel, but it's there." Althea laid a hand on the toe of his boot. "Woman's intuition, Fletcher. That's why you're so damn lucky to have me."

Boyd snatched the box back, knowing Althea could, and would, methodically work her way through to the last piece. "If that woman's insecure, I'll eat my hat."

"You don't have a hat."

"I'll get one and eat it." Dismissing his partner's instincts, he gestured toward the files. "Since our man isn't letting up, we're going to have to go looking elsewhere for him."

"The lady isn't very forthcoming about her past."

"So we push."

Althea considered a moment. Then she shifted her weight gracefully, recrossed her legs. "Want to flip a coin? Because the odds are she'll push back."

Boyd grinned. "I'm counting on it."

"It's your turn in the booth tonight."

"Then you start with Chicago." He handed her the file. "We got the station manager, the landlord." He scanned the sheet himself. He intended to go far beyond what was printed there, but he would start with the facts. "Use that sweet, persuasive voice of yours. They'll spill their guts."

"Thousands have." She glanced over idly as an associate shoved a swearing suspect with a bloody nose into a nearby chair. There was a brief tussle, and a spate of curses followed by mumbled threats. "God, I love this place."

"Yeah, there's no place like home." He snatched up what was left of his coffee before his partner could reach for it. "I'll work from the other end, the first station she worked for. Thea, if we don't come up with something soon, the captain's going to yank us."

She rose. "Then we'll have to come up with something."

He nodded. Before he could pick up the phone, it rang. "Fletcher."

"Slick."

He would have grimaced at the nickname if he hadn't heard the fear first. "Cilla? What is it?"

"I got a call." A quick bubble of laughter worked its way through. "Old news, I guess. I'm at home this time, though, and I— Damn, I'm jumping at shadows."

"Lock your doors and sit tight. I'm on my way. Cilla," he said when there was no response. "I'm on my way."

"Thanks. If you could break a few traffic laws getting here, I'd be obliged."

"Ten minutes." He hung up. "Thea." He caught her before she could complete the first call. "Let's move."

# Chapter 3

She had herself under control by the time they got to her. Above all, she felt foolish to have run to the police—to him—because of a phone call.

Only phone calls, Cilla assured herself as she paced to the window and back. After a week of them she should have a better handle on it. If she could tone down her reaction, convince the caller that what he said and how he said it left her unaffected, they would stop.

Her father had taught her that that was the way to handle bullies. Then again, her mother's solution had been a right jab straight to the jaw. While Cilla saw value in both viewpoints, she thought the passive approach was more workable under the circumstances.

She'd done a lousy job of it with the last call, she admitted. Sometime during his tirade she'd come uncomfortably close to hysteria, shouting back, pleading, meeting threats with threats. She could only be grateful that Deborah hadn't been home to hear it.

Struggling for calm, she perched on the arm of a chair, her body ruler-straight, her mind scrambling. After the call she had turned off the radio, locked the doors, pulled the drapes. Now, in the glow of the lamplight, she sat listening for a sound, any sound, while she scanned the room. The walls she and Deborah had painted, the furniture they had picked out, argued about. Familiar things, Cilla thought. Calming things.

After only six months there was already a scattering of knickknacks, something they hadn't allowed themselves before. But this time the house wasn't rented, the furniture wasn't leased. It was theirs.

Perhaps that was why, though they'd never discussed it, they had begun to fill it with little things, useless things. The china cat who curled in a permanent nap on the cluttered bookshelf. The foolishly expensive glossy white bowl with hibiscus blossoms painted on the rim. The dapper frog in black tie and tails.

They were making a home, Cilla realized. For the first time since they had found themselves alone, they were making a home. She wouldn't let some vicious, faceless voice over the phone spoil that.

What was she going to do? Because she was alone, she allowed herself a moment of despair and dropped her head into her hands. Should she fight back? But how could she fight someone she couldn't see and didn't understand? Should she pretend indifference? But how long could she keep up that kind of pretense, especially if he continued to invade her private hours, as well as her public ones?

And what would happen when he finally wearied of talk and came to her in person?

The brisk knock on the door had her jolting, had her pressing a hand between her breasts to hold in her suddenly frantic heart.

*I'm your executioner. I'm going to make you suffer. I'm going to make you pay.*

"Cilla. It's Boyd. Open the door."

She needed a moment more, needed to cover her face with her hands and breathe deep. Steadier now, she crossed to the door and opened it.

"Hi. You made good time." She nodded to Althea. "Detective Grayson." Cilla gestured them inside, then leaned her back against the closed door. "I feel stupid for calling you all the way out here."

"Just part of the job," Althea told her. The woman was held together by very thin wires, she decided. A few of them had already snapped. "Would you mind if we all sat down?"

"No. I'm sorry." Cilla dragged a hand through her hair. She wasn't putting on a very good show, she thought. And she prided herself on putting on a good show. "I could, ah, make some coffee."

"Don't worry about it." He sat on an oatmeal-colored couch and leaned back against sapphire-blue pillows. "Tell us what happened."

"I wrote it down." The underlying nerves showed in her movements as she walked to the phone to pick up a pad of paper. "A radio habit," she said. "The phone rings and I start writing." She wasn't ready to admit that she didn't want to repeat the conversation out loud. "Some of it's in O'Roarke shorthand, but you should get the drift."

He took the pad from her and scanned the words. His gut muscles tightened in a combination of fury and revulsion. Outwardly calm, he handed the note to his partner.

Cilla couldn't sit. Instead, she stood in the center of the room, twisting her fingers together, dragging them apart again to tug at her baggy sweatshirt. "He's pretty explicit about what he thinks of me, and what he intends to do about it."

"Is this your first call at home?" Boyd asked her.

"Yes. I don't know how he got the number. I— We're not listed."

Althea put the pad aside and took out her own. "Who has your home number?"

"The station." Cilla relaxed fractionally. This was something she could deal with. Simple questions, simple answers. "It would be on file at the college. My lawyer—that's Carl Donnely, downtown. There are a couple of guys that Deb sees. Josh Holden and Darren McKinley. A few girlfriends." She ran through the brief list. "That's about it. What I'm really concerned about is—" She spun around as the door opened behind her. "Deb." Relief and annoyance speared through her. "I thought you had evening classes."

"I did." She turned a pair of big, smoldering blue eyes on Boyd and Althea. "Are you the police?"

"Deborah," Cilla said, "you know better than to cut classes. You had a test—"

"Stop treating me like a child." She slapped the newspaper she was carrying into Cilla's hand. "Do you really expect me to go along like nothing's wrong? Damn it, Cilla, you told me it was all under control."

So she'd made the first page of section B, Cilla thought wearily. Late-night radio princess under siege. Trying to soothe a growing tension headache, she rubbed her fingers at her temple. "It is under control. Stuff like this makes good copy, that's all."

"No, that's not all."

"I've called the police," she snapped back as she tossed the paper aside. "What else do you want?"

There was a resemblance between the two, Boyd noted objectively. The shape of the mouth and eyes. While Cilla was alluring and sexy enough to make a man's head turn a 360, her sister was hands-down gorgeous. Young, he thought. Maybe eighteen. In a few years she'd barely have to glance at a man to have him swallow his tongue.

He also noted the contrasts. Deborah's hair was short and fluffed. Cilla's was long and untamed. The younger sister wore a deep crimson sweater over tailored slacks that were tucked into glossy half boots. Cilla's mismatched sweats bagged and hit on a variety of colors. The top was purple, the bottoms green. She'd chosen thick yellow socks and orange high-tops.

Their tastes might clash, he mused, but their temperaments seemed very much in tune.

And when the O'Roarke sisters were in a temper, it was quite a show.

Shifting only slightly, Althea whispered near his ear. "Obviously they've done this before."

Boyd grinned. If he'd had popcorn and a beer, he would have been content to sit through another ten rounds. "Who's your money on?"

"Cilla," she murmured, crossing one smooth leg. "But the sister's a real up-and-comer."

Apparently weary of beating her head against a brick wall, Deborah turned. "Okay." She poked a finger at Boyd. "You tell me what's going on."

"Ah..."

"Never mind." She zeroed in on Althea. "You."

Biting back a smile, Althea nodded. "We're the investigating officers on your sister's case, Miss O'Roarke."

"So there is a case."

Ignoring Cilla's furious look, Althea nodded again. "Yes. With the station's cooperation, we have a trace on the studio line. Detective Fletcher and I have already interrogated a number of suspects who

have priors for obscene or harassing phone calls. With this latest
development, we'll put a tap on your private line."

"Latest development." It only took Deborah a moment. "Oh,
Cilla, not here. He didn't call you here." Temper forgotten, she threw
her arms around her sister. "I'm sorry."

"It's nothing for you to worry about." When Deborah stiffened,
Cilla drew back. "I mean it, Deb. It's nothing for either of us to
worry about. We've got the pros to do the worrying."

"That's right." Althea rose. "Detective Fletcher and I have over
fifteen years on the force between us. We intend to take good care
of your sister. Is there a phone I can use to make some arrangements?"

"In the kitchen," Deborah said before Cilla could comment. She
wanted a private interview. "I'll show you." She paused and smiled
at Boyd. "Would you like some coffee, Detective?"

"Thanks." He watched her—what man wouldn't?—as she walked
from the room.

"Don't even think about it," Cilla mumbled.

"Excuse me?" But he grinned. It didn't take a detective to recognize a mother hen. "Your sister—Deborah, right?—she's something."

"You're too old for her."

"Ouch."

Cilla picked up a cigarette and forced herself to settle on the arm
of a chair again. "In any case, you and Detective Grayson seem well
suited to each other."

"Thea?" He had to grin again. Most of the time he forgot his
partner was a woman. "Yeah, I'm one lucky guy."

Cilla ground her teeth. She hated to think she could be intimidated
by another woman. Althea Grayson was personable enough, professional enough. Cilla could even handle the fact that she was stunning.
It was just that she was so *together.*

Boyd rose to take the unlit cigarette from her fingers. "Jealous?"

"In your dreams, Slick."

"We'll get into my dreams later." He lifted her chin up with a
fingertip. "Holding on?"

"I'm fine." She wanted to move, but she had the feeling he

wouldn't give her room if she stood. And if she stood it would be much too easy to drop her head on his shoulder and just cave in. She had responsibilities, obligations. And her pride. "I don't want Deb mixed up in this. She's alone here at night while I'm at work."

"I can arrange to have a cruiser stationed outside."

She nodded, grateful. "I hate it that somewhere along the line I've made a mistake that might put her in danger. She doesn't deserve it."

Unable to resist, he spread his fingers to cup her cheek. "Neither do you."

It had been a long time since she'd been touched, allowed herself to be touched, even that casually. She managed to shrug. "I haven't figured that out yet." She gave a little sigh, wishing she could close her eyes and turn her face into that strong, capable hand. "I've got to get ready to go to the station."

"Why don't you give that a pass tonight?"

"And let him think he's got me running scared?" She stood then. "Not on a bet."

"Even Wonder Woman takes a night off."

She shook her head. She'd been right about him not giving her room. Her escape routes were blocked by the chair on one side and his body on the other. Tension quivered through her. Pride kept her eyes level. He was waiting, damn him. And unless he was blind or stupid, he would see that this contact, this connection with him, left her frazzled.

"You're crowding me, Fletcher."

In another minute, just one more minute, he would have given in to impulse and pulled her against him. He would have seen just how close to reality his fantasy was. "I haven't begun to crowd you, O'Roarke."

Her eyes sharpened. "I've had enough threats for one day, thanks."

He wanted to strangle her for that. Slowly, his eyes on hers, he hooked his thumbs in his pockets. "No threat, babe. Just a fact."

Deborah decided she'd eavesdropped long enough and cleared her throat. "Coffee, Detective Fletcher." She passed him a steaming mug. "Thea said black, two sugars."

"Thanks."

"I'm going to hang around," she said, silently daring Cilla to argue with her. "They should be here in an hour or so to hook up the phone." Then, she put her hands on Cilla's shoulders and kissed both of her cheeks. "I haven't missed a class this semester, Simon."

"Simon?" Boyd commented.

"Legree." With a laugh, Deborah kissed Cilla again. "The woman's a slave driver."

"I don't know what you're talking about." Cilla moved aside to gather up her purse. "You ought to catch up on your reading for U.S. studies. Your political science could use a boost. It wouldn't hurt to bone up on Psychology 101." She pulled her coat from the closet. "While you're at it, the kitchen floor needs scrubbing. I'm sure we have an extra toothbrush you could use on it. And I'd like another cord of wood chopped."

Deborah laughed. "Go away."

Cilla grinned as she reached for the doorknob. Her hand closed over Boyd's. She jolted back before she could stop herself. "What are you doing?"

"Hitching a ride with you." He sent Deborah a quick wink as he pulled Cilla out the door.

"This is ridiculous," Cilla said as she strode into the station.

"Which?"

"I don't see why I have to have a cop in the studio with me night after night." She whipped off her coat as she walked—a bit like a bullfighter swirling a cape, Boyd thought. Still scowling, she reached for the door of a small storage room, then shrieked and stumbled back against Boyd as it swung open. "Jeez, Billy, you scared the life out of me."

"Sorry." The maintenance man had graying hair, toothpick arms and an apologetic grin. "I was out of window cleaner." He held up his spray bottle.

"It's okay. I'm a little jumpy."

"I heard about it." He hooked the trigger of the bottle in his belt, then gathered up a mop and bucket. "Don't worry, Cilla. I'm here till midnight."

"Thanks. Are you going to listen to the show tonight?"

"You bet." He walked away, favoring his right leg in a slight limp.

Cilla stepped inside the room and located a fresh bottle of stylus cleaner. Taking a five-dollar bill out of her bag, she slipped it into a pile of cleaning rags.

"What was that for?"

"He was in Vietnam," she said simply, and closed the door again.

Boyd said nothing, knowing she was annoyed he'd caught her. He chalked it up to one more contradiction.

To prep for her shift, she went into a small lounge to run over the daily log for her show, adding and deleting as it suited her. The program director had stopped screaming about this particular habit months before. Another reason she preferred the night shift was the leeway it gave her.

"This new group," she muttered.

"What?" Boyd helped himself to a sugared doughnut.

"This new group, the Studs." She tapped her pencil against the table. "One-shot deal. Hardly worth the airtime."

"Then why play them?"

"Got to give them a fair shake." Intent on her work, she took an absent bite of the doughnut Boyd held to her lips. "In six months nobody will remember their names."

"That's rock and roll."

"No. The Beatles, Buddy Holly, Chuck Berry, Springsteen, Elvis—that's rock and roll."

He leaned back, considering her. "Ever listen to anything else?"

She grinned, then licked a speck of sugar from her top lip. "You mean there *is* something else?"

"Have you always been one-track?"

"Yeah." She pulled a band of fabric out of her pocket. With a couple of flicks of the wrist she had her hair tied back. "So what kind of music do you like?"

"The Beatles, Buddy Holly, Chuck—"

"Well, there's hope for you yet," she interrupted.

"Mozart, Lena Horne, Beaujolais, Joan Jett, Ella Fitzgerald, B.B. King..."

Her brow lifted. "So, we're eclectic."

"We're open-minded."

She leaned back a moment. "You're a surprise, Fletcher. I guess I figured you for the loving-and-hurting, drinking-and-cheating type."

"In music appreciation or personality?"

"Both." She glanced at the clock. "It's show time."

Wild Bob Williams, who had the six-to-ten slot, was just finishing up his show. He was short, paunchy and middle-aged, with the voice of a twenty-year-old stud. He gave Cilla a brief salute as she began sorting through 45s and albums.

"Mmm, the long-legged filly just walked in." He hit a switch that had an echoing heartbeat pounding. "Get ready out there in KHIP land, your midnight star's rising. I'm leaving you with this blast from the past." He potted up "Honky Tonk Woman."

He swung out of his chair and stretched his rubbery leg muscles. "Hey, honey, you okay?"

"Sure." She set her first cut on the turntable and adjusted the needle.

"I caught the paper."

"No big deal, Bob."

"Hey, we're family around here." He gave her shoulder a quick squeeze. "We're behind you."

"Thanks."

"You're the cop?" he asked Boyd.

"That's right."

"Get this guy soon. He's got us all shaking." He gave Cilla another squeeze. "Let me know if you need anything."

"I will. Thanks."

She didn't want to think about it, couldn't afford to think about it, with thirty seconds to air. Taking her seat, she adjusted the mike, took a series of long, deep breaths, ran a one-two-three voice check, then opened her mike.

"All right, Denver, this is Cilla O'Roarke coming to you on number one, KHIP. You've got me from ten till two in the a.m. We're going to start off giving away one hundred and nine dollars. We've got the mystery record coming up. If you can give me the title, the artist and the year, you've got yourself a fistful of cash. That number is 555-5447. Stand by, 'cause we're going to rock.''

The music blasted out, pleasing her. She was in control again.

"Elton John," Boyd said from behind her. "'Honky Cat.' Nineteen seventy...two."

She turned in her chair to face him. He was looking damned pleased with himself, she thought. That half grin on his face, his hands in his pockets. It was a shame he was so attractive, a bloody crying shame. "Well, well, you surprise me, Slick. Remind me to put you down for a free T-shirt."

"I'd rather have a dinner."

"And I'd rather have a Porsche. But there you go— Hey," she said when he took her hand.

"You've been biting your nails." He skimmed a thumb over her knuckles and watched her eyes change. "Another bad habit."

"I've got lots more."

"Good." Instead of sitting back in the corner, he chose a chair beside her. "I didn't have time to get a book," he explained. "Why don't I watch you work?"

"Why don't you—" She swore, then punched a button on the phone. He'd nearly made her miss her cue. "KHIP. Can you name the mystery record?"

It took five calls before she had a winner. Trying to ignore Boyd, she put on another cut while she took the winner's name and address.

As if she didn't have enough on her mind, she thought. How was she supposed to concentrate on her show when he was all but sitting on top of her? Close enough, she realized, that she could smell him. No cologne, just soap—something that brought the mountains to mind one moment and quiet, intimate nights the next.

She wasn't interested in either, she reminded herself. All she wanted was to get through this crisis and get her life back on an even keel. Attractive men came and went, she knew. But success stayed— as long as you were willing to sweat for it.

She shifted, stretching out to select a new record. Their thighs brushed. His were long and as hard as rock. Determined not to jolt, she turned her head to look into his eyes. Inches apart, challenge meeting challenge. She watched as his gaze dipped down to linger on her mouth. And it lifted again, desire flickering. Music pulsed in her ears from the headphones she stubbornly wore so that she wouldn't have to speak to him. They were singing of hot nights and grinding needs.

Very carefully, she moved away. When she spoke into the mike again, her voice was even huskier.

He rose. He'd decided it was his only defense. He'd meant to annoy her, to distract her from the inevitable phone call that would come before the night was over. He'd wanted her mind off it, and on him. He wouldn't deny that he'd wanted her to think of him. But he hadn't known that when he'd succeeded, she would tie him up in knots.

She smelled like midnight. Secret and sinful. She sounded like sex. Hot and inviting. Then you looked into her eyes, really looked, and saw simple innocence. The man that combination wouldn't drive mad either had never been born or was already dead.

A little distance, Boyd told himself as he moved quietly out of the studio. A lot of objectivity. It wouldn't do either one of them any good to allow his emotions to get so tangled up with a woman he was supposed to protect.

When she was alone, Cilla made a conscious effort to relax, muscle by muscle. It was just because she was already on edge. It was a comfort to believe that. Her reaction to Boyd was merely an echo of the tension she'd lived with for more than a week. And he was trying to goad her.

She blew the hair out of her eyes and gave her listeners a treat— two hits in a row. And herself another moment to calm.

She hadn't figured him out yet. He read Steinbeck and recognized Elton John. He talked slow and lazy—and thought fast. He wore scarred boots and three-hundred-dollar jackets.

What did it matter? she asked herself as she set up for the next twenty minutes of her show. She wasn't interested in men. And he was definitely a man. Strike one. She would never consider getting involved with a cop. Strike two. And anyone with eyes could see that he had a close, even intimate relationship with his knockout partner. She'd never been one to poach on someone else's property.

Three strikes and he's out.

She closed her eyes and let the music pour through her. It helped, as it always did, to calm her, or lift her up, or simply remind her how lucky she was. She wasn't sharp and studious like Deborah. She wasn't dedicated, as their parents had been. She had little more than the education required by law, and yet she was here, just where she wanted to be, doing just what she wanted to do.

Life had taught her one vital lesson. Nothing lasted forever. Good times or bad, they passed. This nightmare, however horrid it was at this point in time, would be over eventually. She only had to get through it, one day at a time.

"That was Joan Jett waking you up as we head toward eleven-thirty. We've got a news brief coming up for you, then a double shot of Steve Winwood and Phil Collins to take us into the next half hour. This is KHIP, and the news is brought to you by Wildwood Records."

She punched in the prerecorded cassette, then scanned the printout of the ads and promos she would read. By the time Boyd came back, she was into the next block of music and standing up to stretch her muscles.

He stopped where he was, trying not to groan as she lifted her arms to the ceiling and rotated her hips. In time to the music, he was sure, as she bent from the waist, grabbed her ankles and slowly bent and straightened her knees.

He'd seen the routine before. It was something she did once or twice during her four-hour stint. But she thought she was alone now, and she put a little more rhythm into it. Watching her, he realized that the ten-minute break he'd taken hadn't been nearly long enough.

She sat again, pattered a bit to the audience. Her headphones were around her neck now, as she'd turned the music up for her own pleasure. As it pulsed, she swayed.

When he put a hand on her shoulder, she bolted out of the chair. "Easy, O'Roarke. I brought you some tea."

Her heart was like a trip-hammer in her chest. As it slowed, she lowered to the table. "What?"

"Tea," he repeated, offering her a cup. "I brought you some tea. You drink too much coffee. This is herbal. Jasmine or something."

She'd recovered enough to look at the cup in distaste. "I don't drink flowers."

"Try it. You might not hit the ceiling the next time someone touches you." He sipped a soft drink out of the bottle.

"I'd rather have that."

He took another sip, a long one, then passed the bottle to her. "You're almost halfway there."

Like Boyd, she looked at the clock. It was nearing midnight. This had once been her favorite leg of the show. Now, as she watched the second hand tick away, her palms began to sweat.

"Maybe he won't call tonight, since he got me at home."

He settled beside her again. "Maybe."

"But you don't think so."

"I think we take it a step at a time." He put a soothing hand at the back of her neck. "I want you to try to keep calm, keep him on the line longer. Ask questions. No matter what he says, just keep asking them, over and over. He may just answer one and give us something."

She nodded, then worked her way through the next ten minutes. "There's a question I want to ask you," she said at length.

"All right."

She didn't look at him, but drained the last swallow of the cold drink to ease her dry throat. "How long will they let me have a baby-sitter?"

"You don't have to worry about it."

"Let's just say I know something about how police departments work." It was there in her voice again, that touch of bitterness and regret. "A few nasty calls don't warrant a hell of a lot of attention."

"You're life's been threatened," he said. "It helps that you're a celebrity, and that there's already been some press on it. I'll be around for a while."

"Mixed blessings," she muttered, then opened the request line.

The call came, as she had known it would, but quickly this time. On call number five, she recognized the voice, battled back the urge to scream and switched to music. Without realizing it, she groped for Boyd's hand.

"You're persistent, aren't you?"

"I want you dead. I'm almost ready now."

"Do I know you? I like to think I know everyone who wants to kill me."

She winced a little at the names he spewed at her and tried to concentrate on the steady pressure of Boyd's fingers at the base of her neck.

"Wow. I've really got you ticked off. You know, buddy, if you don't like the show, you've just got to turn it off."

"You seduced him." There was a sound of weeping now, fueled with fury. "You seduced him, tempted him, promised him. Then you murdered him."

"I..." She was more shocked by this than by any of the gutter names he had called her. "Who? I don't know what you're talking about. Please, who—"

The line went dead.

As she sat there, dazed and silent, Boyd snatched up the phone. "Any luck? Damn it." He rose, stuffed his hands in his pockets and began pacing. "Another ten seconds. We'd have had him in another ten seconds. He has to know we've got it tapped." His head snapped around when Nick Peters entered, his hands full of sloshing coffee. "What?"

"I—I—I—" His Adam's apple bobbed as he swallowed. "Mark said it was okay if I stayed through the show." He swallowed again. "I thought Cilla might want some coffee."

Boyd jerked a thumb toward the table. "We'll let you know. Can you help her get through the rest of the show?"

"I don't need help." Cilla's voice was icy-calm. "I'm fine, Nick. Don't worry about it." She put a steady hand on the mike. "That was for Chuck from Laurie, with all her love." She aimed a steady look at Boyd before she punched the phone again. "KHIP, you're on the air."

She got through it. That was all that mattered. And she wasn't going to fall apart the way she had the other night. Cilla was grateful for that. All she needed to do was think it all through.

She hadn't objected when Boyd took the wheel of her car. Relinquishing the right to drive was the least of her worries.

"I'm coming in," Boyd said after he parked the car. She just shrugged and started for the door.

Very deliberately she hung up her coat and pried off her shoes. She sat, still without speaking, and lit a cigarette. The marked cruiser outside had relieved her mind. Deborah was safe and asleep.

"Look," she began once she'd marshaled her thoughts. "There really isn't any use going into this. I think I have it figured out."

"Do you?" He didn't sit down. Her icy calm disturbed him much more than hysterics or anger would have. "Fill me in."

"It's obvious he's made a mistake. He has me mixed up with someone else. I just have to convince him."

"Just have to convince him," Boyd repeated. "And how do you intend to do that?"

"The next time he calls, I'll make him listen." She crossed an arm across her body and began to rub at the chill in her shoulder. "For God's sake, Fletcher, I haven't murdered anyone."

"So you'll tell him that and he'll be perfectly reasonable and apologize for bothering you."

Her carefully built calm was wearing thin. "I'll make him understand."

"You're trying to make yourself believe he's rational, Cilla. He's not."

"What am I supposed to do?" she demanded, snapping the cigarette in two as she crushed it out. "Whether he's rational or not, I have to make him see he's made a mistake. I've never killed anyone." Her laugh was strained as she pulled the band from her hair. "I've never seduced anyone."

"Give me a break."

Anger brought her out of the chair. "What do you see me as, some kind of black widow who goes around luring men, then knocking them off when I'm finished? Get the picture, Fletcher. I'm a voice, a damn good one. That's where it ends."

"You're a great deal more than voice, Cilla. We both know that." He paused, waiting for her to look at him again. "And so does he."

Something trembled inside her—part fear, part longing. She wanted neither. "Whatever I am, I'm no temptress. It's an act, a show, and it has nothing to do with reality. My ex-husband would be the first to tell you I don't even have a sex drive.''

His eyes sharpened. "You never mentioned you'd been married.''

And she hadn't intended to, Cilla thought as she wearily combed a hand through her hair. "It was a million years ago. What does it matter?''

"Everything applies. I want his name and address.''

"I don't know his address. We didn't even last a year. I was twenty years old, for God's sake.'' She began to rub at her forehead.

"His name, Cilla.''

"Paul. Paul Lomax. I haven't seen him for about eight years— since he divorced me.'' She spun to the window, then back again. "The point is, this guy's on the wrong frequency. He's got it into his head I—what?—used my wiles on some guy, and that doesn't wash.''

"Apparently he thinks it does.''

"Well, he thinks wrong. I couldn't even keep one man happy, so it's a joke to think I could seduce legions.''

"That's a stupid remark, even for you.''

"Do you think I like admitting that I'm all show, that I'm lousy in bed?'' She bit off the words as she paced. "The last man I went out with told me I had ice water for blood. But I didn't kill him.'' She calmed a little, amused in spite of herself. "I thought about it, though.''

"I think it's time you start to take this whole business seriously. And I think it's time you start taking yourself seriously.''

"I take myself very seriously.''

"Professionally,'' he agreed. "You know exactly what to do and how to do it. Personally...you're the first woman I've met who was so willing to concede she couldn't make a man dance to her tune.''

"I'm a realist.''

"I think you're a coward.''

Her chin shot up. "Go to hell.''

He wasn't about to back off. He had a point to prove, to both of them. "I think you're afraid to get close to a man, afraid to find out just what's inside. Maybe you'd find out it's something you can't control.''

"I don't need this from you. You just get this man off my back."
She started to storm past him but was brought up short when he
grabbed her arm.

"What do you say to an experiment?"

"An experiment?"

"Why don't you give it a try, O'Roarke—with me? It should be
safe, since you can barely stand the sight of me. A test." He took
her other arm. "Low-risk." He could feel the anger vibrate through
her as he held her. Good. For reasons he couldn't have begun to
name, he was just as angry. "Five to one I don't feel a thing." He
drew her inches closer. "Want to prove me wrong?"

# Chapter 4

They were close. She had lifted one hand in an unconscious defensive gesture and now her fingers were splayed across his chest. She could feel his heartbeat, slow and steady, beneath her palm. She focused her resentment on that even rhythm as her own pulse jerked and scrambled.

"I don't have to prove anything to you."

He nodded. The barely banked fury in her eyes was easier for him to handle than the glaze of fear it replaced. "To yourself, then." Deliberately he smiled, baiting her. "What's the matter, O'Roarke? Do I scare you?"

He'd pushed exactly the right button. They both knew it. He didn't give a damn if it was temper that pushed her forward. As long as she moved.

She tossed her hair back and slowly, purposefully slid her hand from his chest to his shoulder. She wanted a reaction, hang him. He only lifted a brow and, with that faint smile playing around his mouth, watched her.

So he wanted to play games, she thought. Well, she was up for it. Tossing common sense aside, she pressed her lips to his.

His were firm, cool. And unresponsive. With her eyes open, she watched his remain patient, steady, and hatefully amused. As her hand balled into a fist on his shoulder, she snapped her head back.

"Satisfied?"

"Not hardly." His eyes might have been calm. That was training. But if she had bothered to monitor his heartbeat she would have found it erratic. "You're not trying, O'Roarke." He slid a hand down to her hip, shifting her balance just enough to have her sway against him. "You want me to believe that's the best you can do?"

Angry humiliation rippled through her. Cursing him, she dragged his mouth to hers and poured herself into the kiss.

His lips were still firm, but they were no longer cool. Nor were they unresponsive. For an instant the urge to retreat hammered at her. And then needs, almost forgotten needs, surged. A flood of longings, a storm of desires. Overwhelmed by them, she strained against him, letting the power and the heat whip through her, reminding her what it was like to sample passion again.

Every other thought, every other wish, winked out. She could feel the long, hard length of him pressed against her, the slow, deliberate stroke of his hands as they moved up her back and into her hair. His mouth, no longer patient, took and took from hers until the blood pounded like thunder in her head.

He'd known she would pack a punch. He'd thought he was prepared for it. In the days he'd known her he'd imagined tasting her like this dozens of times. He'd imagined what it would be like to hold her against him, to hear her sigh, to catch the fevered scent of her skin as he took his mouth over her.

But reality was much more potent than any dream had been.

Chain lightning. She was every bit as explosive, as turbulent, as potentially lethal. The current sparked and sizzled from her into him, leaving him breathless, dazed and churning. Even as he groaned against the onslaught, he felt her arch away from the power that snapped back into her.

She shuddered against him and made a sound—part protest, part confusion—as she tried to struggle away.

He'd wrapped her hair around his hand. He had only to tug gently to have her head fall back, to have her eyes dark and cloudy on his.

He took his time, letting his gaze skim over her face. He wanted to see in her eyes what he had felt. The reflection was there, that most elemental yearning. He smiled again as her lips trembled open and her breath came fast and uneven.

"I'm not finished yet," he told her, then dragged her against him again and plundered.

She needed to think, but her thoughts couldn't fight their way through the sensations. Layers of them, thin and silky, seemed to cover her, fogging the reason, drugging the will. Before panic could slice through, she was rocketing up again, clinging to him, opening for him, demanding from him.

He knew he could feast and never be full. Not when her mouth was hot and moist and ripe with flavor. He knew he could hold yet never control. Not when her body was vibrating from the explosion they had ignited together. The promise he had heard in her voice, seen in her eyes, was here for the taking.

Unable to resist, he slid his hands under her sweatshirt to find the warmed satin skin beneath. He took, possessed, exploited, until the ache spreading through his body turned to pain.

Too fast, he warned himself. Too soon. For both of them. Holding her steady, he lifted his head and waited for her to surface.

She dragged her eyes open and saw only his face. She gulped in air and tasted only his flavor. Reeling, she pressed a hand to her temple, then let it fall to her side. "I...I want to sit down."

"That makes two of us." Taking her arm, he led her to the couch and sat beside her.

She worked on steadying her breathing, focused on the dark window across the room. Maybe with enough time, enough distance, she would be able to convince herself that what had just happened had not been life-altering.

"That was stupid."

"It was a lot of things," he pointed out. "Stupid doesn't come to mind."

She took one more deep breath. "You made me angry."

"It isn't hard."

"Listen, Boyd—"

"So you *can* say it." Before she could stop him, he stroked a hand down her hair in a casually intimate gesture that made her pulse rate soar again. "Does that mean you don't use a man's name until you've kissed him?"

"It doesn't mean anything." She stood up, hoping she'd get the strength back in her legs quicker by pacing. "Obviously we've gotten off the track."

"There's more than one." He settled back, thinking it was a pleasure to watch her move. There was something just fine and dandy about watching the swing of long feminine legs. As she paced, nervous energy crackling, he tossed an arm over the back of the couch and stretched out his legs.

"There's only one for me." She threw him a look over her shoulder. "You'd better understand that."

"Okay, we'll ride on that one for a while." He could afford to wait, since he had every intention of switching lines again, and soon. "You seem to have some kind of screwy notion that the only thing that attracts men to you is your voice, your act. I think we just proved you wrong."

"What just happened proved nothing." If there was anything more infuriating than that slow, patient smile of his, she had yet to see it. "In any case, that has nothing to do with the man who's calling me."

"You're a smart woman, Cilla. Use your head. He's fixed on you, but not for himself. He wants to pay you back for something you did to another man. Someone you knew," he continued when she stopped long enough to pick up a cigarette. "Someone who was involved with you."

"I've already told you, there's no one."

"No one now."

"No one now, no one before, no one for years."

Having experienced that first wave of her passion, he found that more than difficult to believe. Still, he nodded. "So it didn't mean as much to you. Maybe that's the problem."

"For God's sake, Fletcher, I don't even date. I don't have the time or the inclination."

"We'll talk about your inclinations later."

Weary, she turned away to stare blindly through the glass. "Damn it, Boyd, get out of my life."

"It's your life we're talking about." There was an edge to his voice that had her holding back the snide comment she wanted to make. "If there's been no one in Denver, we'll start working our way back. But I want you to think, and think hard. Who's shown an interest in you? Someone who calls the station more than normal. Who asks to meet you, asks personal questions. Someone who's approached you, asked you out, made a play.''

She gave a short, humorless laugh. ''You have.''

''Remind me to run a make on myself.'' His voice was deceptively mild, but she caught the underlying annoyance and frustration in it. ''Who else, Cilla?''

''There's no one, no one who's pushed.'' Wishing for a moment's, just a moment's, peace of mind, she pressed the heels of her hands against her eyes. ''I get calls. That's the idea. I get some that ask me for a date, some that even send presents. You know, candy-and-flower types. Nothing very sinister about a bunch of roses.''

''There's a lot sinister about death threats.''

She wanted to speak calmly, practically, but she couldn't keep the nastiness out of her voice. ''I can't remember everyone who's called and flirted with me on the air. Guys I turn down stay turned down.''

He could only shake his head. It was a wonder to him that such a sharp woman could be so naive in certain situations. ''All right, we'll shoot for a different angle. You work with men—almost all men—at the station.''

''We're professionals,'' she snapped, and began biting her nails. ''Mark's happily married. Bob's happily married. Jim's a friend—a good one.''

''You forgot Nick.''

''Nick Peters? What about him?''

''He's crazy about you.''

''What?'' She was surprised enough to turn around. ''That's ridiculous. He's a kid.''

After a long study, he let out a sigh. ''You really haven't noticed, have you?''

''There's nothing to notice.'' More disturbed than she wanted to admit, she turned away again. ''Look, Slick, this is getting us nowhere, and I'm...'' Her words trailed off, and her hand crept slowly toward her throat.

''And you're what?''

''There's a man across the street. He's watching the house.''

''Get away from the window.''

"What?"

Boyd was already up and jerking her aside. "Stay away from the windows and keep the door locked. Don't open it again until I get back."

She nodded and followed him to the door. Her lips pressed together as she watched him take out his weapon. That single gesture snapped her back to reality. It had been a smooth movement, not so much practiced as instinctive. Ten years on the force, she remembered. He'd drawn and fired before.

She wouldn't tell him to be careful. Those were useless words.

"I'm going to take a look. Lock the door behind me." Gone was the laid-back man who had taunted her into an embrace. One look at his face and she could see that he was all cop. Their eyes changed, she thought. The emotion drained out of them. There was no room for emotion when you held a gun. "If I'm not back in ten minutes, call 911 for backup. Understood?"

"Yes." She gave in to the need to touch his arm. "Yes," she repeated.

After he slipped out, she shoved the bolt into place and waited.

He hadn't buttoned his coat, and the deep wind of the early hours whipped through his shirt. His weapon, warmed from sitting in its nest against his side, fitted snug in his hand. Sweeping his gaze right, then left, he found the street deserted, dark but for the pools of light from the streetlamps spaced at regular intervals. It was only a quiet suburban neighborhood, cozily asleep in the predawn hours. The night wind sounded through the naked trees in low moans.

He didn't doubt Cilla's words—wouldn't have doubted it even if he hadn't caught a glimpse through her window of a lone figure on the opposite sidewalk.

Whoever had been there was gone now, probably alerted the moment Cilla had spotted him.

As if to punctuate Boyd's thoughts, there was the sound of an engine turning over a block or two away. He swore but didn't bother to give chase. With that much of a lead, it would be a waste of time. Instead, he walked a half block in each direction, then carefully circled the house.

Cilla had her hand on the phone when he knocked.

"It's okay. It's Boyd."

In three hurried strides, she was at the door. "Did you see him?" she demanded the moment Boyd stepped inside.

"No."

"He was there. I swear it."

"I know." He relocked the door himself. "Try to relax. He's gone now."

"Relax?" In the past ten minutes she'd had more than enough time to work herself from upset to frantic. "He knows where I work, where I live. How in God's name am I ever supposed to relax again? If you hadn't scared him off, he might have—" She dragged her hands through her hair. She didn't want to think about what might have happened. Didn't dare.

Boyd didn't speak for a moment. Instead, he watched as she slowly, painfully brought herself under control. "Why don't you take some time off, stay home for a few days? We'll arrange for a black-and-white to cruise the neighborhood."

She allowed herself the luxury of sinking into a chair. "What difference does it make if I'm here or at the station?" She shook her head before he could speak. "And if I stayed home I'd go crazy thinking about it, worrying about it. At least at work I have other things on my mind."

He hadn't expected her to agree. "We'll talk about it later. Right now you're tired. Why don't you go to bed? I'll sleep on the couch."

She wanted to be strong enough to tell him it wasn't necessary. She didn't need to be protected. But the wave of gratitude made her weak. "I'll get you a blanket."

It was almost dawn when he dragged himself home. He'd driven a long time—from one sleepy suburb to another, into an eerily quiet downtown. Covering his trail. The panic had stayed with him for the first hour, but he'd beaten it, made himself drive slowly, carefully. Being stopped by a roving patrol car could have ruined all of his plans.

Under the heavy muffler and cap he was wearing, he was sweating. In the thin canvas tennis shoes, his feet were like ice. But he was too accustomed to discomfort to notice.

He staggered into the bathroom, never turning on a light. With ease he avoided his early-warning devices. The thin wire stretched from the arm of the spindly chair to the arm of the faded couch. The tower of cans at the entrance to his bedroom. He had excellent night vision. It was something he'd always been proud of.

He showered in the dark, letting the water run cold over his tensed body. As he began to relax, he allowed himself to draw in the fragrance of soap—his favorite scent. He used a rough, long-handled brush to violently scrub every inch of his skin.

As he washed, the dark began to lessen with the first watery light of dawn.

Over his heart was an intricate tattoo of two knives, blades crossed in an X. With his fingers he caressed them. He remembered when it had still been new, when he had shown it to John. John had been so impressed, so fascinated.

The image came so clearly. John's dark, excited eyes. His voice— the way he spoke so quickly that the words tumbled into each other. Sometimes they had sat in the dark and talked for hours, making plans and promises. They were going to travel together, do great things together.

Then the world had interfered. Life had interfered. The woman had interfered.

Dripping, he stepped from the shower. The towel was exactly where he had placed it. No one came into this room, into any of his rooms, to disturb his carefully ordered space. Once he was dry, he pulled on faded pajamas. They reminded him of the childhood he'd been cheated out of.

As the sun came up, he made two enormous sandwiches and ate them standing in the kitchen, leaning over the sink so that the crumbs wouldn't fall to the floor.

He felt strong again. Clean and fed. He was outwitting the police, making fools of them. And that delighted him. He was frightening the woman, bringing terror into every day of her life. That excited him. When the time was right, he would do everything he'd told her he would do.

And still it wouldn't be enough.

He went into the bedroom, shut the door, pulled the shades and picked up the phone.

Deborah strolled out of her room in a white teddy, a thin blue robe that reached to mid-thigh, flapping open. Her toenails were shocking pink. She'd painted them the night before to amuse herself as she'd crammed for an exam.

She was muttering the questions she thought would be on the exam she had scheduled at nine. The questions came easily enough, but the answers continued to bog down at some crossroads between the conscious and the unconscious. She hoped to unblock the answers with a quick shot of coffee.

Yawning, she stumbled over a boot, pitched toward the couch, then let out a muffled scream as her hand encountered warm flesh.

Boyd sat up like a shot, his hand already reaching for his weapon. With their faces close, he stared at Deborah—the creamy skin, the big blue eyes, the tumble of dark hair—and relaxed.

"Good morning."

"I—Detective Fletcher?"

He rubbed a hand over his eyes. "I think so."

"I'm sorry. I didn't realize you were here." She cleared her throat and belatedly remembered to close her robe. Still fumbling, she glanced up the stairs and automatically lowered her voice. Her sister wasn't a sound sleeper under the best of circumstances. "Why are you here?"

He flexed a shoulder that had stiffened during his cramped night on the couch. "I told you I was going to look after Cilla."

"Yes, you did." Her eyes narrowed as she studied him. "You take your job seriously."

"That's right."

"Good." Satisfied, she smiled. In the upheaval and confusion of her nineteen years, she had learned to make character judgments quickly. "I was about to make some coffee. I have an early class. Can I get you some?"

If she was anything like her sister, he wouldn't get any more sleep until he'd answered whatever questions were rolling around in her head. "Sure. Thanks."

"I imagine you'd like a hot shower, as well. You're about six inches too long to have spent a comfortable night on that couch."

"Eight," he said, rubbing the back of his stiff neck. "I think it's more like eight."

"You're welcome to all the hot water you want. I'll start on the coffee." As she turned toward the kitchen, the phone rang. Though she knew Cilla would pick it up before the second ring, she stepped toward it automatically. Boyd shook his head. Reaching over, he lifted the receiver and listened.

With her hands clutching the lapels of her robe, Deborah watched him. His face remained impassive, but she saw a flicker of anger in his eyes. Though brief, it was intense enough to make her certain who was on the other end of the line.

Boyd disconnected mechanically, then punched in a series of numbers. "Anything?" He didn't even bother to swear at the negative reply. "Right." After hanging up, he looked at Deborah. She was standing beside the couch, her hands clenched, her face pale. "I'm going upstairs," he said. "I'll take a rain check on that coffee."

"She'll be upset. I want to talk to her."

He pushed aside the blanket and rose, wearing only his jeans. "I'd appreciate it if you'd let me handle it this time."

She wanted to argue, but something in his eyes stopped her. She nodded. "All right, but do a good job of it. She isn't as tough as she likes people to think."

"I know."

He climbed the stairs to the second floor, walked past an open door to a room where the bed was tidily made. Deborah's, he decided, noting the rose-and-white decor and the feminine bits of lace. Pausing at the next door, he knocked, then entered without waiting for an answer.

She was sitting in the middle of the bed, her knees drawn up close to her chest and her head resting on them. The sheets and blankets were tangled, a testimony to the few hours of restless sleep she'd had.

There were no bits of feminine lace here, no soft, creamy colors. She preferred clean lines rather than curves, simplicity rather than flounces. In contrast, the color scheme was electric, and anything but restful. In the midst of the vibrant blues and greens, she seemed all the more vulnerable.

She didn't look up until he sat on the edge of the bed and touched her hair. Slowly she lifted her head. He saw that there were no tears. Rather than the fear he'd expected, there was an unbearable weariness that was even more disturbing.

"He called," she said.

"I know. I was on the extension."

"Then you heard." She looked away, toward the window, where she could see the sun struggling to burn away a low bank of clouds. "It was him outside last night. He said he'd seen me, seen us. He made it sound revolting."

"Cilla—"

"He was watching!" She spit out the words. "Nothing I say, nothing I do, is going to make him stop. And if he gets to me, he's going to do everything he said he'd do."

"He's not going to get to you."

"How long?" she demanded. Her fingers clenched and unclenched on the sheets as her eyes burned into his. "How long can you watch me? He'll just wait. He'll wait and keep calling, keep watching." Something snapped inside her, and she picked up the bedside phone and heaved it across the room. It bounced against the wall, jangling as it thudded to the floor. "You're not going to stop him. You heard him. He said nothing would stop him."

"This is just what he wants." Boyd took her by the arms and gave her one quick shake. "He wants you to fall apart. He wants to know he's made you fall apart. If you do, you're only helping him."

"I don't know what to do," she managed. "I just don't know what to do."

"You've got to trust me. Look at me, Cilla." Her breath was hitching, but she met his eyes. "I want you to trust me," he said quietly, "and believe me when I say I won't let anything happen to you."

"You can't always be there."

His lips curved a little. He gentled his hold to rub his hands up and down her arms. "Sure I can."

''I want—'' She squeezed her eyes shut. How she hated to ask. Hated to need.

''What?''

Her lips trembled as she fought for one last handhold on control. ''I need to hold on to something.'' She let out an unsteady breath. ''Please.''

He said nothing, but he gathered her close to cradle her head on his shoulder. Her hands, balled into fists, pressed against his back. She was trembling, fighting off a wild bout of tears.

''Take five, O'Roarke,'' he murmured. ''Let loose.''

''I can't.'' She kept her eyes closed and held on. He was solid, warm, strong. Dependable. ''I'm afraid once I do I won't be able to stop.''

''Okay, let's try this.'' He tilted her head up and touched his lips gently to hers. ''Think about me. Right here.'' His mouth brushed hers again. ''Right now.'' Easy, patient, he stroked her rigid back. ''Just me.''

Here was compassion. She hadn't known a kiss from a man could hold it. More than gentle, more than tender, it soothed frayed nerves, calmed icy fears, cooled hot despair. Her clenched hands relaxed, muscle by muscle. There was no demand here as his lips roamed over her face. Just understanding.

It became so simple to do as he'd asked. She thought only of him.

Hesitant, she brought a hand to his face, letting her fingers skim along his beard-roughened cheek. Her stomach unknotted. The throbbing in her head quieted. She said his name on a sigh and melted against him.

He had to be careful. Very careful. Her complete and total surrender had his own needs drumming. He ignored them. For now she needed comfort, not passion. It couldn't matter that his senses were reeling from her, the soft give of her body, the rich taste of her mouth. It couldn't matter that the air had thickened so that each breath he took was crowded with the scent of her.

He knew he had only to lay her back on the bed among the tangled sheets. And cover her. She wouldn't resist. Perhaps she would even welcome the heat and the distraction. The temporary respite. He intended to be much more to her.

Battling his own demons, he pressed his lips to her forehead, then rested his cheek on her hair.

"Better?"

On one ragged breath, she nodded. She wasn't sure she could speak. How could she tell him that she wanted only to stay like this, her arms around him, his heart beating against hers? He'd think she was a fool.

"I, uh…didn't know you could be such a nice guy, Fletcher."

He wanted to sigh, but he found himself grinning. "I have my moments."

"Yeah. Well, that was certainly above and beyond."

Maybe, just maybe, she wasn't really trying to needle him. He pulled back, put a hand under her chin and held it steady. "I'm not on duty. When I kiss you, it's got nothing to do with my job. Got it?"

She'd meant to thank him, not annoy him. There was a warning in his eyes that had her frowning. "Sure."

"Sure," he repeated, then rose to jam his hands in his pockets in disgust.

For the first time she noted that he wore only his jeans, unsnapped and riding low. The sudden clutching in her stomach had nothing to do with fear and left her momentarily speechless.

She wanted him. Not just to hold, not just for a few heated kisses. And certainly not just for comfort. She wanted him in bed, the way she couldn't remember ever wanting a man before. She could look at him—the long, lean, golden line of torso, the narrow hips, the dance of muscle in his arms as he balled his hands—and she could imagine what it would be like to touch and be touched, to roll over the bed in one tangled heap of passion. To ride and be ridden.

"What the hell's wrong with you now?"

"What?"

Eyes narrowed, he rocked back on his heels as she blinked at him. "Taking a side trip, O'Roarke?"

"I, ah…" Her mouth was dry, and there was a hard knot of pressure in her gut. What would he say if she told him where her mind had just taken her, taken them? She let her eyes close. "Oh, boy," she whispered. "I think I need some coffee." And a quick dip in a cold lake.

"Your sister was fixing some." He frowned as he studied her. He thought of Deborah for a moment, of how she had nearly fallen on top of him wearing hardly more than a swatch of white lace. He'd appreciated the long, lissome limbs. What man wouldn't? But looking at her hadn't rocked his system.

And here was Cilla—sitting there with her eyes shadowed, wearing a Broncos football jersey that was two sizes too big. The bright orange cotton was hardly seductive lingerie. If he stood there one more moment, he would be on his knees begging for mercy.

"How about breakfast?" His voice was abrupt, not even marginally friendly. It helped to bring her thoughts to order.

"I never eat it."

"Today you do. Ten minutes."

"Look, Slick—"

"Do something with your hair," he said as he walked out of the room. "You look like hell."

He found Deborah downstairs in the kitchen, fully dressed, sipping a cup of coffee. That she was waiting for him was obvious. The moment he stepped into the room, she was out of her chair.

"She's fine," he said briefly. "I'm going to fix her some breakfast."

Though her brow lifted at this information, she nodded. "Look, why don't you sit down? I'll fix some for both of you."

"I thought you had an early class."

"I'll skip it."

He headed for the coffee. "Then she'll be mad at both of us."

She had to smile as he poured a cup, then rooted through a drawer for a spoon for the sugar. "You already know her very well."

"Not well enough." He drank half the cup and felt nearly human again. He had to think of Cilla. It would be safe enough, he hoped, if he kept those thoughts professional. "How much time do you have?"

"About five minutes," she said as she glanced at her watch.

"Tell me about the ex-husband."

"Paul?" There was surprise in her eyes, in her voice. "Why?"

She was shaking her head before he could answer. "You don't think he has anything to do with what's going on here?"

"I'm checking all the angles. The divorce...was it amicable?"

"Are they ever?"

She was young, Boyd thought, nodding, but she was sharp. "You tell me."

"Well, in this case, I'd say it was as amicable—or as bland as they get." She hesitated, torn. If it was a question of being loyal to Cilla or protecting her, she had to choose protection. "I was only about twelve, and Cilla was never very open about it, but my impression was, always has been, that he wanted it."

Boyd leaned back against the counter. "Why?"

Uncomfortable, Deborah moved her shoulders. "He'd fallen in love with someone else." She let out a hiss of breath and prayed Cilla wouldn't see what she was doing as a betrayal. "It was pretty clear that they were having problems before I came to live with them. It was right after our parents had died. Cilla had only been married a few months, but...well, let's say the honeymoon was over. She was making a name for herself in Atlanta, and Paul—he was very conservative, a real straight arrow. He'd decided to run for assemblyman, I think it was, and Cilla's image didn't suit."

"Sounds like it was the other way around to me."

She smiled then, beautifully, and moved over to top off his coffee. "I remember how hard she was working, to hold her job together, to hold everything together. It was a pretty awful time for us. It didn't help matters when the responsibility for a twelve-year-old was suddenly dumped on them. The added strain—well, I guess you could say it hastened the inevitable. A couple of months after I moved in, he moved out and filed for divorce. She didn't fight it."

He tried to imagine how it would have been. At twenty, she'd lost her parents, accepted the care and responsibility of a young girl and watched her marriage crumble. "Sounds to me like she was well rid of him."

"I guess it doesn't hurt to say I never liked him very much. He was inoffensive. And dull."

"Why did she marry him?"

"I think it would be more appropriate to ask me," Cilla said from the doorway.

# Chapter 5

The something she had done with her hair was to pull it back in a ponytail. It left her face unframed, so the anger in her eyes was that much easier to read. Along with the jersey she'd slept in, she'd pulled on a pair of yellow sweatpants. It was a deceptively sunny combination. Her hands were thrust into their deep pockets as she stood, directing all her resentment at Boyd.

"Cilla." Knowing there was a time to argue and a time to soothe, Deborah stepped forward. "We were just—"

"Yes, I heard what you were just." She shifted her gaze to Deborah. The edge of her temper softened. "Don't worry about it. It's not your fault."

"It's not a matter of fault," Deborah murmured. "We care what happens to you."

"Nothing's going to happen. You'd better get going, Deb, or you'll be late. And it appears that Detective Fletcher and I have things to discuss."

Deborah lifted her hands and let them fall. She shot one sympathetic glance toward Boyd, then kissed her sister's cheek. "All right. You'd never listen to reason at this hour anyway."

"Get an A," was all Cilla said.

"I intend to. I'm going to catch a burger and a movie with Josh, but I'll be back before you get home."

"Have a good time." Cilla waited, not moving an inch until she heard the front door close. "You've got a hell of a nerve, Fletcher."

He merely turned and slipped another mug off the hook behind the stove. "Want some coffee?"

"I don't appreciate you grilling my sister."

He filled the mug, then set it aside. "I left my rubber hose in my other suit."

"Let's get something straight." She walked toward him, deliberately keeping her hands in her pockets. She was dead sure she'd hit him if she took them out. "If you have any questions about me, you come to me. Deborah is not involved in any of this."

"She's a lot more forthcoming than her sister. Got any eggs?" he asked as he opened the refrigerator.

She managed to restrain the urge to kick the door into his head. "You know, for a minute upstairs you had me fooled. I actually thought you had some heart, some compassion."

He found a half-dozen eggs, some cheese and a few miserly strips of bacon. "Why don't you sit down, O'Roarke, and drink your coffee?"

She swore at him, viciously. Something shot into his eyes, something dangerous, but he picked up a skillet and calmly began to fry the bacon. "You'll have to do better than that," he said after a moment. "After ten years on the force there's not much you could call me and get a rise."

"You had no right." Her voice had quieted, but the emotion in it had doubled. "No right to dredge all that up with her. She was a child, devastated, scared to death. That entire year was nothing but hell for her, and she doesn't need you to make her remember it."

"She handled herself just fine." He broke an egg into a bowl, then crushed the shell in his hand. "It seems to me you're the one with the problem."

"Just back off."

He had her arm in a tight grip so quickly that she had no chance to evade. His voice was soft, deadly, with temper licking around the edges. "Not a chance."

"What happened back then has nothing to do with what's happening now, and what's happening now is the only thing that concerns you.''

"It's my job to determine what applies." With an effort, he reeled himself in. He couldn't remember when anyone had pushed him so close to the edge so often. "If you want me to put it to rest, then spell it out for me. Ex-spouses are favored suspects."

"It was eight years ago." She jerked away and, needing something to do with her hands, snatched up her coffee. It splattered over the rim and onto the counter.

"I find out from you or I find out from someone else. The end result's the same."

"You want me to spell it out? You want me to strip bare? Fine. It hardly matters at this point. I was twenty, I was stupid. He was beautiful and charming and smart—all the things stupid twenty-year-old girls think they want."

She took a long sip of hot coffee, then automatically reached for a washcloth to mop up the spill. "We only knew each other a couple of months. He was very persuasive, very romantic. I married him because I wanted something stable and real in my life. And I thought he loved me."

She was calmer now. She hadn't realized that the anger had drained away. Sighing, she turned, mechanically reaching for plates and flatware. "It didn't work—almost from day one. He was disappointed in me physically and disillusioned when he saw that I believed my work was as important as his. He'd hoped to convince me to change jobs. Not that he wanted me to quit altogether. He wasn't against my having a career, even in radio—as long as it didn't interfere with his plans."

"Which were?" Boyd asked as he set the bacon aside to drain.

"Politics. Actually, we met at a charity event the station put on. He was trying to charm up votes. I was promoting. That was the basic problem," she murmured. "We met each other's public personalities."

"What happened?"

"We got married—too fast. And things went wrong—too fast. I was even considering his idea that I go into marketing or sales. I figured I should at least give it a shot. Then my parents... I lost my parents, and brought Deborah home.''

She stopped speaking for a moment. She couldn't talk of that time, couldn't even think of the fears and the griefs, the pain and the resentments.

''It must have been rough.''

She shrugged the words away. ''The bottom line was, I couldn't handle another upheaval. I needed to work. The strain ate away at what shaky foundation we had. He found someone who made him happier, and he left me.'' She filled her mug with coffee she no longer wanted. ''End of story.''

What was he supposed to say? Boyd wondered. Tough break, kid? We all make mistakes? You were better off without the jerk? No personal comments, he warned himself. They were both edgy enough.

''Did he ever threaten you?''

''No.''

''Abuse you?''

She gave a tired laugh. ''No. No. You're trying to make him into the bad guy, Boyd, and it won't play. We were simply two people who made a mistake because we got married before we knew what we wanted.''

Thoughtful, Boyd scooped eggs onto her plate. ''Sometimes people hold resentments without even being aware of it. Then one day they bust loose.''

''He didn't resent me.'' Sitting, she picked up a piece of bacon. She studied it as she broke it in two. ''He never cared enough for that. That's the sad, sad truth.'' She smiled, but there wasn't a trace of humor in her eyes. ''You see, he thought I was like the woman he heard on the radio—seductive, sophisticated, sexy. He wanted that kind of woman in bed. And outside the bedroom he wanted a well-groomed, well-mannered, attentive woman to make his home. I was neither.'' She shrugged and dropped the bacon on her plate again. ''Since he wasn't the attentive, reliable and understanding man I thought he was, we both lost out. We had a very quiet, very civilized divorce, shook hands and went our separate ways.''

''If there was nothing more to it, why are you still raw?''

She looked up then, eyes somber. "You've never been married, have you?"

"No."

"Then I couldn't begin to explain. If you want to run a check on Paul, you go ahead, but it's a waste of time. I can guarantee he hasn't given me a thought since I left Atlanta."

He doubted that any man who had ever been close to her would be able to push her completely out of his mind, but he would let that ride for the moment. "You're letting your eggs get cold."

"I told you I don't eat breakfast."

"Humor me." He reached over, scooped up a forkful of eggs from her plate and held them to her lips.

"You're a pest," she said after she swallowed them. "Don't you have to check in or something?"

"I already did—last night, after you went up to bed."

She toyed with the food on her plate, eating a bite or two to keep him from nagging her. He had stayed, she reminded herself, long after his duty shift was over. She owed him for that. And she always paid her debts.

"Look, I appreciate you hanging around, and I know it's your job to ask all kinds of personal and embarrassing questions. But I really want you to leave Deb out of it."

"As much as I can."

"Spring break's coming up. I'm going to try to convince her to head for the beach."

"Good luck." He sipped, watching her over the rim of his mug. "You might pull it off if you went with her."

"I'm not running from this." After pushing her half-eaten breakfast aside, she rested her elbows on the table. "After the call this morning, I was pretty close to doing just that. I thought about it— and after I did I realized it's not going to stop until I figure it out. I want my life back, and that's not going to happen until we know who he is and why he's after me."

"It's my job to find him."

"I know. That's why I've decided to cooperate."

He set his mug aside. "Have you?"

"That's right. From now on, my life's an open book. You ask, I'll answer."

"And you'll do exactly what you're told?"

"No." She smiled. "But I'll do exactly what I'm told if it seems reasonable." She surprised them both by reaching over to touch his hand. "You look tired, Slick. Rough night?"

"I've had better." He linked his fingers with hers before she could withdraw them. "You look damn good in the morning, Cilla."

There it was again—that fluttering that started in her chest and drifted down to her stomach. "A little while ago you said I looked like hell."

"I changed my mind. Before I clock in I'd like to talk to you about last night. About you and me."

"That's not a good idea."

"No, it's not." But he didn't release her hand. "I'm a cop, and you're my assignment. There's no getting around that." She nearly managed a relieved breath before he continued. "Any more than there's any getting around the fact that I want you so much it hurts."

She went very still, so still she could hear the sound of her own heartbeat drumming in her head. Very slowly she moved her eyes, only her eyes, until they met his. They were not so calm now, she thought. There was a fire there, barely banked. It was exciting, terrifyingly exciting.

"Lousy timing," he continued when she didn't speak. "But I figure you can't always pick the right time and the right place. I'm going to do my job, but I think you should know I'm having trouble being objective. If you want someone else assigned to you, you'd better say so now."

"No." She answered too quickly, and she forced herself to backtrack. "I don't think I'm up to breaking in a new cop." Keep it light, she warned herself. "I'm not crazy about having one at all, but I'm almost used to you." She caught herself gnawing on her thumbnail and hastily dropped her hand into her lap. "As for the rest, we're not children. We can...handle it."

He knew he shouldn't expect her to admit the wanting wasn't all one-sided. So he would wait a little while longer.

When he rose, she sprang up so quickly that he laughed. "I'm going to do the dishes, O'Roarke, not jump on you."

"I'll do them." She could have kicked herself. "One cooks, one cleans. O'Roarke rules."

"Fine. You've got a remote at noon, right?"

"How did you know?"

"I checked your schedule. Leave enough time for us to drop by my place so I can shower and change."

"I'm going to be in a mall with dozens of people," she began. "I don't think—"

"I do." With that, he left her alone.

Boyd was lounging on the couch with the paper and a last cup of coffee when Cilla came downstairs. He glanced over, and the casual comment he'd been about to make about her being quick to change died before it reached his tongue. He was glad he was sitting down.

She wore red. Vivid, traffic-stopping red. The short leather skirt was snug at the hips and stopped at midthigh. The jeans she usually wore hadn't given him a true measure of how long her legs were, or how shapely. The matching jacket crossed over her body to side snaps at the waist. It made him wonder what she was wearing beneath it.

She'd done something to her hair. It was still tumbled, but more artfully, and certainly more alluringly. And her face, he noted as he finally stood. She'd fiddled with that, as well—enough to highlight her cheekbones, accent her eyes, slicken her lips.

"Stupid," she muttered as she struggled with an earring. "I can never figure out why hanging things from your ears is supposed to be attractive." On a sigh, she stared down at the dangling columns and the little gold back in her palm. "Either these are defective or I am. Are you any good at this?"

She'd walked to him, her hand held out. Her scent was wheeling in his head. "At what?"

"Putting these in. I don't wear them for weeks at a time, so I've never really gotten the hang of it. Give me a hand, will you?"

He was concentrating on breathing, nice, slow, even breaths. "You want me to put that on for you?"

She rolled her eyes impatiently. "You catch on fast, Slick." She thrust the earring into his hand, then tucked the hair behind her right ear. "You just slide the post through, then fasten the little doodad on the back. That's the part I have trouble with."

He muttered something, then bent to the task. There was a pressure in his chest, and it was building. He knew he would never get that scent out of his system. Swearing softly, he struggled to pinch the tiny fastening with his fingertips.

"This is a stupid system."

"Yeah." She could barely speak. She'd known the minute he touched her that she'd made an enormous mistake. Bursts of sensations, flashes of images, were rushing into her. All she could do was stand still and pray he'd hurry up and finish.

The back of his thumb brushed up and down over her jaw. His fingertips grazed the sensitive area behind her ear. His breath fluttered warm against her skin until she had to bite back a moan.

She lifted an unsteady hand. "Listen, why don't we just forget it?"

"I've got it." Letting out a long breath, he stepped back an inch. He was a wreck. But some of the tension eased when he looked at her and saw that she was far from unaffected. He managed to smile then and flicked a finger over the swaying gold columns. "We'll have to try that again…when we've got more time."

Since no response she could think of seemed safe, she gave none. Instead, she retrieved his coat and her own from the closet. She set his aside and waited while he slipped into his shoulder holster. Watching him give his weapon a quick, routine check brought back memories she wanted to avoid, so she looked away. Pulling open the door, she stepped into the sunlight and left him to follow when he was ready.

He made no comment when he joined her.

"Do you mind if I tune the station in?" she asked as they settled into his car.

"It's on memory. Number three."

Pleased, she turned it on. The morning team was chattering away, punctuating their jokes with sound effects. They plugged an upcoming concert, promised to give another pair of tickets away during the next hour, then invited the listening audience to the mall to see Cilla O'Roarke live and in person.

"She'll be giving away albums, T-shirts and concert tickets," Frantic Fred announced.

"Come on, Fred," his partner broke in. "You know those guys out there don't care about a couple of T-shirts. They want to—" he made loud, panting noises—"see Cilla." There was a chorus of wolf whistles, growls and groans.

"Cute," Boyd muttered, but Cilla only chuckled.

"They're supposed to be obnoxious," she pointed out. "People like absurdity in the morning when they're dragging themselves out of bed or fighting traffic. Last quarter's Arbitron ratings showed them taking over twenty-four percent of the target audience."

"I guess you get a kick out of hearing some guy pant over you."

"Hey, I live for it." Too amused to be offended, she settled back. He certainly had a nice car for a cop. Some sporty foreign job that still smelled new. She was never any good with makes and models. "Come on, Slick, it's part of the act."

He caught himself before he could speak again. He was making a fool of himself. His own investigation had verified that both morning men were married, with tidy homes in the suburbs. Frantic Fred and his wife were expecting their first child. Both men had been with KHIP for nearly three years, and he'd found no cross-reference between their pasts and Cilla's.

Relaxing as the music began, Cilla gazed out the window. The day promised to be warm and sunny. Perhaps this would be the first hint of spring. And her first spring in Colorado. She had a weakness for the season, for watching the leaves bud and grow, the flowers bloom.

Yet in spring she would always think of Georgia. The magnolias, the camellias, the wisterias. All those heady scents.

She remembered a spring when she'd been five or six. Planting peonies with her father on a warm Saturday morning while the radio counted down the Top 40 hits of the week. Hearing the birds without really listening, feeling the damp earth under her hands. He'd told her they would bloom spring after spring and that she would be able to see them from her window.

She wondered if they were still there—if whoever lived in that house cared for them.

"Cilla?"

She snapped back. "What?"

"Are you all right?"

"Sure, I'm fine." She focused on her surroundings. There were big trees that would shade in the summer, trimmed hedges for privacy. A long, gently sloping hill led to a graceful three-story house fashioned from stone and wood. Dozens of tall, slender windows winked in the sunlight. "Where are we?"

"My house. I've got to change, remember?"

"Your house?" she repeated.

"Right. Everyone has to live somewhere."

True enough, she thought as she pushed the door open. But none of the cops she had ever known had lived so well. A long look around showed her that the neighborhood was old, established and wealthy. A country-club neighborhood.

Disconcerted, she followed Boyd up a stone path to an arched door outlined in etched glass.

Inside, the foyer was wide, the floors a gleaming cherry, the ceilings vaulted. On the walls were paintings by prominent twentieth-century artists. A sweep of stairway curved up to the second floor.

"Well," she said. "And I thought you were an honest cop."

"I am." He slipped the coat from her shoulders to toss it over the railing.

She had no doubts as to his honesty, but the house and all it represented made her nervous. "And I suppose you inherited all this from a rich uncle."

"Grandmother." Taking her arm, he led her through a towering arch. The living room was dominated by a stone fireplace topped with a heavy carved mantel. But the theme of the room was light, with a trio of windows set in each outside wall.

There was a scattering of antiques offset by modern sculpture. She could see what she thought was a dining room through another arch.

"That must have been some grandmother."

"She was something. She ran Fletcher Industries until she hit seventy."

"And what is Fletcher Industries?"

He shrugged. "Family business. Real estate, cattle, mining."

"Mining." She blew out a breath. "Like gold?"

"Among other things."

She linked her fingers together to keep from biting her nails. "So why aren't you counting your gold instead of being a cop?"

"I like being a cop." He took her restless hand in his. "Something wrong?"

"No. You'd better change. I have to be there early to prep."

"I won't be long."

She waited until he had gone before she sank onto one of the twin sofas. Fletcher Industries, she thought. It sounded important. Even prominent. After digging in her bag for a cigarette, she studied the room again.

Elegant, tasteful, easily rich. And way out of her league.

It had been difficult enough when she'd believed they were on fairly equal terms. She didn't like to admit it, but the thought had been there, in the back of her mind, that maybe, just maybe, there could be a relationship between them. No, a friendship. She could never be seriously involved with someone in law enforcement.

But he wasn't just a cop now. He was a rich cop. His name was probably listed on some social register. People who lived in houses like this usually had roman numerals after their names.

Boyd Fletcher III.

She was just Priscilla Alice O'Roarke, formerly from a backwater town in Georgia that wasn't even a smudge on the map. True, she had made something of herself, by herself. But you never really pulled out your roots.

Rising, she walked over to toss her cigarette in the fireplace.

She wished he would hurry. She wanted to get out of this house, get back to work. She wanted to forget about the mess her life was suddenly in.

She had to think about herself. Where she was going. How she was going to get through the long days and longer nights until her life was settled again. She didn't have the time, she couldn't afford the luxury of exploring her feelings for Boyd. Whatever she had felt, or thought she was feeling, was best ignored.

If ever there were two people more mismatched, she couldn't imagine them. Perhaps he had stirred something in her, touched something she'd thought could never be touched again. It meant nothing. It only proved that she was alive, still functioning as a human being. As a woman.

It would begin and end there.

The minute whoever was threatening her was caught, they would go their separate ways, back to their separate lives. Whatever closeness they had now was born of necessity. When the necessity passed, they would move apart and forget. Nothing, she reminded herself, lasted forever.

She was standing by the windows when he came back. The light was in her hair, on her face. He had never imagined her there, but somehow, when he looked, when he saw her, he knew he'd wanted her there.

It left him shaken, it left him aching to see how perfectly she fit into his home. Into his life. Into his dreams.

She would argue about that, he thought. She would struggle and fight and run like hell if he gave her the chance. He smiled as he crossed to her. He just wouldn't give her the chance.

"Cilla."

Startled, she whirled around. "Oh. I didn't hear you. I was—"

The words were swallowed by a gasp as he yanked her against him and imprisoned her mouth.

Earthquakes, floods, wild winds. How could she have known that a kiss could be grouped with such devastating natural disasters?

She didn't want this. She wanted it more than she wanted to breathe. She had to push him away. She pulled him closer. It was wrong, it was madness. It was right, it was beautifully mad.

As she pressed against him, as her mouth answered each frenzied demand, she knew that everything she had tried to convince herself of only moments before was a lie. What need was there to explore her feelings when they were all swimming to the surface?

She needed him. However much that might terrify her, for now the knowledge and the acceptance flowed through her like wine. It seemed she had waited a lifetime to need like this. To feel like this. Trembling and strong, dazed and clear-eyed, pliant and taut as a wire.

His hands whispered over the leather as he molded her against him. Couldn't she see how perfectly they fitted? He wanted to hear her say it, to hear her moan it, that she wanted him as desperately as he wanted her.

She did moan as he drew her head back to let his lips race down her throat. The thudding of her pulse heated the fragrance she'd dabbed there. Groaning as it tangled in his senses, he dragged at the snaps of her jacket. Beneath he found nothing but Cilla.

She arched back, her breath catching in her throat as he captured her breasts. At his touch it seemed they filled with some hot, heavy liquid. When her knees buckled, she gripped his shoulders for balance, shuddering as his thumbs teased her nipples into hard, aching peaks.

Mindlessly she reached for him, diving into a deep, intimate kiss that had each of them swaying. She tugged at his jacket, desperate to touch him as he touched her. Her hand slid over the leather of his holster and found his weapon.

It was like a slap, like a splash of ice water. As if burned, she snatched her hand away and jerked back. Unsteady, she pressed the palm of her hand against a table and shook her head.

"This is a mistake." She paced her words slowly, as if she were drunk. "I don't want to get involved."

"Too late." He felt as if he'd slammed full tilt into a wall.

"No." With deliberate care, she snapped her jacket again. "It's not too late. I have a lot on my mind. So do you."

He struggled for the patience that had always been part of his nature. For the first time in days he actively craved a cigarette. "And?"

"And nothing. I think we should go."

He didn't move toward her or away, but simply held up a hand. "Before we do, are you going to tell me you don't feel anything?"

She made herself look at him. "It would be stupid to pretend I'm not attracted to you. You already know you affect me."

"I want to bring you back here tonight."

She shook her head. She couldn't afford, even for an instant, to imagine what it would be like to be with him. "I can't. There are reasons."

"You've already told me there isn't anyone else." He stepped toward her now, but he didn't touch her. "If there was, I wouldn't give a damn."

"This has nothing to do with other men. It has to do with me."

"Exactly. Why don't you tell me what you're afraid of?"

"I'm afraid of picking up the phone." It was true, but it wasn't the reason. "I'm afraid of going to sleep, and I'm afraid of waking up."

He touched her then, just a fingertip to her cheek. "I know what you're going through, and believe me, I'd do anything to make it go away. But we both know that's not the reason you're backing away from me."

"I have others."

"Give me one."

Annoyed, she walked over to grab her purse. "You're a cop."

"And?"

She tossed her head up. "So was my mother." Before he could speak, she was striding back into the foyer to get her coat.

"Cilla—"

"Just back off, Boyd. I mean it." She shoved her arms into her coat. "I can't afford to get churned up like this before a show. For God's sake, my life's screwed up enough right now without this. If you can't let it alone, I'll call your captain and tell him I want someone else assigned. Now you can take me to the mall or I can call a cab."

One more push and she'd be over the edge, he thought. This wasn't the time for her to take that tumble. "I'll take you," he said. "And I'll back off. For now."

# Chapter 6

He was a man of his word, Cilla decided. For the rest of that day, and all of the next, they discussed nothing that didn't relate directly to the case.

He wasn't distant. Far from it. He stuck with her throughout her remote at the mall, subtly screening all the fans who approached her for a word or an autograph, all the winners who accepted their T-shirts or their albums.

It even seemed to Cilla that he enjoyed himself. He browsed through the record racks, buying from the classical, pop and jazz sections, chatted with the engineer about baseball and kept her supplied with a steady supply of cold soft drinks in paper cups.

He talked, but she noted that he didn't talk *to* her, not the way she'd become accustomed to. They certainly had conversations, polite and impersonal conversations. And not once, not even in the most casual of ways, did he touch her.

In short, he treated her exactly the way she'd thought she wanted to be treated. As an assignment, and nothing more.

While he seemed to take the afternoon in stride, even offering to buy her a burger between the end of the remote and the time she was expected back in the studio, she was certain she'd never spent a more miserable afternoon in her life.

It was Althea who sat with her in the booth over her next two shifts, and it was Althea who monitored the calls. Why Boyd's silence, and his absence, made it that much more difficult for her to concentrate, Cilla couldn't have said.

It was probably some new strategy, she decided as she worked. He was ignoring her so that she would break down and make the first move. Well, she wouldn't. She hit her audience with Bob Seger's latest gritty rock single and stewed.

She'd wanted their relationship to be strictly professional, and he was accommodating her. But he didn't have to make it seem so damned easy.

Undoubtedly what had happened between them—or what had almost happened between them—hadn't really meant that much to him. That was all for the best. She would get over it. Whatever it was. The last thing she needed in her life was a cop with a lazy smile who came from a moneyed background.

She wished to God she could go five minutes without thinking about him.

While Cilla juggled turntables, Althea worked a crossword puzzle. She had always been able to sit for hours at a time in contented silence as long as she could exercise her mind. Cilla O'Roarke, she mused, was a different matter. The woman hadn't mastered the fine art of relaxation. Althea filled the squares with her neat, precise printing and thought that Boyd was just the man to teach her how it was done.

Right now, Cilla was bursting to talk. Not to ask questions, Althea thought. She hadn't missed the quick disappointment on Cilla's face when Boyd hadn't been the one to drive her to the station for her night shift.

She's dying to ask me where he is and what he's doing, Althea thought as she filled in the next word. But she doesn't want me to think it matters.

It wasn't possible for her not to smile to herself. Boyd had been pretty closemouthed himself lately. Althea knew he had run a more detailed check on Cilla's background and that he had found answers that disturbed him. Personally, she thought. Whatever he had discovered had nothing to do with the case or he would have shared it with his partner.

But, no matter how close they were, their privacy was deeply respected. She didn't question him. If and when he wanted to talk it through, she would be there for him. As he would be there for her.

It was too bad, she decided, that when sexual tension reared its head, men and women lost that easy camaraderie.

Abruptly Cilla pushed away from the console. "I'm going to get some coffee. Do you want some?"

"Doesn't Nick usually bring some in?"

"He's got the night off."

"Why don't I get it?"

"No." Restlessness seemed to vibrate from her. "I've got nearly seven minutes before the tape ends. I want to stretch my legs."

"All right."

Cilla walked to the lounge. Billy had already been there, she noted. The floor gleamed, and the coffee mugs were washed and stacked. There was the lingering scent of the pine cleaner he always used so lavishly.

She poured two cups and as an afterthought stuck one leftover and rapidly hardening pastry in her pocket.

With a cup in each hand, she turned. In the doorway she saw the shadow of a man. And the silver gleam of a knife. With a scream, she sent the mugs flying. Crockery smashed and shattered.

"Miss O'Roarke?" Billy took a hesitant step into the light.

"Oh, God." She pressed the heel of one hand to her chest as if to force out the air trapped there. "Billy. I thought you were gone."

"I—" He stumbled back against the door when Althea came flying down the hallway, her weapon drawn. In an automatic response, he threw his hands up. "Don't shoot. Don't. I didn't do nothing."

"It's my fault," Cilla said quickly. She stepped over to put a reassuring hand on Billy's arm. "I didn't know anyone was here, and I turned around—" She covered her face with her hands. "I'm sorry," she managed, dropping them again. "I overreacted. I didn't know Billy was still in the station."

"Mr. Harrison had a lunch meeting in his office." He spoke quickly, his eyes darting from Althea to Cilla. "I was just getting to it." He swallowed audibly. "Lots of—lots of knives and forks left over."

Cilla stared at the handful of flatware he held and felt like a fool.

"I'm sorry, Billy. I must have scared you to death. And I've made a mess of your floor."

"That's okay." He grinned at her, relaxing slowly as Althea holstered her weapon. "I'll clean it right up. Good show tonight, Miss O'Roarke." He tapped the headphones that he'd slid around his neck. "You going to play any fifties stuff? You know I like that the best."

"Sure." Fighting nausea, she made herself smile. "I'll pick something out just for you."

He beamed at her. "You'll say my name on the air?"

"You bet. I've got to get back."

She hurried back to the booth, grateful that Althea was giving her a few moments alone. Things were getting pretty bad when she started jumping at middle-aged maintenance men holding dinner knives.

The best way to get through the nerves was to work, she told herself. Keeping her moves precise, she began to set up for what she called the "power hour" between eleven and midnight.

When Althea came back, bearing coffee, Cilla was inviting her audience to stay tuned for more music. "We've got ten hits in a row coming up. This first one's for my pal Billy. We're going back, way back, all the way back to 1958. It ain't Dennis Quaid. It's the real, the original, the awesome Jerry Lee Lewis with 'Great Balls of Fire.'"

After pulling off her headphones, she gave Althea a wan smile. "I really am sorry."

"In your place I probably would have gone through the roof." Althea offered her a fresh mug. "Been a lousy couple of weeks, huh?"

"The lousiest."

"We're going to get him, Cilla."

"I'm hanging on to that." She chose another record, took her time cuing it up. "What made you become a cop?"

"I guess I wanted to be good at something. This was it."

"Do you have a husband?"

"No." Althea wasn't sure where the questions were leading. "A lot of men are put off when a woman carries a gun." She hesitated, then decided to take the plunge. "You might have gotten the impression that there's something between Boyd and me."

"It's hard not to." Cilla lifted a hand for silence, then opened the mike to link the next song. "You two seem well suited."

As if considering it, Althea sat and sipped at her coffee. "You know, I wouldn't have figured you for the type to fall into the clichéd, sexist mind-set that says that if a man and woman work together they must be playing together."

"I didn't." Outraged, Cilla all but came out of her chair. At Althea's bland smile, she subsided. "I did," she admitted. Then her lips curved. "Kind of. I guess you've had to handle that tired line quite a bit."

"No more than you, I imagine." She gestured, both hands palms out, at the confines of the studio. "An attractive woman in what some conceive of as a man's job."

Even that small patch of common ground helped her to relax. "There was a jock in Richmond who figured I was dying to, ah...spin on his turntable."

Understanding and amusement brightened Althea's eyes. "How'd you handle it?"

"During my show I announced that he was hard up for dates and anyone interested should call the station during his shift." She grinned, remembering. "It cooled him off." She turned to her mike to plug the upcoming request line. After an update on the weather, a time check and an intro for the next record, she slipped her headphones off again. "I guess Boyd wouldn't be as easily discouraged."

"Not on your life. He's stubborn. He likes to call it patience, but it's plain mule-headed stubbornness. He can be like a damn bulldog."

"I've noticed."

"He's a nice man, Cilla, one of the best. If you're really not interested, you should make it clear up front. Boyd's stubborn, but he's not obnoxious."

"I don't want to be interested," Cilla murmured. "There's a difference."

"Like night and day. Listen, if the question's too personal, tell me to shut up."

A smile tugged at Cilla's mouth. "You don't have to tell me that twice."

"Okay. Why don't you want to be interested?"

Cilla chose a compact disc, then backed it up with two 45s. "He's a cop."

"So if he was an insurance salesman you'd want to be interested?"

"Yes. No." She let out a huff of breath. Sometimes it was best to be honest. "It would be easier. Then there's the fact that I made a mess of the one serious relationship I've had."

"All by yourself?"

"Mostly." She sent out the cut from the CD. "I'm more comfortable concentrating on my life, and Deborah's. My work and her future."

"You're not the type that would be happy for long with comfortable."

"Maybe not." She stared down at the phone. "But I'd settle for it right now."

So she was running scared, Althea thought as she watched Cilla work. Who wouldn't be? It had to be terrifying to be hounded and threatened by some faceless, nameless man. Yet she was handling it, Althea thought, better than she was handling Boyd and her feelings about him.

She had them, buckets of them. Apparently she just didn't know what to do with them.

Althea kept her silence as the calls began to come in. Cilla was afraid of the phone, afraid of what might be on the other end. But she answered, call after call, moving through them with what sounded like effortless style. If Althea hadn't been in the studio, watching the strain tighten Cilla's face, she would have been totally fooled.

She gave them their music and a few moments of her time. If her hand was unsteady, her finger still pushed the illuminated button.

Boyd had entered her life to protect it, not threaten it. Yet she was afraid of him. With a sigh, Althea wondered why it was that women's lives could be so completely turned upside down by the presence of a man.

If she ever fell in love herself—which so far she'd had the good sense to avoid—she would simply find a way to call the shots.

The tone of Cilla's voice had her snapping back. Recognizing the fear, sympathizing with it, Althea rose to massage her rigid shoulders.

"Keep him talking," she whispered. "Keep him on as long as you can."

Cilla blocked out what he said. She'd found it helped her keep sane if she ignored the vicious threats, the blood-chilling promises. Instead she kept her eye on the elapsed-time clock, grimly pleased when she saw that the one-minute mark had passed and he was still on the line.

She questioned him, forcing herself to keep her voice calm and even. He liked it best when she lost control, she knew. He would keep threatening until she began to beg. Then he would cut her off, satisfied that he had broken her again.

Tonight she struggled not to hear, just to watch the seconds tick away.

"I haven't hurt you," she said. "You know I haven't done anything to you."

"To him." He hissed the words. "He's dead, and it's because of you."

"Who did I hurt? If you'd tell me his name, I—"

"I want you to remember. I want you to say his name before I kill you."

She shut her eyes and tried to fill her head with sound as he described exactly how he intended to kill her.

"He must have been very important to you. You must have loved him."

"He was everything to me. All I had. He was so young. He had his whole life. But you hurt him. You betrayed him. An eye for an eye. Your life for his. Soon. Very soon."

When he cut her off, she turned quickly to send out the next record. She would backsell it, Cilla told herself. Her voice would be strong again afterward. Ignoring the other blinking lights, she pulled out a cigarette.

"They got a trace." Althea replaced the receiver, then moved over to put a hand on Cilla's shoulder. "They got a trace. You did a hell of a job tonight, Cilla."

"Yeah." She closed her eyes. Now all she had to do was get through the next hour and ten minutes. "Will they catch him?"

"We'll know soon. This is the first real break we've had. Just hang on to that."

She wanted to be relieved. Cilla leaned back as Althea drove her home and wondered why she couldn't accept this step as a step forward. They had traced the call. Didn't that mean they would know where he lived? They would have a name, and they would put a face, a person, together with that name.

She would go and see him. She would make herself do that. She would look at that face, into those eyes, and try to find a link between him and whatever she had done in the past to incite that kind of hate.

Then she would try to live with it.

She spotted Boyd's car at the curb in front of her house. He stood on the walk, his coat unbuttoned. Though the calendar claimed it was spring, the night was cold enough for her to see his breath. But not his eyes.

Cilla took a firm grip on the doorhandle, pushed it open. He waited as she moved up the walk toward him.

"Let's go inside."

"I want to know." She saw his eyes now and understood. "You didn't get him."

"No." He glanced toward his partner. Althea saw the frustration held under grim control.

"What happened?"

"It was a phone booth a couple miles from the station. No prints. He'd wiped it clean."

Struggling to hold on for a few more minutes, Cilla nodded. "So we're no closer."

"Yes, we are." He took her hand to warm it in his. "He made his first mistake. He'll make another."

Weary, she looked over her shoulder. Was it just her overworked nerves, or was he out there somewhere, in the shadows, close enough to see? Near enough to hear?

"Come on, let me take you inside. You're cold."

"I'm all right." She couldn't let him come with her. She needed to let go, and for that she needed privacy. "I don't want to talk about any of this tonight. I just want to go to bed. Althea, thanks for the ride, and everything else." She walked quickly to the front door and let herself inside.

"She just needs to work this out," Althea said, placing a hand on his arm.

He wanted to swear, to smash something with his hands. Instead, he stared at the closed door. "She doesn't want to let me help her."

"No, she doesn't." She watched the light switch on upstairs. "Want me to call for a uniform to stake out the house?"

"No, I'll hang around."

"You're off duty, Fletcher."

"Right. We can consider this personal."

"Want some company?"

He shook his head. "No. You need some sleep."

Althea hesitated, then let out a quiet sigh. "You take the first shift. I sleep better in a car than a bed, anyway."

There was a light frost that glittered like glass on the lawn. Cilla sighed as she studied it through her bedroom window. In Georgia the azaleas would be blooming. It had been years, more years than she could remember, since she had yearned for home. In that chill Colorado morning she wondered if she had made a mistake traveling more than halfway across the country and leaving all those places, all those memories of her childhood, behind.

Letting the curtain fall again, she stepped back. She had more to think about than an April frost. She had also seen Boyd's car, still parked at the curb.

Thinking of him, she took more time and more care dressing than was her habit. Not for a moment had she changed her mind about it being unwise to become involved with him. But it seemed it was a mistake she'd already made. The wisdom to face up to her mistakes was something she'd learned very early.

She smoothed her plum-colored cashmere sweater over her hips. It had been a Christmas present from Deborah, and it was certainly more stylish, with its high neck and its generous sleeves, than most of the clothes Cilla chose for herself. She wore it over snug black leggings and on impulse struggled with a pair of star-shaped earrings in glossy silver.

He was spread comfortably over her couch, the newspaper open, a mug of coffee steaming in his hand. His shirt was carelessly unbuttoned to the middle of his chest and wrinkled from being worn all night. His jacket was tossed over the back of the couch, but he still wore his shoulder holster.

She had never known anyone who could melt into his surroundings so easily. At the moment he looked as though he spent every morning of his life in that spot, in her spot, lazily perusing the sports page and drinking a second cup of coffee.

He looked up at her. Though he didn't smile, his utter relaxation was soothing. "Good morning."

"Good morning." Feeling awkward, she crossed to him. She wasn't certain whether she should begin with an apology or an explanation.

"Deborah let me in."

She nodded, then immediately wished she'd worn trousers with pockets. There was nothing to do with her hands but link them together. "You've been here all night."

"Just part of the service."

"You slept in your car."

He tilted his head. Her tone was very close to an accusation. "It wasn't the first time."

"I'm sorry." On a long, shaky breath, she sat on the coffee table across from him. Their knees bumped. He found it a friendly gesture. One of the friendliest she'd made with him. "I should have let you inside. I should have known you would stay. I guess I was—"

"Upset." He passed her his coffee. "You were entitled, Cilla."

"Yeah." She sipped, wincing a bit at the added sugar. "I guess I'd talked myself into believing that you were going to catch him last night. It even—it's weird, but it even unnerved me a bit thinking about finally seeing him, finally knowing the whole story. Then, when we got here and you told me...I couldn't talk about it. I just couldn't."

"It's okay."

Her laugh was only a little strained. "Do you have to be so nice to me?"

"Probably not." Reaching out, he touched her cheek. "Would you feel better if I yelled at you?"

"Maybe." Unable to resist, she lifted a hand to his. "I have an easier time fighting than I do being reasonable."

"I've noticed. Have you ever considered taking a day, just to relax?"

"Not really."

"How about today?"

"I was going to catch up with my paperwork. And I have to call a plumber. We've got a leak under the sink." She let her hand fall to her knees, where it moved restlessly. "It's my turn to do the laundry. Tonight I'm spinning records at this class reunion downtown. Bill and Jim are splitting my shift."

"I heard."

"These reunion things…they can get pretty wild." She was groping, feeling more foolish by the minute. He'd taken the empty cup and set it aside, and was now holding both of her hands lightly in his. "They can be a lot of fun, though. Maybe you'd like to come and…hang around."

"Are you asking me to come and…hang around, like on a date?"

"I'll be working," she began, then subsided. She was getting in deep. "Yes. Sort of."

"Okay. Can I sort of pick you up?"

"By seven," she said. "I have to be there early enough to set up."

"Let's make it six, then. We can have some dinner first."

"I…" Deeper and deeper. "All right. Boyd, I have to tell you something."

"I'm listening."

"I still don't want to get involved. Not seriously."

"Mm-hmm."

"You're completely wrong for me."

"That's just one more thing we disagree on." He held her still when she started to rise. "Don't pace, Cilla. Just take a couple deep breaths."

"I think it's important we understand up front how far this can go, and what limitations there are."

"Are we going to have a romance, Cilla, or a business arrangement?"

He smiled. She frowned.

"I don't think we should call it a romance."

"Why not?"

"Because it's...because a romance has implications."

He struggled against another smile. She wouldn't appreciate the fact that she amused him. "What kind of implications?" Slowly, watching her, he brought her hand to his lips.

"Just..." His mouth brushed over her knuckles, and then, when her fingers went limp, he turned her palm up to press a kiss to its center.

"Just?" he prompted.

"Implications. Boyd—" She shivered when his teeth grazed over her wrist.

"Is that all you wanted to tell me?"

"No. Can you stop that?"

"If I really put my mind to it."

She found that her own lips had curved. "Well, put your mind to it. I can't think."

"Dangerous words." But he stopped nibbling.

"I'm trying to be serious."

"So am I." Once again he stopped her from rising. "Try that deep breath."

"Right." She did, then plunged on. "Last night, when I lay down in the dark, I was afraid. I kept hearing him, hearing that voice, everything he'd said to me. Over and over. I knew I couldn't think of it. If I did, I'd go crazy. So I thought of you." She paused, waiting for the courage to go on. "And when I thought of you, it blocked out everything else. And I wasn't afraid."

His fingers tightened on hers. Her eyes were steady, but he saw that her lips trembled once before she pressed them together. She was waiting, he knew. To see what he would do, what he would say. She couldn't have known, couldn't have had any idea, that at that moment, at that one instant of time, he teetered off the edge he'd been walking and tumbled into love with her.  ·

And if he told her that, he thought as he felt the shock of the emotions vibrate through him, she would never believe it. Some women had to be shown, convinced, not merely told. Cilla was one of them.

Slowly he rose, drawing her up with him. He gathered her close, cradling her head on his shoulder, wrapping his arms around her. He could feel her shiver of relief as he kept the embrace quiet and undemanding.

It was just what she needed. How was it he seemed always to know? To be held, only held, without words, without promises. To feel the solid warmth of his body against her, the firm grip of his hands, the steady beat of his heart.

"Boyd?"

"Yeah." He turned his head just enough to kiss her hair.

"Maybe I don't mind you being nice to me after all."

"We'll give it a trial run."

She thought she might as well go all the way with it. "And maybe I've missed having you around."

It was his turn to take a deep breath and steady himself. "Listen." He slid his hands up to her shoulders. "I've got some calls to make. After, why don't I take a look at that leak?"

She smiled. "I can look at it, Slick. What I want is to have it fixed."

He leaned forward and bit her lower lip. "Just get me a wrench."

Two hours later, Cilla had her monthly finances spread out over the secondhand oak desk in the den that doubled as her office. There were two dollars and fifty-three cents lost somewhere in her checkbook, an amount she was determined to find before she paid the neat stack of bills to her right.

Her sense of order was something she'd taught herself, something she'd clung to during the lean years, the unhappy years, the stormy years. If amid any crisis she could maintain this small island of normalcy, however bland, she believed she would survive.

"Ah!" She found the error, pounced on it. Making the correction, she scrupulously ran her figures again. Satisfied, she filed away her bank statement, then began writing checks, starting with the mortgage.

Even that gave her an enormous sense of accomplishment. It wasn't rent, it was equity. It was hers. The house was the first thing she had ever owned other than the clothes on her back and the occasional secondhand car.

She'd never been poor, but she had learned, growing up in a family where the income was a combination of a cop's salary and the lean monthly earnings of a public defender, to count pennies carefully. She'd grown up in a rented house, and she'd never known the luxury of riding in a new car. College wouldn't have been impossible, but because of the strain it would have added to her parents' income at a time when their marriage was rocky, Cilla had decided to bypass her education in favor of a job.

She didn't regret it often. She resented it only a little, at odd times. But her ability to subsidize Deborah's partial scholarship made her look back to the time when she had made the decision. It had been the right one.

Now they were slowly creeping their way up. The house wasn't simply an acquisition, it was a statement. Family, home, roots. Every month, when she paid the mortgage, she was grateful she'd been given the chance.

"Cilla?"

"What? Oh." She spotted Boyd in the doorway. She started to speak again, then focused. He still had the wrench she'd given him. His hair was mussed and damp. Both his shirt and his slacks were streaked with wet. He'd rolled his sleeves up to the elbows. Water glistened on his forearms. "Oh," she said again, and choked on a laugh.

"I fixed it." His eyes narrowed as he watched her struggle to maintain her dignity. "Problem?"

"No. No, not a thing." She cleared her throat. "So, you fixed it."

"That's what I said."

She had to bite down on her lip. She recognized a frazzled male ego when she heard it. "That's what you said, all right. And since you've just saved me a bundle, the least I can do is fix you lunch. What do you think about peanut butter and jelly?''

"That it belongs in a plastic lunch box with Spiderman on the outside.''

"Well, I've got to tell you, Slick, it's the best thing I cook.'' Forgetting the bills, she rose. "It's either that or a can of tuna fish.'' She ran a fingertip down his shirt experimentally. "Did you know you're all wet?''

He held up one grimy hand, thought about it, then went with the impulse and rubbed it all over her face. "Yeah.''

She laughed, surprising him. Seducing him. He'd heard that laugh before, over the radio, but not once since he'd met her. It was low and rich and arousing as black silk.

"Come on, Fletcher, we'll throw that shirt in the wash while you eat your sandwich.''

"In a minute.'' He kept his hand cupped on her chin, pulling her to him with that subtle pressure alone. When his mouth met hers, her lips were still curved. This time, she didn't stiffen, she didn't protest. With a sigh of acceptance, she opened for him, allowing herself to absorb the taste of his mouth, the alluring dance of his tongue over hers.

There was a warmth here that she had forgotten to hope for. The warmth of being with someone who understood her. And cared, she realized as his fingers skimmed over her cheek. Cared, despite her flaws.

"I guess you were right,'' she murmured.

"Damn right. About what?''

She took a chance, an enormous one for her, and brushed at the hair on his forehead. "It is too late.''

"Cilla.'' He brought his hands to her shoulders again, battling back a clawing need, a ragged desire. "Come upstairs with me. I want to be with you.''

His words sent the passion leaping. He could see the fire of it glow in her eyes before she closed them and shook her head. "Give me some time. I'm not playing games here, Boyd, but the ground's pretty shaky and I need to think it through.'' On a steadying breath, she opened her eyes, and nearly smiled. "You're absolutely everything I swore I'd never fall for."

He brought his hands down to hers and gripped. "Talk to me."

"Not now." But she laced her fingers with his. It was a sign of union that was rare for her. "I'm not ready to dig it all up right now. I'd just like to spend a few hours here like real people. If the phone rings, I'm not going to answer it. If someone comes to the door, I'm going to wait until they go away again. All I want to do is fix you a sandwich and wash your shirt. Okay?"

"Sure." He pressed a kiss to her brow. "It's the best offer I've had in years."

## Chapter 7

There was a wall of noise—the backbeat, the bass, the wail of a guitar riff. There were spinning lights, undulating bodies, the clamor of feet. Cilla set the tone with her midnight voice and stood back to enjoy the results. The ballroom was alive with sound—laughter, music, voices raised in spurts of conversation. Cilla had her finger on the controls. She didn't know any of the faces, but it was her party.

Boyd sipped a club soda and politely avoided a none-too-subtle invitation from a six-foot blonde in a skimpy blue dress. He didn't consider this a trial. He'd spent a large portion of his career watching people, and he'd never gotten bored with it.

It was a hell of a party, and he wouldn't have minded a turn on the dance floor. But he preferred keeping his eye on Cilla. There were worse ways to spend the evening.

She presided over a long table at the front of the ballroom, her records stacked, her amps turned up high. She glittered. Her silver-sequined jacket and black stovepipe pants were a whole new look in tuxedos. Her hair was full and loose, and when she turned her head the silver stars at her ears glistened.

She'd already lured dozens of couples onto the dance floor, and they were bopping and swaying elbow to elbow. Others crowded around the edges in groups or loitered at the banquet tables, lingering over drinks and conversation.

The music was loud, hot and fast. He'd already learned that was how she liked it best. As far as he could tell, the class of 75 was having the time of their lives. From all appearances, Cilla was, too.

She was joking with a few members of the graduating class, most of them male. More than a few of them had imbibed freely at the cash bar. But she was handling herself, Boyd noted. Smooth as silk.

He didn't particularly like it when a man with a lineman's chest put a beefy arm around her and squeezed. But Cilla shook her head. Whatever brush-off she used, she sent the guy off with a smile on his face.

"There's more where that came from, boys and girls. Let's take you back, all the way back to prom night, 1975." She cued up the Eagles' "One Of These Nights," then skimmed the crowd for Boyd.

When she spotted him, she smiled. Fully, so that even with the room between them he could see her eyes glow. He wondered if he could manage to get her to look at him like that when they didn't have five hundred people between them. He had to grin when she put a hand to her throat and mimed desperate thirst.

Lord, he looked wonderful, Cilla thought as she watched him turn toward the bar. Strange, she would have thought a smoke-gray jacket would look too conservative on a man for her tastes. On him, it worked. So well, she mused with a wry smile, that half the female portion of the class of 75 had their eye on him.

Tough luck, ladies, she thought. He's mine. At least for tonight.

A little surprised by where her thoughts had landed, she shook herself back and chose a slip from the pile of requests next to the turntable. A nostalgic crowd, she decided and plucked another fifteen-year-old hit from her stack.

She liked working parties, watching people dance and flirt and gossip. The reunion committee had done a top-notch job on this one. Red and white streamers dripped from the ceiling, competing with a hundred matching balloons. The dance floor glittered from the light of a revolving mirror ball. When the music or the mood called for it, she could flick a switch on a strobe light and give them a touch of seventies psychedelia.

Mixed with the scents of perfume and cologne was the fragrance of the fresh flowers that adorned each table.

"This is for Rick and Sue, those high school sweeties who've been married for twelve years. And they said it was only puppy love. We're 'Rockin' All Over The World.'"

"Nice touch," Boyd commented.

She twisted her head and smiled. "Thanks."

He handed her a soft drink heaped with ice. "I've got a reunion coming up next year. You booked?"

"I'll check my schedule. Wow." She watched as a couple cut loose a few feet away. Other couples spread out as they put the dirty in dirty dancing. "Pretty impressive."

"Mmm. Do you dance?"

"Not like that." She let out a little breath. "I wish I did."

He took her hand before she could reach for another request slip. "Why don't you play one for me?"

"Sure. Name it."

When he poked through her discs, she was too amused to be annoyed. She could reorganize later. After choosing one, he handed it to her.

"Excellent taste." She shifted her mike. "We've got ourself a wild group tonight. Y'all having fun?" The roar of agreement rolled across the dance floor. "We're going to be here until midnight, pumping out the music for you. We've got a request here for Springsteen. 'Hungry Heart.'"

Fresh dancers streamed onto the floor. Couples twined around each other to sway. Cilla turned to speak to Boyd and found herself molded against him.

"Want to dance?" he murmured.

They already were. Body fitted to body, he took her on a long, erotically slow circle. "I'm working."

"Take five." He lowered his head to catch her chin between his teeth. "Until I make love with you, this is the next best thing."

She was going to object. She was sure of it. But she was moving with him, her body fine-tuned to his. In silent capitulation, she slid her arms around his neck. With their faces close, he smiled. Slowly, firmly, he ran his hands over her hips, up, lazily up to the sides of her breasts, then down again.

She felt as though she'd been struck by lightning.

"You've, ah, got some nice moves, Slick."

"Thanks." When their lips were a whisper apart, he shifted, leaving hers hungry as he nuzzled into her neck. "You smell like sin, Cilla. It's just one of the things about you that's been driving me crazy for days."

She wanted him to kiss her. Craved it. She moaned when his hands roamed into her hair, drawing her head back. Her eyes closed in anticipation, but he only brushed those tempting lips over her cheekbone.

Breathless, she clung to him, trying to fight through the fog of pleasure. There were hundreds of people around them, all moving to the erotic beat of the music. She was working, she reminded herself. She was—had always been—a sensible woman, and tonight she had a job to do.

"If you keep this up, I won't be able to work the turntable."

He felt her heart hammering against his. It wasn't enough to satisfy him. But it was enough to give him hope. "Then I guess we'll have to finish the dance later."

When he released her, Cilla turned quickly and chose a record at random. A cheer went up as the beat pounded out. She lifted the hair from the back of her neck to cool it. The press of bodies—or the press of one body—had driven the temperature up. She'd never realized what a dangerous pastime dancing could be.

"Want another drink?" Boyd asked when she drained her glass.

"No. I'm okay." Steadying herself, she reached for the request sheet on top of her pile. "This is a nice group," she said as she glanced across the room. "I like reunions."

"I think I figured that out."

"Well, I do. I like the continuity of them. I like seeing all these people who shared the same experience, the same little block of time. 1975," she mused, the paper dangling from her fingers. "Not the greatest era for music, with the dreaded disco onslaught, but there were a few bright lights. The Doobie Brothers were still together. So were the Eagles."

"Do you always measure time in rock and roll?"

She had to laugh. "Occupational hazard. Anyway, it's a good barometer." Tossing her hair back, she grinned at him. "The first record I spun, as a professional, was the Stones' 'Emotional Rescue.'

That was the year Reagan was elected the first time, the year John Lennon was shot—and the year the Empire struck back.''

"Not bad, O'Roarke."

"It's better than not bad." She considered him. "I bet you remember what was playing on the radio the first time you talked a girl into the back seat of your car."

"'Dueling Banjos.'"

"You're kidding."

"You asked."

She was chuckling as she opened the request sheet. Her laughter died. She thought for a moment her heart had stopped. Carefully she squeezed her eyes shut. But when she opened them again the boldly printed words remained.

I want you to scream when I kill you.

"Cilla?"

With a brisk shake of her head, she passed the note to Boyd.

He was here, she thought, panic clawing as she searched the room. Somewhere in this crowd of laughing, chattering couples, he was watching. And waiting.

He'd come close. Close enough to lay that innocent-looking slip of paper on her table. Close enough to look into her eyes, maybe to smile. He might have spoken to her. And she hadn't known. She hadn't recognized him. She hadn't understood.

"Cilla."

She jolted when Boyd put a hand to her shoulder, and she would have stumbled backward if he hadn't balanced her. "Oh, God. I thought that tonight, just this one night, he'd leave me alone."

"Take a break."

"I can't." Dazed, she clamped her hands together and stared around the room. "I have to—"

"I need to make a call," he told her. "I want you where I can see you."

He could still be here, she thought. Close enough to touch her. Did he have the knife? The long-bladed knife he'd so lovingly described to her? Was he waiting for the moment when the music was loud, when the laughter was at a peak, so that he could plunge it into her?

"Come on."

"Wait. Wait a minute." With her nails biting into her palms, she leaned into the mike. "We're going to take a short break, but don't cool down. I'll be back in ten to start things rocking again." Mechanically she shut off her equipment. "Stay close, will you?" she whispered.

With an arm snug around her waist, he began to lead her through the crowd. Every time they were bumped she shuddered. When a man pushed through the throng and grabbed both of her hands, she nearly screamed.

"Cilla O'Roarke." He had a pleasant, affable face dampened with sweat from a turn on the dance floor. He was beaming as Cilla stood as still as a statue and Boyd tensed beside her. "Tom Collins. Not the drink," he said, still beaming. "That's my name. I'm chairman of the reunion committee. Remember?"

"Oh." She forced her lips to curve. "Yes. Sure."

"Just wanted to tell you how thrilled we are to have you. Got a lot of fans here." He released one of her hands to sweep his arm out. "I'm about the biggest. There's hardly a night goes by I don't catch at least a part of your show. Lost my wife last year."

"I..." She cleared her throat. "I'm sorry."

"No, I mean I lost her. Came home one night and she and the furniture were gone. Never did find her—or the sectional sofa." He laughed heartily while Cilla searched for something to say. "Fact is, your show got me through some pretty lonely nights. Just wanted to thank you and tell you you're doing a hell of a job here tonight." He pressed a business card into her hand. "I'm in appliances. You just call me whenever you need a new refrigerator." He winked. "Give you a good deal."

"Thanks." It should be funny, she thought. Later it would be funny. "Nice seeing you, Tom."

"Pleasure's mine." He watched her walk away and beamed again.

Boyd steered her out of the ballroom and toward the nearest pay phone. "Hang on. Okay?"

She nodded, even managed to smile at a group of women herding toward the ladies' lounge. "I'm better now. I'm going to sit down right over there." She pointed to an arrangement of chairs and a potted plant.

Leaving Boyd digging for change, she walked over, then let her legs collapse under her.

It was a nightmare. She wished it was as simple as a nightmare so that she could wake up with the sun shining in her face. She had nearly gotten through an entire day without thinking of him.

Shaky, she pulled out a cigarette.

Perhaps it had been foolish to let herself believe he would give her a day of peace. But to have come here. The odds of him actually being one of the alumni were slim. Yet he'd gotten inside.

With her back pressed into the chair, she watched people file in and out of the ballroom. It could be any one of them, she thought, straining for some spark of recognition. Would she know him if she saw him, or would he be a complete stranger?

He could be someone standing behind her at the market, someone sitting across from her at a gas pump. He might be the man in front of her at the bank, or the clerk at the dry cleaners.

Anyone, she thought as she closed her eyes. He could be any one of the nameless, faceless people she passed in the course of a day.

Yet he knew her name. He knew her face. He had taken away her peace of mind, her freedom. He wouldn't be satisfied until he'd taken her life.

She watched Boyd hang up the phone and waited until he crossed to her. "Well?"

"Thea's coming by to pick up the paper. We'll send it to the lab." His hand found the tensed muscle at the curve of her neck and soothed. "I don't think we'll get prints."

"No." She appreciated the fact that he didn't give her any false hope. "Do you think he's still here?"

"I don't know." That was its own frustration. "It's a big hotel, Cilla. There's no security to speak of for this event. It wouldn't be very effective to try to close it off and interrogate everyone in it. If you want to take off early, I can tell them you're sick."

"No, I don't want to do that." She took a long last drag on her cigarette. "The only satisfaction I can get is from finishing out. Proving I'm not ready to fold. Especially if he *is* still around, somewhere."

"Okay. Remember, for the next hour, I'm never going to be more than a foot away."

She put a hand in his as she rose. "Boyd, he changed his approach, writing a note. What do you think it means?"

"It could mean a lot of things."

"Such as?"

"Such as it was the most convenient way to contact you tonight. Or he's starting to get sloppy."

"Or impatient," she added, turning to him at the doorway. "Be honest with me."

"Or impatient." He cupped her face in his hands. "He has to get through me first, Cilla. I can promise that won't be an easy job."

She made herself smile. "Cops like to think they're tough."

"No." He kissed her lightly. "Cops have to be tough. Come on. Maybe you've got 'Dueling Banjos' in there. You can play it for me for old times' sake."

"Not on a bet."

She got through it. He'd never doubted that she would, and yet the way she held on despite her fears amazed and impressed him. Not once did she bog down, break down or falter. But he saw the way she studied the crowd, searched the faces as the music raged around her.

Her hands moved constantly, tapping out the beat on the table, shifting through records, fiddling with the sequined studs on her pleated shirt.

She would never be serene, he thought. She would never be soothing. She would pace her way through life driven by nerves and ambition. She would make a demanding and unsettling companion.

Not what he'd had in mind on the rare occasions he'd considered marriage and family. Not even close, he realized with a faint smile. But she was exactly what he wanted and intended to have.

He would protect her with his life. That was duty. He would cherish her for a lifetime. That was love. If the plans he'd made ran smoothly, she would understand the difference very soon.

He, too, was searching the crowd, studying the faces, watching for any sign, any movement, that would bring that quick tensing of the gut called instinct. But the music raged on. The partygoers laughed.

He saw Althea enter. And so, he thought with a shake of his head, did most of the men in the room. He had to chuckle when he saw one woman jab her husband in the ribs as he gawked at the redhead skirting the dance floor.

"You always make an entrance, Thea."

She only shrugged. She was wearing a simple off-the-shoulder cocktail dress in basic black. "I should thank you for getting me out of what turned into an annoying evening. My date had a toothbrush in his pocket and a night of wild sex on his mind."

"Animal."

"Aren't they all?" She glanced past him to Cilla. Amusement faded, to be replaced by concern. "How's she holding up?"

"She's incredible."

She lifted one arched brow. "Partner, my sharp investigative skills lead me to believe that you are seriously infatuated with our assignment."

"I passed infatuation. I'm in love with her."

Thea's lips formed a thoughtful pout. "Is that with a lowercase or uppercase *L*?"

"That's in all caps." He looked away from Cilla to his partner. There were few others with whom he would share his private thoughts. "I'm thinking marriage, Thea. Want to be my best man?"

"You can count on me." Still, she laid a hand on his arm. "I don't want to be a drag, Boyd, but you've got to keep some perspective on this. The lady's in trouble."

He struggled against annoyance. "I can function as a cop and as a man." Because it wasn't something he wanted to discuss at length, he reached in his pocket. "Here's the note, for what it's worth."

She skimmed the message, then slipped it into her bag. "We'll see what the lab boys can do."

He only nodded. "The ex-husband looks clean." An enormous disappointment. "I finished running him through tonight. State Senator Lomax has been married for seven years, and has one point six children. He hasn't been out of Atlanta for three months."

"I finally got ahold of the station manager in Chicago. He had nothing but good things to say about Cilla. I checked out his story about being in Rochester the past week visiting his daughter. It pans. She had a girl. Seven pounds, six ounces. He faxed me the personnel files on the jocks and staff who were at the station when Cilla worked there. So far nothing.''

''When I come in Monday, we'll take a closer look.''

''I figured I'd go over the file this weekend. Stick close to our girl.''

''I owe you one, Thea.''

''You owe me more than one, but who's counting?'' She started out, pausing once, then twice, to refuse the offer of a dance. Then, again, to decline a more intimate offer.

Because a party was appreciated more when it ended on a fever pitch, Cilla chose the last three songs for their beat rather than their sentiment. Jackets were off, ties were undone and careful hairstyles were limp. When the last song ended, the dance floor was jammed.

''Thank you, class of 75, you've been great. I want to see all of you back here for your twentieth.''

''Good job,'' Boyd told her.

She was already stacking records as the crowd split off into groups. Phone numbers and addresses would be exchanged. A few of the goodbyes would be tearful. ''It's not over yet.''

It helped to work. She had to break down the equipment, and with the help of the hotel staff she would load it into Boyd's car. Then there would be a trip back to the station and the unloading. After that, maybe she would allow herself to think again.

''It *was* a good job.''

She looked up, surprised. ''Mark? What are you doing here?''

''I could say I was checking up on one of my jocks.'' He picked up one of the 45s and laughed. ''God, don't tell me you actually played this.''

''It was pretty hot in 75.'' Suspicious, she took it back from him. ''Now, why don't you tell me what you're really doing here?''

Feeling nostalgic himself, he glanced around. He and his wife had met in high school. ''I'm here to get my equipment.''

''Since when does the station manager load equipment?''

''I'm the boss,'' he reminded her. ''I can do whatever I want. And as of now..." he glanced casually at his watch "you're on sick leave."

It was suddenly very clear. She shot an accusing look at Boyd. "I'm not sick."

"You are if I say you are," Mark countered. "If I see you at the station before your shift Monday night, you're fired."

"Damn it, Mark."

"Take it or leave it." Softening the blow, he put his hands on her shoulders. "It's business, Cilla. I've had jocks burn out from a lot less pressure than you're under. I want you for the long haul. And it's personal. You've got a lot of people worried about you."

"I'm handling it."

"Then you should be able to handle a couple of free days. Now get out of here."

"But who's going to—"

Boyd took her arm. "You heard the man."

"I hate being bullied," she muttered as he dragged her along.

"Too bad. I guess you figure KHIP is going to fall apart without you there for a weekend."

Without turning her head, she shifted her eyes and aimed a killing look at him. "That's not the point."

"No, the point is you need a rest, and you're going to get it."

She grabbed her coat before he could help her on with it. "Just what the hell am I supposed to do with myself?"

"We'll think of something."

Seething with resentment, she stalked out to the parking lot. A few stragglers from the reunion loitered around their cars. She plopped into the passenger's seat and scowled.

"Since when did *we* come into it?"

"Since, by an odd coincidence, I've also got the weekend off."

Eyes narrowed, she studied him as he conscientiously buckled her seat belt. "It smells like a conspiracy."

"You haven't seen anything yet."

He deliberately chose a cassette of classical music and popped it into the tape player before driving out of the lot.

"Mozart?" she said with a sneer.

"Bach. It's called cleansing the palate."

On a heavy sigh, she reached for a cigarette. She didn't want people worried about her, didn't want to admit she was tired. Wasn't ready to admit she was relieved. "This stuff always puts me to sleep."

"You could use the rest."

She had her teeth clenched as she punched in the lighter. "I don't appreciate you running to Mark this way."

"I didn't run to Mark. I simply called him and suggested you could use some time."

"I can take care of myself, Slick."

"Your taxes are being used to see that I take care of you."

"Have I mentioned lately how much I dislike cops?"

"Not in the past twenty-four hours."

Apparently he wasn't going to rise to any of the bait she dangled and allow her to purge her annoyance with a fight. Maybe it was for the best after all, she decided. She could use the time to catch up on her reading. The last two issues of *Radio and Records* were waiting for her attention. She also wanted to look through one of the garden magazines that had come in the mail. It would be nice to plant some summer flowers around the house, maybe some bushes. She hadn't a clue what sort of thing suited Denver's climate.

The idea made her smile. She would buy a window box, and maybe one of those hanging baskets. Perhaps that was why she didn't notice they were heading in the wrong direction until Boyd had been driving for twenty minutes.

"Where are we?" She sat up quickly, blinking.

"On 70, heading west."

"Highway 70? What the devil are we doing on 70?"

"Driving to the mountains."

"The mountains." Groggy, she pushed back her tumbled hair. "What mountains?"

"I think they're called the Rockies," he said dryly. "You might have heard of them."

"Don't get smart with me. You're supposed to be driving me home."

"I am—in a manner of speaking. I'm driving you to my home."

"I've seen your home." She jerked her thumb. "It's back that way."

"That's where I live in Denver. This is the place I have in the mountains. It's a very comfortable little cabin. Nice view. We're going for the weekend."

"*We* are not going anywhere for the weekend." She shifted in her seat to glare at him. "I'm spending the weekend at home."

"We'll do that next weekend," he said, perfectly reasonable.

"Look, Fletcher, as a cop you should know when you take somebody somewhere against their will it's considered a crime."

"You can file charges when we get back."

"Okay, this has gone far enough." It wouldn't do any good to lose her temper, she reminded herself. He was immune. "You might think you're doing this for my own good, but there are other people involved. There's no way I'm going to leave Deborah in that house alone while this maniac is running loose looking for me."

"Good point." He glided off at an exit and nearly had her relaxing. "That's why she's spending a couple of days with Althea."

"I—"

"She told me to tell you to have a good time. Oh," he continued while Cilla made incoherent noises, "she packed a bag for you. It's in the trunk."

"Just when did you plan all this?" That fabulous voice of hers was quiet. Too quiet, Boyd decided, bracing for the storm.

"I had some free time today. You'll like the cabin. It's peaceful, not too remote, and like I said, it has a nice view."

"As long as there's a nice high cliff I can throw you off of."

He slowed to navigate the winding road. "There's that, too."

"I knew you had nerve, Fletcher, but this goes beyond. What the hell made you think you could just put me in a car, arrange my sister's life and drive me off to some cabin?"

"Must've had a brainstorm."

"Brain damage is more like it. Get this straight. I don't like the country, I don't like rustic. I am not a happy camper, and I won't go."

"You're already going."

How could he stay so irritatingly calm? "If you don't take me back, right now, I'm going to—"

"What?"

She ground her teeth. "You have to sleep sometime." Her own words made her take a quantum leap. "You creep," she began on a fresh wave of fury. "If this is your way of getting me into bed, you miscalculated. I'll sit in the car and freeze first."

"There's more than one bedroom in the cabin," he said mildly. "You're welcome to share mine, or take any of the others. It's your choice."

She slumped back in her seat, finally speechless.

# Chapter 8

She didn't intend to romanticize it. Being swept away was fine in books about titled ladies and swaggering buccaneers. But it didn't play well in twentieth-century Denver.

She didn't intend to change her attitude. If the only revenge available to her was keeping a frosty distance, she would keep it very well. He wouldn't get one smile or one kind word until the entire ridiculous weekend was over.

That was why it was a shame that her first glimpse of the house was in the moonlight.

He called this a cabin? Cilla was grateful the music masked her surprised gasp. Her idea of a cabin was a squat little log structure in the middle of nowhere lacking all possible conveniences. The kind of place men went when they wanted to grow beards, drink beer and complain about women.

It was built of wood—a soft, aged wood that glowed warm in the dappled moonlight. But it was far from little. Multileveled, with interesting juts of timber and windows, it rested majestically amid the snow-dusted pine. Decks, some covered, some open, promised a breathtaking view from any direction. The metal roof glinted, making her wonder how it would be to sit inside and listen to rain falling.

But she stubbornly bit back all the words of praise and pushed out of the car. The snow came up to midcalf and clogged in her shoes.

"Great," she muttered. Leaving him to deal with whatever luggage they had, she trudged up to the porch.

So it was beautiful, she thought. It didn't make any difference. She still didn't want to be there. But since she was, and hailing a cab wasn't a possibility, she would keep her mouth shut, choose the bedroom farthest away from his and crawl into bed. Maybe she'd stay there for forty-eight hours.

Cilla kept the first part of the vow when he joined her on the porch. The only sounds were the planks creaking under his weight and the calling of something wild in the woods. After setting their bags aside, he unlocked the door and gestured her inside.

It was dark. And freezing. Somehow that made her feel better. The more uncomfortable it was, the more justified her foul temper. Then he switched on the lights. She could only gape.

The main room at the cabin's center was huge, an open gabled structure with rough-hewn beams and a charming granite fireplace. Thick, cushy furniture was arranged around it. Its freestanding chimney rose up through the high, lofted ceiling. Above, a balcony swept the width of the room, keeping with the theme of open space and wood. In contrast, the walls were a simple white, accented with glossy built-in shelves and many-paned doors and windows.

This was nothing like the arches and curves of his house in Denver. The cabin was all straight lines and simplicity. The wide planked floors were bare. A set of gleaming steps marched straight to the next level. Beside the fireplace was an open woodbox stacked with split logs. A touch of whimsy was added by grinning brass dragons that served as andirons.

"It warms up pretty quick," Boyd said, figuring she would start talking to him again when she was ready. He flipped on the heat before he shucked off his coat and hung it on a mirrored rack just inside the door. Leaving her where she was, he crossed to the fireplace and proceeded to arrange kindling and logs.

"The kitchen's through there." He gestured as he touched a match to some crumpled newspaper. "The pantry's stocked, if you're hungry."

She was, but she'd be damned if she'd admit it. She'd been getting a perverse pleasure in watching her breath puff out in front of her.

Sulking, she watched the flames rise up to lick at the logs. He even did that well, she thought in disgust. He'd probably been an Eagle Scout.

When she didn't respond, he stood up, brushing off his hands. As stubborn as she was, he figured he could outlast her. "If you'd rather just go to bed, there are four bedrooms upstairs. Not counting the sleeping porch. But it's a little cold yet to try that."

She knew when she was being laughed at. Setting her chin, she snatched up her bag and stalked up the stairs.

It was hard to tell which room was his. They were all beautifully decorated and inviting. Cilla chose the smallest. Though she hated to admit it, it was charming, with its angled ceiling, its tiny paneled bath and its atrium doors. Dropping her bag on the narrow bed, she dug in to see just what her sister—a partner in this crime—had packed.

The big, bulky sweater and thick cords met with approval, as did the sturdy boots and rag socks. The bag of toiletries and cosmetics was a plus, though she doubted she'd waste her time with mascara or perfume. Instead of her Broncos jersey and frayed chenille robe, there was a swatch of black silk with a matching—and very sheer— peignoir. Pinned to the bodice was a note.

Happy birthday a few weeks early. See you Monday.

Love, Deborah

Cilla blew out a long breath. Her own sister, she thought. Her own baby sister. Gingerly she held up the transparent silk. Just what had Deborah had in mind when she'd packed an outfit like this? she wondered. Maybe that question was best left unanswered. So she'd sleep in the sweater, Cilla decided, but she couldn't resist running her fingertips over the silk.

It felt…well, glorious, she admitted. Rarely did she indulge herself with anything so impractical. A small section of her closet was devoted to outfits like the one she'd worn to the reunion. She thought of them more as costumes than as clothes. The rest were practical, comfortable.

Deborah shouldn't have been so extravagant, she thought. But it was so like her. With a sigh, Cilla let the silk slide through her hands.

It probably wouldn't hurt just to try it on. After all, it was a gift. And no one was going to see it.

Heat was beginning to pour through the vents. Grateful, she slipped out of her coat and kicked off her shoes. She'd indulge herself with a hot bath in that cute claw-footed tub, and then she'd crawl under that very comfortable-looking quilt and go to sleep.

She meant to. Really. But the hot water lulled her. The package of bubble bath Deborah had tucked in the case had been irresistible. Now the night-spice fragrance enveloped her. She nearly dozed off, dreaming, with the frothy, perfumed water lapping over her skin.

Then there was the skylight over the tub, that small square of glass that let the stardust sprinkle through. Indulgent, Cilla thought with a sigh as she sank deeper in the tub. Romantic. Almost sinfully soothing.

It had probably been silly to light the pair of candles that sat in the deep windowsill instead of using the overhead lamp. But it had been too tempting. And as she soaked and dreamed, their scent wafted around her.

She was just making the best of a bad situation, she assured herself as she rose lazily from the tub. Unpinning her hair, she let it swing around her shoulders as she slipped into the teddy Deborah had given her.

It had hardly any back at all, she noted, just a silly little flounce that barely covered the essentials. It laced up the front, thin, glossy ribbons that crisscrossed and ended in a small bow in the center, just below her breasts. Though it barely covered them, as well, some clever structural secret lifted them up, made them look fuller.

Despite her best intentions, she traced a fingertip down the ribbons, wondering what it would be like to have Boyd unlace them. Imagining what it might be like to have his fingers brush over her just-pampered skin. Would he go slowly, one careful hook at a time, or would he simply tear at them until—

Oh Lord.

Cursing herself, she yanked open the door and dashed out of the steamy bath.

It was ridiculous to daydream that way, she reminded herself. She had never been a daydreamer. Always, always, she had known where she was going and how to get there. Not since childhood had she wasted time with fantasies that had no connection with ambition or success.

She certainly had no business fantasizing about a man, no matter how attracted she was to him, when she knew there was no possible way they could become a comfortable reality.

She would go to bed. She would shut off her mind. And she would pray that she could shut off these needs that were eating away at her. Before she could shove her bag on the floor, she saw the glass beside the bed.

It was a long-stemmed crystal glass, filled with some pale golden liquid. As she sampled it, she shut her eyes. Wine, she realized. Wonderfully smooth. Probably French. Turning, she saw herself reflected in the cheval glass in the corner.

Her eyes were dark, and her skin was flushed. She looked too soft, too yielding, too pliant. What was he doing to her? she asked herself. And why was it working?

Before she could change her mind, she slipped the thin silk over her shoulders and went to find him.

He'd been reading the same page for nearly an hour. Thinking about her. Cursing her. Wanting her. It had taken every ounce of self-possession he had to set that wine beside her bed and leave the room when he could hear her splashing lazily in the tub just one narrow door away.

It wasn't as if it were all one-sided, he thought in disgust. He knew when a woman was interested. It wasn't as if it were all physical. He was in love with her, damn it. And if she was too stupid to see that, then he'd just have to beat her over the head with it.

Laying the book on his lap, he listened to the bluesy eloquence of Billie Holiday and stared into the fire. The cheerful flames had cut the chill in the bedroom. That was the practical reason he had built a fire in here, as well as one on the main floor. But there was another, a romantic one. He was annoyed that he had daydreamed of Cilla as he set the logs and lit the kindling.

She had come to him, wearing something thin, flowing, seductive. She had smiled, held out her hands. Melted against him. When he had lifted her into his arms, carried her to the bed, they had...

Keep dreaming, he told himself. The day Cilla O'Roarke came to him of her own free will, with a smile and an open hand, would be the day they built snowmen in hell.

She had feelings for him, damn it. Plenty of them. And if she weren't so bullheaded, so determined to lock up all that incredible passion, she wouldn't spend so much time biting her nails and lighting cigarettes.

Resentful, restrictive and repressed, that was Priscilla Alice O'Roarke, he thought grimly. He picked up his wine for a mock toast. It nearly slid out of his hand when he saw her standing in the doorway.

"I want to talk to you." She'd lost most of her nerve on the short trip down the hall, but she managed to step into the room. She wasn't going to let the fact that he was sitting in front of a sizzling fire wearing nothing but baggy sweats intimidate her.

He needed a drink. After a gulp of wine, he managed a nod. He was almost ready to believe he was dreaming again—but she wasn't smiling. "Yeah?"

She was going to speak, she reminded herself. Say what was on her mind and clear the air. But she needed a sip of her own wine first. "I realize your motives in bringing me here tonight were basically well-intentioned, given the circumstances of the last couple of weeks. But your methods were unbelievably arrogant." She wondered if she sounded like as much of a fool to him as she did to herself. She waited for a response, but he just continued to stare blankly at her. "Boyd?"

He shook his head. "What?"

"Don't you have anything to say?"

"About what?"

A low sound of frustration rumbled in her throat as she stepped closer. She slammed the glass down on a table, and the remaining wine lapped close to the rim. "The least you can do after dragging me all the way up here is to listen when I complain about it."

He was barely capable of breathing, much less listening. In self-defense he took another long sip of wine. "If you had any legs—brains," he corrected, gnashing his teeth, "you'd know that a couple days away from everything would be good for you."

Anger flared in her eyes, making her all the more arousing. Behind her the flames shot high, and the light rippled through the thin silk she wore. "So you just took it on yourself to make the decision for me."

"That's right." In one jerky movement, he set the glass aside to keep it from shattering in his fingers. "If I had asked you to come here for a couple of days, you would have made a dozen excuses why you couldn't."

"We'll never know what I would have done," she countered "because you didn't give me the option of making my own choice."

"I'm doing my damnedest to give you the option now," he muttered.

"About what?"

On an oath, he stood up and turned away. Hands braced on the wall, he began, none too gently, to pound his forehead against it. As she watched him, confusion warred with anger.

"What are you doing?"

"I'm beating my head against the wall. What does it look like I'm doing?" He stopped, letting his forehead rest against the wood.

Apparently she wasn't the only one under too much strain, Cilla mused. She cleared her throat. "Boyd, why are you beating your head against the wall?"

He laughed and, rubbing his hands over his face, turned. "I have no idea. It's just something I've felt obliged to do since I met you." She was standing, a little uncertain now, running nervous fingertips up and down her silk lapel. It wasn't easy, but after a deep breath he found a slippery hold on control. "Why don't you go on to bed, Cilla? In the morning you can tear apart what's left of me."

"I don't understand you." She snapped out the words, then began to pace. Boyd opened his mouth but couldn't even manage a groan as he stared at the long length of her back, bare but for the sheerest of black silk, at the agitated swing of her hips, accented by the sassy little flounce. She was talking again, rapid-fire and irritated, but it was all just a buzzing in his head.

"For God's sake, don't pace." He rubbed the heel of his hand against his heart. In another minute, he was sure, it would explode out of his chest. "Are you trying to kill me?"

"I always pace when I'm mad," she tossed back. "How do you expect me to go quietly to bed after you've got me worked up this way?"

"Got you worked up?" he repeated. Something snapped—he would have sworn he heard it boomerang in his head as he reached out and snatched her arms. "I've got you worked up? That's rich, O'Roarke. Tell me, did you wear this thing in here tonight to make me suffer?"

"I…" She looked down at herself, then shifted uncomfortably. "Deborah packed it. It's all I've got."

"Whoever packed it, it's you who's packed into it. And you're driving me crazy."

"I just thought we should clear all this up." She was going to start stuttering in a minute. "Talk it through, like grown-ups."

"I'm thinking very much like a grown-up at the moment. If you want to talk, there's a chestful of big, thick wool blankets. You can wrap yourself up in one."

She didn't need a blanket. She was already much too warm. If he continued to rub his hands up and down the silk on her arms, the friction was going to cause her skin to burst into flame.

"Maybe I wanted to make you suffer a little."

"It worked." His fingers toyed with the excuse of a robe as it slid from her right shoulder. "Cilla, I'm not going to make this easy on you and drag you to that bed. I'm not saying the idea doesn't appeal to me a great deal. But if we make love, you're going to have to wake up in the morning knowing the choice was yours."

Wasn't that why she had come to him? Hoping he'd take matters out of her hands? That made her a coward—and, in a miserable way, a cheat.

"It's not easy for me."

"It should be." He slid his hands down to hers. "If you're ready."

She lifted her head. He was waiting—every bit as edgy as she, but waiting. "I guess I've been ready since I met you."

A tremor worked through him, and he struggled against his self-imposed leash. "Just say yes."

Saying it wasn't enough, she thought. When something was important, it took more than one simple word.

"Let go of my hands, please."

He held them another long moment, searching her face. Slowly his fingers relaxed and dropped away from hers. Before he could back up, she moved into him, wrapping her arms around his neck. "I want you, Boyd. I want to be with you tonight."

She brought her lips to his. There had already been enough words. Warm and willing, she sank into him.

For a moment, he couldn't breathe. The onslaught on his senses was too overwhelming. Her taste, her scent, the texture of silk against silk. There was her sigh as she rubbed her lips over his.

He remembered taking a kick in the solar plexus from one of his father's prized stallions. This left him just as debilitated. He wanted to savor, to drown, to lose himself, inch by glorious inch. But even as he slipped the robe from her shoulders she was pulling him to the bed.

She was like a whirlwind, hands racing, pressing, tugging, followed by the mad, erotic journey of her mouth. The pressure was building too fast, but when he reached for her she shimmied out of the silk and rushed on.

She didn't want him to regret wanting her. She couldn't have borne it. If she was to throw every shred of caution to the winds for this one night, she needed to know that it would matter. That he would remember.

His skin was hot and damp. She wished she could have lingered over the taste of it, the feel of it under her fingers. But she thought men preferred speed and power.

She heard him groan. It delighted her. When she tugged off his sweats, his hands were in her hair. He was murmuring something— her name, and more—but she couldn't tell. She thought she understood his urgency, the way he pulled her up against him. When he rolled over her, she whispered her agreement and took him inside her.

He stiffened. On an oath, he tried to level himself and draw back. But her hips arched and thrust against him, leaving his body no choice.

Her lips were curved when he lay over her, his face buried in her hair, his breath still shuddering. He wouldn't regret this, she thought, rubbing a soothing hand over his shoulder. And neither would she. It was more than she had ever had before. More than she had ever expected. There had been a warmth when he filled her, and a quiet contentment when she felt him spill into her. She thought how nice it would be to close her eyes and drift off to sleep with his body still warm on hers.

He was cursing himself, steadily. He was enraged by his lack of control, and baffled by the way she had rushed them both from kiss to completion. He'd barely touched her—in more ways than one. Though it was she who had set the pace at a sprint, he knew she hadn't come close to fulfillment.

Struggling for calm, he rolled away from her to stare at the ceiling. She'd set off bombs inside him, and though they had exploded, neither of them had shared the joy.

"Why did you do that?" he asked her.

Her hand paused on its way to stroke his hair. "I don't understand. I thought you wanted to make love."

"I did." He sat up, dragging the hair back from his face. "I thought you did, too."

"But I thought men liked..." She let her eyes close as the warmth drained out of her. "I told you I wasn't very good at it."

He swore, ripely enough to have her jolting. Moving quickly, she scrambled out of bed to struggle back into the peignoir.

"Where the hell are you going?"

"To bed." Because her voice was thick with tears, she lowered it. "We can just chalk this up to one more miscalculation." She reached down for her robe and heard the door slam. Bolting up, she saw Boyd turning a key in the lock, then tossing it across the room. "I don't want to stay here with you."

"Too bad. You already made your choice."

She balled up the robe, hugging it to her chest. So he was angry, she thought. And it was the real thing this time. It wouldn't be the first fight she had had about her inadequacies in bed. Old wounds, old doubts, trickled through her until she stood rigid with embarrassment.

"Look, I did the best I could. If it wasn't good enough, fine. Just let me go."

"Wasn't good enough," he repeated. As he stepped forward, she backed up, ramming into the carved footboard. "Somebody ought to bounce you on your head and knock some sense into it. There are two people in a bed, Cilla, and what happens in it is supposed to be mutual. I wasn't looking for a damn technician."

The angry flush died away from her face until it was marble white. Her eyes filled. Pressing his fingers against his own eyes, he swore. He hadn't meant to hurt her, only to show her that he'd wanted a partner.

"You didn't feel anything."

"I did." She rubbed tears from her cheek, infuriated. No one made her cry. No one.

"Then that's a miracle. Cilla, you barely let me touch you. I'm not blaming you." He took another step, but she evaded him. Searching for patience he stood where he was. "I didn't exactly fight you off. I thought— Let's just say by the time I understood, it was too late to do anything about it. I'd like to make it up to you."

"There's nothing to make up." She had herself under control again, eyes dry, voice steady. She wanted to die. "We'll just forget it. I want you to unlock the door."

He let out a huff of breath, then shrugged. When he turned to the door, she started to follow. But he only turned off the lights.

"What are you doing?"

"We tried it your way." In the moonlight, he moved across the room to light a candle, then another and another. He turned over the record that sat silent on the turntable, engaged the needle. The trembling cry of a tenor sax filled the room. "Now we try it mine."

She was starting to tremble now, from embarrassment and from fear. "I said I wanted to go to bed."

"Good." He swept her up into his arms. "So do I."

"I've had enough humiliation for one night," she said between her teeth.

She saw something in his eyes, something dark, but his voice was quiet when he spoke. "I'm sorry. I never meant to hurt you."

Though she held herself rigid, he lowered her gently to the bed.

With his eyes on hers, he spread out her hair, letting his fingers linger. "I've imagined you here, in the candlelight, with your hair on my pillow." He lowered his lips to brush them across hers. "Moonlight and firelight on your skin. With nothing and no one else but you for miles."

Moved, she turned her head away. She wouldn't be seduced by words and make a fool of herself again. He only smiled and pressed his lips to her throat.

"I love a challenge. I'm going to make love with you, Cilla." He slipped the strap of the peignoir from her shoulder to cruise the slope with his mouth. "I'm going to take you places you've never even dreamed of." He took her hand, pleased that her pulse had quickened. "You shouldn't be afraid to enjoy yourself."

"I'm not."

"You're afraid to relax, to let go, to let someone get close enough to find out what's inside you."

She tried to shift away, but his arms wrapped around her. "We already had sex."

"Yes, we did." He kissed one corner of her mouth, then the other. "Now we're going to make love."

She started to turn her head again, but he cupped her face with his hands. When his mouth came to hers again, her heart leaped into her throat. It was so soft, so tempting. As his fingertips glided across her face, she gave a strangled sigh. He dipped into her parted lips to tease her tongue with his.

"I don't want—" She moaned as his teeth nipped into her bottom lip.

"Tell me what you do want."

"I don't know." Her mind was already hazy. She lifted a hand to push him away, but it only lay limp on his shoulder.

"Then we'll make it multiple-choice." To please himself, and her, he ran a trail of kisses down her throat. "When I'm finished, you can tell me what you like best."

He murmured to her, soft, dreamy words that floated in her head. Then he drugged her with a kiss, long, lazy, luxurious. Though her body had begun to tremble, he barely touched her—just those fingertips stroking along her shoulders, over her face, into her hair.

His tongue slid over the tops of her breasts, just above the fringe of black lace. Her skin was like honey there, he thought, laving the valley between. Her heart jackhammered against him, but when she reached out, he took her hands in his.

Taking his time, his devastating time, he inched the lace down with his teeth. She arched up, offering herself, her fingers tensing like wires against his. He only murmured and, leaving a moist trail, eased the other curve of lace down.

His own breathing was short and shallow, but he fought back the urge to take greedily. With teasing openmouthed kisses he circled her, flicking his hot tongue over her rigid nipple until she shuddered and sobbed out his name. On a groan of pleasure, he suckled.

She felt the pressure deep inside, clenching, unclenching, to the rhythm of his clever mouth. Building, layering, growing, until she thought she would die from it.

Her breath was heaving as she writhed beneath him. Her nails dug hard into the backs of his hands as her body bowed, driven up by a knot of sensation. She heard her own cry, her gasp of relief and torment as something shattered inside her. Hot knives that turned to silky butterfly wings. A pain that brought unreasonable pleasure.

As every muscle in her body went lax, he covered her mouth with his. "Good Lord. You're incredible."

"I can't." She brought a hand up to press a palm to her temple. "I can't think."

"Don't. Just feel."

He straddled her. She was prepared for him to take her. He had already given her more than she had ever had. Shown her more than she had ever imagined. He began to unlace the peignoir with infinite care, infinite patience. His eyes were on her face. He loved being able to see everything she felt as it flickered there. Every new sensation, every new emotion. He heard the whisper of silk against her skin as he drew it down. He felt passion vibrate from her as he pressed his mouth to the quivering flesh of her stomach.

Floating, she stroked his hair, let her mind follow where her body so desperately wanted to go. This was heaven, more demanding, more exciting, more erotic, than any paradise she could have dreamed. She could feel the sheets, hot from her own body, tangled beneath her.

And the shimmer of silk as it slipped slowly, slowly away. His skin, dampened from pleasure, slid over hers. When her lips parted on a sigh, she could still taste him there, rich and male. Candlelight played against her closed lids.

There was so much to absorb, so much to experience. If it went on forever, it would still end too soon.

She was his now, he knew. Much more his than she had been when he had been plunged inside her. Her body was like a wish, long and slim and pale in the moonlight. Her breath was quick and quiet. And it was his name, only his name, she spoke when he touched her. Her hands flexed on his shoulder, urging him on.

He slid down her legs, taking the silk with him, nibbling everywhere as he went. The scent of her skin was a tormenting delight he could have lingered over endlessly. But her body was restless, poised. He knew she must be aching, even as he was.

He stroked a fingertip up her thigh, along that sensitive flesh, close, so close, to where the heat centered. When he slipped inside her, she was wet and waiting.

The breathless moan came first, and then the magic of his hands had her catapulting up, over a new and higher crest. Stunned by the power of it, she arched against him, shuddering again and again as she climbed. Though her hands clutched at him, he continued to drive her with his mouth, with his clever and relentless fingers, until she shot beyond pleasure to delirium.

Then her arms were around him and they were spinning off together, rolling over on the bed like lightning and thunder. The time for patience was over. The time for greed had begun.

He fought for breath as her hands raced over him. As she had the first time, she ripped away his control. But now she was with him, beat for beat and need for need. He saw her eyes glow, dark with passion, depthless with desire. Her slick skin shimmered with it in the shadowy light.

One last time he brought his mouth down on hers, swallowing her stunned cry, as he thrust himself into her. On a half sob she wrapped her arms and legs around him, locking tight so that they could race toward madness together.

\* \* \*

He was exhausted. Weak as a baby. And he was heavy. Using what strength he could find, Boyd rolled, taking Cilla with him so that their positions were reversed. Satisfied, he cradled her head and decided he very much liked the sensation of her body sprawled over his.

She shuddered. He soothed.

"Cold?"

She just shook her head.

Lazy as a cat, he stroked a hand down her naked back. "I might, in an hour or so, find the strength to look for the blankets."

"I'm fine."

But her voice wasn't steady. Frowning, Boyd cupped a hand under her chin and lifted it. He could see a tear glittering on her lashes. "What's this?"

"I'm not crying," she said, almost fiercely.

"Okay. What are you?"

She tried to duck her head again, but he held it firm. "You'll think I'm stupid."

"Probably the only time I couldn't think you were stupid is right after you've turned me inside out." He gave her a quick kiss. "Spill it, O'Roarke."

"It's just that I..." She let out an impatient breath. "I didn't think it was supposed to be that way. Not really."

"What way?" His lips curved. Funny, but it seemed he was getting his strength back. Maybe it was the way she was looking at him. Dazed. Embarrassed. Beautiful. "You mean, like good?" He slid his hands down to caress her bottom casually. "Or very good? Maybe you mean terrific. Or astounding."

"You're making fun of me."

"Uh-uh. I was hoping for a compliment. But you don't want to give me one. I figure you're just too stubborn to admit that my way was better than your way. But that's okay. I also figure I can keep you locked in here until you do."

"Damn it, Boyd, it's not easy for me to explain myself."

"You don't have to." There was no teasing note in his voice now. The look in his eyes made her weak all over again.

"I wanted to tell you that I never...no one's ever made me..." She gave up. "It was terrific."

"Yeah." He cupped a hand on the back of her head and brought her mouth to his. "Now we're going to shoot for astounding."

## Chapter 9

Cilla wrapped her arms across her body to ward off the chill and stared out over the pine and rock. Boyd had been right again. The view was incredible.

From this angle she could see the jagged, snowcapped peaks of the circling mountains. Closer, yet still distant, she caught the faint mist of smoke from a chimney. Evergreens stood, sturdy winter veterans, their needles whistling in the rising wind. There was the harsh whisper of an icy stream. She could catch glimpses of the water, just the glint of it in the fading sun.

The shadows were long, with late afternoon casting a cool blue light over the snow. Earlier she had seen a deer nuzzling her nose into it in search of the grass beneath. Now she was alone.

She'd forgotten what it was to feel so at peace. In truth, she wondered if she had ever known. Certainly not since earliest childhood, when she had still believed in fairy tales and happy endings. It had to be too late, when a woman was nearly thirty, to start believing again.

And yet she doubted things would ever be quite the same again.

He had kept his promise. He had taken her places she had never dreamed of. In one exquisitely long night, he had shown her that love meant you could accept as well as offer, take as well as give. She had learned more than the power of lovemaking in Boyd's bed. She had learned the power of intimacy. The comfort and the glory of it. For the first time in years, she had slept deeply and dreamlessly.

She hadn't felt awkward or uncomfortable on waking with him that morning. She had felt calm. Wonderfully calm. It was almost impossible to believe that there was another world apart from this spot. A world of pain and danger and fear.

Yet there was. And it was a world she would have to face again all too soon. She couldn't hide here—not from a man who wanted her dead, nor from her own miserable memories. But wasn't she entitled to a little more time to pretend that nothing else mattered?

It wasn't right. On a sigh, she lifted her face to the dying sun. No matter how she felt—or perhaps because she had come to feel so deeply—she had to be honest with herself, and with Boyd. She wouldn't let what had started between them go any further. Couldn't, she thought, squeezing her eyes tight. It had to be better to let her heart break a little now than to have it smashed later.

He was a good man, she thought. An honest one, a caring one. He was patient, intelligent and dedicated. And he was a cop.

She shivered and held herself more tightly.

There was a scar just under his right shoulder. Front and back, she remembered. From a bullet—that occupational hazard of law enforcement. She hadn't asked, and wouldn't, how he had come by it, when it had happened, or how near death it had taken him.

But neither could she hide from the fact that the scars she bore were as real as his.

She simply could not delude either of them into believing there was a future for them. She should never have allowed it to progress as far as it had. But that was done. They were lovers. And though she knew that was a mistake, she would always be grateful for the time she had had with him.

The logical thing to do would be to discuss the limitations of their relationship. No strings, no obligations. In all likelihood he would appreciate that kind of practicality. If her feelings had grown too far too fast, she would just have to get a grip on them.

She would simply have to talk herself out of being in love.

He found her there, leaning out on the railing as if she were straining to fly out above the pines, above the snowcapped peaks. The

nerves were coming back, he noted with some frustration. He wondered if she knew how relaxed she had been that morning when she
had stretched against him, waking gradually, turning to him so that
they could make slow, lazy love.

Now, when he touched her hair, she jolted before she leaned back
against his hand.

"I like your place, Slick."

"I'm glad." He intended to come back here with her, year after
year.

Her fingers danced over the railing, then groped in her pockets. "I
never asked you if you bought it or had it built."

"Had it built. Even hammered a few nails myself."

"A man of many talents. It's almost a shame to have a place like
this only for weekends."

"I've been known to break away for more than that from time to
time. And my parents use it now and again."

"Oh. Do they live in Denver?"

"Colorado Springs." He began to massage the tensing muscles in
her shoulders. "But they travel a lot. Itchy feet."

"I guess your father was disappointed when you didn't go into the
family business."

"No. My sister's carrying on the family tradition."

"Sister?" She glanced over her shoulder. "I didn't know you had
a sister."

"There's a lot you don't know." He kissed her lips when they
formed into a pout. "She's a real go-getter. Tough, high-powered
businesswoman. And a hell of a lot better at it than I would have
been."

"But aren't they uneasy about you being a cop?"

"I don't think it's a day-to-day worry. You're getting chilled," he
said. "Come on inside by the fire."

She went with him, moving inside and down the rear steps into
the kitchen. "Mmm... What's that smell?"

"I threw some chili together." He walked over to the center island,
where copper pots hung from the ceiling. Lifting the lid on a pan
simmering on the range, he sniffed. "Be ready in about an hour."

"I would have helped you."

"That's okay." He selected a Bordeaux from the wine rack. "You can cook next time."

She made a feeble attempt at a smile. "So you did like my peanut-butter-and-jelly special."

"Just like Mom used to make."

She doubted that his mother had ever made a sandwich in her life. People who had that kind of money also had a houseful of servants. As she stood feeling foolish, he set the wine on the counter to breathe.

"Aren't you going to take off your coat?"

"Oh. Sure." She shrugged out of it and hung it on a hook by the door. "Is there anything you want me to do?"

"Yes. Relax."

"I am."

"You were." Selecting two glasses from above the rack, he examined them. "I'm not sure what has you tied up again, Cilla, but we're going to talk it through this time. Why don't you go sit by the fire? I'll bring out the wine."

If he read her this easily·after a matter of weeks, Cilla thought as she went into the living room, how much would he see in a year? She settled on a low cushion near·the fire. She wasn't going to think of a year. Or even a month.

When he came in, she offered him a much brighter smile and reached for her wine. "Thanks. It's a good thing I didn't come here before I went house-hunting. I never would have settled on a house without a fireplace."

In silence, he settled beside her. "Look at me," he said at length. "Are you worried about going back to work?"

"No." Then she sighed. "A little. I trust you and Thea, and I know you're doing what you can, but I am scared."

"Do you trust me?"

"I said I did." But she didn't meet his eyes.

He touched a fingertip to her cheek until she faced him again. "Not just as a cop."

She winced, looked away again. "No, not just as a cop."

"And that's the trigger," he mused. "The fact that I am a cop."

"It's none of my business."

"We both know better."

"I don't like it," she said evenly. "I don't expect you to understand."

"I think I do understand." He leaned back against a chair, watching her as he sipped his wine. "I've done some checking, Cilla—necessary to the investigation. But I won't pretend that's the only reason I looked."

"What do you mean?"

"I looked into your background because I need to protect you. And I need to understand you. You told me your mother was a cop. It wasn't hard to track down what happened."

She clutched her glass in both hands and stared straight ahead, into the flames. After all these years, the pain was just as deadly. "So you punched some buttons on your computer and found out my mother was killed. Line of duty. That's what they call it. Line of duty," she repeated, her voice dull. "As if it were part of a job description."

"It is," he said quietly.

There was a flicker of fear in her eyes when she looked at him, then quickly away again. "Yeah. Right. It was just part of her job to be shot that day. Too bad about my father, though. He just happened to be in the wrong place at the wrong time. The old innocent bystander."

"Cilla, nothing's as black-and-white as that. And nothing's that simple."

"Simple?" She laughed and dragged her hair back from her face. "No, the word's *ironic*. The cop and the public defender, who just happen to be married, are going head-to-head over a case. They never agreed. Never once can I remember them looking at any one thing from the same angle. When this happened, they were talking about a separation—again. Just a trial one, they said." With a thoughtful frown, she studied her glass. "Looks like I'm out of wine."

Saying nothing, Boyd poured her more.

"So I guess you read the official report." She swirled the wine, then drank. "They brought this little creep in for interrogation. Three-time loser—armed robbery, assault, drugs. He wanted his lawyer present while the investigating officer questioned him. Talked about making a deal. He knew there wouldn't be any deal. They had him cold, and he was going to do hard time. He had two people to blame for it—in his head, anyway. His lawyer, and the cop who had collared him."

It was painful, still so painful, to remember, to try to picture an event she hadn't seen, one that had so drastically altered her life.

"They caught the guy who smuggled him the gun," she said softly. "He's still doing time." Taking a moment, she soothed her throat with wine. "There they were, sitting across from each other at the table—just as they might have been in our own kitchen— arguing about the law. The sonofabitch took out that smuggled snub-nosed .22 and shot them both."

She looked down at her glass again. "A lot of people lost their jobs over that incident. My parents lost their lives."

"I'm not going to tell you that cops don't die by mistake, unnecessarily, even uselessly."

When she looked at him, her eyes were eloquent. "Good. And I don't want the crap about how proud we're supposed to be of our valiant boys in blue. Damn it, she was my mother."

He hadn't just read the reports, he'd pored over them. The papers had called it a disgrace and a tragedy. The investigation had lasted more than six months, and when it was over eight officials had resigned or been replaced.

But over and above the facts, he remembered a file picture. Cilla, her face blank with grief, standing by the two graves, clutching Deborah's hand in hers.

"It was a horrible way to lose them," he said.

She just shook her head. "Yes. But in most ways I'd already lost my mother the day she joined the force."

"She had an impressive record," Boyd said carefully. "It wasn't easy for a woman back then. And it's always tough on a cop's family."

"How do you know?" she demanded. "You're not the one who sits at home and sweats. From the day I was old enough to understand, I waited for her captain to come to the door and tell us she was dead."

"Cilla, you can't live your life waiting for the worst."

"I lived my life waiting for a mother. The job always came first—

it came before Dad, before me, before Deb. She was never there when I needed her.'' She snatched her hand aside before he could grasp it. ''I didn't care if she baked cookies or folded my socks. I just wanted her to be there when I needed her. But her family was never as important as the masses she'd sworn to serve and protect.''

''Maybe she was too focused on her career,'' he began.

''Don't you compare me with her.''

His brow rose. ''I wasn't going to.'' Now he took her hand despite her resistance. ''It sounds like you are.''

''I've had to be focused. She had people who loved her, who needed her, but she never took time to notice. Cops don't have regular hours, she'd say. Cops don't have regular lives.''

''I didn't know your mother, and I can't comment on the choices she made, but don't you think it's time to cut it loose and get on with your life?''

''I have. I've done what I had to do. I've done what I've wanted to do.''

''And you're scared to death of what you're feeling for me because of my job.''

''It's not just a job,'' she said desperately. ''We both know it's not just a job.''

''Okay.'' He nodded. ''It's what I do, and what I am. We're going to have to find a way to deal with it.''

''It's your life,'' she said carefully. ''I'm not asking you to change anything. I didn't intend to get this involved with you, but I don't regret it.''

''Thanks,'' he muttered, and drained his own glass.

''What I'm trying to say is that if we're reasonable I think we can keep it uncomplicated.''

He set his glass aside. ''No.''

''No what?''

''No, I don't want to be reasonable, and it's already complicated.'' He gave her a long look that was very close to grim. ''I'm in love with you.''

He saw the shock. It flashed into her eyes an instant before she jerked back. The color drained away from her face.

"I see that thrills the hell out of you," he muttered. Rising, he heaved a log on the fire and cursed as he watched the sparks fly.

Cilla thought it best to stay exactly where she was. "Love's a real big word, Boyd. We've only known each other a couple of weeks, and not under the most ideal circumstances. I think—"

"I'm damn tired of you thinking." He turned back to face her. "Just tell me what you feel."

"I don't know." That was a lie, one she knew she would hate herself for. She was terrified. And she was thrilled. She was filled with regrets, and hammered by longings. "Boyd, everything that's happened has happened fast. It's as if I haven't had any control, and that makes me uneasy. I didn't want to be involved with you, but I am. I didn't want to care about you, but I do."

"Well, I finally managed to pry that out of you."

"I don't sleep with a man just because he makes me tingle."

"Better and better." He smiled as he lifted her hand to kiss her fingers. "I make you tingle, and you care about me. Marry me."

She tried to jerk her hand free. "This isn't the time for jokes."

"I'm not joking." Suddenly his eyes were very intense. "I'm asking you to marry me."

She heard a log shift in the grate. Saw the flicker of a new flame as it cast light and shadow over his face. His hand was warm and firm on hers, holding, waiting. Her breath seemed to be blocked somewhere beneath her heart. The effort of dragging in air made her dizzy.

"Boyd—"

"I'm in love with you, Cilla." Slowly, his eyes steady on hers, he pulled her closer. "With every part of you." Soft, persuasive, his lips cruised over hers. "I only want fifty or sixty years to show you." His mouth skimmed down her throat as he lowered her to the hearth rug. "Is that too much to ask?"

"No... Yes." Struggling to clear her mind, she pressed a hand against his chest. "Boyd, I'm not going to marry anyone."

"Sure you are." He nibbled lightly at her lips as his hands began to stroke—soothing and exciting at the same time. "You just have to get used to the fact that it's going to be me." He deepened the kiss, lingering over it until her hand lost its resistance and slid to his

back. "I'm willing to give you time." His lips curved as her murmured protest hummed against them. "A day or two. Maybe a
week."

She shook her head. "I've already made one mistake. I'm not ever
going to repeat it."

He caught her chin in his hand in a movement so quick that her
eyes flew open. In his eyes was a ripe, raging fury that was rare for
him, and all the more dangerous.

"Don't ever compare me with him."

She started to speak, but his fingers tightened once, briefly, and
silenced her.

"Don't ever compare what I feel for you with what anyone else
has felt."

"I wasn't comparing you." Her heart was hammering against his
chest. "It's me. It was my mistake, mine alone. And I'm never going
to make another one like it."

"It takes two people, damn it." Enraged, he braced himself over
her, then took both her hands in his. "If you want to play it that way,
fine. Ask yourself one question, Cilla. Has anyone else made you feel
like this?"

His mouth swooped down to take hers in a hot, rough, frantic kiss
that had her arching against him. In protest? In pleasure? Even she
couldn't tell. Sensations swarmed through her like thousands of swirling stars, all heat and light. Before she could draw and release a
breath, she was tossed into the storm.

No. Her mind all but screamed it. No one. Never. Only he had
ever caused a hunger so sharp and a need so desperate. Even as her
body strained against his, she struggled to remember that it wasn't
enough to want. It wasn't always enough to have.

Whipped by fury and frustration, he crushed his mouth to hers,
again, and then again. If only for this moment, he would prove to
her that what they had together was unique to them. She would think
of no one, remember nothing. Only him.

Her response tore through him, so complete, so right. The small,
helpless sound that purred up from her throat shuddered into him.
Like the flames that rose beside them, what they created burned and
consumed. The gentle loving that had initiated them both during the

night was replaced by a wild and urgent hunger that left no room for tender words and soft caresses.

She didn't want them. This was a new, a frenetic storm of needs that demanded speed and pushed for power. *Hurry.* She tore her hands from his to drag at his shirt. *Touch me.* Twin groans tangled as flesh met flesh. *More.* With a new aggression, she rolled onto him to take her mouth on a frantic race over his body. And still it wasn't enough.

His breath ragged, he stripped the layers of clothing from her, not caring about what he tore. One driving need was prominent. To possess. Hands gripped. Fingers pressed. Mouths devoured.

Agile and electric, she moved over him. Her face glowed, fragile porcelain in the firelight. Her body arched, magnificent in its new power, sheened with passion, shuddering from it, strengthened by it.

For one glorious moment she rose, witchlike, over him, her hands lifting up into her hair, her head thrown back as she lost herself in the wonder. Her body shuddered once, twice, as separate explosions burst within her. Even as she gasped, he gripped her hips and sheathed himself inside her.

He filled her. Not just physically. Even through the wracking pleasure she understood that. He, and only he, had found the key that opened every part of her. He, and only he, had found the way inside her heart, her mind. And somehow, without trying, she had found the way into his.

She didn't want to love him. She reached for his hands and gripped them tight. She didn't want to need him. Opening her eyes, she looked down at him. His eyes were dark and direct on hers. She knew, though she didn't speak, that he understood every thought in her head. On a sigh that was as much from despair as from delight, she bent down to press her mouth to his.

He could taste both the needs and the fears. He was determined to exploit the first and drive away the second. Staying deep inside her, he pushed up so that he could wrap his arms around her. He watched her eyes widen, stunned with pleasure, glazed with passion. Her fingers dug into his back. Her cry of release was muffled against his mouth seconds before he let himself go.

* * *

Bundled in a large, frayed robe, her feet covered with thick rag socks, Cilla sampled the chili. She liked sitting in the warm golden light in the kitchen, seeing the blanket of snow outside the windows, hearing the quiet moan of the wind through the pines. What surprised her, and what she wasn't ready to consider too carefully, was this feeling of regret that the weekend was almost over.

"Well?"

At Boyd's question, she looked back from the window. He sat across from her, his hair still mussed from her hands. Like her, he wore only a robe and socks. Though it made no sense, Cilla found the meal every bit as intimate as their loving in front of the fire.

Uneasy, she broke a piece of the hot, crusty bread on her plate. She was afraid he was going to bring up marriage again.

"Well what?"

"How's the chili?"

"The— Oh." She spooned up another bite, not sure if she was relieved or disappointed. "It's great. And surprising." Nervous again, she reached for her wine. "I'd have thought someone in your position would have a cook and wouldn't know how to boil an egg."

"My position?"

"I mean, if I could afford to hire a cook I wouldn't hassle with making sandwiches."

It amused him that his money made her uncomfortable. "After we're married we can hire one if you want."

Very carefully she set down her spoon. "I'm not going to marry you."

He grinned. "Wanna bet?"

"This isn't a game."

"Sure it is. The biggest in town."

She made a low sound of frustration. Picking up her spoon again, she began to tap it against the wood. "That's such a typically male attitude. It's all a game. You Tarzan, me stupid." His laughter only enraged her further. "Why is it men think women can't resist them— for sex, for companionship, for handling the details of life? Oh, Cilla, you need me. Oh, Cilla, I just want to take care of you. I want to show you what life's all about."

He considered a moment. "I don't remember saying any of those things. I think what I said is I love you and I want to marry you."

"It's the same thing."

"Not even close." He continued to eat, undisturbed.

"Well, I don't want to marry you, but I'm sure that won't make a difference. It never does."

He shot her one brief and dangerous look. "I warned you not to compare me to him. I meant it."

"I'm not just talking about Paul. I wasn't even thinking about Paul." After pushing her bowl aside, she sprang up to find a cigarette. "I hadn't given him a thought in years before all of this." She blew out an agitated stream of smoke. "And if I want to compare you to other men, I will."

He topped off his wine, then hers. "How many others have asked you to marry them?"

"Dozens." It was an exaggeration, but she didn't give a damn. "But somehow I've found the strength to resist."

"You weren't in love with them," he pointed out calmly.

"I'm not in love with you." Her voice had a desperate edge to it, and she had the sinking feeling that they both knew she was lying.

He knew, but it still hurt. The hurt settled into a dull, grinding ache in his belly. Ignoring it, he finished off his chili. "You're crazy about me, O'Roarke. You're just too pigheaded to admit it."

"I'm pigheaded?" Stifling a scream, she crushed out the cigarette. "I'm amazed that even you have the nerve to toss that one out. You haven't listened to a simple no since the day I met you."

"You're right." His gaze skimmed down her. "And look where it's got me."

"Don't be so damn smug. I'm not going to marry you, because I don't want to get married, because you're a cop and because you're rich."

"You are going to marry me," he said, "because we both know you'd be miserable without me."

"Your arrogance is insufferable. It's just as irritating—and just as pathetic—as moon-eyed pleading."

"I'd rather be smug," he decided.

"You know, you're not the first jerk I've had to shake off." She snatched up her wine before she began to pace. "In my business, you get good at it." She whirled back, stabbing a finger at him. "You're almost as bad as this kid I had to deal with in Chicago. Up to now, he's taken the prize for arrogance. But even he didn't sit there with a stupid grin on his face. With him it was flowers and poetry. He was just as much of a mule, though. I was in love with him, too. But I wouldn't admit it. I needed him to take care of me, to protect me, to make my life complete." She spun in a quick circle. "What nerve! Before you, I thought he couldn't be topped. Hounding me at the station," she muttered. "Hounding me at the apartment. Sending me an engagement ring."

"He bought you a ring?"

She paused long enough for a warning look. "Don't get any ideas, Slick."

Boyd kept his voice very cool, very even. "You said he bought you a ring. A diamond?"

"I don't know." She dragged a hand through her hair. "I didn't have it appraised. I sent it back."

"What was his name?"

She waved a hand dismissively. "I don't know how I got off on this. The point I'm trying to make is—"

"I said, what was his name?"

He rose as he asked. Cilla took a confused step back. He wasn't just Boyd now. He was every inch a cop. "I— It was John something. McGill... No, McGillis, I think. Look, he was just a pest. I only brought it up because—"

"You didn't work with a John McGillis in Chicago."

"No." Annoyed with herself, she sat down again. "We're getting off the subject, Boyd."

"I told you to tell me about anyone you were involved with."

"I wasn't involved with him. He was just a kid. Star-struck or something. He listened to the show and got hung up. I made the mistake of being nice to him, and he misunderstood. Eventually I set him straight, and that was that."

"How long?" Boyd asked quietly. "Just how long did he bother you?"

She was feeling more foolish by the minute. She could barely remember the boy's face. "Three or four months, maybe."

"Three or four months," he repeated. Taking her by the arms, he lifted her to her feet. "He kept this up for three or four months and you didn't mention it to me?"

"I never thought of it."

He resisted the temptation to give her a good shake, barely. "I want you to tell me everything you remember about him. Everything he said, everything he did."

"I can't remember."

"You'd better." Releasing her, he stepped back. "Sit down."

She obeyed. He had shaken her more than he realized. She tried to comfort herself with the fact that they were no longer arguing about marriage. But he had reminded her of something she'd allowed herself to forget for hours.

"All right. He was a night stocker at a market, and he listened to the show. He'd call in on his break, and we'd talk a little. I'd play his requests. One day I did a remote—I can't remember where—and he showed up. He seemed like a nice kid. Twenty-three or four, I guess. Pretty," she remembered. "He had a pretty, sort of harmless face. I gave him an autograph. After that he started to write me at the station. Send poems. Just sweet, romantic stuff. Nothing suggestive."

"Go on."

"Boyd, really—"

"Go on."

The best she could do was a muttered oath. "When I realized he was getting in too deep, I pulled back. He asked me out, and I told him no." Embarrassed, she blew out a breath. "A couple of times he was waiting out in the parking lot when I got off my shift. He never touched me. I wasn't afraid of him. He was so pathetic that I felt sorry for him, and that was another mistake. He misunderstood. I guess he followed me home from work, because he started to show up at the apartment. He'd leave flowers and slip notes under the door. Kid stuff," she insisted.

"Did he ever try to get in?"

"He never tried to force his way in. I told you he was harmless."

"Tell me more."

She rubbed her hands over her face. "He'd just beg. He said he loved me, that he would always love me and we were meant to be together. And that he knew I loved him, too. It got worse. He would start crying when he called. He talked about killing himself if I didn't marry him. I got the package with the ring, and I sent it back with a letter. I was cruel. I felt I had to be. I'd already accepted the job here in Denver. It was only a few weeks after the business with the ring that we moved."

"Has he contacted you since you've been in Denver?"

"No. And it's not him who's calling. I know I'd recognize his voice. Besides, he never threatened me. Never. He was obsessed, but he wasn't violent."

"I'm going to check it out." He rose, then held out a hand. "You'd better get some sleep. We're going to head back early."

She didn't sleep. Neither did he. And they lay in the dark, in silence; there was another who kept vigil through the night.

He lit the candles. New ones he'd just bought that afternoon. Their wicks were as white as the moon. They darkened and flared as he set the match against them. He lay back on the bed with the picture pressed against his naked breast—against the twin blades of the tattooed knives.

Though the hour grew late, he remained alert. Anger fueled him. Anger and hate. Beside him the radio hummed, but it wasn't Cilla's voice he heard.

She had gone away. He knew she was with that man, and she would have given herself to that man. She'd had no right to go. She belonged to John. To John, and to him.

She was beautiful, just as John had described her. She had deceptively kind eyes. But he knew better. She was cruel. Evil. And she deserved to die. Almost lovingly, he reached down a hand to the knife that lay beside him.

He could kill her the way he'd been taught. Quick and clean. But there was little satisfaction in that, he knew. He wanted her to suffer first. He wanted her to beg. As John had begged.

When she was dead, she would be with John. His brother would rest at last. And so would he.

# Chapter 10

The heat was working overtime in the precinct, and so was Boyd. While Maintenance hammered away at the faulty furnace, he pored over his files. He'd long since forsaken his jacket. His shoulder holster was strapped over a Denver P.D. T-shirt that had seen too many washings. He'd propped open a window in the conference room so that the stiff breeze from outside fought with the heat still pouring through the vents.

Two of his ongoing cases were nearly wrapped, and he'd just gotten a break in an extortion scam he and Althea had been working on for weeks. There was a court appearance at the end of the week he had to prepare for. He had reports to file and calls to make, but his attention was focused on O'Roarke, Priscilla A.

Ignoring the sweat that dribbled down his back, he read over the file on Jim Jackson, KHIP's all-night man. It interested and annoyed him.

Cilla hadn't bothered to mention that she had worked with Jackson before, in Richmond. Or that Jackson had been fired for drinking on the job. Not only had he broadcast rambling streams of consciousness, but he had taken to nodding off at the mike and leaving his audience with that taboo of radio. Dead air.

He'd lost his wife, his home and his prime spot as the morning jock and program director on Richmond's number-two Top 40 station.

When he'd gotten the ax, Cilla had taken over his duties as program director. Within six months, the number-two station had been number one. And Jackson had been picked up for drunk and disorderly.

As Althea stepped into the conference room carrying two dripping cans of soda, Boyd tossed the Jackson file across the table. Saying nothing, she passed one can to Boyd, popped the top on the second, then glanced at the file.

"He's clean except for a couple of D and D's," Althea commented.

"Revenge is high on the list for this kind of harassment. Could be he's carrying a grudge because she replaced him in Richmond and outdid him." Boyd took a swig of the warming soda. "He's only had the night spot in Denver for three months. The station manager in Richmond claims Jackson got pretty bent when they let him go. Tossed around some threats, blamed Cilla for undermining his position. Plus, you add a serious drinking problem to the grudge."

"You want to bring him in?"

"Yeah. I want to bring him in."

"Okay. Why don't we make it a doubleheader?" She picked up the file on Nick Peters. "This guy looks harmless—but then I've dated harmless-looking guys before and barely escaped with my skin. He doesn't date at all." She shrugged out of her turquoise linen jacket and draped it carefully over her chair back. "It turns out that Deborah has a couple of classes with him. Over the weekend she mentioned that he pumps her for information on Cilla all the time. Personal stuff. What kind of flowers does she like? What's her favorite color? Is she seeing anyone?"

She reached in her skirt pocket and drew out a bag of jelly beans. Carefully, and after much thought, she selected a yellow one. "Apparently he got upset when Deborah mentioned that Cilla had been married before. Deborah didn't think much of it at the time—put it down to his being weird. But she was worried enough to mention it over the weekend. She's a nice kid," Althea put in. "Real sharp. She's totally devoted to Cilla." Althea hesitated. "Over the course of the weekend, she told me about their parents."

"We've already covered that ground."

"I know we did." Althea picked up a pencil, ran it through her fingers, then set it aside again. "Deborah seems to think you're good for her sister." She waited until Boyd looked up. "I just wonder if her sister's good for you."

"I can take care of myself, partner."

"You're too involved, Boyd." She lowered her voice, though it couldn't have carried over the noise outside of the closed door. "If the captain knew you were hung up, personally, with an assignment, he'd yank you. He'd be right."

Boyd kicked back in his chair. He studied Althea's face, a face he knew as well as his own. Resentment simmered in him, but he controlled it. "I can still do my job, Thea. If I had any doubts about that, I'd yank myself."

"Would you?"

His eyes narrowed. "Yeah, I would. My first priority is my assignment's safety. If you want to go to the captain, that's your right. But I'm going to take care of Cilla, one way or the other."

"You're the one who's going to get hurt," she murmured. "One way or the other."

"My life. My problem."

The anger she'd hoped to control bubbled to the surface. "Damn it, Boyd, I care about you. It was one thing when you were infatuated by her voice. I didn't even see it as a problem when you met her and had a few sparks flying. But now you're talking serious stuff like marriage, and I know you mean it. She's got trouble, Boyd. She *is* trouble."

"You and I are assigned to take care of the trouble she's got. As for the rest, it's my business, Thea, so save the advice."

"Fine." Irked, she flipped open another file. "Bob Williams— Wild Bob—is so clean he squeaks. I haven't turned up a single connection with Cilla other than the station. He has a good marriage, goes to church, belongs to the Jaycees and for the last two weeks has been accompanying his wife to Lamaze classes."

"Nothing's turned up on the morning guys." Boyd took another swallow of the soda and wished it was an ice-cold beer.

"KHIP's just one big happy family."

"So it seems," Boyd mumbled. "Harrison looks solid, but I'm

still checking. He's the one who hired her, and he actively pursued her, offering her a hefty raise and some tidy benefits to persuade her to move to Denver and KHIP.''

Althea meticulously chose a red jelly bean. ''What about the McGillis guy?''

''I'm expecting a call from Chicago.'' He opened another file. ''There's the maintenance man. Billy Lomus. War veteran—Purple Heart and a Silver Star in Nam. Did two tours of duty before the leg mustered him out. He seems to be a loner. Never stays in one place more than a year or so. He did drop down in Chicago for a while a couple years back. No family. No close friends. Settled in Denver about four months ago. Foster homes as a kid.''

Althea didn't look up. ''Rough.''

''Yeah.'' Boyd studied her bent head. There weren't many who knew that Althea Grayson had been shuffled from foster home to foster home as a child. ''It doesn't look like we're going to have much luck inside the station.''

''No. Maybe we'll do better with McGillis.'' She looked up, face calm, voice even. Only one who knew her well would have seen that she was still angry. ''You want to start with Jackson or Peters?''

''Jackson.''

''Okay. We'll try it the easy way first. I'll call and ask him to come in.''

''Thanks. Thea,'' he added before she could rise, ''you have to be hit before you can understand. I can't turn off my feelings, and I can't turn back from what I've been trained to do.''

She only sighed. ''Just watch your step, partner.''

He intended to. And while he was watching his step, he was going to watch Cilla's. She wouldn't care for that, Boyd thought as he continued to study the files. From the moment he had told her that he loved her, she'd been trying to pull back.

But she wasn't afraid of him, he mused. She was afraid of herself. The deeper her feelings for him went, the more afraid she became to acknowledge them. Odd, but he hadn't known he would need the words. Yet he did. More than anything he could remember, he needed to have her look at him and tell him that she loved him.

A smile, a touch, a moan in the night—it wasn't enough. Not with

Cilla. He needed the bond, and the promise, that verbal connection. Three words, he thought. A simple phrase that came easily, often too easily—and could change the structure of people's lives.

They wouldn't come easily to Cilla. If she ever pushed them through the self-doubts, the barrier of defense, the fear of being hurt, she would mean them with all of her heart. It was all he needed, Boyd decided. And he would never let her take them back.

For now he had to put aside his own wants and needs and be a cop. To keep her safe, he had to be what she feared most. For her sake, he couldn't afford to think too deeply about where their lives would go once he closed the files.

"Boyd?" Althea poked her head back in the door. "Jackson's on his way in."

"Good. We should be able to catch Peters before he checks in at the station. I want to—" He broke off when the phone rang beside him. "Fletcher." He held up a hand to wave Althea inside. "Yeah. I appreciate you checking into it for me." He muffled the phone for a moment. "Chicago P.D. That's right," he continued into the receiver. "John McGillis." Taking up a pencil, he began making notes on a legal pad. In midstroke he stopped, fingers tightening. "When?" His oath was strong and quiet. "Any family? He leave a note? Can you fax it? Right." On the legal pad he wrote in bold letters: Suicide.

In silence, Althea lowered a hip to the table.

"Anything you can get me. You're sure he didn't have a brother? No. I appreciate it, Sergeant." He hung up and tapped the pencil against the pad. "Son of a bitch."

"We're sure it's the same McGillis?" Althea asked.

"Yeah. Cilla gave me the information she had on him, plus a physical description. It's the same guy. He cashed himself in almost five months ago." He let out a long breath. "Slit his wrists with a hunting knife."

"It fits, Boyd." Althea leaned over to check his notes. "You said McGillis was obsessing on Cilla, that he'd threatened to kill himself if she didn't respond. The guy over the phone is blaming her for the death of his brother."

"McGillis didn't have a brother. Only child, survived by his mother."

"Brother could be an emotional term. A best friend."

"Maybe." He knew it fit. What worried him was how Cilla would react. "The Chicago police are cooperating. They're sending us what information they've got. But I think it might be worth a trip east. We might get a lead from the mother."

Althea nodded. "Are you going to tell Cilla?"

"Yeah, I'm going to tell her. We'll talk to Jackson and Peters first, see if we can make a connection to McGillis."

Across town, Cilla dashed from the shower to the phone. She wanted it to be Boyd. She wanted him to tell her that he'd found John McGillis happily stocking shelves in Chicago. With her hair dripping down her back, she snatched up the phone.

"Hello."

"Did you sleep with him? Did you let him touch you?"

Her damp hands shook as she gripped the receiver. "What do you want?"

"Did you make promises to him the way you made promises to my brother? Does he know you're a whore and a murderer?"

"No. I'm not. I don't know why—"

"He'll have to die, too."

Her blood froze. The fear she thought she'd come to understand clawed viciously at her throat. "No! Boyd has nothing to do with this. It's—it's between you and me, just as you've said all along."

"He's involved now. He made his choice, like you made yours when you killed my brother. When I'm finished with him, I'm coming for you. Do you remember what I'm going to do to you? Do you remember?"

"You don't have to hurt Boyd. Please. Please, I'll do anything you want."

"Yes, you will." There was laughter, too, long, eerily lilting. "You'll do anything."

"Please. Don't hurt him." She continued to shout into the phone long after the connection went dead. With a sob tearing at her throat, she slammed the receiver down and raced to the bedroom to dress.

She had to talk to Boyd. To see him, face-to-face. To make certain he was unharmed. And to warn him, she thought frantically. She wouldn't, couldn't, lose someone else she loved.

With her hair still streaming wet, she dashed down the stairs and yanked open the door. She nearly ran over Nick Peters.

"Oh, God." Her hands clutched at her chest. "Nick."

"I'm sorry." With fumbling hands, he pushed up his glasses. "I didn't mean to scare you."

"I have to go." She was already digging in her purse for her keys. "He called. I have to get to Boyd. I have to warn him."

"Hold on." Nick picked up the keys, which she'd dropped on the stoop. "You're in no shape to drive."

"I've got to get to Boyd," she said desperately, gripping Nick by his coat. "He said he would kill him."

"You're all worked up about the cop." Nick's mouth thinned. "He looks like he can handle himself."

"You don't understand," she began.

"Yeah, I understand. I understand just fine. You went away with him." The note of accusation surprised her, and unnerved her enough that she glanced toward the black-and-white sitting at her curb. Then she shook herself. It was foolish, absolutely foolish, to be afraid of Nick.

"Nick, I'm sorry, but I don't have time to talk right now. Can we get into this later, at the station?"

"I quit." He bit off the words. "I quit this morning."

"Oh, but why? You're doing so well. You have a future at KHIP."

"You don't even know," he said bitterly. "And you don't care."

"But I do." When she reached out to touch his arm, he jerked back.

"You let me make a fool of myself over you."

Oh, God, not again. She shook her head. "Nick, no."

"You wouldn't even let me get close, and then he comes along and it's all over before you let it begin. Now they want me to come down to the police station. They want to question me." His lips trembled. "They think I'm the one who's been calling you."

"There has to be a mistake—"

"How could you?" he shouted. "How could you believe I'd want to hurt you?" He dropped the keys back into her hand. "I just came by to let you know I'd quit, so you don't have to worry about me bothering you again.''

"Nick, please. Wait." But he was already striding off to his car. He didn't look back.

Because her knees were weak, Cilla lowered herself to the stoop. She needed a moment, she realized. A moment to steady herself before she got behind the wheel of a car.

How could she have been so stupid, so blind, that she couldn't see that Nick's pride and ego were on the line? Now she had hurt him, simply by being unaware. Somehow she had to straighten out this mess her life had become. Then she had to start making amends.

Steadier, she rose, carefully locked the door, then walked to her car.

She hated police stations—had from the first. Fingering her plastic visitor's badge, she walked down the corridor. It had been scrubbed recently, and she caught the scent of pine cleaner over the ever-present aroma of coffee.

Phones rang. An incessant, strident, whirl of sound punctuated by voices raised to a shout or lowered to a grumble. Cilla turned into a doorway, to the heart of the noise, and scanned the room.

It was different from the cramped quarters where her mother had worked. And died. There was more space, less grime, and there was the addition of several computer work stations. The clickety-clack of keyboards was an underlying rhythm.

There were men and women, jackets off, shirts limp with sweat, though it was a windy fifty-five outside.

On a nearby bench, a woman rocked a fretful baby while a cop tried to distract it by jiggling a pair of handcuffs. Across the room, a young girl, surely just a teenager, related information to a trim woman cop in jeans and a sweatshirt. Silent tears coursed down the girl's face.

And Cilla remembered.

She remembered sitting in a corner of a squad room, smaller, hotter, dingier, than the one she stood in now. She had been five or six, and the baby-sitter had canceled because she'd been suffering from stomach flu. Cilla's mother had taken her to work—something about a report that couldn't wait to be written. So Cilla had sat in a corner with a doll and a Dr. Seuss book, listening to the phones and the voices. And waiting for her mother to take her home.

There had been a water cooler, she remembered. And a ceiling fan. She had watched the bubbles glug in the water and the blades whirl sluggishly. For hours. Her mother had forgotten her. Until, suffering from the same bug as her sitter, Cilla had lost her breakfast all over the squad room floor.

Shaky, Cilla wiped a hand over her damp brow. It was an old memory, she reminded herself. And not all of it. After she had been sick, her mother had cleaned her up, held her, taken her home and pampered her for the rest of the day. It wasn't fair to anyone to remember only the unhappy side.

But as she stood there she could feel all too clearly the dragging nausea, the cold sweat, and the misery of being alone and forgotten.

Then she saw him, stepping from another room. His T-shirt was damp down the front. Jackson was behind him, his hat in place, his face sheened with sweat and nerves. Flanking him was Althea.

Jackson saw her first. He took a hesitant step toward her, then stopped and shrugged. Cilla didn't hesitate. She walked to him to take his hand in both of hers.

"You okay?"

"Sure." Jackson shrugged again, but his fingers held tight on hers. "We just had to clear some things up. No big deal."

"I'm sorry. Look, if you need to talk, you can wait for me."

"No, I'm okay. Really." He lifted a hand to adjust his cap. "I guess if you screw up once you've got to keep paying for it."

"Oh, Jim."

"Hey, I'm handling it." He gave her a quick smile. "I'll catch you tonight."

"Sure."

"We appreciate your cooperation, Mr. Jackson," Althea put in.

"I told you, anything I can do to help Cilla, I'll do. I owe you," he said to Cilla, cutting her off before she could shake her head. "I owe you," he repeated, then crossed the room into the corridor.

"I could have told you that you were wasting your time with him," Cilla stated.

Boyd only nodded. "You could have told us a lot of things."

"Maybe." She turned back to him. "I need to talk to you, both of you."

"All right." Boyd gestured toward the conference room. "It's a little quieter in here."

"You want something cold?" Althea began before they settled. "I think they've finally fixed the furnace, but it's still like an oven in here."

"No, thanks. This won't take long." She sat, Althea across from her, Boyd at the table's head. She wanted to choose her words carefully. "Can I ask why you brought Jackson in?"

"You worked together in Richmond." Boyd shoved a file aside. "He had a drinking problem that got him fired, and you took over his job. He wasn't too happy about it at the time."

"No, he wasn't."

"Why didn't you tell us about it, Cilla?"

"I didn't think of it." She lifted a hand. "I honestly didn't think of it. It was a long time ago, and Jackson's come a long way. I'm sure he told you he's been in AA for over three years. He made a point of coming to see me when I was doing my run in Chicago. He wanted me to know he didn't blame me for what had happened. He's been putting his life back together."

"You got him the job at KHIP," Boyd added.

"I put in a good word for him," she said. "I don't do the hiring. He was a friend, he needed a break. When he's sober, Jackson's one of the best. And he wouldn't hurt a fly."

"And when he's drunk, he breaks up bars, threatens women and drives his car into telephone poles."

"That was a long time ago," Cilla said, struggling for calm. "And the point is, he is sober. There are some things you have to forgive and forget."

"Yes." He watched her carefully. "There are."

She thought of her mother again, and of that painful memory of the squad room. "Actually, I didn't come here to talk to you about Jackson. I got another call at home."

"We know." Althea's voice was brisk and professional. "They relayed the information to us here."

"Then you know what he said." Finding Althea's cool gaze unsympathetic, Cilla turned to Boyd. "He wants to hurt you now. He knows you're involved with me, and he's dragged you into whatever sick plans he has."

"They traced the call to another phone booth, just a couple of blocks from your house," Boyd began.

"Didn't you hear me?" Cilla slapped a fist on the table. Pencils jumped. "He's going to try to kill you, too."

He didn't reach for her hand to soothe her. At the moment, he thought, she needed him more professionally than personally. "Since I'm protecting you, he would have had to try all along. Nothing's changed."

"Everything's changed," she burst out. "It doesn't matter to him if you're with the police or not, it only matters that you're with me. I want you off the case. I want you reassigned. I don't want you anywhere near me until this is over."

Boyd crushed a disposable cup in his hand and tossed it in a wastebasket. "Don't be ridiculous."

"I'm not being ridiculous. I'm being practical." She turned to Althea, her eyes full of pleas. "Talk to him. He'll listen to you."

"I'm sorry," she said after a moment. "I agree with him. We both have a job to do, and at the moment you're it."

Desperate, Cilla whipped back to Boyd. "I'll go to your captain myself."

"He already knows about the call."

She sprang up. "I'll tell him I'm sleeping with you."

"Sit down, Cilla."

"I'll insist he take you off the case."

"Sit down," Boyd repeated. His voice was still mild, but this time she relented and dropped back in her chair. "You can go to the captain and request another officer. You can demand one. It won't make any difference. If he takes me off the case, I'll just turn in my badge."

Her head snapped up at that. "I don't believe you."

"Try me."

He was too calm, Cilla realized. And too determined. Like a brick wall, she thought in despair. Going head-to-head with him when he was like this was futile. "Boyd, don't you realize I couldn't handle it if anything happened to you?"

"Yes," he said slowly. "I think I do. Then you should realize I'm just as vulnerable where you're concerned."

"That's the whole point." She broke down enough to take his hands. "You are vulnerable. Listen to me." Desperate, she pulled his hand to her cheek. "For eight years I've wondered if it had been anyone else in the room with my mother that day, anyone else but my father, would she have been sharper, would she have been quicker. Would her concentration have been more focused. Don't make me have to ask that same question about you for the rest of my life."

"Your mother wasn't prepared. I am."

"Nothing I say is going to change your mind."

"No. I love you, Cilla. One day soon you're going to have to learn to accept that. In the meantime, you're going to have to trust me."

She took her hand away to drop it into her lap. "Then there's nothing more to say."

"There's this." He pulled a file closer. She was already upset, he mused. Already on edge. But they couldn't afford to wait. "John McGillis."

Her head aching, Cilla pressed the heels of her hands to her eyes. "What about him?"

"He's dead."

Slowly she lowered her hands. "Dead?" she repeated dully. "But he was just a kid. Are you sure? Are you sure it's the same one?"

"Yes." The man wished he could spare her this. The cop knew he couldn't. "He committed suicide about five months ago."

For a moment she only stared. The blood drained out of her face, inch by inch, until it was bone white. "Oh, God. Oh, dear God. He— He threatened, but I didn't believe—"

"He was unstable, Cilla. He'd been in and out of therapy since he was fourteen. Trouble with his mother, in school, with his contemporaries. He'd already attempted suicide twice before."

"But he was so quiet. He tried so hard to make me—" She stopped, squeezing her eyes shut. "He killed himself after I left Chicago to come here. Just as he said he would."

"He was disturbed," Althea said gently. "Deeply disturbed. A year before he contacted you, he was involved with a girl. When she broke things off, he swallowed a fistful of barbiturates. He was in a clinic for a while. He'd only been out for a few weeks when he made the connection with you."

"I was cruel to him." Cilla turned her purse over and over on her lap. "Really cruel. At the time I thought it was the best way to handle it. I thought he would be hurt, maybe hate me for a little while, then find some nice girl and... But he won't."

"I'm not going to tell you it wasn't your fault, because you're smart enough to know that yourself." Boyd's voice was deliberately devoid of sympathy. "What McGillis did, he did to himself. You were just an excuse."

She gave a quick, involuntary shudder. "It's not as easy for me. I don't live with death the way you do."

"It's never easy, not for anyone." He opened the file. "But there are priorities here, and mine is to make the connection between McGillis and the man we're after."

"You really think John's the reason I'm being threatened?"

"It's the only thing that fits. Now I want you to tell us everything you remember about him."

She released her death grip on the bag, then carefully folded her hands on the table. As clearly as possible, she repeated everything she'd already told him.

"Did you ever see him with anyone?" Boyd asked. "Did he ever talk about his friends, his family?"

"He was always alone. Like I told you, he used to call the station. I didn't meet him face-to-face for weeks. After I did, all he really talked about was the way he felt about me. The way he wanted us to be together." Her fingers twisted together. "He used to send me notes, and flowers. Little presents. It isn't that unusual for a fan to develop a kind of fantasy relationship with a jock. But then I began to see that it wasn't—" she cleared her throat "—it wasn't the normal kind of weird, if you know what I mean."

Boyd nodded and continued to write on the pad. "Go on."

"The notes became more personal. Not sexual so much as emotional. The only time he got out of hand was when he showed me

his tattoo. He had these knives tattooed on his chest. It seemed so
out of character for him, and I told him I thought it was foolish for
him to mark up his body that way. We were out in the parking lot.
I was tired and annoyed, and here was this kid pulling open his shirt
to show me this stupid tattoo. He was upset that I didn't like it.
Angry, really. It was the only time I saw him angry. He said that if
it was good enough for his brother, it was good enough for him.''

"His brother?" Boyd repeated.

"That's right."

"He didn't have a brother."

She stopped twisting her fingers. "Yes, he did. He mentioned him
a couple of times."

"By name?"

"No." She hesitated, tried to think. "No," she repeated, more
certain now. "He just mentioned that his brother was living out in
California. He hadn't seen him for a couple of months. He wanted
me to meet him. Stuff like that."

"He didn't have a brother." Althea turned the file around to skim
the top sheet again. "He was an only child."

Cilla shook her head. "So he made it up."

"No." Boyd sat back, studying his partner and Cilla in turn. "I
don't think the man we're after is a figment of John McGillis's imagination."

# Chapter 11

Her head was pounding in a dull, steady rhythm that made her ears ring. It was too much to absorb all at once. The phone call, Nick's visit, the reminders at the station house. John McGillis's suicide.

For the first time in her life, Cilla was tempted to shut herself in her room, lock the door and escape into a drugged sleep. She wanted peace, a few hours of peace, without guilt, without dreams, without fears.

No, she realized. More than that, much more than that, she wanted control over her life again. She'd taken that control for granted once, but she would never do so again.

She could think of nothing to say to Boyd as he followed her into the house. She was much too tired to argue, particularly since she knew the argument would be futile on her side. He wouldn't take himself off the case. He wouldn't believe her when she told him they could have no future. He refused to understand that in both instances she was looking out for his best interests.

Going to the kitchen, she went directly to the cupboard above the sink. From a bottle she shook out three extra-strength aspirin.

Boyd watched her fill a glass from the tap and swallow the pills. Her movements were automatic and just a little jerky. As she rinsed the glass, she stared out the window at the backyard.

There were daffodils, their yellow blooms still secreted in the protective green. Along the low fence they sprang up like slender spears, promising spring. She hadn't known they were there when she'd bought the house.

She wished they were blooming now so that she could see those cheerful yellow trumpets waving in the breeze. How bad could life be if you could look through your own window and see flowers blooming?

"Have you eaten?" he asked her.

"I don't remember." She folded her arms and looked out at the trees. There was the faintest hint of green along the branches. You had to look hard to see it. She wondered how long it would take for the leaves to unfurl and make shade. "But I'm not hungry. There's probably something around if you are."

"How about a nap?" He brought his hands to her shoulders and massaged them gently.

"I couldn't sleep yet." On a quiet sigh, she lifted a hand up to lay it over his. "In a few weeks I'll have to cut the grass. I think I'll like that. I've never had a lawn to mow before."

"Can I come over and watch?"

She smiled, as he'd wanted her to. "I love it here," she murmured. "Not just the house, though it means a lot to stand here, just here, and look out at something that belongs to me. It's this place. I haven't really felt at home anywhere since I left Georgia. It wasn't even something I realized until I came here and felt at home again."

"Sometimes you find what you want without looking."

He was talking of love, she knew. But she was afraid to speak of it.

"Some days the sky is so blue that it hurts your eyes. If you're downtown on one of those days when the wind has swept through and cleared everything, the buildings look painted against the sky. And you can see the mountains. You can stand on the corner in the middle of rush hour and see the mountains. I want to belong here."

He turned her to him. "You do."

"I never really believed that things could last. But I was beginning to, before this. I'm not sure I can belong here, or anywhere, until I can stop being afraid. Boyd." She lifted her hands to his face. Intense, she studied him, as if to memorize every plane, every angle. "I'm not just talking about belonging to a place, but to a person. I care for you more than I've cared for anyone in my life but Deborah. And I know that's not enough.''

"You're wrong." He touched his lips to hers. "It's exactly enough.''

She gave him a quick, frustrated shake of her head. "You just won't listen.''

"Wrong again. I listen, Cilla. I just don't always agree with what you say.''

"You don't have to agree, you just have to accept.''

"Tell you what—when this is over, you and I will have a nice, long talk about what we both have to accept.''

"When this is over, you might be dead." On impulse, she gripped him harder. "Do you really want to marry me?''

"You know I do.''

"If I said I'd marry you, would you take yourself off the case? Would you let someone else take over and go up to your cabin until it's done?''

He struggled against a bitter anger. "You should know better than to try to bribe a public servant.''

"I'm not joking.''

"No." His eyes hardened. "I wish you were.''

"I'll marry you, and I'll do my best to make you happy if you do this one thing for me.''

He set her aside and stepped back. "No deal, O'Roarke.''

"Damn it, Boyd.''

He jammed his hands into his pockets before he exploded. "Do you think this is some kind of trade-off? What you want for what I want? Damn you, we're talking about marriage. It's an emotional commitment and a legal contract, not a bartering tool. What's next?'' he demanded. "I give up my job and you agree to have my child?''

Shock and shame robbed her of speech. She held up both hands, palms out. "I'm sorry. I'm sorry," she managed. "I didn't mean for it to sound like that. I just keep thinking of what he said today. How he said it. And I can imagine what it would be like if you weren't here." She shut her eyes. "It would be worse than dying.''

"I am here." He reached for her again. "And I'm going to stay here. Nothing's going to happen to either of us.''

She pulled him close, pressed her face to his throat. "Don't be angry. I just haven't got a good fight in me right now."

He relented and lifted a hand to her hair. "We'll save it for later, then."

She didn't want to think about later. Only now. "Come upstairs," she whispered. "Make love with me."

Hand in hand they walked through the empty house, up the stairs. In the bedroom she closed the door, then locked it. The gesture was a symbol of her need to lock out everything but him for this one moment in time.

The sun came strong through the windows, but she felt no need for dim lights or shadows. There would be no secrets between them here. With her eyes on his, she began to unbutton her shirt.

Only days before, she thought, she would have been afraid of this. Afraid she would make the wrong move, say the wrong word, offer too much, or not enough. He had already shown her that she had only to hold out a hand and be willing to share.

They undressed in silence, not yet touching. Did he sense her mood? she wondered. Or did she sense his? All she knew was that she wanted to look, to absorb the sight of him.

There was the way the light streamed through the window and over his hair—the way his eyes darkened as they skimmed over her. She wanted to savor the line of his body, the ridges of muscle, the smooth, taut skin.

Could she have any idea how exciting she was? he wondered. Standing in the center of the room, her clothes pooled at her feet, her skin already flushed with anticipation, her eyes clouded and aware?

He waited. Though he wanted to touch her so badly his fingers felt singed, he waited.

She came to him, her arms lifted, her lips parted. Slim, soft, seductive, she pressed against him. Still, he waited. His name was a quiet sigh as she brought her mouth to his.

Home. The thought stirred inside her, a trembling wish. He was home to her. The strength of his arms, the tenderness of his hands, the unstinting generosity of his heart. Tears burned the backs of her lids as she lost herself in the kiss.

He felt the change, the slow and subtle yielding. It aroused unbearably. Strong, she was like a flame, smoldering and snapping with life and passion. In surrender, she was like a drug that seeped silently into his blood.

Lured by, lost in, her total submission, he lowered her to the bed. Her body was his. And so for the first time, he felt, was her mind, and her heart. He was careful to treat each gently.

So sweet, she thought dreamily. So lovely. The patient stroke of his fingers, the featherbrush of his lips, turned the bright afternoon into the rich secrets of midnight. Now that she knew where he could take her, she craved the journey all the more.

No dark thoughts. No nagging fears. Like flowers on the verge of blooming, she wanted to celebrate life, the simplicity of being alive and capable of love.

He aroused her thoroughly, thoughtfully, torturously. Her answering touch and her answering kiss were just as generous. What she murmured to him were not demands, but promises she desperately wanted to keep.

They knelt together in the center of the bed, lips curved as they touched, bodies almost painfully in tune. Her hair flowed through his fingers. His skin quivered at her light caress.

Soft, quiet sighs.

Heart-to-heart, they lowered again. Mouth teased mouth. Their eyes were open when he slid into her. Joined, they held close, absorbing a fresh riot of sensation. When they moved, they moved together, with equal wonder.

The booth seemed like another world. Cilla sat at the console, studying the controls she knew so well. Both her mind and body were sluggish. The clear-sighted control she had felt for a short time with Boyd that afternoon had vanished. She wanted only for the night to be over.

He had mentioned going to Chicago the next day. She intended to encourage him. If she couldn't convince him to be reassigned, at least she would have the satisfaction of knowing he would be miles away for a day or two. Away from her, and safe, she thought.

He, whoever he was, was closing in. She could feel it. When he struck, she wanted Boyd far away.

If this man was determined to punish her for what had happened to John McGillis, she would deal with it. Boyd had been right, to a point. She didn't blame herself for John's suicide. But she did share in the responsibility. And she couldn't keep herself from grieving for a young, wasted life.

The police would protect her, she thought as she cued up the next song. And she would protect herself. The new fear, the grinding fear, came from the fact that she didn't know how to protect Boyd.

"You're asleep at the switch," Boyd commented.

She shook herself. "No, just resting between bouts." She glanced at the clock. It was nearly midnight. Nearly time for the request line.

Once again the station was locked. There was only the two of them.

"You're nearly halfway home," he pointed out. "Look, why don't you come back to my place tonight? We can listen to my Muddy Waters records."

She decided to play dumb, because she knew it amused him. "Who?"

"Come on, O'Roarke."

It helped, a great deal, to see him grin at her. It made everything seem almost normal. "Okay, I'll listen to Muddy Whatsis—"

"Waters."

"Right—if you can answer these three music trivia questions."

"Shoot."

"Hold on." She set the next record, did a quick intro. She ruffled through her papers. "Okay, you've got three-ten to come up with them. Number one, what was the first British rock group to tour the States?"

"Ah, a trick question. The Dave Clark Five. The Beatles were the second."

"Not bad for an amateur. Number two. Who was the last performer at Woodstock?"

"Jimi Hendrix. You'll have to do better, O'Roarke."

"I'm just lulling you into complacency. Number three, and this is the big one, Fletcher. What year was Buddy Holly and the Crickets' hit 'That'll Be the Day' released?"

"Going back a ways, aren't you?"

"Just answer the question, Slick."

"Fifty-six."

"Is that 1956?"

"Yeah, that's 1956."

"Too bad. It was 57. You lose."

"I want to look it up."

"Go ahead. Now you'll have to come back to my place and listen to a Rolling Stones retrospective." She yawned hugely.

"If you stay awake that long." It pleased him that she had taken a moment out to play. "Want some coffee?"

She shot him a grateful look. "Only as much as I want to breathe."

"I'll get it."

The station was empty, he thought. Since Nick Peters had gotten his ego bruised and quit, there had been no one around to brew that last pot of the evening. He, too, glanced at the clock. He wanted to have it done and be back beside her before the phones started to ring.

He'd grab her a doughnut while he was at it, Boyd decided as he checked the corridor automatically. A little sugar would help her get through the night.

Before going to the lounge, he moved to the front of the building to check the doors. The locks were in place, and the alarm was engaged. His car was alone on the lot. Satisfied, he walked through the building and gave the same careful check to the rear delivery doors before he turned into the lounge.

It wasn't going to go on much longer. With the McGillis lead, Boyd had every confidence they would tie someone to the threats in a matter of days. It would be good to see Cilla without those traces of fear in her eyes, that tension in the set of her shoulders.

The restlessness would remain, he thought. And the energy. They were as much a part of her as the color of her hair.

He added an extra scoop of coffee to the pot and listened to her voice over the speaker as she segued from one record to the next.

That magic voice, he thought. He'd had no idea when he first heard it, when he was first affected by it, that he would fall in love with the woman behind it.

It was Joan Jett now, blasting out "I Love Rock and Roll." Though the lounge speaker was turned down to little more than a murmur, the feeling gritted out. It should be Cilla's theme song, he mused. Though he'd learned in their two days in his cabin that she was just as easily fascinated by the likes of Patsy Cline or Ella Fitzgerald.

What they needed was a good solid week in the mountains, he decided. Without any outside tensions to interfere.

He took an appreciative sniff of the coffee as it began to brew and hoped that he could get to Chicago, find the answers he needed and make the trip back quickly.

He whirled, disturbed by some slight sound in the corridor. A rustle. A creak of a board. His hand was already on the butt of his weapon. Drawing it, turning his back to the side wall, he took three careful strides to the doorway, scanning.

Getting jumpy, he told himself when he saw nothing but the empty halls and the glare of security lights. But instinct had him keeping the gun in his hand. He'd taken the next step when the lights went out.

Cursing under his breath, he moved fast. Though he held his weapon up for safety, he was prepared to use it. Above, from the speakers, the passionate music continued to throb. Up ahead he could see the faint glow of lights from the booth. She was there, he told himself. Safe in those lights. Keeping his back to the wall, skimming his gaze up and down the darkened hallway, he moved toward her.

As he rounded the last turn in the hallway before the booth, he heard something behind him. He saw the storeroom door swing open as he whirled. But he never saw the knife.

"That was Joan Jett and the Blackhearts coming at you. It's 11:50, Denver, and a balmy forty-two degrees." Cilla frowned at the clock and wondered why Boyd was taking so long. "A little reminder that you can catch KHIP's own Wild Bob tomorrow at the Brown Palace Hotel downtown on 17th. And hey, if you've never been there, it's a very classy place. Tickets are still available for the banquet benefiting abused children. So open your wallets. It's twenty dollars stag, forty if you take your sweetie. The festivities start at seven o'clock, and Wild Bob will be spinning those discs for you." She potted up the next song. "Now get ready for a doubleheader to take you to midnight. This is Cilla O'Roarke. We've got the news, then the request line, coming up.''

She switched off her mike. Shrugging her shoulders to loosen them, she slipped off the headphones. She was humming to herself as she checked the program director's hot clock. A canned ad was next, then she'd *seg* into the news at the top of the hour. She pushed away from the console to set up for the next segment.

It was then that she saw that the corridor beyond the glass door was dark. At first she only stared, baffled. Then the blood rushed to her head. If the security lights were out, the alarm might be out, as well.

He was here. Sweat pearled cold on her brow as she gripped the back of her chair. There would be no call tonight, because he was here. He was coming for her.

A scream rose in her throat to drown in a flood of panic.

Boyd. He had also come for Boyd.

Propelled by a new terror, she hit the door at a run.

''Boyd!'' She shouted for him, stumbling in the dark. Her forward motion stopped when she saw the shadow move toward her. Though it was only a shape, formless in the darkened corridor, she knew. Groping behind her, she stepped back. ''Where's Boyd? What have you done with him?'' She stepped back again. The lights from the booth slanted through the glass and split the dark in two.

She started to speak again, to beg, then nearly fainted with relief. ''Oh, God, it's you. I didn't know you were here. I thought everyone had left.''

''Everyone's gone,'' he answered. He moved fully into the light. And smiled. Cilla's relief iced over. He held a knife, a long-bladed hunting knife already stained with blood.

''Boyd,'' she said again.

''He can't help you now. No one can. We're all alone. I've waited a long time for us to be alone.''

''Why?'' She was beyond fear now. It was Boyd's blood on the blade, and grief left no room for fear. ''Why, Billy?''

''You killed my brother.''

''No. No, I didn't.'' She stepped back, into the booth. Hot hysteria bubbled in her throat. A cold chill sheened her skin. "I didn't kill John. I hardly knew him."

"He loved you." He limped forward, the knife in front of him, his eyes on hers. His feet were bare. He wore only camouflage pants and a dark stocking cap pulled low over his graying hair and brows. Though he had smeared his face and chest and arms with black, she could see the tattoo over his heart. The twin to the one she had seen over John McGillis's.

"You were going to marry him. He told me."

"He misunderstood." She let out a quick gasp as he jabbed with the knife. Her chair toppled with a crash as she fell back against the console.

"Don't lie to me, you bitch. He told me everything, how you told him you loved him and wanted him." His voice lowered, wavered, whispered, like the voice over the phone, and had her numbed heart racing. "How you seduced him. He was so young. He didn't understand about women like you. But I do. I would have protected him. I always protected him. He was good." Billy wiped his eyes with the hand holding the knife, then drew a gun out of his pocket. "Too good for you." He fired, ramming a bullet into the board above the controls. Cilla pressed both hands to her mouth to hold back a scream. "He told me how you lied, how you cheated, how you flaunted yourself."

"I never wanted to hurt John." She had to stay calm. Boyd wasn't dead. She wouldn't believe he was dead. But he was hurt. Somehow she had to get help. Bracing herself on the console, she reached slowly behind her and opened her mike, all the while keeping her eyes on his face. "I swear, Billy, I never wanted to hurt your brother."

"Liar," he shouted, lifting the knife to her throat. She arched back, struggling to control her shuddering. "You don't care about him. You never cared. You just used him. Women like you love to use."

"I liked him." She sucked in her breath as the knife nicked her throat. Blood trickled warm along her skin. "He was a nice boy. He—he loved you."

"I loved him." The knife trembled in his hand, but he pulled it back an inch. Cilla let out a long, quiet breath. "He was the only person I ever loved, who ever loved me. I took care of him."

"I know." She moistened her dry lips. Surely someone would come. Someone was listening. She didn't dare take her eyes from his to glance around to the phone, where the lights were blinking madly.

"He was only five when they sent me to that house. I would have hated it there, like I'd hated all the other places they'd sent me. But John lived there. He looked up to me. He cared. He needed me. So I stayed until I was eighteen. It was only a year and a half, but we were brothers."

"Yes."

"I joined the Army. When I'd have leave he'd sneak out to see me. His pig of a mother didn't want him to have anything to do with me, 'cause I'd gotten in some trouble." He fired again, randomly, and shattered the glass in the top of the door. "But I liked the army. I liked it fine, and John liked my uniform."

His eyes glazed over a moment, as he remembered. "They sent us to Nam. Messed up my leg. Messed up my life. When we came back, people wanted to hate us. But not John. He was proud of me. No one else had ever been proud of me."

"I know."

"They tried to put him away. Twice." Again he squeezed the trigger. A bullet plowed into the reel-to-reel six inches from Cilla's head. Sweaty fear dried to ice on her skin. "They didn't understand him. I went to California. I was going to find us a nice place there. I just needed to find work. John was going to write poetry. Then he met you." The glaze melted away from his eyes, burned away by hate. "He didn't want to come to California anymore. He didn't want to leave you. He wrote me letters about you, long letters. Once he called. He shouldn't have spent his money, but he called all the way to California to tell me he was getting married. You wanted to get married at Christmas, so he was going to wait. I was coming back for it, because he wanted me there."

She could only shake her head. "I never agreed to marry him. Killing me isn't going to change that," she said when he leveled the gun at her. "You're right, he didn't understand me. And I guess I didn't understand him. He was young. He imagined I was something I wasn't, Billy. I'm sorry, terribly sorry, but I didn't cause his death.''

"You killed him.'' He ran the flat of the blade down her cheek. "And you're going to pay.''

"I can't stop you. I won't even try. But please, tell me what you've done with Boyd.''

"I killed him.'' He smiled a sweet, vacant smile that made the weapons he carried incongruous.

"I don't believe you.''

"He's dead.'' Still smiling, he held the knife up to the light. "It was easy. Easier than I remembered. I was quick,'' he assured her. "I wanted him dead, but I didn't care if he suffered. Not like you. You're going to suffer. I told you, remember? I told you what I was going to do.''

"If you've killed Boyd,'' she whispered, "you've already killed me.''

"I want you to beg.'' He laid the knife against her throat again. "I want you to beg the way John begged.''

"I don't care what you do to me.'' She couldn't feel the knife against her flesh. She couldn't feel anything. From a long way off came the wail of sirens. She heard them without emotion, without hope. They were coming, but they were coming too late. She looked into Billy's eyes. She understood that kind of pain, she realized. It came when the person who meant the most was taken from you.

"I'm sorry,'' she said, prepared to die. "I didn't love him.''

On a howl of rage, he struck her a stunning blow against the temple with the knife handle. He had planned and waited for weeks. He wouldn't kill her quickly, mercifully. He wouldn't. He wanted her on her knees, crying and screaming for her life.

She landed in a heap, driven down by the explosive pain. She would have wept then, with her hands covering her face and her body limp. Not for herself, but for what she had lost.

They both turned as Boyd staggered to the doorway.

Seconds. It took only seconds. Her vision cleared, her heart almost burst. Alive. He was alive.

Her sob of relief turned to a scream of terror as she saw Billy raise the gun. Then she was on her feet, struggling with him. Records crashed to the floor and were crushed underfoot as they rammed into a shelf. His eyes burned into hers. She did beg. She pleaded even as she fought him.

Boyd dropped to his knees. The gun nearly slipped out of his slickened fingers. Through a pale red mist he could see them. He tried to shout at her, but he couldn't drag his voice through his throat. He could only pray as he struggled to maintain a grip on consciousness and the gun. He saw the knife come up, start its vicious downward sweep. He fired.

She didn't hear the crashing glass or the clamor of feet. She didn't even hear the report as the bullet struck home. But she felt the jerk of his body as the knife flew out of his hand. She lost her grip on him as he slammed back into the console.

Wild-eyed, she whirled. She saw Boyd swaying on his knees, the gun held in both hands. Behind him was Althea, her weapon still trained on the figure sprawled on the floor. On a strangled cry, Cilla rushed over as Boyd fell.

"No." She was weeping as she brushed the hair from his eyes, as she ran a hand down his side and felt the blood. "Please, no." She covered his body with hers.

"You've got to move back." Althea bit down on panic as she urged Cilla aside.

"He's bleeding."

"I know." And badly, she thought. Very badly. "There's an ambulance coming."

Cilla stripped off her shirt to make a pressure bandage. Kneeling in her chemise, she bent over Boyd. "I'm not going to let him die."

Althea's eyes met hers. "That makes two of us."

# Chapter 12

There had been a sea of faces. They seemed to swim inside Cilla's head as she paced the hospital waiting room. It was so quiet there, quiet enough to hear the swish of crepe-soled shoes on tile or the whoosh of the elevator doors opening, closing. Yet in her head she could still hear the chaos of sirens, voices, the crackle of static on the police cruisers that had nosed together in the station's parking lot.

The paramedics had come. Hands had pulled her away from Boyd, pulled her out of the booth and into the cool, fresh night.

Mark, she remembered. It was Mark who had held her back as she'd run the gamut from hysteria to shock. Jackson had been there, steady as a rock, pushing a cup of some hot liquid into her hand. And Nick, white-faced, mumbling assurances and apologies.

There had been strangers, dozens of them, who had heard the confrontation over their radios. They had crowded in until the uniformed police set up a barricade.

Then Deborah had been there, racing across the lot in tears, shoving aside cops, reporters, gawkers, to get to her sister. It was Deborah who had discovered that some of the blood on Cilla was her own.

Now, dully, Cilla looked down at her bandaged hand. She hadn't felt the knife slice into it during the few frantic seconds she had fought with Billy. The scratch along her throat where the blade had nicked her was more painful. Shallow wounds, she thought. They were only shallow wounds, nothing compared to the deep gash in her heart.

She could still see how Boyd had looked when they had wheeled him out to the ambulance. For one horrible moment, she'd been afraid he was dead. So white, so still.

But he was alive. Althea had told her. He'd lost a lot of blood, but he was alive.

Now he was in surgery, fighting to stay that way. And she could only wait.

Althea watched her pace. For herself, she preferred to sit, to gather her resources and hold steady. She had her own visions to contend with. The jolt when Cilla's voice had broken into the music. The race from the precinct to the radio station. The sight of her partner kneeling on the floor, struggling to hold his weapon. He had fired only an instant before her.

She'd been too late. She would have to live with that.

Now her partner, her friend, her family, was lying on an operating table. And she was helpless.

Rising, Deborah walked across the room to put an arm around her sister. Cilla stopped pacing long enough to stare out the window.

"Why don't you lie down?" Deborah suggested.

"No, I can't."

"You don't have to sleep. You could just stretch out on the couch over there."

Cilla shook her head. "So many things are going through my mind, you know? The way he'd just sit there and grin after he'd gotten me mad. How he'd settle down in the corner of the booth with a book. The calm way he'd boss me around. I spent most of my time trying to push him away, but I didn't push hard enough. And now he's—"

"You can't blame yourself for this."

"I don't know who to blame." She looked up at the clock. How could the minutes go by so slowly? "I can't really think about that now. The cause isn't nearly as important as the effect."

"He wouldn't want you to take this on, Cilla."

She nearly smiled. "I haven't made a habit of doing what he wanted. He saved my life, Deb. How can I stand it if the price of that is his?"

There seemed to be no comfort she could offer. "If you won't lie down, how about some coffee?"

"Sure. Thanks."

She crossed to a pot of stale coffee resting on a hot plate. When Althea joined her, Deborah poured a second cup.

"How's she holding up?" Althea asked.

"By a thread." Deborah rubbed her gritty eyes before she turned to Althea. "She's blaming herself." Studying Althea, she offered the coffee. "Do you blame her, too?"

Athlea hesitated, bringing the coffee to her lips first. She'd long since stopped tasting it. She looked over to the woman still standing by the window. Cilla wore baggy jeans and Mark Harrison's tailored jacket. She wanted to blame Cilla, she realized. She wanted to blame her for involving Boyd past the point of wisdom. She wanted to blame her for being the catalyst that had set an already disturbed mind on the bloody path of revenge.

But she couldn't. Neither as a cop nor as a woman.

"No," she said with a sigh. "I don't blame her. She's only one of the victims here."

"Maybe you could tell her that." Deborah passed the second cup to Althea. "Maybe that's what she needs to hear."

It wasn't easy to approach Cilla. They hadn't spoken since they had come to the waiting room. In some strange way, Althea realized, they were rivals. They both loved the same man. In different ways, perhaps, and certainly on different levels, but the emotions were deep on both sides. It occurred to her that if there had been no emotion on Cilla's part, there would have been no resentment on hers. If she had remained an assignment, and only an assignment, Althea would never have felt the need to cast blame.

It seemed Boyd had not been the only one to lose his objectivity.

She stopped beside Cilla, stared at the same view of the dark studded with city lights. "Coffee?"

"Thanks." Cilla accepted the cup but didn't drink. "They're taking a long time."

"It shouldn't be much longer."

Cilla drew in a breath and her courage. "You saw the wound. Do you think he'll make it?"

*I don't know.* She almost said it. They both knew she'd thought it. "I'm counting on it."

"You told me once he was a good man. You were right. For a long time I was afraid to see that, but you were right." She turned to face Althea directly. "I don't expect you to believe me, but I would have done anything to keep him from being hurt."

"I do believe you. And you did what you could." Before Cilla could turn away again, Althea put a hand on her arm. "Opening your mike may have saved his life. I want you to think about that. With a wound as serious as Boyd's, every second counted. With the broadcast, you gave us a fix on the situation, so there was an ambulance on the scene almost as quickly as we were. If Boyd makes it, it's partially due to your presence of mind. I want you to think about that."

"Billy only went after him because of me. I have to think about that, as well."

"You're trying to logic out an irrational situation. It won't work." The sympathy vanished from her voice. "If you want to start passing out blame, how about John McGillis? It was his fantasy that lit the fuse. How about the system that allowed someone like Billy Lomus to bounce from foster home to foster home so that he never knew what it was like to feel loved or wanted by anyone but a young, troubled boy? You could blame Mark for not checking Billy's references closely enough. Or Boyd and me for not making the connection quicker. There's plenty of blame to pass around, Cilla. We're all just going to have to live with our share."

"It doesn't really matter, does it? No matter who's at fault, it's still Boyd's life on the line."

"Detective Grayson?"

Althea snapped to attention. The doctor who entered was still in surgical greens damped down the front with sweat. She tried to judge his eyes first. They were a clear and quiet gray and told her nothing.

"I'm Grayson."

His brow lifted slightly. It wasn't often you met a police detective who looked as though she belonged on the cover of *Vogue*. "Dr. Winthrop, chief of surgery."

"You operated on Boyd, Boyd Fletcher?"

"That's right. He's your partner?"

"Yes." Without conscious thought on either side, Althea and Cilla clasped hands. "Can you tell us how he is?"

"I can tell you he's a lucky man," Winthrop said. "If the knife had gone a few inches either way, he wouldn't have had a chance. As it is, he's still critical, but the prognosis is good."

"He's alive." Cilla finally managed to force the words out.

"Yes." Winthrop turned to her. "I'm sorry, are you a relative?"

"No, I... No."

"Miss O'Roarke is the first person Boyd will want to see when he wakes up." Althea gave Cilla's hand a quick squeeze. "His family's been notified, but they were in Europe and won't be here for several hours yet."

"I see. He'll be done in Recovery shortly. Then we'll transfer him to ICU. O'Roarke," he said suddenly. "Of course. My son's a big fan." He lifted her bandaged hand gently. "I've already heard the story. If you were my patient, you'd be sedated and in bed."

"I'm fine."

Frowning, he studied her pupils. "To put it in unprofessional terms, not by a long shot." His gaze skimmed down the long scratch on her throat. "You've had a bad shock, Miss O'Roarke. Is there someone who can drive you home?"

"I'm not going home until I see Boyd."

"Five minutes, once he's settled in ICU. Only five. I can guarantee he won't be awake for at least eight hours."

"Thank you." If he thought she would settle for five minutes, he was very much mistaken.

"Someone will come by to let you know when you can go down." He walked out rubbing the small of his back and thinking about a hot meal.

"I need to call the captain." It infuriated Althea that she was close to tears. "I'd appreciate it if you'd come back for me after you've seen him. I'd like a moment with him myself."

"Yes, of course. Thea." Letting her emotions rule, Cilla wrapped her arms around Althea. The tears didn't seem to matter. Nor did pride. They clung together and held on to hope. They didn't speak.

They didn't have to. When they separated, Althea walked away to call her captain. Cilla turned blindly to the window.

"He's going to be okay," Deborah murmured beside her.

"I know." She closed her eyes. She did know. The dull edge of fear was gone. "I just need to see him, Deb. I need to see him for myself."

"Have you told him you love him?"

She shook her head.

"Now might be a good time."

"I was afraid I wouldn't get the chance, and now...I don't know."

"Only a fool would turn her back on something so special."

"Or a coward." Cilla pressed her fingers to her lips. "Tonight, all night, I've been half out of my mind thinking he might die. Line of duty." She turned to face her sister. "In the line of duty, Deborah. If I let myself go, if I don't turn my back, how many other times might I stand here wondering if he'll live or die?"

"Cilla—"

"Or open the door one day and have his captain standing there, waiting to tell me that he was already gone, the way Mom's captain came to the door that day."

"You can't live your life waiting for the worst, Cilla. You have to live it hoping for the best."

"I'm not sure I can." Weary, she dragged her hands through her hair. "I'm not sure of anything right now except that he's alive."

"Miss O'Roarke?" Both Cilla and Deborah turned toward the nurse. "Dr. Winthrop said to bring you to ICU."

"Thank you."

Her heart hammered in her ears as she followed the nurse toward the corridor. Her mouth was dry, and her palms were damp. She tried to ignore the machines and monitors as they passed through the double doors into Intensive Care. She wanted to concentrate on Boyd.

He was still so white. His face was as colorless as the sheet that covered him. The machines blipped and hummed. A good sound, she tried to tell herself. It meant he was alive. Only resting.

Tentatively she reached out to brush at his hair. It was so warm and soft. As was his skin when she traced the back of her knuckles over his cheek.

"It's all over now," she said quietly. "All you have to do is rest and get better." Desperate for the contact, she took his limp hand in hers, then pressed it to her lips. "I'm going to stay as close as they'll let me. I promise." It wasn't enough, not nearly enough. She brushed her lips over his hair, his cheek, his mouth. "I'll be here when you wake up."

She kept her word. Despite Deborah's arguments, she spent the rest of the night on the couch in the waiting room. Every hour they allowed her five minutes with him. Every hour she woke and took what she was given.

He didn't stir.

Dawn broke, shedding pale, rosy light through the window. The shifts changed. Cilla sipped coffee and watched the night staff leave for home. New sounds began. The clatter of the rolling tray as breakfast was served. Bright morning voices replaced the hushed tones of night. Checking her watch, she set the coffee aside and walked out to sit on a bench near the doors of ICU. It was almost time for her hourly visit.

While she waited to be cleared, a group of three hurried down the hall. The man was tall, with a shock of gray hair and a lean, almost cadaverous face. Beside him was a trim woman, her blond hair ruffled, her suit wrinkled. They were clutching hands. Walking with them was another woman. The daughter, Cilla thought with dazed weariness. She had her father's build and her mother's face.

There was panic in her eyes. Even through the fatigue Cilla saw it and recognized it. Beautiful eyes. Dark green, just like…Boyd's.

"Boyd Fletcher," the younger woman said to the nurse. "We're his family. They told us we could see him."

The nurse checked her list. "I'll take you. Only two at a time, please."

"You go." Boyd's sister turned to her parents. "I'll wait right here."

Cilla wanted to speak, but as the woman sat on the opposite end of the bench she could only sit, clutching her hands together.

What could she say to them? To any of them? Even as she searched for words, Boyd's sister leaned back against the wall and shut her eyes.

Ten minutes later, the Fletchers came out again. There were lines of strain around the woman's eyes, but they were dry. Her hand was still gripping her husband's.

"Natalie." She touched her daughter's shoulder. "He's awake. Groggy, but awake. He recognized us." She beamed a smile at her husband. "He wanted to know what the hell we were doing here when we were supposed to be in Paris." Her eyes filled then, and she groped impatiently for a handkerchief. "The doctor's looking at him now, but you can see him in a few minutes."

Natalie slipped an arm around her mother's waist, then her father's. "So what were we worried about?"

"I still want to know exactly what happened." Boyd's father shot a grim look at the double doors. "Boyd's captain has some explaining to do."

"We'll get the whole story," his wife said soothingly. "Let's just take a few minutes to be grateful it wasn't worse." She dropped the handkerchief back in her purse. "When he was coming around, he asked for someone named Cilla. That's not his partner's name. I don't believe we know a Cilla."

Though her legs had turned to jelly, Cilla rose. "I'm Cilla." Three pairs of eyes fixed on her. "I'm sorry," she managed. "Boyd was...he was hurt because...he was protecting me. I'm sorry," she said again.

"Excuse me." The nurse stood by the double doors again. "Detective Fletcher insists on seeing you, Miss O'Roarke. He's becoming agitated."

"I'll go with you." Taking charge, Natalie steered Cilla through the doors.

Boyd's eyes were closed again, but he wasn't asleep. He was concentrating on reviving the strength he'd lost in arguing with the doctor. But he knew the moment she entered the room, even before she laid a tentative hand on his. He opened his eyes and looked at her.

"Hi, Slick." She made herself smile. "How's it going?"

"You're okay." He hadn't been sure. The last clear memory was of Billy holding the knife and Cilla struggling.

"I'm fine." Deliberately she put her bandaged hand behind her back. Natalie noted the gesture with a frown. "You're the one hooked up to machines.'' Though her voice was brisk, the hand that brushed over his cheek was infinitely tender. ''I've seen you looking better, Fletcher.''

He linked his fingers with hers. ''I've felt better.''

''You saved my life.'' She struggled to keep it light, keep it easy. ''I guess I owe you.''

''Damn right.'' He wanted to touch her, but his arms felt like lead. ''When are you going to pay up?''

''We'll talk about it. Your sister's here.'' She glanced across the bed at Natalie.

Natalie leaned down and pressed a kiss to his brow. ''You jerk.''

''It's nice to see you, too.''

''You just couldn't be a pushy, uncomplicated business shark, could you?''

''No.'' He smiled and nearly floated off again. ''But you make a great one. Try to keep them from worrying.''

She sighed a little as she thought of their parents. ''You don't ask for much.''

''I'm doing okay. Just keep telling them that. You met Cilla.''

Natalie's gaze skimmed up, measuring. ''Yes, we met. Just now.''

''Make her get the hell out of here.'' Natalie saw the shocked hurt in Cilla's eyes, saw her fingers tighten convulsively on the bedguard.

''She doesn't have to make me go.'' With her last scrap of pride, she lifted her chin. ''If you don't want me around, I'll—''

''Don't be stupid,'' Boyd said in that mild, slightly irritated voice that made her want to weep. He looked back at his sister. ''She's dead on her feet. Last night was rough. She's too stubborn to admit it, but she needs to go home and get some sleep.''

''Ungrateful slob,'' Cilla managed. ''Do you think you can order me around even when you're flat on your back?''

''Yeah. Give me a kiss.''

''If I didn't feel sorry for you, I'd make you beg.'' She leaned close to touch her lips to his. At the moment of contact she realized with a new panic that she was going to break down. ''Since you want me to clear out, I will. I've got a show to prep for.''

''Hey, O'Roarke.''

She got enough of a grip on control to look over her shoulder. "Yes?"

"Come back soon."

"Well, well…" Natalie murmured as Cilla hurried away.

"Well, well…" her brother echoed. He simply could not keep his eyes open another moment. "She's terrific, isn't she?"

"I suppose she must be."

"As soon as I can stay awake for more than an hour at a time, I'm going to marry her."

"I see. Maybe you should wait until you can actually stand up for an hour at a time."

"I'll think about it. Nat." He found her hand again. "It is good to see you."

"You bet," she said as he fell asleep.

Cilla was almost running when she hit the double doors. She didn't pause, not even when Boyd's parents both rose from the bench. As her breath hitched and her eyes filled, she hurried down the hall and stumbled into the ladies' room.

Natalie found her there ten minutes later, curled up in a corner, sobbing wretchedly. Saying nothing, Natalie pulled out a handful of paper towels. She dampened a few, then walked over to crouch in front of Cilla.

"Here you go."

"I hate to do this," Cilla said between sobbing breaths.

"Me too." Natalie wiped her own eyes, and then, without a thought to her seven-hundred-dollar suit, sat on the floor. "The doctor said they'd probably move him to a regular room by tomorrow. They're hoping to downgrade his condition from critical to serious by this afternoon."

"That's good." Cilla covered her face with the cool, wet towel. "Don't tell him I cried."

"All right."

There was silence between them as each worked on control.

"I guess you'd like to know everything that happened," Cilla said at length.

"Yes, but it can wait. I think Boyd had a point when he told you to go home and get some sleep."

With very little effort she could have stretched out on the cool tile floor and winked out like a light. "Maybe."

"I'll give you a lift."

"No, thanks. I'll call a cab."

"I'll give you a lift," Natalie repeated, and rose.

Lowering the towel, Cilla studied her. "You're a lot like him, aren't you?"

"So they say." Natalie offered a hand to help Cilla to her feet. "Boyd told me you're getting married."

"So he says."

For the first time in hours, Natalie laughed. "We really will have to talk."

She all but lived in the hospital for the next week. Boyd was rarely alone. Though it might have frustrated him from time to time that he barely had a moment for a private word with her, Cilla was grateful.

His room was always filled with friends, with family, with associates. As the days passed and his condition improved, she cut her visits shorter and kept them farther apart.

They both needed the distance. That was how she rationalized it. They both needed time for clear thinking. If she was to put the past—both the distant past and the near past—behind her, she needed to do it on her own.

It was Thea who filled her in on Billy Lomus. In his troubled childhood, the only bright spot had been John McGillis. As fate would have it, they had fed on each other's weaknesses. John's first suicide attempt had occurred two months after Billy left for Viet Nam. He'd been barely ten years old.

When Billy had returned, bitter and wounded, John had run away to join him. Though the authorities had separated them, they had always managed to find each other again. John's death had driven Billy over the fine line of reason he had walked.

"Delayed stress syndrome," Althea said as they stood together in the hospital parking lot. "Paranoid psychosis. Obsessive love. It doesn't really matter what label you put on it."

"Over these past couple of weeks, I've asked myself dozens of times if there was anything I could have done differently with John

McGillis.'' She took in a deep breath of the early spring air. ''And there wasn't. I can't tell you what a relief it is to finally be sure of that.''

''Then you can put it behind you.''

''Yes. It's not something I can forget, but I can put it behind me. Before I do, I'd like to thank you for everything you did, and tried to do.''

''It was my job,'' Althea said simply. ''We weren't friends then. I think maybe we nearly are now.''

Cilla laughed. ''Nearly.''

''So, as someone who's nearly your friend, there's something I'd like to say.''

''Okay.''

''I've been watching you and Boyd since the beginning. Observation's also part of the job.'' Her eyes, clear and brown and direct, met Cilla's. ''I still haven't decided if I think you're good for Boyd. It's not really my call, but I like to form an opinion.''

Cilla looked out beyond the parking lot to a patch of green. The daffodils were blooming there, beautifully. ''Thea, you're not telling me anything I don't already know.''

''My point is, Boyd thinks you're good for him. That's enough for me. I guess the only thing you've got to decide now is if he's good for you.''

''He thinks he is,'' she murmured.

''I've noticed.'' In an abrupt change of mood, Althea looked toward the hospital. ''I heard he was getting out in a couple of days.''

''That's the rumor.''

''You've already been up, I take it.''

''For a few minutes. His sister's there, and a couple of cops. They brought in a flower arrangement shaped like a horseshoe. The card read Tough break, Lucky. They tried to tell him they'd confiscated it from some gangster's funeral.''

''Wouldn't surprise me. Funny thing about cops. They usually have a sense of humor, just like real people.'' She gave Cilla an easy smile. ''I'm going to go up. Should I tell him I ran into you and you're coming back later?''

"No. Not this time. Just—just tell him to listen to the radio. I'll see if I can dig up 'Dueling Banjos.'"

"'Dueling Banjos'?"

"Yeah. I'll see you later, Thea."

"Sure." Althea watched Cilla walk to her car and was grateful, not for the first time, not to be in love.

Though the first couple of nights in the booth after the shooting had been difficult, Cilla had picked up her old routine. She no longer got a flash of Boyd bleeding as he knelt by the door, or of Billy, his eyes wild, holding a knife to her throat.

She'd come to enjoy the request line again. The blinking lights no longer grated on her nerves. Every hour she was grateful that Boyd was recovering, and so she threw herself into her work with an enthusiasm she had lost for too long.

"Cilla."

She didn't jolt at the sound of her name, but swiveled easily in her chair and smiled at Nick. "Hey."

"I, ah, decided to come back."

She kept smiling as she accepted the cup of coffee he offered. "I heard."

"Mark was real good about it."

"You're an asset to the station, Nick. I'm glad you changed your mind."

"Yeah, well..." He let his words trail off as he studied the scar on the palm of her hand. The stitches had come out only days earlier. "I'm glad you're okay."

"Me too. You want to get me the Rocco's Pizza commercial?"

He nearly jumped for it, sliding it out of place and handing it to her. Cilla popped the tape in, then potted it up.

"I wanted to apologize," he blurted out.

"You don't have to."

"I feel like a jerk, especially after I heard...well, the whole story about Billy and that guy from Chicago."

"You're nothing like John, Nick. And I'm flattered that you were attracted to me—especially since you have a class with my incredibly beautiful sister."

"Deborah's nice. But she's too smart."

Cilla had her first big laugh of the month. "Thanks a lot, kid. Just what does that make me?"

"I didn't mean—" He broke off, mortally embarrassed. "I only meant—"

"Don't bury yourself." Giving him a quick grin, she turned on her mike. "Hey, Denver, we're going to keep it rocking for you for the next quarter hour. It's 10:45 on this Thursday night, and I'm just getting started." She hit them with a blast of "Guns 'n' Roses". "Now that's rock and roll," she said to herself. "Hey, Nick, why don't you..." Her words trailed off when she saw Boyd's mother in the doorway. "Mrs. Fletcher." She sprang up, nearly strangling herself with her headphones.

"I hope I'm not disturbing you." She smiled at Cilla, nodded to Nick.

"No, no, of course not." Cilla brushed uselessly at her grimy jeans. "Um...Nick, why don't you get Mrs. Fletcher a cup of coffee?"

"No, thank you, dear. I can only stay a moment."

Nick made his excuses and left them alone.

"So," Mrs. Fletcher said after a quick study. She blinked at the posters on the wall and examined the equipment. "This is where you work?"

"Yes. I'd, ah...give you a tour, but I've got—"

"That's perfectly all right." The lines of strain were no longer around her eyes. She was a trim, attractive and perfectly groomed woman. And she intimidated the hell out of Cilla. "Don't let me interrupt you."

"No, I...I'm used to working with people around."

"I missed you at the hospital the past few days, so I thought I'd come by here and say goodbye."

"You're leaving?"

"Since Boyd is on the mend, we're going back to Paris. It's business, as well as pleasure."

Cilla made a noncommittal noise and cued up the next record. "I know you must be relieved that Boyd...well, that he's all right. I'm sure it was dreadful for you."

"For all of us. Boyd explained it all to us. You've had a horrible ordeal."

"It's over now."

"Yes." She lifted Cilla's hand and glanced at the healing wound. "Experiences leave scars. Some deeper than others." She released Cilla's hand to wander around the tiny booth. "Boyd tells me you're to be married."

"I..." She shook off the shock, cleared her throat. "Excuse me a minute." Turning to the console she segued into the next record, then pushed another switch. "It's time for our mystery record," she explained. "The roll of thunder plays over the song, then people call in. The first caller who can give me the name of the song, the artist and the year of the recording wins a pair of concert tickets. Wc've got Madonna coming in at the end of the month."

"Fascinating." Mrs. Fletcher smiled, a smile precisely like Boyd's. "As I was saying, Boyd tells me you're to be married. I wondered if you'd like any help with the arrangements."

"No. That is, I haven't said... Excuse me." She pounced on a blinking light. "KHIP. No, I'm sorry, wrong answer. Try again." She struggled to keep her mind clear as the calls came through. The fourth caller's voice was very familiar.

"Hey, O'Roarke."

"Boyd." She sent his mother a helpless look. "I'm working."

"I'm calling. You got a winner yet?"

"No, but—"

"You've got one now. 'Electric Avenue,' Eddy Grant, 1983."

She had to smile. "You're pretty sharp, Slick. Looks like you've got yourself a couple of concert tickets. Hold on." She switched on her mike. "We've got a winner."

Patient, Mrs. Fletcher watched her work, smiling as she heard her son's voice over the speakers.

"Congratulations," Cilla said after she'd potted up a new record.

"So, are you going to the concert with me?"

"If you're lucky. Gotta go."

"Hey!" he shouted before she could cut him off. "I haven't heard 'Dueling Banjos' yet."

"Keep listening." After a long breath, she turned back to his mother. "I'm very sorry."

"No problem, no problem at all." In fact, she'd found the interlude delightful. "About the wedding?"

"I don't know that there's going to be a wedding. I mean, there isn't a wedding." She dragged a hand through her hair. "I don't think."

"Ah, well…" That same faint, knowing smile hovered around her mouth. "I'm sure you or Boyd will let us know. He's very much in love with you. You know that?"

"Yes. At least I think I do."

"He told me about your parents. I hope you don't mind."

"No." She sat again. "Mrs. Fletcher—"

"Liz is fine."

"Liz. I hope you don't think I'm playing some sort of game with Boyd. I wouldn't ask him to change. I could never ask him to change, and I just don't know if I can live with what he does."

"Because you're afraid of his being a policeman? Afraid he might die and leave you, as your parents did?"

Cilla looked down at her hands, spread her fingers. "I guess when you trim away all the fat, that's it."

"I understand. I worry about him," she said quietly. "I also understand he's doing what he has to do."

"Yes, it is what he has to do. I've given that a lot of thought since he was hurt." Cilla looked up again, her eyes intense. "How do you live with it?"

Liz took Cilla's restless hand in hers. "I love him."

"And that's enough?"

"It has to be. It's always difficult to lose someone you love. The way you lost your parents was tragic—and, according to Boyd, unnecessary. My mother died when I was only six. I loved her very much, though I had little time with her."

"I'm sorry."

"She cut herself in the garden one day. Just a little nick on the thumb she paid no attention to. A few weeks later she was dead of blood poisoning. All from a little cut on the thumb with a pair of rusty garden shears. Tragic, and unnecessary. It's hard to say how and when a loved one will be taken from us. How sad it would be not to allow ourselves to love because we were afraid to lose." She touched a hand to Cilla's cheek. "I hope to see you again soon."

"Mrs. Fletcher—Liz," Cilla said as she stopped at the door. "Thank you for coming."

"It was my pleasure." She glanced at a poster of a bare-chested rock star with shoulder-length hair and a smoldering sneer. "Though I do prefer Cole Porter."

Cilla found herself smiling as she slipped in another tape. After the ad, she gave her listeners fifteen uninterrupted minutes of music and herself time to think.

When the request line rolled around, she was as nervous as a cat, but her mind was made up.

"This is Cilla O'Roarke for KHIP. It's five minutes past midnight and our request lines are open. Before I take a call, I've got a request of my own. This one goes to Boyd. No, it's not 'Dueling Banjos,' Slick. You're just going to have to try a new memory on for size. It's an old one by the Platters. 'Only You.' I hope you're listening, because I want you to know—" For the first time in her career, she choked on the air. "Oh, boy, it's a lot to get out. I guess I want to say I finally figured out it's only you for me. I love you, and if the offer's still open, you've got a deal."

She sent the record out and, with her eyes closed, let the song flow through her head.

Struggling for composure, she took call after call. There were jokes and questions about Boyd, but none of the callers *was* Boyd. She'd been so certain he would phone.

Maybe he hadn't even been listening. The thought of that had her dropping her head in her hands. She had finally dragged out the courage to tell him how she felt, and he hadn't been listening.

She got through the next two hours step-by-step. It had been a stupid move, she told herself. It was unbelievably foolish to announce that you loved someone over the radio. She'd only succeeded in embarrassing herself.

The more she thought about it, the angrier she became. She'd told him to listen, damn it. Couldn't he do anything she asked him to do? She'd told him to go away, he'd stayed. She'd told him she wasn't going to marry him, he'd told everyone she was. She'd told him to listen to the radio, he'd shut it off. She'd bared her soul over the public airwaves for nothing.

"That was a hell of a request," Jackson commented when he strolled into the booth just before two.

"Shut up."

"Right." He hummed to himself as he checked the programmer's clock for his shift. "Ratings should shoot right through the roof."

"If I wanted someone to be cheerful in here, I'd have brought along Mickey Mouse."

"Sorry." Undaunted, he continued to hum.

With her teeth on edge, Cilla opened her mike. "That's all for tonight, Denver. It's 1:58. I'm turning you over to my man Jackson. He'll be with you until six in the a.m. Have a good one. And remember, when you dream of me, dream good." She kicked her chair out of the way. "And if you're smart," she said to Jackson, "you won't say a word."

"Lips are sealed."

She stalked out, snatching up her jacket and digging for her keys as she headed for the door. She was going to go home and soak her head. And if Deborah had been listening and was waiting up, it would just give her someone to chew out.

Head down, hands in her pockets, she stomped to her car. She had her hand on the doorhandle before she saw that Boyd was sitting on the hood.

"Nice night," he said.

"What—what the hell are you doing here?" Anger forgotten, she rushed around the car. "You're supposed to be in the hospital. They haven't released you yet."

"I went over the wall. Come here."

"You jerk. Sitting out here in the night air. You were nearly dead two weeks ago, and—"

"I've never felt better in my life." He grabbed her by the front of her jacket and hauled her against him for a kiss. "And neither have you."

"What?"

"You've never felt better in my life, either."

She shook her head to clear it and stepped back. "Get in the car. I'm taking you back to the hospital."

"Like hell." Laughing, he pulled her against him again and devoured her mouth.

She went weak and hot and dizzy. On a little sigh, she clung to him, letting her hands rush over his face, into his hair. Just to touch him, to touch him and know he was whole and safe and hers.

"Lord, do you know how long it's been since you've kissed me like that?" He held her close, waiting for his heart rate to level. His side was throbbing in time with it. "Those chaste little pecks in the hospital weren't enough."

"We were never alone."

"You never stayed around long enough." He pressed his lips to the top of her head. "I liked the song."

"What song? Oh." She stepped back again. "You were listening."

"I liked the song a lot." He took her hand and pressed his mouth to the scar. "But I liked what you said before it even better. How about saying it again, face-to-face?"

"I..." She let out a huff of breath.

Patient, he cupped her face in his hands. "Come on, O'Roarke." He smiled. "Spit it out."

"I love you." She said it so quickly, and with such obvious relief, that he laughed again. "Damn it, it's not funny. I really love you, and it's your fault for making it impossible for me to do anything else."

"Remind me to pat myself on the back later. You've got a hell of a voice, Cilla." He wrapped his arms around her, comfortably. "And you've never sounded better than tonight."

"I was scared."

"I know."

"I guess I'm not anymore." She rested her head against his shoulder. "It feels right."

"Yeah. Just right. The offer still holds, Cilla. Marry me."

She took her time, not because she was afraid, but because she wanted to savor it. She wanted to remember every second. The moon was full, the stars were out. She could just catch the faintest drift of those fragile spring flowers.

"There's one question I have to ask you first."

"Okay."

"Can we really hire a cook?"

He laughed and lowered his mouth to hers. "Absolutely."

"Then it's a deal."

# Night Shadow

With thanks to Isabel and Dan

# Chapter 1

He walked the night. Alone. Restless. Ready. Clad in black, masked, he was a shadow among shadows, a whisper among the murmurs and mumbles of the dark.

He was watchful, always, for those who preyed on the helpless and vulnerable. Unknown, unseen, unwanted, he stalked the hunters in the steaming jungle that was the city. He moved unchallenged in the dark spaces, the blind alleys and violent streets. Like smoke, he drifted along towering rooftops and down into dank cellars.

When he was needed, he moved like thunder, all sound and fury. Then there was only the flash, the optical echo that lightning leaves after it streaks the sky.

They called him Nemesis, and he was everywhere.

He walked the night, skirting the sound of laughter, the cheerful din of celebrations. Instead he was drawn to the whimpers and tears of the lonely and the hopeless pleas of the victimized. Night after night, he clothed himself in black, masked his face and stalked the wild, dark streets. Not for the law. The law was too easily manipulated by those who scorned it. It was too often bent and twisted by those who claimed to uphold it. He knew, oh, yes, he knew. And he could not forget.

When he walked, he walked for justice—she of the blind eyes.

With justice, there could be retribution and the balancing of scales.

Like a shadow, he watched the city below.

* * *

Deborah O'Roarke moved quickly. She was always in a hurry to catch up with her own ambitions. Now her neat, sensible shoes clicked rapidly on the broken sidewalks of Urbana's East End. It wasn't fear that had her hurrying back toward her car, though the East End was a dangerous place—especially at night—for a lone, attractive woman. It was the flush of success. In her capacity as assistant district attorney, she had just completed an interview with a witness to one of the drive-by shootings that were becoming a plague in Urbana.

Her mind was completely occupied with the need to get back to her office and write her report so that the wheels of justice could begin to turn. She believed in justice, the patient, tenacious and systematic stages of it. Young Rico Mendez's murderers would answer for their crime. And with luck, she would be the one to prosecute.

Outside the crumbling building where she had just spent an hour doggedly pressuring two frightened young boys for information, the street was dark. All but two of the streetlights that lined the cracked sidewalk had been broken. The moon added only a fitful glow. She knew that the shadows in the narrow doorways were drunks or pushers or hookers. More than once she had reminded herself that she could have ended up in one of those sad and scarred buildings—if it hadn't been for her older sister's fierce determination to see that she had a good home, a good education, a good life.

Every time Deborah brought a case to trial, she felt she was repaying a part of that debt.

One of the doorway shadows shouted something at her, impersonally obscene. A harsh feminine cackle followed it. Deborah had only been in Urbana for eighteen months, but she knew better than to pause or to register that she had heard at all.

Her strides long and purposeful, she stepped off the curb to get into her car. Someone grabbed her from behind.

"Ooh, baby, ain't you sweet."

The man, six inches taller than she and wiry as a spring, stank. But not from liquor. In the split second it took her to read his glassy eyes, she understood that he wasn't pumped high on whiskey but on chemicals that would make him quick instead of sluggish. Using both hands, she shoved her leather briefcase into his gut. He grunted and

his grip loosened. Deborah wrenched away and ran, digging frantically for her keys.

Even as her hand closed over the jingling metal in her pocket, he
grabbed her, his fingers digging in at the collar of her jacket. She
heard the linen rip and turned to fight. Then she saw the switchblade,
its business end gleaming once before he pressed it against the soft
skin under her chin.

"Gotcha," he said, and giggled.

She went dead still, hardly daring to breathe. In his eyes she saw
a malicious kind of glee that would never listen to pleading or logic.
Still she kept her voice low and calm.

"I've only got twenty-five dollars."

Jabbing the point of the blade against her skin, he leaned intimately
close. "Uh-uh, baby, you got a lot more than twenty-five dollars."
He twisted her hair around his hand, jerking once, hard. When she
cried out, he began to pull her toward the deeper dark of the alley.

"Go on and scream." He giggled in her ear. "I like it when they
scream. Go on." He nicked her throat with the blade. "Scream."

She did, and the sound rolled down the shadowed street, echoing
in the canyons of the buildings. In doorways people shouted encouragement—to the attacker. Behind darkened windows people kept
their lights off and pretended they heard nothing.

When he pushed her against the damp wall of the alleyway, she
was icy with terror. Her mind, always so sharp and open, shut down.
"Please," she said, though she knew better, "don't do this."

He grinned. "You're going to like it." With the tip of the blade,
he sliced off the top button of her blouse. "You're going to like it
just fine."

Like any strong emotion, fear sharpened her senses. She could feel
her own tears, hot and wet on her cheeks, smell his stale breath and
the overripe garbage that crowded the alley. In his eyes she could
see herself pale and helpless.

She would be another statistic, she thought dully. Just one more
number among the ever increasing victims.

Slowly, then with increasing power, anger began to burn through
the icy shield of fear. She would not cringe and whimper. She would
not submit without a fight. It was then she felt the sharp pressure of

her keys. They were still in her hand, closed tight in her rigid fist. Concentrating, she used her thumb to push the points between her stiff fingers. She sucked in her breath, trying to channel all of her strength into her arm.

Just as she raised it, her attacker seemed to rise into the air, then fly, arms pinwheeling, into a stand of metal garbage cans.

Deborah ordered her legs to run. The way her heart was pumping, she was certain she could be in her car, doors locked, engine gunning, in the blink of an eye. But then she saw him.

He was all in black, a long, lean shadow among the shadows. He stood over the knife-wielding junkie, his legs spread, his body tensed.

"Stay back," he ordered when she took an automatic step forward. His voice was part whisper, part growl.

"I think—"

"Don't think," he snapped without bothering to look at her.

Even as she bristled at his tone, the junkie leaped up, howling, bringing his blade down in a deadly arc. Before Deborah's dazed and fascinated eyes, there was a flash of movement, a scream of pain and the clatter of the knife as it skidded along the concrete.

In less than the time it takes to draw and release a single breath, the man in black stood just as he had before. The junkie was on his knees, moaning and clutching his stomach.

"That was…" Deborah searched her whirling brain for a word, "impressive. I—I was going to suggest that we call the police."

He continued to ignore her as he took some circular plastic from his pocket and bound the still-moaning junkie's hands and ankles. He picked up the knife, pressed a button. The blade disappeared with a whisper. Only then did he turn to her.

The tears were already drying on her cheeks, he noted. And though there was a hitch in her breath, she didn't appear to be ready to faint or shoot off into hysterics. In fact, he was forced to admire her calm.

She was extraordinarily beautiful, he observed dispassionately. Her skin was pale as ivory against a disheveled cloud of ink-black hair. Her features were soft, delicate, almost fragile. Unless you looked at her eyes. There was a toughness in them, a determination that belied the fact that her slender body was shaking in reaction.

Her jacket was torn, and her blouse had been cut open to reveal the icy-blue lace and silk of a camisole. An interesting contrast to the prim, almost mannish business suit.

He summed her up, not as man to woman, but as he had countless other victims, countless other hunters. The unexpected and very basic jolt of reaction he felt disturbed him. Such things were more dangerous than any switchblade.

"Are you hurt?" His voice was low and unemotional, and he remained in shadow.

"No. No, not really." There would be plenty of bruises, both on her skin and her emotions, but she would worry about them later. "Just shaken up. I want to thank you for—" She had stepped toward him as she spoke. In the faint backsplash from the streetlight, she saw that his face was masked. As her eyes widened, he saw they were blue, a brilliant electric blue. "Nemesis," she murmured. "I thought you were the product of someone's overworked imagination."

"I'm as real as he is." He jerked his head toward the figure groaning among the garbage. He saw that there was a thin trickle of blood on her throat. For reasons he didn't try to understand, it enraged him. "What kind of a fool are you?"

"I beg your pardon?"

"This is the sewer of the city. You don't belong here. No one with brains comes here unless they have no choice."

Her temper inched upward, but she controlled it. He had, after all, helped her. "I had business here."

"No," he corrected. "You have no business here, unless you choose to be raped and murdered in an alley."

"I didn't choose anything of the sort." As her emotions darkened, the faint hint of Georgia became more prominent in her voice. "I can take care of myself."

His gaze skimmed down, lingered on the shredded blouse then returned to her face. "Obviously."

She couldn't make out the color of his eyes. They were dark, very dark. In the murky light, they seemed black. But she could read the dismissal in them, and the arrogance.

"I've already thanked you for helping me, even though I didn't need any help. I was just about to deal with that slime myself."

"Really?"

"That's right. I was going to gouge his eyes out." She held up her keys, lethal points thrusting out. "With these."

He studied her again, then gave a slow nod. "Yes, I believe you could do it."

"Damn right I could."

"Then it appears I've wasted my time." He pulled a square of black cloth from his pocket. After wrapping the knife in it, he offered it to her. "You'll want this for evidence."

The moment she held it, she remembered that feeling of terror and helplessness. With a muffled oath, she bit back her temper. Whoever, whatever he was, he had risked his life to help her. "I am grateful."

"I don't look for gratitude."

Her chin came up as he threw her words back in her face. "For what then?"

He stared at her, into her. Something came and went in his eyes that made her skin chill again as she heard his words, "For justice."

"This isn't the way," she began.

"It's my way. Weren't you going to call the police?"

"Yes." She pressed the heel of her hand to her temple. She was a little dizzy, she realized. And more than a little sick to her stomach. This wasn't the time or the place to argue morality and law enforcement with a belligerent masked man. "I have a phone in my car."

"Then I suggest you use it."

"All right." She was too tired to argue. Shivering a bit, she started down the alley. At the mouth of it, she saw her briefcase. She picked it up with a sense of relief and put the switchblade in it.

Five minutes later, after calling 911 and giving her location and the situation, she walked back into the alley. "They're sending a cruiser." Weary, she pushed the hair back from her face. She saw the junkie, curled up tight on the concrete. His eyes were wide and wild. Nemesis had left him with the promise of what would happen to him if he was ever caught again attempting to rape.

Even through the haze of drugs, the words had rung true.

"Hello?" With a puzzled frown, she looked up and down the alley. He was gone.

"Damn it, where did he go?" On a hiss of breath, she leaned back against the clammy wall. She hadn't finished with him yet, not by a long shot.

He was almost close enough to touch her. But she couldn't see him. That was the blessing, and the curse, the repayment for the lost days.

He didn't reach out and was curious why he wanted to. He only watched her, imprinting on his memory the shape of her face, the texture of her skin, the color and sheen of her hair as it curved gently beneath her chin.

If he had been a romantic man, he might have thought in terms of poetry or music. But he told himself he only waited and watched to make certain she was safe.

When the sirens cut the night, he could see her rebuild a mask of composure, layer by layer. She took deep, steadying breaths as she buttoned the ruined jacket over her slashed blouse. With a final breath, she tightened her grip on her briefcase, set her chin and walked with confident strides toward the mouth of the alley.

As he stood alone in his own half world between reality and illusion, he could smell the subtle sexiness of her perfume.

For the first time in four years, he felt the sweet and quiet ache of longing.

Deborah didn't feel like a party. In her fantasy, she wasn't all glossed up in a strapless red dress with plastic stays digging into her sides. She wasn't wearing pinching three-inch heels. She wasn't smiling until she thought her face would split in two.

In her fantasy, she was devouring a mystery novel and chocolate chip cookies while she soaked in a hot bubble bath to ease the bruises that still ached a bit three days after her nasty adventure in the East End alley.

Unfortunately, her imagination wasn't quite good enough to keep her feet from hurting.

As parties went, it was a pretty good one. Maybe the music was a bit loud, but that didn't bother her. After a lifetime with her sister, a first-class rock and roll fanatic, she was well indoctrinated into the world of loud music. The smoked salmon and spinach canapés weren't chocolate chip cookies, but they were tasty. The wine that she carefully nursed was top-notch.

There was plenty of glitz and glamour, lots of cheek bussing and glad-handing. It was, after all, a party thrown by Arlo Stuart, hotel magnate, as a campaign party for Tucker Fields, Urbana's mayor. It was Stuart's, and the present administration's hope, that the campaign would end in November with the mayor's reelection.

Deborah was as yet undecided whether she would pull the lever for the incumbent, or the young upstart challenger, Bill Tarrington. The champagne and pâté wouldn't influence her. Her choice would be based on issues, not party affiliations—either social or political. Tonight she was attending the party for two reasons. The first was that she was friends with the mayor's assistant, Jerry Bower. The second was that her boss had used the right combination of pressure and diplomacy to push her through the gilded swinging doors of the Stuart Palace.

"God, you look great." Jerry Bower, trim and handsome in his tux, his blond hair waving around his tanned, friendly face, stopped beside Deborah to press a quick kiss to her cheek. "Sorry I haven't had time to talk. There was a lot of meeting and greeting to do."

"Things are always busy for the big boss's right arm." She smiled, toasting him. "Quite a bash."

"Stuart pulled out all the stops." With a politician's eye, he scanned the crowd. The mix of the rich, famous and influential pleased him. There were, of course, other aspects to the campaign. Visibility, contact with shop owners, factory workers—the blue, the gray and the white collars, press conferences, speeches, statements. But Jerry figured if he could spend a small slice of one eighteen-hour day rubbing silk elbows and noshing on canapés, he'd make the best of it.

"I'm properly dazzled," Deborah assured him.

"Ah, but it's your vote we want."

"You might get it."

"How are you feeling?" Taking the opportunity in hand, he began to fill a plate with hors d'oeuvres.

"Fine." She glanced idly down at the fading bruise on her forearm. There were other, more colorful marks, hidden under the red silk.

"Really?"

She smiled again. "Really. It's an experience I don't want to repeat, but it did bring it home, straight home to me that we've got a lot more work to do before Urbana's streets are safe."

"You shouldn't have been out there," he mumbled.

He might as well have nudged a soapbox under her feet. Her eyes lit up, her cheeks flushed, her chin angled. "Why? Why should there be any place, any place at all in the city where a person isn't safe to walk? Are we supposed to just accept the fact that there are portions of Urbana that are off-limits to nice people? If we're—"

"Hold it, hold it." He held up a surrendering hand. "The only person someone in politics can't comfortably outtalk is a lawyer. I agree with you, okay?" He snagged a glass of wine from a passing waiter and reminded himself it could be his only one of the long evening. "I was stating a fact. It doesn't make it right, it just makes it true."

"It shouldn't be true." Her eyes had darkened in both annoyance and frustration.

"The mayor's running on a tough anticrime campaign," Jerry reminded her, and gave smiling nods to constituents who wandered by. "Nobody in this city knows the statistics better than I do. They're nasty, no doubt, and we're going to push them back. It just takes time."

"Yeah." Sighing, she pulled herself away from the brink of the argument she'd had with Jerry more times than she could count. "But it's taking too much time."

He bit into a carrot slice. "Don't tell me you're going to step over to the side of this Nemesis character? 'If the law won't deal with it quickly enough, I will'?"

"No." On that she was firm. The law would mete out justice in a proper fashion. She believed in the law, even now, when it was so totally overburdened. "I don't believe in crusades. They come too close to vigilantism. Though I have to admit, I'm grateful he was tilting at windmills in that alley the other night."

"So am I." He touched her lightly on the shoulder. "When I think of what might have happened—"

"It didn't." That helpless fear was still much too close to the surface to allow her to dwell on it. "And in spite of all the romantic press he's been getting, up close and in person, he's rude and abrupt." She took another sip of wine. "I owe him, but I don't have to like him."

"Nobody understands that sentiment more than a politician."

She relaxed and laughed up at him. "All right, enough shoptalk. Tell me who's here that I should know and don't."

Jerry entertained her. He always did. For the next few minutes he gulped down canapés and put names and tax brackets to the faces crowding the Royal Stuart ballroom. His clever and pithy comments made her chuckle. When they began to stroll through the crowd, she hooked her arm easily through his. It was a matter of chance that she turned her head and, in that sea of people, focused on one single face.

He was standing in a group of five or six, with two beautiful women all but hanging on his arms. Attractive, yes, she thought. But the room was filled with attractive men. His thick, dark hair framed a long, lean, somewhat scholarly face. Prominent bones, deep-set eyes—brown eyes, she realized, dark and rich like bittersweet chocolate. They seemed faintly bored at the moment. His mouth was full, rather poetic looking, and curved now in the barest hint of a smile.

He wore his tux as if he'd been born in one. Easily, casually. With one long finger he brushed a fiery curl off the redhead's cheek as she leaned closer to him. His smile widened at something she said.

Then, without turning his head, he merely shifted his gaze and locked on Deborah.

"....and she bought the little monsters a wide-screen TV."

"What?" She blinked, and though she realized it was absurd, she felt as though she had broken out of a spell. "What?"

"I was telling you about Mrs. Forth-Wright's poodles."

"Jerry, who is that? Over there. With the redhead on one side and the blonde on the other."

Glancing over, Jerry grimaced, then shrugged. "I'm surprised he doesn't have a brunette sitting on his shoulders. Women tend to stick to him as though he was wearing flypaper instead of a tux."

She didn't need to be told what she could see with her own eyes. "Who is he?"

"Guthrie, Gage Guthrie."

Her eyes narrowed a bit, her mouth pursed. "Why does that sound familiar?"

"It's splashed liberally through the society section of the *World* almost every day."

"I don't read the society section." Well aware it was rude, Deborah stared stubbornly at the man across the room. "I know him," she murmured. "I just can't place how."

"You've probably heard his story. He was a cop."

"A cop." Deborah's brows lifted in surprise. He looked much too comfortable, much too much a part of the rich and privileged surroundings to be a cop.

"A good one, apparently, right here in Urbana. A few years ago, he and his partner ran into trouble. Big trouble. The partner was killed, and Guthrie was left for dead."

Her memory jogged then homed in. "I remember now. I followed his story. My God, he was in a coma for…"

"Nine or ten months," Jerry supplied. "He was on life-support, and they'd just about given him up, when he opened his eyes and came back. He couldn't hack the streets anymore, and turned down a desk job with UPD. He'd come into a plump inheritance while he was in the *Twilight Zone,* so I guess you could say he took the money and ran."

It couldn't have been enough, she thought. No amount of money could have been enough. "It must have been horrible. He lost nearly a year of his life."

Jerry picked through the dwindling supply on his plate, looking for something interesting. "He's made up for lost time. Apparently women find him irresistible. Of course that might be because he turned a three-million-dollar inheritance into thirty—and counting." Nipping a spiced shrimp, Jerry watched as Gage smoothly disentangled himself from the group and started in their direction. "Well, well," he said softly. "Looks like the interest is mutual."

Gage had been aware of her since the moment she'd stepped into the ballroom. He'd watched, patient, as she'd mingled then separated herself. He'd kept up a social patter though he'd been wholly and uncomfortably aware of every move she'd made. He'd seen her smile at Jerry, observed the other man kiss her and brush a casually intimate hand over her shoulder.

He'd find out just what the relationship was there.

Though it wouldn't matter. Couldn't matter, he corrected. Gage had no time for sultry brunettes with intelligent eyes. But he moved steadily toward her.

"Jerry," Gage smiled. "It's good to see you again."

"Always a pleasure, Mr. Guthrie. You're enjoying yourself?"

"Of course." His gaze flicked from Jerry to Deborah. "Hello."

For some ridiculous reason, her throat snapped shut.

"Deborah, I'd like to introduce you to Gage Guthrie. Mr. Guthrie, Assistant District Attorney Deborah O'Roarke."

"An A.D.A." Gage's smile spread charmingly. "It's comforting to know that justice is in such lovely hands."

"Competent," she said. "I much prefer competent."

"Of course." Though she hadn't offered it, he took her hand and held it for a brief few seconds.

*Watch out!* The warning flashed into Deborah's mind the instant her palm met his.

"Will you excuse me a minute?" Jerry laid a hand on Deborah's shoulder again. "The mayor's signaling."

"Sure." She summoned up a smile for him, though she was ashamed to admit she'd forgotten he was beside her.

"You haven't been in Urbana long," Gage commented.

Despite her uneasiness, Deborah met his eyes straight on. "About a year and a half. Why?"

"Because I'd have known."

"Really? Do you keep tabs on all the A.D.A's?"

"No." He brushed a finger over the pearl drop at her ear. "Just the beautiful ones." The instant suspicion in her eyes delighted him. "Would you like to dance?"

"No." She let out a long, quiet breath. "No, thanks. I really can't stay any longer. I've got work to do."

He glanced at his watch. "It's already past ten."

"The law doesn't have a time clock, Mr. Guthrie."

"Gage. I'll give you a lift."

"No." A quick and unreasonable panic surged to her throat. "No, that's not necessary."

"If it's not necessary, then it must be a pleasure."

He was smooth, she thought, entirely too smooth for a man who had just shrugged off a blonde and a redhead. She didn't care for the idea of being the brunette to round out the trio.

"I wouldn't want to take you away from the party."

"I never stay late at parties."

"Gage." The redhead, her mouth pouty and moist, swayed up to drag on his arm. "Honey, you haven't danced with me. Not once."

Deborah took the opportunity to make a beeline for the exit.

It was stupid, she admitted, but her system had gone haywire at the thought of being alone in a car with him. Pure instinct, she supposed, for on the surface Gage Guthrie was a smooth, charming and appealing man. But she sensed something. Undercurrents. Dark, dangerous undercurrents. Deborah figured she had enough to deal with; she didn't need to add Gage Guthrie to the list.

She stepped out into the steamy summer night.

"Hail you a cab, miss?" the doorman asked her.

"No." Gage cupped a firm hand under her elbow. "Thank you."

"Mr. Guthrie," she began.

"Gage. My car is just here, Miss O'Roarke." He gestured to a long sleek limo in gleaming black.

"It's lovely," she said between her teeth, "but a cab will suit my needs perfectly."

"But not mine." He nodded at the tall, bulky man who slipped out of the driver's seat to open the rear door. "The streets are dangerous at night. I'd simply like to know you've gotten where you want to go, safely."

She stepped back and took a long careful study, as she might of a mug shot of a suspect. He didn't seem as dangerous now, with that half smile hovering at his mouth. In fact, she thought, he looked just a little sad. Just a little lonely.

She turned toward the limo. Not wanting to soften too much, she shot a look over her shoulder. "Has anyone ever told you you're pushy, Mr. Guthrie?"

"Often, Miss O'Roarke."

He settled beside her and offered a single long-stemmed red rose.

"You come prepared," she murmured. Had the blossom been waiting for the blonde, she wondered, or the redhead?

"I try. Where would you like to go?"

"The Justice Building. It's on Sixth and—"

"I know where it is." Gage pressed a button, and the glass that separated them from the driver slid open noiselessly. "The Justice Building, Frank."

"Yes, sir." The glass closed again, cocooning them.

"We used to work on the same side," Deborah commented.

"Which side is that?"

"Law."

He turned to her, his eyes dark, almost hypnotic. It made her wonder what he had seen when he had drifted all those months in that strange world of half life. Or half death.

"You're a defender of the law?"

"I like to think so."

"Yet you wouldn't be adverse to making deals and kicking back charges."

"The system's overburdened," she said defensively.

"Oh, yes, the system." With a faint movement of his shoulders, he seemed to dismiss it all. "Where are you from?"

"Denver."

"No, you didn't get cypress trees and magnolia blossoms in your voice from Denver."

"I was born in Georgia, but my sister and I moved around quite a bit. Denver was where I lived before I came east to Urbana."

Her sister, he noted. Not her parents, not her family, just her sister. He didn't press. Not yet. "Why did you come here?"

"Because it was a challenge. I wanted to put all those years I studied to good use. I like to think I can make a difference." She thought of the Mendez case and the four gang members who had been arrested and were even now awaiting trial. "I have made a difference."

"You're an idealist."

"Maybe. What's wrong with that?"

"Idealists are often tragically disappointed." He was silent a moment, studying her. The streetlamps and headlights of oncoming traffic sliced into the car, then faded. Sliced, then faded. She was beautiful in both light and shadow. More than beauty, there was a kind of power in her eyes. The kind that came from the merging of intelligence and determination.

"I'd like to see you in court," he said.

She smiled and added yet one more element to the power and the beauty. Ambition. It was a formidable combination.

"I'm a killer."

"I bet you are."

He wanted to touch her, just the skim of a fingertip on those lovely white shoulders. He wondered if it would be enough, just a touch. Because he was afraid it wouldn't, he resisted. It was with both relief and frustration that he felt the limo glide to the curb and stop.

Deborah turned to look blankly out of the window at the old, towering Justice Building. "That was quick," she murmured, baffled by her own disappointment. "Thanks for the lift." When the driver opened her door, she swung her legs out.

"I'll see you again."

For the second time, she looked at him over her shoulder. "Maybe. Good night."

He sat for a moment against the yielding seat, haunted by the scent she had left behind.

"Home?" the driver asked.

"No." Gage took a long, steadying breath. "Stay here, take her home when she's finished. I need to walk."

## Chapter 2

Like a boxer dazed from too many blows, Gage fought his way out of the nightmare. He surfaced, breathless and dripping sweat. As the grinding nausea faded, he lay back and stared at the high ornate ceiling of his bedroom.

There were 523 rosettes carved into the plaster. He had counted them day after day during his slow and tedious recuperation. Almost like an incantation, he began to count them again, waiting for his pulse rate to level.

The Irish linen sheets were tangled and damp around him, but he remained perfectly still, counting. Twenty-five, twenty-six, twenty-seven. There was a light, spicy scent of carnations in the room. One of the maids had placed them on the rolltop desk beneath the window. As he continued to count, he tried to guess what vase had been used. Waterford, Dresden, Wedgwood. He concentrated on that and the monotonous counting until he felt his system begin to level.

He never knew when the dream would reoccur. He supposed he should have been grateful that it no longer came nightly, but there was something more horrible about its capricious visits.

Calmer, he pressed the button beside the bed. The drapes on the wide arching window slid open and let in the light. Carefully he flexed his muscles one by one, assuring himself he still had control.

Like a man pursuing his own demons, he reviewed the dream. As always, it sprang crystal clear in his mind, involving all his senses.

They worked undercover. Gage and his partner, Jack McDowell. After five years, they were more than partners. They were brothers. Each had risked his life to save the other's. And each would do so again without hesitation. They worked together, drank together, went to ball games, argued politics.

For more than a year, they had been going by the names of Demerez and Gates, posing as two high-rolling dealers of cocaine and its even more lethal offspring, crack. With patience and guile, they had infiltrated one of the biggest drug cartels on the East Coast. Urbana was its center.

They could have made a dozen arrests, but they, and the department, agreed that the goal was the top man.

His name and face remained a frustrating mystery.

But tonight they would meet him. A deal had been set painstakingly. Demerez and Gates carried five million in cash in their steel-reinforced briefcase. They would exchange it for top-grade coke. And they would only deal with the man in charge.

They drove toward the harbor in the customized Maserati Jack was so proud of. With two dozen men for backup, and their own cover solid, their spirits were high.

Jack was a quick-thinking, tough-talking veteran cop, devoted to his family. He had a pretty, quiet wife and a young pistol of a toddler. With his brown hair slicked back, his hands studded with rings and the silk suit fitting creaselessly over his shoulders, he looked the part of the rich, conscienceless dealer.

There were plenty of contrasts between the two partners. Jack came from a long line of cops and had been raised in a third-floor walk-up in the East End by his divorced mother. There had been occasional visits from his father, a man who had reached for the bottle as often as his weapon. Jack had gone straight into the force after high school.

Gage had come from a business family filled with successful men who vacationed in Palm Beach and golfed at the country club. His parents had been closer to working class by the family standard, preferring to invest their money, their time, and their dreams in a small, elegant French restaurant on the upper East side. That dream had ultimately killed them.

After closing the restaurant late one brisk autumn night, they had been robbed and brutally murdered not ten feet from the doorway.

Orphaned before his second birthday, Gage had been raised in style and comfort by a doting aunt and uncle. He'd played tennis instead of streetball, and had been encouraged to step into the shoes of his late father's brother, as president of the Guthrie empire.

But he had never forgotten the cruelty, and the injustice of his parents' murder. Instead, he had joined the police force straight out of college.

Despite the contrasts in their backgrounds, the men had one vital thing in common—they both believed in the law.

"We'll hang his ass tonight," Jack said, drawing deeply on his cigarette.

"It's been a long time coming," Gage murmured.

"Six months prep work, eighteen months deep cover. Two years isn't much to give to nail this bastard." He turned to Gage with a wink. "'Course, we could always take the five mil and run like hell. What do you say, kid?"

Though Jack was only five years older than Gage, he had always called him "kid." "I've always wanted to go to Rio."

"Yeah, me, too." Jack flicked the smoldering cigarette out of the car window where it bounced on asphalt and sputtered. "We could buy ourselves a villa and live the high life. Lots of women, lots of rum, lots of sun. How 'bout it?"

"Jenny might get annoyed."

Jack chuckled at the mention of his wife. "Yeah, that would probably tick her off. She'd make me sleep in the den for a month. Guess we'd just better kick this guy's butt." He picked up a tiny transmitter. "This is Snow White, you copy?"

"Affirmative, Snow White. This is Dopey."

"Don't I know it," Jack muttered. "We're pulling in, Pier Seventeen. Keep a bead on us. That goes for Happy and Sneezy and the rest of you dwarfs out there."

Gage pulled up in the shadows of the dock and cut the engine. He could smell the water and the overripe odor of fish and garbage. Following the instructions they'd been given, he blinked his headlights twice, paused, then blinked them twice again.

"Just like James Bond," Jack said, then grinned at him. "You ready, kid?"

"Damn right."

He lit another cigarette, blew smoke between his teeth. "Then let's do it."

They moved cautiously, Jack holding the briefcase with its marked bills and microtransmitter. Both men wore shoulder holsters with police issue .38s. Gage had a backup .25 strapped to his calf.

The lap of water on wood, the skitter of rodents on concrete. The dim half-light of a cloudy moon. The sting of tobacco on the air from Jack's cigarette. The small, slow-moving bead of sweat between his own shoulder blades.

"Doesn't feel right," Gage said softly.

"Don't go spooky on me, kid. We're going to hit the bell tonight."

With a nod, Gage fought off the ripple of unease. But he reached for his weapon when a small man stepped out of the shadows. With a grin, the man held up his hands, palms out.

"I'm alone," he said. "Just as agreed. I am Montega, your escort."

He had dark shaggy hair, a flowing moustache. When he smiled, Gage caught the glint of gold teeth. Like them, he was wearing an expensive suit, the kind that could be tailored to disguise the bulk of an automatic weapon. Montega lowered one hand carefully and took out a long, slim cigar. "It's a nice night for a little boat ride, *sí?*"

"*Sí.*" Jack nodded. "You don't mind if we pat you down? We'd feel better holding all the hardware until we get where we're going."

"Understandable." Montega lit the cigar with a slender gold lighter. Still grinning, he clamped the cigar between his teeth. Gage saw his hand slip the lighter casually back into his pocket. Then there was an explosion, the sound, the all too familiar sound of a bullet ripping out of a gun. There was a burning hole in the pocket of the fifteen-hundred-dollar suit. Jack fell backward.

Even now, four years later, Gage saw all the rest in hideous slow motion. The dazed, already dead look in Jack's eyes as he was thrown backward by the force of the bullet. The long, slow roll of the briefcase as it wheeled end over end. The shouts of the backup teams as they started to rush in. His own impossibly slow motion as he reached for his weapon.

The grin, the widening grin, flashing with gold as Montega had turned to him.

"Stinking cops," he said, and fired.

Even now, Gage could feel the hot tearing punch that exploded in his chest. The heat, unbearable, unspeakable. He could see himself flying backward. Flying endlessly. Endlessly into the dark.

And he'd been dead.

He'd known he was dead. He could see himself. He'd looked down and had seen his body sprawled on the bloody dock. Cops were working on him, packing his wound, swearing and scrambling around like ants. He had watched it all passionlessly, painlessly.

Then the paramedics had come, somehow pulling him back into the pain. He had lacked the strength to fight them and go where he wanted to go.

The operating room. Pale blue walls, harsh lights, the glint of steel instruments. The beep, beep, beep of monitors. The labored hiss and release of the respirator. Twice he had slipped easily out of his body—like breath, quiet and invisible—to watch the surgical team fight for his life. He'd wanted to tell them to stop, that he didn't want to come back where he could hurt again. Feel again.

But they had been skillful and determined and had dragged him back into that poor damaged body. And for a while, he'd returned to the blackness.

That had changed. He remembered floating in some gray liquid world that had brought back primordial memories of the womb. Safe there. Quiet there. Occasionally he could hear someone speak. Someone would say his name loudly, insistently. But he chose to ignore them. A woman weeping—his aunt. The shaken, pleading sound of his uncle's voice.

There would be light, an intrusion really, and though he couldn't feel, he sensed that someone was lifting his eyelids and shining a bead into his pupils.

It was a fascinating world. He could hear his own heartbeat. A gentle, insistent thud and swish. He could smell flowers. Only once in a while, then they would be overpowered by the slick, antiseptic smell of hospital. And he would hear music, soft, quiet music. Beethoven, Mozart, Chopin.

Later he learned that one of the nurses had been moved enough to bring a small tape player into his room. She often brought in discarded flower arrangements and sat and talked with him in a quiet, motherly voice.

Sometimes he mistook her for his own mother and felt unbearably sad.

When the mists in that gray world began to part, he struggled against it. He wanted to stay. But no matter how deep he dived, he kept floating closer to the surface.

Until at last, he opened his eyes to the light.

That was the worst part of the nightmare, Gage thought now. When he'd opened his eyes and realized he was alive.

Wearily Gage climbed out of bed. He had gotten past the death wish that had haunted him those first few weeks. But on the mornings he suffered from the nightmare, he was tempted to curse the skill and dedication of the medical team that had brought him back.

They hadn't brought Jack back. They hadn't saved his parents who had died before he'd even known them. They hadn't had enough skill to save his aunt and uncle, who had raised him with unstinting love and who had died only weeks before he had come out of the coma.

Yet they had saved him. Gage understood why.

It was because of the gift, the curse of a gift he'd been given during those nine months his soul had gestated in that gray, liquid world. And because they had saved him, he had no choice but to do what he was meant to do.

With a dull kind of acceptance, he placed his right hand against the pale green wall of his bedroom. He concentrated. He heard the hum inside his brain, the hum no one else could hear. Then, quickly and completely, his hand vanished.

Oh, it still existed. He could feel it. But even he couldn't see it. There was no outline, no silhouette of knuckles. From the wrist up, the hand was gone. He had only to focus his mind, and his whole body would do the same.

He could still remember the first time it had happened. How it had terrified him. And fascinated him. He made his hand reappear and studied it. It was the same. Wide palmed, long fingered, a bit rough with callus. The ordinary hand of a man who was no longer ordinary.

A clever trick, he thought, for someone who walks the streets at night, searching for answers.

He closed the hand into a fist, then moved off into the adjoining bathroom to shower.

At 11:45 a.m., Deborah was cooling her heels at the twenty-fifth precinct. She wasn't particularly surprised to have been summoned there. The four gang members who had gunned down Rico Mendez were being held in separate cells. That way they would sweat out the charges of murder one, accessory to murder, illegal possession of firearms, possession of controlled substances, and all the other charges on the arrest sheet. And they could sweat them out individually, with no opportunity to corroborate each other's stories.

She'd gotten the call from Sly Parino's public defense attorney at nine sharp. This would make the third meeting between them. At each previous encounter, she had held firm against a deal. Parino's public defender was asking for the world, and Parino himself was crude, nasty and arrogant. But she had noted that each time they sat in the conference room together, Parino sweated more freely.

Instinct told her he did indeed have something to trade but was afraid.

Using her own strategy, Deborah had agreed to the meeting, but had put it off for a couple of hours. It sounded like Parino was ready to deal, and since she had him cold, with possession of the murder weapon and two eye witnesses, he'd better have gold chips to ante up.

She used her time waiting for Parino to be brought in from lockup by reviewing her notes on the case. Because she could have recited them by rote, her mind wandered back to the previous evening.

Just what kind of man was Gage Guthrie? she wondered. The type who bundled a reluctant woman into his limo after a five-minute acquaintance. Then left that limo at her disposal for two and a half hours. She remembered her baffled amusement when she had come out of the Justice Building at one o'clock in the morning only to find the long black limo with its taciturn hulk of a driver patiently waiting to take her home.

Mr. Guthrie's orders.

Though Mr. Guthrie had been nowhere to be seen, she had felt his presence all during the drive from midtown to her apartment in the lower West End.

A powerful man, she mused now. In looks, in personality, and in basic masculine appeal. She looked around the station house, trying to imagine the elegant, just slightly rough-around-the-edges man in the tuxedo working here.

The twenty-fifth was one of the toughest precincts in the city. And where, Deborah had discovered when she'd been driven to satisfy her curiosity, Detective Gage Guthrie had worked during most of his six years with UPD.

It was difficult to connect the two, she mused. The smooth, obstinately charming man, with the grimy linoleum, harsh fluorescent lights, and odors of sweat and stale coffee underlaid with the gummy aroma of pine cleaner.

He liked classical music, for it had been Mozart drifting through the limo's speakers. Yet he had worked for years amid the shouts, curses and shrilling phones of the twenty-fifth.

From the information she'd read once she'd accessed his file, she knew he'd been a good cop—sometimes a reckless one, but one who had never crossed the line. At least not on record. Instead, his record had been fat with commendations.

He and his partner had broken up a prostitution ring which had preyed on young runaways, were given credit for the arrest of three prominent businessmen who had run an underground gambling operation that had chastised its unlucky clients with unspeakable torture, had tracked down drug dealers, small and large, and had ferreted out a crooked cop who had used his badge to extort protection money from small shop owners in Urbana's Little Asia.

Then they had gone undercover to break the back of one of the largest drug cartels on the eastern seaboard. And had ended up broken themselves.

Was that what was so fascinating about him? Deborah wondered. That it seemed the sophisticated, wealthy businessman was only an illusion thinly covering the tough cop he had been? Or had he simply returned to his privileged background, his years as a policeman the aberration? Who was the real Gage Guthrie?

She shook her head and sighed. She'd been thinking a lot about illusions lately. Since the night in the alley when she'd been faced with the terrifying reality of her own mortality. And had been saved—though she firmly believed she would have saved herself— by what many people thought was no more than a phantom.

Nemesis was real enough, she mused. She had seen him, heard him, even been annoyed by him. And yet, when he came into her mind, he was like smoke. If she had reached out to touch him, would her hand have passed right through?

What nonsense. She was going to have to get more sleep if over- work caused her mind to take fantasy flights in the middle of the day.

But somehow, she was going to find that phantom again and pin him down.

"Miss O'Roarke."

"Yes." She rose and offered her hand to the young, harried- looking public defender. "Hello again, Mr. Simmons."

"Yes, well..." He pushed tortoiseshell glasses up on his hooked nose. "I appreciate you agreeing to this meeting."

"Cut the bull." Behind Simmons, Parino was flanked by two uni- formed cops. He had a sneer on his face and his hands in cuffs. "We're here to deal, so let's cut to the chase."

With a nod, Deborah led the way into the small conference room. She settled her briefcase on the table and sat behind it. She folded her hands. In her trim navy suit and white blouse she looked every inch the Southern belle. She'd been taught her manners well. But her eyes, as dark as the linen of her suit, burned as they swept over Parino. She had studied the police photos of Mendez and had seen what hate and an automatic weapon could do to a sixteen-year-old body.

"Mr. Simmons, you're aware that of the four suspects facing in- dictment for the murder of Rico Mendez, your client holds the prize for the most serious charges?"

"Can we lose these things?" Parino held out his cuffed hands. Deborah glanced at him.

"No."

"Come on, babe." He gave her what she imagined he thought was a sexy leer. "You're not afraid of me, are you?"

"Of you, Mr. Parino?" Her lips curved, but her tone was frigidly sarcastic. "Why, no. I squash nasty little bugs every day. You, however, should be afraid of me. I'm the one who's going to put you away." She flicked her gaze back to Simmons. "Let's not waste time, again. All three of us know the score. Mr. Parino is nineteen and will be tried as an adult. It is still to be determined whether the others will be tried as adults or juveniles." She took out her notes, though she didn't need them as more than a prop. "The murder weapon was found in Mr. Parino's apartment, with Mr. Parino's fingerprints all over it."

"It was planted," Parino insisted. "I never saw it before in my life."

"Save it for the judge," Deborah suggested. "Two witnesses place him in the car that drove by the corner of Third and Market at 11:45, June 2. Those same witnesses have identified Mr. Parino, in a lineup, as the man who leaned out of that car and fired ten shots into Rico Mendez."

Parino began to swear and shout about squealers, about what he would do to them when he got out. About what he would do to her. Not bothering to raise her voice, Deborah continued, her eyes on Simmons.

"We have your client, cold, murder one. And the state will ask for the death penalty." She folded her hands on her notes and nodded at Simmons. "Now, what do you want to talk about?"

Simmons tugged at his tie. The smoke from the cigarette Parino was puffing was drifting in his direction and burning his eyes. "My client has information that he would be willing to turn over to the D.A.'s office." He cleared his throat. "In return for immunity, and a reduction of the current charges against him. From murder one, to illegal possession of a firearm."

Deborah lifted a brow, let the silence take a beat. "I'm waiting for the punch line."

"This is no joke, sister." Parino leaned over the table. "I got something to deal, and you'd better play."

With deliberate motions, Deborah put her notes back into her brief-case, snapped the lock then rose. "You're slime, Parino. Nothing, nothing you've got to deal is going to put you back on the street again. If you think you can walk over me, or the D.A.'s office, then think again."

Simmons bobbed up as she headed for the door. "Miss O'Roarke, please, if we could simply discuss this."

She whirled back to him. "Sure, we'll discuss it. As soon as you make me a realistic offer."

Parino said something short and obscene that caused Simmons to lose his color and Deborah to turn a cold, dispassionate eye on him.

"The state is going for murder one and the death penalty," she said calmly. "And believe me when I say I'm going to see to it that your client is ripped out of society just like a leech."

"I'll get off," Parino shouted at her. His eyes were wild as he lunged to his feet. "And when I do, I'm coming looking for you, bitch."

"You won't get off." She faced him across the table. Her eyes were cold as ice and never wavered. "I'm very good at what I do, Parino, which is putting rabid little animals like you away in cages. In your case, I'm going to pull out all the stops. You won't get off," she repeated. "And when you're sweating in death row, I want you to think of me."

"Murder two," Simmons said quickly, and was echoed by a savage howl from his client.

"You're going to sell me out, you sonofabitch."

Deborah ignored Parino and studied Simmons's nervous eyes. There was something here, she could smell it. "Murder one," she repeated, "with a recommendation for life imprisonment rather than the death penalty—if you've got something that holds my interest."

"Let me talk to my client, please. If you could give us a minute."

"Of course." She left the sweaty public defender with his scream-ing client.

Twenty minutes later, she faced Parino again across the scarred table. He was paler, calmer, as he smoked a cigarette down to the filter.

"Deal your cards, Parino," she suggested.

"I want immunity."

"From whatever charges might be brought from the information you give me. Agreed." She already had him where she wanted him.

"And protection." He'd begun to sweat.

"If it's warranted."

He hesitated, fiddling with the cigarette, the scorched plastic ashtray. But he was cornered, and knew it. Twenty years. The public defender had said he'd probably cop a parole in twenty years.

Twenty years in the hole was better than the chair. Anything was. And a smart guy could do pretty well for himself in the joint. He figured he was a pretty smart guy.

"I've been doing some deliveries for some guys. Heavy hitters. Trucking stuff from the docks to this fancy antique shop downtown. They paid good, too good, so I knew something was in those crates besides old vases." Awkward in the cuffs, he lit one cigarette from the smoldering filter of another. "So I figured I'd take a look myself. I opened one of the crates. It was packed with coke. Man, I've never seen so much snow. A hundred, maybe a hundred and fifty pounds. And it was pure."

"How do you know?"

He licked his lips, then grinned. "I took one of the packs, put it under my shirt. I'm telling you, there was enough there to fill up every nose in the state for the next twenty years."

"What's the name of the shop?"

He licked his lips again. "I want to know if we got a deal?"

"If the information can be verified, yes. If you're pulling my chain, no."

"Timeless. That's the name. It's over on Seventh. We delivered once, maybe twice a week. I don't know how often we were taking in coke or just fancy tables."

"Give me some names."

"The guy I worked with at the docks was Mouse. Just Mouse, that's all I know."

"Who hired you?"

"Just some guy. He came into Loredo's, the bar in the West End where the Demons hang out. He said he had some work if I had a strong back and knew how to keep my mouth shut. So me and Ray, we took him up on it."

"Ray?"

"Ray Santiago. He's one of us, the Demons."

"What did he look like, the man who hired you?"

"Little guy, kinda spooky. Big mustache, couple of gold teeth. Walked into Loredo's in a fancy suit, but nobody thought to mess with him."

She took notes, nodded, prompted until she was certain Parino was wrung dry. "All right, I'll check it out. If you've been straight with me, you'll find I'll be straight with you." She rose, glancing at Simmons. "I'll be in touch."

When she left the conference room, her head was pounding. There was a tight, sick feeling in her gut that always plagued her when she dealt with Parino's type.

He was nineteen, for God's sake, she thought as she tossed her visitor's badge to the desk sergeant. Barely even old enough to vote, yet he'd viciously gunned down another human being. She knew he felt no remorse. The Demons considered drive-bys a kind of tribal ritual. And she, as a representative of the law, had bargained with him.

That was the way the system worked, she reminded herself as she stepped out of the stuffy station house into the steamy afternoon. She would trade Parino like a poker chip and hope to finesse bigger game. In the end, Parino would pay by spending the rest of his youth and most of his adult life in a cage.

She hoped Rico Mendez's family would feel justice had been served.

"Bad day?"

Still frowning, she turned, shaded her eyes and focused on Gage Guthrie. "Oh. Hello. What are you doing here?"

"Waiting for you."

She lifted a brow, cautiously debating the proper response. Today he wore a gray suit, very trim and quietly expensive. Though the humidity was intense, his white shirt appeared crisp. His gray silk tie was neatly knotted.

He looked precisely like what he was. A successful, wealthy businessman. Until you looked at his eyes, Deborah thought. When you did, you could see that women were drawn to him for a much more basic reason than money and position.

She responded with the only question that seemed apt. "Why?"

He smiled at that. He had seen her caution and her evaluation clearly and was as amused as he was impressed by it. "To invite you to lunch."

"Oh. Well, that's very nice, but—"

"You do eat, don't you?"

He was laughing at her. There was no mistaking it. "Yes, almost every day. But at the moment, I'm working."

"You're a dedicated public servant, aren't you, Deborah?"

"I like to think so." There was just enough sarcasm in his tone to put her back up. She stepped to the curb and lifted an arm to hail a cab. A bus chugged by, streaming exhaust. "It was kind of you to leave your limo for me last night." She turned and looked at him. "But it wasn't necessary."

"I often do what others consider unnecessary." He took her hand and, with only the slightest pressure, brought her arm down to her side. "If not lunch, dinner."

"That sounds more like a command than a request." She would have tugged her hand away, but it seemed foolish to engage in a childish test of wills on a public street. "Either way, I have to refuse. I'm working late tonight."

"Tomorrow then." He smiled charmingly. "A request, Counselor."

It was difficult not to smile back when he was looking at her with humor and—was it loneliness?—in his eyes. "Mr. Guthrie. Gage." She corrected herself before he could. "Persistent men usually annoy me. And you're no exception. But for some reason, I think I'd like to have dinner with you."

"I'll pick you up at seven. I keep early hours."

"Fine. I'll give you my address."

"I know it."

"Of course." His driver had dropped her off at her doorstep the night before. "If you'll give me back my hand, I'd like to hail a cab."

He didn't oblige her immediately, but looked down at her hand. It was small and delicate in appearance, like the rest of her. But there was strength in the fingers. She kept her nails short, neatly rounded with a coating of clear polish. She wore no rings, no bracelets, only a slim, practical watch that he noted was accurate to the minute.

He looked up from her hand, into her eyes. He saw curiosity, a touch of impatience and again, the wariness. Gage made himself smile as he wondered how a simple meeting of palms could have jolted his system so outrageously.

"I'll see you tomorrow." He released her and stepped away.

She only nodded, not trusting her voice. When she slipped into a cab, she turned back. But he was already gone.

It was after ten when Deborah walked up to the antique store. It was closed, of course, and she hadn't expected to find anything. She had written her report and passed the details of her interview with Parino on to her superior. But she hadn't been able to resist a look for herself.

In this upscale part of town, people were lingering over dinner or enjoying a play. A few couples wandered by on their way to a club or a restaurant. Streetlights shot out pools of security.

It was foolish, she supposed, to have been drawn here. She could hardly have expected the doors to have been opened so she could walk in and discover a cache of drugs in an eighteenth-century armoire.

The window was not only dark, it was barred and shaded. Just as the shop itself was under a triple cloak of secrecy. She had spent hours that day searching for the name of the owner. He had shielded himself well under a tangle of corporations. The paper trail took frustrating twists and turns. So far, every lead Deborah had pursued had come up hard at a dead end.

But the shop was real. By tomorrow, the day after at the latest, she would have a court order. The police would search every nook and cranny of Timeless. The books would be confiscated. She would have everything she needed to indict.

She walked closer to the dark window. Something made her turn quickly to peer out at the light and shadow of the street behind her.

Traffic rolled noisily by. Arm in arm, a laughing couple strolled along the opposite sidewalk. The sound of music through open car windows was loud and confused, punctuated by the honking of horns and the occasional squeak of brakes.

Normal, Deborah reminded herself. There was nothing here to cause that itch between her shoulder blades. Yet even as she scanned the street, the adjoining buildings, to assure herself no one was paying any attention to her, the feeling of being watched persisted.

She was giving herself the creeps, Deborah decided. These little licks of fear were left over from her night in the alley, and she didn't care for it. It wasn't possible to live your life too spooked to go out at night, so paranoid you looked around every corner before you took that last step around it. At least it wasn't possible for her.

Most of her life she had been cared for, looked after, even pampered by her older sister. Though she would always be grateful to Cilla, she had made a commitment when she had left Denver for Urbana. To leave her mark. That couldn't be done if she ran from shadows.

Determined to fight her own uneasiness, she skirted around the building, walking quickly through the short, narrow alley between the antique store and the boutique beside it.

The rear of the building was as secure and unforthcoming as the front. There was one window, enforced with steel bars, and a pair of wide doors, triple bolted. Here, there were no streetlamps to relieve the dark.

"You don't look stupid."

At the voice, she jumped back and would have tumbled into a line of garbage cans if a hand hadn't snagged her wrist. She opened her mouth to scream, brought her fist up to fight, when she recognized her companion.

"You!" He was in black, hardly visible in the dark. But she knew.

"I would have thought you'd had your fill of back alleys." He didn't release her, though he knew he should. His fingers braceleted her wrist and felt the fast, hot beat of her blood.

"You've been watching me."

"There are some women it's difficult to look away from." He pulled her closer, just a tug on her wrist, and stunned both of them. His voice was low and rough. She could see anger in the gleam of his eyes. She found the combination oddly compelling. "What are you doing here?"

Her mouth was so dry it ached. He had pulled her so close that their thighs met. She could feel the warm flutter of his breath on her lips. To insure some distance and some control, she put a hand to his chest.

Her hand didn't pass through, but met a warm, solid wall, felt the quick, steady beat of a heart.

"That's my business."

"Your business is to prepare cases and try them in court, not to play detective."

"I'm not playing—" She broke off, eyes narrowing. "How do you know I'm a lawyer?"

"I know a great deal about you, Miss O'Roarke." His smile was thin and humorless. "That's my business. I don't think your sister worked to put you through law school, and saw you graduate at the top of your class to have you sneaking around back entrances of locked buildings. Especially when that building is a front for some particularly ugly commerce."

"You know about this place?"

"As I said, I know a great deal."

She would handle his intrusion into her life later. Now, she had a job to do. "If you have any information, any proof about this suspected drug operation, it's your duty to give that information to the D.A.'s office."

"I'm very aware of my duty. It doesn't include making deals with scum."

Heat rushed to her cheeks. She didn't even question how he knew about her interview with Parino. It was enough, more than enough, that he was holding her integrity up to inspection. "I worked within the law," she snapped at him. "Which is more than you can say.

You put on a mask and play Captain America, making up your own rules. That makes you part of the problem, not part of the solution.''

In the slits of his mask, his eyes narrowed. ''You seemed grateful enough for my solution a few nights ago.''

Her chin came up. She wished she could face him on her own ground, in the light. ''I've already thanked you for your help, unnecessary though it was.''

''Are you always so cocky, Miss O'Roarke?''

''Confident,'' she corrected.

''And do you always win in court?''

''I have an excellent record.''

''Do you always win?'' he repeated.

''No, but that's not the point.''

''That's exactly the point. There's a war in this city, Miss O'Roarke.''

''And you've appointed yourself general of the good guys.''

He didn't smile. ''No, I fight alone.''

''Don't you—''

But he cut her off swiftly, putting a gloved hand over her mouth. He listened, but not with his ears. It wasn't something he heard, but something he felt, as some men felt hunger or thirst, love or hate. Or, from centuries ago when their senses were not dulled by civilization, danger.

Before she had even begun to struggle against him, he pulled her aside and shoved her down beneath him behind the wall of the next building.

''What the hell do you think you're doing?''

The explosion that came on the tail of her words made her ears ring. The flash of light made her pupils contract. Before she could close her eyes against the glare, she saw the jagged shards of flying glass, the missiles of charred brick. Beneath her, the ground trembled as the antique store exploded.

She saw, with horror and fascination, a lethal chunk of concrete crash only three feet from her face.

''Are you all right?'' When she didn't answer, only trembled, he took her face in his hand and turned it to his. ''Deborah, are you all right?''

He repeated her name twice before the glassy look left her eyes. "Yes," she managed. "Are you?"

"Don't you read the papers?" There was the faintest of smiles around his mouth. "I'm invulnerable."

"Right." With a little sigh, she tried to sit up. For a moment he didn't move, but left his body where it was, where it wanted to be. Fitted against hers. His face was only inches away. He wondered what would happen—to both of them—if he closed that distance and let his mouth meet hers.

He was going to kiss her, Deborah realized and went perfectly still. Emotion swarmed through her. Not anger, as she'd expected. But excitement, raw and wild. It pumped through her so quickly, so hugely, it blocked out everything else. With a little murmur of agreement, she lifted her hand to his cheek.

Her fingers brushed his mask. He pulled back from her touch as if he'd been slapped. Shifting, he rose then helped her to her feet. Fighting a potent combination of humiliation and fury, she stepped around the wall toward the rear of the antique shop.

There was little left of it. Brick, glass and concrete were scattered. Inside the crippled building, fire raged. The roof collapsed with a long, loud groan.

"They've beaten you this time," he murmured. "There won't be anything left for you to find—no papers, no drugs, no records."

"They've destroyed a building," she said between her teeth. She hadn't wanted to be kissed, she told herself. She'd been shaken up, dazed, a victim of temporary insanity. "But someone owns it, and I'll find out who that is."

"This was meant as a warning, Miss O'Roarke. One you might want to consider."

"I won't be frightened off. Not by exploding buildings or by you." She turned to face him, but wasn't surprised that he was gone.

# Chapter 3

It was after one in the morning when Deborah dragged herself down the hallway toward her apartment. She'd spent the best part of two hours answering questions, giving her statement to the police, and avoiding reporters. Even through the fatigue was a nagging annoyance toward the man called Nemesis.

Technically he'd saved her life again. If she'd been standing within ten feet of the antique shop when the bomb had gone off, she would certainly have met a nasty death. But then he'd left her holding the bag, a very large, complicated bag she'd been forced to sort through, assistant D.A. or not, for the police.

Added to that was the fact he had shown in the short, pithy conversation they'd had, that he held no respect for her profession or her judgment. She had studied and worked toward the goal of prosecutor since she'd been eighteen. Now with a shrug, he was dismissing those years of her life as wasted.

No, she thought as she dug in her purse for her keys, he preferred to skulk around the streets, meting out his own personal sense of justice. Well, it didn't wash. And before it was over, she was going to prove to him that the system worked.

And she would prove to herself that she hadn't been the least bit attracted to him.

"You look like you had a rough night."

Keys in hand, Deborah turned. Her across-the-hall neighbor, Mrs.

Greenbaum, was standing in her open doorway, peering out through a pair of cherry-red framed glasses.

"Mrs. Greenbaum, what are you doing up?"

"Just finished watching David Letterman. That boy cracks me up." At seventy, with a comfortable pension to buffer her against life's storms, Lil Greenbaum kept her own hours and did as she pleased. At the moment she was wearing a tatty terry-cloth robe, Charles and Di bedroom slippers and a bright pink bow in the middle of her hennaed hair. "You look like you could use a drink. How about a nice hot toddy?"

Deborah was about to refuse, when she realized a hot toddy was exactly what she wanted. She smiled, dropped the keys into her jacket pocket and crossed the hall. "Make it a double."

"Already got the hot water on. You just sit down and kick off your shoes." Mrs. Greenbaum patted her hand then scurried off to the kitchen.

Grateful, Deborah sank into the deep cushions of the couch. The television was still on, with an old black-and-white movie flickering on the screen. Deborah recognized a young Cary Grant, but not the film. Mrs. Greenbaum would know, she mused. Lil Greenbaum knew everything.

The two-bedroom apartment—Mrs. Greenbaum kept a second bedroom ready for any of her numerous grandchildren—was both cluttered and tidy. Tables were packed with photographs and trinkets. There was a lava lamp atop the television, with a huge brass peace symbol attached to its base. Lil was proud of the fact that she'd marched against the establishment in the sixties. Just as she had protested nuclear reactors, Star Wars, the burning of rain forests and the increased cost of Medicare.

She liked to protest, she'd often told Deborah. When you could argue against the system, it meant you were still alive and kicking.

"Here we are." She brought out two slightly warped ceramic mugs—the product of one of her younger children's creativity. She flicked a glance at the television. "*Penny Serenade,* 1941, and oh, wasn't that Cary Grant something?" After setting down the mugs, she picked up her remote and shut the TV off. "Now, what trouble have you been getting yourself into?"

"It shows?"

Mrs. Greenbaum took a comfortable sip of whiskey-laced tea. "Your suit's a mess." She leaned closer and took a sniff. "Smells like smoke. Got a smudge on your cheek, a run in your stocking and fire in your eyes. From the look in them, there's got to be a man involved."

"The UPD could use you, Mrs. Greenbaum." Deborah sipped at the tea and absorbed the hot jolt. "I was doing a little legwork. The building I was checking out blew up."

The lively interest in Mrs. Greenbaum's eyes turned instantly to concern. "You're not hurt?"

"No. Few bruises." They would match the ones she'd gotten the week before. "I guess my ego suffered a little. I ran into Nemesis." Deborah hadn't mentioned her first encounter, because she was painfully aware of her neighbor's passionate admiration for the man in black.

Behind the thick frames, Mrs. Greenbaum's eyes bulged. "You actually saw him?"

"I saw him, spoke to him and ended up being tossed to the concrete by him just before the building blew up."

"God." Lil pressed a hand to her heart. "That's even more romantic than when I met Mr. Greenbaum at the Pentagon rally."

"It had nothing to do with romance. The man is impossible, very likely a maniac and certainly dangerous."

"He's a hero." Mrs. Greenbaum shook a scarlet-tipped finger at Deborah. "You haven't learned to recognize heroes yet. That's because we don't have enough of them today." She crossed her feet so that Princess Di grinned up at Deborah. "So, what does he look like? The reports have all been mixed. One day he's an eight-foot black man, another he's a pale-faced vampire complete with fangs. Just the other day I read he was a small green woman with red eyes."

"He's not a woman," Deborah muttered. She could remember, a bit too clearly, the feel of his body over hers. "And I can't really say what he looks like. It was dark and most of his face was masked."

"Like Zorro?" Mrs. Greenbaum said hopefully.

"No. Well, I don't know. Maybe." She gave a little sigh and

decided to indulge her neighbor. "He's six-one or six-two, I suppose, lean but well built."

"What color is his hair?"

"It was covered. I could see his jawline." Strong, tensed. "And his mouth." It had hovered for one long, exciting moment over hers. "Nothing special," she said quickly, and gulped more tea.

"Hmm." Mrs. Greenbaum had her own ideas. She'd been married and widowed twice, and in between had enjoyed what she considered her fair share of affairs and romantic entanglements. She recognized the signs. "His eyes? You can always tell the make of a man by his eyes. Though I'd rather look at his tush."

Deborah chuckled. "Dark."

"Dark what?"

"Just dark. He keeps to the shadows."

"Slipping through the shadows to root out evil and protect the innocent. What's more romantic than that?"

"He's bucking the system."

"My point exactly. It doesn't get bucked enough."

"I'm not saying he hasn't helped a few people, but we have trained law enforcement officers to do that." She frowned into her mug. There hadn't been any cops around either time she had needed help. They couldn't be everywhere. And she probably could have handled both situations herself. Probably. She used her last and ultimate argument. "He doesn't have any respect for the law."

"I think you're wrong. I think he has great respect for it. He just interprets it differently than you do." Again she patted Deborah's hand. "You're a good girl, Deborah, a smart girl, but you've trained yourself to walk down a very narrow path. You should remember that this country was founded on rebellion. We often forget, then we become fat and lazy until someone comes along and questions the status quo. We need rebels, just as we need heroes. It would be a dull, sad world without them."

"Maybe." Though she was far from convinced. "But we also need rules."

"Oh, yes." Mrs. Greenbaum grinned. "We need rules. How else could we break them?"

* * *

Gage kept his eyes closed as his driver guided the limo across town. Through the night after the explosion and the day that followed, he had thought of a dozen reasons why he should cancel his date with Deborah O'Roarke.

They were all very practical, very logical, very sane reasons. To offset them had been only one impractical, illogical and potentially insane reason.

He needed her.

She was interfering with his work, both day and night. Since the moment he'd seen her, he hadn't been able to think of anyone else. He'd used his vast network of computers to dig out every scrap of available information on her. He knew she'd been born in Atlanta, twenty-five years before. He knew she had lost her parents, tragically and brutally, at the age of twelve. Her sister had raised her, and together they had hopscotched across the country. The sister worked in radio and was now station manager at KHIP in Denver where Deborah had gone to college.

Deborah had passed the bar the first time and had applied for a position in the D.A.'s office in Urbana, where she had earned a reputation for being thorough, meticulous and ambitious.

He knew she had had one serious love affair in college, but he didn't know what had ended it. She dated a variety of men, none seriously.

He hated the fact that that one last piece of information had given him tremendous relief.

She was a danger to him. He knew it, understood it and seemed unable to avoid it. Even after their encounter the night before when she had come within a hair's breadth of making him lose control—of his temper and his desire—he wasn't able to shove her out of his mind.

To go on seeing her was to go on deceiving her. And himself.

But when the car pulled to the curb in front of her building, he got out, walked into the lobby and took the elevator up to her floor.

When Deborah heard the knock, she stopped pacing the living room. For the past twenty minutes she'd been asking herself why she had agreed to go out with a man she barely knew. And one with a reputation of being a connoisseur of women but married to his business.

She'd fallen for the charm, she admitted, that smooth, careless charm with the hint of underlying danger. Maybe she'd even been intrigued, and challenged, by his tendency to dominate. She stood for a moment, hand on the knob. It didn't matter, she assured herself. It was only one evening, a simple dinner date. She wasn't naïve and wide-eyed, and expected no more than good food and intelligent conversation.

She wore blue. Somehow he'd known she would. The deep midnight-blue silk of her dinner suit matched her eyes. The skirt was snug and short, celebrating the length of long, smooth legs. The tailored, almost mannish jacket made him wonder if she wore more silk, or simply her skin, beneath it. The lamp she had left on beside the door caught the gleam of the waterfall of blue and white stones she wore at her ears.

The easy flattery he was so used to dispensing lodged in his throat. "You're prompt," he managed.

"Always." She smiled at him. "It's like a vice." She closed the door behind her without inviting him in. It seemed safer that way.

A few moments later, she settled back in the limo and vowed to enjoy herself. "Do you always travel this way?"

"No. Just when it seems more convenient."

Unable to resist, she slipped off her shoes and let her feet sink into the deep pewter carpet. "I would. No hassling for cabs or scurrying to the subway."

"But you miss a lot of life on, and under, the streets."

She turned to him. In his dark suit and subtly striped tie he looked elegant and successful. There were burnished gold links at the cuffs of his white shirt. "You're not going to tell me you ride the subway."

He only smiled. "When it seems most convenient. You don't believe that money should be used as an insulator against reality?"

"No. No, I don't." But she was surprised he didn't. "Actually, I've never had enough to be tempted to try it."

"You wouldn't be." He contented himself, or tried, by toying with the ends of her hair. "You could have gone into private practice with a dozen top firms at a salary that would have made your paycheck at the D.A.'s office look like pin money. You didn't.''

She shrugged it off. ''Don't think there aren't moments when I question my own sanity.'' Thinking it would be safer to move to more impersonal ground, she glanced out the window. ''Where are we going?''

''To dinner.''

''I'm relieved to hear that since I missed lunch. I meant where.''

''Here.'' He took her hand as the limo stopped. They had driven to the very edge of the city, to the world of old money and prestige. Here the sound of traffic was only a distant echo, and there was the light, delicate scent of roses in bloom.

Deborah stifled a gasp as she stepped onto the curb. She had seen pictures of his home. But it was entirely different to be faced with it. It loomed over the street, spreading for half a block.

It was Gothic in style, having been built by a philanthropist at the turn of the century. She'd read somewhere that Gage had purchased it before he'd been released from the hospital.

Towers and turrets rose up into the sky. High mullioned windows gleamed with the sun that was lowering slowly in the west. Terraces jutted out, then danced around corners. The top story was dominated by a huge curving glass where one could stand and look out over the entire city.

''I see you take the notion that a man's home is his castle literally.''

''I like space, and privacy. But I decided to postpone the moat.'' With a laugh, she walked up to the carved doors at the entrance.

''Would you like a tour before we eat?''

''Are you kidding?'' She hooked her arm through his. ''Where do we start?''

He led her through winding corridors, under lofty ceilings, into rooms both enormous and cramped. And he couldn't remember enjoying his home more than now, seeing it through her eyes.

There was a two-level library packed with books—from first editions to dog-eared paperbacks. Parlors with curvy old couches and delicate porcelain. Ming vases, Tang horses, Lalique crystal and Mayan pottery. Walls were done in rich, deep colors, offset by gleaming wood and Impressionist paintings.

The east wing held a tropical greenery, an indoor pool and a fully equipped gymnasium with a separate whirlpool and sauna. Through another corridor, up a curving staircase, there were bedrooms furnished with four-posters or heavy carved headboards.

She stopped counting rooms.

More stairs, then a huge office with a black marble desk and a wide sheer window that was growing rosy with sundown. Computers silent and waiting.

A music room, complete with a white grand piano and an old Wurlitzer jukebox. Almost dizzy, she stepped into a mirrored ballroom and stared at her own multiplied reflection. Above, a trio of magnificent chandeliers blazed with sumptuous light.

"It's like something out of a movie," she murmured. "I feel as though I should be wearing a hooped skirt and a powdered wig."

"No." He touched her hair again. "I think it suits you just fine as it is."

With a shake of her head, she stepped further inside, then went with impulse and turned three quick circles. "It's incredible, really. Don't you ever get the urge to just come into this room and dance?"

"Not until now." Surprising himself as much as her, he caught her around the waist and swung her into a waltz.

She should have laughed—have shot him an amused and flirtatious look and have taken the impulsive gesture for what it was. But she couldn't. All she could do was stare up at him, stare into his eyes as he spun her around and around the mirrored room.

Her hand lay on his shoulder, her other caught firmly in his. Their steps matched, though she gave no thought to them. She wondered, foolishly, if he heard the same music in his head that she did.

He heard nothing but the steady give and take of her breathing. Never in his life could he remember being so totally, so exclusively aware of one person. The way her long, dark lashes framed her eyes. The subtle trace of bronze she had smudged on the lids. The pale, moist gloss of rose on her lips.

Where his hand gripped her waist, the silk was warm from her body. And that body seemed to flow with his, anticipating each step, each turn. Her hair fanned out, making him ache to let his hands dive into it. Her scent floated around him, not quite sweet and utterly tempting. He wondered if he would taste it if he pressed his lips to the long, white column of her throat.

She saw the change in his eyes, the deepening, the darkening of them as desire grew. As her steps matched his, so did her need. She felt it build and spread, like a living thing, until her body thrummed with it. She leaned toward him, wondering.

He stopped. For a moment they stood, reflected dozens and dozens of times. A man and a woman caught in a tentative embrace, on the brink of something neither of them understood.

She moved first, a cautious half-step in retreat. It was her nature to think carefully before making any decision. His hand tightened on hers. For some reason she thought it was a warning.

"I…my head's spinning."

Very slowly his hand slipped away from her waist and the embrace was broken. "Then I'd better feed you."

"Yes." She nearly managed to smile. "You'd better."

They dined on sautéed shrimp flavored with orange and rosemary. Though he'd shown her the enormous dining room with its heavy mahogany servers and sideboards, they took their meal in a small salon at a table by a curved window. Between sips of champagne, they could watch the sunset over the city. On the table, between them, were two slender white candles and a single red rose.

"It's beautiful here," she commented. "The city. You can see all its possibilities, and none of its problems."

"Sometimes it helps to take a step back." He stared out at the city himself, then turned away as if dismissing it. "Or else those problems can eat you alive."

"But you're still aware of them. I know you donate a lot of money to the homeless and rehabilitation centers, and other charities."

"It's easy to give money away when you have more than you need."

"That sounds cynical."

"Realistic." His smile was cool and easy. "I'm a businessman, Deborah. Donations are tax deductible."

She frowned, studying him. "It would be a great pity, I think, if people were only generous when it benefited them."

"Now you sound like an idealist."

Riled, she tapped a finger against the champagne goblet. "That's the second time in a matter of days you've accused me of that. I don't think I like it."

"It wasn't meant as an insult, just an observation." He glanced up when Frank came in with individual chocolate soufflés. "We won't need anything else tonight."

The big man shrugged. "Okay."

Deborah noted that Frank moved with a dancer's grace, an odd talent in a man who was big and bulky. Thoughtful, she dipped a spoon into the dessert. "Is he your driver or your butler?" she asked.

"Both. And neither." He topped off her wine. "You might say he's an associate from a former life."

Intrigued, she lifted a brow. "Which means?"

"He was a pickpocket I collared a time or two when I was a cop. Then he was my snitch. Now...he drives my car and answers my door, among other things."

She noted that Gage's fingers fit easily around the slender stem of the crystal glass. "It's hard to imagine you working the streets."

He grinned at her. "Yes, I suppose it is." He watched the way the candlelight flickered in her eyes. Last night, he had seen the reflection of fire there, from the burning building and her own smothered desires.

"How long were you a cop?"

"One night too long," he said flatly, then reached for her hand. "Would you like to see the view from the roof?"

"Yes, I would." She pushed back from the table, understanding that the subject of his past was a closed book.

Rather than the stairs, he took her up in a small smoked-glass elevator. "All the comforts," she said as they started their ascent. "I'm surprised the place doesn't come equipped with a dungeon and secret passageways."

"Oh, but it does. Perhaps I'll show you...another time."

Another time, she thought. Did she want there to be another time? It had certainly been a fascinating evening, and with the exception of that moment of tension in the ballroom, a cordial one. Yet despite his polished manners, she sensed something restless and dangerous beneath the tailored suit.

That was what attracted her, she admitted. Just as that was what made her uneasy.

"What are you thinking?"

She decided it was best to be perfectly honest. "I was wondering who you were, and if I wanted to stick around long enough to find out."

The doors to the elevator whispered open, but he stayed where he was. "And do you?"

"I'm not sure." She stepped out and into the topmost turret of the building. With a sound of surprise and pleasure, she moved toward the wide curve of glass. Beyond it, the sun had set and the city was all shadow and light. "It's spectacular." She turned to him, smiling. "Just spectacular."

"It gets better." He pushed a button on the wall. Silently, magically, the curved glass parted. Taking her hand, he led her onto the stone terrace beyond.

Setting her palms on the stone railing, she leaned out into the hot wind that stirred the air. "You can see the trees in City Park, and the river." Impatiently she brushed her blowing hair out of her eyes. "The buildings look so pretty with their lights on." In the distance, she could see the twinkling lights of the Dover Heights suspension bridge. They draped like a necklace of diamonds against the dark.

"At dawn, when it's clear, the buildings are pearly gray and rose. And the sun turns all the glass into fire."

She looked at him and the city he faced. "Is that why you bought the house, for the view?"

"I grew up a few blocks from here. Whenever we walked in the park, my aunt would always point it out to me. She loved this house. She'd been to parties here as a child—she and my mother. They had been friends since childhood. I was the only child, for my parents, and then for my aunt and uncle. When I came back and learned they were gone...well, I couldn't think of much of anything at first. Then I began to think about this house. It seemed right that I take it, live in it."

She laid a hand over his on the rail. "There's nothing more difficult, is there, than to lose people you love and need?"

"No." When he looked at her, he saw that her eyes were dark and glowing with her own memories and with empathy for his. He brought a hand to her face, skimming back her hair with his fingers, molding her jawline with his palm. Her hand fluttered up to light on his wrist and trembled. Her voice was just as unsteady.

"I should go."

"Yes, you should." But he kept his hand on her face, his eyes on hers as he shifted to trap her body between his and the stone parapet. His free hand slid gently up her throat until her face was framed. "Have you ever been compelled to take a step that you knew was a mistake? You knew, but you couldn't stop."

A haze was drifting over her mind, and she shook her head to clear it. "I—no. No, I don't like to make mistakes." But she already knew she was about to make one. His palms were rough and warm against her skin. His eyes were so dark, so intense. For a moment she blinked, assaulted by a powerful sense of déjà vu.

But she'd never been here before, she assured herself as he skimmed his thumbs over the sensitive skin under her jawline.

"Neither do I."

She moaned and shut her eyes, but he only brushed his lips over her brow. The light whisper of contact shot a spear of reaction through her. In the hot night she shuddered while his mouth moved gently over her temple.

"I want you." His voice was rough and tense as his fingers tightened in her hair. Her eyes were open again, wide and aware. In his she could see edgy desire. "I can barely breathe from wanting you. You're my mistake, Deborah. The one I never thought I would make."

His mouth came down on hers, hard and hungry, with none of the teasing seduction she had expected and told herself she would have resisted. There was nothing of the smooth and sophisticated man she had dined with here. This was the reckless and dangerous man she had caught only glimpses of.

He frightened her. He fascinated her. He seduced her.

With no hesitation, no caution, no thought, she responded, meeting power for power and need for need.

She didn't feel the rough stone against her back, only the hard long length of him as his body pressed to hers. She could taste the zing of wine on his tongue and something darker, the potent flavor of passion barely in check. With a groan of pleasure, she pulled him closer until she could feel his heart thudding against hers. Beat for beat.

She was more than he had dreamed. All silk and scent and long limbs. Her mouth was heated, yielding against his, then demanding. Her hands slid under his jacket, fingers flexing even as her head fell back in a taunting surrender that drove him mad.

A pulse hammered in her throat, enticing him to press his lips there and explore the new texture, the new flavor, before he brought his mouth back to hers. With teeth he nipped, with tongue he soothed, pushing them closer and closer to the edge of reason. He swallowed her gasp as he stroked his hands down her, seeking, cupping, molding.

He felt her shudder, then his own before he forced himself to grip tight to a last thin line of control. Very cautiously, like a man backing away from a sheer drop, he stepped away from her.

Dazed, Deborah brought a hand to her head. Fighting to catch her breath, she stared at him. What kind of power did he have, she wondered, that he could turn her from a sensible woman into a trembling puddle of need?

She turned, learning over the rail and gulping air as though it were water and she dying of thirst. "I don't think I'm ready for you," she managed at length.

"No. I don't think I'm ready for you, either. But there won't be any going back."

She shook her head. Her palms were pressed so hard into the rail that the stone was biting her skin. "I'll have to think about that."

"Once you've turned certain corners, there's no place to go but forward."

Calmer, she turned back to him. It was time, past time, to set the ground rules. For both of them. "Gage, however it might appear after what just happened, I don't have affairs with men I hardly know."

"Good." He, too, was calmer. His decision was made. "When we have ours, I want it to be exclusive."

Her voice chilled. "Obviously I'm not making myself clear. I haven't decided if I want to be involved with you, and I'm a long way from sure if I'd want that involvement to end up in bed."

"You are involved with me." Reaching out, he cupped the back of her neck before she could evade. "And we both want that involvement to end up in bed."

Very deliberately, she reached up and removed his hand. "I realize you're used to women falling obligingly at your feet. I have no intention of joining the horde. And I make up my own mind."

"Should I kiss you again?"

"No." She threw a hand up and planted it solidly against his chest. In an instant she was reminded of how she had stood, just like this, with the man called Nemesis. The comparison left her shaken. "No. It was a lovely evening, Gage." She took a long steadying breath. "I mean that. I enjoyed the company, the dinner and…and the view. I'd hate to see you spoil it completely by being arrogant and argumentative."

"It's not being either to accept the inevitable. I don't have to like it to accept it." Something flickered in his eyes. "There is such a thing as destiny, Deborah. I had a long time to consider, and to come to terms with that." His brows drew together in a frown as he looked at her. "God help both of us, but you're part of mine." He looked back, then offered a hand. "I'll take you home."

## Chapter 4

Groaning, her eyes firmly shut, Deborah groped for the shrilling phone on her nightstand. She knocked over a book, a brass candlestick and a notepad before she managed to snag the receiver and drag it under the pillow.

"Hello?"

"O'Roarke?"

She cleared her throat. "Yes."

"Mitchell here. We've got a problem."

"Problem?" She shoved the pillow off her head and squinted at her alarm clock. The only problem she could see was that her boss was calling her at 6:15 a.m. "Has the Slagerman trial been postponed? I'm scheduled for court at nine."

"No. It's Parino."

"Parino?" Scrubbing a hand over her face, she struggled to sit up. "What about him?"

"He's dead."

"Dead." She shook her head to clear her groggy brain. "What do you mean he's dead?"

"As in doornail," Mitchell said tersely. "Guard found him about half an hour ago."

She wasn't groggy now, but was sitting ramrod straight, brain racing. "But—but how?"

"Knifed. Looks like he went up to the bars to talk to someone, and they shoved a stiletto through his heart."

"Oh, God."

"Nobody heard anything. Nobody saw anything," Mitchell said in disgust. "There was a note taped to the bars. It said, 'Dead birds don't sing.'"

"Somebody leaked that he was feeding us information."

"And you can bet that I'm going to find out who. Listen, O'Roarke, we're not going to be able to muzzle the press on this one. I figured you'd want to hear it from me instead of on the news during your morning coffee."

"Yeah." She pressed a hand to her queasy stomach. "Yeah, thanks. What about Santiago?"

"No show yet. We've got feelers out, but if he's gone to ground, it might be a while before we dig him up."

"They'll be after him, too," she said quietly. "Whoever arranged for Parino to be murdered will be after Ray Santiago."

"Then we'll just have to find him first. You're going to have to shake this off," he told her. "I know it's a tough break all around, but the Slagerman case is your priority now. The guy's got himself a real slick lawyer."

"I can handle it."

"Never figured otherwise. Give him hell, kid."

"Yeah. Yeah, I will." Deborah hung up and stared blankly into space until her alarm went off at 6:30.

"Hey! Hey, beautiful." Jerry Bower charged up the courthouse steps after Deborah. "Boy, that's concentration," he panted when he finally snagged her arm and stopped her. "I've been calling you for half a block."

"Sorry. I'm due in court in fifteen minutes."

He gave her a quick, smiling going-over. She'd pinned her hair back into a simple twist and wore pearl buttons at her ears. Her red linen suit was severely tailored and still managed to show off each subtle curve. The result was competent, professional and completely feminine.

"If I was on the jury, I'd give you a guilty verdict before you finished your opening statement. You look incredible."

"I'm a lawyer," she said tightly. "Not Miss November."

"Hey." He had to race up three more steps to catch her. "Hey, look, I'm sorry. That was a poorly phrased compliment."

She found a slippery hold on her temper. "No, I'm sorry. I'm a little touchy this morning."

"I heard about Parino."

With a grim nod, Deborah continued up the steps to the high carved doors of city courthouse. "News travels fast."

"He was a walking statistic, Deb. You can't let it get to you."

"He deserved his day in court," she said as she crossed the marble floor of the lobby and started toward a bank of elevators. "Even he deserved that. I knew he was afraid, but I didn't take it seriously enough."

"Do you think it would have mattered?"

"I don't know." It was that single question she would have to live with. "I just don't know."

"Look, the mayor's got a tough schedule today. There's this dinner tonight, but I can probably slip out before the brandy and cigar stage. How about a late movie?"

"I'm lousy company, Jerry."

"You know that doesn't matter."

"It matters to me." A ghost of a smile touched her lips. "I'd bite your head off again and hate myself." She stepped into the elevator.

"Counselor." Jerry grinned and gave her a thumbs-up before the doors slid shut.

The press was waiting for her on the fourth floor. Deborah had expected no less. Moving quickly, she waded through them, dispensing curt answers and no comments.

"Do you really expect to get a jury to convict a pimp for knocking around a couple of his girls?"

"I always expect to win when I go into court."

"Are you going to put the prostitutes on the stand?"

"Former prostitutes," she corrected, and let the question go unanswered.

"Is it true Mitchell assigned you to this case because you're a woman?"

"The D.A. doesn't choose his prosecutors by their sex."

"Do you feel responsible for the death of Carl Parino?"

That stopped her on the threshold of the courtroom. She looked around and saw the reporter with curly brown hair, hungry brown eyes and a sarcastic smirk. Chuck Wisner. She'd run foul of him before and would again. In his daily column in the *World,* he preferred the sensational to the factual.

"The D.A.'s office regrets that Carl Parino was murdered and not allowed his day in court."

In a quick, practiced move, he blocked her way. "But do you feel responsible? After all, you're the one who turned the deal."

She choked back the urge to defend herself and met his eyes levelly. "We're all responsible, Mr. Wisner. Excuse me."

He simply shifted, crowding her back from the door. "Any more encounters with Nemesis? What can you tell us about your personal experiences with the city's newest hero?"

She could feel her temper begin to fray, strand by strand. Worse, she knew that was exactly what he was hoping for. "Nothing that could compete with your fabrications. Now if you'll move aside, I'm busy."

"Not too busy to socialize with Gage Guthrie. Are you and he romantically involved? It makes a wild kind of triangle, doesn't it? Nemesis, you, Guthrie."

"Get a life, Chuck," she suggested, then elbowed him aside.

She barely had enough time to settle behind the prosecutor's table and open her briefcase when the jury filed in. She and the defense counsel had taken two days to select them, and she was satisfied with the mix of genders and races and walks of life. Still, she would have to convince those twelve men and women that a couple of prostitutes deserved justice.

Turning slightly, she studied the two women in the first row. They had both followed her instructions and dressed simply, with a minimum of makeup and hair spray. She knew they were on trial today, as much as the man charged with assault and battery. They huddled together, two young, pretty women who might have been mistaken for college students. Deborah sent them a reassuring smile before she shifted again.

James P. Slagerman sat at the defense table. He was thirty-two, dashingly blond and handsome in a dark suit and tie. He looked precisely like what he claimed he was, a young executive. His escort service was perfectly legitimate. He paid his taxes, contributed to charity and belonged to the Jaycees.

It would be Deborah's primary job to convince the jury that he was no different than a street pimp, taking his cut from the sale of a woman's body. Until she did that, she had no hope of convicting him on assault.

As the bailiff announced the judge, the courtroom rose.

Deborah kept her opening statement brief, working the jury, dispensing facts. She didn't attempt to dazzle them. She was already aware that this was the defense counsel's style. Instead, she would underplay, drawing their attention with the contrast of simplicity.

She began her direct examination by calling the doctor who had attended Marjorie Lovitz. With a few brief questions she established the extent of Marjorie's injuries on the night she and Suzanne McRoy had been brought into Emergency. She wanted the jury to hear of the broken jaw, the blackened eyes, the cracked ribs, even before she entered the photographs taken of the women that night into evidence.

She picked her way slowly, carefully through the technicalities, doctors, ambulance attendants, uniformed cops, social workers. She weathered her opponent's parries. By the noon recess, she had laid her groundwork.

She hustled Marjorie and Suzanne into a cab and took them across town for lunch and a last briefing.

"Do I have to go on the stand today, Miss O'Roarke?" Marjorie fidgeted in her seat and ate nothing. Though her bruises had faded over the weeks since the beating, her jaw still tended to ache. "Maybe what the doctors and all said was enough, and Suzanne and I won't have to testify."

"Marjorie." She laid a hand over the girl's and found it ice-cold and trembly. "They'll listen to the doctors, and they'll look at the pictures. They'll believe you and Suzanne were beaten. But it's you, both of you, who will convince them that Slagerman was the one who did it, that he is not the nice young businessman he pretends to be. Without you, he'll walk away and do it again."

Suzanne bit her lip. "Jimmy says he's going to get off anyway. That people will know we're whores, even though you helped us get regular jobs. He says when it's over he's going to find us, and hurt us real bad."

"When did he say that?"

"He called last night." Marjorie's eyes filled with tears. "He found out where we're living and he called. He said he was going to mess us up." She wiped at a tear with the heel of her hand. "He said he was going to make us wish we'd never started this. I don't want him to hurt me again."

"He won't. I can't help you unless you help me. Unless you trust me."

For the next hour, she talked, soothing, bullying, cajoling and promising. At two o'clock, both frightened women were back in court.

"The State calls Marjorie Lovitz," Deborah announced, and flicked a cool glance at Slagerman.

Gage slipped into the courtroom just as she called her first witness for the afternoon session. He'd had to cancel two meetings in order to be there. The need to see her had been a great deal stronger than the need to hear quarterly reports. It had been, Gage admitted, stronger than any need he had ever experienced.

For three days he'd kept his distance. Three very long days.

Life was often a chess match, he thought. And you took what time you needed to work out your next move. He chose a seat in the rear of the courtroom and settled back to watch her work.

"How old are you, Marjorie?" Deborah asked.

"Twenty-one."

"Have you always lived in Urbana?"

"No, I grew up in Pennsylvania."

With a few casual questions, she helped Marjorie paint a picture of her background, the poverty, the unhappiness, the parental abuse.

"When did you come to the city?"

"About four years ago."

"When you were seventeen. Why did you come?"

"I wanted to be an actress. That sounds pretty dumb, but I used to be in plays in school. I thought it would be easy."

"Was it?"

"No. No, it was hard. Real hard. Most of the time I didn't even get to audition, you know? And I ran out of money. I got a job waiting tables part-time, but it wasn't enough. They turned off the heat, and the lights."

"Did you ever think of going home?"

"I couldn't. My mother said if I took off then she was done with me. And I guess I thought, I still thought I could do okay, if I just got a break."

"Did you get one?"

"I thought I did. This guy came into the grill where I worked. We got kind of friendly, talking, you know. I told him how I was an actress. He said he'd known it as soon as he'd seen me, and what was I doing working in a dump like that when I was so pretty, and so talented. He told me he knew lots of people, and that if I came to work for him, he'd introduce me. He gave me a business card and everything."

"Is the man you met that night in the courtroom, Marjorie?"

"Sure, it was Jimmy." She looked down quickly at her twisting fingers. "Jimmy Slagerman."

"Did you go to work for him?"

"Yeah. I went the next day to his offices. He had a whole suite, all these desks and phones and leather chairs. A real nice place, uptown. He called it Elegant Escorts. He said I could make a hundred dollars a night just by going to dinner and parties with these businessmen. He even bought me clothes, pretty clothes and had my hair done and everything."

"And for this hundred dollars a night, all you had to do was go to dinner or parties?"

"That's what he told me, at first."

"And did that change?"

"After a while...he took me out to nice restaurants and places. Dress rehearsals, he called them. He bought me flowers and..."

"Did you have sex with him?"

"Objection. Irrelevant."

"Your Honor, the witness's relationship, her physical relationship with the defendant is very relevant."

"Overruled. You'll answer the question, Miss Lovitz."

"Yes. I went to bed with him. He treated me so nice. After, he gave me money—for the bills, he said."

"And you accepted it?"

"Yes. I guess I knew what was going on. I knew, but I pretended I didn't. A few days later, he told me he had a customer for me. He said I was to dress up real nice, and go out to dinner with this man from D.C."

"What instructions were you given by Mr. Slagerman?"

"He said, 'Marjorie, you're going to have to earn that hundred dollars.' I said I knew that, and he told me I was going to have to be real nice to this guy. I said I would."

"Did Mr. Slagerman define 'nice' for you, Marjorie?"

She hesitated, then looked down at her hands again. "He said I was to do whatever I was told. That if the guy wanted me to go back to his hotel after, I had to go or I wouldn't get my money. It was all acting, he said. I acted like I enjoyed the guy's company, like I was attracted to him, and I acted like I had a great time in bed with him."

"Did Mr. Slagerman specifically tell you that you would be required to have sex with this customer?"

"He said it was part of the job, the same as smiling at bad jokes. And if I was good at it, he'd introduce me to this director he knew."

"And you agreed?"

"He made it sound okay. Yes."

"And were there other occasions when you agreed to exchange sex for money in your capacity as an escort for Mr. Slagerman's firm?"

"Objection."

"I'll rephrase." She flicked a glance at the jury. "Did you continue in Mr. Slagerman's employ?"

"Yes, ma'am."

"For how long?"

"Three years."

"And were you satisfied with the arrangement?"

"I don't know."

"You don't know if you were satisfied?"

"I got used to the money," Marjorie said, painfully honest. "And after a while you get so you can forget what you're doing, if you think about something else when it's going on."

"And was Mr. Slagerman happy with you?"

"Sometimes." Fearful, she looked up at the judge. "Sometimes he'd get real mad, at me or one of the other girls."

"There were other girls?"

"About a dozen, sometimes more."

"And what did he do when he got mad?"

"He'd smack you around."

"You mean he'd hit you?"

"He'd just go crazy and—"

"Objection."

"Sustained."

"Did he ever strike you, Marjorie?"

"Yes."

Deborah let the simplicity of the answer hang over the jury. "Will you tell me the events that took place on the night of February 25 of this year?"

As she'd been instructed, Marjorie kept her eyes on Deborah and didn't let them waver back to Slagerman. "I had a job, but I got sick. The flu or something. I had a fever and my stomach was really upset. I couldn't keep anything down. Suzanne came over to take care of me."

"Suzanne?"

"Suzanne McRoy. She worked for Jimmy, too, and we got to be friends. I just couldn't get up and go to work, so Suzanne called Jimmy to tell him." Her hands began to twist in her lap. "I could hear her arguing with him over the phone, telling him I was sick. Suzanne said he could come over and see for himself if he didn't believe her."

"And did he come over?"

"Yes." The tears started, big silent drops that cruised down her cheeks. "He was really mad. He was yelling at Suzanne, and she was yelling back, telling him I was really sick, that I had a fever like a hundred and two. He said—" She licked her lips. "He said we were both lazy, lying sluts. I heard something crash and she was crying. I got up, but I was dizzy." She rubbed the heel of her hands under her eyes, smearing mascara. "He came into the bedroom. He knocked me down."

"You mean he bumped into you?"

"No, he knocked me down. Backhanded me, you know?"

"Yes. Go on."

"Then he told me to get my butt up and get dressed. He said the customer had asked for me, I was going to do it. He said all I had to do was lie on my back and close my eyes anyway." She fumbled for a tissue, blew her nose. "I told him I was sick, that I couldn't do it. He was yelling and throwing things. Then he said he'd show me how it felt to be sick. And he started hitting me."

"Where did he hit you?"

"Everywhere. In the face, in the stomach. Mostly my face. He just wouldn't stop."

"Did you call for help?"

"I couldn't. I couldn't hardly breathe."

"Did you try to defend yourself?"

"I tried to crawl away, but he kept coming after me, kept hitting me. I passed out. When I woke up, Suzanne was there, and her face was all bloody. She called an ambulance."

Gently Deborah continued to question. When she took her seat at the prosecutor's table, she prayed that Marjorie would hold up under cross-examination.

After almost three hours on the witness stand, Marjorie was pale and shaky. Despite the defense counselor's attempt to destroy her character, she stepped down looking young and vulnerable.

And it was that picture, Deborah thought with satisfaction, that would remain in the jury's mind.

"Excellent job, Counselor."

Deborah turned her head and, with twin pricks of annoyance and pleasure, glanced up at Gage. "What are you doing here?"

"Watching you work. If I ever need a lawyer..."

"I'm a prosecutor, remember?"

He smiled. "Then I'll just have to make sure I don't get caught breaking the law." When she stood, he took her hand. A casual gesture, even a friendly one. She couldn't have said why it seemed so possessive. "Can I offer you a lift? Dinner, dessert? A quiet evening?"

And she'd said he wouldn't tempt her again. Fat chance. "I'm sorry, I have something to do."

Tilting his head, he studied her. "I think you mean it."

"I do have work."

"No, I mean that you're sorry."

His eyes were so deep, so warm, she nearly sighed. "Against my better judgment, I am." She started out of the courtroom into the hall.

"Just the lift then."

She sent him a quick, exasperated look over her shoulder. "Didn't I tell you once how I felt about persistent men?"

"Yes, but you had dinner with me anyway."

She had to laugh. After all the tense hours in court, it was a relief. "Well, since my car's in the shop, I could use a lift."

He stepped into the elevator with her. "It's a tough case you've taken on here. And a reputation maker."

Her eyes cooled. "Really?"

"You're getting national press."

"I don't take cases for clippings." Her voice was as frigid as her eyes.

"If you're going to be in for the long haul, you'll have to develop a thicker skin."

"My skin's just fine, thanks."

"I noticed." Relaxed, he leaned back against the wall. "I think anyone who knows you realizes the press is a by-product, not the purpose. You're making a point here, that no one, no matter who or what they are, should be victimized. I hope you win."

She wondered why it should have unnerved her that he understood precisely what she was reaching for. "I will win."

She stepped out of the elevator into the marble lobby.

"I like your hair that way," he commented, pleased to see he'd thrown her off. "Very cool, very competent. How many pins would I have to pull out to have it fall loose?"

"I don't think that's—"

"Relevant?" he supplied. "It is to me. Everything about you is, since I don't seem to be able to stop thinking about you."

She kept walking quickly. It was typical, she imagined, that he would say such things to a woman in a lobby swarming with people—and make her feel as though they were completely alone. "I'm sure you've managed to keep busy. I noticed a picture of you in this morning's paper—there was a blonde attached to your arm. Candidate Tarrington's dinner party." She set her teeth when he kept smiling. "You switch your allegiances quickly, politically speaking."

"I have no allegiances, politically speaking. I was interested to hear what Fields's opposition had to say. I was impressed."

She remembered the lush blonde in the skinny black dress. "I bet."

This time he grinned. "I'm sorry you weren't there."

"I told you before I don't intend to be part of a horde." At the wide glass doors, she stopped, braced. "Speaking of hordes." Head up, she walked into the crowd of reporters waiting on the courthouse steps.

They fired questions. She fired answers. Still, as annoyed as she was with him, she was grateful to see Gage's big black limo with its hulk of a driver waiting at the curb.

"Mr. Guthrie, what's your interest in this case?"

"I enjoy watching justice at work."

"You enjoy watching gorgeous D.A.s at work." Wisner pushed his way through his associates to shove a recorder into Gage's face. "Come on, Guthrie, what's happening between you and Darling Deb?"

Hearing her low snarl, Gage put a warning hand on Deborah's arm and turned to the reporter. "I know you, don't I?"

Wisner smirked. "Sure. We ran into each other plenty in those bad old days when you worked for the city instead of owning it."

"Yeah. Wisner." He summed the man up with one quick, careless look. "Maybe my memory's faulty, but I don't recall you being as big a jerk then as you are now." He bundled a chuckling Deborah into the limo.

"Nicely done," she said.

"I'll have to consider buying *The World,* just to have the pleasure of firing him."

"I have to admire the way you think." With a sigh, she slipped out of her shoes and shut her tired eyes. She could get used to traveling this way, she thought. Big cushy seats and Mozart playing softly in the speakers. A pity it wasn't reality. "My feet are killing me. I'm going to have to buy a pedometer to see how many miles I put in during an average day in court."

"Will you come home with me if I promise you a foot massage?"

She opened one eye. He'd be good at it, she thought. At massaging a woman's foot—or anything else that happened to ache. "No." She shut her eye again. "I have to get back to my office. And I'm sure there are plenty of other feet you can rub."

Gage opened the glass long enough to give Frank their destination. "Is that what concerns you? The other…feet in my life?"

She hated the fact that it did. "They're your business."

"I like yours. Your feet, your legs, your face. And everything in between."

She ignored, tried to ignore, the quick frisson of response. "Do you always try to seduce women in the back of limos?"

"Would you prefer someplace else?"

She opened both eyes. Some things, she thought, were better handled face-to-face. "Gage, I've done some thinking about this situation."

His mouth curved charmingly. "Situation?"

"Yes." She didn't chose to call it a relationship. "I'm not going to pretend I'm not attracted to you, or that I'm not flattered you seem to be attracted to me. But—"

"But?" He picked up her hand, rubbed his lips over her knuckles. The skin there smelled as fresh and clear as rainwater.

"Don't." Her breath caught when he turned her hand over to press a slow, warm kiss in the palm. "Don't do that."

"I love it when you're cool and logical, Deborah. It makes me crazy to see how quickly I can make you heat up." He brushed his lips over her wrist and felt the fast thud of her pulse. "You were saying?"

Was she? What woman could be cool and logical when he was

looking at her? Touching her. She snatched her hand away, reminding herself that was precisely the problem. "I don't want this—situation to go any further, for several good reasons."

"Mmm-hmm."

She knocked his hand away when he began to toy with the pearl at her ear. "I mean it. I realize you're used to picking and discarding women like poker chips, but I'm not interested. So ante up with someone else."

Yes, she was heating up nicely. "That's a very interesting metaphor. I could say that there are some winnings I prefer to hold on to rather than gamble with."

Firing up, she turned to him. "Let's get this straight. I'm not this week's prize. I have no intention of being Wednesday's brunette following Tuesday's blonde."

"So, we're back to those feet again."

"You might consider it a joke, but I take my life, personally and professionally, very seriously."

"Maybe too seriously."

She stiffened. "That's my business. The bottom line here is that I'm not interested in becoming one of your conquests. I'm not interested in becoming tangled up with you in any way, shape or form." She glanced over when the limo glided to the curb. "And this is my stop."

He moved quickly, surprising them both, dragging her across the seat so that she lay across his lap. "I'm going to see to it that you're so tangled up you'll never pull free." Hard and sure, his mouth met hers.

She didn't struggle. She didn't hesitate. Every emotion she had felt along the drive had been honed down to one: desire. Irrevocable. Instantaneous. Irresistible. Her fingers dived into his hair as her mouth moved restless and hungry under his.

She wanted, as she had never wanted before. Never dreamed of wanting. The ache of it was so huge it left no room for reason. The rightness of it was so clear it left no room for doubt. There was only the moment—and the taking.

He wasn't patient as he once had been. Instead, his mouth was fevered as it raced over her face, streaked down her throat. With an urgent murmur, she pulled his lips back to hers.

Never before had he known anyone who had matched his needs so exactly. There was a fire burning in her, and he had only to touch to make it leap and spark. He'd known desire before, but not this gnawing, tearing desperation.

He wanted to drag her down on the seat, pull and tug at that slim, tidy suit until she was naked and burning beneath him.

But he also wanted to give her comfort and compassion and love. He would have to wait until she was ready to accept it.

With real regret, he gentled his hands and drew her away. "You're everything I want," he told her. "And I've learned to take what I want."

Her eyes were wide. As the passion faded from them, it was replaced by a dazed fear that disturbed him. "It's not right," she whispered. "It's not right that you should be able to do this to me."

"No, it's not right for either of us. But it's real."

"I won't be controlled by my emotions."

"We all are."

"Not me." Shaky, she reached down for her shoes. "I've got to go."

He reached across her to unlatch the door. "You will belong to me."

She shook her head. "I have to belong to myself first." Climbing out, she bolted.

Gage watched her retreat before he opened his fisted hand. He counted six hairpins and smiled.

Deborah spent the evening with Suzanne and Marjorie in their tiny apartment. Over the Chinese takeout she'd supplied, she discussed the case with them. It helped, pouring herself into her work helped. It left little time to brood about Gage and her response to him. A response that worried her all the more since she had felt much the same stunning sexual pull toward another man.

Because she wanted to turn to both, she couldn't turn to either. It was a matter of ethics. To Deborah, when a woman began to doubt her ethics, she had to doubt everything.

It helped to remind herself that there were things she could control. Her work, her life-style, her ambitions. Tonight she hoped to do something to control the outcome of the case she was trying.

Each time the phone rang, she answered it herself while Marjorie and Suzanne sat on the sofa, hands clutched. On the fifth call, she hit pay dirt.

"Marjorie?"

She took a chance. "No."

"Suzanne, you bitch."

Though a grim smile touched her lips, she made her voice shake. "Who is this?"

"You know damn well who it is. It's Jimmy."

"I'm not supposed to talk to you."

"Fine. Just listen. If you think I messed you up before, it's nothing to what I'm going to do to you if you testify tomorrow. You little slut, I picked you up off the street where you were earning twenty a trick and set you up with high rolling johns. I own you, and don't you forget it. Do yourself a favor, Suze, tell that tight-assed D.A. that you've changed your mind, that you and Marjorie lied about everything. Otherwise, I'll hurt you, real bad. Understand?"

"Yes." She hung up and stared at the phone. "Oh, yeah. I understand." Deborah turned to Marjorie and Suzanne. "Keep your door locked tonight and don't go out. He doesn't know it yet, but he just hanged himself."

Pleased with herself, she left them. It had taken a great deal of fast talking to get a tap on Marjorie and Suzanne's line. And it would take more to subpoena Slagerman's phone records. But she would do it. When Slagerman took the stand in a few days, both he and his defense counsel were in for a surprise.

She decided to walk a few blocks before trying to hunt up a cab. The night was steamy. Even the buildings were sweating. Across town there was a cool room, a cool shower, a cool drink waiting. But she didn't want to go home, alone, yet. Alone it would be too easy to think about her life. About Gage.

She had lost control in his arms in the afternoon. That was becoming a habit she didn't care for. It wasn't possible to deny that she was attracted to him. More, pulled toward him in a basic, almost primitive way that was all but impossible to resist.

Yet, she also felt something, a very strong something, for a man who wore a mask.

How could she, who had always prized loyalty, fidelity, above all else, have such deep and dramatic feelings for two different men?

She hoped she could blame her own physicality. To want a man wasn't the same as to need one. She wasn't ready to need one, much less two.

What she needed was control, over her emotions, her life, her career. For too much of her life she had been a victim of circumstance. Her parents' tragic deaths, and the depthless well of fear and grief that had followed it. The demands of her sister's job that had taken them both from city to city to city.

Now she was making her own mark, in her own way, in her own time. For the past eighteen months she had worked hard, with a single-minded determination to earn and deserve the reputation as a strong and honest representative of the justice system. All she had to do was keep moving forward on the same straight path.

As she stepped into the shadows of the World Building, she heard someone whisper her name. She knew that voice, had heard it in her dreams—dreams she'd refused to acknowledge.

He seemed to flow out of the dark, a shadow, a silhouette, then a man. She could see his eyes, the gleam of them behind the mask. The longing came so quickly, so strongly, she nearly moaned aloud.

And when he took her hand to draw her into the shadows, she didn't resist.

"You seem to be making it a habit to walk the streets at night alone."

"I had work." Automatically she pitched her voice low to match his. "Are you following me?"

He didn't answer, but his fingers curled around hers in a way that spoke of possession.

"What do you want?"

"It's dangerous for you." She'd left her hair down, he saw, so that it flowed around her shoulders. "Those who murdered Parino will be watching you.'' He felt her pulse jump, but not with fear. He recognized the difference between fear and excitement.

''What do you know about Parino?''

''They won't be bothered by the fact you're a woman, not if you're in their way. I don't want to see you hurt.''

Unable to help herself, she leaned toward him. ''Why?''

As helpless as she, he lifted both of her hands to his lips. He clutched them there, his grip painfully tight. His eyes met hers over them. ''You know why.''

''It isn't possible.'' But she didn't, couldn't step away when he brushed a hand over her hair. ''I don't know who you are. I don't understand what you do.''

''Sometimes neither do I.''

She wanted badly to step into his arms, to learn what it was like to be held by him, to have his mouth hot on hers. But there were reasons, she told herself as she held back. Too many reasons. She had to be strong, strong enough not only to resist him, but to use him.

''Tell me what you know. About Parino, about his murder. Let me do my job.''

''Leave it alone. That's all I have to tell you.''

''You know something. I can see it.'' With a disgusted breath, she stepped back. She needed the distance, enough of it so that she could hear her brain and remember that she was an officer of the court and he a wrench in the system in which she believed fervently. ''It's your duty to tell me.''

''I know my duty.''

She tossed back her hair. Attracted to him? Hell, no, she was infuriated by him. ''Sure, skulking around shadows, dispensing your own personal sense of justice when and where the whim strikes. That's not duty, Captain Bonehead, it's ego.'' When he didn't respond, she let out a hiss of breath and stepped toward him again. ''I could bring you up on charges for withholding information. This is police business, D.A.'s business, not a game.''

''No, it isn't a game.'' His voice remained low, but she thought she caught hints of both amusement and annoyance. ''But it has pawns. I wouldn't like to see you used as one.''

"I can take care of myself."

"So you continue to say. You're out of your league this time, Counselor. Leave it alone." He stepped back.

"Just hold on." She rushed forward, but he was gone. "Damn it, I wasn't finished arguing with you." Frustrated, she kicked the side of the building, missing his shin by inches. "Leave it alone," she muttered. "Not on your life."

# Chapter 5

Dripping, swearing, Deborah rushed toward the door. Knocks at 6:45 a.m. were the same as phone calls at three in the morning. They spelled trouble. When she opened the door and found Gage, she knew her instincts had been on target.

"Get you out of the shower?" he asked her.

She pushed an impatient hand through her wet hair. "Yes. What do you want?"

"Breakfast." Without waiting for an invitation, he strolled inside. "Very nice," he decided.

She'd used the soft cream of ivory with slashes of color—emerald, crimson, sapphire—in the upholstery of the low sofa, in the scatter of rugs on the buffed wood floor. He noted, too, that she had left a damp trail on that same floor.

"Looks like I'm about five minutes early."

Realizing the belt of her robe was loose, she snapped it tight. "No, you're not, because you shouldn't be here at all. Now—"

But he cut her off with a long, hard kiss. "Mmm, you're still wet."

She was surprised the water wasn't steaming off her. Surprised with the sudden urge that poured through her just to lay her head against his shoulder. "Look, I don't have time for this. I have to be in court—"

"In two hours," he said with a nod. "Plenty of time for breakfast."

"If you think I'm going to fix you breakfast, you're doomed to disappointment."

"I wouldn't dream of it." He skimmed a glance down her short silky robe. The single embrace had made him achingly aware that she wore nothing else. "I like you in blue. You should always wear blue."

"I appreciate the fashion advice, but—" She broke off when another knock sounded.

"I'll get it," he offered.

"I can answer my own door." She stomped over to it, her temper fraying. She was never at her best in the morning, even when she only had herself to deal with. "I'd like to know who hung out the sign that said I was having an open house this morning." Wrenching the door open, she was confronted by a white-jacketed waiter pushing an enormous tray.

"Ah, that would be breakfast. Over by the window, I think," Gage said, gesturing the waiter in. "The lady likes a view."

"Yes, sir, Mr. Guthrie."

Deborah set her hands on her hips. It was difficult to take a stand before seven in the morning, but it had to be done. "Gage, I don't know what you're up to, but it isn't going to work. I've tried to make my position clear, and at the moment, I don't have the time or the inclination...is that coffee?"

"Yes." Smiling, Gage lifted the big silver pot and poured a cup. The scent of it seduced her. "Would you like some?"

Her mouth moved into a pout. "Maybe."

"You should like this blend." Crossing to her, he held the cup under her nose. "It's one of my personal favorites."

She sipped, shut her eyes. "You don't play fair."

"No."

She opened her eyes to study the waiter, who moved briskly about his business. "What else is there?"

"Shirred eggs, grilled ham, croissants, orange juice—fresh, of course."

"Of course." She hoped she wasn't drooling.

"Raspberries and cream."

"Oh." She folded her tongue inside her mouth to keep it from hanging out.

"Would you like to sit?"

She wasn't a weak woman, Deborah assured herself of that. But there were rich and wonderful smells filling her living room. "I guess." Giving up, she took one of the ladder-back chairs the waiter had pulled up to the table.

Gage passed the waiter a bill and gave him instructions to pick up the dishes in an hour. She couldn't bring herself to complain when Gage topped off her cup.

"I suppose I should ask what brought all this on."

"I wanted to see what you looked like in the morning." He poured juice out of a crystal pitcher. "This seemed like the best way. For now." He toasted her with his cup, his eyes lingering on her face, free of makeup and unframed by her slicked-back hair. "You're beautiful."

"And you're charming." She touched the petals of the red rose beside her plate. "But that doesn't change anything." Thoughtful, she tapped a finger on the peach-colored cloth. "Still, I don't see any reason to let all this food go to waste."

"You're a practical woman." He'd counted on it. "It's one of the things I find most attractive about you."

"I don't see what's attractive about being practical." She cut a small slice of ham and slipped it between her lips. His stomach muscles tightened.

"It can be...very attractive."

She did her best to ignore the tingles sprinting through her system and concentrate on a safer kind of hunger. "Tell me, do you always breakfast this extravagantly?"

"When it seems appropriate." He laid a hand over hers. "Your eyes are shadowed. Didn't you sleep well?"

She thought of the long and restless night behind her. "No, I didn't."

"The case?"

She only shrugged. Her insomnia had had nothing to do with the case and everything to do with the man she had met in the shadows.

Yet now she was here, just as fascinated with, just as frustrated by the man she sat with in the sunlight.

"Would you like to talk about it?"

She glanced up. In his eyes she saw patience, understanding and something beneath it all she knew would burn to the touch. "No." Cautious, she drew her hand away again.

He found himself enjoying the not-so-subtle pursuit and retreat. "You work too hard."

"I do what I have to do. What about you? I don't even know what you do, not really."

"Buy and sell, attend meetings, read reports."

"I'm sure it's more complicated than that."

"And often more boring."

"That's hard to believe."

Steam and fragrance erupted when he broke open a flaky croissant. "I build things, buy things."

She wouldn't be put off that easily. "Such as?"

He smiled at her. "I own this building."

"Trojan Enterprises owns this building."

"Right. I own Trojan."

"Oh."

Her reaction delighted him. "Most of the Guthrie money came from real estate, and that's still the basis. We've diversified quite a bit over the past ten years. So, one branch handles the shipping, another the mining, another the manufacturing."

"I see." He wasn't an ordinary man, she thought. Then again she didn't seem to be attracted to ordinary men lately. "You're a long way from the twenty-fifth."

"Yeah." A shadow flickered into his eyes. "Looks that way." He lifted a spoonful of berries and cream and offered it.

Deborah let the fruit lie on her tongue a moment. "Do you miss it?"

He knew if he kissed her now she would taste sharp, fresh, alive. "I don't let myself miss it. There's a difference."

"Yes." She understood. It was the same way she didn't let herself miss her family, those who were gone and those who were so many miles away.

"You're very appealing when you're sad, Deborah." He trailed a finger over the back of her hand. "In fact, irresistible."

"I'm not sad."

"You are irresistible."

"Don't start." She made a production out of pouring more coffee. "Can I ask you a business question?"

"Sure."

"If the owner, or owners, of a particular piece of property didn't want that ownership publicized, could they hide it?"

"Easily. Bury it in paper corporations, in different tax numbers. One corporation owns another, another owns that, and so on. Why?"

But she leaned forward, waving his question aside. "How difficult would it be to track down the actual owners?"

"That would depend on how much trouble they'd gone to, and how much reason they had to keep their names off the books."

"If someone was determined enough, and patient enough, those names could be found?"

"Eventually. If you found the common thread."

"Common thread?"

"A name, a number, a place. Something that would pop up over and over." He would have been concerned by her line of questioning if he hadn't been one step ahead of her. Still, it was best to be cautious. "What are you up to, Deborah?"

"My job."

Very carefully, he set his cup back in its saucer. "Does this have anything to do with Parino?"

Her eyes sharpened. "What do you know about Parino?"

"I still have contacts at the twenty-fifth. Don't you have enough to do with the Slagerman trial?"

"I don't have the luxury of working on one case at a time."

"This is one you shouldn't be working on at all."

"Excuse me?" Her tone had dropped twenty degrees.

"It's dangerous. The men who had Parino murdered are dangerous. You don't have any idea what you're playing with."

"I'm not playing."

"No, and neither are they. They're well protected, and well-informed. They'll know what your next move is before you do." His eyes darkened, seemed to turn inward. "If they see you as an obstacle, they'll remove you, very quickly, very finally."

"How do you know so much about the men who killed Parino?"

He brought himself back. "I was a cop, remember? This isn't something you should be involved in. I want you to turn it over to someone else."

"That's ridiculous."

He gripped her hand before she could spring up. "I don't want you hurt."

"I wish people would stop saying that to me." Pulling her hand away, she rose. "This is my case, and it's going to stay mine."

His eyes darkened, but he remained seated. "Ambition is another attractive trait, Deborah. Until you let it blind you."

She turned back to him slowly, fury shimmering around her. "All right, part of it is ambition. But that's not all of it, not nearly. I believe in what I do, Gage, and in my ability to do it well. It started out with a kid named Rico Mendez. He wasn't a pillar of the community. In fact, he was a petty thief who had already done time, and would have done more. But he was gunned down while standing on a street corner. Because he belonged to the wrong gang, wore the wrong colors."

She began to pace, her hands gesturing and emphasizing. "Then his killer is killed, because he talked to me. Because I made a deal with him. So when does it stop, when do we stop and say this is not acceptable, I'll take the responsibility and change it?"

He stood then and came toward her. "I'm not questioning your integrity, Deborah."

"Just my judgment?"

"Yes, and my own." His hands slid up, inside the sleeves of her robe. "I care about you."

"I don't think—"

"No, don't. Don't think." He covered her mouth with his, his fingers tightening on her arms as he pulled her against him.

Instant heat, instant need. How was she to fight it? His body was so solid against hers, his lips were so skilled. And she could feel the waves, not just of desire, but of something deeper and truer, pouring out of him and into her. As if he were already inside her.

She was everything. When he held her he didn't question the power she had to both empty his mind and fill it, to sate his hunger even as she incited it. She made him strong; she left him weak. With her, he began, almost, to believe in miracles again.

When he stepped away, his hands were still on her arms. She struggled for balance. How could he do this to her each time, every time, with only a touch?

"I'm not ready for this," she managed.

"Neither am I. I don't think it matters." He brought her close again. "I want to see you tonight." He crushed his mouth to hers. "I want to be with you tonight."

"No, I can't." She could hardly breathe. "The trial."

He bit back an oath. "All right. After the trial is over. Neither one of us can keep walking away from this."

"No." He was right. It was time to resolve it. "No, we can't. But I need time. Please don't push me."

"I may have to." He turned for the door, but paused with his hand on the knob. "Deborah, is there someone else?"

She started to deny it, but found she could only be honest with him. "I don't know."

Nodding, he closed the door at his back. With a bitter kind of irony, he realized he was competing with himself.

She worked late that night, poring over papers and law books at the desk in her bedroom. After court she had spent hours cleaning her already clean apartment. It was one of the best ways she knew to relieve tension. Or to ignore it. The other was work, and she had dived into it, knowing sleep was impossible.

As she reached for her mug of coffee, the phone rang.

"Hello."

"O'Roarke? Deborah O'Roarke?"

"Yes, who is this?"

"Santiago."

Instantly alert, she grabbed a pencil. "Mr. Santiago, we've been looking for you."

"Yeah. Right."

"I'd like very much to talk to you. The D.A.'s office is prepared to offer you cooperation and protection."

"Like Parino got?"

She smothered the quick pang of guilt. "You'll be safer with us than on your own."

"Maybe." There was fear in his voice, tight and nervy.

"I'm willing to set up an interview any time you agree to come in."

"No way. I'm not going nowhere. They'd hit me before I got two blocks." He began to talk quickly, words tumbling over each other. "You come to me. Listen, I got more than Parino had. Lots more. I got names, I got papers. You want to hear about it, sister, you come to me."

"All right. I'll have the police—"

"No cops!" His voice turned vicious with terror. "No cops or no deal. You come, and you come alone. That's it."

"We'll do it your way then. When?"

"Now, right now. I'm at the Darcy Hotel, 38 East 167th. Room 27."

"Give me twenty minutes."

"You're sure this is where you want to go, lady?" Though his fare was wearing worn jeans and a T-shirt, the cabbie could see she had too much class for an armpit like the Darcy.

Deborah looked through the hard mean rain that was falling. She could see the dark windows, the scarred surface of the building and the deserted street. "Yes. I don't suppose I could convince you to wait."

"No, ma'am."

"I didn't think so." She pushed a bill through the slot in the thick security glass. "Keep it." Taking a breath, holding it, she plunged into the rain and up the broken steps to the entrance.

In the lobby she stood, dripping. The check-in desk was behind rusty iron bars and was deserted. There was a light, shooting its yellow beam over the sticky linoleum floor. The air smelled of sweat and garbage and something worse. Turning, she started up the stairs.

A baby was crying in long, steady wails. The sound of misery rolled down the graffiti-washed stairwell. Deborah watched something small and quick scuttle past her foot and into a crack. With a shudder, she continued up.

She could hear a man and woman, voices raised in a vicious argument. As she turned into the hallway of the second floor, a door creaked open. She saw a pair of small, frightened eyes before it creaked shut again and a chain rattled into place.

Her feet crunched over broken glass that had once been the ceiling light. Down the dim hall, she heard the bad-tempered squeal of brakes from a television car chase. Lightning flashed outside the windows as the storm broke directly overhead.

At Room 27, she stopped. The raucous television boomed on the other side of the door. Lifting a hand, she knocked hard.

"Mr. Santiago."

When she received no response, she knocked and called again. Cautious, she tried the knob. The door opened easily.

In the gray, flickering light of the television, she saw a cramped room with one dingy window. There were heaps of clothes and garbage. The single dresser had a drawer missing. There was the stench of beer gone hot and food gone bad.

She saw the figure stretched across the bed and swore. Not only would she have the pleasure of conducting an interview in this hellhole, she would have to sober up her witness first.

Annoyed, she switched off the television so that there was only the sound of drumming rain and the shouts of the argument down the hall. She spotted a stained sink bolted to the wall, a chunk of its porcelain missing. It would come in handy, she thought, if she could manage to hold Santiago's head in it.

"Mr. Santiago." She raised her voice as she picked her way across the room, trying to avoid greasy take-out bags and spilled beer. "Ray." Reaching him, she started to shake him by the shoulder, then noted his eyes were open. "I'm Deborah O'Roarke," she began. Then she realized he wasn't looking at her. He wasn't looking at all. Lifting her trembling hand, she saw it was wet with blood.

"Oh, God." She took one stumbling step back, fighting down the hot nausea that churned in her stomach. Another drunken step, then another. She turned and all but ran into a small well-built man with a mustache.

*"Señorita,"* he said quietly.

"The police," she managed. "We have to call the police. He's dead."

"I know." He smiled. She saw the glint of gold in his mouth. And the glint of silver when he lifted the stiletto. "Miss O'Roarke. I've been waiting for you."

He grabbed her by the hair when she lunged toward the door. She cried out in pain, then was silent, deathly still as she felt the prick of the knife at the base of her throat.

"No one listens to screams in a place such as this," he said, and the gentleness in his voice made her shudder as he turned her to face him. "You are very beautiful, *señorita*. What a pity it would be to damage that cheek." Watching her, he laid the shaft of the knife against it. "You will tell me, *por favor,* what Parino discussed with you before his...accident. All names, all details. And with whom you shared this information."

Struggling to think through her terror, she looked into his eyes. And saw her fate. "You'll kill me anyway."

He smiled again. "Wise and beautiful. But there are ways, and ways. Some are very slow, very painful." He glided the blade lightly down her cheek. "You will tell me what I need to know."

She had no names, nothing to bargain with. She had only her wits. "I wrote them down, I wrote all of it down and locked it away."

"And told?"

"No one." She swallowed. "I told no one."

He studied her for a moment, twirling the stiletto. "I think you lie. Perhaps after I show you what I can do with this, you'll be willing to cooperate. Ah, that cheek. Like satin. What a pity I must tear it."

Even as she braced, there was another flash of lighting and the sound of the window glass crashing.

He was there, all in black, illuminated by a new spear of lightning. This time the thunder shook the room. Before she could so much as breathe, the knife was at her throat and a beefy arm banded her waist.

"Come closer," her captor warned, "and I will slit her throat from ear to ear."

Nemesis stood where he was. He didn't look at her. Didn't dare. But in his mind's eye he could see her, face pale with fear. Eyes glazed with it. Was it her fear, or his own that had made him unable to concentrate, unable to come into the room as a shadow instead of a man? If he was able to do so now, to divorce himself from his fear for her and vanish, would it be a weapon, or would it cause the stiletto to strike home before he could act? He hadn't been quick enough to save her. Now he had to be clever enough.

"If you kill her, you lose your shield."

"A risk we both take. No closer." He slid the blade more truly against her throat until she whimpered.

There was fear now, and fury. "If you hurt her, I will do things to you that even in your own nightmares you have never imagined."

Then he saw the face, the full looping mustache, the gleam of gold. He was back, back on the docks with the smell of fish and garbage, the sound of water lapping. He felt the hot explosion in his chest and nearly staggered.

"I know you, Montega." His voice was low, harsh. "I've been looking for you for a long time."

"So, you have found me." Though his tone was arrogant, Deborah could smell his sweat. It gave her hope. "Put down your weapon."

"I don't have a weapon," Nemesis said, his hands held out from his sides. "I don't need one."

"Then you are a fool." Montega eased his arm from around Deborah's waist and slipped a hand into his pocket. Just as the shot rang out, Nemesis lunged to the side.

It happened so fast. Afterward, Deborah couldn't be sure who had moved first. She saw the bullet smash into the stained wallpaper and plaster of the wall, saw Nemesis fall. With a strength fueled by rage and terror, she slammed her elbow into Montega's stomach.

More concerned with his new quarry than her, he shoved her away. Her head struck the edge of the sink. There was another flash of lightning. Then the dark.

"Deborah. Deborah, I need you to open your eyes. Please."

She didn't want to. Small vicious explosions were going off behind them. But the voice was so desperate, so pleading. She forced her eyelids to lift. Nemesis swam into focus.

He was holding her, cradling her head, rocking her. For a moment, she could only see his eyes. Beautiful eyes, she thought dizzily. She had fallen in love with them the first time she'd seen them. She had looked through the crowd of people through the dazzle of lights and had seen him, seen them.

With a little groan, she lifted a hand to the knot already forming on her temple. She must be concussed, she thought. The first time she had seen Nemesis she had been in a dark alley. And there had been a knife. Like tonight.

"A knife," she murmured. "He had a knife."

Stunned by relief, he lowered his brow to hers. "It's all right. He didn't get a chance to use it."

"I thought he'd killed you." She lifted a hand to his face, found it warm.

"No."

"Did you kill him?"

His eyes changed. Concern rushed out as fury rushed in. "No." He had seen Deborah crumpled on the floor and had known such blank terror, the kind he thought he'd forgotten how to feel. It had been easy for Montega to get away. But there would be another time. He promised himself that. And he would have his justice. And his revenge.

"He got away?"

"For now."

"You knew him." Over the pounding in her head, she tried to think. "You called him by name."

"Yes, I knew him."

"He had a gun." She squeezed her eyes tight, but the pain continued to roll. "Where did he have a gun?"

"In his pocket. He makes it a habit to ruin his suits."

That was something she would have to consider later. "We have to call the police." She put a hand on his arm for balance and felt the warm stickiness on her fingers. "You're bleeding."

He glanced down to where the bullet had grazed him. "Some."

"How badly?" Ignoring the throbbing in her temple, she pushed away. Before he could answer, she was ripping his sleeve to expose the wound. The long, ugly graze had her stomach doing flip-flops. "We need to stop the bleeding."

She couldn't see his lifted brow, but heard it in his voice. "You could tear your T-shirt into a tourniquet."

"You should be so lucky." She glanced around the room, scrupulously avoiding looking at the form sprawled over the bed. "There's nothing in here that wouldn't give you blood poisoning."

"Try this." He offered her a square of black cloth.

She fumbled with the bandage. "It's my first gunshot wound, but I think this should be cleaned."

"I'll see to it later." He enjoyed having her tend to him. Her fingers were gentle on his skin, her brows drawn together in concentration. She had found a murdered man, had nearly been murdered herself. But she had bounced back and was doing competently what needed to be done.

Practicality. His lips curved slightly. Yes, it could be very attractive. Added to that, he could smell her hair as she bent close, feel the softness of it as it brushed against his cheek. He heard her breathing, slow, steady, under the sound of the quieting rain.

Having done her best, Deborah sat back on her heels. "Well, so much for invulnerability."

He smiled and stopped her heart. "There goes my reputation."

She could only stare, spellbound as they knelt on the floor of the filthy little room. She forgot where she was, who she was. Unable to stop herself, she lowered her gaze to his mouth. What tastes would she find there? What wonders would he show her?

He could barely breathe when she lifted her eyes to his again. In hers he saw passion smoldering, and an acceptance that was terrifying. Her fingers were still on his skin, gently stroking. He could see each quick beat of her heart in the pulse that hammered at her throat.

"I dream of you." He reached out to bring her unresistingly against him. "Even when I'm awake I dream of you. Of touching you." His hands slid up to cup, to caress her breasts. "Of tasting you." Compelled, he buried his mouth at her throat where the flavor and the scent were hot.

She leaned toward him, into him, stunned and shattered by the wildly primitive urges beating in her blood. His lips were like a brand on her skin. And his hands… Oh, Lord, his hands. With a deep, throaty moan, she arched back, eager and willing.

And Gage's face swam in front of her eyes.

"No." She jerked away, shocked and shamed. "No, this isn't right."

He cursed himself. Her. Circumstance. How could he have touched her now, here? "No, it isn't." He rose, stepped away. "You don't belong here."

Because she was on the verge of tears, her voice was sharp. "And you do?"

"More than you," he murmured. "Much more than you."

"I was doing my job. Santiago called me."

"Santiago's dead."

"He wasn't." She pressed her fingers to her eyes and prayed for composure. "He called, asked me to come."

"Montega got here first."

"Yes." Telling herself she was strong, she lowered her hands and looked at him. "But how? How did he know where to find Santiago? How did he know I was coming here tonight? He was waiting for me. He called me by name."

Interested, Nemesis studied her. "Did you tell anyone you were coming here tonight?"

"No."

"I'm beginning to believe you are a fool." He swung away from her. "You come here, to a place like this, alone, to see a man who would as soon put a bullet in your brain as speak to you."

"He wouldn't have hurt me. He was terrified, ready to talk. And I know what I'm doing."

He turned back. "You don't begin to know."

"But you do, of course." She pushed at her tousled hair and had fresh pain shooting through her head. "Oh, why the hell don't you go away? Stay away? I don't need this kind of grief from you. I've got work to do."

"You need to go home, leave this to others."

"Santiago didn't call others," she snapped. "He called me, talked to me. And if I had gotten to him first I would know everything I need to know. I don't..." She trailed off as a thought struck. "My phone. Damn it, they've got a tap on my phone. They knew I was coming here tonight. My office phone, too. That's how they knew I was about to get a court order to deal with the antique shop." Her eyes blazed. "Well, we can fix that in a hurry."

She sprang up. The room spun. He caught her before she slid to the floor again.

"You're not going to be doing anything in a hurry for a day or two." Smoothly he hooked an arm under her knees and lifted her.

She liked the feeling of being carried by him, a bit too much. "I walked into this room, Zorro, I'll walk out."

He carried her into the hall. "Are you always so thickheaded?"

"Yes. I don't need your help."

"I can see you're doing just dandy on your own."

"I may have had some trouble before," she said as he started down the stairs. "But now I have a name. Montega. Five-eight, a hundred and sixty. Brown hair, brown eyes, brown mustache. Two gold incisors. It shouldn't be too hard to run a make on him."

He stopped and his eyes were ice. "Montega's mine."

"The law doesn't make room for personal vendettas."

"You're right. The law doesn't." He shifted her slightly as he came to the base of the stairs.

There was something in his tone—disillusionment?—that had her lifting a hand to his cheek. "Was it very bad?"

"Yes." God, how he wished he could turn to her, bury his face in her hair and let her soothe him. "It was very bad."

"Let me help you. Tell me what you know and I swear I'll do everything I can do to see that Montega and whoever is behind him pays for what they've done to you."

She would try. Realizing it moved something in him, even as it frightened him. "I pay my own debts, my own way."

"Damn it, talk about thickheaded." She squirmed as he carried her into the rain. "I'm willing to bend my principles and work with you, to form a partnership, and you—"

"I don't want a partner."

She could feel him stiffen with the words, all but feel the pain rush through him. But she wouldn't soften. Not again. "Fine, just great. Oh, put me down, you can hardly carry me a hundred blocks."

"I don't intend to." But he could have. He could imagine carrying her through the rain to her apartment, inside, to the bed. Instead, he walked to the end of the block, toward the lights and the traffic. At the curb he stopped. "Hail a cab."

"Hail a cab? Like this?"

He wondered why she could make him burn and want to laugh at the same time. He turned his head and watched the heat flare in her eyes as their lips hovered an inch apart. "You can still lift your arm, can't you?"

"Yes, I can lift my arm." She did so, stewing as they stood and waited. After five soaking minutes, a cab cruised up the curb. Miffed as she was, she had to bite back a smile at the way the driver's mouth fell open when he got a load of her companion.

"Jeez, you're him, ain't ya? You're Nemesis. Hey, buddy, want a ride?"

"No, but the lady does." Effortlessly he slid Deborah into the back seat. His gloved hand brushed once over her cheek, like a memory. "I'd try an ice pack and some aspirin."

"Thanks. Thanks a lot. Listen, I'm not finished—"

But he stepped back, disappearing into the dark, thin rain.

"That was really him, wasn't it?" The cabbie craned his neck around to Deborah, ignoring the bad-tempered honks around him. "What'd he do, save your life or something?"

"Or something," she muttered.

"Jeez. Wait till I tell the wife." Grinning, he switched off the meter. "This ride's on me."

# Chapter 6

Grunting, his body running with sweat, Gage lifted the weights again. He was on his back on the bench press, stripped down to a pair of jogging shorts. His muscles were singing, but he was determined to reach his quota of a hundred presses. Perspiration soaked his sweatband and ran into his eyes as he concentrated on one small spot on the ceiling. There was a satisfaction even in pain.

He remembered, too well, when he'd been so weak he'd barely been able to lift a magazine. There had been a time when his legs had turned to rubber and his breath had been ragged at trying to walk the length of the hospital corridor. He remembered the frustration of it, and more, the helplessness.

He'd resisted therapy at first, preferring to sit alone and brood. Then he'd used it, like a punishment because he'd been alive and Jack had been dead. The pain had been excruciating.

And one day, weak, sick, darkly depressed, he'd stood weaving in his hospital room, braced against the wall. He'd wished with all of his strength, with all of his will, that he could simply vanish.

And he had.

He'd thought he'd been hallucinating. Going mad. Then, terrified and fascinated, he'd tried it again and again, going so far as to tilt a mirror across the room so that he could watch himself fade back, fade into the pastel wall beside his bed.

He would never forget the morning a nurse came in with his breakfast tray, walked right past him without seeing him, grumbling about patients who didn't stay in bed where they belonged.

And he'd known what he'd brought out of the coma with him. He'd known it had come with him for a purpose.

So therapy had become like a religion, something he'd dedicated every ounce of strength to, every particle of will. He'd pushed himself harder, harder still, until his muscles had toned and firmed. He had thrown himself into lessons in the martial arts, spent hours with weight lifting, the treadmills, the punishing laps in the pool every day.

He had exercised his mind, as well, reading everything, pushing himself to understand the myriad businesses he had inherited, spending hours day after·day until he was skilled with complex computer systems.

Now he was stronger, faster, sharper than he had been during his years on the force. But he would never wear a badge again. He would never take another partner.

He would never be helpless.

His breath hissed out, and he continued to lift when Frank strolled in with a tall glass of iced juice.

Setting the glass on the table beside the bench press, Frank watched in silence for a moment. "Pushing it a bit today," he commented. "'Course you pushed it a bit yesterday, too, and the day before." Frank grinned. "What is it about some women that makes guys go out and lift heavy objects?"

"Go to hell, Frank."

"She's a looker, all right," he said, unoffended. "Smart, too, I guess, being a lawyer and all. Must be hard to think about her mind, though, when she looks at you with those big, blue eyes."

With a last grunt, Gage set the bar in the safety. "Go lift a wallet."

"Now, you know I don't do that anymore." His wide face split with a new grin. "Nemesis might get me." He plucked up a towel from the neatly folded pile beside the bench.

Saying nothing, Gage took it and swiped at the sweat on his face and chest.

"How's the arm?"

"Fine." Gage didn't bother to glance at the neat white bandage Frank had used to replace Deborah's effort.

"Must be getting slow. Never known you to catch one before."

"Do you want to be fired?"

"Again? Nah." He waited, patient, while Gage switched to leg presses. "I'm looking for job security. If you go out and get yourself killed, I'll have to go back to fleecing tourists."

"Then I'll have to stay alive. The tourists have enough trouble in Urbana."

"Wouldn't have happened if I'd been with you."

Gage flashed him a look and continued to push. "I work alone. You know the deal."

"She was there."

"And that was the problem. She doesn't belong on the streets, she belongs in a courtroom."

"You don't want her in a courtroom, you want her in the bedroom."

The weights came down with a crash. "Drop it."

He'd known Gage too long to be intimidated. "Look, you're crazy about her, and it's throwing you off, messing up your concentration. It isn't good for you."

"I'm not good for her." He stood and grabbed the glass of juice. "She has feelings for me, and she has feelings for Nemesis. It's making her unhappy."

"So, tell her she's only got feelings for one guy, and make her happy."

"What the hell am I supposed to do?" He drained the glass and barely prevented himself from heaving it against the wall. "Take her out to dinner, and over cocktails I could say, oh, by the way, Deborah, besides being a businessman and a pillar of the damn community, I have this sideline. An alter ego. The press likes to call him Nemesis. And we're both nuts about you. So, when I take you to bed, do you want it with the mask or without?"

Frank considered a moment. "Something like that."

With a half laugh, Gage set down the glass. "She's a straight arrow, Frank. I know, because I used to be one myself. She sees things in black and white—the law and the crime." Suddenly tired, he looked out over the sparkling water of the pool. "She'd never understand what I do or why I do it. And she'd hate me for lying to her, because every time I'm with her, I'm deceiving her."

"I don't think you're giving her enough credit. You've got reasons for what you do."

"Yeah." Absently he touched the jagged scar on his chest. "I've got reasons."

"You could make her understand. If she really does have feelings for you, she'd have to understand."

"Maybe, just maybe she'd listen, even accept without agreeing. She might even forgive the lies. But what about the rest?" He set his hand down on the bench, waited, watched it disappear into the damp leather. "How do I ask her to share her life with a freak?"

Frank swore once, violently. "You're not a freak. You've got a gift."

"Yeah." Gage lifted his hand, flexed his fingers. "But I'm the one who has to live with it."

At twelve-fifteen sharp, Deborah walked into City Hall. She made her way to the mayor's office, walking under the stern-faced portraits of former mayors, governors, presidents. She moved past marble busts of the country's founding fathers. The current mayor of Urbana liked having his walls lined with tradition, his floor carpeted in red.

She didn't begrudge him. In fact, Deborah appreciated the hushed, reverential feel of tradition. She enjoyed walking past the doors and hearing the quiet hum of keyboards, the click of copiers, the muted phone conversations as people worked for the city.

She paused in the reception area. Tucker Fields's secretary glanced up and, recognizing her, smiled. "Miss O'Roarke. He's expecting you. Just let me buzz him."

Within an efficient twenty seconds, she was escorted into the mayor's office. Fields sat behind his desk, a trim and tidy man with a fringe of snowy hair and the ruddy outdoor complexion of his farmer forebears. Beside him, Jerry looked like a preppy executive.

Fields had earned a reputation during his six years in office as a man not afraid to get his hands dirty to keep his city clean.

At the moment, his jacket was off, his white shirt-sleeves rolled up his sinewy forearms. His tie was askew and he reached up to straighten it as Deborah entered.

"Deborah, always a pleasure to see you."

"Good to see you, Mayor. Hello, Jerry."

"Have a seat, have a seat." Fields gestured her to a chair as he settled back against the cushy leather of his own. "So, how's the Slagerman trial going?"

"Very well. I think he'll take the stand after the noon recess."

"And you're ready for him."

"More than."

"Good, good." He waved in his secretary as she came to the door with a tray. "I thought since I'm making you miss lunch, I could at least offer you some coffee and a Danish."

"Thank you." She took the cup, exchanged idle conversation, though she knew she hadn't been sent for to drink coffee and chat.

"Heard you had some excitement last night."

"Yes." It was no more than she'd expected. "We lost Ray Santiago."

"Yes, I heard. It's unfortunate. And this Nemesis character, he was there, as well?"

"Yes, he was."

"He was also there the night the antique store on Seventh blew up." Steepling his fingers, Fields sat back. "One might begin to think he was involved."

"No, not in the way you mean. If he hadn't been there last night, I wouldn't be sitting here now." Though it annoyed her, she was compelled to defend him. "He's not a criminal—at least not in the standard sense."

The mayor merely lifted a brow. "In whatever sense, I prefer to have the police enforce the law in my city."

"Yes, I agree."

Satisfied, he nodded. "And this man..." He pushed through the papers on his desk. "Montega?"

"Enrico Montega," Deborah supplied. "Also known as Ricardo Sanchez and Enrico Toya. A Colombian national who entered the U.S. about six years ago. He's suspected of the murder of two drug merchants in Columbia. He was based in Miami for a while, and

Vice there has a fat file on him. As does Interpol. Allegedly, he is the top enforcer on the East Coast. Four years ago, he murdered a police officer, and seriously wounded another." She paused, thinking of Gage.

"You've been doing your homework," Fields commented.

"I always like a firm foundation when I go after someone."

"Hmm. You know, Deborah, Mitchell considers you his top prosecutor." Fields grinned. "Not that he'd admit it. Mitch doesn't like to hand out compliments."

"I'm aware of that."

"We're all very pleased with your record, and particularly with the way the Slagerman case seems to be going. Both Mitch and I agree that we want you to concentrate more fully on your litigation. So, we've decided to take you off this particular case."

She blinked, stunned. "I beg your pardon?"

"We've decided you should turn your notes, your files over to another D.A."

"You're pulling me?"

He held up a hand. "We're simply beefing up the police investigation. With your caseload, we prefer to have you turn over your files on this to someone else."

She set her cup down with a snap. "Parino was mine."

"Parino is dead."

She shot a glance at Jerry, but he only lifted his hands. She rose, fighting to hold her temper. "This sprang out of that. All of it. This is my case. It has been all along."

"And you've endangered yourself, and the case, twice already."

"I've been doing my job."

"Someone else will be doing it, this part of it, after today." He spread his hands. "Deborah, this isn't a punishment, merely a shifting of responsibilities."

She shook her head and snatched up her briefcase. "Not good enough, not nearly. I'm going to speak with Mitchell myself." Turning, she stormed out. She had to struggle to maintain her dignity and not give in to the urge to slam the door behind her.

Jerry caught up with her at the elevators. "Deb, wait."

"Don't even try it."

"What?"

"To soothe and placate." After jamming the Down button, she whirled on him. "What the hell is this, Jerry?"

"Like the mayor said—"

"Don't hand me that. You knew, you knew what was going on, why I was being called in, and you didn't tell me. Not even a warning so I could prepare myself."

"Deb—" He laid a hand on her shoulder, but she shrugged it off. "Look, not that I don't agree with everything the mayor said—"

"You always do."

"I didn't know. I didn't know, damn it," he repeated when she only stared at him. "Not until ten o'clock this morning. And whatever I think, I would have told you."

She stopped pounding her fist against the Down button. "Okay, I'm sorry I jumped all over you. But it's not right. Something's not right about all this."

"You nearly got yourself killed," he reminded her. "When Guthrie came in this morning—"

"Gage?" she interrupted. "Gage was here?"

"The ten-o'clock appointment."

"I see." Hands fisted, she whirled back to the elevator. "So he's behind it."

"He was concerned, that's all. He suggested—"

"I get the picture." She cut him off again and stepped into the elevator. "This isn't finished. And you can tell your boss I said so."

She had to bank her temper when she walked into court. Personal feelings, personal problems had no place here. There were two frightened young women and the justice system depending on her.

She sat, taking careful notes as the defense counsel questioned Slagerman. She blanked Gage and his handiwork out of her mind.

When it came time for cross-examination, she was ready. She remained seated a moment, studying Slagerman.

"You consider yourself a businessman, Mr. Slagerman?"

"Yes."

"And your business consists of hiring escorts, both male and female, for clients?"

"That's right. Elegant Escorts provides a service, finding suitable companions for other businessmen and women, often from out of town.''

She let him ramble a few moments, describing his profession. ''I see.'' Rising, she strolled past the jury. ''And is it in—let's say the job description—of any of your employees to exchange sex for money with these clients?''

''Absolutely not.'' Attractive and earnest, he leaned forward. ''My staff is well-screened and well-trained. It's a firm policy that if anyone on staff develops this kind of a relationship with a client, it would result in termination.''

''Are you aware that any of your employees have indeed exchanged sex for money?''

''I am now.'' He aimed a pained look at Suzanne and Marjorie.

''Did you request that Marjorie Lovitz or Suzanne McRoy entertain a client on a sexual level?''

''No.''

''But you're aware that they did so?''

If he was surprised by her train of questioning, he didn't bat an eye. ''Yes, of course. They admitted to it under oath.''

''Yes, they were under oath, Mr. Slagerman. Just as you are. Have you ever struck an employee?''

''Certainly not.''

''Yet both Miss Lovitz and Miss McRoy claim, under oath, that you did.''

''They're lying.'' And he smiled at her.

''Mr. Slagerman, didn't you go to Miss Lovitz's apartment on the night of February 25th, angry that she was unable to work, and in your anger, beat her?''

''That's ridiculous.''

''You swear that, under oath?''

''Objection. Asked and answered.''

''Withdrawn. Mr. Slagerman, have you contacted either Miss Lovitz or Miss McRoy since this trial began?''

''No.''

''You have not telephoned either of them?''

''No.''

Nodding, she walked back to her table and picked up a stack of papers. "Is the number 555-2520 familiar to you?"

He hesitated. "No."

"That's odd. It's your private line, Mr. Slagerman. Shouldn't you recognize your own private telephone number?"

Though he smiled, she saw the icy hate in his eyes. "I call from it, not to it, so I don't have to remember it."

"I see. And did you, on the night of June 18, use that private line to call the apartment where both Miss Lovitz and Miss McRoy now live?"

"No."

"Objection, Your Honor. This is leading nowhere."

Deborah shifted again, facing the judge and leaving the jury's view of Slagerman unobstructed. "Your Honor. I'll show you where it leads in just a moment."

"Overruled."

"Mr. Slagerman, perhaps you could explain why, according to your phone records, a call was placed from your private line to the number at Miss Lovitz and Miss McRoy's apartment at 10:47 p.m. on June 18?"

"Anybody could have used my phone."

"Your private line?" She lifted a brow. "It's hardly worth having a private line if anyone can use it. The caller identified himself as Jimmy. You are known as Jimmy, aren't you?"

"Me and a lot of other people."

"Did you speak to me on the phone on the night of June 18?"

"I've never spoken with you on the phone."

She smiled coolly and moved closer to the chair. "Have you ever noticed, Mr. Slagerman, how to some men, all women's voices sound alike? How, to some men, all women look alike? How, to some men, women's bodies are for one purpose?"

"Your Honor." Defense counsel leaped to his feet.

"Withdrawn." Deborah kept her eyes level with Slagerman's. "Can you explain, Mr. Slagerman, how someone using your private line, using your name, called Miss McRoy on the night of June 18? And how when I answered the phone, this person, using your line and your name, mistook my voice for hers, and threatened Miss

McRoy?'' She waited a beat. ''Would you like to know what that person said?''

Sweat was beading on his upper lip. ''You can make up whatever you want.''

''That's true. Fortunately we had a tap on Miss McRoy's phone. I have the transcript.'' She turned over a sheet of paper. ''Should I refresh your memory?''

She had won. Though there were still closing arguments to take place, she knew she had won. Now, as she stormed through the Justice Building, she had other business to tend to.

She found Mitchell in his office, a phone to his ear. He was a big bull-chested man who had played linebacker in college. Pictures of him in his jersey were scattered on the wall among his degrees. He had short red hair and a sprinkling of freckles that did nothing to soften his leathered looks.

When he spotted Deborah, he waved her in, gestured toward a chair. But she remained standing until he'd completed his call.

''Slagerman?''

''I've got him nailed.'' She took a step closer to the desk. ''You sold me out.''

''That's bull.''

''What the hell do you call it? I get pulled into the mayor's office and get the brush-off. Damn it, Mitch, this is my case.''

''It's the state's case,'' he corrected, chomping on the end of his unlit cigar. ''You're not the only one who can handle it.''

''I made Parino, I made the deal.'' She slapped her palms down on his desk so they were eye to eye. ''I'm the one who's been busting my tail over this.''

''And you've been overstepping your bounds.''

''You're the one who taught me that trying a case takes more than putting on a pin-striped suit and dancing in front of a jury. I know my job, damn it.''

''Going to see Santiago alone was an error in judgment.''

''Now, that *is* bull. He called me. He asked for me. You tell me what you'd have done if he'd called you.''

He scowled at her. ''That's entirely different.''

"That's entirely the same," she snapped back, certain from the look in his eyes that he knew it. "If I'd screwed things up I'd expect to get bumped, but I haven't. I'm the one who's been sweating and frying my brains over this case. Now when I get a lead, I find out Guthrie chirps up and you and the mayor keel over. Still the old boys' network, is it, Mitch?"

He stabbed the cigar toward her face. "Don't pull that feminist crap on me. I don't care what way you button your shirt."

"I'm telling you, Mitch, if you pull me off this without good cause, I'm gone. I can't work for you if I can't depend on you, so I might as well go out on my own and take on divorce cases for three hundred an hour."

"I don't like ultimatums."

"Neither do I."

He leaned back, measuring her. "Sit down."

"I don't want—"

"Damn it, O'Roarke, sit."

Tight-lipped and fuming, she did. "So?"

He rolled the cigar between his fingers. "If Santiago had called me, I would have gone, just like you. But," he continued before she could speak, "your handling of this case isn't the only reason I've considered pulling you."

"Considered" took her position back several notches. Calming a bit, she nodded. "Well, then?"

"You've been getting a lot of press on this."

"I hardly see what that has to do with it."

"Did you see this morning's paper?" He snatched it up from his desk and waved it in her face. "Read the headline?" Because she had, and had winced over it already, she simply shrugged. Darling Deb Swept Through City In Arms of Nemesis.

"So, some cab driver wanted his name in the paper, what does that have to do with the case?"

"When my prosecutors start having their names linked with the masked marauder, it has everything to do with everything." He popped the cigar back in his mouth, gnashing it. "I don't like the way you keep running into him."

Neither did she. "Look, if the police can't stop him, I can hardly be responsible for his popping up all over the place. And I'd hate to think you'd take me off a case because some jerk had to fill his column."

Personally Mitch hated the weasely reporter. And he hadn't cared for the strong-arm tactics the mayor had used. "You've got two weeks."

"That's hardly enough time to—"

"Two weeks, take it or leave it. You bring me something we can take to a jury, or I pass the ball. Got it?"

"Yeah." She rose. "I got it."

She stormed out, past snickering associates. A paper was tacked on the door of her office. Someone had used magic markers and highlighter pens to draw a caricature of Deborah being carried in the arms of a lantern-jawed, muscle-bound masked man. Under it was a caption. The Continuing Adventures Of Darling Deb.

On a snarl, she ripped it down, balling it into her pocket as she stomped out. She had another stop to make.

She kept her finger pressed to the button of Gage's doorbell until Frank pulled the door open.

"Is he in?"

"Yes, ma'am." He stepped back as she pushed past him. He'd seen furious women before. Frank would have preferred to have faced a pack of hungry wolves.

"Where?"

"He's up in his office. I'll be glad to tell him you're here."

"I'll announce myself," she said as she started up the steps.

Frank looked after her, lips pursed. He considered buzzing Gage on the intercom and giving him fair warning. But he only grinned. Surprises were good for you.

Deborah didn't bother to knock, but pushed open the door and strode in. Gage was behind his desk, a phone in one hand, a pen in the other. Computer screens blinked. Across from him sat a trim, middle-aged woman with a steno pad. At Deborah's unannounced entrance she rose and glanced curiously at Gage.

"I'll get back to you," he said into the receiver before lowering it to the cradle. "Hello, Deborah."

She tossed her briefcase onto a chair. "I think you might prefer to have this conversation in private."

He nodded. "You can transcribe those notes tomorrow, Mrs. Brickman. It's late. Why don't you go home?"

"Yes, sir." She gathered her things and made a fast, discreet exit.

Deborah hooked her thumbs in the pockets of her skirt. Like a gunfighter hooking thumbs in a holster. He'd seen her take that pose in court. "It must be nice," she began, "sitting up here in your lofty tower and dispensing orders. I bet it feels just dandy. Not all of us are so fortunate. We don't have enough money to buy castles, or private planes or thousand-dollar suits. We work on the streets. But most of us are pretty good at our jobs, and happy enough." As she spoke, she walked slowly toward him. "But you know what makes us mad, Gage? You know what really ticks us off? That's when someone in one of those lofty towers sticks his rich, influential nose in our business. It makes us so mad that we think real hard about taking a punch at that interfering nose."

"Should we break out the boxing gloves?"

"I prefer my bare hands." As she had in Mitchell's office, she slapped them down on his desk. "Who the hell do you think you are, going to the mayor, pressuring him to take me off this case?"

"I went to the mayor," he said slowly, "and gave him my opinion."

"Your opinion." She blew a breath between her teeth and snatched up an onyx paperweight from the desk. Though she gave careful consideration to heaving it through the plate glass at his back, she contented herself with passing it from hand to hand. "And I bet he just fell all over himself to accommodate you and your thirty million."

Gage watched her pace and waited until he was sure he could speak rationally. "He agreed with me that you're more suitable to a courtroom than a murder scene."

"Who are you to say what's more suitable for me?" she whirled back, her voice rich with fury. "I say it, not you. All my life I've prepared myself for this job and I'm not having anyone come along and tell me I'm not suitable for any case I take on." She snapped the paperweight back on the desk, a hard crack of stone against stone. "You stay out of my business, and out of my life."

No, he realized, he wasn't going to be able to be rational. "Are you finished?"

"No. Before I leave I want you to know that it didn't work. I'm still on this case, and I'm staying on. So you wasted your time, and mine. And lastly, I think you're arrogant, officious and overbearing."

His hands were fisted beneath the desk. "Are you finished?" he asked again.

"You bet I am." She snatched up her briefcase, turned on her heel and headed for the door.

Gage pushed a button under the desk and had the locks snap into place. "I'm not," he said quietly.

She hadn't known she could be more furious. But as she spun back to him, a red haze formed in front of her eyes. "Unlock that door immediately, or I'll have you up on charges."

"You've had your say, Counselor." He rose. "Now I'll have mine."

"Not interested."

He came around the desk, but only leaned back against it. He didn't trust himself to approach her, not yet. "You've got all the evidence, don't you, Counselor? All your neat little facts. So, I'll save time and plead guilty as charged."

"Then we have nothing more to say."

"Isn't the prosecution interested in motive?"

She tossed back her head, bracing as he crossed to her. Something about the way he moved just then, slowly, soundlessly, set off a flash of memory. But it was gone, overwhelmed by her own temper.

"Motive isn't relevant in this case, results are."

"You're wrong. I went to the mayor, I asked him to use his influence to have you taken off the case. But I'm guilty of more than that—I'm guilty of being in love with you."

Her tensed hands went limp at her side so that the briefcase fell to the floor. Though she opened her mouth to speak, she could say nothing.

"Amazing." His eyes were dark and furious as he took that final step toward her. "A sharp woman like you being surprised by that. You should have seen it every time I looked at you. You should have seen it every time I touched you." He put his hands on her shoulders. "You should have tasted it, every time I kissed you."

Pushing her back against the door, he brushed his mouth over hers, once, twice. Then he devoured her lips.

Her knees were weak. She hadn't thought it was possible, but they were shaking so she had to hold on to him or slide bonelessly to the floor. Even clinging, she was afraid. For she had seen it, had felt it, had tasted it. But that was nothing compared to hearing him say it, or to hearing the echo of her own voice repeating the words inside her mind.

He was lost in her. And the more she opened to him, the deeper he fell. He took his hands over her face, through her hair, down her body, wanting to touch all of her. And to know as he did, that she trembled in response.

When he lifted his head, she saw the love, and she saw the desire. With them was a kind of war she didn't understand.

"There were nights," he said quietly, "hundreds of nights when I lay awake sweating and waiting for morning. I'd wonder if I'd ever find someone I could love, that I could need. No matter how I drew the fantasy, it's nothing compared to what I feel for you."

"Gage." She lifted her hands to his face, wishing with all her heart. Knowing well that heart was already lost to him. But she remembered that she had swayed close to another man only the night before. "I don't know what I'm feeling."

"Yes, you do."

"All right, I do, but I'm afraid to feel it. It's not fair. I'm not being fair, but I have to ask you to let me think this through."

"I'm not sure I can."

"A little while longer, please. Unlock the door, and let me go."

"It is unlocked." He stepped back to open it for her. But he blocked her exit for one last moment. "Deborah. I won't let you go the next time."

She looked up again and saw the truth of his words in his eyes. "I know."

## Chapter 7

The jury was out. Deborah spent their deliberating time in her office, using both her telephone and computer to try to track down what Gage had referred to as the common thread. The antique shop, Timeless, had been owned by Imports Incorporated, whose address was a vacant lot downtown. The company had filed no insurance claim on the loss, and the manager of the shop had vanished. The police had yet to locate the man Parino had referred to as Mouse.

More digging turned up the Triad Corporation, based in Philadelphia. A phone call to Triad put Deborah in touch with a recording telling her that the number had been disconnected. As she placed a call to the D.A.'s office in Philadelphia, she inputted all of her known data into the computer.

Two hours later, she had a list of names, social security numbers and the beginnings of a headache.

Before she could make her next call, the receiver rang under her hand. "Deborah O'Roarke."

"Is this the same Deborah O'Roarke who can't keep her name out of the paper?"

"Cilla." At the sound of her sister's voice, the headache faded a bit. "How are you?"

"Worried about you."

"What else is new?" Deborah rolled her shoulders to relieve the stiff muscles, then leaned back in the chair. Coming tinnily through the earpiece was the music Deborah imagined was pulsing in Cilla's office at the radio station. "How's Boyd?"

"That's Captain Fletcher to you."

"Captain?" She sat straight again. "When did that happen?"

"Yesterday." The pride and pleasure came through clearly. "I guess I'll really have to watch myself now, sleeping with a police captain."

"Tell him I'm proud of him."

"I will. We all are. Now—"

"How are the kids?" Deborah had learned to stall and evade long before taking the bar exam.

"It's dangerous to ask a mother how her kids are during summer vacation—no elementary school, no kindergarten, so they outnumber me and the cop three to two." Cilla gave a rich, warm laugh. "All three members of the demon brigade are fine. Allison pitched a shut-out in a Little League game last week—then got into a wrestling match with the opposing pitcher."

"Sounds like he was a rotten loser."

"Yeah. And Allison's always been a rotten winner. I practically had to sit on her to make her give over. Let's see…Bryant knocked out a tooth roller-skating, then, being a clever little capitalist, sold it to the boy next door for fifty cents. Keenan swallowed it."

"Swallowed what?"

"The fifty cents. Five dimes. My youngest son eats anything. I'm thinking about putting in a hot line to the Emergency room. Now let's talk about you."

"I'm fine. How are things at KHIP?"

"About as chaotic as they are around the house. All in all, I'd rather be in Maui." Cilla recognized the delaying tactics well and pushed a little harder. "Deborah, I want to know what you're up to."

"Work. In fact, I'm about to win a case." She glanced at the clock and calculated how long the jury had been out. "I hope."

Sometimes, Cilla mused, you just had to be direct. "Since when have you started dating guys in masks?"

Stalling couldn't last forever, she thought with regret. "Come on, Cilla, you don't believe everything you read in the paper."

"Right. Or everything that comes over the wire, even though we ran your latest adventure at the top of every hour yesterday. Even if I didn't go to the trouble to get the Urbana papers, I'd have heard all the noise. You're making national news out there, kid, and I want to know what's going on. That's why I'm asking you.''

It was usually easier to evade if you added a couple of dashes of truth. ''This Nemesis character is a nuisance. The press is glorifying him—and worse. Just this morning at a shop two blocks from the courthouse, I saw a display of Nemesis T-shirts.''

''Isn't merchandising wonderful?'' But Cilla wasn't about to be distracted again. ''Deborah, I've been in radio too long not to be able to read voices—especially my baby sister's. What's between you?''

''Nothing,'' she insisted, wanting it to be true. ''I've simply run into him a couple of times during this investigation I'm doing. The press plays it up.''

''I've noticed, Darling Deb.''

''Oh, please.''

''I do want to know what's going on, but it's more to the point right now why you're involved in something so dangerous. And why I had to read in the paper that some maniac had a knife to my sister's throat.''

''It's exaggerated.''

''Oh, so no one held a knife to your throat?''

No matter how well she lied, Deborah thought, Cilla would know. ''It wasn't as dramatic as it sounds. And I wasn't hurt.''

''Knives at your throat,'' Cilla muttered. ''Buildings blowing up in your face. Damn it, Deb, don't you have a police force out there?''

''I was just doing some legwork. Don't start,'' she said quickly. ''Cilla, do you know how frustrating it is to have to keep repeating that you know what you're doing, that you can take care of yourself and do your job?''

Cilla let out a long breath. ''Yeah. I can't stop worrying about you, Deborah, just because you're a couple thousand miles away. It's taken me years to finally accept what happened to Mom and Dad. If I lost you, I couldn't handle it.''

''You're not going to lose me. Right now, the most dangerous thing I'm facing is my computer.''

''Okay. Okay.'' Arguing with her sister wouldn't change a thing,

Cilla knew. And whatever answers Deborah gave her, she would keep right on worrying. "Listen, I also saw a picture of my little sister with some millionaire. I'm going to have to start a scrapbook. Anything you want to tell me?"

The automatic no caught in her throat. "I don't know. Things are pretty complicated right now and I haven't had time to think it through."

"Is there something to think through?"

"Yes." The headache was coming back. She reached into her drawer for a bottle of aspirin. "A couple of things," she murmured, thinking of Gage and of Nemesis. That was something not even Cilla could help her with. But there were other matters. "Cilla, since you're married to a police captain, how about using your influence to have him do me a favor?"

"I'll threaten to cook. He'll do anything I want."

With a laugh, Deborah picked up one of her printouts. "I'd like him to check out a couple of names for me. George P. Drummond and a Charles R. Meyers, both with Denver addresses." She spelled out both names, then added social security numbers. "Got it?"

"Mmm-hmm," Cilla murmured as she scribbled the information.

"And there's a Solar Corporation, also based in Denver. Drummond and Meyers are on the board of directors. If Boyd could run these through the police computer, it would save me several steps through the bureaucracy."

"I'll threaten him with my pot roast."

"That should do the trick."

"Deb, you will be careful, won't you?"

"Absolutely. Give everyone a hug for me. I miss you. All of you." Mitchell came to the door and signaled. "I've got to go, Cilla. The jury's coming back."

Deep in the recesses of his home, in an echoing cavern of a room, Gage studied a bank of computers. There was some work he couldn't do in his office. Some work he preferred to do in secret. With his hands hooked in the pockets of his jeans, he watched the monitors. Names and numbers flashed by.

He could see on one of the monitors just what Deborah had inputted in her computer across town. She was making progress, he thought. Slow, it was true, but it still worried him. If he could follow the steps she was taking, so could others.

Eyes intent, face sober, he took his fingers flying over one keyboard, then another and still another. He had to find the link. Once he did, he would carefully, systematically locate the name of the man responsible for Jack's death. As long as he found it before Deborah, she was safe.

The computers offered him one way. Or he could take another. Leaving the machines to their work, he turned, pressed a button. On the wall on the far side of the high-ceilinged, curving room a huge map slid into place. Crossing to it, he studied a very large-scaled detail of the city of Urbana.

Using yet another keyboard, he had colored lights blinking at various parts of the city. Each represented a major drug exchange, many of which were as yet unknown to the UPD.

They flashed in the East End, and the West, in the exclusive neighborhoods uptown, in the barrios, in the financial district. There seemed to be no pattern. Yet there was always a pattern. He had only to find it.

As he studied the map, his gaze lit and lingered on one building. Deborah's apartment. Was she home yet? he wondered. Was she safe inside? Was she wearing her blue robe and studying files, the television news murmuring in the background?

Was she thinking of him?

Gage rubbed his hands over his face. Frank was right, she was interfering with his concentration. But what could he do about it? Every attempt he made to see that she withdrew from the case had failed. She was too stubborn to listen.

He smiled a bit. He hadn't believed he would ever fall in love. How inconvenient, he thought wryly, that when he did, it was with a dedicated public servant. She wouldn't budge. He knew it. And neither would he. But however much discipline he had over his body and his mind, he seemed to have none over his heart.

It wasn't just her beauty. Though he had always loved beautiful things and had grown up learning to appreciate them for no more than their existence. After he'd come out of the coma, he had found a certain comfort in surrounding himself with beauty. All that color, all that texture after so much flat gray.

It wasn't just her mind. Though he respected intelligence. As a cop and as a businessman, he had learned that a sharp mind was the most powerful and the most dangerous weapon.

There was something, some indefinable something beyond her looks and her mind that had captured him. Because he was just as much her prisoner as he was of his own fate. And he had no idea how to resolve the two.

He was only sure that the first step would be to find the key himself, to find the name and to find the justice. When this was behind him, and her, there might be a chance for a future.

Clearing his mind, he studied the lights then, bending over a computer, went to work.

Balancing a pizza box, a bottle of Lambrusco and a briefcase full of paperwork, Deborah stepped off the elevator. As she wondered how she would manage to dig for her keys, she glanced up at the door of her apartment. Colorful draping letters crossed the door. CONGRATULATIONS, DEBORAH.

Mrs. Greenbaum, she thought with a grin. Even as she turned toward her neighbor's apartment, Mrs. Greenbaum's door opened.

"I heard it on the six-o'clock news. You put that little weasel away." Mrs. Greenbaum adjusted the hem of her tie-dyed T-shirt. "How do you feel?"

"Good. I feel good. How about some celebratory pizza?"

"You twisted my arm." Mrs. Greenbaum let her door slam, then crossed the hall in her bare feet. "I guess you noticed the air-conditioning's on the fritz again."

"I got the picture during my steam bath in the elevator."

"This time I think we should mobilize the rest of the tenants." She gave Deborah a shrewd look. "Especially if we had some sharp, fast-talking lawyer lead the way."

"You're already leading the way," Deborah said as she shifted the wine. "But if it's not on within twenty-four hours, I'll contact the landlord and put on the pressure." She fumbled around in her pocket. "Now if I could just get my keys."

"I've got the copy you gave me." Reaching into the pocket of her baggy jeans, Mrs. Greenbaum produced a key ring crowded with keys. "Here we go."

"Thanks." Inside, Deborah set the pizza box on a table. "I'll get some glasses and plates."

Lil lifted the lid and saw with approval that the pizza was loaded with everything. "You know, a pretty young girl like you should be celebrating with some pretty young boy on a Friday night instead of with an old woman."

"What old woman?" Deborah called from the kitchen and made Lil laugh.

"With a slightly above-middle-aged woman then. What about that mouth-watering Gage Guthrie?"

"I can't imagine him eating pizza and drinking cheap wine." She walked back in, carrying the bottle and two glasses, paper plates and napkins tucked under her arm. "He's more the caviar type."

"Something wrong with that?"

"No." She frowned. "No, but I'm in the mood for pizza. And after I gorge myself, I have work."

"Honey, don't you ever let up?"

"I've got a deadline," Deborah said, and found she still resented it. She poured two glasses, handed one to her friend. "To justice," she said. "The most beautiful lady I know."

Just as they sat, gooey slices of pizza split between them, there was a knock on the door. Licking sauce from her fingers, Deborah went to answer. She saw a huge basket of red roses that appeared to have legs.

"Delivery for Deborah O'Roarke. Got someplace I can put this thing, lady?"

"Oh…yes, ah. Here." She stood on tiptoe and got a glimpse of the deliveryman's head under the blossoms. "On the coffee table."

They not only sat on the coffee table, Deborah noted as she signed the clipboard, they covered it from end to end. "Thanks." She dug into her wallet for a bill.

"Well?" Lil demanded when they were alone again. "Who are they from?"

Though she already knew, Deborah picked up the card.

Nice work, Counselor.
Gage

She couldn't prevent the softening, or the smile that bloomed on her lips. "They're from Gage."

"The man knows how to make a statement." Behind her lenses, Lil's eyes sparkled. There was nothing she liked better than romance—unless it was a good protest rally. "Must be five dozen in there."

"They're beautiful." She slipped the card into her pocket. "I suppose I'll have to call him and thank him."

"At least." Lil bit into the pizza. "Why don't you do it now, while it's on your mind?" And while she could eavesdrop.

Deborah hesitated, the scent of the flowers surrounding her. No, she thought with a shake of her head. If she called him now, while his gesture weakened her, she might do or say something rash. "Later," she decided. "I'll call him later."

"Stalling," Lil said over a mouthful of pizza.

"Yeah." Not ashamed to admit it, Deborah sat again. She ate for a moment in silence, then picked up her wine. "Mrs. Greenbaum," she began, frowning into her glass. "You were married twice."

"So far," Lil answered with a grin.

"You loved both of them?"

"Absolutely. They were good men." Her sharp little eyes became young and dreamy. "Both times I thought it was going to be forever. I was about your age when I lost my first husband in the war. We only had a few years together. Mr. Greenbaum and I were a bit luckier. I miss both of them."

"Have you ever wondered...I guess it's an odd sort of question, but have you ever wondered what would have happened if you'd met both of them at the same time?"

Lil arched her eyebrows, intrigued with the notion. "That would have been a problem."

"You see what I mean. You loved both of them, but if they had come into your life at the same time, you couldn't have loved both of them."

"There's no telling what tricks the heart will play."

"But you can't love two men the same way at the same time." She leaned forward, her own conflict showing clearly on her face. "And if somehow you did, or thought you did, you couldn't make a commitment to either one, without being unfaithful to the other."

Taking her time, Lil topped off both glasses. "Are you in love with Gage Guthrie?"

"I might be." Deborah glanced back at the basket bursting with roses. "Yes, I think I am."

"And with someone else?"

With her glass cupped in her hand, Deborah pushed away from the table and rose to pace. "Yes. But that's crazy, isn't it?"

Not crazy, Lil thought. Nothing to do with love was ever crazy. And for some, such a situation would be delightful and exciting. Not for Deborah. For Deborah, she understood it would only be painful.

"Are you sure it's love on either side, and not just sex?"

After letting out a long breath, Deborah sat again. "I thought it was just physical. I wanted it to be. But I've thought about it, tried to be honest with myself, and I know it's not. I even get them mixed up in my mind. Not just comparisons, but well, as if I'm trying to make them one man, so it would be simpler." She drank again. "Gage told me he loves me, and I believe him. I don't know what to do."

"Follow your heart," Lil told her. "I know that sounds trite, the truest things often do. Let your mind take a back seat and listen to your heart. It usually makes the right choice."

At eleven, Deborah switched on the late news. She wasn't displeased to see her victory in the Slagerman case as the top story. She watched her own image give a brief statement on the courthouse steps, frowning a bit when Wisner pushed through to ask his usual nonsense about Nemesis.

The news team segued from that into Nemesis's latest exploits— the liquor store robbery he had scotched, the mugger he had captured, the murder he had prevented.

"Busy man," Deborah muttered, and drained the last of the wine. If Mrs. Greenbaum hadn't spent most of the evening with her, Deborah thought, she would have contented herself with one glass of wine rather than half the bottle.

Well, tomorrow was Saturday, she thought with a shrug, as the anchorman reported on the upcoming mayoral debates. She could sleep a little late before she went into the office. Or, if she was lucky, she would uncover something that evening. But she wouldn't get anything done if she continued to sit in front of the television.

She waited long enough to hear the weather report, which promised continuing heat, raging humidity and chances of thunderstorms. Switching off the set, she went to the bedroom to settle at her desk.

She'd left the window open in the vain hope of catching a breeze. The traffic noise was a steady din from five stories down. The heat rose from the street, intensifying on its upward journey. She could all but see it.

Hot nights. Hot needs.

She walked to the window, hoping for a breath of air to ease the aching even the wine hadn't dulled. But it remained, a deep, slow throb. Was he out there? she wondered, then put a hand to her temple. She wasn't even sure which man she was thinking of. And it would be best, she knew, if she thought of neither.

Turning on her desk lamp, she opened a file, then glanced at the phone.

She'd called Gage an hour before, only to be told by the taciturn Frank that Mr. Guthrie was out for the evening. She could hardly call him again, she thought. It would look as though she were checking up on him. Something she had no right to do—especially since she was the one who had asked for the time and space.

That was what she wanted, she assured herself. What she had to have. And thinking of him wouldn't help her find the answers that were buried somewhere in the papers on her desk.

She began to read through them again, making notations on a legal pad. As she worked, time slipped past and thunder muttered in the distance.

He shouldn't have come. He knew it wasn't right. But as he had walked the streets, his steps had taken him closer and closer to her apartment. Draped in shadows, he looked up and saw the light in her window. In the heat-drenched night he waited, telling himself if the light switched off, he would leave. He would go.

But it remained, a pale yet steady beacon.

He wondered if he could convince himself he wanted only to see her, to speak with her. It was true that he needed to find out how much she knew, how close she was. Facts on her computer didn't take in her intuition or her suspicions. The closer she came to answers, the more jeopardy she was in.

Even more than he wanted to love her, he needed to protect her.

But that wasn't why he crossed the street, why he swung himself onto the fire escape and began to climb. What he did he did because he couldn't stop himself.

Through the open window, he saw her. She was seated at a desk, the slant of light directed onto the papers she read through. A pencil moved quickly in her hand.

He could smell her. The tauntingly sexy scent she wore reached out to him like an invitation. Or a dare.

He could see only her profile, the curve of her cheek and jaw, the shape of her mouth. Her short blue robe was loosely tied, and he could see the long white column of her throat. As he watched, she lifted a hand to rub at the back of her neck. The robe shifted, sliding up her thighs, parting gently as she crossed her legs and bent over her work again.

Deborah read the same paragraph three times before she realized her concentration had been broken. She rubbed her eyes, intending to begin again. And her whole body stiffened. Heat rushed over her skin. Slowly she turned and saw him.

He was standing inside the window, away from the light. Her heart was hammering—not in shock, she realized. In anticipation.

"Taking a break from crime fighting?" she asked, hoping the sharp tone of her voice would cover her trembling. "According to the eleven-o'clock news, you've been busy."

He hadn't bothered to concentrate. This time, at least this time, he'd needed to come to her whole. "So have you."

"And I still am." She pushed at her hair and discovered her hand wasn't quite steady. "How did you get in?" When he glanced toward the window, she nodded. "I'll have to remember to keep that locked."

"It wouldn't have mattered. Not after I saw you."

Every nerve in her body was on edge. Telling herself it would add more authority, she rose. "I'm not going to let this go on."

"You can't stop it." He stepped toward her. "Neither can I." His gaze shifted to the papers on her desk. "You haven't listened."

"No. I don't intend to. I'll wade through all the lies, navigate all the dead ends until I find the truth. Then I'll finish it." Her stance was tense and watchful. Her eyes challenged him. "If you want to help me, then tell me what you know."

"I know I want you." He hooked a hand in the belt of her robe to hold her still. At that moment, she was his only need, his only quest, his only hunger. "Now. Tonight."

"You have to go." She could do nothing to prevent the shudder of response or the flare of desire. Integrity warred with passion. "You have to leave."

"Do you know how I ache for you?" His voice was harsh as he jerked her against him. "There is no law I wouldn't break, no value I wouldn't sacrifice to have you. Do you understand that kind of need?"

"Yes." It was clawing her. "Yes. It's wrong."

"Right or wrong, it's tonight." With one sweep of his hand, he sent the lamp crashing to the floor. As the room was plunged into darkness, he lifted her into his arms.

"We can't." But her fingers dug hard into his shoulder, negating the denial.

"We will."

Even as she shook her head, his mouth came down on hers, fast and fevered, strong and seductive. The power of it slammed into her, leaving her reeling and rocky—and helpless, helpless to resist her own answering need. Her lips softened without yielding, parted without surrendering. As she tumbled deaf and blind into the kiss, her mind heard what her heart had been trying to tell her.

He pressed her into the mattress, his mouth frantic and impatient as it roamed her face, his hands already tearing at the thin robe that covered her. Beneath it she was just as he'd dreamed. Hot and smooth and fragrant. Stripping off his gloves he let himself feel what he had craved.

Like a river she flowed under his hands. He could have drowned in her. Though he burned to see what he was making his, he contented himself with texture, with taste, with scent. In the hot storm-haunted night, he was relentless.

He was still a shadow, but she knew him. And wanted him. With all reason, all rationality aside, she clung to him, mouth seeking mouth as they rolled over the bed. Desperate to feel him against her, to feel the wild beat of his heart match the wild beat of hers, she pulled at his shirt. There were harshly whispered words against her lips, against her throat, her breast, as she frantically undressed him.

Then he was as vulnerable as she, his skin as slick, his hands as greedy. Thunder rumbled, lightning flickered in the moonless night. The scent of roses and passion hung heavy in the air. She shuddered, mindless with the pleasures he so recklessly showed her.

It was all heat, all ache, all glory. Even as she wept with it, she strained against him, demanding more. Before she could demand, he gave, sending her soaring again. Dark, secret delights. Moans and whispers. Bruising caresses. Insatiable hungers.

When she thought she would surely go mad, he plunged inside her. And it was madness. She gave herself to it, to him, with all her strength, all her eagerness.

''I love you.'' She wrapped tight around him as the words poured out.

They filled him, even as he filled her. They moved him even as their bodies moved together. He buried his face in her hair. Her nails dug into his back. He felt his own shattering release, then hers as she cried out his name.

He lay in the dark. The roaring in his head gradually subsided until all he heard was the sound of traffic on the street below and Deborah's deep, unsteady breaths. Her arms were no longer tight around him, but had slid off. She was still now, and quiet.

Slowly, unnerved by his own weakness, he shifted from her. She didn't move, didn't speak. In the dark, he touched a hand to her face and found it damp. And he hated that part of him that had caused her grief.

"How long have you known?"

"Not until tonight." Before he could touch her again, she turned away and groped for her robe. "Did you think I wouldn't know when you kissed me? Didn't you realize that no matter how dark it was, no matter how confused you made me, once this happened I would know?"

It wasn't just anger in her voice, but pain. He could have withstood the anger. "No, I didn't think of it."

"Didn't you?" She switched on the bedside lamp and stared at him. "But you're so clever, Gage, so damn clever to have made such a mistake."

He looked at her. Her hair was tumbled, her pale skin still flushed and warm from his hands. There were tears in her eyes, and behind them a bright anger. "Maybe I did know. Maybe I just didn't want to let it matter." He rose and reached for her. "Deborah—"

She slapped him once, then twice. "Damn you, you lied to me. You made me doubt myself, my values. You knew, you had to know I was falling in love with you." With a half-laugh she turned away. "With both of you."

"Please listen." When he touched her on the shoulder, she jerked away.

"It wouldn't be wise to touch me just now."

"All right." He curled his hand into a fist. "I fell in love with you so fast, I couldn't think. All I knew was that I needed you, and that I wanted you to be safe."

"So, you put on your mask and looked out for me. I won't thank you for it. For any of it."

The finality in her voice had panic racing through him. "Deborah, what happened here tonight—"

"Yes, what happened here. You trusted me enough for this." She gestured to the bed. "But not for the rest. Not for the truth."

"No, I didn't. I couldn't because I know how you feel about what I'm doing."

"That's a whole different story, isn't it?" She swiped away tears.

The anger was dying away to misery. "If you knew you had to lie to me, why didn't you just stay away from me?"

He forced himself not to reach for her again. He had lied and, by lying, hurt her. Now he could only offer the truth and hope it would begin to heal. "You're the only thing in four years I haven't been able to overcome. You're the only thing in four years I've needed as much as I've needed to live. I don't expect you to understand or even accept, but I need you to believe me."

"I don't know what to believe. Gage, since I met you I've been torn in two different directions, believing I was falling in love with two different men. But it's just you. I don't know what to do." On a sigh, she shut her eyes. "I don't know what's right."

"I love you, Deborah. Nothing's righter than that. Give me a chance to show you, time to explain the rest."

"I don't seem to have much choice. Gage, I can't condone—" She opened her eyes and for the first time focused on the long, jagged scars on his chest. Pain slammed into her, all but bringing her to her knees. Dulled with horror, her eyes lifted to his. "They did that to you?" she whispered.

His body stiffened. "I don't want pity, Deborah."

"Be quiet." She moved quickly, going to him, wrapping her arms around him. "Hold me." She shook her head. "No, tighter. I might have lost you all those years ago before I ever had the chance to have you." There were tears in her eyes again as she lifted her head. "I don't know what to do, or what's right. But tonight it's enough that you're here. You'll stay?"

He touched his lips to hers. "As long as you want."

# Chapter 8

Deborah always awakened reluctantly. She snuggled into sleep, easily blocking out the honks and gunning engines from the street. A jackhammer was machine-gunning the concrete, but she only yawned and shifted. If she put her mind to it, she could sleep through an atomic bomb.

It wasn't the noise that had her opening her groggy eyes. It was the faint and glorious scent of brewing coffee.

Ten-thirty, she noted, peering at the clock. *Ten-thirty!* Deborah struggled to sit up and discovered she was alone in bed.

Gage, she thought, pressing the heels of her hands to her eyes. Had he ordered breakfast again? Eggs Benedict? Belgian waffles? Strawberries and champagne? God, what she would have given for a simple cup of black coffee and a stale doughnut.

Pushing herself from the bed, she reached down for her robe, which was lying in a heap on the floor. Beneath it was a swatch of black cloth. She picked it up, then lowered herself to the bed again.

A mask. She balled the material in her hand. So, it hadn't been a dream. It was real, all of it. He had come to her in the night, loved her in the night. Both of her fantasies. The charming businessman, the arrogant stranger in black. They were one man, one lover.

On a low groan, she buried her face in her hands. What was she going to do? How the hell was she going to handle this? As a woman? As a D.A.?

God, she loved him. And by loving him, she betrayed her principles. If she revealed his secret, she betrayed her heart.

And how could she love him without understanding him?

Yet she did, and there was no way she could take back her heart.

They had to talk, she decided. Calmly and sensibly. She could only pray she would find the strength and the right words. It wouldn't be enough to tell him she disapproved. He already knew it. It wouldn't be enough to tell him she was afraid. That would only prompt him to reassure. Somehow, she had to find the words to convince him that the path he had taken was not only dangerous, but wrong.

Deborah braced herself, prepared.

When the phone rang, she muttered an oath. Struggling into her robe, she climbed across the bed to snatch up the receiver.

"…Deborah's sister." Cilla's voice held both amusement and curiosity. "And how are you?"

"Fine, thanks," Gage said. "Deborah's still sleeping. Would you like me to—"

"I'm right here." Sighing, Deborah pushed at her tousled hair. "Hello, Cilla."

"Hi."

"Goodbye, Cilla." Deborah heard Gage set the phone on the hook. There was a moment of humming silence.

"Ah…I guess I called at a bad time."

"No. I was just getting up. Isn't it a bit early in Denver?"

"With three kids, this is the middle of the day. Bryant, take that basketball outside. *Out!* No dribbling in the kitchen. Deb?"

"Yes?"

"Sorry. Anyway, Boyd checked out those names, and I thought you'd like the information right away."

"That's great." She picked up a pen.

"I'll let Boyd fill you in." The phone rattled. "No, I'll take him. Keenan, don't put that in your mouth. Good grief, Boyd, what's all over his face?" There was some giggling, a crash as the receiver hit the kitchen floor and the sound of running feet.

"Deb?"

"Congratulations, Captain Fletcher."

"Thanks. I guess Cilla's been bragging again. How's it going?"

She looked down at the mask she still held in her hand. "I'm not at all sure." Shaking off the mood, she smiled into the phone. "Things sound normal out there."

"Nothing's ever normal out here. Hey, Allison, don't let that dog—" There was another crash and a flurry of barking. "Too late."

Yes, it sounded perfectly normal. "Boyd, I appreciate you moving so fast on this."

"No problem. It sounded important."

"It is."

"Well, it isn't much. George P. Drummond was a plumber, owned his own business—"

"Was?" Deborah interrupted.

"Yeah. He died three years ago. Natural causes. He was eighty-two and had no connection with a Solar Corporation or any other."

She shut her eyes. "And the other?"

"Charles R. Meyers. High school science teacher and football coach. Deceased five years. They were both clean as a whistle."

"And the Solar Corporation?"

"We can't find much so far. The address you gave Cilla was non-existent."

"I should have guessed. Every time I turn a corner on this, I run into a dead end."

"I know the feeling. I'll do some more digging. Sorry I can't be more helpful."

"But you have been."

"Two dead guys and a phony address? Not much. Deborah, we've been following the papers out here. Can you tell me if this business has anything to do with your masked phantom?"

She balled the black cloth in her hand again. "Off the record, yes."

"I imagine Cilla's already said it, but be careful, okay?"

"I will."

"She wants to talk to you again." There was some muttering, a chuckle. "Something about a man answering your phone." Boyd laughed again, and Deborah could almost see them wrestling over the receiver.

"I just want to know—" Cilla was breathless. "Boyd, cut it out.

Go feed the dog or something. I just want to know,'' she repeated into the receiver, "who owns the terrific, sexy voice."

"A man."

"I figured that out. Does he have a name?"

"Yes."

"Well, do you want me to guess? Phil, Tony, Maximillion?"

"Gage," Deborah muttered, giving up.

"The millionaire? Nice going."

"Cilla—"

"I know, I know. You're a grown woman. A sensible woman with a life of her own. I won't say another word. But is he—"

"Before you take this any further, I should warn you I haven't had coffee yet."

"Okay. But I want you to call me, and soon. I need details."

"I'll let you know when I have them. I'll be in touch."

"You'd better."

She hung up and sat a moment. It seemed she was back to square one, all around. But first things first, she reminded herself, and followed the scent of coffee into the kitchen.

Gage was at the stove, in jeans and bare feet, his shirt unbuttoned. She wasn't surprised to see him there, but she was surprised at what he was doing.

"You're cooking?" she said from the doorway.

He turned. The impact of seeing her there in the strong sunlight, her eyes sleepy and cautious, nearly bowled him over. "Hi. Sorry about the phone, I thought I could get it before it woke you up."

"It's all right. I was...awake." Feeling awkward, she took a mug from a hook over the sink and poured coffee. "It was my sister."

"Right." He put his hands on her shoulders, running his hands gently down to her elbows and back. When she stiffened, he felt the pain knife into him. "Would you rather I wasn't here?"

"I don't know." She drank without turning around. "I guess we have to talk." But she couldn't bring herself to face it yet. "What are you making?"

"French toast. You didn't have much in the fridge, so I went down to the corner and picked some things up."

So normal, she thought as her stomach clenched. So easy. "How long have you been up?"

"Two or three hours."

When he walked back to the stove, she turned around. "You didn't get much sleep."

His eyes met hers. She was holding back, he thought, on both the hurt and the anger. But they were there. "I don't need much—not anymore." He added two eggs to the milk he already had in a bowl. "I spent the better part of a year doing nothing but sleeping. After I came back, I didn't seem to need more than four hours a night."

"I guess that's how you manage to run your businesses, and...the other."

"Yeah." He continued to mix ingredients, then dunked bread into the bowl. "You could say my metabolism changed—among other things." Coated bread sizzled when he placed it in the skillet. "Do you want me to apologize for what happened last night?"

She didn't speak for a moment, then opened a cupboard. "I'll get some plates."

He bit off an oath. "Fine. This only takes a few minutes."

He waited until they were seated by the window. Deborah said nothing while she toyed with her breakfast. Her silence and the miserable look in her eyes were more disturbing to him than a hundred shouted accusations.

"It's your call," he said quietly.

Her eyes lifted to his. "I know."

"I won't apologize for being in love with you. Or for making love with you. Being with you last night was the most important thing that's ever happened to me."

He waited, watching her. "You don't believe that, do you?"

"I'm not sure what I believe. What I can believe." She cupped her hands around her mug, her fingers tense. "You've lied to me, Gage, from the very beginning."

"Yes, I have." He banked down on the need to reach out for her, just to touch her. "Apologies for that really don't matter much. It was deliberate, and if it had been possible, I would have continued to lie to you."

She pushed away from the table to wrap her arms around herself. "Do you know how that makes me feel?"

"I think I do."

Hurting, she shook her head. "You couldn't possibly know. You made me doubt myself on the most basic of levels. I was falling in love with you—with both of you, and I was ashamed. Oh, I can see now that I was a fool not to have realized it sooner. My feelings were exactly the same for what I thought were two different men. I would look at you, and think of him. Look at him, and think of you." She pressed her fingers to her lips. The words were pouring out too quickly.

"That night, in Santiago's room, after I came to and you were holding me. I looked up into your eyes and remembered the first time I had seen you in the ballroom at the Stuart Palace. I thought I was going crazy."

"It wasn't done to hurt you, only to protect you."

"From what?" she demanded. "From myself, from you? Every time you touched me, I..." Her breath hitched as she fought for composure. That was her problem, after all. Her emotions. "I don't know if I can forgive you, Gage, or trust you. Even loving you, I don't know."

He sat where he was, knowing she would resist if he tried to approach her. "I can't make up for what was done. I didn't want you, Deborah. I didn't want anyone who could make me vulnerable enough to make a mistake." He thought of his gift. His curse. "I don't even have the right to ask you to take me as I am."

"With this?" She pulled the mask from the pocket of her robe. "No, you don't have the right to ask me to accept this. But that's just what you're doing. You're asking me to love you. And you're asking me to close my eyes to what you're doing. I dedicated my life to the law. Am I supposed to say nothing while you ignore it?"

His eyes darkened. "I nearly lost my life to the law. My partner died for it. I've never ignored it."

"Gage, this can't be personal."

"The hell it can't. It's all personal. Whatever you read in your law books, whatever precedents or procedures you find, it all comes down to people. You know that. You feel that. I've seen you work."

"Within the law," she insisted. "Gage, you must see what you're doing is wrong, not even to mention dangerous. You have to stop."

His eyes were very dark, very clear. "Not even for you."

"And if I go to Mitchell, to the police commissioner, to Fields?"

"Then I'll do whatever I have to do. But I won't stop."

"Why?" She crossed to him, the mask fisted in her hand. "Damn it, why?"

"Because I don't have a choice." He rose, his hands gripping her shoulders hard before he let go and turned away. "There's nothing I can do to change it. Nothing I would do."

"I know about Montega." When he turned back, she saw the pain. "I'm sorry, Gage, so sorry for what happened to you. For what happened to your partner. We'll bring Montega in, I swear it. But revenge isn't the answer for you. It can't be."

"What happened to me four years ago changed my life. That's not trite. That's reality." He laid his hand against the wall, stared at it, then pulled it back to stick it into his pocket. "You read the reports of what happened the night Jack was killed?"

"Yes, I read them."

"All the facts," he murmured. "But not all the truth. Was it in the report that I loved him? That he had a pretty wife and a little boy who liked to ride a red tricycle?"

"Oh, Gage." She couldn't prevent her eyes from filling, or her arms from reaching out. But he shook his head and moved away.

"Was it in the report that we had given nearly two years of our lives to break that case? Two years of dealing with the kind of slime who have big yachts, big houses, fat portfolios all from the money they earn selling drugs to smaller dealers, who pay the rent by putting it out on the streets, and the playgrounds and the projects. Two years working our way in, our way up. Because we were cops and we believed we could make a difference."

He put his hands on the back of the chair, fingers curling, uncurling. She could only stand and watch in silence as he remembered.

"Jack was going to take a vacation when it was over. Not to go anywhere, just to sit around the house, mow the grass, fix a leaky sink, spend time with Jenny and his kid. That's what he said. I was thinking about going to Aruba for a couple of weeks, but Jack, he didn't have big dreams. Just ordinary ones.''

He looked up, out the window, but he didn't see the sunlight or the traffic crowding the streets. Effortlessly he slid into the past. ''We got out of the car. We had a case full of marked bills, plenty of backup and a solid cover. What could go wrong? We were both ready, really ready. We were going to meet the man in charge. It was hot. You could smell the water, hear it lapping against the docks. I was sweating, not just because of the heat, but because it didn't feel right. But I didn't listen to my instincts. And then Montega...''

Gage could see him, standing in the shadows of the docks, gold glinting in his grin.

*Stinking cops.*

''He killed Jack before I could even reach for my weapon. And I froze. Just for an instant, just for a heartbeat, but I froze. And he had me.''

She thought of the scars on his chest and could hardly breathe. To have watched his partner murdered. To have had that moment, that instant of time to see his own death coming. The sharp, shuddering pain that ripped through her was all for him.

''Don't. What good does it do to go back and remember? You couldn't have saved Jack. No matter how quick you had been, no matter what you had done, you couldn't have saved him.''

He looked back at her. ''Not then. I died that night.''

The way he said it, so flat, so passionlessly, had her blood going cold. ''You're alive.''

''Death's almost a technical term these days. Technically, I died. And part of me slipped right out of my body.'' Her face grew only paler as he spoke, but she had to know. He had to tell her. ''I watched them working on me, there on the docks. And again in the operating room. I almost—almost floated free. And then...I was trapped.''

''I don't understand.''

''Back in my body, but not *back*.'' He lifted his hands, spread them. He'd never tried to explain it to anyone before, and wasn't certain he could. ''Sometimes I could hear—voices, the classical music the nurse left playing by the bed, crying. Or I'd smell flowers. I couldn't speak, I couldn't see. But more than that I couldn't feel anything.'' He let his hands drop again. ''I didn't want to. Then I came back—and I felt too much.''

It was impossible to imagine, but she felt the pain and the despair in her own heart. ''I won't say I understand what you went through. No one could. But it hurts me to think of it, of what you're still going through.''

He looked at her, watched a tear slide down her cheek. ''When I saw you that night, in the alley, my life changed again. I was just as helpless to stop it as I had been the first time.'' His gaze shifted down to the mask she held tight. ''Now, my life's in your hands.''

''I wish I knew what was right.''

He came to her again, lifting his hands to her face. ''Give me some time. A few more days.''

''You don't know what you're asking me.''

''I do,'' he said, holding her still when she would have turned away. ''But I don't have a choice. Deborah, if I don't finish what I've started I might as well have died four years ago.''

Her mouth opened to argue, to protest, but she saw the truth of his words in his eyes. ''Isn't there another way?''

''Not for me. A few more days,'' he repeated. ''After that, if you feel you have to take what you know to your superiors, I'll accept it. And take the consequences.''

She shut her eyes. She knew what he could not. That she would have given him anything. ''Mitchell gave me two weeks,'' she said dully. ''I can't promise you any longer.''

He knew what it cost her and prayed he would find the time and the place to balance the scales. ''I love you.''

She opened her eyes, looked into his. ''I know,'' she murmured, then laid her head against his chest. The mask dangled from her fingers. ''I know you do.''

She felt his arms around her, the solid reality of them. She lifted her head again to meet his lips with hers, to let the kiss linger, warm and promising, even while her conscience waged a silent battle.

What was going to happen to them? Afraid, she tightened her grip and held on. ''Why can't it be simple?'' she whispered. ''Why can't it be ordinary?''

He couldn't count the times he had asked himself the same questions. "I'm sorry."

"No." Shaking her head, she drew away. "I'm sorry. It doesn't do any good to stand here whining about it." With a sniffle, she brushed away tears. "I may not know what's going to happen, but I know what has to be done. I have to go to work. Maybe I can find a way out of this thing." She lifted a brow. "Why are you smiling?"

"Because you're perfect. Absolutely perfect." As he had the night before, he hooked a hand in the belt of her robe. "Come to bed with me. I'll show you what I mean."

"It's nearly noon," she said as he lowered his head to nibble at her ear. "I have work."

"Are you sure?"

Her eyes drifted closed. Her body swayed toward his. "Ah...yes." She pulled away, holding both palms out. "Yes, really. I don't have much time. Neither of us do."

"All right." He smiled again when her lips moved into a pout at his easy acquiescence. Perhaps, with luck, he could give her something ordinary. "On one condition."

"Which is?"

"I have a charity function tonight. A dinner, a couple of performers, dancing. At the Parkside."

"The Parkside." She thought of the old, exclusive and elegant hotel overlooking City Park. "Are you talking about the summer ball?"

"Yeah, that's it. I'd considered skipping it, but I've changed my mind. Will you go with me?"

She lifted a brow. "You're asking me at noon, if I'll go with you to the biggest, glitziest event in the city—which begins eight hours from now. And you're asking me when I've got to go to work, have absolutely no hope of getting an appointment at a hairdresser, no time to shop for the right dress."

"That about covers it," he said after a moment.

She blew out a breath. "What time are you going to pick me up?"

At seven, Deborah stepped under a steaming hot shower. She didn't believe it could possibly ease all the aches, and she was over her quota of aspirin for the day. Six hours in front of a computer terminal, a phone receiver at her ear, had brought her minimal results.

Each name she had checked had turned out to belong to someone long dead. Each address was a blind alley, and each corporation she investigated led only to a maze of others.

The common thread, as Gage had termed it, seemed to be frustration.

More than ever she needed to find the truth. It wasn't only a matter of justice now. It was personal. Though she knew that warped her objectivity, it couldn't be helped. Until this was resolved, she couldn't begin to know where her future, and Gage's, lay.

Perhaps nowhere, she thought as she bundled into a towel. They had come together like lightning and thunder. But storms passed. She knew that an enduring relationship required more than passion. Her parents had had passion—and no understanding. It required even more than love. Her parents had loved, but they had been unhappy.

Trust. Without trust, love and passion faded, paled and vanished.

She wanted to trust him. And to believe in him. Yet he didn't trust her. There were things he knew that could bring her closer to the truth in the case they were both so involved in. Instead, he kept them to himself, determined that his way and only his way was the right one.

With a sigh, she began to dry her hair. Wasn't she just as determined that her way, only her way, was the right one?

If they were so opposed on this one fundamental belief, how could love be enough?

But she had agreed to see him that night. Not because she wanted to go to a fancy ball, she thought. If he had asked her for hot dogs and bowling, she would have gone. Because she couldn't stay away. If she was honest, she would admit she didn't want to stay away.

She would give herself tonight, Deborah thought, carefully applying blusher. But like Cinderella, when the ball was over, she would have to face reality.

Moving briskly, she walked into the bedroom. Spread over the bed was the dress she had bought less than an hour before. Fate, she mused, running a hand over its shimmering sequins. He'd said he liked her in blue. When she'd rushed into the dress shop, frantic, it had been there, waiting. A liquid column of rich, royal blue, studded with silvery sequins. And it fit like a glove from its high-banded collar to its ankle-skimming hem.

Deborah had winced at the price tag, then had gritted her teeth. She'd thrown caution and a month's pay to the winds.

Now, looking in the mirror, she couldn't regret it. The rhinestone swirls at her ears were the perfect match. With her hair swept up and back, her shoulders were bare. She shifted. So was most of her back.

She was just slipping on her shoes when Gage knocked.

His smile faded when she opened the door. Her own lips curved at the sudden and intense desire she saw in his eyes. Very slowly she turned a full circle.

"What do you think?"

He discovered, if he did so very slowly, he could breathe. "I'm glad I didn't give you more time to prepare."

"Why?"

"I couldn't have handled it if you were any more beautiful."

She tilted her chin. "Show me."

He was almost afraid to touch her. Very gently he laid his hands on her shoulders, lowered his mouth to hers. But the taste of her punched into his system, making his fingers tighten, his mouth greedy. With a murmur, he shifted, reaching out to shut the door.

"Oh, no." She was breathless, and unsteady enough to have to lean back against the door. But she was also determined. "For what I paid for this dress, I want to take it out in public."

"Always practical." He gave her one last, lingering kiss. "We could be late."

She smiled at him. "We'll leave early."

When they arrived, the ballroom was already crowded with the glamorous, the influential, the wealthy. Over champagne and appetizers, Deborah scanned the tables and the table-hoppers.

She saw the governor glad-handing a well-known actress, a publishing tycoon cheek-bussing an opera star, the mayor exchanging grins and guffaws with a bestselling author.

"Your usual crowd?" Deborah murmured, smiling at Gage.

"A few acquaintances." He touched his glass to hers.

"Mmm. That's Tarrington, isn't it?" She nodded her head toward a young, earnest-looking man. "What do you think his chances are in the debates?"

"He has a lot to say," Gage commented. "Sometimes a bit tactlessly, but he has a point. Still, he'll have a hard time swaying the over-forty vote."

"Gage." Arlo Stuart stopped at their table, patting his hand on Gage's shoulder. "Good to see you."

"Glad you could make it."

"Wouldn't have missed it." A tall, tanned man with a wavy mane of snowy hair and clear green eyes, he gestured with his glass of Scotch. "You've done nice things in here. I haven't been in since you finished the renovations."

"We like it."

It took Deborah only a minute to realize they were talking about the hotel. And that the hotel belonged to Gage. She glanced up at the opulent crystal chandeliers. She should have known.

"I like knowing my competition has class." His gaze flicked to Deborah. "Speaking of class. Your face is very familiar. And I'm too old for you to consider that a line."

"Arlo Stuart, Deborah O'Roarke."

He took Deborah's hand, holding it in a hearty squeeze. "O'Roarke—O'Roarke." His eyes were both friendly and crafty. "You're the hot lawyer, aren't you? The D.A. who knocked that little creep Slagerman down a peg. The newspaper pictures aren't even close."

"Mr. Stuart."

"The mayor has good things to say about you. Very good things. We'll have to have a dance later so you can tell me all you know about our friend, Nemesis."

Her hand jerked in his, but she managed to keep her eyes level. "It would be a short conversation."

"Not according to our favorite journalist. Of course Wisner's an ass." He had yet to release her hand. "Where did you meet our up-and-coming D.A., Gage? I must be frequenting the wrong places."

"At your hotel," he said easily. "The mayor's fund-raiser."

Stuart gave a hearty laugh. "Well, that will teach me to run around drumming up votes for Fields, won't it? Don't forget that dance."

"I won't," she said, grateful to have her hand, sore fingers and all, back in her lap.

When he walked away, Deborah wiggled her fingers. "Is he always so…exuberant?"

"Yes." Gage picked up her hand and kissed it. "Anything broken?"

"I don't think so." Content to have her hand in his, she glanced around the room. Lush palms, a musical fountain, mirrored ceilings. "This is your hotel?"

"Yeah. Do you like it?"

"It's okay." She gave a little shrug when he grinned. "Shouldn't you be socializing?"

"I am." He touched his lips to hers.

"If you keep looking at me like that—"

"Go on. Please."

She let out one long, unsteady breath. "I think I'll take a trip to the powder room."

Halfway across the ballroom, she was waylaid by the mayor. "I'd like a moment, Deborah."

"Of course."

With an arm around her waist, flashing a broad political smile, he steered her expertly through the crowd and through the high ballroom doors.

"I thought we could use a little privacy."

Glancing back, she noted that Jerry was moving their way. At a signal from the mayor, he stopped, sent Deborah an apologetic look and merged back with the crowd.

"It's quite an elaborate event," Deborah began, schooled enough to know the mayor preferred to launch a topic himself.

"I was surprised to see you here." He nudged her away from the doors toward an alcove that held potted plants and pay phones. "Then again, perhaps I shouldn't have been, since your and Guthrie's names have been linked so often lately."

"I'm seeing Gage," she said coolly. "If that's what you mean.

On a personal level.'' She was already weary of playing politics. ''Is that what you wanted to talk to me about, Mayor? My social life?''

''Only as it affects your professional one. I was disturbed and disappointed to learn that against my wishes you're remaining on this investigation.''

''Your wishes?'' she countered. ''Or Mr. Guthrie's?''

''I respected and agreed with his viewpoint.'' There was a flash of anger in his eyes he rarely showed outside of the privacy of his own offices. ''Frankly, I'm displeased with your performance on this matter. Your excellent record in the courtroom does not override your reckless mistakes outside of it.''

''Reckless? Believe me, Mayor Fields, I haven't begun to be reckless. I'm following my superior's orders in pursuing this matter. I began it, and I intend to finish it. Since we're supposed to be on the same side, I'd think you'd be pleased with the dedication of the D.A.'s office in this case, not only with our persistence in tracking down and prosecuting the men trafficking drugs, but in finding Montega, a known cop killer, and bringing him to justice.''

''Don't tell me whose side I'm on.'' Clearly on the edge of losing control, he wagged a finger in her face. ''I've worked for this city since before you could tie your own shoes. You don't want to make an enemy of me, young lady. I run Urbana, and I intend to keep right on running it. Young, overeager prosecutors are a dime a dozen.''

''Are you threatening to have me fired?''

''I'm warning you.'' With an obvious effort of will, he brought himself under control. ''You either work with the system, or you work against it.''

''I know that.'' Her fingers tightened on her evening bag.

''I admire you, Deborah,'' he said more calmly. ''But while you have enthusiasm, you lack experience, and a case like this requires more experienced hands and minds.''

She stood her ground. ''Mitchell gave me two weeks.''

''I'm aware of that. Make sure you play by the book for the time you have left.'' Though his eyes were still hot, he laid an avuncular hand on her arm. ''Enjoy yourself this evening. The menu's excellent.''

When he left her, she stood there for a moment, quietly shaking with rage. Grappling for control, she strode toward the ladies' room. Inside, she stormed through two arching ficus trees and into the adjoining room with its rose-colored chairs and mint-green counters. Still seething, she tossed her bag onto the counter and plopped down into a chair in front of one of the oval lighted mirrors.

So the mayor was displeased, she thought. He was disappointed. He was disturbed. She grabbed a lipstick out of her purse and concentrated on painting her lips. What he was, she thought, was spitting mad because she had bucked him.

Did he think there was only one way to do things, only one route to take? What the hell was wrong with taking a few detours, as long as they led to the same destination? Especially if they got you there quicker.

She tossed the lipstick back into her purse and reached for her compact. In the glass, she met her own eyes.

What was she thinking? Only twenty-four hours before, she had been sure there was only one way, only one route. And though she wouldn't have appreciated the mayor's tactics, she would have applauded his sentiments.

And now? She dropped her chin on her hand. And now she just wasn't sure. Wasn't she, even at this moment, veering outside of the system that she believed in? Wasn't she allowing her feelings, her personal feelings for Gage, to interfere with her professional ethics?

Or did it all come down to a matter of right and wrong, with her not knowing which was which? How could she continue, how could she function as a lawyer, if she couldn't see clearly what was right?

Maybe it was time to examine the facts, along with her own conscience, and ask herself if it wouldn't be better for everyone if she did withdraw.

As she sat studying her own face and her own values, the lights went out.

# Chapter 9

Deborah clutched her evening bag and set one hand on the counter to orient herself. Big, fancy hotel like this, she thought, and it blows a fuse. Though she tried to see the humor of it as she stood, her heart was pounding. She swore when her hip bumped the chair as she groped through the dark.

Though it was foolish, she was afraid, and felt both trapped and smothered by the dark.

The door creaked open. There was a shaft of light, then blackness.

"Hey, pretty lady."

She froze, holding her breath.

"I got a message for you." The voice was high and piping with a giggle at the end of each sentence. "Don't worry. I'm not going to hurt you. Montega wants you all for himself, and he'd get real mad if I messed you up any first."

Her skin iced over. He couldn't see her, Deborah reminded herself as she fought the paralyzing fear. That evened the odds. "Who are you?"

"Me?" Another giggle. "You've been looking for me, but I'm hard to find. That's why they call me Mouse. I can get in and out of anyplace."

He was moving toward her soundlessly. Deborah could only guess at the direction of his voice. "You must be very clever." After she spoke, she too moved, shifting a careful foot to the left.

"I'm good. I'm the best. Ain't nobody better than old Mouse. Montega wanted me to tell you he's real sorry you didn't get to talk more before. He wants you to know he's keeping an eye on you. All the time. And on your family."

For an instant her blood stopped flowing. Her thoughts of outmaneuvering him, of slipping past him to the door vanished. "My family?"

"He knows people in Denver, too. Real slick people." He was closer now, so close she could smell him. But she didn't move away. "If you cooperate, he'll make sure your sister and the rest stay safe and snug in their beds tonight. Get the picture?"

She reached into her bag, felt the cool metal in her hand. "Yes, I get the picture." Pulling it out, she aimed in the direction of his voice and fired.

Screaming, he crashed into the chairs. Deborah sprinted around him, ramming her shoulder against one wall, then another until she located the door. Mouse was weeping and cursing as she tugged and found the door jammed.

"Oh, God. Oh, God." Panicked, she continued to pull.

"Deborah!" She heard her name shouted. "Get away from the door. Step back from the door."

She took one stumbling step backward and heard the heavy thud. Another, and the door crashed open. She ran into the light and Gage's arms.

"You're all right?" His hands were running over her, checking for hurts.

"Yes. Yes." She buried her face in his shoulder, ignoring the gathering crowd. "He's inside." When he started to push away, Deborah held on tighter. "No, please."

His face grim, Gage nodded to a pair of security guards. "Come and sit down."

"No, I'm okay." Though her breath was still shuddering, she drew away to look at his face. She saw murder there and tightened her hold on him. "Really. He didn't even touch me. He was trying to frighten me, Gage. He didn't hurt me."

His voice was low as he studied her pale face. "Is that supposed to make me want to kill him less?"

With a burly guard on each arm, the weeping Mouse stumbled out, his hands covering his face. Deborah noted he was wearing a waiter's uniform.

Alarmed by the look in Gage's eyes, she pulled his attention back to her. "He's in a lot worse shape than I am. I used this." With an unsteady hand, Deborah held up a can of Mace. "I've been carrying it with me since that night in the alley."

Gage wasn't sure if he should laugh or swear. Instead, he pulled her against him and kissed her. "It looks as though I can't let you out of my sight."

"Deborah." Jerry elbowed through the onlookers. "Are you all right?"

"I am now. The police?"

"I called them myself." Jerry glanced up at Gage. "You should get her out of here."

"I'm fine," Deborah insisted, glad the full-length dress concealed her knocking knees. "I'll have to go down to the police station and make a statement. But I need to make a phone call first."

"I'll call whomever you like." Jerry gave her hand a quick squeeze.

"Thanks, but I need to do this." Behind him, she spotted the mayor. "You could do me a favor and hold Fields off my back for a while."

"Done." He looked at Gage again. "Take care of her."

"I intend to." Keeping Deborah tight at his side, Gage led her away from the crowd. He moved quickly across the lobby and toward a bank of elevators.

"Where are we going?"

"I keep an office here, you can make the call from there." Inside the elevator, he turned her to him again and held tight. "What happened?"

"Well, I didn't get to powder my nose." She turned her face into his collar, breathing deeply. "First, Fields waylaid me and read me the riot act. He's not pleased with my performance." When the elevator doors opened, she loosened her hold so they could walk into the hallway. "When we parted ways, I was seeing red. I sat down in the powder room to repair my makeup and my composure." She was calming, and grateful the shaking had stopped. "Very elegant, by the way."

He shot her a look as he slid a key into a lock. "I'm glad you approve."

"I liked it a lot." She stepped into the parlor of a suite and crossed the thick oatmeal-colored carpet. "Until the lights went out. I was just orienting myself when the door opened, and he came in. The elusive Mouse," she said as her stomach began to churn again. "He had a message for me from Montega."

The name, just the name, had Gage's muscles tensing. "Sit down. I'll get you a brandy."

"The phone?"

"Right there. Go ahead."

Gage was fighting his own demons as he moved to the bar for the decanter and two snifters. She'd been alone, and however resourceful she was, she'd been vulnerable. When he'd heard the screaming... His fingers went white on the decanter. If it had been Montega instead of his messenger boy, she could have been dead. And he would have been too late.

Nothing that had happened to him before, nothing that could happen to him in the future would be more devastating than losing her.

She was sitting now, very straight, very tense, her face too pale, her eyes too dark. In one hand she held the receiver while the other vised around the cord. She was talking fast, to her brother-in-law, Gage realized after a moment.

They had threatened her family. He could see the possibility they would be harmed was more terrifying to her than any attempt on her own life.

"I need you to call me every day," she insisted. "You'll make sure Cilla has guards at the radio station. The children..." She covered her face with her hand. "God, Boyd." She listened a moment, nodding, trying to smile. "Yes, I know, I know. You didn't make captain for nothing. I'll be fine. Yes, and careful. I love you. All of you." She paused again, inhaling deeply. "Yes, I know. Bye."

She replaced the receiver. Saying nothing, Gage pushed the snifter into her hands. She cupped it a moment, staring down at the amber liquid. On another deep breath, she tipped the glass to her lips and drank deeply. She shuddered, drank again.

"Thanks."

"Your brother-in-law's a good cop. He won't let anything happen to them."

"He saved Cilla's life years ago. That's when they fell in love." Abruptly she looked up, her eyes wet and eloquent. "I hate this, Gage. They're my family, all I have left of family. The idea that something I've done, something I'm doing could—" She broke off, pulling herself back from the unthinkable. "When I lost my parents, I didn't think anything would ever be as bad. But this..." With a shake of her head, she looked down at the brandy again. "My mother was a cop."

He knew. He knew it all, but he only covered her hand with his and let her talk.

"She was a good one, or so I was told. I was only twelve when it happened. I didn't know her very well, not really. She wasn't cut out to be a mother."

She shrugged it off, but even in that casual, dismissive gesture, he saw the scars.

"And my father," she continued. "He was a lawyer. A public defender. He tried hard to keep it all together, the family—the illusion of family. But he and my mother just couldn't pull it off." She sipped the brandy again, grateful for its numbing smoothness. "Two uniforms came to school that day, picked me up, took me back to the house. I guess I knew. I knew my mother was dead. They told me, as gently as possible, that it was both of them. Both of them. Some creep my father was defending managed to smuggle in a gun. When they were in the conference room, he cut loose."

"I'm sorry, Deborah. I know how hard it is to lose family."

She nodded, setting the empty snifter aside. "I guess that's why I was determined to be a lawyer, a prosecutor. Both of my parents dedicated their lives, and lost them defending the law. I didn't want it to have been for nothing. Do you understand?"

"Yes." He brought her hands to his lips. "For whatever reason you chose to be a lawyer, it was the right decision. You're a good one."

"Thanks."

"Deborah." He hesitated, wanting to phrase his thoughts carefully. "I respect both your integrity and your abilities."

"I feel a *but* coming on."

"I want to ask you again to back off from this. To leave the rest to me. You'll have your chance to do what you do best, and that's prosecute Montega and the rest of them."

She gave herself a moment, wanting, as he had, to make her thoughts clear. "Gage, tonight, after the mayor came down on me, I sat in the powder room. Once I got over being mad, I started to think, to examine my position, and my motives. I began to think maybe the mayor was right, maybe it would be better if I turned this over to someone with more experience and less personal involvement." Then she shook her head. "And I can't, especially now. They threatened my family. If I stepped back, I'd never be able to trust myself again, to believe in myself. I have to finish this." Before he could speak, she put her hands on his shoulders. "I don't agree with you. I don't know if I ever can, but I understand, in my heart, what you're doing and why you have to do it. That's all I'm asking from you."

How could he refuse? "Then I guess we have a stalemate, for now."

"I have to go down and make my statement." She rose, held out a hand. "Will you come with me?"

They wouldn't let her talk to Mouse. Deborah figured she could work around that eventually. By Monday, she would have the police reports if nothing else. With Mouse under tight security, it was unlikely the same kind of accident could befall him as it had Parino.

For the answers she needed, she would bargain with Mouse, just as she would have bargained with the devil.

She gave her statement, wearily waited while it was typed for her signature. On Saturday night, the station was hopping. Hookers and pimps, dealers and mugging victims, gang members and harried public defenders. It was reality, an aspect of the system she represented and believed in. But it was with relief that she stepped outside.

"Long night," she murmured.

"You handled yourself very well." He laid a hand on her cheek. "You must be exhausted."

"Actually, I'm starving." Her lips curved. "We never did have dinner."

"I'll buy you a hamburger."

With a laugh, she threw her arms around him. Perhaps some things, some very precious things, could be simple. "My hero."

He pressed his lips to the side of her throat. "I'll buy you a dozen hamburgers," he murmured. "Then for God's sake, Deborah, come home with me."

"Yes." She turned her lips to his. "Yes."

He knew how to set the stage. Perfectly. When Deborah walked into the bedroom beside him, there was moonlight drifting through the windows, stardust filtering through the skylight, candle glow warming the shadows. Roses—the scent of them sweetened the air. The sound of a hundred violins romanced it.

She didn't know how he'd managed it all with the single phone call he'd made from the noisy little diner where they had eaten. She didn't care. It was enough to know he would have thought of it.

"It's lovely." She was nervous, she realized, ridiculously so after the passion of the previous night. But her legs were unsteady as she crossed to where a bottle of champagne sat nestled in a crystal bowl of ice. "You thought of everything."

"Only of you." His lips brushed her shoulder before he poured the wine. "I've pictured you here a hundred times. A thousand." He offered her a glass.

"So have I." Her hand trembled as she lifted her glass. Desire, fighting to break free. "The first time you kissed me, up in the tower, whole worlds opened up. It's never been like that for me before."

"I nearly begged you to stay that night, even though you were angry." He slipped off one of her earrings, then let his fingers rub over the sensitive lobe. "I wonder if you would have."

"I don't know. I would have wanted to."

"That's almost enough." He drew off her other earring, set them both on the table. Slowly he slid out one of her hairpins, then another, watching her. Always watching her. "You're shivering."

His hands were so gentle, his eyes so urgent. "I know."

He took the glass from her limp fingers and set it aside. With his eyes on hers, he continued to free her hair. The whisper of his fingertips on the nape of her neck. "You're not afraid of me?"

"Of what you can do to me."

Something flared in his eyes, dark and dangerous. But he lowered his head to gently kiss her temple.

Heavy-eyed and sultry, she looked up at him. "Kiss me, Gage."

"I will." His mouth trailed over her face, teasing, never satisfying her. "I am."

Her breath was already coming fast. "You don't have to seduce me."

He ran a finger up and down her bare spine, smiling when she shuddered. "It's my pleasure." And he wanted it to be hers.

The night before, all the passion, all the fierce and angry needs had clawed their way out of him. Tonight he wanted to show her the softer side of love. When she swayed against him, he withstood the swift arrows of desire.

"We made love in the dark," he murmured as his fingers flicked open the trio of buttons at the back of her neck. "Tonight I want to see you."

The dress shimmered down her, a glittery blue pool at her feet. She wore only a lacy woman's fancy that lifted her breasts and skimmed transparent to her hips. Her beauty struck him breathless.

"Every time I look at you, I fall in love again."

"Then don't stop looking." She reached up to undo the formal tie. Her fingers slid down to unfasten the unfamiliar studs. "Don't ever stop." She parted his shirt with her hands, then pressed her mouth to the heated skin beneath. The tip of her tongue left a moist trail before she lifted her head, let it fall back in invitation. Her eyes were a rich blue gleam beneath her lashes. "Kiss me now."

As seduced as she, he branded her lips with his. Twin moans, low and throaty, shuddered through the room. Her hands slid slowly up his chest to his shoulders to push the dinner jacket aside. Her fingers tightened, then went bonelessly lax as he softened the kiss, deepened it, gentled it.

He lifted her into his arms as though she were fragile crystal rather than flesh and blood. With his eyes on hers, he held her there a moment, letting his mouth tease and torment hers. He continued those feather-light kisses as he carried her to the bed.

He sat, holding her cradled in his lap. His mouth continued its quiet devastation of her reason. He could almost see her float. Her eyes drifted shut. Her limbs were fluid. In arousing contrast, her heart pounded under his hand. He wanted her like this. Totally pleasured. Totally his. As he drew more and more of that warm exotic flavor from her mouth, he thought he could stay just so for hours. For days.

She felt each impossibly tender touch, the stroke of a fingertip, the brush of his palm, the oh-so-patient quest of his lips. Her body seemed as light as the rose-scented air, yet her arms were too heavy to lift. The music and his murmurs merged in her mind into one seducing song. Beneath it was the violent roar of her own speeding pulse.

She knew she had never been more vulnerable or more willing to go wherever he chose to take her.

And this was love—a need more basic than hunger, than thirst.


One quiet, helpless gasp escaped her when his lips whispered over the tops of her breasts. Slowly, erotically, his tongue slid under the lace to tease her hardened nipples. His fingers played over the skin above her stockings, lightly, so lightly, gliding beneath the sheer triangle of material.

With one touch, he sent her over the first towering peak. She arched like a bow, and the pleasure arrowed out of her into him. Then she seemed to melt in his arms.

Breathless, almost delirious, she reached for him. "Gage, let me…"

"I will." He covered her next stunned cry with his mouth. And while she was still shuddering, he laid her on the bed.

Now, he thought. He could take her now, while she lay hot and damp in surrender. There was moonlight on her skin, on her hair. The white lace she wore was like an illusion. When she looked at him from beneath those heavy lashes, he saw the dark flicker of desire.

He had more to show her.

His knuckles brushed her skin, making her jolt as he unhooked her stocking. Almost lazily, he slid it down her leg, following the route with soft, openmouthed kisses. His tongue glided over the back of her knee, down her calf until she was writhing in mindless pleasures.

Trapped in gauzy layers of sensation, she reached for him again, only to have him evade and repeat each devastating delight on her other leg. His mouth journeyed up, lingering, pausing, until it found her. His name burst from her lips as she reared up. Nearly weeping, she grasped him against her.

And at the first touch, the strength seemed to pour into her.

Furnace hot, her flesh met his. But it wasn't enough. Urgent, her fingers pulled at his open shirt, tearing seams in her desperation to find more of him. As she ripped the silk away, her teeth nipped into his shoulder. She felt his stomach muscles quiver, heard the quick intake of his breath as she pulled at the waistband of his trousers. Buttons popped off.

"I want you." Her mouth fixed ravenously to his. "Oh, Lord, I want you."

The control he had held so tightly slipped through his tensed fingers. Desire overpowered him. She overpowered him with her desperate hands, her greedy mouth. The breath was clogging in his lungs, burning as he struggled out of his clothes.

Then they were kneeling in the middle of the ravaged bed, bodies trembling, eyes locked. He hooked a hand in the bodice of the lace and rent it ruthlessly down the center. With his fingers digging into her hips, he pulled her against him.

During the rough, reckless ride, she arched back. Her hands slid down his slick shoulders, then found purchase. She sobbed out his name as she tumbled off the razor's edge of sanity. He gripped her hair in his hand and drove her up again. Again. Then he closed his mouth over hers and followed.

Weak, she lay on the bed, one arm tossed across her eyes, the other hanging limply off the mattress. She knew she couldn't move, wasn't sure she could speak, doubted that she was even breathing.

Yet when he pressed a kiss to her shoulder, she shuddered again.

"I meant to be gentle with you."

She managed to open her eyes. His face was close. She felt his fingers move in her hair. "Then I guess you'll just have to try again until you get it right."

A smile curved his mouth. "I have a feeling that's going to take a long time."

"Good." She traced his smile with a fingertip. "I love you, Gage. That's the only thing that seems to matter tonight."

"It's the only thing that matters." He put a hand over hers. There was a bond in the touch, every bit as deep and as intimate as their lovemaking. "I'll get you some wine."

With a contented sigh, she settled back as he got up. "I never thought it could be like this. I never thought I could be like this."

"Like what?"

She caught a glimpse of herself in the wide mirror across the room—sprawled naked over pillows and rumpled sheets. "So wanton, I guess." She laughed at her choice of words. "In college I had a reputation for being very cool, very studious and very unapproachable."

"School's out." He sat on the bed, handed her a glass then tapped his against it.

"I guess. But even after, when I started in the D.A.'s office, the reputation remained." She wrinkled her nose. "Earnest O'Roarke."

"I like it when you're earnest." He sipped. "I can see you in a law library, poring over thick, dusty books, scribbling notes."

She made a face. "That's not exactly the image I prefer at the moment."

"I like it." He lowered his head to capture her chin gently between his teeth. "You'd be wearing one of those conservatively tailored suits, in those very unconservative colors you like." She frowned a bit, making him chuckle. "Sensible shoes and very discreet jewelry."

"You make me sound like a prude."

"And under it all would be something thin and sexy." He hooked a finger in a torn swatch of lace and lifted it to the light. "A very personal choice for a very proper attorney. Then you'd start quoting precedents and making me crazy."

"Like *Warner v. Kowaski?*"

"Mmm." He switched to her ear. "Just like. And I'd be the only one who knew that it takes six pins to hold your hair back in that very proper twist.''

"I know I can be too serious," she murmured. "It's only because what I do is so important to me." She looked down at her wine. "I have to know what I'm doing is right. That the system I represent works." When he drew away to study her, she sighed. "I know part of it's ego and ambition, but another part of it is so basic, Gage, so ingrained. That's why I worry how you and I are going to resolve this."

"We won't resolve it tonight."

"I know, but—"

"Not tonight," he said, laying a finger over her lips. "Tonight it's just you and me. I need that, Deborah. And so do you."

She nodded. "You're right. I'm being too earnest again."

"We can fix that." He grinned and held up his glass to the light. The champagne bubbled.

"By getting drunk?" she said, brow lifted.

"More or less." When his eyes met hers, there was a smile in them. "Why don't I show you a...less serious way to drink champagne?" He tilted his glass and had a trickle of cool wine sliding over her breast.

# Chapter 10

Gage lost track of time as he watched her sleep. The candles had gutted out in their own hot, fragrant wax so that their scent drifted, quiet as a memory. She had a hand in his, holding lightly even in sleep.

The shadows lifted, fading in the pearl gray of dawn. He watched the growing light fall over her hair, her face, her shoulders. Just as softly, he followed its path with his lips. But he didn't want to wake her.

There was too much to be done, too much he still refused to make her a part of. He knew that over a matter of weeks, the goals he carried inside him for more than four years had become mixed. It was not enough now to avenge his partner's death. It was not enough now to seek and find payment for the time and the life that had been stolen from him. Even justice, that driving force, was not enough.

He would have to move quickly now, for each day that passed without answers was another day Deborah was in jeopardy. There was nothing more important than keeping her safe.

He slid away from her, moving soundlessly from the bed to dress. There was time to make up, all the hours he had spent with her rather than on the streets or at his work. He glanced back when she shifted and snuggled deeper into the pillow. She would sleep through the morning. And he would work.

He pushed a button beneath the carved wood on the wall farthest from the bed. A panel slid open. Gage stepped into the dark and let it close again at his back.

With the husky morning greeting still on her tongue, Deborah blinked sleepily. Had she been dreaming? she wondered. She would have sworn Gage had stepped into some kind of secret passageway. Baffled, she pushed up on her elbows. In sleep she had reached for him and, finding him gone, had awakened just at the moment when the wall had opened.

Not a dream, she assured herself. For he wasn't beside her, and the sheets where he had lain were already cooling.

More secrets, she thought and felt the sorrow of his distrust envelop her. After the nights they had spent together, the love he had shown her, he still wouldn't give her his trust.

So she would take it, Deborah told herself as she pushed herself out of bed. She would not sit and sulk or wish and whine, but demand. Fumbling in his closet, she located a robe. Soft cotton in steel gray, it hit her mid-calf. Impatient, she bundled the sleeves up out of her way and began to search for the mechanism that opened the panel.

Even knowing the approximate location, it took her ten frustrating minutes to find it and another two to figure out how it worked. Her breath hissed out in satisfaction as the panel slid open. Without hesitation, she stepped into the dark, narrow corridor.

Keeping one hand on the wall for guidance, she started forward. There was no dank, disused smell as she might have expected. The air was clean, the wall smooth and dry. Even when the panel behind her closed her completely into the dark, she wasn't uneasy. There would be no scratching or skittering sounds here. It was obvious Gage used the passage, and whatever it led to, often.

She picked her way along, straining her eyes and ears. Corridors veered off, twisting like snakes from the main passage, but she followed instinct and kept to the same straight path. After a moment, she saw a dim glow up ahead and moved a bit more quickly. A set of stone stairs with pie-shaped treads curved into a tight semicircle as it plunged downward. With one hand tight on the thin iron rail, she wove her way to the bottom, where she was faced with three tunnels leading in different directions.

The lady or the tiger, she thought, then shook her head at her own fancy. "Damn you, Gage. Where did you go?" Her whisper echoed faint and hollow, then died.

Bracing her shoulders, she started through one archway, changed her mind and backtracked to the middle. Again she hesitated. Then she heard it, dim and dreamy down the last tunnel. Music.

She plunged into the dark again, following the sound, moving cautiously down the sloping stone floor. She had no idea how deep she was traveling underground, but the air was cooling rapidly. The music grew in volume as degree by faint degree the tunnel's light increased. She heard a mechanical hum, and a clatter—like typewriter keys hitting a platen.

When she stepped into the mouth of the tunnel, she could only stand and stare.

It was an enormous room with curving stone walls. Cavernlike with its arching ceiling and echoes, it spread more than fifty feet in every direction. But it wasn't primitive, she thought as she gathered Gage's robe close around her throat. Rather than appearing gloomy, it was brilliantly lit, equipped with a vast computer system, printers and monitors blinking away. Television screens were bolted to one wall. An enormous topographic map of Urbana spread over another. Music, eerily romantic, poured out of speakers she couldn't see. Granite-gray counters held work stations, telephones, stacks of photographs and papers.

There was a control panel, studded with switches and buttons and levers. Gage sat in front of it, his fingers moving. Over the map, lights blinked on. He shifted, working the controls. On a computer screen, the map was reproduced.

He looked like a stranger, his face grimly set and intense. She wondered if his choice of a black sweater and jeans had been deliberate.

She stepped forward, down a trio of stone steps. "Well," she began as he turned quickly, "you didn't include this on my tour."

"Deborah." He stood, automatically turning off the monitor. "I'd hoped you'd sleep longer."

"I'm sure you did." She stuck her tensed hands into the deep pockets of his robe. "Apparently I've interrupted your work. An interesting…getaway," she decided. "Nemesis's style, I'd say. Dramatic, secretive.'' She moved past a bank of computers toward the map. ''And thorough,'' she murmured. ''Very thorough.'' She whirled around. ''One question. Just the one that seems to matter the most at the moment. Who am I sleeping with?''

''I'm the same man you were with last night.''

''Are you? Are you the same man who told me he loved me, who showed me he did in dozens of beautiful ways? Is that the same man who left me in bed to come down here? How long are you going to lie to me?''

''It isn't a matter of lying to you. This is something I have to do. I thought you understood that.''

''Then you were wrong. I didn't understand that you would keep this from me. That you would work without me, holding information from me.''

He seemed to change before her eyes, growing distant and cool and aloof. ''You gave me two weeks.''

''Damn you, I gave you more than that. I gave you everything.'' Her eyes were brilliant with emotion as hurt and anger battled for priority. But she flung up a hand before he could cross to her. ''No, don't. You won't use my feelings this time.''

''All right.'' Though his own were straining for release. ''It isn't a matter of feelings, but logic. You should appreciate that, Deborah. This is my work. Your presence here is as unnecessary as mine would be in the courtroom with you.''

''Logic?'' She spat out the word. ''It's only logical if it suits your purposes. Do you think I'm a fool? Do you think I can't see what's happening here?'' She gestured sharply toward one of the monitors. ''And we'll keep it strictly professional. You have all the information I've been painfully digging up. All the names, all the numbers, and more, much more than I've been able to uncover. Yet you haven't told me. And wouldn't have.''

The cloak came around him again, impenetrable. ''I work alone.''

''Yes, I'm aware of that.'' The bitterness seeped into her voice as she walked toward him. ''No partners. Except in bed. I'm good enough to be your partner there.''

''One has nothing to do with the other.''

''Everything,'' she all but shouted. ''One has everything to do with the other. If you can't trust me, in every way, respect me, in every way and be honest with me, in every way, then there's nothing between us.''

"Damn it, Deborah, you don't know everything." He gripped her arms. "You don't understand everything."

"No, I don't. Because you won't let me."

"Can't let you," he corrected, holding her still when she would have pulled away. "There's a difference between lying to you and holding back information. This isn't black-and-white."

"Yes, it is."

"These are vicious men. Without conscience, without morals. They've already tried to kill you, and you'd hardly broken the surface. I won't risk you. If you want black-and-white, there it is." He shook her, punctuating each word. "I will not risk you."

"You can't prevent me from doing my job, or what I feel is right."

"By God, if I have to lock you upstairs until I'm done with this to keep you safe, I will."

"And then what? Will the same thing happen the next time, and the next?"

"I'll do whatever it takes to protect you. That won't change."

"Maybe you've got a nice little plastic bubble you could stick me in." She put her hands on his forearms, willing him to understand. "If you love me, then you have to love the whole person I am. I demand that, just as I demand to know and love the whole person you are." She saw something flicker in his eyes and pushed her point. "I can't become something different for you, someone who sits and waits to be taken care of."

"I'm not asking you to."

"Aren't you? If you can't accept me now, you never will. Gage, I want a life with you. Not just a few nights in bed, but a life. Children, a home, a history. But if you can't share with me what you know, and who you are, there can't be a future for us." She broke away from him. "And if that's the case, it would be better for both of us if I left now."

"Don't." He reached out for her before she could turn away. However deep his own need for survival ran, it was nothing compared to the possibility of life without her. "I need your word." His fingers tightened on hers. "That you won't take any chances, and that you'll move in here with me at least until it's over. Whatever we find here has to stay here. You can't risk taking it to the D.A. Not yet."

"Gage, I'm obligated to—"

"No." He cut her off. "Whatever we do, whatever we find stays here until we're ready to move. I can't give you more than that, Deborah. I'm only asking for a compromise."

And it was costing him. She could see that. "All right. I won't take anything to Mitchell until we're both sure. But I want it all, Gage. Everything." Her voice calmed, her hands gentled. "Don't you see I know you're holding something back from me, something basic that has nothing to do with secret rooms or data? I know, and it hurts me."

He turned away. If he was to give her everything, he had no choice but to begin with himself. The silence stretched between them before he broke it. "There are things you don't know about me, Deborah. Things you may not like or be able to accept."

The tone of his voice had her mouth growing dry and her pulse beating irregularly. "Do you have such little faith in me?"

He was putting all his faith in her, he thought. "I've had no right to let things go as far as they have between us without letting you know what I am." He reached out to touch her cheek, hoping it wouldn't be the last time. "I didn't want to frighten you."

"You're frightening me now. Whatever you have to tell me, just tell me. We'll work it out."

Without speaking, he walked away from her, toward the stone wall. He turned and, with his eyes on her, vanished.

Deborah's mouth opened, but the only sound she could make was a strangled gasp. With her eyes riveted to where Gage should be— had to be, her confused brain insisted—she stumbled back. Her unsteady hand gripped the arm of a chair as she let her numbed body slide into it.

Even while her mind rejected what her eyes had seen, he returned—materializing ten feet from where he had disappeared. For an instant she could see through him, as if he were no more than the ghost of the man who stood in front of her.

Deborah started to rise, decided against it, then cleared her throat. "It's an odd time for magic tricks."

"It isn't a trick." Her eyes were still huge with shock as he walked toward her, wondering if she would stiffen or jerk away. "At least not the way you mean."

"All these gadgets you've got down here," she said, clinging desperately to the lifeline of logic in a sea of confusion. "Whatever you're using, it produces quite an optical illusion." She swallowed. "I imagine the Pentagon would be very interested."

"It's not an illusion." He touched her arm, and though she didn't pull away as he'd feared she would, her skin was cold and clammy. "You're afraid of me now."

"That's absurd." But her voice was shaking. She forced herself to stand. "It was just a trick, an effective one, but—"

She broke off when he placed his hand, palm down on the counter beside them. It vanished to the wrist. Dark and dazed, her eyes lifted to his.

"Oh, God. It's not possible." Terrified, she pulled his arm and was almost faint with relief when she saw his hand, whole and warm.

"It's possible." He brought the hand gently to her face. "It's real."

She lifted her trembling fingers to his. "Give me a minute." Moving carefully, she turned and walked a few steps away. Rejection sliced through him, a dull, angry blade.

"I'm sorry." With great effort he controlled his voice, kept it even. "I didn't know of a better way, an easier way, to show you. If I had tried to explain, you wouldn't have believed me."

"No, no, I wouldn't have." She had seen it. Yet her mind still wanted to argue that she could not have seen it. A game, a trick, nothing more. Though there was a comfort in the denial, she remembered how time and again, Nemesis had seemed to vanish before her eyes.

She turned back and saw that he was watching her, his body tensed and ready. No game. When she accepted the truth her trembling only increased. Briskly, she rubbed her hands up and down her arms, hoping to warm and steady the muscles.

"How do you do this?"

"I'm not completely sure." He opened his hands, stared at them, then fisted them to push them impotently into his pockets. "Something·happened to me when I was in the coma. Something changed me. A few weeks after I came back I discovered it, almost by accident. I had to learn to accept it, to use it, because I know it was given to me for a reason."

"And so—Nemesis."

"Yes, and so Nemesis." He seemed to steady himself. Deborah saw that his eyes were level and curiously blank when he looked at her. "I have no choice in this, Deborah. But you do."

"I don't think I understand." She lifted a hand to her head and gave a quick, shaky laugh. "I know I don't understand."

"I wasn't honest with you, about what I am. The man you fell in love with was normal."

Baffled, she let her hand fall to her side again. "I'm not following you. I fell in love with you."

"Damn it, I'm not normal." His eyes were suddenly furious. "I'll never be. I'll carry this thing with me until I die. I can't tell you how I know, I just do."

"Gage—" But when she reached out to him, he backed away.

"I don't want your pity."

"You don't have it," she snapped back. "Why should you? You're not ill. You're whole and you're healthy. If anything, I'm angry because you held *this* back from me, too. And I know why." She dragged both hands through her hair as she paced away from him. "You thought I'd walk, didn't you? You thought I was too weak, too stupid, or too fragile to handle it. You didn't trust me to love you." Her fury built so quickly, she was all but blind with it. "You didn't trust me to love you," she repeated. "Well, the hell with you. I do, and I always will."

She turned, sprinting for the stairs. He caught her at the base of them, turning her back to him and pulling her close while she cursed at him and struggled.

"Call me anything you like." He grabbed her shoulders and shook once. "Slap me again if you want. But don't leave."

"You expected me to, didn't you?" she demanded. She tossed her head back as she strained away from him. "You expected me to turn around and walk away."

"Yes."

She started to shout at him. Then she saw what was in his eyes, what he held back with such rigid control. It was fear. Accusations melted away. "You were wrong," she said quietly. With her eyes still on his, she lifted her hands to his face, rose on her toes and kissed him.

A shudder. From him, from her. Twin waves of relief. He drew her closer, crushing, consuming. As huge as his fear had been, a need sprang up to replace it. It was not pity he tasted on her lips, but passion.

Small, seductive sounds hummed in her throat as she struggled out of the robe. It was more than an offering of herself. It was a demand that he take her as she was, that he allow himself to be taken. With an oath that ended in a groan, he moved his hands over her. He was caught in the madness, a purifying madness.

Impatient, she tugged at his shirt. "Make love with me." Her head fell back and her eyes were as challenging as her voice. "Make love with me now."

She pulled at his clothes even as they lowered to the floor.

Frenzied and frantic. Heated and hungry. They came together. Power leaped like wind-fed flames. It was always so between them, she thought as her body shuddered, shuddered, shuddered. Yet now there was more. Here was a unity. Here was compassion, trust, vulnerability to mix with hungers. She had never wanted him more.

Her hands clenched in his dark hair as she rose above him. She needed to see his face, his eyes. "I love you." The breath tore in her throat. "Let me show you how I love you."

Agile, quick, greedy, she moved over him, taking her mouth down his throat, over his chest, down to where his taut stomach muscles quivered under her moist, seeking lips. The blood pounded in his head, his heart, his loins.

She was a miracle, the second he'd been given in a lifetime. When he reached for her, he reached for love and for salvation.

They rolled, a tangle of limbs and needs, unmindful of the hard, unyielding floor, the clatter and hum of machines blindly working.

Breath came fast, heartbeats galloped. Each taste, each touch seemed more potent, more pungent than ever before.

His fingers dug into her hips when he lifted her. She sheathed him, surrounded him. The pleasure speared them both. Their hands slid toward each other's, palm against palm, then fingers locked tight.

They held on, eyes open, bodies joined, until they took the final leap together.

Boneless, she slid down to him. Her mouth brushed his once, then again, before she lay her head on his shoulder. Never had she felt more beautiful, more desirable, more complete, than in feeling his heart thunder wildly beneath hers.

Her lips curved as she turned and pressed them to his throat. "That was my way of saying you're stuck with me."

"I like the way you get your point across." Gently he ran a hand up and down her spine. She was his. He'd been a fool to ever doubt it, or her. "Does this mean I'm forgiven?"

"Not necessarily." Bracing her hands on his shoulders, she pushed herself up. "I don't understand who you are. Maybe I never will. But understand this. I want all, or I want nothing. I saw what evasions, denials, refusals did to my parents' marriage. I won't live with that."

He put a hand on hers, very lightly. "Is that a proposal?"

She didn't hesitate. "Yes."

"Do you want an answer now?"

Her eyes narrowed. "Yes. And don't think you can get out of it by disappearing. I'll just wait until you come back."

He laughed, amazed that she could joke about something he'd been so sure would repel her. "Then I guess you'll have to make an honest man out of me."

"I intend to." She kissed him briefly, then shifted away to bundle into the robe. "No long engagement."

"Okay."

"As soon as we put a cap on this thing and Cilla and Boyd can arrange to bring the kids out, we get married."

"Agreed." Humor danced in his eyes. "Anything else?"

"I want children right away."

He hitched on his jeans. "Any particular number?"

"One at a time."

"Sounds reasonable."

"And—"

"Shut up a minute." He took her hands. "Deborah, I want to be married to you, to spend the rest of my life knowing when I reach out, I'll find you there. And I want a family, our family." He pressed his lips to the fingers that curled over his. "I want forever with you." He watched her blink back tears and kissed her gently. "Right now I want something else."

"What?"

"Breakfast."

With a strangled laugh, she threw her arms around him. "Me, too."

They ate in the kitchen, laughing and cozy, as if they always shared the first meal of the day together. The sun was bright, the coffee strong. Deborah had dozens of questions to ask him, but she held them back. For this one hour, she wanted them to be two ordinary people in love.

Ordinary, she thought. Strange, but she felt they were and could be ordinary, even with the very extraordinary aspects of their lives. All they needed were moments like this, where they could sit in the sunshine and talk of inconsequential things.

When Frank walked in, he paused at the kitchen doorway and gave Deborah a polite nod. "Is there anything you need this morning, Mr. Guthrie?"

"She knows, Frank." Gage laid a hand over Deborah's. "She knows everything."

A grin split Frank's wide, sober face. "Well, it's about time." All pretense of formality dropped as he lumbered across the room to pluck up a piece of toast. He took a seat at the semicircular breakfast nook, bit into the toast and gestured with the half that was left. "I told him you wouldn't head for the hills when you found out about his little vanishing act. You're too tough for that."

"Thank you. I think." Deborah chuckled and the rest of the toast disappeared in one healthy bite.

"I know people," Frank said, taking the tray of bacon Gage passed him. "In my profession—my former profession—you had to be able to make somebody quick. And I was good, real good, right, Gage?"

"That's right, Frank."

"I could spot a patsy two blocks away." He wagged a piece of bacon at Deborah. "You ain't no patsy."

And she'd thought of him as the strong, silent type, Deborah mused. She was fascinated by the way he made up for lost time, rattling quickly as he steam-shoveled food away. "You've been with Gage a long time."

"Eight years—not counting the couple of times he sent me up."

"Kind of like Kato to his Green Hornet."

He grinned again, then let out a series of guffaws. "Hey, I like her, Gage. She's okay. I told you she was okay."

"Yes, you did. Deborah's going to be staying, Frank. How would you like to be best man?"

"No kidding?" Deborah didn't think Frank's grin could stretch any wider. Then she saw the gleam of tears in his eyes. At that moment, her heart was lost to him.

"No kidding." She shifted, took his big face in her hands and kissed him firmly on the mouth. "There, you're first to kiss the bride-to-be."

"How about that." Deborah had to bite back a chuckle as a beet-red blush stained Frank's face. "How about that."

"I'd like Deborah to move in a few things today," Gage put in.

She glanced down at the robe. Besides the borrowed garment, she had an evening dress, a pair of stockings and an evening bag. "I could use a few things." But she was thinking of the big room downstairs, the computers, the information Gage had at his fingertips.

Gage had little trouble following the direction of her thoughts. "Do you have someone who could put what you need together? Frank could go by your apartment and pick them up."

"Yes." She thought of Mrs. Greenbaum. "I'll just make a call."

Within a half an hour, she was back in Gage's secret room, wearing a pair of his jeans hitched up with the belt of his robe and a crisply pressed linen shirt skimming her thighs. Hands on her hips, she studied the map as Gage explained.

"These are drop points, major drug deals. I've been able to run makes on a handful of the messengers."

"Why haven't you fed this information to the police?"

He glanced at her briefly. On this point they might never agree. "It wouldn't help them get any closer to the top men. Right now, I'm working on the pattern." He moved to one of the computers and, after a moment, signaled to her. "None of the drops are less than twenty blocks apart." He motioned to the reproduction on the monitor. "The time span between them is fairly steady." He punched a few buttons. A list of dates rolled onto the screen. "Two weeks, sometimes three."

Frowning in concentration, she studied the screen. "Can I have a printout of this?"

"Why?"

"I'd like to run it through my computer at the office. See if I can find any correlation."

"It isn't safe." Before she could argue, he took her hand and led her to another work station. He tapped a code in the keyboard and brought up a file. Deborah's mouth opened in surprise as she saw her own work reproduced on the screen.

"You've tapped into my system," she murmured. "In more ways than one."

"The point is, if I can, so can someone else. Anything you need, you can find here."

"Apparently." She sat, far from sure how she felt about Gage or anyone else peeking over her shoulder as she worked. "Am I on the right track?"

Saying nothing, he tapped in a new code. "You've been going after the corporations, and the directors. A logical place to start. Whoever set up the organization knows business. Four years ago, we didn't have the information or the technology to get this close, so we had to go in and physically infiltrate." Names flipped by, some she recognized, some she didn't. They were all tagged Deceased. "It didn't work because there was a leak. Someone who knew about the undercover operation passed the information to the other side. Montega was waiting for us, and he knew we were cops." Though Deborah felt a chill, he said it calmly. "He also had to know exactly how we were set up that night, to the man. Otherwise he could never have slipped through the backup.''

"Another cop?"

"It's a possibility. We had ten handpicked men on the team that night. I've checked out every one of them, their bank accounts, their records, their life-style. So far, I haven't found a thing.''

"Who else knew?"

"My captain, the commissioner, the mayor.'' He made a restless movement with his shoulders. "Maybe more. We were only cops. They didn't tell us everything.''

"When you find the pattern, what then?''

"I wait, I watch, and I follow. The man with the money leads me to the man in charge. And he's the one I want.''

She suppressed a shudder, promising herself she would somehow convince him to let the police take over when they had enough information. "While you're looking for that, I'd like to concentrate on finding names—that common thread.''

"All right." He ran a hand over her hair until it rested on her shoulder. "This machine is similar to the one you use in the office. It has a few more—''

"How do you know?" she interrupted.

"How do I know what?''

"What machine I use in the office?''

He had to smile. "Deborah...'' Lightly, lingering, he bent down to kiss her. "There's nothing about you I don't know.''

Uncomfortable, she shifted away, then rose. "Will I find my name programmed on one of these machines?''

He watched her, knowing he would have to tread lightly. "Yes. I told myself it was routine, but the truth was I was in love with you and greedy for every detail. I know when you were born, to the minute, and where. I know you broke your wrist falling off a bike when you were five, that you moved in with your sister and her husband after the death of your parents. And when your sister divorced, you moved with her. Richmond, Chicago, Dallas. Finally Denver where you zipped through college in three years, *cum laude,* drove yourself through law school to graduate in the top five percent of your class, and passed your bar on the first attempt. With enough finesse to bring you offers from four of the top law firms in the country. But you chose to come here, and work in the D.A.'s office.''

She rubbed her palms over the thighs of her jeans. ''It's odd to hear an encapsulated version of my life story.''

''There were things I couldn't learn from the computer.'' The important things, he thought. The vital things. ''The way your hair smells, the way your eyes go to indigo when you're angry or aroused. The way you make me feel when you touch me. I won't deny I invaded your privacy, but I won't apologize for it.''

''No, you wouldn't,'' she said after a moment. She let out a little breath. ''And I suppose I can't be overly offended, since I ran a make on you, too.''

He smiled. ''I know.''

She laughed, shaking her head. ''Okay. Let's get to work.''

They had hardly settled when one of the three phones on the long counter rang. Deborah barely glanced over as Gage lifted a receiver.

''Guthrie.''

''Gage, it's Frank. I'm at Deborah's apartment. You'd better get over here.''

# Chapter 11

Her heart beating erratically, Deborah sprinted out of the elevator and down the hall one step in front of Gage. Frank's phone call had had them shooting across town in Gage's Aston Martin in record time.

The door was open. Deborah's breath stopped as she stood on the threshold and saw the destruction of her apartment. Curtains slashed, mementos crushed, tables and chairs viciously broken and tossed in pieces on the floor. The first groan escaped before she spotted Lil Greenbaum propped on the remains of the torn and tattered sofa, her face deathly white.

"Oh, God." Kicking debris aside, she rushed over to drop to her knees. "Mrs. Greenbaum." She took the cold, frail hand in hers.

Lil's thin lids fluttered up, and her myopic eyes struggled to focus without the benefit of her glasses. "Deborah." Though her voice was weak, she managed a faint smile. "They never would have done it if they hadn't caught me by surprise."

"They hurt you." She looked up as Frank came out of the bedroom carrying a pillow. "Did you call an ambulance?"

"She wouldn't let me." Gently he slipped the pillow under Lil's head.

"Don't need one. Hate hospitals. Just a bump on the head," Lil said, and squeezed Deborah's hand. "I've had one before."

"Do you want me to worry myself sick?" As she spoke, Deborah slipped her fingers down to monitor Lil's pulse.

"Your apartment's in worse shape than I am."

"It's easy to replace my things. How would I replace you?" She kissed Lil's gnarled knuckles. "Please. For me."

Defeated, Lil let out a sigh. "Okay, I'll let them poke at me. But I won't stay in the hospital."

"Good enough." She turned, but Gage was already lifting the phone.

"It's dead."

"Mrs. Greenbaum's apartment is right across the hall."

Gage nodded to Frank.

"The keys—" Deborah began.

"Frank doesn't need keys." He crossed over to crouch beside Deborah. "Mrs. Greenbaum, can you tell us what happened?"

She studied him, narrowing and widening her eyes until she brought him into shaky focus. "I know you, don't I? You picked Deborah up last night, all spiffed up in a tux. You sure can kiss."

He grinned at her, but his hand slipped to her wrist just as Deborah's had. "Thanks."

"You're the one with pots of money, right?"

She may have had a bump on the head, Gage thought, but her mind seemed to work quickly enough. "Right."

"She liked the roses. Mooned over them."

"Mrs. Greenbaum." Deborah sat back on her heels. "You don't have to play matchmaker—we've taken care of it ourselves. Tell us what happened to you."

"I'm glad to hear it. Young people today waste too much time."

"Mrs. Greenbaum."

"All right, all right. I had the list of things you'd called for. I was in the bedroom, going through the closet. Neat as a pin, by the way," she said to Gage. "The girl's very tidy."

"I'm relieved to hear it."

"I was just taking out the navy pin-striped suit when I heard a sound behind me." She grimaced, more embarrassed now than shaken. "I'd have heard it before, but I turned on the radio when I came in. That'll teach me to listen to the Top 40 countdown. I started to turn, and, boom. Somebody put my lights out."

Deborah lowered her head to Lil's hand. Emotions screamed through her, tangled and tearing. Fury, terror, guilt. She was an old woman, Deborah thought as she struggled for control. What kind of person strikes a seventy-year-old woman?

"I'm sorry," she said as levelly as she could. "I'm so sorry."

"It's not your fault."

"Yes, it is." She lifted her head. "This was all for my benefit. All of it. I knew they were after me, and I asked you to come in here. I didn't think. I just didn't think."

"Now, this is nonsense. I'm the one who got bashed, and I can tell you I'm damn mad about it. If I hadn't been caught off guard, I'd have put some of my karate training into use." Lil's mouth firmed. "I'd like to have another go at it. Wasn't too many years ago I could deck Mr. Greenbaum, and I'm still in shape." She glanced up as the paramedics came through the door. "Oh, Lord," she said in disgust. "Now I'm in for it."

With Gage's arm around her shoulders, Deborah stood back while Lil ordered the paramedics around, complaining about every poke and prod. She was still chattering when they lifted her onto a stretcher and carried her out.

"She's quite a woman," Gage commented.

"She's the best." When tears threatened, she bit her lip. "I don't know what I'd do if..."

"She's going to be fine. Her pulse was strong, her mind was clear." He gave her a quick squeeze then turned to Frank. "What's the story?"

"The door wasn't locked when I got here." The big man jerked his thumb toward the opening. "They did a messy job forcing it. I walked into this." He gestured around the chaos of the living room. "I thought I should check out the rest of the place before I called you, and found the lady in the bedroom. She was just coming to. Tried to take a swing at me." He smiled at Deborah. "She's one tough old lady. I calmed her down, then I called you." His mouth tightened. There had been a time he hadn't been above pinching a purse from a nice little old lady, but he'd never laid a finger on one.

"I figure I missed them by ten or fifteen minutes." His big fists bunched. "Otherwise they wouldn't have walked out of here."

Gage nodded. "I have a couple of things I'd like you to do." He turned back to Deborah, gently cradling her face in his hands. "I'll have him call the police," he said, knowing how her mind worked. "Meanwhile, why don't you see if you can salvage anything you might need until tomorrow?"

"All right." She agreed because she needed a moment alone. In the bedroom, she pressed her hands to her mouth. There had been such viciousness here, such fury, yet there was a cold kind of organization to the destruction that made it all the more frightening.

Her clothes were torn and shredded, the little antique bottles and jars she'd collected over the years broken and smashed over the heaps of silk and cotton. Her bed had been destroyed, her desk littered with ugly words someone had carved deeply in the wood with a knife. Everything she owned had been pulled out or torn down.

Kneeling, she picked up a ragged scrap of paper. It had once been a photograph, one of the many of her family she had treasured.

Gage came in quietly. After a moment, he knelt beside her and laid a hand on her shoulder. "Deborah, let me take you out of here."

"There's nothing left." She pressed her lips together, determined to keep her voice from shaking. "I know they're only things, but there's nothing left." Slowly she curled her fingers around the remains of the photograph. "My parents—" She shook her head, then turned her face into his shoulder.

His own anger was a bright steady flame in his chest. He held her, letting her grieve while he promised himself he would find the men who had hurt her. And all the while he couldn't get past the sick terror that lodged in his throat.

She might have been there. She might have been alone in this room when they'd come in. Instead of trinkets and mementos, he could have found her broken on the floor.

"They'll pay," he promised her. "I swear it."

"Yes, they will." When she lifted her head, he saw that her grief had passed into fury. It was just as deep, just as sharp. "Whatever I have to do, I'm going to bring them down." After pushing back her hair, she stood up. "If they thought they could scare me away by doing this, they're going to be disappointed.'' She kicked at the remains of her favorite red suit. "Let's go to work.''

They spent hours in the cavern beneath his house, checking data, inputting more. Deborah's head was throbbing in time with the machines, but she continued to push. Gage busied himself across the room, but they rarely spoke. They didn't need to. Perhaps for the first time, their purposes meshed and their differences in viewpoints no longer seemed to matter.

They were both anxious to make up the time lost while talking to the police—and evading the enterprising Wisner, who had shown up at the apartment in their wake. She'd be a Monday-morning headline again, Deborah thought impatiently. The press would only bring more pressure from City Hall. She was ready for it.

She no longer swore when she slammed into a dead end, but meticulously backtracked with a patience she hadn't been aware of possessing. When the phone rang, she didn't even hear it. Gage had to call her name twice before she broke out of her concentrated trance.

"Yes, what?''

"It's for you." He held up the receiver. "Jerry Bower.''

With a frown for the interruption, she walked over to take the call. "Jerry.''

"Good God, Deborah, are you all right?''

"Yes, I'm fine. How did you know where I was?''

She could hear him take two long breaths. "I've been trying to reach you for hours, to make sure you were okay after last night. I finally decided just to go by your place and see for myself. I ran into a pack of cops and that little weasel Wisner. Your place—''

"I know. I wasn't there.''

"Thank God. What the hell's going on, Deb? We're supposed to have a handle on these things down at City Hall, but I feel like I'm boxing in the dark. The mayor's going to blow when he hears this. What am I supposed to tell him?''

"Tell him to concentrate on the debates next week." She rubbed her temple. "I already know his stand on this, and he knows mine. You're only going to drive yourself crazy trying to arbitrate.''

"Look, I work for him, but you're a friend. There might be something I can do.''

"I don't know." She frowned at the blinking lights on the map. "Someone's sending me a message, loud and clear, but I haven't worked out how to send one back. You can tell the mayor this. If I manage to work this out before the election, he's going to win by a landslide."

There was a slight hesitation. "I guess you're right," Jerry said thoughtfully. "That might be the best way to keep him from breathing down your neck. Just be careful, okay?"

"I will."

She hung up, then tilted her head from one side to the other to work out kinks.

Gage glanced over. "I wouldn't mind taking out a full page ad in the *World* to announce our engagement."

Confused, she blinked. Then laughed. "Jerry? Don't be stupid. We're just pals."

"Mmm-hmm."

She smiled, then walked over to hook her arms around his waist. "Not one big, sloppy kiss between us. Which is exactly what I could use right now."

"I guess I've got at least one in me." He lowered his head.

When his lips met hers, she felt the tension seep out of her, layer by layer, degree by degree. With a murmur, she slid her hands up his back, gently kneading the muscles, soothing them as his lips soothed her.

Quiet, content, relaxed. She could bring him to that, just as she could make him shudder and ache. With a soft sound of pleasure, he changed the angle of the kiss and deepened it for both of them.

"Sorry to break this up." Frank came through the tunnel, bearing a large tray. "But since you're working so hard..." He grinned hugely. "I figured you should eat to keep up your strength."

"Thanks." Deborah drew away from Gage and took a sniff. "Oh, Lord, what is it?"

"My special burn-through-the-ribs chili." He winked at her. "Believe me, it'll keep you awake."

"It smells incredible."

"Dig in. You got a couple of beers, a thermos of coffee and some cheese nachos."

Deborah rolled a chair over. "Frank, you are a man among men."
He blushed again, delighting her. She took her first bite, scorched her
mouth, her throat and her stomach lining. "And this," she said with
real pleasure, "is a bowl of chili."

He shuffled his feet. "Glad you like it. I put Mrs. Greenbaum in
the gold room," he told Gage. "I thought she'd get a kick out of the
bed curtains and stuff. She's having some chicken soup and watching
*King Kong* on the VCR."

"Thanks, Frank." Gage scooped up his own spoon of chili.

"Just give me a ring if you need anything else."

Deborah listened to the echo of Frank's footsteps in the tunnel.
"You had her brought here?" she said quietly.

"She didn't like the hospital." He shrugged. "Frank talked to the
doctor. She only had a mild concussion, which was a miracle in
someone her age. Her heart's strong as an elephant. All she needs is
some quiet and pampering for a few days."

"So you had her brought here."

"She shouldn't be alone."

She leaned over and kissed his cheek. "I love you very much."

When they had finished and were back to work, Deborah couldn't
stop her mind from wandering in his direction. He was such a complicated man. Arrogant as the devil when it suited him, rude when it
pleased him, and as smooth and charming as an Irish poet when the
mood struck him. He ran a multimillion-dollar business. And he
walked the streets at night to ward off muggers, thieves, rapists. He
was the lover every woman dreamed about. Romantic, erotic, yet
solid and dependable as granite. Yet he carried something intangible
inside him that allowed him to vanish like smoke into the wall, slip
without a shadow through the night.

She shook her head. She was far from ready, far from able to dwell
on that aspect of him.

How could he, a man she knew to be flesh and blood, become
insubstantial at will? Yet she had seen it with her own eyes. She
pressed her fingers against those eyes for a moment and sighed.
Things weren't always what they seemed.

Straightening her shoulders, she doubled her concentration. If numbers began to blur, she downed more coffee. Already she had a half

dozen more names, names she was sure she would find attached to death certificates.

It seemed hopeless. But until this avenue was exhausted, she had no other. Mumbling to herself, she punched up screen after screen. Abruptly she stopped. Cautious, eyes sharpened, she backtracked— one screen, two. She held back a smile, afraid to believe she'd finally broken through. After another five minutes of careful work, she called Gage.

"I think I've found something."

So had he, but he chose to keep his information to himself. "What?"

"This number." When he bent over her shoulder, she ran a finger below it on the screen. "It's all mixed with the corporation number, the tax number, and all the other identification numbers of this company." When he lifted a hand to rub at the base of her neck, she leaned back into the massage gratefully. "A supposedly bankrupt corporation, by the way. Out of business for eighteen months. Now look at this." She punched up a new screen. "Different company, different location, different names and numbers. Except...this one." She tapped a finger on the screen. "It's in a different place here, but the number's the same. And here." She showed him again, screen after screen. "It's the corporation number on one, the company branch on another, tax ID here, a file code there."

"Social security number," Gage muttered.

"What?"

"Nine digits. I'd say it's a social security number. An important one." He turned to walk quickly to the control board.

"What are you doing?"

"Finding out who it belongs to."

She blew out a breath, a bit annoyed that he hadn't seemed more enthusiastic about her find. Her eyes were all but falling out of her head, and she didn't even get a pat on the back. "How?"

"It seems worth going to the main source." The screen above him began to blink.

"Which is?"

"The IRS."

"The—" She was out of her chair like a shot. "You're telling me you can tap into the IRS computers?"

"That's right." His concentration was focused on the panel. "Almost got it."

"That's illegal. A federal offense."

"Mmm-hmm. Want to recommend a good lawyer?"

Torn, she gripped her hands together. "It's not a joke."

"No." But his lips curved as he followed the information on the screen. "All right. We're in." He shot her a look. The internal war she was waging showed clearly on her face. "You could go upstairs until I've finished."

"That hardly matters. I know what you're doing. That makes me a part of it." She closed her eyes and saw Lil Greenbaum lying pale and hurt on her broken couch. "Go ahead," she said, and put a hand on his arm. "We're in this together."

He tapped in the numbers she had found, pushed a series of buttons and waited. A name flashed up on the screen.

"Oh, God." Deborah's fingers dug into Gage's shoulder.

He seemed to be made of stone at that moment, unmoving, almost unbreathing, his muscles hard as rock.

"Tucker Fields," he murmured. "Son of a bitch."

Then he moved so quickly, Deborah nearly stumbled. With a strength born of desperation, she grabbed him. "Don't. You can't." She saw his eyes burn, as she had seen them behind the mask. They were full of fury and deadly purpose. "I know what you want," she said quickly, clinging. "You want to go find him right now. You want to tear him apart. But you can't. That isn't the way."

"I'm going to kill him." His voice was cold and flat. "Understand that. Nothing's going to stop me."

The breath was searing and clogging in her lungs. If he left now, she would lose him. "And accomplish what? It won't bring Jack back. It won't change what happened to you. It won't even finish what you both started that night on the docks. If you kill Fields, someone will replace him, and it'll go on. We need to break the back of the organization, Gage, to bring it all out to the public so that people will see. If Fields is responsible—"

"If?"

She took a careful, steadying breath and kept her grip on him tight. "We don't have enough, not yet. I can build a case if you give me time, and bring them down. Bring them all down."

"My God, Deborah, do you really think you'll get him in court? A man with that much power? He'll slip through your fingers like sand. The minute you start an investigation, he'll know, and he'll cover himself."

"Then you'll do the investigating here, and I'll throw dust in his eyes from my office." She spoke quickly, desperate to convince him and, she was sure, to save them both. "I'll make him think I'm on the wrong track. Gage, we have to be sure. You must see that. If you go after him now, like this, everything you've worked for, everything we've started to build together, will be destroyed."

"He tried to have you killed." Gage put his hands to her face, and though his touch was light, she could feel the tension in each finger. "Don't you understand that nothing, not even Jack's murder, signed his death warrant more indelibly?"

She brought her hands to his wrists. "I'm here, with you. That's what's important. We have more work to do, to prove that Fields is involved, to find out how far down the line the corruption runs. You'll have justice, Gage. I promise."

Slowly he relaxed. She was right—at least in some ways she was right. Killing Fields with his bare hands would have been satisfying, but it wouldn't complete the job he had begun. So he could wait for that. There was another stone to uncover, and he had less than a week to wait until he did so.

"All right." He watched the color seep slowly back into her face. "I didn't mean to frighten you."

"Well, I hope you never mean to, because you scared me to death." She turned her head, pressing her lips to his palm, then managed a shaky smile. "Since we've already broken a federal law, why don't we go a step forward and look at the mayor's tax records for the last few years?"

Minutes later, she was seated beside Gage at the console.

"Five hundred and sixty-two thousand," she murmured, when she read Fields's declared income for the previous tax year. "A bit more than the annual salary for Urbana's mayor."

"It's hard to believe he's stupid enough to put that much on record." Gage flipped back another year. "I imagine he's got several times that much in Swiss accounts."

"I never liked him, personally," Deborah put in. "But I always respected him." She rose to pace. "When I think about the kind of position he's been in, a direct line to the police, to the D.A.'s office, to businesses, utilities. Nothing goes on in Urbana he doesn't know about. And he can put his people everywhere. How many city officials are on his private payroll, how many cops, how many judges?"

"He thinks he's got it covered." Gage pushed away from the console. "What about Bower?"

"Jerry?" Deborah sighed and rubbed her stiff neck. "Loyal to the bone, and with political aspirations of his own. He might overlook a few under-the-table machinations, but nothing so big as this. Fields was clever enough to pick someone young and eager, with a good background and unblemished reputation." She shook her head. "I feel badly that I can't pass this along to him."

"Mitchell?"

"No, I'd bet my life on Mitch. He's been around a long time. He's never been Fields's biggest fan but he respects the office. He's by the book because he believes in the book. He even pays his parking tickets. What are you doing?"

"It doesn't hurt to check."

To Deborah's consternation, he pulled up Jerry's then Mitchell's tax returns. Finding nothing out of the ordinary, he moved toward another console.

"We can start pulling up bank accounts. We need a list of people who work at City Hall, the department, the D.A.'s office." He glanced up at her. "You've got a headache."

She realized she was rubbing at her temple. "Just a little one."

Instead of turning on the machine, he shut the others down. "You've been working too hard."

"I'm fine. We've got a lot to do."

"We've already done a lot." And he was cursing himself for pushing her so hard for so long. "A couple of hours off won't change anything." He slipped an arm around her waist. "How about a hot bath and a nap?"

"Mmm." She leaned her head against his shoulder as they started down the tunnel. "That sounds incredible."

"And a back rub."

"Yes. Oh, yes."

"And why don't I give you that foot rub that's long overdue."

She smiled. Had she ever really been worried about something as foolish as other women? "Why don't you?"

Deborah was already half-asleep by the time they came through the panel into Gage's bedroom. She stopped in mid-yawn and stared at the boxes covering the bed.

"What's all this?"

"At the moment all you have is my shirt on your back. And though I like it—" he flicked a finger down the buttons "—a lot, I thought you might want some replacements."

"Replacements?" She pushed at her tumbled hair. "How?"

"I gave Frank a list. He can be very enterprising."

"Frank? But it's Sunday. Half the stores are closed." She pressed a hand to her stomach. "Oh, God, he didn't steal them, did he?"

"I don't think so." Then he laughed and caught her in his arms. "How am I going to live with such a scrupulously honest woman? No, they're paid for, I promise. It's as easy as making a few calls. You'll notice the boxes are from Athena's."

She nodded. It was one of the biggest and slickest department stores in the city. And the light dawned. "You own it."

"Guilty." He kissed her. "Anything you don't like can go back. But I think I know your style and your size."

"You didn't have to do this."

From the tone of her voice, he understood she wished he hadn't done it. Patient, he tucked her tumbled hair behind her ear. "This wasn't an attempt to usurp your independence, Counselor."

"No." And she was sounding very ungrateful. "But—"

"Be practical. How would it look for you to show up at the office tomorrow in my pants?" He tugged the belt loose and had the jeans sliding to her feet.

"Outrageous," she agreed, and smiled when he lifted her up and set her down beside the heap of denim.

"And my shirt." He began to undo the buttons.

"Ridiculous. You're right, you were being very practical." She took his hands to still them before he could distract her. "And I appreciate it. But it doesn't feel right, you buying my clothes."

"You can pay me back. Over the next sixty or seventy years." He cupped her chin when she started to speak again. "Deborah, I've got more money than any one man needs. You're willing to share my problems, then it should follow that you'll share my fortunes."

"I don't want you to think that the money matters to me, that it makes any difference in the way I feel about you."

He studied her thoughtfully. "You know, I didn't realize you could come up with anything quite that stupid."

She lifted her chin, but when he smiled at her she could only sigh. "It is stupid. I love you even though you do own hotels, and apartment buildings, and department stores. And if I don't open one of these boxes, I'm going to go crazy."

"Why don't you keep your sanity then, and I'll go run the bath?"

When he walked into the adjoining room, she grabbed one at random, shook it, then pulled off the lid. Under the tissue paper she found a long, sheer sleeping gown in pale blue silk.

"Well." She held it up, noting the back was cut below the waist. "Frank certainly has an eye for lingerie. I wonder what the boys in the office will say if I wear this in tomorrow."

Unable to resist, she stripped off the shirt and let the cool thin silk slide over her head and shoulders. A perfect fit, she mused, running her hands over her hips. Delighted, she turned to the mirror just as Gage came back into the room.

He couldn't speak any more than he could take his eyes from her. The long, sleek shimmer of silk whispered against her skin as she turned to him. Her eyes were dark as midnight and glistening with a woman's secret pleasure.

Her lips curved slowly. Was there a woman alive who didn't dream about having the man she loved stare at her with such avid hunger? Deliberately she tilted her head and lifted one hand to run her fingertips lazily down the center of the gown—and just as lazily up again—watching his eyes follow the movement.

"What do you think?"

His gaze trailed up until it met hers again. "I think Frank deserves a very large raise."

As she laughed, he came toward her.

# Chapter 12

Over the next three days and the next three evenings, they worked together. Piece by steady piece they built a case against Tucker Fields. At her office Deborah pursued avenues she knew would lead nowhere, carefully laying a false trail.

As she worked, she continued to fight the rugged tug-of-war inside her. Ethics versus instinct.

Each night, Gage would slip out of bed, clothe himself in black and roam the streets. They didn't speak of it. If he knew how often Deborah lay awake, anxious and torn until he returned just before dawn, he offered no excuses or apologies. There were none he could give her.

The press continued to herald Nemesis's exploits. Those secret nocturnal activities were never mentioned and stood between them like a thick, silent wall that couldn't be breached on either side.

She understood, but couldn't agree.

He understood, but couldn't acquiesce.

Even as they worked toward a single goal, their individual beliefs forced them at cross-purposes.

She sat in her office, the evening paper beside a stack of law books.

Nemesis Bags East End Ripper

She hadn't read the copy, couldn't bring herself to read it. She already knew about the man who had killed four people in the past ten days, with his favored weapon, a hunting knife. The headline was enough to tell her why she had found traces of blood in the bathroom sink.

When was it going to end? she asked herself. When was he going to stop? A psychotic with a knife had nothing to do with Fields and the drug cartel. How much longer could they go on pretending that their relationship, their future, could be normal?

He wasn't pretending, Deborah admitted with a sigh. She was.

"O'Roarke." Mitchell slapped a file on her desk. "The city doesn't pay you this princely salary to daydream."

She looked at the file that had just landed on a pile of others. "I don't suppose it would do any good to remind you that my caseload has already broken the world's record."

"So's the city's crime rate." Because she looked exhausted, he walked over to her coffee machine to pour her a cup of the bitter bottom-of-the-pot brew. "Maybe if Nemesis would take some time off, we wouldn't be so overworked."

Her frown turned into a grimace as she sipped the coffee. "That sounded almost like a compliment."

"Just stating facts. I don't have to approve of his methods to like the results."

Surprised, she looked up into Mitchell's round, sturdy face. "Do you mean that?"

"This Ripper character carved up four innocent people and was starting on a fifth when Nemesis got there. It's hard to complain when anybody, even a misguided masked wonder, drops a creep like that in our laps and saves the life of an eighteen-year-old girl."

"Yes." Deborah murmured. "Yes, it is."

"Not that I'm going out and buying a T-shirt and joining his fan club." Mitchell pulled out a cigar and ran it through his stubby fingers. "So, making any progress on your favorite case?"

She shrugged evasively. "I've got another week."

"You're hardheaded, O'Roarke. I like that."

Her brows rose. "Now, that was definitely a compliment."

"Don't let it swell your pinstripes. The mayor's still unhappy with you—and the polls are happy with him. If he knocks Tarrington out in the debates tomorrow, you could have a hard road until the next election.''

"The mayor doesn't worry me.''

"Suit yourself. Wisner's still pumping your name into copy.'' He held up a hand before she could snarl. "I'm holding Fields off, but if you could keep a lower profile—''

"Yeah, it was really stupid of me to have my apartment trashed.''

"Okay, okay.'' He had the grace to flush. "We're all sorry about that, but if you could try to keep out of trouble for a while, it would make it easy on everyone.''

"I'll chain myself to my desk,'' she said between her teeth. "And the minute I get the chance, I'm going to kick Wisner right in his press card.''

Mitchell grinned. "Get in line. Hey, ah, let me know if you need a few extra bucks before the insurance takes over.''

"Thanks, but I'm fine.'' She looked at the files. "Besides, with all this, who needs an apartment?''

When he left her alone, Deborah opened the new case file. And dropped her head in her hands. Was it a twisted kind of irony or fate that she'd been assigned to prosecute the East End Ripper? Her chief witness, she thought, her lover, was the one man she couldn't even discuss it with.

At seven Gage waited for her at a quiet corner table in a French restaurant skirting City Park. He knew it was almost over and that when it was, he would have to explain to Deborah why he hadn't trusted her with all the details.

She would be hurt and angry. Rightfully so. But he preferred her hurt and angry, and alive. He was well aware how difficult the past few days—and nights—had been for her. If there had been a choice, he would have given up everything, including his conscience, to keep her happy.

But he had no choice, hadn't had a choice since the moment he'd come out of the coma.

He could do nothing but tell her and show her how completely he loved her. And to hope that between the very strong and opposing forces that drove each of them, there could be a compromise.

He saw her come in, slim and lovely in a sapphire-colored suit trimmed and lined with chartreuse. Flashy colors and sensible shoes. Was there lace or silk or satin beneath? He had an urge to sweep her up then and there, take her away and discover the answer for himself.

"I'm sorry I'm late," she began, but before the mâitre d' could seat her, Gage had risen to pull her to him. His kiss was not discreet, not brief. Before he released her, nearby diners were looking on with curiosity and envy.

The breath she hadn't been aware of holding rushed out between her parted lips. Her eyes were heavy, her body vibrating.

"I—I'm awfully glad I wasn't on time."

"You worked late." There were shadows under her eyes. He hated seeing them. Knowing he'd caused them.

"Yes." Still breathless, she took her seat. "I had another case dumped on my desk just before five."

"Anything interesting?"

Her gaze came to his and held. "The East End Ripper."

He watched her unwaveringly. "I see."

"Do you, Gage? I wonder if you do." She drew her hand from his and laid it in her lap. "I felt I should disqualify myself, but what reason could I give?"

"There is no reason, Deborah. I stopped him, but it's your job to see that he pays for the crimes. One does not have to interfere with the other."

"I wish I could be sure." She took up her napkin, pleating it between her fingers. "Part of me sees you as a vigilante, another part a hero."

"And the truth lies somewhere in between." He reached for her hand again. "Whatever I am, I love you."

"I know." Her fingers tightened on his. "I know, but, Gage—" She broke off when the waiter brought over the champagne Gage had ordered while waiting for her.

"The drink of the gods," the waiter said in a rich French accent. "For a celebration, *n'est-ce pas?* A beautiful woman. A beautiful wine." At Gage's nod of approval, he popped the cork with a flourish that had the bubbling froth lapping at the lip of the bottle before teasingly retreating. "*Monsieur* will taste?" He poured a small amount into Gage's glass.

"Excellent," Gage murmured, but his eyes were on Deborah.

"*Mais, oui.*" The waiter's gaze slid approvingly over Deborah before he filled her glass, then Gage's. "*Monsieur* has the most exquisite taste." When the waiter bowed away, Deborah chuckled and touched her glass to Gage's.

"You're not going to tell me you own this place, too?"

"No. Would you like to?"

Though she shook her head, she had to laugh. "Are we celebrating?"

"Yes. To tonight. And to tomorrow." He took a small velvet box from his pocket and offered it to her. When she only stared at it, his fingers tensed. Panic rushed through him, but he kept his voice light. "You asked me to marry you, but I felt this privilege was mine."

She opened the box. In the candlelight, the center sapphire glittered a deep and dark blue. Surrounding that bold square was a symphony of ice-white diamonds. They flashed triumphantly in the setting of pale gold.

"It's exquisite."

He'd chosen the stones himself. But he had hoped to see pleasure in her eyes, not fear. Nor had he thought to feel fear himself.

"Are you having doubts?"

She looked up at him and let her heart speak. "Not about the way I feel about you. I never will. I'm afraid, Gage. I've tried to pretend I'm not, but I'm afraid. Not only of what you do, but that it might take you away from me."

He wouldn't make her promises that could be impossible to keep. "I was brought out of that coma the way I was brought out for a reason. I can't give you logic and facts on this one, Deborah. Only feelings and instinct. If I turned my back on what I'm meant to do, I'd die again."

Her automatic protest clogged in her throat. "You believe that?"

"I know that."

How could she look at him and not see it, too? How many times had she looked in his eyes and seen—something? Different, special, frightening. She knew he was flesh and blood, yet he was more. It

wouldn't be possible to change that. And for the first time, she realized she didn't want to.

"I fell in love with you twice. With both sides of you." She looked
down at the ring, took it out of its box where it flashed like lightning
in her hand. "Until then, I was sure of my direction, of what I
wanted, needed, and was working for. I was certain, so certain that
when I fell in love it would be with a very calm, very ordinary man."
She held the ring out to him. "I was wrong. You didn't come back
just to fight for your justice, Gage. You came back for me." Then
she smiled and held her hand out to him. "Thank God."

He slipped the ring on her finger. "I want to take you home."
Even as he brought her hand to his lips, the waiter bounced back to
their table.

"I knew it. Henri is never wrong." Deborah chuckled as he made
a business out of topping off their glasses. "You have chosen my
table. So, you have chosen well. You must leave the menu to me.
You must! I will make a night such as you will never forget. It is
my pleasure. Ah, *monsieur,* you are the most fortunate of men." He
grabbed Deborah's hand and kissed it noisily.

Deborah was still laughing as he hurried away, but when she
looked at Gage, she saw his attention was elsewhere. "What is it?"

"Fields." Gage lifted his glass, but his eyes followed the mayor's
progress across the room. "He just came in with Arlo Stuart and a
couple of other big guns with your friend Bower bringing up the
rear."

Tensed, Deborah turned her head. They were heading for a table
for eight. She recognized a prominent actress and the president of a
major auto manufacturer. "Power meeting," she muttered.

"He's got the theater, industry, finance and the art worlds all represented neatly at one table. Before the evening's over, someone will
come along and take a few 'candid' shots."

"It won't matter." She covered Gage's hand with hers. "In another week, it won't matter."

In less than that, he thought, but nodded. "Stuart's coming over."

"Well, now." Stuart clamped a hand on Gage's shoulder. "This
is a nice coincidence. You look stunning as always, Miss O'Roarke."

"Thank you."

"Great restaurant this. Nobody does snails better." He beamed at both of them. "Hate to waste them talking business and politics. Now, you've got the right idea here. Champagne, candlelight." His sharp gaze fell on Deborah's ring hand. "Well, that's a pretty little thing." He grinned at Gage. "Got an announcement to make?"

"You caught us in the act, Arlo."

"Glad to hear it. You take your honeymoon in any of my hotels." He winked at Deborah. "On the house." Still grinning, he signaled to the mayor. It wouldn't hurt Fields's image, he thought, to be in on the first congratulations to one of the city's top businessmen and the most recognizable D.A.

"Gage, Deborah." Though Fields's smile was broad, his nod of greeting was stiff. "Nice to see you. If you haven't ordered, perhaps you'd like to join us."

"Not tonight." Stuart answered before Gage could. "We've got ourselves a newly engaged couple here, Tuck. They don't want to waste the evening talking campaign strategy."

Fields glanced down at Deborah's ring, the smile still in place. But he wasn't pleased. "Congratulations."

"I like to think we brought them together." Always exuberant, Stuart tossed an arm around Fields's shoulder. "After all, they met at my hotel during your fund-raiser."

"I guess that makes us one big, happy family." Fields looked at Gage. He needed Guthrie's support. "You're marrying a fine woman, a tough lawyer. She's given me a few headaches, but I admire her integrity."

Gage's voice was cool, but perfectly polite. "So do I."

Stuart gave another booming laugh. "I've admired more than her integrity." He winked at Deborah again. "No offense. Now we'll get back to politics and leave you two alone."

"Bastard," Deborah mumbled when they were out of earshot. She snatched up her wine. "He was sucking up to you."

"No." Gage tapped his glass to hers. "To both of us." Over her shoulder, he saw the minute Jerry Bower heard the news. The man jolted, glanced up and over. Gage could almost hear him sigh as he stared at Deborah's back.

"I can't wait until we nail him."

There was such venom in her voice that Gage covered her hand with his and squeezed. "Just hold on. It won't take much longer."

She was so lovely. Gage lingered in bed, just looking at her. He knew she was sleeping deeply, sated by love, exhausted from passion. He wanted to know that she would dream content until morning.

He hated knowing there were times she woke in the middle of the night to find him gone. But tonight, when he could all but feel the danger tripping through his blood, he needed to be sure she would sleep, safe.

Silently he rose to dress. He could hear her breathing, slow and steady, and it soothed him. In the sprinkle of moonlight, he saw his reflection in the mirror. No, not a reflection, he thought. A shadow.

After flexing his hands in the snug black gloves, he opened a drawer. Inside was a .38, a regulation police issue revolver whose grip was as familiar to him as a brother's handshake. Yet he had not carried it since the night on the docks four years before.

He had never needed to.

But tonight, he felt that need. He no longer questioned instinct, but tucked the gun into a holster and belted it on so that the weapon fit at the small of his back.

He opened the panel, then paused. He wanted to see her again, sleeping. He could taste the danger now—bitter on his tongue, in his throat. His only respite from it was knowing she wouldn't be affected. He would come back. He promised himself, and her. Fate could not deal such a killing blow twice in one lifetime.

He slipped away in the dark.

More than an hour later, the phone rang, pulling Deborah from sleep. Out of habit, she groped for it, murmuring to Gage as she rattled the receiver from the hook.

"Hello."

"*Señorita.*"

The sound of Montega's voice had her icy and awake. "What do you want?"

"We have him. The trap was so easily sprung."

"What?" Panicked, she reached out for Gage. But even before her hands slid over empty sheets, she knew. Terror made her voice shake. "What do you mean?"

"He's alive. We want to keep him alive, for now. If you wish the same you'll come, quickly and alone. We'll trade him for all your papers, all your files. Everything you have."

She pressed a hand to her mouth, trying to stall until she could think. "You'll kill us both."

"Possibly. But I will surely kill him if you don't come. There is a warehouse on East River Drive. Three twenty-five East River Drive. It will take you thirty minutes. Any longer and I remove his right hand."

A rancid sickness heaved her stomach. "I'll come. Don't hurt him. Please, let me talk to him first—"

But the phone went dead.

Deborah sprang out of bed. Dragging on a robe, she rushed out to Frank's room. When one glance told her it was empty, she bounded down the hall to find Mrs. Greenbaum sitting up in bed with an old movie and a can of peanuts.

"Frank. Where is he?"

"He went out to the all-night video store, and for pizza. We decided to have a Marx Brothers festival. What's wrong?"

But Deborah only covered her face with her hands and rocked. She had to think.

"He'll be back in twenty minutes."

"That's too late." She dropped her hands. She couldn't waste another moment. "You tell him I got a call, I had to go. Tell him it involves Gage."

"You're in trouble, tell me."

"Just tell him, please. The moment he comes in. I've gone to 325 East River Drive."

"You can't." Lil was climbing out of bed. "You can't go there at this time of night by yourself."

"I have to. Tell Frank I had to." She gripped Lil's hands. "It's life or death."

"We'll call the police—"

"No. No, just Frank. Tell him everything I said, and tell him what time I left. Promise me."

"Of course, but—"

But Deborah was already racing out.

It took several precious minutes to throw on clothes and to push stacks of printouts in her briefcase. Her hands were slick with sweat when she reached her car. In her mind, like a chant, she said Gage's name over and over as she streaked down the streets. Sickness stayed lodged in her throat as she watched the clock on the dash tick away the minutes.

Like a ghost, Nemesis watched the exchange of drugs for money. Thousands of bills for thousands of pounds of pain. The buyer slit one sample bag open, scooped out a touch of white powder and tapped it into a vial to test the purity. The seller flipped through stacks of bills.

When both were satisfied, the deal was made. There were few words exchanged. It was not a friendly business.

He watched the buyer take his miserable product and walk away. Even though Nemesis understood he would find the man again, and quickly, there was regret. If he had not been stalking larger game, it would have given him great pleasure to have thrown both merchants and their product into the river.

Footsteps echoed. The acoustics were good in the high, spreading cinderblock building. Boxes and crates were piled beside walls and on long metal shelves. Tools and two-by-fours crowded work-benches. A large forklift was parked by the aluminum garage doors, there to lift the stacks of lumber stored within. Though the scent of sawdust remained, the enormous saws were silent.

He saw, with blood-boiling fury, Montega walk into the room.

"Our first prize tonight." He strode to the suitcase of cash, waving the underlings aside. "But we have richer coming." He closed the suitcase, locked it. "When he comes, show him here."

As he stood, as insubstantial as the air he breathed, Nemesis fisted his hands. It was now, he thought. It was tonight. A part of him that thirsted only for revenge burned to take the gun he carried and fire it. Cold-blooded.

But his blood was too hot for such a quick and anonymous solu-

tion. His lips curved humorlessly. There were better ways. More ju-
dicious ways.

Even as he opened his mouth to speak, he heard voices, the sound
of shoes rushing over the concrete floor. His heart froze to a ball of
ice in his chest.

He had left her sleeping.

While his blood ran cold, the sweat of terror pearled on his brow.
The danger he had tasted. Not for himself. Dear God, not for himself,
but for her. He watched Deborah rush into the room, followed by
two armed guards. For an instant, he slipped, wavering between Nemesis's world of shadows and hers.

"Where? Where is he?" She faced Montega like a tigress, head
back, eyes blazing. "If you've hurt him, I'll see you dead. I swear
it."

With an inclination of his head, Montega tapped his hands together
in applause. "Magnificent. A woman in love."

There was no room for fear of him, not when all her fear was for
Gage. "I want to see him."

"You are prompt, *señorita,* but have you come with what I asked
for?"

She heaved the briefcase at him. "Take it to hell with you."

Montega passed the briefcase to a guard and, with a jerk of his
head, had the man take it into an adjoining room.

"Patience," Montega said, holding up a hand. "Would you like
to sit?"

"No. You have what you want, now give me what I came for."

The door opened again. Eyes wide, she stared. "Jerry?" Over surprise came the first wave of relief. Not Gage, she thought. They had
never had Gage. It had been Jerry. Moving quickly, she went over
to take his hands. "I'm sorry, I'm so sorry this happened. I had no
idea."

"I know." He squeezed her hands. "I knew you'd come. I was
counting on it."

"I wish I thought it was going to help either of us."

"It already has." He put an arm around her shoulder as he faced
Montega. "The deal went smoothly, I take it."

"As expected, Mr. Bower."

"Excellent." Jerry gave Deborah's shoulder a friendly pat. "We have to talk."

She knew the color had drained from her face. She had felt it. "You—you're not a hostage here at all, are you?"

He allowed her to step away, even holding up a hand to signal the guards back. There was nowhere for her to go, and he was feeling generous. "No, and unfortunately, neither are you. I regret that."

"I don't believe it." Shaken, she lifted both hands to her temples. "I knew, I knew how blindly you stood behind Fields, but this—in the name of God, Jerry, you can't possibly let yourself be a part of this. You know what he's doing? The drugs, the murders? This isn't politics, it's madness."

"It's all politics, Deb." He smiled. "Mine. You don't honestly believe that a spineless puppet like Fields is behind this organization?" This time he laughed and signaled for a chair. "But you did. You did, because I laid a nice, neat trail of bread crumbs for you and anyone else who decided to look." Putting a hand on her shoulder, he pushed her into the chair.

"You?" She stared at him, head reeling. "You're telling me you're in charge? That Fields—"

"Is no more than a pawn. For more than six years I've stood two paces behind him, picking up all the flack—and pushing all the buttons. Fields couldn't run a dime store much less a city. Or the state..." He took a seat himself. "As I will in five years."

She wasn't afraid. Fear couldn't penetrate the numbness. This was a man she had known for nearly two years, one she had considered a friend and who she had judged as honest, if a bit weak. "How?"

"Money, power, brains." He ticked the three points off on his fingers. "I had the brains. Fields supplied the power. Believe me, he's been more than willing to leave the details, administrative and otherwise, to me. He makes a hell of a speech, knows whose butt to kick and whose to kiss. The rest of it, I do, and have since I was put in his office six years ago."

"By whom?"

"You are sharp." Still smiling, he gave her an admiring nod. "Arlo Stuart—he's the money. The problem has been that his businesses—the legitimate ones—dug a bit deeper into his profits than he cared for. Being a businessman, he saw another way to make that profit margin sing."

"The drugs."

"Right again." Casually he crossed his legs and gave an almost disinterested glance at his watch. There was time yet to indulge her, he thought. Since this was the last time. "He's been the head man on the East Coast for over twelve years. And it pays. I worked my way up in the organization. He likes initiative. I had the knowledge—law, political science—and he had Fields."

Questions, she ordered herself. She had to think of questions and keep him answering. Until…would Gage come? she wondered. Was there a way for Frank to contact him?

"So the three of you worked together," she said.

"Not Fields—I'd hate to give him credit in your mind, because I do respect your mind. He's nothing but a handy pawn and he hasn't a clue about our enterprise. Or if he does, he's wise enough to overlook it." He moved his shoulders. It didn't matter either way. "When the time is right, we'll expose the tax information and so forth that you've already discovered. No one will be more surprised than Fields. Since I'll be the one who righteously and regretfully exposes him, it should be very simple to step into his place. Then beyond."

"It won't work. I'm not the only one who knows."

"Guthrie." Jerry linked his fingers over his knee. "Oh, I intend to see to Guthrie. I ordered Montega to remove him four years ago, and the job was incomplete."

"You?" she whispered. "You ordered?"

"Arlo leaves that kind of detail to me." He leaned forward so only she could hear him. "I like details—such as what your new fiancé does in his spare time." His lips curved when her color drained. "You led me to him this time, Deborah."

"I don't know what you're talking about."

"I'm a good judge of people. I have to be. And you are a very predictable person. You, a woman of integrity, intelligence and fierce loyalties, involved with two men? It didn't seem likely. Tonight, I became sure of what I've suspected for several weeks. There's only one man, one man who would have recognized Montega, one man who would have won your heart, one man with enough reason to fanatically pursue me.'' He patted her hand when she remained silent. ''That's our little secret. I enjoy secrets.''

His eyes chilled again as he rose. ''And though I regret it, sincerely, only one of us can walk out of here tonight with that secret. I've asked Montega to be quick. For old times' sake.''

Though her body was shaking, she made herself stand. ''I've learned to believe in destiny, Jerry. You won't win. He'll see to that. You'll kill me, and he'll come after you like a Fury. You think you know him, but you don't. You don't have him, and you never will.''

''If it gives you comfort.'' He stepped away from her. ''We don't have him—at the moment.''

''You're wrong.''

Every head in the room turned at the voice. There was nothing but blank walls and piles of lumber. Deborah's knees went so weak she almost folded to the ground.

Then everything seemed to happen at once.

A guard standing beside the wall jerked back, his eyes bright with surprise. While his body struggled and strained, the rifle he was holding began to spray bullets. Men shouted, diving for cover. The guard screamed, stumbled away from the wall. His own men cut him down.

Dashing behind a line of shelves, Deborah searched frantically for a weapon. Laying her hands on a crowbar, she stepped back, ready to defend herself. Before her astonished eyes, a weapon was grappled away from a goggle-eyed guard. Mad with fear, he raced away, screaming.

''Stay back.'' The voice floated out toward her.

''Thank God, I thought that—''

''Just stay back. I'll deal with you later.''

She stood, gripping the crowbar. Nemesis was back, she thought, and gritted her teeth. And as arrogant as ever. Sliding a box aside, she peeked through the opening to the melee beyond. There were five men left—the guards, Montega and Jerry. They were firing wildly, as terrified as they were confused. When one of the bullets plowed into the wall a scant foot from her head, she crouched lower.

Someone screamed. The sound made her squeeze her eyes shut. A hand grabbed her hair, dragging her up.

"What is he?" Jerry hissed in her ear. Though his hand was shaking, it maintained a firm grip. "What the hell is he?"

"He's a hero," she said, looking defiantly into his wild eyes. "Something you'll never understand."

"He'll be a dead one before this is over. You're coming with me." He jerked her in front of him. "If you try anything, I'll shoot you in the back and take my chances."

Deborah took a deep breath and slammed the crowbar into his stomach. When he keeled over, retching, she raced out, weaving and dodging around workbenches and shelving. He recovered quickly, half running, half crawling until his hand reached out and slipped over her ankle. Cursing, she kicked him off, knowing any minute she could feel a bullet slam into her back. She scrambled up a graduated hack of lumber, thinking if she could climb to safety, he couldn't use her as a shield.

She could hear him clambering behind her, gaining ground as he got back his wind. Desperate, she imagined herself like a lizard, quick and sure, clinging to the wood. She couldn't fall. All she knew was that she couldn't fall. Splinters dug into her fingers, unfelt.

With all her strength, she heaved the crowbar at him. It struck him on the shoulder, making him curse and falter. Knowing better than to look back, she set her teeth and jumped from the stack of lumber to a narrow metal ladder. Sweaty, her hands slipped, but she clung, climbing up to the next level. Her breath was coming fast as she raced across the steel landing crowded with rolls of insulation and building material.

But there was no place to go. As she reached the far side, she saw that she was trapped. He had nearly reached the top. She couldn't go down, had no hope of making the five-foot leap to the overhang of metal shelving that held more supplies.

He was breathing hard, and there was blood on his mouth. And a gun in his hand. Deborah took an unsteady step back, looking down twenty-five feet to where Nemesis battled three to one. She couldn't call to him, she realized. To distract him even for an instant could mean his death.

Instead, she turned and faced her one-time friend. "You won't use me to get him."

With the back of his hand he wiped blood and spittle from his lip. "One way or another."

"No." She stepped back again and bumped into a hoist chain. It was thick and hooked and heavy, used, she realized quickly, to lift the huge stacks of material to the next level for storage. "No," she said again and, using all her strength, swung the chain at his face.

She heard the sound of bones breaking. And then his scream, one horrible scream before she covered her own face.

He had whittled things down to Montega when Nemesis looked up and saw her, white as a ghost and swaying on the brink of a narrow metal ledge. He didn't spare a glance for the man who had fallen screaming to the concrete below. As he sprinted toward her, he heard a bullet whistle past his head.

"No!" she shouted at him, pushing aside the faintness. "He's behind you." She saw with relief, and Montega with disbelief, that he veered left and disappeared.

Cautious, wanting to draw Montega's attention from Deborah, Nemesis moved along the wall. He would call tauntingly, then move right or left before Montega could aim his trembling gun and fire.

"I will kill you!" Shaking with fear, Montega fired again and again into the walls. "I've seen you bleed. I will kill you."

It wasn't until he was certain Deborah was down and safely huddled in the shadows that he reappeared, six feet from Montega. "You've already killed me once." Nemesis held his gun steady at Montega's heart. He had only to pull the trigger, he thought. And it would be over. Four years of hell would be over.

But he saw Deborah, her face white and sheened with sweat. Slowly his finger relaxed on the trigger.

"I came back for you, Montega. You'll have a long time to wonder why. Drop your weapon."

Speechless, he did so, sending it clattering onto the concrete. Pale but steady, Deborah stepped forward to pick it up.

"Who are you?" Montega demanded. "What are you?" A scream of warning burst from Deborah's lips as Montega slipped a hand into his pocket.

Two more gunshots ripped the air. Even as they echoed, Montega sprawled lifelessly on the floor. Staring at him, Nemesis stepped closer. "I'm your destiny," he whispered, then turned and caught Deborah in his arms.

"They said they had you. They were going to kill you."

"You should have trusted me." He turned her away, determined to shield her from the death surrounding them.

"But you were here," she said, then stopped. "Why were you here? How did you know?"

"The pattern. Sit down, Deborah. You're shaking."

"I have a feeling it's going to be from anger in a minute. You knew they would be here tonight."

"Yes, I knew. Sit. Let me get you some water."

"Stop it, just stop it." She snatched at his shirtfront with both hands. "You knew, and you didn't tell me. You knew about Stuart, about Jerry."

"Not about Jerry." And he would always regret it. "Until he walked in here tonight and I heard what he told you, I was focused on Fields."

"Then why were you here?"

"I broke the pattern a few days ago. Every drop had been made in a building Stuart owned. And each drop was at least two weeks apart in a different section of the city. I spent a couple of nights casing a few other spots, but honed in here. And I didn't tell you," he continued when her eyes scraped at him, "because I wanted to avoid exactly what happened here tonight. Damn it, when I'm worried about you I can't concentrate. I can't do my job."

Her body was braced as she held out her hand. "Do you see this ring? You gave this to me only hours ago. I'm wearing it because I love you, and because I'm teaching myself how to accept you, your feelings and your needs. If you can't do the same for me, you'll have to take it back."

Behind his mask his eyes were dark and flat. "It's not a matter of doing the same—"

"It's exactly that. I killed a man tonight." Her voice shook, but she pushed him away when he would have held her again. "I killed a man I knew. I came here tonight ready, willing to exchange not only my ethics but my life for yours. Don't you ever protect me, pamper me, or think for me again."

"Are you through?"

"No." But she did lean against the chair. "I know you won't stop what you do. That you can't. I'll worry about you, but I won't stand in your way. You won't stand in mine, either."

He nodded. "Is that all?"

"For now."

"You're right."

She opened her mouth, shut it, then blew out a long breath. "Would you say that again?"

"You're right. I kept things from you and instead of protecting you, I put you in more danger. For that, I'm sorry. And besides admitting that, I think you should know I wasn't going to kill him." He looked down at Montega, but cupped Deborah's chin in his hand before she could follow his direction. "I wanted to. For an instant, I tasted it. But if he had surrendered, I would have turned him over to the police."

She saw the truth of it in his eyes. "Why?"

"Because I looked at you and I knew I could trust you to see there was justice." He held out a hand. "Deborah, I need a partner."

She was smiling even as her eyes overflowed. "So do I." Instead of taking his hand, she launched herself into his arms. "Nothing's going to stop us," she murmured. In the distance, she heard the first sirens. "I think Frank's bringing the cavalry." She kissed him. "I'll explain later. At home. You'd better go." With a sigh, she stepped back. "It's going to take a good lawyer to explain all of this."

At the sound of rushing feet, he moved back, then into the wall behind her. "I'll be here."

She smiled, spreading her palm on the wall, knowing he was doing the same on the shadowy other side. "I'm counting on it."

# Nightshade

For Dan

# Prologue

It was a hell of a place to meet a snitch. A cold night, a dark street, with the smell of whiskey and sweat seeping through the pores of the bar door at his back. Colt drew easily on a slim cigar as he studied the spindly bag of bones who'd agreed to sell him information. Not much to look at, Colt mused—short, skinny, and ugly as homemade sin. In the garish light tossed fitfully by the neon sign behind them, his informant looked almost comical.

But there was nothing funny about the business at hand.

"You're a hard man to pin down, Billings."

"Yeah, yeah…" Billings nibbled on a grimy thumb, his gaze sweeping up and down the street. "A guy keeps healthy that way. Heard you were looking for me." He studied Colt, his eyes flying up, then away, soaring on nerves. "Man in my position has to be careful, you know? What you want to buy, it don't come cheap. And it's dangerous. I'd feel better with my cop. Generally I work through the cop, but I ain't been able to get through all day."

"I'd feel better without your cop. And I'm the one who's paying." To illustrate his point, Colt drew two fifties from his shirt pocket. He watched Billings's eyes dart toward the bills and linger greedily. Colt might be a man who'd take risks, but buying a pig in a poke wasn't his style. He held the money out of reach.

"Talk better if I had a drink." Billings jerked his head toward the doorway of the bar behind them. A woman's laugh, high and shrill, burst through the glass like a gunshot.

"You talk just fine to me." The man was a bundle of raw nerves, Colt observed. He could almost hear the thin bones rattle together as Billings shifted from foot to foot. If he didn't press his point now, the man was going to run like a rabbit. And he'd come too far and had too much at stake to lose him now. "Tell me what I need to know, then I'll buy you a drink."

"You're not from around here."

"No." Colt lifted a brow, waited. "Is that a problem?"

"Nope. Better you aren't. They get wind of you..." Billings swiped the back of his hand over his mouth. "Well, you look like you can handle yourself okay."

"I've been known to." He took one last drag before flicking the cigar away. Its single red eye gleamed in the gutter. "Information, Billings." To show good faith, Colt held out one of the bills. "Let's do business."

Even as Billings's eager fingers reached out, the frigid air was shattered by the shriek of tires on pavement.

Colt didn't have to read the terror in Billings's eyes. Adrenaline and instinct took over, with a kick as quick and hard as a mule's. He was diving for cover as the first shots rang out.

# Chapter 1

Althea didn't mind being bored. After a rough day, a nice spot of tedium could be welcome, giving both mind and body a chance to recharge. She didn't really mind coming off a tough ten-hour shift after an even more grueling sixty-hour week and donning cocktail wear or slipping her tired feet into three-inch heels. She wouldn't even complain about being stuck at a banquet table in the ballroom of the Brown House while speech after droning speech muddled her head.

What she *did* mind was having her date's hand slide up her thigh under cover of the white linen tablecloth.

Men were so predictable.

She picked up her wineglass and, shifting in her seat, nuzzled her date's ear. "Jack?"

His fingers crept higher. "Mmm-hmm?"

"If you don't move your hand—say, within the next two seconds—I'm going to stab it, really, really hard, with my dessert fork. It would hurt, Jack." She sat back and sipped her wine, smiling over the rim as he arched a brow. "You wouldn't play racket ball for a month."

Jack Holmsby, eligible bachelor, feared prosecutor, and guest of honor at the Denver Bar Association Banquet, knew how to handle women. And he'd been trying to get close enough to handle this particular woman for months.

"Thea..." He breathed her name, gifting her with his most charming, crooked smile. "We're nearly done here. Why don't we go back to my place? We can..." He whispered into her ear a suggestion that was descriptive, inventive and possibly anatomically impossible.

Althea was saved from answering—and Jack was spared minor surgery—by the sound of her beeper. Several of her tablemates began shifting, checking pockets and purses. Inclining her head, she rose.

"Pardon me. I believe it's mine." She walked away with a subtle switch of hips, a long flash of leg. The compact body in the backless purple dress glinting with silver beading caused more than one head to turn. Blood pressures were elevated. Fantasies were woven.

Not unaware, but certainly unconcerned, Althea strode out of the ballroom and into the lobby, toward a bank of phones. Opening her beaded evening bag, which contained a compact, lipstick, ID, emergency cash and her nine-millimeter, she fished out a quarter and made her call.

"Grayson." While she listened, she pushed back her fall of flame-colored hair. Her eyes, a tawny shade of brown, narrowed. "I'm on my way."

She hung up, turned and watched Jack Holmsby hurry toward her. An attractive man, she thought objectively. Nicely polished on the outside. A pity he was so ordinary on the inside.

"Sorry, Jack. I have to go."

Irritation scored a deep line between his brows. He had a bottle of Napoleon brandy, a stack of apple wood and a set of white satin sheets waiting at home. "Really, Thea, can't someone else take the call?"

"No." The job came first. It always came first. "It's handy I had to meet you here, Jack. You can stay and enjoy yourself."

But he wasn't giving up that easily. He dogged her through the lobby and out into the brisk fall night. "Why don't you come by after you've finished? We can pick up where we left off."

"We haven't left off, Jack." She handed her parking stub to an attendant. "You have to start to leave off, and I have no intention of starting anything with you."

She only sighed as he slipped his arms around her. "Come on, Thea, you didn't come here tonight to eat prime rib and listen to a bunch of lawyers make endless speeches.'' He lowered his head and murmured against her lips, ''You didn't wear a dress like that to keep me at arm's length. You wore it to make me hot. And you did.''

Mild irritation became brittle and keen. ''I came here tonight because I respect you as a lawyer.'' The quick elbow to his ribs had his breath woofing out and allowed her to step back. ''And because I thought we could spend a pleasant evening together. What I wear is my business, Holmsby, but I didn't choose it so that you'd grope me under the table or make ludicrous suggestions as to how I might spend the rest of my evening.''

She wasn't shouting, but neither was she bothering to keep her voice down. Anger glinted in her voice, like ice under fog. Appalled, Jack tugged at the knot of his tie and darted glances right and left.

''For God's sake, Althea, keep it down.''

''Exactly what I was going to suggest to you,'' she said sweetly.

Though the attendant was all eyes and ears, he politely cleared his throat. Althea turned to accept her keys. ''Thank you.'' She offered him a smile and a generous tip. The smile had his heart skipping a beat, and he didn't glance at the bill before tucking it into his pocket. He was too busy dreaming.

''Ah...drive carefully, miss. And come back soon. Real soon.''

''Thanks.'' She tossed her hair back, then slid gracefully behind the wheel of her reconditioned Mustang convertible. ''See you in court, Counselor.'' Althea gunned the engine and peeled out.

Murder scenes, whether indoors or out, in an urban, suburban or pastoral setting, had one thing in common: the aura of death. As a cop with nearly ten years' experience, Althea had learned to recognize it, absorb it and file it away, while going about the precise and mechanical business of investigation.

When Althea arrived, a half block had been secured. The police photographer had finished recording the scene and was already packing up his gear. The body had been identified. That was why she was here.

Three black-and-whites sat, their lights flashing blue and their radios coughing static. Spectators—for death always drew them—were straining against the yellow police tape, greedy, Althea knew, for a glimpse of death to reaffirm that they were alive and untouched.

Because the night was cool, she grabbed the wrap she'd tossed into the back seat of her car. The emerald-green silk kept the chill off her arms and back. Flashing her badge to the rookie handling crowd control, she slipped under the barricade. She was grateful when she spotted Sweeney, a hard-bitten cop who had twice her years on the job and was in no hurry to give up his uniform.

"Lieutenant." He nodded to her, then took out a handkerchief and made a valiant attempt to clear his stuffy nose.

"What have we got here, Sweeney?"

"Drive-by." He stuffed the handkerchief back into his pocket. "Dead guy was standing in front of the bar, talking." He gestured to the shattered window of the Tick Tock. "Witnesses say a car came by, moving north, fast. Sprayed the area with bullets and kept going."

She could still smell the blood, though it was no longer fresh. "Any bystanders hit?"

"Nope. Couple of cuts from flying glass, that's all. They hit their mark." He glanced over his shoulder, and down. "He didn't have a chance, Lieutenant. Sorry."

"Yeah, me too." She stared down at the form sprawled on the stained concrete. There'd been nothing much to him to begin with, she thought. Now there was less. He'd been five-five, maybe a hundred and ten soaking wet, spindly bones and had had a face even a mother would have been hard-pressed to love.

Wild Bill Billings, part-time pimp, part-time grifter and full-time snitch.

And, damn it, he'd been hers.

"Forensics?"

"Been and gone," Sweeney confirmed. "We're ready to put him on ice."

"Then do it. Got a list of witnesses?"

"Yeah, mostly useless. It was a black car, it was a blue car. One drunk claims it was a chariot driven by flaming demons." He swore with inventive expertise, knowing Althea well enough not to worry about her taking offense.

"We'll take what we can get." She scanned the crowd—bar types, teenagers looking for action, a scattering of the homeless and—

Her antenna vibrated as she locked in on one man. Unlike the others, he wasn't goggle-eyed with either revulsion or excitement. He stood at his ease, his leather bomber jacket open to the wind, revealing a chambray shirt, a glint of silver on a chain. His rangy build made her think he'd be fast on his feet. Snug, worn jeans rode down long legs and ended at scuffed boots. Hair that might have been dark blond or brown ruffled in the breeze and curled well over his collar.

He smoked a thin cigar, his eyes scanning the scene as hers had. The light wasn't good, but she decided he looked tanned, which suited the sharply defined face. The eyes were deep-set, and the nose was long, and just shy of being narrow. The mouth was strong, the kind that looked as though it could thin into a sneer easily.

Some instinct had her dubbing him a pro before his eyes shifted and locked on hers with an impact like a bare-fisted punch.

"Who's the cowboy, Sweeney?"

"The— Oh." Sweeney's tired face creased in what might have been a smile. Damned if she hadn't called it, he thought. The guy looked as though he should be wearing a Stetson and riding a mustang. "Witness," he told her. "Victim was talking to him when he got hit."

"Is that so?" She didn't look around when the coroner's team dealt with the body. There was no need to.

"He's the only one to give us a coherent account." Sweeney pulled out his pad, wet his thumb and flipped pages. "Says it was a black '91 Buick sedan, Colorado plates Able Charlie Frank. Says he missed the numbers 'cause the plate lights were out and he was a little busy diving for cover. Says the weapon sounded like an AK-47."

"Sounded like?" Interesting, she thought. She'd kept her eyes level with her witness's. "Maybe—" She broke off when she spotted her captain crossing the street. Captain Boyd Fletcher walked directly to the witness, shook his head, then grinned and enveloped the other man in the masculine equivalent of an embrace. There was a lot of back-thumping.

"Looks as though the captain's handling him for now." Althea pocketed her curiosity as she would a treat to be saved for later. "Let's finish up here, Sweeney."

Colt had watched her from the moment one long, smooth leg swung out of the door of the Mustang. A lady like that was worth watching—well worth it. He'd liked the way she moved—with an athletic and economical grace that wasted neither time nor energy. Certainly he'd liked the way she looked. Her neat, sexy little body had just enough curves to whet a man's appetite, and with all that green-and-purple silk rippling in the wind... The sunburst of hair, blowing away from a cool cameo face, brought much more interesting things to a man's mind than his grandmother's heirloom jewelry.

It was a cold night, and one look at that well-packed number had Colt thinking about heat.

It wasn't such a bad way to keep warm while he waited. He wasn't a man who waited well under the best of circumstances.

He hadn't been particularly surprised to see her flash ID to the baby-faced cop at the barricade. She carried authority beautifully on her luscious swimmer's shoulders. Idly lighting a cigar, he decided she was an assistant D.A., then realized his error when she went into conference with Sweeney.

The lady had *cop* written all over her.

Late twenties, he figured, maybe five-four without those ankle-wrecking heels, and a tidy one-ten.

They sure were making cops in interesting packages these days.

So he waited, sizing up the scene. He didn't have any feelings one way or the other about the remains of Wild Bill Billings. The man was no good to him now.

He'd dig up something, or someone, else. Colt Nightshade wasn't a man to let murder get in his way.

When he felt her watching him, he drew smoke in lazily, chuffed it out. Then he shifted his gaze until it met hers. The tightening in his gut was unexpected—it was raw and purely sexual. The one fleeting instant when his mind was wiped clean as glass was more than unexpected. It was unprecedented. Power slapped against power. She took a step toward him. He let out the breath he'd just realized he was holding.

His preoccupation made it easy for Boyd to come up behind him and catch him unawares.

"Colt! Son of a bitch!"

Colt turned, braced and ready for anything. But the flat intensity in his eyes faded into a grin that might have melted any woman within twenty paces.

"Fletch." With the easy warmth he reserved for friends, Colt returned the bear hug before stepping back to take stock. He hadn't seen Boyd in nearly ten years. It relieved him to see that so little had changed. "Still got that pretty face, don't you?"

"And you still sound like you've just ridden in off the range. God, it's good to see you. When'd you get into town?"

"Couple of days ago. I wanted to take care of some business before I got in touch."

Boyd looked past him to where the coroner's van was being loaded. "Was that your business?"

"Part of it. I appreciate you coming down like this."

"Yeah." Boyd spotted Althea, acknowledging her with an imperceptible nod. "Did you call a cop, Colt, or a friend?"

Colt looked down at the stub of his cigar, dropped it near the gutter and crushed it with his boot. "It's handy, you being both."

"Did you kill that guy?"

It was asked so matter-of-factly that Colt grinned again. He knew Boyd wouldn't have turned a hair if he'd confessed then and there. "Nope."

Boyd nodded again. "Going to fill me in?"

"Yep."

"Why don't you wait in the car? I'll be with you in a minute."

"*Captain* Boyd Fletcher." Colt shook his head and chuckled. Though it was after midnight, he was as alert as he was relaxed, a cup of bad coffee in his hand and his scruffy boots propped on Boyd's desk. "Ain't that just something?"

"I thought you were raising horses and cattle in Wyoming."

"I do." His voice was a drawl, with the faintest whisper of a twang. "Now and again I do."

"What happened to the law degree?"

"Oh, it's around somewhere."

"And the air force?"

"I still fly. Just don't wear a uniform anymore. How long's it going to take for that pizza to get here?"

"Just long enough for it to be cold and inedible." Boyd leaned back in his chair. He was comfortable in his office. He was comfortable on the street. And, as he had been twenty years ago, in their prep school days, he was comfortable with Colt.

"You didn't get a look at the shooter?"

"Hell, Fletch, I was lucky to make the car before I was diving for cover and chewing asphalt. Not that that's going to help much. Odds are it was stolen."

"Lieutenant Grayson's tracking it. Now, why don't you tell me what you were doing with Wild Bill?"

"He contacted me. I've bee—" He broke off when Althea strolled in. She hadn't bothered to knock, and she was carrying a flat cardboard box.

"You two order pizza?" She dropped the box onto Boyd's desk, held out a hand. "Ten bucks, Fletcher."

"Althea Grayson, Colt Nightshade. Colt's an old friend." Boyd dug ten dollars out of his wallet. After folding the bill neatly and tucking it in a pocket of her purse, she set her beaded bag on a stack of files.

"Mr. Nightshade."

"Ms. Grayson."

"*Lieutenant* Grayson," she corrected. Popping up the lid on the box, she perused the contents, chose a slice. "I believe you were at my crime scene."

"Sure did look that way." He lowered his legs so that he could lean forward and take a piece himself. He caught her scent over the aroma of cooling sausage pizza. It was a whole lot more tantalizing.

"Thanks," she murmured when Boyd passed her a napkin. "I wonder what you were doing there, getting shot at with my snitch."

Colt's eyes narrowed. "Your snitch?"

"That's right." Like his hair, his eyes couldn't seem to decide what color they should be, Althea thought. They were caught somewhere between blue and green. And at the moment they were as cold as the wind whipping at the window.

"Bill told me he tried to reach his police contact off and on all day."

"I was in the field."

Colt's brow arched as he skimmed his gaze over the swirl of emerald silk. "Some field."

"Lieutenant Grayson spent all day putting the cap on a drug operation," Boyd interjected. "Now, kids, why don't we start over, and at the beginning?"

"Fine." Setting her half-eaten slice down, Althea wiped her fingers, then removed her wrap. Colt clenched his teeth to keep his tongue from falling out. Because she was turned away from him, Colt had the painful pleasure of gauging just how alluring a naked back could be when it was slim, straight and framed in purple silk.

After laying her coat over a file cabinet, Althea reclaimed her pizza and sat on the corner of Boyd's desk.

She knew just what she did to a man, Colt realized. He could see that smug, faintly amused female knowledge in her eyes. Colt had always figured every woman knew her own arsenal down to the last eyelash, but it was tough on a man when the woman was as heavily armed as this.

"Wild Bill, Mr. Nightshade..." Althea began. "What were you doing with him?"

"Talking." He knew his answer was obstinate, but at the moment he was trying to judge whether there was anything between the sexy lieutenant and his old friend. His old *married* friend, Colt mused. He was relieved, and more than a little surprised not to scent even a whiff of attraction between them.

"About?" Althea's voice was still patient, even pleasant. As if, Colt thought, she were questioning a small boy who was mentally deficient.

"The victim was Thea's snitch," Boyd reminded Colt. "If she wants the case—"

"And I do."

"Then it's hers."

To buy himself time, Colt reached for another slice of pizza. He was going to have to do something he hated, something that stuck in his craw like bad beef jerky. He was going to have to ask for help. And to get it he was going to have to share what he knew.

"It took me two days to track down Billings and get him to agree to talk to me." It had also cost him two hundred in bribes to clear the path, but he wasn't one to count the cost until the final tally. "He was nervous, didn't really want to talk unless he had his police contact with him. So I made it worth his while."

He glanced back at Althea. The lady was wiped out, he realized. The fatigue was hard to spot, but it was there—in the slight drooping of her eyelids, the faint shadows under them.

"I'm sorry you lost him, but I don't think your being there would have changed anything."

"We won't know that, will we?" She wouldn't let the regret color her voice, or her judgment. "Why did you go to so much trouble to contact Bill?"

"He used to have a girl working for him. Jade. Probably her street name."

Althea let her mind click back, nodded. "Yeah. Little blonde, babyface. She took a couple of busts for solicitation. I'll have to check, but I don't think she's worked the stroll for four or five weeks."

"That'd be about right." Colt rose to fill his cup with more of the sludge from the automatic brewer. "It would have been about that long ago that Billings got her a job. In the movies." If he was going to drink poison, he'd take it like a man, without any cream or sugar to cut the bite. Sipping, he turned back. "I ain't talking Hollywood. This was the down-and-dirty stuff, for private viewers who have the taste and the money to buy thrills. Videotapes for hard-core connoisseurs." He shrugged and sat again. "Can't say it bothers me any, if we're talking about consenting adults. Though I prefer my sex in the flesh."

"But we're not talking about you, Mr. Nightshade."

"Oh, you don't have to call me *mister,* Lieutenant. Seems cold, when we're discussing such warm topics." Smiling, he leaned back. He had yet to ruffle her feathers, and for reasons he wasn't going to take the time to explore, he wanted to ruffle them good and proper. "Well, as it happens, something spooked Jade and she lit out. I'm not one to think a hooker's got a heart of gold, but this one at least had a conscience. She sent off a letter to a Mr. and Mrs. Frank Cook.'' He shifted his gaze to Boyd. ''Frank and Marleen Cook.''

''Marleen?'' Boyd's brows shot up. ''Marleen and Frank?''

''The same.'' Colt's smile was wry. ''More old friends, Lieutenant. As it happens, I was what you might call intimate friends with Mrs. Cook about a million years ago. Being a woman of sound judgment, she married Frank, settled down in Albuquerque and had herself a couple of beautiful kids.''

Althea shifted, crossed her legs with a rustle of silk. The silver dangling over his shirt was a Saint Christopher medal, she noted. The patron saint of travelers. She wondered if Mr. Nightshade felt the need for spiritual protection.

''I assume this is leading somewhere other than down memory lane?''

''Oh, it's leading right back to your professional front door, Lieutenant. I just prefer the circular route now and then.'' He took out a cigar, running it through his long fingers before reaching for his lighter. ''About a month ago, Marleen's oldest girl—that's Elizabeth. You ever meet Liz, Boyd?''

Boyd shook his head. He didn't like where this was heading. Not one bit. ''Not since she was in diapers. What is she, twelve?''

''Thirteen. Just.'' Colt flicked his lighter on, sucked his cigar to life. Though he knew, all too well, that the tang of smoke wouldn't cloud the bitter taste in his throat. ''Pretty as a picture, like her mama. Got Marleen's hair-trigger temper, too. There was some trouble at home, the kind I imagine most families have some time or other. But Liz got her back up and took off.''

''She ran away?'' Althea understood the runaway's mind well. Too well.

''Tossed a few things in her backpack and took off. Needless to say, Marleen and Frank have been living in hell the past few weeks. They contacted the police, but the official route wasn't getting them very far.'' He blew out smoke. ''No offense. Ten days ago they called me.''

''Why?'' Althea asked.

''Told you. We're friends.''

"Do you usually track down pimps and dodge bullets for friends?"

She had a way with sarcasm, all right, Colt mused. It was one more weapon in the arsenal. "I do favors for people."

"Are you a licensed investigator?"

Pursing his lips, Colt studied the tip of his cigar. "I'm not big on licenses. I put out some feelers, had a little luck tracing her north. Then the Cooks got Jade's letter." Clamping his cigar between his teeth, he drew a folded sheet of floral stationery from his inside jacket pocket. "Save time if you read it yourself," he said, and passed it to Boyd. Althea rose, going behind Boyd's back, laying a hand on his shoulder as she read with him.

It was a curiously intimate and yet asexual gesture. One, Colt decided, that spoke of friendship and trust.

The handwriting was as girlishly fussy as the paper. But the content, Althea noted, had nothing to do with flowers and ribbons and childhood fancies.

Dear Mr. and Mrs. Cook,
I met Liz in Denver. She is a nice kid. I know she is really sorry she ran away and would come back now if she could. I would help her out, but I got to get out of town. Liz is in trouble. I would go to the cops, but I'm scared and I don't think they listen to someone like me. She is not cut out for the life, but they won't let her go. She is young and so pretty, and they are making lots of money from the movies I think. I have been in the life for five years, but some of the stuff they want us to do for the camera gives me the creeps. I think they killed one of the girls, so I am getting out before they kill me. Liz gave me your address and asked me to write and say she was sorry. She's real scared and I hope you find her okay.

Jade

P.S. They have a place up in the mountains where they do the movies. And there is an apartment on Second Avenue.

Boyd didn't give the letter back, but laid it on his desk. He had a daughter of his own. He thought of Allison, sweet, feisty and six, and had to swallow a hot ball of sick rage.

"You could have come to me with this. You *should* have come to me."

"I'm used to working alone." Colt drew on his cigar again before tamping it out. "In any case, I intended to come to you after I put a few things together. I got the name of Jade's pimp, and I wanted to shake him down."

"And now he's dead." Althea's voice was flat as she turned to stare out of Boyd's window.

"Yeah." Colt studied her profile. It wasn't just anger he felt from her. There was a lot more mixed up with it. "Word must have gotten back that I was looking for him, and that he was willing to talk to me. Leads me to think that we're dealing with well-connected slime, and slime that doesn't blink at murder."

"This is a police matter, Colt," Boyd said quietly.

"No argument." Ready to deal, he spread his hands. "It's also a personal matter. I'm going to keep digging, Fletch. There's no law against it. I'm the Cooks' representative—their lawyer, if we need a handle."

"Is that what you are?" Her emotions under control again, Althea turned back to him. "A lawyer?"

"When it suits me. I don't want to interfere with your investigation," he said to Boyd. "I want the kid back—safely back—with Marleen and Frank. I'll cooperate completely. Anything I know, you'll know. But it has to be quid pro quo. Give me a cop to work with on this, Boyd." He smiled a little—just a quirk at the corner of his mouth, as if he were amused at himself. "And you of all people know how much I hate asking for an official partner on a job. But it's Liz that matters, all that matters. You know I'm good." He leaned forward. "You know I won't back off. Let me have your best man, and let's get these bastards."

Boyd pressed his fingers to his tired eyes. He could, of course, order Colt to back off. And he'd be wasting his breath. He could refuse to cooperate, could refuse to share any information the department unearthed. And Colt would work around him. Yes, he knew Colt was good, and he had some idea of the kind of work he'd done while in the military.

It would hardly be the first time Boyd Fletcher had bent the rules. His decision made, he gestured toward Althea.

''She's my best man.''

## Chapter 2

If a man had to have a partner, she might as well be easy on the eyes. In any case, Colt didn't intend to work *with* Althea so much as *through* her. She would be his conduit to the official end of the investigation. He'd keep his word—he always did, except when he didn't—and feed her whatever information he gleaned. Not that he expected her to do much with it.

There were only a handful of cops Colt respected, with Boyd topping the list. As far as Lieutenant Grayson was concerned, Colt figured she'd be decorative, marginally helpful and little else.

The badge, the bod and the sarcasm would probably be useful when it came to interviewing any possible connections.

At least he'd had a decent night's sleep—all six hours of it. He hadn't protested when Boyd insisted he check out of his hotel and check into the Fletcher household for the duration of his stay. Colt liked families—other people's, in any case—and he'd been curious about Boyd's wife.

He'd missed their wedding. Though he wasn't particularly fond of the spit and polish ceremonies called for, he would have gone. But it was a long way from Beirut to Denver, and he'd been busy with terrorists at the time.

He was delighted with Cilla. The woman hadn't turned a hair at having her husband bring home a strange man at 2:00 a.m. Bundled in a terry-cloth robe, she'd offered him the guest room, with the suggestion that if he wanted to sleep in he should put the pillow over his head. The kids apparently rose at seven to get ready for school.

He'd slept like a rock, and when he'd awakened to the sounds of shouts and clomping feet, he'd taken his hostess's advice and had caught another hour of sleep with his head buried.

Now, fortified by an excellent breakfast and three cups of first-class coffee prepared by the Fletchers' housekeeper, he was ready to roll.

His agreement with Boyd made the precinct house his first stop. He'd check in with Althea, grill her on any associates of Billings's, then go his own way.

It seemed to him that his old friend ran a tight ship. There was the usual din of ringing phones, clattering keyboards and raised voices inside the station. There were the usual scents of coffee, industrial-strength cleaners and sweaty bodies. But there was also an underlying sense of organization and purpose.

The desk sergeant had Colt's name, and he handed him a visitor's badge and directed him to Althea's office. Past the bull pen, and two doors down a narrow corridor he found her door. It was shut, so he rapped once before pushing it open. He knew she was there before he saw her. He scented her, as a wolf scents his mate. Or his prey.

Gone were the bold silks, but she still looked more the fashion plate than the cop. The tailored slacks and jacket in smoke gray did nothing to suggest masculinity. Nor did he think she chose to deny her sex, for she'd accented the suit with a soft pink blouse and a star-shaped jeweled lapel pin. Her mass of hair had been trained back in some complicated braid that left her face softly framed. Two heavy twists of gold glinted at her ears.

The result was as neat as any maiden aunt could want, and still had the knockout punch of frosted sex.

A lesser man might have licked his lips.

"Grayson."

"Nightshade." She gestured toward a chair. "Have a seat."

There was only one to spare, straight-backed and wood. Colt turned it around and straddled it. As he did, he noted that her office was less than half the size of Boyd's, and ruthlessly organized. File drawers were neatly closed, papers properly stacked, pencils sharpened to lethal points. There was a plant on one of the rear corners of the desk that he was sure was meticulously watered. There were no pictures of family or friends. The only spot of color in the small, windowless room was a painting, an abstract in vivid blues, greens and reds. Slashes of colors that clashed and warred, rather than melded.

Some instinct told him it suited her down to the ground.

"So." He folded his arms over the back of the chair and leaned forward. "You run the shooter's car through Motor Vehicles?"

"Didn't have to. It was on this morning's hot sheet." She took her copy and offered it. "Reported stolen at eleven o'clock last night. Owners had been out for dinner, came out of the restaurant and found the car gone. Dr. and Dr. Wilmer, a couple of dentists celebrating their fifth anniversary. Looks like they're clean."

"Probably." He tossed the sheet back onto her desk. He hadn't really believed he'd find a connection through the car. "Don't guess it's turned up?"

"Not yet. I've got Jade's rap sheet, if you're interested." After replacing the hot sheet in its proper place, she picked up a file. "Janice Willowby. Age twenty-two. Couple of busts for solicitation—a few charges as a juvie for more of the same. One possession arrest, also as a juvenile, when she got rousted with a couple of joints in her purse. Went through the social services route, a halfway house, counseling, then turned twenty-one and went back on the streets."

It wasn't a new story. "Have we got any family? She might head home."

"A mother in Kansas City—or she was in Kansas City as of eighteen months ago. I'm trying to track her down."

"You've been busy."

"Not all of us start our day at—" she looked down at her watch "—ten."

"I do better at night, Lieutenant." He took out a cigar.

Althea eyed it, shook her head. "Not in here, pal."

Agreeably Colt tapped the cigar back into his pocket. "Who did Billings trust, other than you?"

"I don't know that he trusted anybody." But it hurt, because she knew he had trusted somebody. He'd trusted her, and somehow she'd missed a step. And now he was dead. "We had an arrangement. I gave him money, he gave me information."

"What kind?"

"With Wild Bill, it came in a variety pack. He had his fingers in a lot of pies. Little pies, mostly." She shifted some papers on her desk, tapping the edges neatly together. "He was strictly small-time, but he had big ears, knew how to fade into the background so you forgot he was around. People talked around him, because he looked like his brain would fit in a teacup. But he was smart." Her voice changed, tipping Colt off to something she had yet to admit even to herself. She was grieving. "Smart enough to keep from crossing the line that would send him up to hard time. Smart enough to keep from stepping on the wrong toes. Until last night."

"I didn't make any secret of the fact I was looking for him, and for information he could give me. But I sure as hell didn't want him dead."

"I'm not blaming you."

"No?"

"No." She pushed away from the desk far enough to allow her to swivel the chair around and face him. "People like Bill, no matter how smart, have short life expectancies. If he'd have been able to contact me, I might have met him at the same spot you did, with the same results." She'd thought that through, carefully, ruthlessly. "I might not like your style, Nightshade, but I'm not pinning this on you."

She sat very still, he noted, no gestures, no shrugs, no restless tapping. Like the painting on the wall behind her, she communicated vibrant passion without movement.

"And just what is my style, Lieutenant?"

"You're a renegade. The kind who doesn't just refuse to play by the rules, but rejoices in breaking them." Her eyes stayed level with his, and were cool as lake water. He wondered what it would take to warm them up. "You start things, but you don't always finish them. Maybe that means you bore easily, or you just run out of energy. Either way, it doesn't say much about your dependability."

Her rundown of his personality annoyed him, but when he spoke again, his slow southwestern drawl was amused. "You figured all that out since last night?"

"I ran a make on you. The prep school where you hung out with Boyd surprised me." Her lips curved, but the eyes had yet to warm. "You don't look like the preppie type."

"My parents thought it would tame me." He grinned. "Guess not."

"Neither did Harvard, where you got your law degree—which you haven't put to much use. Parts of your military career were classified, but all in all, I got the picture." There was a dish of sugared almonds on her desk. Althea leaned over and, after careful deliberation, chose the one she wanted. "I don't work with someone I don't know."

"Me either. So why don't you fill me in on Althea Grayson?"

"I'm the cop," she said simply. "And you're not. I assume you have a recent picture of Elizabeth Cook?"

"Yeah, I got one." But he didn't reach for it. He didn't have to take this kind of bull from some glamourpuss with a badge. "Tell me, Lieutenant, just who jammed a stick up your—"

The phone cut him off, which, considering the flash in Althea's eyes, might have been for the best. At least he knew how to defrost those eyes now.

"Grayson." She waited a beat, then jotted something down on a pad. "Notify Forensics. I'm on my way." She rose, tucking the pad into a snakeskin purse. "We found the car." She was frowning when she slung the bag over her shoulder. "Since Boyd wants you in, you can come along for the ride—as an observer only. Got it?"

"Oh, yeah. I got it fine."

He followed her out, then quickly moved up so that they walked side by side. The woman had the best rear view this side of the Mississippi, and Colt didn't care to be distracted.

"I didn't have much time to play catch-up with Boyd last night," he began. "I wondered how it was that you're on such...easy terms with your captain."

She was walking down the stairs to the garage, and she stopped, turned, aimed one razor-sharp glance.

"What?" he demanded as she assessed him silently.

"I'm trying to decide if you're insulting me and Boyd—in which case I'd have to hurt you—or if you simply phrased your question badly."

He lifted a brow. "Try the second choice."

"All right." She continued down. "We were partners for over seven years." She reached the bottom of the steps and turned sharply to the right. The flat heels of her suede half boots clicked busily on the concrete. "When you trust someone with your life on a day-to-day basis, you'd better be on easy terms."

"Then he made captain."

"That's right." After taking out her keys, she unlocked her car. "Sorry, but the passenger seat's stuck all the way forward. I haven't had time to take it in and get it fixed."

Colt looked down at the spiffy sports car with some regret. A sexy car, sure, but with the seat in that position, he was going to have to fold himself up like an accordion and sit with his chin on his knees. "And you don't have a problem with that—Boyd's being captain?"

Althea slid in gracefully, smirking a bit as Colt grunted and arranged himself beside her. "No. Am I ambitious? Yes. Do I resent having the best cop I ever worked with as my superior? No. Do I expect to make captain myself within another five years? You bet your butt." She pushed mirrored aviator sunglasses over her eyes. "Fasten your seat belt, Nightshade." With that, she peeled out, shooting up the ramp of the garage and out onto the street.

He had to admire her driving. He had no choice, since she was behind the wheel and his life was in her hands. Easy terms? he wondered. Yeah, right. "So, you and Boyd are friends."

"That's right. Why?"

"I just wanted to establish that it wasn't all good-looking men of a certain age who put your back up." He grinned at her as she downshifted around a corner. "I like knowing it's just me. Makes me feel kind of special, you know?"

She smiled then and shot him what could have been a friendly look. It certainly was no more than friendly, and it really shouldn't have had his heart doing a slow roll in his chest. "I wouldn't say you put my back up, Nightshade. I just don't trust hotdoggers. But since we're both after the same thing here, and since Boyd's a pal on both sides, we can try to get along."

"Sounds reasonable. We've got the job and Boyd in common. Maybe we can find a couple of other things." Her radio was turned down low. Colt flicked the volume up and nodded approval at the slow, pulse-pumping blues. "There, that's one more thing. How do you feel about Mexican food?"

"I like my chili hot and my margaritas cold."

"Progress." He tried to shift in his seat, rapped his knee on the dash, and swore. "If we're going to do any more driving together, we take my four-wheel."

"We'll discuss it." She turned the music down again when she heard the police radio squawk to life.

"All units in the vicinity of Sheridan and Jewell, 511 in progress."

Althea swore as the dispatcher continued to call for assistance. "That's only a block down." She turned left and aimed a quick, dubious look at Colt. "Shots fired," she told him. "Police business, got it?"

"Sure."

"This is unit six responding," she said into the transmitter. "I'm on the scene." After squealing to a halt behind her black-and-white, she shoved open her door. "Stay in the car." With that terse order, she drew her weapon and headed for the entrance of a four-story apartment building.

She paused at the door, sucking in her breath. The minute she bolted through, she heard the blast of another gunshot.

One floor up, she thought. Maybe two. With her body braced and flattened against the wall, she scanned the cramped, deserted entryway, then started up. Screaming— No, she thought, crying. A child. Her mind cold, her hands steady, she swung her weapon toward the first landing, then followed it. A door opened to her left. Crouching, she aimed toward the movement and stared into the face of an elderly woman with terrified eyes.

"Police," Althea told her. "Stay inside."

The door shut. A bolt turned. Althea shifted toward the second staircase. She saw them then, the cop who was down, and the cop who was huddled over him.

"Officer." There was the snap of authority in her voice when she dropped a hand on the uninjured cop's shoulder. "What's the status here?"

"He shot Jim. He came running out with the kid and opened up."

The uniformed cop was sheet-white, she noted, as pale as his partner, who was bleeding on the stairway. She couldn't tell which of them was shaking more violently. "What's your name?"

"Harrison. Don Harrison." He was pressing a soaked handkerchief to the gaping wound low on his partner's left shoulder.

"Officer Harrison, I'm Lieutenant Grayson. Give me the situation here, and make it fast."

"Sir." He took two short, quick breaths. "Domestic dispute. Shots fired. A white male assaulted the woman in apartment 2-D. He opened fire on us and headed upstairs with a small female child as a shield."

As he finished, a woman stumbled out of the apartment above. Where she clutched her side, blood trickled through her fingers. "He took my baby. Charlie took my baby. Please, God…" She fell weeping to her knees. "He's crazy. Please, God…"

"Officer Harrison." A sound on the stairs had Althea moving fast, then swearing. She should have known Colt wouldn't stay in the car. "Get on the horn, now," she continued. "Call for backup. Officer and civilian down. Hostage situation. Now tell me what he was carrying."

"Looked like a .45."

"Make the call, then get in here and back me up." She spared one look at Colt. "Make yourself useful. Do what you can for these two."

She raced up the stairs. She could hear the baby crying again, long terrified wails that echoed in the narrow corridors. By the time she reached the top floor, she heard the slam of a door. The roof, she decided. Braced on one side of the door, she turned the knob, kicked it open and went in low.

He fired once, wildly. The bullet sang more than a foot to her right. Althea took her stand, and faced him.

"Police!" she shouted. "Put down your weapon!"

He stood near the edge of the roof, a big man. Linebacker-size, she noted, his skin flushed with rage, his eyes glazed by chemicals.

That she could handle. It was a .45 he was carrying. She could handle that, as well. But it was the child, the little girl of perhaps two that he was holding by one foot over the edge of the roof, that she wasn't sure she could deal with.

"I'll drop her!" He shouted it, like a chant against the brisk wind. "I'll do it! I'll do it! I swear to God, I'll drop her like a stone!" He shook the child, who continued to scream. One of her little pink tennis shoes flew off and fell five long stories.

"You don't want to make a mistake, do you, Charlie?" Althea inched away from the door, sidestepping slowly, her nine-millimeter aimed at the broad chest. "Bring her back from the edge."

"I'm going to drop the little bitch." He grinned when he said it, his teeth bared, his eyes glittering. "She's just like her mother. Whining and crying all the damn time. Thought they could get away from me. I found them, didn't I? Linda's real sorry now, isn't she? Real damn sorry now."

"Yes, she is." She had to get to the kid. There had to be a way to get to the child. Unbidden an old, obscene memory flashed through her head. The shouting, the threats, the fear. Althea tramped on them as she would a roach. "You hurt the little girl and it's all over, Charlie."

"Don't tell me it's over!" Enraged, he swung the child like a sack of laundry. Althea's heart stopped, and so did the screaming. The little girl was merely sobbing now, quietly, helplessly, her arms dangling limply, her huge blue eyes fixed and glazed. "She tried to tell me it was over. It's over, Charlie," he mimicked in a singsong voice. "So I knocked her around some. God knows she deserved it, nagging me about getting work, nagging about every damn thing. And as soon as the kid came along, everything changed. I got no use for bitches in my life. But *I* say when it's over."

The wail of sirens rose up in the air. Althea sensed movement behind her, but didn't turn. Didn't dare. She needed the man focused on her, only on her. "Bring the kid in and you might get away. You want to get away, don't you, Charlie? Come on. Give her to me. You don't need her."

"You think I'm stupid?" His lips curled into a snarl. "You're just one more bitch."

"I don't think you're stupid." She caught a movement out of the corner of her eye, and would have sworn if she'd dared. It wasn't Harrison. It was Colt, slipping like a shadow toward the man's blind side. "I don't think you'd be stupid enough to hurt the kid." She was closer now, five feet away. Althea knew that it might as well be fifty.

"I'm going to kill her!" he shouted. "And I'm going to kill you, and I'm going to kill anybody who gets in my way! Nobody says it's over till I say it's over!"

It happened then, fast, like a blur at the corner of a dream. Colt lunged, wrapping one arm around the child's waist. Althea caught the flash of metal in his hand and recognized it as a .32. He might have used it, if saving the child hadn't been his priority. He pivoted back, swinging the child so that his body was her shield, and by the time he'd brought his weapon to bear it was over.

Althea watched the .45 arch from her toward Colt and the girl. And she fired. The bullet drove him back. His knees hit the low curbing at the edge of the roof. He was the one who dropped like a stone.

Althea didn't permit herself even a sigh. She holstered her weapon and strode to where Colt was cuddling the weeping child. "She okay?"

"Looks like." In a move so natural she would have sworn he'd spent his life doing it, he settled the girl on his hip and kissed her damp temple. "You're okay now, baby. Nobody's going to hurt you."

"Mama." Choking on tears, she buried her face in Colt's shoulder. "Mama."

"We'll take you to your mama, honey, don't you worry." Colt still held his gun, but his other hand was busy stroking the girl's wispy blond hair. "Nice work, Lieutenant."

Althea glanced over her shoulder. Cops were already pounding up the stairs. "I've done better."

"You kept him talking so the kid had a shot, then you took him down. It doesn't get better than that." And there had been a look in her eyes, from the moment she'd started up the steps with a cop's blood on her hands. And it hadn't faded yet. A look he'd seen before, Colt mused. One he'd always termed a warrior's look.

Her eyes held his for another minute. "Let's get her out of here" was all she said.

"Fine." They started toward the door.

"Just one thing, Nightshade."

He smiled a little, certain this was the moment she'd thank him. "What's that?"

"Have you got a permit for that gun?"

He stopped, stared. Then his smile exploded into a deep, rich laugh. Charmed, the little girl looked up, sniffled, and managed a watery smile.

She didn't think about killing. Didn't permit herself. She'd killed before, and knew she would likely do so again. But she didn't think about it. She knew that if she reflected too deeply on that aspect of the job, she could freeze, or she could drink or she could grow callous. Or, worse—infinitely worse—she could grow to enjoy it.

So she filed her report and put it out of her mind. Or tried to.

She hand-carried a copy of the report to Boyd's office, laid it on his desk. His eyes flicked down to it, then back to hers. "The cop—Barkley—he's still in surgery. The woman's out of danger."

"Good. How's the kid?"

"She has an aunt in Colorado Springs. Social Services contacted her. The creep was her father. History of battering and drugs. His wife took the kid about a year ago and went to a women's shelter. Filed for divorce. She moved here about three months ago, got herself a job, started a life."

"And he found her."

"And he found her."

"Well, he won't find her again." She turned toward the door, but Boyd was up and walking around the desk. "Thea." He shut the door, cutting off most of the din from the bull pen. "Are you okay?"

"Sure. I don't see IAD hassling me on this one."

"I'm not talking about Internal Affairs." He tilted his head. "A day or two off wouldn't hurt."

"It wouldn't help, either." She lifted her shoulders, let them fall.

To Boyd she could say things she could never say to anyone else. "I didn't think I'd get to her in time. I didn't get to her," she added. "Colt did. And he shouldn't have been there."

"He was there." Gently Boyd laid his hands on her shoulders. "Oh-oh, it's the supercop complex. I can see it coming. Dodging bullets, filing reports, screaming down dark alleys, selling tickets to the Policemen's Ball, ridding the world of bad guys and saving cats from the tops of trees. She can do it all."

"Shut up, Fletcher." But she smiled. "I draw the line at saving cats."

"Want to come to dinner tonight?"

She rested a hand on the knob. "What's to eat?"

He shrugged, grinned. "Can't say. It's Maria's night off."

"Cilla's cooking?" She gave him a pained, sorrowful look. "I thought we were friends."

"We'll send out for tacos."

"Deal."

When she walked back into the bull pen, she spotted Colt. He had his boots up on a desk and a phone at his ear. She strolled over, sat on the corner and waited for him to finish the call.

"Paperwork done?" he asked her.

"Nightshade, I don't suppose I have to point out that this desk, this phone, this chair, are department property, and off-limits to civilians."

He grinned at her. "Nope. But go right ahead, if you want to. You look good enough to eat when you're spouting proper procedure."

"Why, your compliments just take my breath away." She knocked his feet off the desk. "The stolen car's been impounded. The lab boys are going over it, so I don't see the point in rushing to take a look."

"Got a different plan?"

"Starting with the Tick Tock, I'm going to hit a few of Wild Bill's hangouts, talk to some people."

"I'm with you."

"Don't rub it in."

When she started toward the garage, he took her arm. "My car this time, remember?"

With a shrug, she went with him out to the street. His rugged black four-wheeler had a parking ticket on the windshield. Colt stuffed it in his pocket. "I don't suppose I can ask you to fix this."

"No." Althea climbed in.

"That's okay. Fletch'll do it."

She slanted him a look, and what might have been a smile, before turning to stare out of the windshield again. "You did good with that kid today." It galled her a bit to admit it, but it had to be done. "I don't think she'd have made it without you."

"Us," he said. "Some people might have called it teamwork."

She fastened her belt with a jerk of her wrist. "Some people."

"Don't take it so hard, Thea." Whistling through his teeth, he shoved the gearshift into First and cruised into traffic. "Now, where were we before we were interrupted? Oh, yeah, you were telling me about yourself."

"I don't think so."

"Okay, I'll tell me about you. You're a woman who likes structure, depends on it. No, no, it's more that you insist on it," he said. "That's why you're so good at your job, all that law and order."

She snorted. "You should be a psychiatrist, Nightshade. Who could have guessed a cop would prefer law and order?"

"Don't interrupt, I'm on a roll. You're what—twenty-seven, twenty-eight?"

"Thirty-two. You lost your roll."

"I'll pick it up again." He glanced down at her naked ring finger. "You're not married."

"Another brilliant deduction."

"You have a tendency toward sarcasm, and an affection for wearing silk and expensive perfume. Real nice perfume, Thea, the kind that seduces a man's mind before his body gets involved."

"Maybe you should be writing ad copy."

"There's nothing subtle about your sexuality. It's just there, in big capital letters. Now, some women would exploit it, some would disguise it. You don't do either, so I figure you've decided somewhere along the line that it's up to a man to deal with it. And that's not only smart, it's wise."

· She didn't have an answer to that, he thought. Or didn't choose to give him one.

"You don't waste time, you don't waste energy. That way, when you need either one, you've got them. There's a cop's brain inside there, so you can size up a situation fast and act on it. And I figure you can handle a man every bit as coolly as you do your gun."

"An interesting analysis, Nightshade."

"You didn't flinch when you took that guy out today. It bothered you, but you didn't flinch." He pulled up in front of the Tick Tock and turned off the ignition. "If I've got to work with somebody, with the possibility of heading into a nasty situation, I like knowing she doesn't flinch."

"Well, gee, thanks. Now I can stop worrying that you don't approve of me." Her temper on the boil, she slammed out of the car.

"Finally..." Colt reached her in a few long-legged strides and swung his arm over her shoulder. "A little heat. It's a relief to see there's some temper in there, too."

She surprised them both by ramming an elbow into his gut. "You wouldn't be relieved if I cut it loose. Take my word for it."

They spent the next two hours going from bar to pool hall to grubby diner. It wasn't until they tried a hole-in-the-wall called Clancy's that they made some progress.

The lights were dim, a sop to the early drinkers, who liked to forget that the sun was still up. A radio behind the bar scratched out country music that told a sad tale of cheating and empty bottles. Several of those early customers were already scattered at the bar or at tables, most of them doing their drinking steadily and solo.

The liquor was watered, and the glasses were dingy, but the whiskey came cheap and the atmosphere was conducive to getting seriously drunk.

Althea walked to the end of the bar and ordered a club soda she had no intention of sampling. Colt opted for the beer on tap. She lifted a brow.

"Had a tetanus shot recently?" She took out a twenty, but kept her finger on the corner of the bill as their drinks were served. "Wild Bill used to come in here pretty regular."

The bartender glanced down at the bill, and back at Althea. Bloodshot eyes and the map of broken capillaries over his broad face attested to the fact that he swallowed as much as he served.

Althea prompted him. "Wild Bill Billings."

"So?"

"He was a friend of mine."

"Looks like you lost a friend."

"I was in here with him a couple of times." Althea drew the twenty back a fraction. "Maybe you remember."

"My memory's real selective, but it don't have no trouble making a cop."

"Good. Then you probably figured out that Bill and I had an arrangement."

"I probably figured out the arrangement got him splattered all over the sidewalk."

"You'd have figured that one wrong. He wasn't snitching for me when he got hit, and me, I'm just the sentimental type. I want who did him, and I'm willing to pay." She shoved the bill forward. "A lot more than this."

"I don't know nothing about it." But the twenty disappeared into his pocket.

"But you might know people who know people who know something." She leaned forward, a smile in her eyes. "If you put the word out, I'd appreciate it."

He shrugged, and would have moved away, but she put a hand on his arm. "I think that twenty's worth a minute or two more. Bill had a girl named Jade. She's skipped. He had a couple others, didn't he?"

"A couple. He wasn't much of a pimp."

"Got a name?"

He took out a dirty rag and began to wipe the dirty bar. "A black-haired girl named Meena. She worked out of here sometimes. Haven't seen her lately."

"If you do, you give me a call." She took out a card and dropped it onto the bar. "You know anything about movies? Private movies, with young girls?"

He looked blank and shrugged, but not before Althea saw the flash of knowledge in his eyes. "I ain't got time for movies, and that's all you get for twenty."

"Thanks." Althea strolled out. "Give him a minute," she said under her breath to Colt. Then she peered through the dirty window. "Look at that. Funny that he'd get an urge to make a call just now."

Colt watched the bartender hurry to the wall phone, drop in a quarter. "I like your style, Lieutenant."

"Let's see how much you like it after a few hours in a cold car. We've got a stakeout tonight, Nightshade."

"I'm looking forward to it."

# Chapter 3

She was right about the cold. He didn't mind it so much, not with long johns and a sheepskin jacket to ward it off. But he did mind the dragging inactivity. He'd have sworn that Althea thrived on it.

She was settled comfortably in the passenger seat, working a crossword puzzle by the dim glow of the glove-compartment light. She worked methodically, patiently, endlessly, he thought, while he tried to stave off boredom with the B. B. King retrospective on the radio.

He thought of the evening they'd both missed at the Fletchers'. Hot food, blazing fire, warm brandy. It had even occurred to him that Althea might have defrosted a bit in unofficial surroundings. It might not have helped matters to think of her that way—the ice goddess melting—but it did something for his more casual fantasies.

In his current reality, she was all cop, and emotionally as distant from him as the moon. But in the daydream, assisted by the slow blues on the radio, she was all woman—seductive as the black silk he imagined her wearing, enticing as the crackling fire he pictured burning low in a stone hearth, soft as the white fur rug they lowered themselves to.

And her taste, once his mouth sampled hers, was honeyed whiskey. Drugging, sweet, potent. Her scent tangled up with her flavor in his senses until they were one and the same. An opiate a man could drown in.

The silk slipped away, inch by seductive inch, revealing the alabaster flesh beneath. Rose-petal smooth, flawless as glass, firm and soft as water. And when she reached for him, drew him in, her lips moved against his ear in whispered invitation.

"Want more coffee?"

"Huh?" He snapped back, swiveling his head around to stare at her in the shadowed car. She held a thermos out to him. "What?"

"Coffee?" Intrigued by the look on his face, she picked up his cup herself and filled it halfway. At first glance, she would have said there was temper in his eyes, ripe and ready to rip. But she knew that look, and knew it well. This was desire, equally ripe, equally ready. "Taking a side trip, Nightshade?"

"Yeah." He accepted the cup and drank deep, wishing it was whiskey. But his lips curved, his amusement with himself and the ridiculous situation easing the discomfort in his gut. "One hell of a trip."

"Well, try to keep up with our tour, will you?" She sipped from her own cup and offered him a share of her bag of candy. "There goes another one." Efficient, she set aside her cup and picked up her camera. She took two quick shots of the man entering the bar. He was only the second who had gone in during the past hour.

"They don't exactly do a thriving business down here, do they?"

"Most people like a little ambience with their liquor."

"Ferns and canned music?"

She set the camera aside again. "Clean glasses, for a start. I doubt we're going to see one of our moviemakers down here."

"Then why are we sitting in a cold car looking at a dive at eleven o'clock at night?"

"Because it's my job." She chose a single piece of candy, popped it into her mouth. "And because I'm waiting for something else."

It was the first he'd heard of it. "Want to clue me in?"

"No." She chose another piece and went back to her crossword puzzle.

"Okay, that tears it." He ripped the paper out of her hands. "You want to play games, Grayson? Let me tell you how I play. I get peeved when people hold out on me. I get especially peeved when I'm bored senseless while they're doing it. Then I get mean."

"Excuse me," she said, in a mild tone that was in direct contrast to the fire in her eyes. "I can hardly speak for the ball of terror in my throat."

"You want to be scared?" He moved fast, eerily so. She wouldn't have been able to evade him if she'd tried. So she submitted without any show of resistance when he grabbed her by the shoulders. "I figure I ought to be able to put the fear of God into you, Thea, and liven things up a bit for both of us."

"Back off. If you've finished your imitation of machismo, what I've been waiting for is about to walk into the bar."

"What?"

He turned his head, which presented Althea with the perfect opportunity to grab his thumb and twist it viciously. When he swore, she released him. "Meena. Wild Bill's other girl." Althea lifted her camera and took another shot. "I got her picture out of the files this afternoon. She's done time. Solicitation, running a confidence game, possession with intent to sell, disorderly behavior."

"A sweet girl, our Meena."

"*Your* Meena," Althea told him. "Since you play the big, bad type so well, you can go on in and charm Meena, get her out here so we can talk." Opening her purse, Althea took out an envelope with five crisp ten-dollar bills. "And if your charm fails, offer her fifty."

"You want me to go in and convince her I'm looking to party?"

"That's the ticket."

"Fine." He'd certainly done worse in his career than play the eager john in a seedy bar. But he shoved the envelope back into her lap. "I've got my own money."

Althea watched him cross the street, waiting until he'd disappeared inside. Then she leaned back and indulged herself for one moment by closing her eyes and letting out a long, long breath.

A dangerous man, Colt Nightshade, she thought. A deadly man. She hadn't felt simple anger when he lunged toward her and grabbed. She hadn't felt simple anything. What she'd experienced was complex, convoluted and confusing.

What she'd felt was arousal, gut-deep, red-hot, soul-searing arousal, mixed with a healthy dose of primal fear and teeth-baring fury.

It wasn't like her, she told herself as she took the time alone to gather her wits. Coming that close to losing control because a man pushed the wrong buttons—or the right ones—was uncharacteristic of her.

*She* pushed the buttons. That was Althea Grayson's number one hard-and-fast rule. And if Colt thought he could break that one, he was in for a big disappointment.

She'd worked too hard forming herself into what she was, laying out the stages of her life and following them. She'd come from chaos, and she'd beaten it back. Certainly it was necessary from time to time to change the pattern. She wasn't rigid. But nothing, absolutely nothing, jarred that pattern.

It was the case itself, she supposed. The child being held by strangers, almost certainly being abused.

Another pattern, she thought bitterly. All too familiar to her.

And the child that morning, she remembered. Helplessly trapped by the adults around her.

She shook that off, picked up the crumpled newspaper to fold it neatly and set it aside.

She was just tired, she told herself. The drug bust the week before had been vicious. And to tumble from that into this would have shaken anyone. What she needed was a vacation. She smiled to herself, imagining a warm white-sand beach, blue water, a tall spear of glistening hotel behind her. A big bed, room service, mud packs, and a private whirlpool.

And that was just what she was going to have when she capped this case and sent Colt Nightshade back to his cattle or his law practice or whatever the hell he called his profession.

Glancing toward the bar again, she was forced to nod in approval. Less than ten minutes had passed, and he was coming out, Meena in tow.

"Oh, a group thing?" Meena studied Althea through heavily kohled eyes. She pushed back her stiff black curls and smirked. "Well, now, honey, that's going to cost you extra."

"No problem." Gallantly Colt helped her into the back seat.

"I guess a guy like you can handle the two of us." She settled back, reeking of floral cologne.

"I don't think that'll be necessary." Althea took out her badge, flashed it.

Meena swore, shot Colt a look of intense dislike, then folded her arms. "Haven't you cops got anything better to do than roust us working girls?"

"We won't have to take you in, Meena, if you answer a few questions. Drive around a little, will you, Colt?" As he obliged, Althea turned in her seat. "Wild Bill was a friend of mine."

"Yeah, right."

"He did some favors for me. I did some for him."

"Yeah, I bet—" Meena broke off, narrowed her eyes. "You the cop he snitched for? The one he called classy." Meena relaxed a little. There was a pretty good chance she wouldn't be spending the night in lockup after all. "He said you were okay. Said you always slipped him a few without whining about it."

Althea noted Meena's greedy little smile and lifted a brow. "I'm touched. Maybe he should've said I paid when he had something worth buying. Do you know Jade?"

"Sure. She hasn't been around for a few weeks. Bill said she skipped town." Meena dug in her red vinyl purse and pulled out a cigarette. When Colt clicked on his lighter and offered the flame, she cupped her hand over his and slanted him a warm look under thickly blackened lashes. "Thanks, honey."

"How about this girl?" Colt took the snapshot of Elizabeth out of his pocket. After turning on the dome light, he offered it to Meena.

"No." She started to pass it back, then frowned. "I don't know. Maybe." While she considered, she blew out a stream of smoke, clouding the car. "Not on the stroll. Seems like maybe I saw her somewhere."

"With Bill?" Althea asked.

"Hell, no. Bill didn't deal in jailbait."

"Who does?"

Meena shifted her eyes to Colt. "Georgie Cool's got a few young ones in his stable. Nobody as fresh as this, though."

"Did Bill get you a gig, Meena? A movie gig?" Althea asked.

"Maybe he did."

"The answer's yes, or the answer's no." Althea took back the photo of Liz. "You waste my time, I don't waste my money."

"Well, hell, it don't bother me if some guy wants to take videos while I work. They paid extra for it."

"Have you got a name?"

Meena snorted in Althea's direction. "We didn't exchange business cards, sweetie."

"But you can give me a description. How many were involved. Where it went down."

"Probably." The sly look was back as Meena blew out smoke. "If I had some incentive."

"Your incentive's not to spend time in a cell with a two-hundred-pound Swede named Big Jane," Althea said mildly.

"You can't send me up. I'll scream entrapment."

"Scream all you want. With your record, the judge will just chuckle."

"Come on, Thea." Colt's drawl seemed to have thickened. "Give the lady a break. She's trying to cooperate. Aren't you, Meena?"

"Sure." Meena butted out her cigarette, licked her lips. "Sure I am."

"What she's trying to do is hose me." Althea realized she and Colt had picked up the good cop—bad cop routine without missing a beat. "And I want answers."

"She's giving them to us." He smiled at Meena in the rearview mirror. "Just take your time."

"There were three of them," Meena said, and set her cherry-red lips in a pout. "The guy running the camera, another guy sitting back in a corner. I couldn't see him. And the guy who was, like, performing with me, you know? The guy with the camera was bald. A black guy, really big—like a wrestler or something. I was there about an hour, and he never opened his mouth once."

Althea flipped open her notebook. "Did they call each other by name?"

"No." Meena thought it through, shook her head. "No. That's funny, isn't it? They didn't talk to each other at all, as I remember. The one I was working with was a little guy—except for certain vital parts." She chuckled and reached for another cigarette. "Now, *he* did some talking. Trash talk, get it? Like for the camera. Some guys like that. He was, I don't know…in his forties, maybe, skinny, had his hair pulled back in a ponytail that hit his shoulder blades. He wore this Lone Ranger mask.''

"I'm going to want you to work with a police artist," Althea told her.

"No way. No more cops."

"We don't have to do it at the station." Althea played her trump card. "If you give us a good enough description, one that helps us nail these film buffs, there's an extra hundred for you."

"Okay." Meena brightened. "Okay."

Althea tapped her pencil against her pad. "Where did you shoot?"

"Shoot? Oh, you mean the movie? Over on Second. Real nice place. It had one of them whirlpool tubs in the bathroom, and mirrors for walls." Meena leaned forward to brush her fingertips over Colt's shoulder. "It was…stimulating."

"The address?" Althea said.

"I don't know. One of those big condo buildings on Second. Top floor, too. Like the penthouse."

"I bet you'd recognize the building if we drove by it, wouldn't you, Meena?" Colt's tone was all friendly encouragement, as was the smile he shot her over his shoulder.

"Yeah, sure I would."

And she did. Minutes later she was pointing out the window. "That place, there. See the one up top, with the big windows and the balcony thing? It was in there. Real class joint. White carpet. This really sexy bedroom, with red curtains and a big round bed. There was gold faucets in the bathroom, shaped like swans. Jeez. I woulda loved to go back."

"You only went once?" Colt asked her.

"Yeah. They told Billy I wasn't the right type." With a sound of disgust, she reached for yet another cigarette. "Get this. I was too old. I just had my twenty-second birthday, and those creeps tell Billy I'm too old. It really ticked me— Oh, yeah…'' Suddenly inspired, she rapped Colt on the shoulder. "The kid. The one in the picture? That's where I saw her. I was leaving, but I went back 'cause I left

my smokes. She was sitting in the kitchen. I didn't recognize her in
the picture right off, 'cause she was all made-up when I saw her.''

"Did she say anything to you?" Colt asked, struggling to keep his
voice quiet and even. "Do anything?"

"No, just sat there. She looked stoned to me."

Because she sensed he needed something, Althea slid her hand
across the seat and covered Colt's. His was rigid. She was surprised,
but didn't protest, when he turned his hand over and gripped hers,
palm to palm.

"I'm going to want to talk to you again." With her free hand,
Althea reached into her purse for enough money to ensure Meena's
continued cooperation. "I need a number where I can reach you."

"No sweat." Meena rattled it off while she counted her money.
"I guess Billy had it right. You're square. Hey, maybe you could
drop me at the Tick Tock. I think I'll go in and drink one for Wild
Bill.''


"We can't do anything without a warrant." Althea was repeating
the statement for the third time as they stepped out of the elevator
on the top floor of the building Meena had pointed out.

"You don't need a warrant to knock on a door."

"Right." With a sigh, Althea slipped a hand inside her jacket in
an automatic check of her weapon. "And they're going to invite us
in for coffee. If you give me a couple of hours—"

When he whirled, her jaw dropped. After the cool, matter-of-fact
manner in which he'd handled everything up to this point, the raw
fury on his face was staggering. "Get this, Lieutenant—I'm not waiting another two *minutes* to see if Liz is in there. And if she is, if
anybody is, I'm not going to need a damn warrant."

"Look, Colt, I understand—"

"You don't understand diddley."

She opened her mouth, then shut it again, shocked that she'd been
about to shout that she did understand. Oh, yes, she understood very,
very well. "We'll knock," she said tightly, and strode to the door of
the penthouse and did so.

"Maybe they're hard of hearing." Colt used his fist to hammer.

When the summons went unanswered, he moved so fast Althea didn't have time to swear. He'd already kicked the door in.

"Good, real good, Nightshade. Subtle as a brick."

"Guess I slipped." He pulled his gun out of his boot. "And look at this, the door's open."

"Don't—" But he was already inside. Cursing Boyd and all his boyhood friends, Althea drew her weapon and went in the door behind him, instinctively covering his back. She didn't need the light Colt turned on to see that the room was empty. It had a deserted feel. There was nothing left but the carpet, and the drapes at the windows.

"Split," Colt muttered to himself as he moved quickly from room to room. "The bastards split."

Satisfied she wouldn't need it, Althea replaced her gun. "I guess we know who our friendly bartender called this afternoon. We'll see what we can get from the rental contract, the neighbors..." Yet she thought if their quarry had been this slick so far, what they got would be close to useless.

She stepped into the bathroom. It was as Meena had described, the big whirlpool tub, the swan-shaped faucets—brass, not gold—the all-around mirrors. "You've just jeopardized the integrity of a possible crime scene, Nightshade. I hope you're satisfied."

"She could have been here," he said from behind her.

She looked over, saw their reflections trapped in the mirrored tiles. It was the expression on his face, one she hadn't expected to see there, that softened her. "We're going to find her, Colt," she said quietly. "We're going to see that she gets back home."

"Sure." He wanted to break something, anything. It took every ounce of his will not to smash his fist through the mirrors. "Every day they've got her is a day she's going to have to live with, forever." Bending, he slipped his gun back in his boot. "God, Thea, she's just a child."

"Children are tougher than most people think. They close things off when they have to. And it's going to be easier because she has family who loves her."

"Easier than what?"

Than having no one but yourself, she thought. "Just easier." She couldn't help it. She reached out, laid a hand on his cheek. "Don't let it eat at you, Colt. You'll mess up if you do."

"Yeah." He drew it back, that dangerous emotion that led to dangerous mistakes. But when she started to drop her hand and move past him, Colt snagged her wrist. "You know something?" Maybe it was only because he needed contact, but he tugged her an inch closer. "For a minute there, you were almost human."

"Really?" Their bodies were almost brushing. A bad move, she thought. But it would be cowardly to pull back. "What am I usually?"

"Perfect." He lifted his free hand—because he'd wanted to almost from the first moment he'd seen her—and tangled his fingers in her hair. "It's scary," he said. "It's the whole package—that face, the hair, the body, the mind. A man doesn't know whether to bay at the moon or whimper at your feet."

She had to tilt her head back to keep her eyes level with his. If her heart was beating a bit faster, she could ignore it. It had happened before. If she felt the little pull of curiosity, even of lust, it wasn't the first time, and it could be controlled. But what was difficult, very difficult, to channel, was the unexpected clouding of her senses. That would have to be fought.

"You don't strike me as the type to do either," she said, and smiled, a cool, tight-lipped smirk that had most men backing off babbling.

Colt wasn't most men.

"I never have been. Why don't we try something else?" He said it slowly, then moved like lightning to close his mouth over hers.

If she had protested, if she had struggled—if there had been even a token pulling back—he would have released her and counted his losses. Maybe.

But she didn't. That surprised them both.

She could have, should have. She would think later. She could have stopped him cold with any number of defensive or offensive moves. She would think later. But there was such raw heat in his lips, such steely strength in his arms, such whirling pleasure in her own body.

Oh, yes, she would think later. Much later.

It was exactly as he'd imagined it. And he'd imagined it a lot. That tart, flamboyant flavor she carried on her lips was the twin of the one he'd sampled in his mind. It was as addicting as any opiate. When she opened for him, he dived deeper and took more.

She was as small, as slim, as supple, as any man could wish. And as strong. Her arms were locked hard around him, and her fingers were clutching at his hair. The low, deep sound of approval that vibrated in her throat had his blood racing like a fast-moving river.

Murmuring her name, he spun her around, ramming her against the mirrors, covering her body with his. His hands ran over her in a greedy sprint to take and touch and possess. Then his fingers were jerking at the buttons on her blouse in a desperate need to push aside the first barrier.

He wanted her now. No, no, he needed her now, he realized. The way a man needed sleep after a vicious day of hard labor, the way he needed to eat after a long, long fast.

He tore his mouth from hers to press it against her throat, reveling in the sumptuous taste of flesh.

Half-delirious, she arched back, moaning at the thrill of his hungry mouth on her heated skin. Without the wall for support, she knew, she would already have sunk to the floor. And it was there, just there, that he would take her, that they would take each other. On the cool, hard tile, with dozens of mirrors tossing back reflections of their desperate bodies.

Here and now.

And like a thief sneaking into a darkened house, an image of Meena, and what had gone on in that apartment, crept into her mind.

What was she doing? Good Lord, what was she *doing?* she raged at herself as she levered herself away.

She was a cop, and she had been about to indulge in some wild bout of mindless sex in the middle of a crime scene.

"Stop!" Her voice was harsh with arousal and self-disgust. "I mean it, Colt. Stop. Now."

"What?" Like a diver surfacing from fathoms-deep, he shook his head, nearly swayed. Good Lord, his knees were weak. To compensate, he braced a hand on the wall as he stared down at her. He'd loosened her hair, and it spilled rich and red over her shoulders. Her eyes were more gold than brown now, huge, and seductively misted. Her mouth was full, reddened by the pressure and demand of his, and her skin was flushed a pale, lovely rose.

"You're beautiful. Impossibly beautiful." Gently he skimmed a finger down her throat. "Like some exotic flower behind glass. A man just has to break that glass and take it."

"No." She grabbed his hand to keep from losing her mind again. "This is insane, completely insane."

"Yeah." He couldn't have agreed more. "And it felt great."

"This is an investigation, Nightshade. And we're standing in what is very possibly the scene of a major crime."

He smiled and lifted her hand to nip at her fingers. Just because this was a dead end for their investigation didn't mean all activity had to come to a halt. "So, let's go someplace else."

"We are going someplace else." She shoved him away, and quickly, competently redid her blouse. "Separately." She wasn't steady, she realized. Damn him, damn her, she wasn't steady.

He felt that the safest place for his hands at the moment was his pockets, so he shoved them in. She was right, one hundred percent right, and that was the worst of it.

"You want to pretend this didn't happen?"

"I don't pretend anything." Settling on dignity, she pushed her tumbled hair back, smoothed down her rumpled jacket. "It happened, now it's done."

"Not by a long shot, Lieutenant. We're both grown-ups, and though I can only speak for myself, that kind of connection just doesn't happen every day."

"You're right." She inclined her head. "You can only speak for yourself." She made it back to the living room before he grabbed her arm and spun her around to face him.

"You want me to press the point now?" His voice was quiet, deadly quiet. "Or do you want to be straight with me?"

"All right, fine." She could be honest, because lies wouldn't work. "If I were interested in a quick, hot affair, I'd certainly give you a call. As it happens, I have other priorities at the moment."

"You've got a list, right?"

She had to take a moment to get her temper back under wraps.

"Do you think that insults me?" she asked sweetly. "I happen to prefer organizing my life."

"Compartmentalizing."

She arched a brow. "Whatever. For better or worse, we have a professional relationship. I want that girl found, Colt, every bit as much as you do. I want her back with her family, eating hamburgers and worrying over her latest math test. And I want to bring down the bastards who have her. More than you could possibly understand."

"Then why don't you help me understand?"

"I'm a cop," she told him. "That's enough."

"No, it's not." There had been passion in her face, the same kind of passion he'd felt when he had her in his arms. Fierce and ragged and at the edge of control. "Not for you, or for me, either."

He let out a deep breath and rubbed the base of his neck, where most of his tension had lodged. They were both tired, he realized, tired and strung out. It wasn't the time and it wasn't the place to delve into personal reasons. He'd need to find some objectivity if he wanted to figure out Althea Grayson.

"Look, I'd apologize for back there if I was out of line. But we both know I wasn't. I'm here to get Liz back, and nothing's going to stop me. And after a taste of you, Thea, I'm going to be just as determined to have more."

"I'm not the soup du jour, Nightshade," she said wearily. "You'll only get what I give."

His grin flashed, quick and easy. "That's just the way I want it. Come on, I'll drive you home."

Saying nothing, Althea stared after him. She had the uncomfortable feeling that they hadn't resolved matters precisely as she'd wanted.

# Chapter 4

Armed with a second cup of coffee, Colt stood at the edge of a whirlwind. It was obvious to him that getting three kids out of the house and onto a school bus was an event of major proportions. He could only wonder how a trio of adults could handle the orchestration on a daily basis and remain sane.

"I don't like this cereal," Bryant complained. He lifted a spoonful and, scowling, let the soggy mess plop back into his bowl. "It tastes like wet trees."

"You picked it out, because it had a whistle inside," Cilla reminded him as she slapped peanut-butter-and-jelly sandwiches together. "You eat it."

"Put a banana on it," Boyd suggested while he struggled to bundle Allison's pale, flyaway hair into something that might have passed for a braid.

"Ouch! Daddy, you're pulling!"

"Sorry. What's the capital of Nebraska?"

"Lincoln," his daughter said with a sigh. "I hate geography tests." While she pouted over it, she practiced her pliés for ballet class. "How come I have to know the stupid states and their stupid capitals, anyway?"

"Because knowledge is sacred." With his tongue caught in his teeth, Boyd fought to band the wispy braid. "And once you learn something, you never really forget it."

"Well, I can't remember the capital of Virginia."

"It's, ah..." As the sacred knowledge escaped him, Boyd swore under his breath. What the hell did he care? He lived in Colorado. One of the major problems with having kids, as he saw it, was that the parents were forced to go back to school. "It'll come to you."

"Mom, Bry's feeding Bongo his cereal." Allison sent her brother a smug, smarmy smile of the kind that only a sister can achieve.

Cilla turned in time to see her son thrusting his spoon toward their dog's eager mouth. "Bryant Fletcher, you're going to be wearing that cereal in a minute."

"But look, Mom, even Bongo won't eat it. It's crap."

"Don't say 'crap,'" Cilla told him wearily. But she noted that the big, scruffy dog, who regularly drank out of toilet bowls, had turned up his nose after one sample of soggy Rocket Crunchies. "Eat the banana, and get your coat."

"Mom!" Keenan, the youngest, scrambled into the room. He was shoeless and sockless, and was holding one grubby high-top sneaker in his hand. "I can't find my other shoe. It's not anywhere. Somebody musta stole it."

"Call a cop," Cilla muttered as she dumped the last peanut-butter-and-jelly sandwich into a lunch box.

"I'll find it, *señora*." Maria wiped her hands on her apron.

"Bless you."

"Bad guys took it, Maria," Keenan told her, his voice low and serious. "They came in the middle of the night and swiped it. Daddy'll go out and lock them up."

"Of course he will." Equally sober, Maria took his hand to lead him toward the stairs. "Now we go look for clues, *sí?*"

"Umbrellas." Cilla turned from the counter, running a hand through her short crop of brown hair. "It's raining. Do we have umbrellas?"

"We used to have umbrellas." His hairstyling duties completed, Boyd poured himself another cup of coffee. "Somebody stole them. Probably the same gang who stole Keenan's shoe and Bryant's spelling homework. I've already put a task force on it."

"Big help you are." Cilla went to the kitchen doorway. "Maria! Umbrellas!" She turned back, tripping over the dog, swore, then grabbed three lunch boxes. "Coats," she ordered. "You've got five minutes to make the bus."

There was a mad scramble, impeded by Bongo, who decided this was the perfect time to jump on everyone in sight.

"He hates goodbyes," Boyd told Colt as he deftly collared the mutt.

"The shoe was in the closet," Maria announced as she hustled Keenan into the kitchen.

"The thieves must have hidden it there. It's too diabolical." She offered him his lunch box. "Kiss."

Keenan grinned and planted a loud smack on her lips. "I get to be the milk monitor all week."

"It's a tough job, but I know you're up to it. Bry, the banana peel goes in the trash." As she handed him his lunch box, she hooked an arm around his throat, making him giggle as she kissed him goodbye. "Allison, the capital of Virginia's Richmond. I think."

"Okay."

After everyone exchanged kisses—including, Colt noted with some amusement, Bongo—Cilla held up one hand.

"Anyone leaving their umbrella at school will be immediately executed. Scram."

They all bolted. The door slammed. Cilla closed her eyes. "Ah, another quiet morning at the Fletchers'. Colt what can I offer you? Bacon, eggs? Whiskey?"

"I'll take the first two. Reserve the last." Grinning, he took the chair Bryant had vacated. "You put on this show everyday?"

"With matinees on Saturdays." She ruffled her hair again, checked the clock on the stove. "I'd like to hang around with you guys, but I've got to get ready for work. I've got a meeting in an hour. If you find yourself at loose ends, Colt, stop by the radio station. I'll show you around."

"I might just do that."

"Maria, do you need me to pick up anything?"

"No, *señora*." She already had the bacon sizzling. "*Gracias.*"

"I should be home by six." Cilla paused by the table to run a hand over her husband's shoulder. "I hear there's a big poker game here tonight."

"That's the rumor." Boyd tugged his wife down to him, and Colt saw their lips curve before they met. "You taste pretty good, O'Roarke."

"Strawberry jelly. Catch you later, Slick." She gave him one last, lingering kiss before she left him.

Colt listened to her race up the stairs. "You hit the bull's-eye, didn't you, Fletch?"

"Hmm?"

"Terrific wife, great kids. And the first time out."

"Looks that way. I guess I knew Cilla was it for me almost from the first." Remembering made him smile. "Took a little while to convince her she couldn't live without me, though."

It was tough not to envy that particular smile, Colt mused. "You and Althea, you were partners when you met Cilla, right?"

"Yeah. All three of us were working nights in those days. Thea was the first woman I'd ever partnered with. Turned out to be the best cop I'd ever partnered with, as well."

"I have to ask—you don't have to answer, but I have to ask." And how best to pose the question? Colt wondered as he picked up a fork and tapped it on the edge of the table. "You and Thea...before Cilla, there was nothing...personal?"

"There's plenty personal when you're partners, working together, sometimes around the clock." He picked up his coffee, his smile easy. "But there was nothing romantic, if that's what you're dancing around."

"It's none of my business." Colt shrugged, annoyed by just how much Boyd's answer relieved him. "I was curious."

"Curious why I didn't try to move in on a woman with her looks? Her brains? Her—what's the best word for it?" Amused by Colt's obvious discomfort, he chuckled as Maria silently served their breakfast. "Thanks, Maria. We'll call it style, for lack of something better. It's simple, Colt. I'm not going to say I didn't think about it. Could be Thea gave it a couple moments of her time, too. But we clicked as partners, we clicked as friends, and it just didn't take us down any of those other alleys." He scooped up some eggs, arched a brow. "You thinking about it?"

Colt moved his shoulders again, toyed with his bacon. "I can't say we've clicked as partners—or as friends, for that matter. But I figure we've already turned down one of those other alleys."

Boyd didn't pretend to be surprised. Anyone who said oil and water didn't mix just hadn't stirred them up enough. "There are some women who get under your skin, some that get into your head. And some who do both."

"Yeah. So what's the story on her?"

"She's a good cop, a person you can trust. Like anybody else, she's got some baggage, but she carries it well. If you want to know personal stuff, you'll have to ask her." He lifted his cup. "And she'd get the same answer from me about you."

"Has she asked?"

"Nope." Boyd sipped to hide his grin. "Now, why don't you tell me your progress in finding Liz?"

"We got a tip on the place on Second Avenue, but they'd already split." It still frustrated him. The whole bloody business frustrated him. "Figured I'd talk to the apartment manager, the neighbors. There's a witness who might be able to ID one or more of our movie moguls."

"That's a good start. Anything I can do to help?"

"I'll let you know. They've already had her a couple of weeks, Fletch. I'm going to get her back." He lifted his gaze, and the quiet rage in it left no room for doubt. "What worries me is what shape she'll be in when I do."

"Take it one step at a time."

"That sounds like the lieutenant." Colt preferred to take leaps, rather than steps. "I can't hook up with her until later this afternoon. She's in court or something."

"In court?" Boyd frowned, then nodded. "Right. The Marsten trial. Armed robbery, assault. She made a good collar on that one. Do you want me to send a uniform with you to Second Avenue?"

"No. I'd just as soon handle it myself."

It was good to be back on his own, Colt decided. Working alone meant you didn't have to worry about stepping on your partner's toes or debating strategy. And as far as Althea was concerned, it meant he didn't have to work overtime trying to keep himself from thinking of her as a woman.

First he rousted the apartment manager, Nieman, a short, balding man who obviously thought his position required him to wear a three-piece suit, a brutally knotted tie, and an ocean of pine-scented aftershave.

"I've already given my statement to the other officer," he informed Colt through the two-inch crack provided by the security chain on his door.

"Now you'll have to give it to me." Colt saw no need to disabuse Nieman of the notion that he was with the police. "Do you want me to shout my questions from out in the hall, Mr. Nieman?"

"No." Nieman shot the chain back, clearly annoyed. "Haven't I already had enough trouble? I was hardly out of my bed this morning before you people were banging on my door. Now the phone has been ringing off the hook with tenants calling, demanding to know what the police are doing sealing off the penthouse. The resulting publicity will take weeks for me to defuse."

"You got a real tough job, Mr. Nieman." Colt scanned the apartment as he entered. It wasn't as plush or as large as the empty penthouse, but it would do in a pinch. Nieman had furnished it in fussy French rococo. Colt knew his mother would have adored it.

"You can't imagine it." Resigned, Nieman gestured toward an ornately carved chair. "Tenants are such children, really. They need someone to guide them, someone to slap their hands when they break the rules. I've been a resident apartment manager for ten years, three in this building, and the stories I could tell..."

Because Colt was afraid he would do just that, he cut Nieman off. "Why don't you tell me about the penthouse tenants?"

"There's very little I can tell." Nieman plucked at the knees of his slacks before sitting. He crossed his legs at the ankles and revealed patterned argyle socks. "As I explained to the other detective, I never actually met them. They were only here four months."

"Don't you show the apartment to tenants, Mr. Nieman? Take their applications?"

"As a rule, certainly. In this particular case, the tenant sent references and a certified check for first and last month's rent via the mail.''

"Is it usual for you to rent an apartment that way?"

"Not usual, no…" After clearing his throat, Nieman fiddled with the knot of his tie. "The letter was followed up with a phone call. Mr. Davis—the tenant—explained that he was a friend of Mr. and Mrs. Ellison. They had the penthouse before, for three years. Lovely couple, elegant taste. They moved to Boston. As he'd been acquainted with them, he had no need to view the apartment. He claimed to have attended several dinner parties and other affairs in the penthouse. He was quite anxious to have it, you see, and as his references were impeccable…''

"You checked them out?"

"Of course." Lips pursed, Nieman drew himself up. "I take my responsibilities seriously."

"What did this Davis do for a living?"

"He's an engineer with a local firm. When I contacted the firm, they had nothing but the highest regard for him."

"What firm?"

"I still have the file out." Nieman reached to the coffee table for a slim folder. "Foxx Engineering," he began, then recited the address and phone number. "Naturally, I contacted his landlord, as well. We apartment managers have a code of ethics. I was assured that Mr. Davis was an ideal tenant, quiet, responsible, tidy, and that his rent was always timely. This proved to be the case."

"But you never actually saw Mr. Davis?"

"This is a large building. There are several tenants I don't see. It's the troublemakers you meet regularly, and Mr. Davis was never any trouble."

Never any trouble, Colt thought grimly as he completed the slow process of door-to-door. He carried with him copies of the lease, the references, and Davis's letter. It was past noon, and he'd already interviewed most of the tenants who'd answered his knock. Only three of them claimed to have seen the mysterious Mr. Davis. Colt now had three markedly different descriptions to add to his file.

The police seal on the penthouse door had barred his entrance. He could have picked the lock and cut the tape, but he'd doubted he'd find anything worthwhile.

So he'd started at the top and was working his way down. He was currently canvassing the third floor, with a vicious case of frustration and the beginnings of a headache.

He knocked at 302 and felt himself being sized up through the peephole. The chain rattled, the bolt turned. Now he was being sized up, face-to-face, by an old woman with a wild mop of hair dyed an improbable orange. She had bright blue eyes that sprayed into dozens of wrinkles as she squinted to peer at him. Her Denver Broncos sweatshirt was the size of a tent, covering what Colt judged to be two hundred pounds of pure bulk. She had two chins and was working on a third.

"You're too good-looking to be selling something I don't want."

"No, ma'am." If Colt had had a hat, he'd have tipped it. "I'm not selling anything at all. The police are conducting an investigation. I'd like to ask you a few questions regarding some of your neighbors in the building."

"Are you a cop? You'd have a badge if you were."

It looked as though she were a great deal sharper than Nieman. "No, ma'am, I'm not a cop. I'm working privately."

"A detective?" The blue eyes brightened like light bulbs. "Like Sam Spade? I swear, that Humphrey Bogart was the sexiest man ever born. If I'd have been Mary Astor, I wouldn't have thought twice about some dumb bird when I could have had him."

"No, ma'am." It took Colt a moment, but he finally caught on to her reference to *The Maltese Falcon*. "I kind of went for Lauren Bacall, myself. They sure did set things humming in *The Big Sleep*."

Pleased, she let out a loud, lusty laugh. "Damned if they didn't. Well, come on in. No use standing here in the doorway."

Colt entered and immediately had to start dodging furniture and cats. The apartment was packed with both. Tables, chairs, lamps, some of them superior antiques, others yard-sale rejects, were set helter-skelter throughout the wide living room. Half a dozen cats of all descriptions were curled, draped and stretched out with equal abandon.

"I collect," she told him, then plopped herself down on a Louis

XV love seat. Her girth took up three-quarters of the cushions, so Colt wisely chose a ratty armchair with a faded pattern of colonial soldiers fighting redcoats. "I'm Esther Mavis."

"Colt Nightshade." Colt took it philosophically when a lean gray cat sprang into his lap and another leapt onto a wing of the chair to sniff at his hair.

"Well, just what are we investigating, Mr. Nightshade?"

"We're doing a check on the tenant who occupied the penthouse."

"The one who just moved out?" She scratched one of her chins. "Saw a bunch of burly men carrying stuff out to a van yesterday."

So had several other people, Colt thought. No one had bothered to note whether the van had carried the name of a moving company.

"Did you notice what kind of van, Mrs. Mavis?"

"Miss," she told him. "A big one. They didn't act like any movers I ever saw."

"Oh?"

"They worked fast. Not like people who get paid by the hour. You know. Moved out some good pieces, too." Her bright eyes scanned her living room. "I like furniture. There was this Belker table I'd have liked to get my hands on. Don't know where I'd put it, but I always find room."

"Could you describe any of the movers?"

"Don't notice men unless there's something special about them." She winked slyly.

"How about Mr. Davis? Did you ever see him?"

"Can't say for sure. I don't know most of the people in the building by name. Me and my cats keep to ourselves. What did he do?"

"We're looking into it."

"Playing it close to the vest, huh? Well, Bogey would've done the same. So, he's moved out?"

"It looks that way."

"I guess I won't be able to give him his package, then."

"Package?"

"Just came yesterday. Messenger brought it, dropped it here by mistake. Davis, Mavis..." She shook her head. "People don't pay enough attention to details these days."

"I know what you mean." Colt cautiously plucked a cat from his shoulder. "What sort of a package, Miss Mavis?"

"A package package." With a few grunts and whistles, she hauled herself to her feet. "Put it back in the bedroom. Meant to take it up to him today." She moved with a kind of tanklike grace through the narrow passages between the furniture and came back with a sealed, padded bag.

"Ma'am, I'd like to take that with me. If you have a problem with that, you can call Captain Boyd Fletcher, Denver PD."

"No skin off my nose." She handed Colt the package. "Maybe when you've cracked the case, you'll come let me know what's what."

"I'll just do that." On impulse, he took out the photo of Liz. "Have you seen this girl?"

Miss Mavis looked at it, frowned over it, then shook her head. "No, not that I recollect. Is she in trouble?"

"Yes, ma'am."

"Does it have something to do with upstairs?"

"I think so."

She handed the photo back. "She's a pretty little thing. I hope you find her real soon."

"So do I."

It wasn't his usual operating procedure. Colt couldn't have said why he made the exception, why he felt he had to. Instead of opening the package and dealing with its contents immediately, he left it sealed and drove to the courthouse.

He was just in time to hear the defense's cross of Althea. She was dressed in a rust-colored suit that should have been dull. Instead, the effect was subtly powerful, with her vibrant hair twisted up off her neck and a single strand of pearls at her throat.

Colt took a seat at the back of the courtroom and watched as she competently, patiently and devastatingly ripped the defense to shreds. She never raised her voice, never stumbled over words. Anyone looking or listening, including the jury, would have judged her a cool, detached professional.

And so she was, Colt mused as he stretched out his legs and

waited. Certainly no one watching her now would imagine her flaming like a rocket in a man's arms. His arms.

No one would picture this tidy, controlled woman arching and straining as a man's hands—his hands—raced over her.

But he was damned if he could forget it.

And studying her now, when she was unaware of him and completely focused on the job at hand, he began to notice other things, little things.

She was tired. He could see it in her eyes. Now and again there was the faintest whisper of impatience in her voice as she was called on to repeat herself. She shifted, crossing her legs. It was a smooth movement, economical, as always. But he sensed something else beneath it. Not nerves, he realized. Restlessness. She wanted this over with.

When the cross was complete, the judge called for a fifteen-minute recess. She winced as the gavel struck. It was just a flicker of a movement across her face, but he caught it.

Jack Holmsby caught her arm before she could move by him. "Nice job, Thea."

"Thanks. You shouldn't have any trouble nailing him."

"I'm not worried about it." He shifted, just enough to block her path. "Listen, I'm sorry things didn't work out the other night. Why don't we give it another shot? Say, dinner tomorrow night, just you and me?"

She waited a beat, not so much amazed by his gall as fatigued by it. "Jack, do the words *no way in hell* have any meaning for you?"

He only laughed and gave her arm an intimate little squeeze. For one wild moment, she considered decking him and taking the rap for assault.

"Come on, Althea. I'd like a chance to make it up to you."

"Jack, we both know you'd like a chance to make me. And it isn't going to happen. Now let go of my arm while we're both on the same side of the law."

"There's no need to be—"

"Lieutenant?" Colt drawled out the word. He let his gaze sweep over Holmsby. "Got a minute?"

"Nightshade." It annoyed the hell out of her that he'd witnessed the little tussle. "Excuse me, Jack. I've got work to do."

She strode out of the courtroom, leaving Colt to follow. "If you've got something that's worth my time, spill it," she ordered. "I'm not real pleased with lawyers at the moment."

"Darling, I don't have any briefs with me—except the ones I'm wearing."

"You're a riot, Nightshade."

"You look like a lady who could use a laugh." He took her arm, and felt his own temper peak when she stiffened. Battling it down, he steered her toward the doors. "My car's out front. Why don't we take a ride while we catch up?"

"Fine. I walked over from the precinct. You can take me back."

"Right." He found another ticket on his windshield. Not surprising, since he'd parked in a restricted zone. He pocketed it, and climbed in. "Sorry I interrupted your mating ritual."

"Kiss my butt." She snapped her seat belt into place.

"Lieutenant, I've been dreaming of doing just that." Reaching over, he popped open the glove compartment. This time she didn't stiffen at the contact, only seemed to withdraw. "Here."

"What?" She glanced down at the bottle of aspirin.

"For your headache."

"I'm fine." It wasn't exactly a lie, she thought. What she had couldn't be termed a mere headache. It was more like a freight train highballing behind her eyes.

"I hate a martyr."

"Leave me alone." She closed her eyes and effectively cut him off.

She was far from fine. She hadn't slept. Over the years, she'd become accustomed to rolling on two or three hours a night. But last night she hadn't slept at all, and she was too proud to lay the blame where it belonged. Right at Colt's door.

She'd thought of him. And she'd berated herself. She'd run over the impossible scene in the penthouse, and she'd ached. Then she'd berated herself again. She'd tried a hot bath, a boring book, yoga, warm brandy. Nothing had done the trick.

So she'd tossed and turned, and eventually she'd crawled out of bed to roam restlessly through her apartment. And she'd watched the sun come up.

Since dawn, she'd worked. It was now slightly past one, and she'd been on the job for nearly eight hours without a break. And what made it worse, what made it next to intolerable, was that she could very well be stuck with Colt for another eight.

She opened her eyes again when he stopped with a jerk of brakes. They were parked in front of a convenience store.

"I need something," he muttered, and slammed out.

Fine, terrific, she thought, and shut her eyes again. Don't bother to ask if maybe *I* need something. Like a chain saw to slice off my head, for instance.

She heard him coming back. Odd, she mused, that she recognized the sound of his stride, the click of his boot heels, after so short a time. In defense, or simply out of obstinacy, she kept her eyes shut.

"Here." He pushed something against her hand. "Tea," he told her when she opened her eyes to stare down at the paper cup. "To wash down the aspirin." He popped the top on the bottle himself and shook out the medication. "Now take the damn pills, Althea. And eat this. You probably haven't eaten anything all day, unless it's chocolate bits or candied nuts. I've never seen a woman pick her way through a pound bag of candy the way you do."

"Sugar's loaded with energy." But she took the pills, and the tea. The package of cheese and crackers earned a frown. "Didn't they have any cupcakes?"

"You need protein."

"There's probably protein in cupcakes." The tea was too strong, and quite bitter, but it helped nonetheless. "Thanks." She sipped again, then broke down and opened the package of crackers. It was important to remember that she was responsible for her own actions, her own reactions and her own emotions. If she hadn't slept, it was her own problem. "The lab boys should have finished at the penthouse by now."

"They have. I've been there."

She muttered over a mouthful, "I'd rather you didn't go off on your own."

"I can't please everybody, so I please myself. I talked to the little weasel who manages the place. He never set eyes on the top-floor tenant.''

While Althea chewed her way through the impromptu meal, he filled her in.

''I knew about Davis,'' she told him when he finished. ''I got Nieman out of bed this morning. Already called the references. Phone disconnect on both. There is no Foxx Engineering at that address, or at any other address in Denver. Same for the apartment Davis used as a reference. Mr. and Mrs. Ellison, the former tenants, have never heard of him.''

''You've been busy.'' Watching her, he tapped a finger on the steering wheel. ''What was that you meant about not going off on your own?''

She smiled a little. The headache was backing off. ''I carry a badge,'' she said, deadpan. ''You don't.''

''Your badge didn't get you into Miss Mavis's apartment.''

''Should it have?''

''I think so.'' Darkly pleased to be one up on her, Colt reached into the back and showed Althea the package. ''Messenger delivered it to the cat lady by mistake.''

''Cat lady?''

''You had to be there. Uh-uh.'' He snatched it out of reach as she made a move toward it. ''My take, darling. I'm willing to share.''

Her temper spiked, then leveled off when she noticed that the package was still intact. ''It's still sealed.''

''Seemed fair,'' he said, meeting her eyes. ''I figured we should open it together.''

''Looks like you figured right this time. Let's have a look.''

Colt reached down and drew a knife out of his boot. As he slit open the package, Althea narrowed her eyes.

''I don't think that toy's under the legal limit, champ.''

''Nope,'' he said easily, and slid the knife back into his boot. Reaching into the package, he pulled out a videotape and a single sheet of paper.

Final edit. Okay for dupes? Heavy snows expected by weekend. Supplies good. Next drop send extra tapes and beer. Roads may be closed.

Althea held the sheet by a corner, then dug a plastic bag out of her purse. "We'll have it checked for prints. We could get lucky."

"It might tell us who. It won't tell us where." Colt slid the tape back into the bag. "Want to go to the movies?"

"Yeah." Althea set the bag on her lap, tapped it. "But I think this one calls for a private screening. I've got a VCR at home."

She also had a comfortable couch crowded with cushy pillows. Gleaming hardwood floors were accented by Navaho rugs. The art deco prints on the walls should have been at odds with the southwestern touches, but they weren't. Neither were the homey huddle of lush green plants on the curvy iron tea cart, the two goldfish swimming in a tube-shaped aquarium, or the footstool fashioned to resemble a squat, grinning gnome.

"Interesting place" was the best Colt could do.

"It does the job." She walked to a chrome-and-glass entertainment center, stepping out of her shoes on the way.

Colt decided that single gesture told him more about Althea Grayson than a dozen in-depth reports would have.

With her usual efficiency, she popped in the tape and flicked both the VCR and TV on.

There was no need to fast-forward past the FBI warning, because there wasn't one. After a five-second lag, the tape faded from gray.

And the show began.

Even for a man with Colt's experience, it was a surprise. He tucked his hands in his pockets and rocked back on his heels. It was foolish, he supposed, seeing as they were both adults, both professionals, but he felt an undeniable tug of embarrassment.

"I, ah, guess they don't believe in whetting the audience's appetite."

Althea tilted her head, studying the screen with a clinical detachment. It wasn't lovemaking. It wasn't even sex, according to her definition. It was straight porn, more pathetic than titillating.

"I've seen hotter stuff at bachelor parties."

Colt took his eyes from the screen long enough to arch a brow at her. "Oh, really?"

"Tape's surprisingly good quality. And the camera work, if you can call it that, seems pretty professional." She listened to the moans. "Sound, too." She nodded as the camera pulled back for a long shot. "Not the penthouse."

"Must be the place in the mountains. High-class rustic, from the paneling. Bed looks like a Chippendale."

"How do you know?"

"My mother's big on antiques. Look at the lamp by the bed. It's Tiffany, or a damn fine imitation. Ah, the plot thickens...."

They both watched as another woman walked into the frame. A few lines of dialogue indicated that she had come upon her lover and her best friend. The confrontation turned violent.

"I don't think that's fake blood." Althea hissed through her teeth as the first woman took a hard blow to the face. "And I don't think she was expecting that punch."

Colt swore softly as the rest of the scene unfolded. The mixture of sex and violence—violence that was focused on the women—made an ugly picture. He had to clench his fists to keep himself from slamming the television off.

It was no longer a matter of amused embarrassment. It was a matter of revulsion.

"You handling this, Nightshade?" Althea laid a hand on his arm. They both knew what he feared most—that Liz would come on-screen.

"I don't guess I'll be wanting any popcorn."

Instinctively Althea left her hand where it was and moved closer.

There was a plot of sorts, and she began to follow it. A weekend at a ski chalet, two couples who mixed and mingled in several ways. She moved beyond that, picking up the details. The furnishings. Colt had been right—they were first-class. Different camera angles showed that it was a two-story with an open loft and high beamed ceilings. Stone fireplace, hot tub.

In a few artistic shots, she saw that it was snowing lightly. She caught glimpses of screening trees and snow-capped peaks. In one outdoor scene that must have been more than uncomfortable for the actors, she noted that there was no other house or structure close by.

The tape ended without credits. And without Liz. Colt didn't know whether he was relieved or not.

"I don't think it's got much of a shot in the Oscar race." Althea kept her voice light as she rewound the tape. "You okay?"

He wasn't okay. There was a burning in his gut that needed some sort of release. "They were rough on the women," he said carefully. "Really vicious."

"Offhand, I'd say the main customers for this kind of thing would be guys who fantasize about dominance—physical and emotional."

"I don't think you can apply the word fantasy in conjunction with something like this."

"Not all fantasies are pretty," she murmured, thinking. "You know, the quality was good, but some of the acting—and I use the term loosely—was downright pitiful. Could be they let some of their clients live out those fantasies on film."

"Lovely." He took one careful, cleansing breath. "Jade's letter mentioned that she thought one of the girls had been killed. Looks like she might have been right."

"Sadism's a peculiar sexual tool—and one that can often get out of hand. We might be able to make the general area from the outside shots."

She started to eject the tape, but he whirled her around. "How can you be so damn clinical? Didn't that get to you? Doesn't anything?"

"Whatever does, I deal with it. Let's leave personalities out of this."

"No. It goes back to knowing who you're working with. We're talking about the fact that some girl might have been killed for the camera." There was a fury in him that he couldn't control, and a terrible need to vent it. "We've just seen two women slapped, shoved, punched, and threatened with worse. I want to know what watching that did to you."

"It made me sick," she snapped back, jerking away. "And it made me angry. And if I'd let myself, it would have made me sad. But all that matters, all that really matters, is that we have our first piece of hard evidence." She snatched out the tape and replaced it in its bag. "Now, if you want to do me a favor, you'll drop me back at the precinct so that I can turn this over. Then you can give me some space."

"Sure, Lieutenant." He strode to the door to yank it open. "I'll give you all the space you need."

# Chapter 5

Colt was holding three ladies. And he thought it was really too bad that the lady he wanted was sitting across the table from him, upping his bet.

"There's your twenty-five, Nightshade, and twenty-five more." Althea tossed chips into the kitty. She held her cards close to her vest, like her thoughts.

"Ah, well..." Sweeney heaved a sigh and studied the trash in his hand as if wishing alone might turn it to gold. "Too rich for my blood."

From her seat between Sweeney and a forensic pathologist named Louie, Cilla considered her pair of fives. "What do you think, Dead-eye?"

Keenan, dressed for bed in a Denver Nuggets jersey, bounced on her lap. "Throw the money in."

"Easy for you to say." But her chips clattered onto the pile.

After a personal debate that included a great deal of muttering, shifting and head shaking, Louie tossed in his chips, as well.

"I'll see your twenty-five," Colt drawled. He kept his cigar clamped between his teeth as he counted out chips. "And bump it again."

Boyd just grinned, pleased that he'd folded after the draw. The bet made the rounds again, with only Althea, Cilla and Colt remaining in.

"Three pretty queens," he announced, and laid down his cards.

Althea's eyes glinted when they met his. "Nice. But we don't have room for them in my full house." She spread her cards, revealing three eights and a pair of deuces.

"That puts my two fives to shame." Cilla sighed as Althea raked in the pot. "Okay, kid, you cost me seventy-five cents. Now you have to die." She hauled a giggling Keenan up as she rose.

"Daddy!" He spread his arms and grinned. "Help me! Don't let her do it!"

"Sorry, son." Boyd ruffled Keenan's hair and gave him a solemn kiss. "Looks like you're doomed. We're going to miss you around here."

Always ready to prolong the inevitable, Keenan hooked his arms around Colt's neck. "Save me!"

Colt kissed the waiting lips and shook his head. "Only one thing in this world scares me, partner, and that's a mama. You're on your own."

Levering in Cilla's arms, the boy made the rounds of the table. When he got to Althea, his eyes gleamed. "Okay? Can I?"

It was an old game, one she was willing to play. "For a nickel."

"I can owe you."

"You already owe me eight thousand dollars and fifteen cents."

"I get my allowance Friday."

"Okay, then." She took him onto her lap for a hug, and he sniffed her hair like a puppy. Colt saw her face soften, watched her hand slide up to stroke the tender nape of the boy's neck.

"It's good," Keenan announced, taking one last exaggerated sniff.

"Don't forget that eight thousand on Friday. Now beat it." After a kiss, she passed him back to Cilla.

"Deal me out," Cilla suggested, and, settling her son on her hip, she carried him upstairs to bed.

"A boy who can talk his way into a woman's lap's a boy to be proud of." Sweeney grinned as he gathered the cards. "My deal. Ante up."

During the next hour, Althea's pile of chips grew slowly, steadily. She enjoyed the monthly poker games that had become a routine shortly after Cilla and Boyd were married. The basic challenge of outwitting her opponents relaxed her almost as much as the domestic atmosphere that had seeped into every corner of the Fletcher home.

She was a cautious player, one who gambled only when satisfied with the odds, and who bet meticulously, thoughtfully, even then. She noted that Colt's pile multiplied, as well, but in fits and starts. He wasn't reckless, she decided. *Ruthless* was the word. Often he bumped the pot when he had nothing, or sat back and let others do the raising when he had a handful of gold.

No pattern, she mused, which she supposed was a pattern of its own.

After Sweeney won a piddling pot with a heart flush, she pushed back from the table. "Anybody want a beer?"

Everybody did. Althea strolled into the kitchen and began to pop tops. She was pouring herself a glass of wine when Colt walked in.

"Thought you could use some help."

"I can handle it."

"I don't figure there's much you can't handle." Damn, the woman was prickly, he thought. "I just thought I'd lend a hand."

Maria had prepared enough sandwiches to satisfy a hungry platoon on a long march. For lack of anything better to do Colt shifted some from platter to plate. He had to get it out, he decided. Now that they were alone and he had the opportunity, he wasn't sure how to start.

"I've got something to say about this afternoon."

"Oh?" Her tone frosty, Althea turned to the refrigerator and took out a bowl of Maria's incomparable guacamole dip.

"I'm sorry."

And nearly dropped it. "Excuse me?"

"Damn it, I'm sorry. Okay?" He hated to apologize—it meant he had made a mistake, one that mattered. "Watching that tape got to me. It made me want to smash something, someone. The closest I could come to it was ripping into you."

Because it was the last thing she would have expected, she was caught off guard. She stood with the bowl in her hand, unsure of her next move. "All right."

"I was afraid I'd see Liz," he continued, compelled to say it all. "I was afraid I wouldn't." At a loss, he picked up one of the opened beers and took a long swallow. "I'm not used to being scared like this."

There was very little he could have said, and nothing he could have done, that would have gotten through her defenses more thoroughly. Touched, and shaken, she set the bowl on the counter and opened a bag of chips.

"I know. It got to me, too. It's not supposed to, but it did." She poured the chips into the bowl, wishing there was something else she could do. Anything else. "I'm sorry things aren't moving faster, Colt."

"They haven't been standing still, either. And I've got you to thank for most of that." He lifted a hand, then dropped it. "Thea, there was something else I wanted to do this afternoon besides punching somebody. I wanted to hold you." He saw the wariness flash into her eyes, quick as a heartbeat, and had to grind down his temper. "Not jump you, Thea. Hold you. There's a difference."

"Yes, there is." She let out a long, quiet breath. There was need in his eyes. Not desire, just need. The need for contact, for comfort, for compassion. That she understood. "I guess I could have used it, too."

"I still could." It cost him to make the first move, this sort of move. But he stepped toward her and held out his arms.

It cost her, as well, to respond, to move into his arms and encircle him with her own.

And when they were close, when her cheek was resting against his shoulder and his against her hair, they both sighed. The tension drained away like water through a broken dam.

He didn't understand it, wasn't sure he could accept it, but he realized it felt right. Very simply right. Unlike the first time he'd held her, there was no punch of lust, no molten fire in his blood. But there was a warmth, sweet and spreading and solid.

He could have held her like that, just like that, for hours.

She didn't often let herself relax so completely, not with a man, and certainly not with a man who attracted her. But this was so easy, so natural. The steady thudding of his heart lulled her. She nearly nuzzled. The urge was there—to rub her cheek against him, to close her eyes and purr. When she felt him sniffing her hair, she laughed.

"The kid's right," he murmured. "It's good."

"That's going to cost you a nickel, Nightshade."

"Put it on my tab," he told her as she lifted her head to smile at him.

Was it because she'd never looked at him quite that way that it hit him so hard? He couldn't be sure. All he knew was that she was outrageously beautiful, her hair loose and tumbling into his hands, glinting like flame in the hard kitchen light. Her eyes were smiling, deep and tawny and warm with humor. And her mouth—unpainted, curved, slightly parted. Irresistible.

He tilted his head, lowered it, waiting for her to stiffen or draw back. She did neither. Though the humor in her eyes had turned to awareness, the warmth remained. So he touched his lips to hers, gently testing, an experiment in emotions. With their eyes open, they watched each other, as if each were waiting for the other to move back, or leap forward.

When she remained pliant in his arms, he changed the angle, nipping lightly. He felt her tremble, only once, as her eyes darkened, clouded. But they remained open and on his.

She wanted to see him. Needed to. She was afraid that if she closed her eyes she might fall into whatever pit it was that yawned before her. She had to see who he was, to try to understand what there was about this one man that made him capable of turning her system to mush.

No one had done so before. And she'd been proud of her ability to resist, or to control, and smugly amused by men and women who fell under the spell of another. In falling they had suffered the torments of love. She had never been certain the joys balanced those torments.

But as he deepened the kiss, slowly, persuasively deepened it so that not only her lips, but also her mind, her heart, her body, were involved in that contact, she wondered what she had missed by never allowing surrender to mix with power.

"Althea..." He whispered her name as he again, teasingly, changed the angle of the kiss. "Come with me...."

She understood what he was asking. He wanted her to let go, to tumble with him wherever the moment took them. To yield to him, even as he yielded to her.

To gamble, when she wasn't sure of the odds.

He closed his eyes first. The soft, drowsy warmth slid seamlessly into a numbing ache, an ache that was all pleasure. Her eyes fluttered closed on a sigh.

"Hey! How about those beers— Oops!" Boyd winced and struggled not to grin. He slipped his hands into his pockets, and had to prevent himself from whistling a tune as his old friend and his former partner jumped apart like thieves caught in a bust.

"Sorry, guys." He strolled over to gather up the beer bottles himself. It occurred to him that in all the years he'd known Althea, he'd never seen that bemused, punch-drunk look on her face. "Must be something about this kitchen," he added as he headed for the door. "Can't tell you how many times I've found myself occupied the same way in here."

The door swung shut behind him. Althea blew out a long breath.

"Oh, boy" was the best she could manage.

Colt laid a hand on her shoulder. Not for balance, he assured himself, though his legs were weak. Just to keep things nice and light. "He looked pretty damned pleased with himself, didn't he?"

"He'll razz me about this," she muttered. "And he'll tell Cilla, so she can razz me, too."

"They've probably got better things to do."

"They're married," she shot back. "Married people love talking about other people's—"

"Other people's what?"

"Stuff."

The more unraveled she became, the more Colt liked it. He was positive that only a privileged few had ever seen the cool lieutenant flustered. He wanted to savor every moment of the experience. Grinning, he leaned back against the counter.

"So? If you really want to drive them crazy, you could let me come home with you tonight."

"In your dreams, Nightshade."

He lifted a brow. Her voice hadn't been quite steady. He liked that—a whole lot. "Well, there's truth in that, darling. Might as well be straight and tell you I'm not willing to wait much longer to turn that dream into reality."

She needed to calm down, needed to do something with her hands. Killing two birds with one stone, she picked up her wine and sipped. "Is that a threat?"

"Althea." There was a world of patience in his voice. That amused him. He couldn't recall ever having been patient about anything before. "We both know what just went on here can't be turned into a threat. It was nice." He flicked a finger down her hair. "If we'd been alone somewhere, it would have turned out a lot nicer." The intent flickered in his eyes too quickly for her to avoid the result. His hand fisted in her hair, held her still. "I want you, Althea, and I want you bad. You can make out of that whatever you choose."

She felt a skip of something sprint down her spine. It wasn't fear. She'd been a cop long enough to recognize fear in all its forms. And she'd lived her life her own way long enough to remain cautious. "It seems to me that you want a great many things. You want Liz back, you want the men responsible for keeping her from her parents caught and punished. You want to do those things your way, with my cooperation. And—" she sipped her wine again, her eyes cool and level "—you want to go to bed with me."

She was amazing, Colt reflected. She had to be feeling some portion of the need and the desperation he was experiencing. Yet she might have been discussing a change in the weather. "That about sums it up. Why don't you tell me what you want?"

She was afraid she knew exactly what she wanted, and it was standing almost close enough to taste. "The difference between you and me, Nightshade, is that I know you don't always get what you want. Now I'm going to pack it in. I've had a long day. You can check with me tomorrow. We'll have the sketches from Meena. Something might turn up when we run them."

"All right." He'd let her go—for now, he thought. The trouble with a woman like Althea, he mused, was that a man would always be tempted to seduce her, and he would always crave her coming to him freely.

"Thea?"

She paused at the kitchen door, looked back. "Yes?"

"What are we going to do about this?"

She felt a sigh building—not one of weariness, one of longing—and choked it off. "I don't know," she said, as truthfully as she could. "I wish I did."

By nine-thirty the following morning, Colt was cooling his heels in Althea's office. There wasn't much room in her cubbyhole to cool anything. Out of sheer boredom, he flipped through some of the papers on her desk. Reports, he noted, in that peculiar language cops used, a language that was both concise and florid. Vehicles proceeded in a southwesterly direction, alleged perpetrators created disturbances, arresting officers apprehended suspects after responding to 312s and 515s.

She wrote a damn good report, if you were into such bureaucratic hogwash. Which, he decided, she obviously was. Rules-and-Regulations Grayson, he thought, and closed the file. Maybe his biggest problem was that he'd seen that there was a lot more to her than the straight-arrow cop.

He'd seen her hold a gun, steady as a rock, while her eyes were alive with fear and determination. He'd felt her respond like glory to an impulsive and urgent embrace. He'd watched her cuddle a child, soften with compassion and freeze like a hailstone.

He'd seen too much, and he knew he hadn't seen nearly enough.

Liz was his priority, had to be. Yet Althea remained lodged inside him, like a bullet in the flesh. Hot, painful, and impossible to ignore.

It made him angry. It made him itchy. And when she swept into the room, it made him snarl.

"I've been waiting for the best part of a damn hour. I haven't got time for this."

"That's a shame." She dropped another file onto her desk, noting immediately that her papers had been disturbed. "Could be you're watching too much TV, Nightshade. That's the only place a cop gets to work on one case at a time."

"I'm not a cop."

"That's more than obvious. And next time you have to wait for me, keep your nose out of my papers."

"Listen, Lieutenant—" He broke off, swearing, when her phone rang.

"Grayson." She slipped into her chair as she spoke, her hand already reaching for a pencil. "Yeah. Yeah, I got it. That was quick work, Sergeant. I appreciate it. I'll be sure to do that if I get over your way. Thanks again." She broke the connection and immediately began to dial again. "Kansas City located Jade's mother," she told Colt. "She'd moved from the Kansas side to Missouri."

"Is Jade with her?"

"That's what I'm going to try to find out." As she completed the call, Althea checked her watch. "She waits tables at night. Odds are I'll catch her at home at this hour."

Before Colt could speak again, Althea shot up a hand for silence.

"Hello, I'd like to speak with Janice Willowby." A sleepy and obviously irritated voice informed her that Janice didn't live there. "Is this Mrs. Willowby? Mrs. Willowby, this is Lieutenant Grayson, Denver Police— No, ma'am, she hasn't done anything. She isn't in any trouble. We believe she might be of some help to us on a case. Have you heard from your daughter in the last few weeks?" She listened patiently as the woman denied having been in contact with Janice and irritably demanded information. "Mrs. Willowby, Janice isn't a fugitive from justice, or under any sort of suspicion. However, we are anxious to contact her." Her eyes hardened, quickly, coldly. "Excuse me? Since I'm not asking you to turn your daughter in, I don't see a reward as being applicable. If—"

Colt thrust a hand over the receiver. "Five thousand," he stated. "If she gets us Jade, and Jade leads us to Liz." He saw the spitting denial in her eyes, but held firm. "It's not up to you. The reward's private."

Althea sucked in her disgust. "Mrs. Willowby, there is a private party authorizing the sum of five thousand for information on Janice, on the condition that this then results in the satisfactory close of the investigation. Yes, I'm quite sure you can have it in cash. Oh, yes, I'm sure you will see what you can do. You can reach me twenty-four hours a day, at this number." She repeated it twice. "Collect, of course. That's Lieutenant Althea Grayson, Denver. I hope you do."

After hanging up the phone, she sat simmering. "It's no wonder girls like Jade take off and end up on the streets. She didn't give a damn about her daughter, just wanted to be sure no backlash was going to come her way. If Jade had been in any trouble, she'd have been willing to trade her for cash in the blink of an eye."

"Not everybody has the maternal instincts of Donna Reed."

"You're telling me." Because emotions would interfere with the job at hand, Althea shelved them. "Meena's been working with the police artist, and she's come up with some pretty good likenesses. One of them matches one of the stars from the production we watched yesterday."

"Which one?"

"The guy in the red leather G-string. We're running a make through Vice to start. It'll take time."

"I don't have time."

She set aside the pencil, folded her hands. She wouldn't lose her temper, she promised herself. Not again. "Do you have a better way?"

"No." He turned away, then swung back. "Any prints on the car used to hit Billings?"

"Clean."

"The penthouse?"

"No prints. Some hair fibers. They won't help us catch them, but they'll be good for tying it up in court. The lab's working on the tape, and the note. We could get lucky."

"How about missing persons? A Jane Doe at the morgue? Jade said she thought one of the girls was killed."

"Nothing's turned up. If they did kill someone, and she'd been in the life for a while, a missing-persons report's unlikely. I've checked all the unidentified and suspicious deaths over the last three months. Nobody fits the profile."

"Any luck in the homeless shelters, runaway hostels, halfway houses?"

"Not yet." She hesitated, then decided it was best that they talk it through. "There's something I've been kicking around."

"Go ahead, kick it my way."

"We've got a couple of babyfaces on the force. Good cops. We can put them undercover, out on the street. See if they get a movie offer.''

Colt rolled it around in his head. That, too, would take time, he mused. But at least it was a chance. ''It's a tricky spot. Do you have anyone good enough to handle it?''

''I said I did. I'd do it myself—''

''No.'' His abrupt denial was like the lash of a whip.

Althea inclined her head and continued without a flinch. ''I said, I'd do it myself, but I can't pass for a teenager. Apparently our producer prefers kids. I'll set it in motion.''

''Okay. Can you get me a dupe of the tape?''

She smiled. ''Evenings too dull for you?''

''Very funny. Can you?''

She thought it through. It wasn't strictly procedure, but it couldn't do any harm. ''I'll check with the lab. Meanwhile, I'm going to roust the bartender at Clancy's. I'm betting he's the one who tipped off the bunch on Second Avenue. We might sweat something out of him.''

''I'll go with you.''

She shook her head. ''I'm taking Sweeney.'' She smiled, fully, easily. ''A big Irish cop, a bar called Clancy's. It just seems to fit.''

''He's a lousy poker player.''

''Yeah, but a darlin' man,'' she said, surprising him by slipping into a perfect Irish brogue.

''How about I go along anyway?''

''How about you wait for me to call you?'' She rose, pulled a navy blazer from the back of her chair. She wore pleated slacks of the same color and texture and a paler blue blouse in a silky material. Her shoulder harness and weapon looked so natural on her, they might have been fashion accessories.

''You will call me.''

''I said I would.''

Because it seemed right, he laid his hands on her shoulders, and briefly rested his brow on hers. ''Marleen called me this morning. I don't like to think I was giving her false hope, but I told her we were getting closer. I had to tell her that.''

''Whatever eases her mind is the right thing to say.'' She couldn't help it. She pressed a hand briefly to his cheek in comfort, then let it drop. "Hang tough, Nightshade. We've gathered a lot of information in a short amount of time."

"Yeah." He lifted his head and slid his hands down her arms until he could link fingers with her. "I'll let you go find your intimidating Irishman. But there's one more thing." He raised their linked hands, studying the contrast of texture, tone and size. "Sooner or later, we'll be going off the clock." His gaze shifted to meet hers. "Then we'll have to deal with other things."

"Then we'll deal with them. But you may not like the way it shakes down."

He caught her chin in one hand, kissed her hard, then released her before she could do more than hiss. "Same goes. You be careful out there, Lieutenant."

"I was born careful, Nightshade." She walked away, shrugging into the blazer as she went.

Ten hours later, she parked her car in her building's garage and headed for the elevator. She was ready for a hot bath pregnant with bubbles, a glass of icy white wine, and some slow blues, heavy on the bass.

As she rode to her floor, she leaned against the back wall and shut her eyes. They hadn't gotten very far with the bartender, Leo Dorsetti. Bribes hadn't worked, and veiled threats hadn't, either. Althea didn't doubt he had connections with the pornography ring. Nor did she doubt that he was worried that the same fate might befall him that had Wild Bill.

So she needed more than a threat. She needed to dig up something on Leo Dorsetti. Something solid enough that she could drag him downtown and into interrogation.

Once she had him, she could crack him. She was damn sure of that.

She jingled her keys as she walked through the open elevator doors and into the hall. Now it was time to put the cop on hold, at least for an hour or two. Obsessing over a case usually equalled making mistakes on a case. So she'd pack it away into a corner of her mind, let it sit, let it ripen, while the woman indulged in a purely selfish evening.

She'd already unlocked the door, pushed it open, when the alarm went off in her head. She didn't question what tripped it, just whipped out her weapon. Automatically she followed standard entry procedure, checking in corners and behind the door.

Her eyes scanned the room, noting that nothing was out of place—unless she counted the Bessie Smith record currently playing on the turntable. And the scent. She took a quick whiff, identifying cooking, something spicy. It made her mouth water in response, even as her mind stayed alert.

A sound from the kitchen had her whirling in that direction, ending in the spread-legged police stance, her weapon steady in both hands.

Colt stopped in the doorway, wiping his hands on a dishcloth. Smiling, he leaned back against the jamb. "Hi there, darling. And how was your day?"

## Chapter 6

Althea lowered her gun. She didn't raise her voice. The words she chose, quiet and precise, made her feelings known with more clarity than a shout could have.

When she'd finished, Colt could only shake his head in admiration. "I don't believe I've ever been cussed out with more style. Now, I'd be obliged if you'd holster that gun. Not that I figure you'd use it and risk getting blood all over your floor."

"It might be worth it." She slapped her gun back in place, but her eyes never left his. "You have the right to remain silent...." she began.

Wisely, Colt stifled a chuckle. He held up a hand. "What're you doing?"

"I'm reading you your rights before I haul your butt in for night-time breaking and entering."

He didn't doubt she'd do it. She'd have him booked, fingerprinted and photographed without breaking stride. "I'll waive them, providing you listen to an explanation."

"It better be good." Shrugging out of her blazer, she tossed it over the back of the chair. "How did you get in here?"

"I, ah… Through the door?"

Her eyes narrowed. "You have the right to an attorney."

Obviously humor wasn't going to do the trick. "Okay, I'm

busted.'' He tossed up both hands in a gesture of surrender. ''I picked the lock. It's a damn good one, too. Or maybe I'm getting rusty.''

''You picked the lock.'' She nodded, as if it were no more than she'd expected. ''You carry a concealed weapon—an ASP nine-millimeter...''

''Good eye, Lieutenant.''

''And a knife that likely exceeds the legal limit,'' she continued. ''Now it appears you also carry lock picks.''

''They come in handy.'' And it was something he preferred not to dwell on when she was in this sort of mood. ''Now, I figured you had a rough day, and you deserved coming home to a hot meal and some cold wine. I also figured you'd be a little testy coming in and finding me here. But I have to believe you'll come around after you've had a taste of my linguine.''

Maybe, she thought, maybe if she closed her eyes for a minute, it would all go away. But when she tried it, he was still there, grinning at her. ''Your linguine?''

''Linguine marinara. I'd claim it was my sainted mother's recipe, but she never boiled an egg in her life. How about that wine?''

''Sure. Why the hell not?''

''That's the way.'' He stepped back into the kitchen. Deciding she could always kill him later, Althea followed. The aromas drifting through the air were heaven. ''You like white,'' he said as he poured two glasses, using her best crystal. ''This is a nice, full-bodied Italian that won't embarrass my sauce. Bold, but classy. See if it suits you.''

She accepted the glass, allowed him to clink his against hers, then sipped. The wine tasted like liquid heaven. ''Who the hell are you, Nightshade?''

''Why, I'm the answer to your prayers. Why don't we go in and sit down? You know you want to take your shoes off.''

She did, but she obstinately kept them on as she walked back and lowered herself onto the couch. ''Explain.''

''I just did.''

''If you cannot afford an attorney—''

''God, you're tough.'' He let out a long breath and stretched out beside her. ''Okay, I have a couple of reasons. One, I know you've been putting in a lot of extra time on my business....''

"It's my—"

"Job?'' he finished for her. "Maybe. But I know when someone's taking those extra steps, the kind that eat into personal time, and fixing you dinner's just a way of saying thanks."

It was a damn nice gesture, too, she thought, though she wasn't willing to say so. Yet. "You might have mentioned the idea to me earlier."

"It was an impulse. You ever have them?"

"Don't push your luck, Nightshade."

"Right. Well, to get back to the whys. There's also the fact that I haven't been able to snatch more than an hour at a time to clear this whole mess out of my head. Cooking helps me recharge. Maria wasn't likely to turn her stove over to me, so I thought of you." He reached out to curl a lock of her hair around his finger. "I think of you a lot. And finally, and simply, I wanted the evening with you."

He was getting to her. Althea wanted to believe that it was the glorious scents sneaking out of the kitchen that were weakening her. But she didn't believe it. "So you broke into my home and invaded my privacy."

"The only thing I poked into was your kitchen cupboards. It was tempting," he admitted, "but I didn't go any farther than that."

Frowning, Althea swirled the wine in her glass. "I don't like your methods, Nightshade. But I think I'm going to like your linguine."

She didn't like it. She adored it. It was difficult to harbor resentments when her palate was being so thoroughly seduced. She'd had men cook for her before, but she couldn't remember ever being so completely charmed.

Here was Colt Nightshade, very possibly armed to the teeth beneath his faded jeans and chambray shirt, serving her pasta by candlelight. Not that it was romantic, she thought. She was too smart to fall for any conventional trappings. But it was funny, and oddly sweet.

By the time she'd worked her way through one helping and was starting on a second, she'd filled him in on her progress. The lab reports were expected within twenty-four hours, the bartender at

Clancy's was under surveillance, and an undercover officer was being prepped to hit the streets.

Colt filed her information away and traded it for some of his own. He'd talked to some of the local working girls that afternoon. Whether due to his charm or to the money that had changed hands, he'd learned that a girl who went by the street name Lacy hadn't been seen in any of her usual haunts for the past several weeks.

"She fits the profile," he continued, topping off Althea's wineglass. "Young, tiny. Girls said she was a brunette, but liked to wear a blond wig."

"Did she have a pimp?"

"Uh-uh. Free-lancer. I went by the rooms she'd been renting." Colt broke a piece of garlic bread in two and passed Althea half. "Talked to the landlord—a prince of a guy. Since she'd missed a couple of weekly rent payments, he'd packed up her stuff. Pawned what was worth anything, trashed the rest."

"I'll see if anybody at Vice knows about her."

"Good. I hit some of the shelters again," he went on. "The half-way houses, showing Liz's picture around, and the police sketches." He frowned, toying with the rest of his meal. "I couldn't get anyone to ID. Had a hard enough time convincing any of the kids that they should look at the pictures. Most of the kids want to act tough, invincible, and all you see is the confusion in their eyes."

"When you're dealing with that kind of confusion, you have to be tough. Most of them come from homes that are torn apart by drugs, drinking, physical and sexual abuse. Or they got into substance abuse all on their own and don't know how to get out again." She moved her shoulders. "Either way, running seems like the best way out."

"It wasn't like that for Liz."

"No," she agreed. It was time for him to turn it off, as well, she decided. If only for a few minutes. She scraped a last bite from her plate. "You know, Nightshade, you could give up playing the adventurer and go into catering. You'd make a fortune."

He understood what she was doing, and he put some effort into accommodating her. "I prefer small, private parties."

Her gaze flicked up to his, then back to her glass. "So, if it wasn't your sainted mother who taught you to make world-class linguine, who did?''

"We had this terrific Irish cook when I was growing up. Mrs. O'Malley.''

"An Irish cook who taught you Italian cuisine.''

"She could make anything—from lamb stew to coq au vin. 'Colt, me boy,' she used to tell me, 'the best thing a man can do for himself is to learn to feed himself well. Depending on a woman to fill your belly's a mistake.''' The memory made him grin. "When I'd gotten into trouble, which was most of the time, she'd sit me down in the kitchen. I'd get lectures on behavior, and the proper way to debone a chicken.''

"Quite a combination.''

"The stuff on behavior didn't stick.'' He toasted her. "But I make a hell of a chicken pot pie. And when Mrs. O'Malley retired—oh, almost ten years ago now—my mother went into a dark state of depression.''

Althea's lips curved on the rim of her glass. "And hired another cook.''

"A French guy with a bad attitude. She loves him.''

"A French chef in Wyoming.''

"I live in Wyoming,'' he said. "They live in Houston. We get along better that way. What about your family? Are they from around here?''

"I don't have one. What about your law degree? Why haven't you done anything with it?''

"I didn't say I hadn't.'' He studied her for a moment. She'd certainly dropped his question like a hot coal. It was something he'd have to come back to. "I found out I wasn't suited to spending hours hunched over law books, trying to outwit justice on technicalities.''

"So you went into the air force.''

"It was a good way to learn how to fly.''

"But you're not a pilot.''

"Sometimes I am.'' He smiled. "Sorry, Thea, I don't fit into a slot. I've got enough money that I can do what suits me when it suits me.''

That wasn't good enough. "And the military didn't suit you?''

"For a while it did. Then I had enough." He shrugged and sat back. The candlelight flickered on his face and in his eyes. "I learned some things. Just like I learned from Mrs. O'Malley, and from prep school, from Harvard, and from this old Indian horse trainer I met in Tulsa some years back. You never know when you're going to use what you've learned."

"Who taught you to pick locks?"

"You're not going to hold that against me, are you?" He leaned forward to flick a finger over her hair, and to pour more wine. "I picked it up in the service. I was in what you might call a special detachment."

"Covert operations," she said, translating. It was no surprise. "That's why so much of your record's classified."

"It's old news, should be declassified by now. But that's the way of it, isn't it? Bureaucrats like secrets almost as much as they like red tape. What I did was gather information, or plant information, maybe defuse certain volatile situations, or stir them up, depending on the orders." He drank again. "I guess we could say I started doing favors for people—only these people ran the government." His lip curled. "Or tried to."

"You don't like the system, do you?"

"I like what works." For an instant only, his eyes darkened. "I saw plenty that didn't work. So..." He shrugged, and the mood was gone. "I got out, bought myself a few horses and cows, played rancher. Looks like old habits die hard, because now I do favors for people again. Only now I have to like them first."

"Some people might say that you've had a hard time deciding what you want to do when you grow up."

"Some people might. I figure I've been doing it. What about you? What's the back story on Althea Grayson?"

"It's nothing that would sell to the movies." Relaxed, she rested her elbows on the table, running a finger around the rim of her glass until the crystal sang. "I went straight into the academy when I was eighteen. No detours."

"Why?"

"Why a cop?" She mulled over her answer. "Because I do like the system. It's not perfect, but if you keep at it, you can make it work. And the law...there are people out there who want to make it work. Too many lives get lost in the cracks. It means something when you can pull one out.''

"I can't argue with that." Without thinking about it, he laid a hand over hers. "I could always see that Boyd was meant to make law and order work. Until recently, he was about the only cop I respected enough to trust.''

"I think you just gave me a compliment.''

"You can be sure of it. The two of you have a lot in common. A clear-sightedness, a stubborn kind of valor, a steady compassion." He smiled, toying with her fingers. "The kid we got off the roof—I went to see her, too. She had a lot to say about the pretty lady with the red hair who brought her a baby doll.''

"So I did a follow-up. It's my job to—''

"Bull." Delighted with her response, he picked up her hand, kissed it. "It had nothing to do with duty, and everything to do with you. Having a soft side doesn't make you less of a cop, Thea. It just makes you a kinder one.''

She knew where this was leading, but she didn't pull her hand away. "Just because I have a soft spot for kids doesn't mean I've got one for you.''

"But you do," he murmured. "I get to you." Watching her, he skimmed his lips down to her wrist. The pulse there beat steady, but it also beat fast. "I'm going to keep getting to you.''

"Maybe you do." She was too smart to continue to deny the obvious. "That doesn't mean anything's going to come of it. I don't sleep with every man who attracts me.''

"I'm glad to hear it. Then again, you're going to do a lot more than sleep with me." He chuckled and kissed her hand again. "God, I love it when you smirk, Thea. It drives me crazy. What I was going to say was, when we get each other to bed, sleeping's not going to be a priority. So maybe you should catch some shut-eye." He rose, pulling her to her feet. "Kiss me good-night, and I'll let you get some now.''

The surprise in her eyes made him grin again. He'd wait until later to pat himself on the back for his strategy.

"You thought I cooked you dinner and kept you company so I

could use it as a springboard to seduction.'' On a windy sigh, he shook his head. ''Althea, I'm wounded. Close to crushed.''

She laughed, keeping a friendly hand in his. ''You know, Nightshade, sometimes I almost like you. Almost.''

''See, that's just a couple of short steps away from you being nuts about me.'' He gathered her close, and the instant twisting in his gut mocked his light tone. ''If I'd bothered to make dessert, you'd be begging for me.''

Amused, she tucked her tongue in her cheek. ''Your loss. Everybody knows cannoli turns me into a wild woman.''

''I'll sure as hell remember that.'' He kissed her lightly, watched her smile. And felt his heart turn over. ''There must be a bakery around here where I can pick up some Italian pastries.''

''Nope. You missed your shot.'' She brought a hand to his chest, telling herself she was going to end the interlude now, while she could still feel her legs under her. ''Thanks for the pasta.''

''Sure.'' But he continued to stare down at her, his eyes sharpening, focusing, as if he were struggling to see past the ivory skin, the delicate bones. Something was happening here, he realized. Something internal that he couldn't quite get a grip on. ''You have something in your eyes.''

Her nerves were dancing. ''What?''

''I don't know.'' He spoke slowly, as if measuring each word. ''Sometimes I can almost see it. When I do, it makes me wonder where you've been. Where we're going.''

Her lungs were backing up. She took a careful breath to clear them. ''*You* were going home.''

''Yeah. In a minute. Too easy to tell you you're beautiful,'' he murmured, as if speaking to himself. ''You hear that too much, and it's too superficial to carry any weight with you. It should be enough for me, but there's something else in there. I keep coming back to it.'' Still seeking, he drew her closer. ''What is it about you, Althea? What is it I can't shake loose?''

''There's nothing. You're too used to looking for shadows.''

''No, you've got them.'' Slowly he slid a hand up to cup her cheek. ''And what I have is a problem.''

''What problem?''

"Try this."

He lowered his mouth to hers and had every muscle in her body going lax. It wasn't demanding, it wasn't urgent. It was devastating. The kiss tumbled her deeper, deeper, bombarding her with emotions she had no defense against. His feelings were free and ripe and poured over her, into her, so that she was covered and filled and surrounded by them.

No escape, she thought, and heard her own muffled sound of despair with a dull acceptance. He'd breached a defense she had taken for granted, one she might never fully shore up again.

She could tell herself again and again that she wouldn't fall in love, that she couldn't fall in love with a man she hardly knew. But her heart was already laughing at logic.

He felt her give—not all the way, not yet, but give yet another degree of self. There was more than heat here, though, sweet heaven, there was heat. But there was a kind of discovery, as well. For Colt, it was a revelation to discover that one woman—this woman—could tangle up his mind, rip open his heart, and leave him helpless.

"I'm losing ground here." He kept his hands firm on her shoulders as he pulled back. "I'm losing it fast."

"It's too much." It was a poor response, but the best she could summon.

"You're telling me." There was tension in her shoulders again, and in his. It compelled him to step away. "I've never felt like this before. And that's no line," he said when she turned away from him.

"I know. I wish it were." She gripped the back of the chair, where her shoulder holster hung. A symbol of duty, she thought. Of control, of what she had made of herself. "Colt, I think we're both getting in deeper than we might like."

"Maybe we've been treading water long enough."

She was very much afraid that she was ready, willing, even eager, to sink. "I don't let personal business interfere with my job. If we can't keep this under control, you should consider working with someone else."

"We've been working together just fine," he said between his teeth. "Don't pull out any lame excuses because you don't want to face up to what's going on between us."

"It's the best I've got." Her knuckles had turned white on the chair. "And it's not an excuse, only a reason. You want me to say you scare me. All right. You scare me. This scares me. And I don't think you want a partner who can't focus because you make her nervous."

"Maybe I'm happier with that than with one who's so focused it's hard to tell if she's human." She wasn't going to pull away from him now. He'd be damned if he'd let her. "Don't tell me you can't work on two levels, Thea, or that you can't function as a cop when you've got a problem in your personal life."

"Maybe I just don't want to work with you."

"That's tough. You're stuck. If you want to put this on hold, I'll try to oblige you. But you're not backing off from Liz because you're afraid to let yourself feel something for me."

"I'm thinking about Liz, and what's best for her."

"How the hell would you know?" he exploded, and if it was unreasonable, he didn't give a damn. He was on the edge of falling in love with a woman who was calmly telling him she didn't want him in any area of her life. He was desperate to find a frightened girl, and the person who'd helped him make progress toward doing so was threatening to pull out. "How the hell would you know about her or anyone else? You've got yourself so wrapped up in regulations and procedure that you can't feel. No, not can't. Won't. You won't feel. You'll risk your life, but one brush with emotion and up goes the shield. Everything's so tidy for you, isn't it, Althea? There's some poor scared kid out there, but she's just another case for you, just another job."

"*Don't* you tell me how I feel." Her control snapped as she shoved the chair aside, clattering to the floor between them. "Don't tell me what I understand. You can't possibly know what's inside me. Do you think you know Liz, or any of those girls you talked with today? You've walked into shelters and halfway houses, and you think you understand?"

Her eyes glinted, not with tears, but with a rage so sharp he could only stand and let it slice at him. "I know there are plenty of kids who need help, and not always enough help to go around."

"Oh, that's so easy." She strode across the room and back in a rare show of useless motion. "Write a check, pass a bill, make a speech. It's so effortless. You haven't a clue what it's like to be alone, to be afraid or to be caught up in that grinding machine we toss displaced kids into. I spent most of my life in that machine, so don't tell me I don't feel. I know what it's like to want out so bad you run even when there's no place to go. And I know what it's like to be yanked back, to be helpless, to be abused and trapped and miserable. I understand plenty. And I know that Liz has a family that loves her, and we'll get her back to them. No matter what, we'll get her back, and she won't be caught in that cycle. So don't you tell me she's just another case, because she matters. They all matter."

She broke off, running a shaky hand through her hair. At the moment, she wasn't sure which was bigger, her embarrassment or her anger. "I'd like you to go now," she said quietly. "I'd really like you to go."

"Sit down." When she didn't respond, he walked over and pressed her into a chair. She was trembling, and the fact that he'd played a part in causing that made him feel as if he'd punched a hole in something precious and fragile. "I'm sorry. That's a record for me, apologizing to the same person twice in one day." He started to brush a hand over her hair, but stopped himself. "Do you want some water?"

"No. I just want you to leave."

"I can't do it." He lowered himself to the footstool in front of her so that their eyes were level. "Althea..."

She sat back, her eyes shut. She felt as though she'd raced to the top of a mountain and leapt off. "Nightshade, I'm not in the mood to tell you my life story, so if that's what you're waiting for, you know where the door is."

"That'll keep." He took a chance and reached for her hand. It was steady now, he noted, but cold. "Let's try something else. What we've got here are two separate problems. Finding Liz is number one. She's an innocent, a victim, and she needs help. I could find her on my own, but that would take too long. Every day that goes by... Well, too many days have gone by already. I need you to work with me, because you can cut through channels it would take me twice as long to circumvent. And because I trust you to put everything you've got into getting her home.''

"All right." She kept her eyes closed, willing the tension away. "We'll find her. If not tomorrow, the next day. But we'll find her."

"Second problem." He looked down at their hands, studying the way the second hand on her watch ticked off the time. "I think…ah, and since this is a new area for me, I want to qualify it by saying that it's only an opinion…"

"Nightshade." She opened her eyes again, and there was a ghost of a smile in them. "I swear you sound just like a lawyer."

He winced, shifted. "I don't think you should insult a man who's about to tell you he's pretty sure he's in love with you." She jolted. He'd have bet the farm that he could pull a gun and she wouldn't flinch. But mention love and she jumped six inches off the chair. "Don't panic," he continued while she searched for her voice. "I said 'I think.' That leaves us with a safe area to play with."

"Sounds more like a mine field to me." Because she was afraid it might start shaking again, she drew her hand away from his. "I think it would be wise, under the circumstances, to table that for the time being."

"Now who sounds like a lawyer?" He grinned, not at all sure why it seemed so appropriate to laugh at himself. "Darling, you think it puts the fear of God into you? Picture what it does to me. I only brought it up because I'm hoping that'll make it easier to deal with. For all I know, it's just a touch of the flu or something."

"That would be good." She choked back a laugh, terrified it would sound giddy. "Get plenty of rest, drink fluids."

"I'll give that a try." He leaned forward, not displeased to see the wariness in her eyes or the bracing of her shoulders. "But if it's not the flu, or some other bug, I'm going to do something about it. Whatever that might be can wait until we've settled the first problem. Until we do, I won't bring up love, or all the stuff that generally follows along after it—you know, like marriage and family and a two-car garage."

For the first time since he'd known her, he saw her totally at a loss. Her eyes were huge, and her mouth was slack. He would have sworn that if he tapped her, she'd keel over like a sapling in a storm.

"Guess it's just as well I don't, since talking about them in the abstract sense seems to have put you in a coma."

"I..." She managed to close her mouth, swallow, then speak. "I think you've lost your mind."

"Me, too." Lord knew why he felt so cheerful about it. "So for now let's concentrate on digging up those bad guys. Deal?"

"And if I agree, you're not going to sneak in any of that other stuff?"

His smile spread slowly. "Are you willing to take my word on it?"

"No." She steadied herself and smiled back. "But I'm willing to bet I can deflect anything you toss out."

"I'll take that bet." He held out a hand. "Partner." They shook, solemnly. "Now, why don't we—"

The phone interrupted what Althea was sure would have been an unprofessional suggestion. She slipped by Colt and picked up the extension in the kitchen.

It gave him a moment to think about what he'd started. To smile. To think about how he'd like to finish it. Before he'd wound his fantasy up, she was striding back. She righted the chair, snagged her shoulder harness.

"Our friend Leo, the bartender? We just busted him for selling coke out of his back room." The warrior look was back on her face as she shrugged into the harness. "They're bringing him in for interrogation."

"I'm right behind you."

"Behind me is just where you'll stay, Nightshade," she said as she slipped into her blazer. "If Boyd clears it, you can observe through the glass, but that's the best deal you'll get."

He chafed at the restraint. "Let me sit in. I'll keep my mouth shut."

"Don't make me laugh." She grabbed her purse on the way to the door. "Take it or leave it—partner."

He swore at her, and slammed the door behind him. "I'll take it."

## Chapter 7

Colt's initial frustration at being stuck behind the two-way glass faded as he watched Althea work. Her patient, detail-by-detail interrogation had a style all its own. It surprised Colt to label that style not only meticulous, but relentless, as well.

She never allowed Leo to draw her off track, never betrayed any reaction to his sarcasm, and never—not even when Leo tried abusive language and veiled threats—raised her voice.

She played poker the same way, he remembered. Coolly, methodically, without a flicker of emotion until it was time to cash in her chips. But Colt was beginning to see through the aloof shell into the woman behind it.

Certainly he'd been able to surprise many varied emotions from the self-contained lieutenant. Passion, anger, sympathy, even speechless shock. He had a feeling he'd only scratched the surface. There was a wealth of emotions beneath that tidy, professional and undeniably stunning veneer. He intended to keep digging until he unearthed them all.

"Long night." Boyd came up behind him bearing two mugs of steaming coffee.

"I've had longer." Colt accepted the mug, sipped. "This stuff's strong enough to do the tango." He winced and drank again. "Does the captain usually come in for a routine interrogation?"

"The captain does when he has a personal interest." Fletcher watched Althea a moment, noting that she sat, serene and unruffled, as Leo jerkily lit one cigarette from the butt of another. "Is she getting anything?"

With some effort, Colt restrained an urge to beat against the glass just to prove he could do something. "He's still tap dancing."

"He'll wear out long before she does."

"I've already figured that out for myself." They both lapsed into silence as Leo snarled out a particularly foul insult and Althea responded by asking if he'd like to repeat that statement for the record. "She doesn't ruffle," Colt commented. "Fletch, have you ever seen the way a cat'll sit outside a mouse hole?" He flicked a glance at Boyd, then looked back through the glass. "That cat just sits there, hardly blinking, maybe for hours. Inside the hole, the mouse starts to go crazy. He can smell that cat, see those eyes staring in at him. After a while, I guess, the mouse circuits in his brain overload, and he makes a break for it. The cat just whips out one paw, and it's over."

Colt sipped more coffee, nodded at the glass. "That's one gorgeous cat."

"You've gotten to know her pretty well in a short amount of time."

"Oh, I've got a ways to go yet. All those layers," he murmured, almost to himself. "Can't say I've ever run into a woman who had me just as interested in peeling the layers of her psyche as peeling off her clothes."

The image had Boyd scowling into his coffee. Althea was a grown woman, he reminded himself, and more than able to take care of herself. Boyd remembered he'd been amused to find Colt and his former partner in a clinch in his kitchen. But the idea of it going further, of his friends leaping into the kind of quick, physical relationship that could leave them both battered at the finish, disturbed him.

Particularly when he thought of Colt's talent with women. It was a talent they both had, and both of them had enjoyed the benefits of that talent over the years. But they weren't discussing just any woman this time. This was Althea.

"You know," Boyd began, feeling his way with the care of a blind man in a maze, "Thea's special. She can handle pretty much anything that comes her way."

"And does," Colt added.

"Yeah, and does. But that's not to say that she doesn't have her vulnerabilities. I wouldn't want to see her hurt. I wouldn't like that at all."

Mildly surprised, Colt lifted a brow. "A warning? Sounds like the same kind you gave me about your sister Natalie about a million years ago."

"Comes to the same thing. Thea's family."

"And you think I could hurt her."

Boyd let out a weary breath. He wasn't enjoying this conversation. "I'm saying, if you did, I'd have to bruise several of your vital organs. I'd be sorry, but I'd have to do it."

Colt acknowledged that with a thoughtful nod. "Who won the last time we went at it?"

Despite his discomfort, Boyd grinned. "I think it was a draw."

"Yeah, that's how I remember it. It was over a woman then, too, wasn't it?"

"Cheryl Anne Madigan." This time Boyd's sigh was nostalgic.

"Little blonde?"

"Nope, tall brunette. Big…blue eyes."

"Right." Colt laughed, shook his head. "I wonder whatever happened to pretty Cheryl Anne."

They fell into a comfortable silence for a moment, reminiscing. Through the speakers they could hear Althea's calm, relentless questioning.

"Althea's a long way from Cheryl Anne Madigan," Colt murmured. "I wouldn't want to hurt her, but I can't promise it won't happen. The thing is, Fletch, for the first time I've run into a woman who matters enough to hurt me back." Colt took another bracing sip. "I think I'm in love with her."

Boyd choked and was forced to set down his mug before he dumped the contents all over his shirt. He waited a beat, tapped a hand against his ear as if to clear it. "You want to say that again? I don't think I caught it."

"You heard me," Colt muttered. Leave it to a friend, he thought, to humiliate you at an emotionally vulnerable moment. ''I got almost the same reaction from her when I told her.''

''You told her?'' Boyd struggled to keep one ear on the interrogation while he absorbed this new and fascinating information. ''What did she say?''

''Not much of anything.''

The frustration in Colt's voice tickled Boyd so much, he had to bite the tip of his tongue to keep from grinning. ''Well, at least she didn't laugh in your face.''

''She didn't seem to think it was very funny.'' Colt blew out a breath and wished Boyd had thought to lace the coffee with a good dose of brandy. ''She just sat there, going pale, kind of gaping at me.''

''That's a good sign.'' Boyd patted Colt's shoulder comfortingly. ''It's real hard to throw her off that way.''

''I figured it was best if it was out, you know? It would give us both time to decide what to do about it.'' He smiled through the glass at Althea, who continued to sit, cool and unruffled, while Leo gulped down water with a trembling hand. ''Though I've pretty much figured out what I'm going to do about it.''

''Which is?''

''Well, unless I wake up some morning real soon and realize I've had some sort of brain seizure, I'm going to marry her.''

''Marry her?'' Boyd rocked back on his heels and chuckled. ''You and Thea? Lord, wait until I tell Cilla.''

The murderous look Colt aimed at him only made Boyd's grin widen.

''I can't thank you enough for your support here, Fletch.''

Boyd gamely swallowed another chuckle, but he couldn't defeat the grin. ''Oh, you've got it, pal. All the way. It's just that I never thought I'd be using the word *marriage* in the same sentence with *Colt Nightshade.* Or *Althea Grayson,* for that matter. Believe me, I'm with you all the way.''

Inside the interrogation room, Althea continued to wear down her quarry. She scented his fear, and used it ruthlessly.

''You know, Leo, a little cooperation would go a long way.''

"Sure, a long way to seeing me greased like Wild Bill."

Althea inclined her head. "As much as it pains me to offer it, you'd have protection."

"Right." Leo snorted out smoke. "You think I want cops on my butt twenty-four hours a day? You think it would work if I did?"

"Maybe not." She used her disinterest as another tool, slowing down the pace of the interview until Leo was squirming in his chair. "But, then again, no cooperation, no shield. You go out of here naked, Leo."

"I'll take my chances."

"That's fine. You'll make bail on the drug charges—probably deal them down so you won't do any time to speak of. But it's funny how word spreads on the street, don't you think?" She let that thought simmer in his brain. "Interested parties already know you've been tagged, Leo. And when you walk out, they won't be real sure about what you might have spilled while you were inside."

"I didn't tell you anything. I don't know anything."

"That's too bad. Because it might work against you, this ignorance. You see, we're closing in, and those same interested parties might wonder if you helped out." Casually she opened a file and revealed the police sketches. "They might wonder if I got the descriptions of these suspects from you."

"I didn't give you anything." Sweat popped out on Leo's forehead as he stared at the sketches. "I never seen those guys before."

"Well, that may be. But I'd have to say—if the subject came up—that I talked with you. A long time. And that I have detailed sketches of suspects. You know, Leo," she added, leaning toward him, "some people add two and two and get five. Happens all the time."

"That ain't legal." He moistened his lips. "It's blackmail."

"Don't hurt my feelings. You want me to be your friend, Leo." She nudged the sketches toward him. "You see, it's all a matter of attitude, and whether or not I care if you walk out of here and end up a smear on the sidewalk. Can't say I do at the moment." She smiled, chilling him. "Now, if you were my friend, I'd do everything I could to make sure you lived a long and happy life. Maybe not in Denver, maybe someplace new. You know, Leo, a change of scene can work wonders. Change your name, change your life."

Something flickered in his eyes. She knew it was doubt. "You talking witness protection program?"

"I could be. But if I'm going to ask for something that big, I have to be able to prime the pump." When he hesitated, she sighed. "You better choose sides, pal. Remember Wild Bill? All he did was meet a guy. They might have been talking about the Broncos' chances for the Superbowl. Nobody gave him the benefit of the doubt. They just iced him."

The fear was back, running in the sweat down his temples. "I get immunity. And you drop the drug charges."

"Leo, Leo..." Althea shook her head. "A smart man like you knows how life works. You give me something, if it's good enough, I give you something back. It's the American way."

He licked his lips again, lit yet another cigarette. "Maybe I've seen these two before."

"These two?" Althea tapped the sketches, and then, like a cat, she pounced. "Tell me."

It was 2:00 a.m. before she was finished. She'd questioned Leo, listened to his long, rambling story, made notes, made him backtrack, repeat, expand. Then she'd called in a police stenographer and had Leo go over the same ground again, making an official statement for the tape.

She was energized as she strode back to her office. She had names now, names to run through the computer. She had threads—thin threads, perhaps, but threads nonetheless, tying an organization together.

Much of what Leo had told her was speculation and gossip. But Althea knew that a viable investigation could be built on less.

Peeling off her jacket, she sat at her desk and booted up her computer. She was peering at the screen when Colt walked in and stuck a cup under her nose.

"Thanks." She sipped, winced and spared him a glance. "What is this? It tastes like a meadow."

"Herbal tea," he told her. "You've had enough coffee."

"Nightshade, you're not going to spoil our relationship by thinking you have to take care of me, are you?'' She set the cup aside and went back to the screen.

"You're wired, Lieutenant."

"I know how much I can take before the system overloads. Aren't you the one who keeps saying time's what we don't have?''

"Yeah." From his position behind her chair, he lowered his hands to her shoulders and began to rub. "You did a hell of a job with Leo," he said before she could shrug his hands off. "If I ever decide to go back to law, I'd hate to have you take on one of my clients."

"More compliments." His fingers were magic, easing without weakening, soothing without softening. "I didn't get as much as I wanted, but I think I got all he had."

"He's small-time," Colt agreed. "Passing a little business to the big boys, taking his commission."

"He doesn't know the main player. I'm sure he was telling the truth about that. But he ID'd the two Meena described. Remember the cameraman she'd told us about—the big African-American? Look." She gestured toward the screen. "Matthew Dean Scott, alias Dean Miller, alias Tidal Wave Dean."

"Catchy."

"He played some semipro football about ten years ago. Made a career out of unnecessary roughness. He broke an opposing quarterback's leg."

"These things happen."

"After the game."

"Ah, a poor sport. What else have we got on him?"

"I'll tell you what else *I've* got on him," she said, but she couldn't resist leaning back against his massaging hands. "He was fired for breaking training—having a woman in his room."

"Boys will be boys."

"This particular woman was tied up and screaming her lungs out. They dealt it down from rape to assault, but Scott's football days were over. After that, we've got him on a couple more assaults, indecent exposure, drunk and disorderly, petty larceny, lewd behavior." She punched another button on the keyboard. "That was up to four years ago. After that, nothing."

"You figure he turned over a new leaf? Became a pillar of the community?"

"Sure, just like I believe men read girlie magazines because of the erudite articles."

"That's what motivates me." Grinning, he leaned down to kiss the top of her head.

"I bet. We've got a similar history on contestant number two," she continued. "Harry Kline, a small-time actor from New York whose rap sheet includes drunk and disorderly, possession, sexual assault, several DWIs. He drifted into porno films about eight years ago, and was, incredibly enough, fired from several jobs because of his violent and erratic behavior. He headed west, got a few similar gigs in California, then was arrested for raping one of his costars. The defense pleaded it down and, due to the victim's line of work, made it all go away. The victim's only justice came from the fact that Harry was finished in film—blue or otherwise. Nobody even partially legit would touch him. That was five years ago. There's been nothing on him since."

"Once again, one would think our friends either became solid citizens or died in their sleep."

"Or found a handy hole to hide in. Leo claimed that he was first approached—by Kline—two, maybe three years ago. He knows it was at least two. Kline wanted women, young women who were interested in making private films. Citing free enterprise, Leo obliged him and took his commission. The number he was given to contact Kline is out of service. I'll run it through the phone company to see if it was the penthouse or another location."

"He never saw the other man, the one Meena said sat off in the corner?"

"No. His only contacts were Scott and Kline. Apparently Scott would drop in for a few drinks and brag about how good he was with a camera, and how much money he was pulling in."

"And about the girls," Colt said under his breath. The fingers rubbing Althea's shoulders went rigid. "How he and his friends had— How did he put it? The pick of the litter?"

"Don't think about it." Instinctively she lifted a hand to cover his.

"Don't, Colt. You'll mess up if you do. We're a big step closer to finding her. That's what you have to concentrate on."

"I am." He turned away and paced to the far wall. "I'm also concentrating on the fact that if I find out either of those slime touched Liz, I'm going to kill them." He turned back, his eyes blank. "You won't stop me, Thea."

"Yes, I will." She rose and went to him to take both of his fisted hands in hers. "Because I understand how much you'll want to. And that if you do, it won't change what happened. It won't help Liz. But we'll cross that bridge after we find her." She gave his hands a hard squeeze. "Don't go renegade on me now, Nightshade. I'm just starting to like working with you."

He pulled himself back, let himself look down at her. Though her eyes were shadowed and her cheeks were pale with fatigue, he could feel energy vibrating from her. She was offering him something. Compassion—with restrictions, of course. And hope, without any. The viciousness of his anger faded into the very human need for the comfort of contact.

"Althea..." His hands relaxed. "Let me hold you, will you?" She hesitated, her brow lifting in surprise. He could only smile. "You know, I'm beginning to read you pretty well. You're worried about your professional image, snuggling up against a guy in your office." Sighing, he brushed a hand through her hair. "Lieutenant, it's almost three in the morning. There's nobody here to see. And I really need to hold you."

Once again she let instinct rule, and she moved into his arms. Every time, she mused as she settled her head in the curve of his neck, every time they stood like this, they fitted perfectly. And each time it was easier to admit it.

"Feel better?" she asked, and felt him move his head against her hair.

"Yeah. He didn't know anything about Lacy, the girl who's missing?"

"No." Without thinking, she stroked his back, soothing muscles there as he had soothed hers. "And when I mentioned the possibility of murder, he was genuinely shaken. He wasn't faking that. That's why I'm certain he gave us everything he had."

"The house in the mountains." Colt let his eyes close. "He couldn't give us much."

"West or maybe north of Boulder, near a lake." She moved her shoulders. "It's a little better than we had before. We'll narrow it down, Colt."

"I feel like I'm not putting the pieces together."

"We're putting the pieces we have together," she told him. "And you're feeling that way because you're tired. Go home." She eased back so that she could look up at him. "Get some sleep. We'll start fresh in the morning."

"I'd rather go home with you."

Amused, exasperated, she could only shake her head. "Don't you ever quit?"

"I didn't say I expected to, only that I'd rather." Lifting his hands, he framed her face, stroking his thumbs over her cheekbones, then back to her temples. "I want time with you, Althea. Time when there isn't so much on my mind, or on yours. Time to be with you, and time to figure out what it is about you, just you, that makes me start thinking of long-term, permanent basis."

Instantly wary, she backed out of his arms. "Don't start that now, Nightshade."

Instantly relaxed, he grinned. "That sure does make you nervous. I never knew anyone so spooked by the thought of marriage—unless it was me. Makes me wonder why—and whether I should just sweep you right off your feet and find out the reasons after I've got a ring on your finger. Or—" he moved toward her, backing her against the desk "—if I should take things real slow, real easy, sliding you into the *I do*'s so slick that you wouldn't know you were hitched until it was over and done."

"Either way, you're being ridiculous." There was something lodged in her throat. Althea recognized it as nerves, and bitterly resented it. Feigning indifference, she picked up the tea and sipped. Now it tasted like cold flowers. "It's late," she said. "You go ahead. I can requisition a unit and drive myself home."

"I'll take you." He caught her chin in his hand and waited until her eyes were level with his. "And I mean that, Thea. Any way I can get you. But you're right—it's late. And I owe you."

"You don't—" Her denial ended on a moan when his mouth swooped down to cover hers.

She tasted frustration in the kiss, a jagged need that was barely restrained. And most difficult of all to resist, she tasted the sweetness of affection, like a thin, soothing balm over the pulsing heat.

"Colt." Even as she murmured his name against his mouth, she knew she was losing. Her arms had already lifted to wrap around him, to bring him closer, to accept and to demand.

Her body betrayed her. Or was it her heart? She could no longer tell the two apart, as the needs of one so closely matched the needs of the other. Her fingers dug deep into his shoulders as she struggled to regain her balance. Then they went lax as she allowed herself one moment of madness.

It was Colt who drew back—for himself, and for her. She'd become more important than the satisfactions of the moment. "I owe you," he said again, carefully spacing the words as he stared down into her eyes. "If I didn't, I wouldn't let you go tonight. I don't think I could. I'll drive you home." He picked up her jacket, offered it to her. "Then I'm probably going to spend the rest of the night wondering what it would have been like if I'd just locked that door there and let nature take its course."

Shaken, she draped her jacket over her shoulders before walking to the door. But she'd be damned if she'd be outdone or outmaneuvered. She paused and sent one slow smile over her shoulder. "I'll tell you what it would have been like, Nightshade. It would have been like nothing you've ever experienced. And when I'm ready—if I'm ever ready—I'll prove it."

Stunned by the punch of that single cool smile, he watched her saunter off. Letting out a long breath, he pressed a hand to the knot in his gut. Sweet God, he thought, this was the woman for him. The only woman for him. And damned if *he* wasn't ready to prove it.

With four hours' sleep, two cups of black coffee and a cherry Danish under her belt, Althea was ready to roll. By 9:00 a.m., she was at her desk, putting through a call to the telephone company with an official request for a check on the number she'd gotten from Leo.

By 9:15, she had a name and address, and the information that the customer had cancelled the service only forty-eight hours before.

Though she didn't expect to find anything, she was putting in a request for a search warrant when Colt walked in.

"You don't let moss grow under your feet, do you?"

Althea hung up the phone. "I don't let anything grow under my feet. I've got a line on the number from Leo. The customer canceled the service. I imagine we'll find the place cleaned out, but I can pick up a search warrant within the hour."

"That's what I love about you, Lieutenant—no wasted moves." He eased a hip down on her desk—and was delighted to discover she smelled as good as she looked. "How'd you sleep?"

She slanted a look up at him. Direct challenge. "Like a rock. You?"

"Never better. I woke up this morning with a whole new perspective. Can you be ready to roll by noon?"

"Roll where?"

"This idea I had. I ran it by Boyd, and he—" He scowled down at her shrilling phone. "How many times a day does that ring?"

"Often enough." She plucked up the receiver. "Grayson. Yes, this is Lieutenant Althea Grayson." Her head snapped up. "Jade." With a nod for Colt, Althea covered the receiver. "Line two," she whispered. "And keep your mouth shut." She continued to listen as Colt shot from the room to pick up an extension. "Yes, we have been looking for you. I appreciate you calling in. Can you tell me where you are?"

"I'd rather not." Jade's voice was thin, jumping with nerves. "I only called because I don't want any trouble. I'm getting a job and everything. A straight job. If there's trouble with the cops, I'll lose it."

"You're not in any trouble. I contacted your mother because you can be of some help on a case I'm investigating." Althea swiveled her chair to the right so that she could see Colt through the doorway. "Jade, you remember Liz, don't you? The girl whose parents you wrote?"

"I...I guess. Maybe."

"It took a lot of courage to write that letter, and to get out of the situation you'd found yourself in. Liz's parents are very grateful to you.''

''She was a nice kid. Didn't really know the score, you know? She wanted out.'' Jade paused, and Althea heard the sound of a scraping match, a deep intake of breath. ''Listen, there was nothing I could do for her. We only had a couple of minutes alone once or twice. She slipped me the address, asked me if I'd write her folks. Like I said, she was a nice kid in a bad spot.''

''Then help me find her. Tell me where they've got her.''

''I don't know. Man, I really don't. They took a couple of us up in the mountains a few times. Really out there, you know. Wilderness stuff. They had this really classy cabin, though. First-rate, with a Jacuzzi, and a big stone fireplace, and this big-screen TV.''

''Which way did you go out of Denver? Can you remember that?''

''Well, yeah, sort of. It was like Route 36, toward Boulder, but we just kept going on it forever. Then we took this other little road for a while. Not a highway. One of those two-lane winding jobs.''

''Do you remember going by any towns? Anything that sticks out in your mind?''

''Boulder. After that there wasn't much.''

''Did you go up in the morning, afternoon, night?''

''The first time it was in the morning. We got a really early start.''

''After Boulder, was the sun in front of you, or behind?''

''Oh, I get it. Ah…I guess it was kind of behind us.''

Althea continued to press for details, about the location, the routine, descriptions of the people Jade had seen. As a witness, Jade proved vague but cooperative. Still, Althea had no problem recognizing Scott and Kline from Jade's descriptions. There was again a mention of a man who stayed in the background, keeping to the shadows, watching.

''He was creepy, you know?'' Jade continued. ''Like a spider, just hanging there. The job paid good, so I went back a couple of times. Three hundred for one day, and a fifty-dollar bonus if they needed you for two. I… You know you just can't make that kind of money on the street.''

''I know. But you stopped going.''

''Yeah, because sometimes they got really rough. I had bruises all over me, and one of the guys even split my lip while we were doing this scene. I got scared, because it didn't seem like they were acting. It seemed like they wanted to hurt you. I told Wild Bill, and he said how I shouldn't go back. And that he wasn't going to send any more girls. He said he was going to do some checking into it, and if it was bad, he was going to talk to his cop. I knew that was you, so that's why I called back when I got the message. Bill thinks you're okay."

Wearily Althea rubbed a hand over her brow. She didn't tell Jade that she should be using the past tense as far as Wild Bill was concerned. She didn't have the heart. "Jade, you said something in your letter about thinking they'd killed one of the girls."

"I guess I did." Her voice quavered, weakened. "Listen, I'm not going to testify or anything. I'm not going back there."

"I can't promise anything, only that I'll try to keep you out of it. Tell me why you think they killed one of the girls."

"I told you how they could get rough. And it wasn't no playacting, either. The last time I was up, they really hurt me. That's when I decided I wasn't going back. But Lacy, that's a girl I hung with some, she said how she could handle it, and how the money was too good to pass up. She went up again, but she never came back. I never saw her again."

She paused, another match scraped. "It's not like I can prove anything. It's just... She left all her stuff in her room, 'cause I checked. Lacy was real fond of her things. She had this collection of glass animals. Real pretty, crystal, like. She wouldn't have left them behind. She'd have come back for them, if she could. So I thought she was dead, or they were keeping her up there, like with Liz. And I figured I better split before they tried something with me."

"Can you give me Lacy's full name, Jade? Any other information about her?"

"She was just Lacy. That's all I knew. But she was okay."

"All right. You've been a lot of help. Why don't you give me a number where I can contact you?"

"I don't want to. Look, I've told you all I know. I want out of it. I told you, I'm starting over out here."

Althea didn't press. It was a simple matter to get the number from the phone company. "If you think of anything else, no matter how insignificant it seems, will you call me back?"

"I guess. Look, I really hope you get the kid out of there, and give those creeps what they deserve."

"We will. Thanks."

"Okay. Say hi to Wild Bill."

Before Althea could think of a reply, Jade broke the connection. When she looked up, Colt was standing in her doorway. His eyes held that blank, dangerous look again.

"You can get her back here. Material witness."

"Yeah, I could." Althea dialed the phone again. She'd get the number now. Keep it for backup. "But I won't." She held up a hand for silence before Colt could speak, and made the official request to the operator.

"A 212 area code," Colt noted as Althea scribbled on her pad. "You can get the NYPD to pick her up."

"No," she said simply, then slipped the pad into her purse and rose.

"Why the hell not?" Colt grabbed her arm as she reached for her coat. "If you can get that much out of her on the phone, you'd get that much more face-to-face."

"It's because I got that much out of her." Resentful of his interference, she jerked away. "She gave me everything she had, just for the asking. No threats, no promises, no maneuvering. I asked, she answered. I don't betray trusts, Nightshade. If I need her to drop the hammer on these bastards, then I'll use her. But not until then, and not if there's another way. And not," she added deliberately, "without her consent. Is that clear?"

"Yeah." He scrubbed his hands over his face. "Yeah, it's clear. And you're right. So, you want to pick up that warrant, check that other address?"

"Yes. Do you intend to tag along?"

"You bet. We should have just enough time to finish that before we take off."

She stopped in the doorway. "Take off?"

"That's right, Lieutenant. You and I are taking a little trip. I'll tell you all about it on the way."

# Chapter 8

"I think we've all lost our minds." Althea gripped her seat as the nose of the Cessna rose into the soft autumn sky.

Comfortable at the controls, Colt spared her a glance. "Come on, tough stuff, don't you like planes?"

"Sure I like planes." A tricky patch of cross-currents sent the Cessna rocking. "But I like them with flight attendants."

"There's stuff in the galley. Once we level off, you can serve yourself."

That wasn't precisely what she'd meant, but Althea said nothing, just watched the land tilt away. She enjoyed flying, really. It was just that she had a routine. She would strap in, adjust her headset to the music of her choice, open a book and zone out for the length of the flight.

She didn't like to think of all the gauges over which she had no control.

"I still think this is a waste of time."

"Boyd didn't argue," Colt pointed out. "Look, Thea, we know the general location of the cabin. I studied that damn tape until my eyes bugged out. I'll recognize it when I see it, and plenty of the surrounding landmarks. This is worth a shot."

"Maybe" was all she'd give him.

"Think about it." Colt banked the plane and set his course. "They know the heat's on. That's why they pulled out of the penthouse.

They're going to be wondering where that tape ended up, and if they try to contact Leo, they won't find him, since you've got him stashed in a safe house.''

"So they'll stay out of Denver," she agreed. The engines were an irritating roar in her ears. "They might even pull up stakes and move on."

"That's just what I'm afraid of." Colt's mouth thinned as they left Denver behind. "What happens to Liz if they do? None of the options have a happy ending."

"No." That, and Boyd's approval, had convinced her to go with Colt. "No, they don't."

"I have to think they'd stick to the cabin for the time being. Even if they figure we know it exists, they wouldn't think we'd know its location. They don't know about Jade."

"I'll give you that, Nightshade. But it seems to me that you're relying on blind luck to guide you there."

"I've been lucky before. Better?" he asked when the plane leveled. "It's pretty up here, don't you think?"

There was snow on the peaks to the north, and there were broad, flat valleys between the ridges. They were cruising low enough that she could make out cars along the highway, communities that were little huddles of houses, and the deep, thick green of the forest to the west.

"It has its points." A thought erupted in her mind, making her swivel her head in his direction. "Do you have a pilot's license, Nightshade?"

He glanced over, stared, then nearly collapsed with laughter. "Lord, I'm crazy about you, Lieutenant. Do you want one of those big blowout weddings or the small, intimate kind?"

"You're crazy, period," she muttered, and shifted deliberately to stare out through the windscreen. She'd check on his license when they got back to Denver. "And you said you weren't going to bring up that kind of thing."

"I lied." He said it cheerfully. Despite the worry that never quite dissipated, he didn't think he'd ever felt better in his life. "I've got a problem with that. A woman like you could probably cure me of it."

"Try a psychiatrist."

"Thea, we're going to make a hell of a pair. Wait until my family gets a load of you."

"I'm not meeting your family." She attributed the sudden hollowness in her stomach to another spot of turbulence.

"Well, you're probably right about that—at least until we're ready to walk down the aisle. My mother tends to manage everything, but you can handle her. My father likes spit and polish, which means the two of you would get along like bacon and eggs. A regulation type, that's the admiral."

"Admiral?" she repeated, despite her vow to remain stubbornly silent.

"Navy man. Broke his heart when I joined the air force." Colt shrugged. "That's probably why I did it. Then I have this aunt... Well, better you should meet them for yourself."

"I'm not meeting your family," she said again, annoyed that the statement sounded more petulant than firm. She unstrapped herself and marched back into the tiny galley, rooting about until she found a can of nuts and a bottle of mineral water. Curiosity had her opening the small refrigerated compartment and studying a tin of caviar and a bottle of Beaujolais. "Whose plane is this?"

"Some friend of Boyd's. A weekend jockey who likes to take women up."

Her answer to that was a grunt as she came back to take her seat. "Must be Frank the lecher. He's been after me to fly the sexy skies for years." She chose a cashew.

"Oh, yeah? Not your type?"

"He's so obvious. But then, men tend to be."

"I'll have to remind myself to be subtle. You going to share those?"

She offered the can. "Is that Boulder?"

"Yep. I'm going to track northwest from here, circle around some. Boyd tells me he has a cabin up here."

"Yes. Lots of people do. They like to escape from the city on weekends and tramp through the snow."

"Not your speed?"

"I don't see any purpose for snow unless you're skiing. And the main purpose of skiing, as far as I'm concerned, is coming back to a lodge and having hot buttered rum in front of a fire.''

"Ah, you're the adventurous type.''

"I live for adventure. Actually, Boyd's place does have a nice view,'' she admitted. "And the kids get a big kick out of it.''

"So you've been there.''

"A few times. I like it better in late spring, early summer, when there isn't much chance of the roads being closed.'' She glanced down at the patchy snow in the foothills. "I hate the thought of being stuck.''

"It might have its advantages.''

"Not for me.'' She was silent for a time, watching hills and trees take over from city and suburbs. "It is pretty,'' she conceded. "Especially from up here. Like a segment on public television.''

He grinned at that. "Nature at a distance? I thought city girls always yearned for a country retreat.''

"Not this city girl. I'd rather—'' There was a violent bump that sent nuts flying and had Althea grabbing for a handhold. "What the hell was that?''

Narrow-eyed, Colt studied his gauges while he fought to bring the nose of the plane back up. "I don't know.''

"You don't know? What do you mean, you don't know? You're supposed to know!''

"Shh!'' He tilted his head to listen hard to the engines. "We're losing pressure,'' he said, with the icy calm that had kept him alive in war-torn jungles, in deserts and in skies alive with flak.

Once she understood that the trouble was serious, Althea responded in kind. "What do we do?''

"I'm going to have to set her down.''

Althea looked down, studying the thick trees and rocky hills fatalistically. "Where?''

"According to the map, there's a valley a few degrees east.'' Colt adjusted the course, fighting the wheel as he jiggled switches. "Watch for it,'' he ordered, then flipped on his radio. "Boulder tower, this is Baker Able John three.''

"There.'' Althea pointed to what looked to be a very narrow spit of flat land between jagged peaks. Colt nodded, and continued to inform the tower of his situation.

"Hang on," he told her. "It's going to be a little rough."

She braced herself, refusing to look away as the land rushed up to meet them. "I heard you were good, Nightshade."

"You're about to find out." He cut speed, adjusting for the drag of currents as he finessed the plane toward the narrow valley.

Like threading a needle, Althea thought. Then she sucked in her breath at the first vicious thud of wheels on land. They bounced, teetered, shook, then rolled to a gentle halt.

"You okay?" Colt asked instantly.

"Yeah." She let out a breath. Her stomach was inside out, but apart from that she thought she was all in one piece. "Yeah, I'm fine. You?"

"Dandy." He reached out, grabbed her face in both of his hands and dragged her, straining against her seat belt, close enough to kiss. "By damn, Lieutenant," he said, and kissed her again, hard. "You never flinched. Let's elope."

"Can it." When a woman was used to level emotions, it was difficult to know what to do when she had the urge to laugh and scream simultaneously. She shoved him away. "You want to let me out of this thing? I could use some solid ground under my feet."

"Sure." He released the door, even helped her alight. "I'm going to radio in our position," he told her.

"Fine." Althea took a deep gulp of fresh, cold air and tried out her legs. Not too wobbly, she discovered, pleased. All in all, she'd handled her first—and hopefully last—forced landing rather well. She had to give Colt credit, she mused as she looked around. He'd chosen his spot, and he'd made it work.

She didn't get down on her knees and kiss the ground, but she was grateful to feel it under her. As an added bonus, the view was magnificent. They were cupped between mountain and forest, sheltered from the wind, low enough to look up at the snow cascading down from the rocky peaks without being inconvenienced by it.

There was a good clean scent to the air, a clear blue sky overhead, and a bracing chill that stirred the blood. With any luck, a rescue could be accomplished within the hour, so she could afford to enjoy the scenery without being overwhelmed by the solitude.

She was feeling in tune with the world when she heard Colt clamber out of the cockpit. She even smiled at him.

"So, when are they coming to get us?"

"Who?"

"Them. Rescue people. You know, those selfless heroes who get people out of tricky situations such as this."

"Oh, them. They're not." He dropped a tool chest on the ground, then went back inside for a short set of wooden steps.

"Excuse me?" Althea managed when she found her voice. She knew it was an illusion, but the mountains suddenly seemed to loom larger. "Did you say no one's coming to get us? Isn't the radio working?"

"Works fine." Colt climbed on the steps and uncovered the engine. He'd already stuck a rag in the back pocket of his jeans. "I told them I'd see if I could do the repairs on-site and keep in contact."

"You told them—" She moved fast, before either of them understood her intention. Her first swing caught him in the kidneys and had him tumbling off the steps. "You *idiot!* What do you mean, you'll do the repairs?" She swung again, but he dodged, more baffled than annoyed. "This isn't a Ford broken down on the highway, Nightshade. We haven't got a damn flat tire."

"No," he said carefully, braced and ready for her next move. "I think it's the carburetor."

"You think it's—" Her breath whistled out through her teeth, and her eyes narrowed. "That's it. I'm going to kill you with my bare hands."

She launched herself at him. Colt made a split-second decision, pivoted, and let her momentum carry them both to the ground. It only took him another second to realize the lady was no slouch at hand-to-hand. He took one on the chin that snapped his teeth together. It looked like it was time to get serious.

He scissored his legs around her and managed, after a short, grunting tussle, to roll her onto her back. "Hold on, will you? Somebody's going to get hurt!"

"You're damn right."

Since reason wouldn't work, he used his weight, levering himself over her as he cuffed her wrists with his hands. She bucked twice, then went still. They both knew she was only biding her time until she found an opening.

"Listen." He gave himself another moment to catch his breath, then spoke directly into her ear. "It was the most logical alternative."

"That's bull."

"Let me explain. If you still disagree afterward, we'll go for two falls out of three. Okay?" When she didn't respond, Colt set his teeth. "I want your word you won't take another punch at me until I finish."

It was a pity he couldn't see her expression at that moment. "Fine," Althea said tightly. Cautious, Colt eased back until he could watch her face. He was halfway into a sitting position when she brought her knee solidly into his crotch.

He didn't have the breath to curse her as he rolled into a ball.

"That wasn't a punch," she pointed out. She took the time to smooth back her hair, brush down her parka, before she rose. "Okay, Nightshade, let's hear it."

He only lifted a hand, made a couple of woofing noises, and waited for the stars to fade from behind his eyes. "You may have endangered our bloodline, Thea." He got creakily to his knees, breathing shallowly. "You fight dirty."

"It's the only way to fight. Spill it."

As his strength returned, he shot her a killing look. "I owe you. I owe you big. We're not injured," he ground out. "At least I wasn't until you started on me. The plane's undamaged. If you'll take a look around, you'll see that there isn't room to land another plane safely. They could send a copter, lift us out, but for what? Odds are, if I make a few minor adjustments I can fly us out."

Maybe it made sense, Althea thought. Maybe. But it didn't alter one simple fact. "You should have consulted me. I'm here, too, Nightshade. You had no right to make that decision on your own."

"My mistake." He turned to walk—limp—back to the steps. "I figured you were the logical type and, being a public servant, wouldn't want to see other public servants pulled out for an unnecessary rescue. And, damn it, Liz might be over that ridge." With a violent clatter, he pulled a wrench from the toolbox. "I'm not going back without her."

Oh, he would have to push that button, Althea thought as she turned away to stare into the deep green of the neighboring forest. He would have to let her hear that terrible worry in his voice, see the fire of it in his eyes.

He would have to be perfectly and completely right.

Pride was the hardest of all pills to swallow. Making the effort, she turned back and walked to stand beside the steps. "I'm sorry. I shouldn't have lost my temper."

His response was a grunt.

"Does it still hurt?"

He looked back down at her then, with a gleam in his eyes that would have made lesser women grovel. "Only when I breathe."

She smiled and patted his leg. "Try to think about something else. Do you want me to hand you tools or something?"

His eyes only narrowed farther, until they were thin blue slits. "Do you know the difference between a ratchet and a torque wrench?"

"No." She tossed her hair back. "Why should I? I have a perfectly competent mechanic to look after my car."

"And if you break down on the highway?"

She sent him a pitying look. "What do you think?"

He ground his teeth and went back to the carburetor. "If I made a comment like that, you'd call it sexist."

She grinned behind his back, but when she spoke, her voice was sober. "Why is calling a tow truck sexist? I think there's some instant coffee in the galley," she continued. "I'll make some."

"It isn't smart to use the battery," he muttered. "We'll make do with soft drinks."

"No problem."

When she returned twenty minutes later, Colt was cursing the engine. "This friend of Boyd's should be shot for taking such haphazard care of his equipment."

"Are you going to fix it or not?"

"Yeah, I'm going to fix it." He found several interesting names to call a bolt he was fighting to loosen. "It's just going to take a little longer than I expected.'' Prepared for some pithy comment, he glanced down. She merely stood there patiently, the breeze ruffling her hair. ''What's that?'' he asked, nodding down at her hands.

''I think it's called a sandwich.'' She held up the bread and cheese for his inspection. ''Not much of one, but I thought you might be hungry.''

''Yeah, I am.'' The gesture mollified him somewhat. He lifted his hands and showed her palms and fingers streaked with grease. ''I'm a little handicapped.''

''Okay. Bend over.'' When he obeyed, she brought the bread to his mouth. They watched each other over it as he took a bite.

''Thanks.''

''You're welcome. I found a beer.'' She pulled the bottle out of her pocket and tipped it back. ''We'll share.'' Then she held it to his lips.

''Now I know I love you.''

''Just eat.'' She fed him more of the sandwich. ''Do you have any idea how much longer it's going to take you to get us airborne?''

''Yeah.'' And because he did, he made sure he got his full share of the beer and the sandwich before he told her. ''It'll be an hour, maybe two.''

She blinked. ''Two hours? We'll have run out of daylight by then. You don't plan to fly this out of here in the dark?''

''No, I don't.'' Though he remained braced for a sneak attack, he went back to the engine. ''It'll be safer to wait until morning.''

''Until morning,'' she repeated, staring at his back. ''And just what are we supposed to do until morning?''

''Pitch a tent, for starters. There's one in the cabin, in the overhead. I guess old Frank likes to take his ladies camping.''

''That's great. Just great. You're telling me we have to sleep out here?''

''We could sleep in the plane,'' he pointed out. ''But it wouldn't be as comfortable, or as warm, as stretching out in a tent beside a fire.'' He began to whistle as he worked. He'd said he owed her one. He hadn't realized he'd be able to pay her back so soon, or so well. ''I don't suppose you know how to start a campfire.''

''No, I don't know how to start a damn campfire.''

"Weren't you ever a Girl Scout?"

She made a sound like steam escaping a funnel. "No. Were you?"

"Can't say I was—but I was friendly with a few of them. Well, you go on and gather up some twigs, darling. I'll talk you through your first merit badge."

"I am not going to gather twigs."

"Okay, but it's going to get cold once that sun goes down. A fire keeps the chill—and other things—away."

"I'm not—" She broke off, looked uneasily around. "What other things?"

"Oh, you know. Deer, elk...wildcats..."

"Wildcats." Her hand went automatically to her shoulder rig. "There aren't any wildcats around here."

He lifted his head and glanced around as if considering. "Well, it might be too early in the year yet. But they do start coming down from the higher elevations near winter. Of course, if you want to wait until I've finished here, I'll get a fire going. May be dark by then, though."

He was doing it on purpose. She was sure of it. But then again... She cast another look around, toward the forest, where the shadows were lengthening. "I'll get the damn wood," she muttered, and stomped off toward the trees. After she checked her weapon.

He watched her, smiling. "We're going to do just fine together," he said to himself. "Just fine."

Following Colt's instructions, Althea managed to start a respectable fire within a circle of stones. She didn't like it, but she did it. Then, because he claimed to be deeply involved in the final repairs to the plane, she was forced to rig the tent.

It was a lightweight bubble that Colt declared would nearly erect itself. After twenty minutes of struggle and swearing, she had it up. A narrow-eyed study showed her that it would shelter the two of them—as long as they slept hip to hip.

She was still staring at it, ignoring the chill of the dusk, when she heard the engine spring to life.

"Good as new," Colt shouted, then shut off the engines. "I have to clean up," he told her. He leapt out of the cabin, holding a jug of water. He used it sparingly, along with a can of degreaser from the toolbox. "Nice job," he said, nodding toward the tent.

"Thanks a bunch."

"There are blankets in the plane. We'll do well enough." Still crouched, he drew in a deep breath, tasting smoke and pine and good, crisp air. "Nothing quite like camping out in the hills."

She shoved her hands into her pockets. "I'll have to take your word for it."

He finished scrubbing his hands with a rag before he rose. "Don't tell me you've never done any camping."

"All right, I won't tell you."

"What do you do for a vacation?"

She arched a brow. "I go to a hotel," she said precisely. "Where they have room service, hot and cold running water and cable TV."

"You don't know what you're missing."

"I suppose I'm about to find out." She shivered once, sighed. "I could use a drink."

In addition to the Beaujolais, they feasted on rich, sharp cheese, caviar and thin crackers spread with a delicate pâté.

All in all, Althea decided, it could have been worse.

"Not like any camp meal I ever had," Colt commented as he scooped more caviar onto a cracker. "I thought I'd have to go kill us a rabbit."

"Please, not while I'm eating." Althea sipped more wine and found herself oddly relaxed. The fire did indeed keep the chill away. And it was soothing to watch it flicker and hiss. Overhead, countless stars wheeled and winked, stabbing the cloudless black sky. A quarter-moon silvered the trees and lent a glow to the snow capping the peaks that circled them.

She'd stopped jerking every time an owl hooted.

"Pretty country." Colt lit an after-dinner cigar. "I never spent much time here before."

Neither had she, Althea realized, though she'd lived in Denver for a dozen years. "I like the city," she said, more to herself than Colt. She picked up a stick to stir the fire, not because it needed it, but because it was fun to watch the sparks fly.

"Why?"

"I guess because it's crowded. Because you can find anything you want. And because I feel useful there."

"And that's important to you, feeling useful."

"Yeah, it's important."

He watched the way the flames cast shadow and light over her face, highlighting her eyes, sharpening her cheekbones, softening her skin. "It was rough on you, growing up."

"It's over." When he took her hand, she neither resisted nor responded. "I don't talk about it," she said flatly. "Ever."

"All right." He could wait. "We'll talk about something else." He brought her hand to his lips, and felt a response, just a slight flexing, then relaxing, of her fingers. "I guess you never told stories around the campfire."

She smiled. "I guess not."

"I could probably think of one—just to pass the time. Lie or truth?"

She started to laugh, but then she shot to her feet, whipping out her weapon. Colt's reaction was lightning-fast. In an instant he was beside her, shoving her back, his own gun slapped from his boot into his palm.

"What?" he demanded, his eyes narrowed and searching every shadow.

"Did you hear that? There's something out there."

He cocked an ear, while she instinctively shifted to guard his back. After a moment of throbbing silence, he heard a faint rustling, then the far-off cry of a coyote. The plaintive call had Althea's blood drumming.

Colt swore, but at least he didn't laugh. "Animals," he told her, bending to replace his gun.

"What kind?" Her eyes were still scanning the perimeter, wary, watchful.

"Small ones," he assured her. "Badgers, rabbits." He laid a hand over the ones that gripped her weapon. "Nothing you have to put a hole in, Deadeye."

She wasn't convinced. The coyote called again, and an owl hooted in counterpoint. "What about those wildcats?"

He started to respond, thought better of it, and tucked his tongue in his cheek. "Well, now, darling, they aren't likely to come too close to the fire."

Frowning, she replaced her weapon. "Maybe we should have a bigger fire."

"It's big enough." He turned her toward him, running his hands up and down her arms. "I don't think I've ever seen you so spooked."

"I don't like being this exposed. There's too much here, out here." And the sterling truth was that she would rather face a hopped-up junkie in a dark alley than one small, furry creature with fangs. "Don't grin at me, damn it!"

"Was I grinning?" He ran his tongue around his teeth and struggled to look sober. "It looks like you're going to have to trust me to get you through this."

"Oh, am I?"

He tightened his grip when she started to back away. The look in his eyes changed so quickly, from amusement to desire, that it took her breath away. "There's just you and me, Althea."

She let the clogged air slowly out of her lungs. "It looks like."

"I don't figure I have to tell you again how I feel about you. Or how much I want you."

"No." Tension flooded into her when he brushed his lips over her temple. And heat, a frightening spear of it, stabbed up her spine.

"I can make you forget where you are." He trailed his lips down to her jawline and nibbled up the other side. "If you'll let me."

"You'd have to be damn good for that."

He laughed, because there had been a challenge in the statement, even though her breath had caught on the words. "It's a long time until morning. I'm betting I can convince you before sunrise."

Why was she resisting something she wanted so terribly? Hadn't she told herself long ago never again to let fear cloud her desires? And hadn't she learned to sate those desires without penalty?

She could do so now, with him, and erase this grinding ache.

"All right, Nightshade." Fearlessly she linked her arms around his neck, met his eyes straight on. "I'll take that bet."

His hand fisted in her hair, dragged her head back. For one long, humming moment, they stared at each other. Then he plundered.

Her mouth was hot and honeyed under his, as demanding as hunger, as wild as the night. He plunged into the kiss, using tongue and teeth, knowing he could gorge himself on her and never be filled. So he took more, relentlessly savaging her mouth while she met demand with demand and power with power.

It was like the first time, she realized giddily. The first time he'd dragged her to him and made her taste what he had to offer. Like some fatal drug, the taste had her pulses pounding, her blood swimming fast and her mind spinning away from reason.

She wondered how she had expected to come away whole. And then she forgot to care.

She no longer wanted to be safe, to be in control. Now, here, with him, she wanted only to feel, to experience everything that had once seemed impossible, or at least unwise. And if she sacrificed survival, so be it.

Driven by greed, she tore at his coat, desperate to feel the hard, solid body beneath. He didn't have to be stronger than she, but if he was, she would accept the vulnerability that came with being a woman. And the power that raced alongside it.

She was like a volcano ready to erupt, and she wanted nothing more than to be joined with him when the tremors came.

She was stripping him of his sanity, layer by layer. Those wild lips, those frantic hands. On an oath that was almost a prayer, he half carried, half dragged her toward the tent, feeling like some primeval hunter flinging his chosen mate into his cave.

They tumbled into the small shelter together, a tangle of limbs, a tangle of needs. He yanked her coat down her shoulders, fighting for breath as he raced greedy kisses down her throat.

He felt the vibration of her groan against his lips as he fought her shoulder rig, tearing aside that symbol of control and violence, knowing he was losing control, overwhelmed by a violence of feelings that he couldn't suppress.

He wanted her naked and straining. And screaming.

Her breath caught in gasps as she tugged, pulled, ripped, at his clothes. The firelight glowed orange through the thin material of the tent, and she could see his eyes, the dark, dangerous purpose in them. She reveled in it, in the panicked excitement that racked her body where he groped and possessed. He would ravage her tonight, she knew. And be ravaged in turn.

Levering himself back, he dragged her sweater up and over her head and tossed it aside. She wore lace beneath, a snow-white fancy that in a saner place, in a saner time, would have aroused him by its blatant femininity. He might have toyed with the straps, skimmed his fingers over her subtle peaks. Now he only ripped it apart in one jerky move to free her breasts for his greedy mouth.

The flavor of that warm, scented flesh hit his system like a blow. And her response, the lovely arching of her body against his, the long, throaty moan, the quick, helpless quiver, drove him toward a summit of pleasure he had never dreamed of.

He feasted.

A whimper caught in her throat. She dug her nails into the naked flesh of his shoulders, needing to drive him on, terrified of where he was taking her. She clutched at him for balance, moved under him in sinuous invitation, arching once more as he peeled her slacks away, skimming those impossibly clever fingers down her thighs.

The triangle of lace that shielded her tore jaggedly. Once again his mouth feasted.

Her cry of stunned release rippled through his blood. She shot up like a rocket, exploding, imploding, feeling herself scatter and burn. But where the release should have peaked and leveled, he gave her no respite. She clutched at the blanket while he battered her system with sensations that had no name, no form.

When he rose over her, every muscle trembling, he found her eyes open and on his. He watched her face, filled himself with it even as he buried himself inside her in one desperate stroke. Her eyes glazed, closed. His own vision grayed before he buried his face in her hair.

His body took over, matching the fast, furious rhythm of her hips. They rode each other like fury, greedy children gorging themselves on forbidden fruit. Her final cry of dark pleasure echoed through the air seconds before his own.

Strength sapped, he collapsed onto her, gulping in air as he felt her tremble beneath him from the aftershocks.

"Who won?" he managed after a moment.

She hadn't thought it possible to laugh at such a time, but a chuckle rumbled into her throat. "Let's call it a draw."

"Good enough for me." He thought about lifting himself off her, but was afraid he might shatter if he tried to move. "Plenty good enough. I'm going to kiss you in a minute," he murmured, "but first I have to drum up the strength."

"I can wait." Althea let her eyes close again, and savored the closeness. His body continued to radiate heat, and his heart was far from steady. She stroked her hand down his back for the simple pleasure of the contact, frowning a bit when her fingers ran over a raised scar. "What's this?"

"Hmm?" He stirred himself, surprised that he'd nearly fallen asleep on top of her. "Desert Storm."

She hadn't realized he'd been there. It occurred to her that there was quite a bit about him that lay in shadows. "I thought you'd retired before that went down."

"I had. I agreed to do a little job—sort of a side job."

"A favor."

"You could call it that. Caught a little flak—nothing to worry about." He tilted his head, nuzzling. "You have the most gorgeous shoulders. Have I mentioned that?"

"No. Do you still do favors for the government?"

"Only if they ask nicely." He grunted and rolled so that he could shift her on top of him. "Better?"

"Mmm...." She rested her cheek on his chest. "But I think we might freeze to death."

"Not if we keep active." He grinned when she lifted her head to look down at him. "Survival methods, Lieutenant."

"Of course." Her lips curved into a smile. "I have to say, Nightshade, I like your methods."

"That so?" Gently he combed his fingers through her hair, tested its weight with his hand.

"That's very so. How soon do we have to add wood to that fire?"

"Oh, we've got a little while yet."

"Then we shouldn't waste time, should we?" Still smiling, she lowered her mouth to his.

"Nope." He felt himself hardening again inside her, and prepared to let her take the lead. As his lips curved against hers, he was struck by a stab of love so sharp it stole his breath. He clutched her close, held on. "I know it's a tired line, Thea, but it's never been like this for me before. Not with anyone."

That frightened her, and what frightened her more than the words was the flush of warmth they brought to her. "You talk too much."

"Thea..."

But she shook her head and rose up, taking him deep inside her, tantalizing his body so that the need for words slipped away.

# Chapter 9

Colt awakened quickly. An old habit. He registered his surroundings—the pale light of dawn creeping into the tent, the rough blanket and hard ground beneath his back, and the soft, slender woman curled on top of him. It made him smile, remembering the way she'd rolled over him during the night, seeking a place more comfortable than the unyielding floor of the valley.

At the time, they'd both been too exhausted to do more than cuddle up and sleep. Now the sun had brought a reminder of the outside world, and their duties in it. Still, he took a moment to enjoy the lazy intimacy, and to imagine other times, other places, where it would once again be only the two of them.

Gently he tugged the blanket over her bare shoulder and let his fingers trail down over her hair where it lay pooled across her cheek and throat.

She shifted, her eyes opening and locking on his.

"Good reflexes, Lieutenant."

She ran her tongue over her teeth, letting her mind and body adjust to the situation. "I guess it's morning."

"Right the first time. Sleep okay?"

"I've slept better." Every muscle in her body ached, but she figured a couple of aspirin and some exercise would handle that. "You?"

"Like a baby," he said. "Some of us are used to roughing it."

She only lifted a brow, then rolled off him. "Some of us want coffee." The moment she left his warmth, the chill stung her skin. Shivering, she groped for her sweater.

"Hey." Before she could bundle up in the sweater, he grabbed her around the waist and hauled her to him. "You forgot something." His hand slid up her back to cup her head as his mouth met hers.

Her body went fluid, sweetly so, and her lips parted in invitation. She could feel herself melting into him, and wondered at it. All through the night they had come together, again and again, each time like lightning, with flashes of greed. But this was softer, steadier, stronger, like a candle that remained alight long after a raging fire had burned itself out.

"You sure are nice to wake up to, Althea."

She wanted to burrow into him, to grab hold and hang on as though her life depended on it. Instead, she flicked a finger down the stubble on his chin. "You're not so bad, Nightshade."

She moved away quickly, a little too quickly, to give herself the time and space to settle. Because he was beginning to read her very well, he smiled.

"You know, once we're married, we should get ourselves one of those king-size beds, so we'll have plenty of room to roll around and get tangled up."

She tugged the sweater on. When her head emerged, her eyes were cool. "Who's making the coffee?"

He nodded thoughtfully. "That is something we'll have to decide. Keeping those little routines straight helps a marriage run smooth."

She bit back a laugh and reached for her slacks. "You owe me some underwear."

He watched her pull the slacks up her long, smooth legs. "Buying it for you is going to be pure pleasure." He shrugged into his shirt while Althea hunted for her socks. Knowing the value of timing, he waited until she'd found them both. "Darling, I've been thinking...."

She answered with a grunt as she tugged on her shoes.

"How do you feel about getting hitched on New Year's Eve? Kind of romantic, starting out the next year as husband and wife."

This time she hissed out her breath. "I'll make the damn coffee," she muttered, and crawled out of the tent.

Colt gave her retreating bottom a friendly pat and chuckled to himself. She was coming around, he decided. She just didn't know it yet.

By the time Althea got the fire started again, she'd had more than enough of the great outdoors. Maybe it was beautiful, she thought as she rummaged through the small supply of pots they'd found on the plane. Maybe it was even magnificent, with its rugged, snow-capped peaks and densely forested slopes. But it was also cold, and hard and deserted.

They had a handful of nuts between them, and not a restaurant in sight.

Too impatient to wait until it boiled, she heated water until it was hot to the touch, then dumped in a generous amount of instant coffee. The scent was enough to make her drool.

"Now that's a pretty sight." Colt stood just outside the tent, watching her. "A beautiful woman bending over a campfire. And you do have a nice way of bending, Thea."

"Stuff it, Nightshade."

He strolled to her grinning. "Cranky before your coffee, darling?"

She knocked aside the hand he'd lifted to toy with her hair. He was charming her again, and it was just going to have to stop. "Here's breakfast." She shoved the can of nuts at him. "You can pour your own coffee."

Obligingly he crouched down and poured the mixture into two tin mugs. "Nice day," he said conversationally. "Low wind, good visibility."

"Yeah, great." She accepted the mug he offered. "God, I'd kill for a toothbrush."

"Can't help you there." He sampled the coffee, grimaced. It was mud, he decided, but at least it packed a punch. "Don't you worry, we'll be back in civilization before much longer. You can brush your teeth, have yourself a nice hot bubble bath, go to the hairdresser."

She started to smile—it was the bubble bath that did it—but then she whipped her head up and scowled. "Leave my hair out of this." Setting the mug down, she knelt and began to rummage through her purse. Once she found her brush, she sat cross-legged on the ground, her back to Colt, and began to drag it through her tangled hair.

"Here now." He sat behind her, snuggling her back into the vee of his legs. "Let me do that."

"I can do it myself."

"Yeah, but you're about to brush yourself bald." After a short tussle, he snatched the brush away. "You should take more care with this," he murmured, gently working out the tangles. "It's the most beautiful head of hair I've ever seen. Up close like this, I can see a hundred different shades of red and gold and russet."

"It's just hair." But if Althea had a point of vanity, Colt was stroking it now. And it felt wonderful. She couldn't resist a sigh as he brushed and lifted, caressed and smoothed. They might be in the middle of nowhere, but for that moment Althea felt as though she were in the lap of luxury.

"Look," Colt whispered against her ear. "At three o'clock."

Responding instinctively to the direction, Althea turned her head. There, just at the verge of the forest, stood a deer. No, not a deer, she realized. Surely no deer could be so huge. His shoulders were nearly as high as a man, and massive. His head was lifted, scenting the air, with his high crown of antlers spearing upward.

"It's, ah…"

"Wapiti," Colt murmured, wrapping his arms companionably around her waist. "American elk. That's one beautiful bull."

"Big. Big is what he is."

"Close to seven hundred pounds, by the look of him. There, he's caught our scent."

Althea felt her heart jolt when the elk turned his great head and looked at her. He seemed both arrogant and wise as he studied the humans who were trespassing on his territory.

And suddenly there was an aching in her throat, a response to beauty, a trembling deep inside, a kind of wonder. For a moment the three of them remained poised, measuring each other. A lark called, a searingly beautiful cascade of notes.

The elk turned, vanished into the shadowed trees.

"I guess he didn't want coffee and cashews," Althea said quietly. She couldn't say why she was moved. She only knew that she was, deeply. Relaxed against Colt, cradled in his arms, she was completely and inexplicably content.

"Can't say I blame him." Colt rubbed his cheek against her hair. "It's a hell of a way to start the day."

"Yeah." She turned, impulsively winding an arm around his neck, pressing her lips to his. "This is better."

"Much better," he agreed, sinking in when she deepened the kiss. He nuzzled, and was amused when she laughed and shoved his unshaven face away from the tender curve of her throat. "Once we're back in Denver, I want you to remind me where we left off."

"I might do that." With some regret, she drew away. "We'd better—what do you call it? Break camp? And, by the way," she added, shrugging into her shoulder rig, "you owe me more than new lingerie—you owe me breakfast."

"Put it on my tab."

Twenty minutes later, they were strapped into the cockpit. Colt checked his gauges while Althea applied blusher to her cheekbones.

"We ain't going to a party," he commented.

"I may not be able to brush my teeth," she said, and crunched down on a mint she'd found in her purse. "I may not be able to take a shower. But, by damn, I haven't lost all sense of propriety."

"I like your cheeks pale." He started the engines. "Kind of fragile."

After one narrow-eyed stare, she deliberately added more blusher. "Just fly, Nightshade."

"Yes, sir, Lieutenant."

He didn't see the point in telling her it would be a tricky takeoff. While she was occupied braiding her hair, he maneuvered the plane into the best position for taxiing. After touching a finger to the medal that rested under his shirt, he let her rip.

They jolted, bounced, shuddered and finally lifted, degree by degree. Colt fought the crosscurrents, dipping one wing, leveling off, nosing upward. Finally they cleared the ridge and shot over the tops of the trees.

"Not too shabby, Nightshade." Althea flipped her braid behind her back. When he glanced over, he saw the awareness in her eyes.

The hands that were currently uncapping a tube of mascara were rock-steady, but she knew. He should have realized she would know.

"Boyd was right, Thea. You're a hell of a partner."

"Just try to hold this thing steady for a few minutes, will you?" Smiling to herself, she angled her purse mirror and began to do her lashes. "So, what's the plan?"

"Same as before. We circle this area. Look for cabins. The one we want has a sloped drive."

"That certainly narrows things down."

"Shut up. It's also a two-story with a covered wraparound deck and a trio of windows on the front, facing west. The sun was going down in one scene in the video," he explained. "According to the other information we have, there's a lake somewhere in the general area. I also saw fir and spruce, which gives us the elevation. The cabin was whitewashed logs. It shouldn't be that hard to spot."

He might be right about that, but Althea knew there was something else that needed to be said. "She might not be there, Colt."

"We're going to find out." He banked the plane and headed west.

Because she could see the worry come into his eyes, Althea changed tacks. "Tell me, what rank were you in the air force?"

"Major." He drummed up a smile. "Looks like I outrank you."

"You're retired," she reminded him. "I bet you looked swell in uniform."

"I wouldn't mind seeing you in dress blues. Look."

Following his direction, she spotted a cabin below. It was a three-level structure fashioned from redwood. She noted two others, separated from each other by lines of trees.

"None of them fit."

"No," he agreed. "But we'll find the one that does."

They continued to search, with Althea peering through binoculars. Hideaways were snuggled here and there, most of them seemingly unoccupied. A few had smoke puffing out of a chimney and trucks or four-wheel-drive vehicles parked outside.

Once she saw a man in a bright red shirt splitting wood. She spotted a herd of elk grazing in a frosty meadow, and the flash of White-tail deer.

"There's nothing," she said at length. "Unless we want to do a documentary on— Wait.'' A glint of white caught her attention, then was lost. "Circle around. Four o'clock.'' She continued to scan, searching the snow-dusted ridges.

And there it was, two stories of whitewashed logs, a trio of windows facing west, the deck. At the end of the sloping gravel drive sat a muscular-looking truck. As further proof of habitation, smoke was spiraling out of the chimney.

"That could be it.''

"I'm betting it is.'' Colt circled once, then veered off.

"I might take that bet.'' She unhooked the radio mike. "Give me the position. I'll call it in, get a surveillance team up here so we can go back and talk a judge into issuing a warrant.''

Colt gave her the coordinates. "Go ahead and call it in. But I'm not waiting for a piece of paper.''

"What the hell do you think you can do?''

His eyes flashed to hers, then away. "I'm setting the plane down, and I'm going in.''

"No,'' she said, "you're not.''

"You do what you have to.'' He angled for the meadow where Althea had spotted the grazing elk. "There's a good chance she's in there. I'm not leaving her.''

"What are you going to do?'' she demanded, too incensed to noticed the perilous descent. "Break in, guns blazing? That's movie stuff, Nightshade. Not only is it illegal, but it puts the hostage in jeopardy.''

"You've got a better idea?'' He braced himself. They were going to slide once the wheels hit. He hoped to God they didn't roll.

"We'll get a team up here with surveillance equipment. We figure out who owns the cabin, get the paperwork pushed through.''

"Then we break in? No thanks. You said you'd been skiing, right?''

"What?''

"You're about to do it in a plane. Hold on.''

She jerked her head around, gaped through the windscreen as the glittering meadow hurled toward them. She had time for an oath—a vicious one—but then she lost her breath at the impact.

They hit, and went sliding. Snow spewed up the side of the plane, splattering the windows. Althea watched almost philosophically as they hurtled toward a wall of trees. Then the plane spun in two wicked circles before coming to a grinding stop.

"You maniac!" She took deep breaths, fighting back the worst of her temper. She would have let it loose, but there wasn't enough room to maneuver in the cabin. And when she murdered him she wanted to do it right.

"I landed a plane in the Aleutians once, when the radar was down. It was a lot worse than this."

"What does that prove?" she demanded.

"That I'm still a hell of a pilot?"

"Grow up!" she shouted. "This isn't fantasyland. We're closing in on suspected kidnappers, suspected murderers, and there's very possibly an innocent kid caught in the middle. We're going to do this right, Nightshade."

With one jerk, he unstrapped himself, then grabbed both her hands at the wrists. "You listen to me." She would have winced at the way his fingers dug into her flesh, but the fury in his eyes stopped her. "I know what's real, Althea. I've seen enough reality in my life— the waste of it, and the cruelty of it. I know that girl. I held her when she was a baby, and I'm not leaving her welfare up to paperwork and procedure."

"Colt—"

"Forget it." He shoved her hands aside, jerked back. "I'm not asking for your help, because I'm trying to respect your ideas of rules and regulations. But I'm going after her, Thea, and I'm going now."

"Wait." She held up a hand, then dragged it through her hair. "Let me think a minute."

"You think too damn much." But when he started to rise, she shoved a fist into his chest.

"I said wait." Then she tipped her head back, closed her eyes and thought it through.

"How far is it to the cabin?" she asked after a moment. "Half a mile?"

"More like three-quarters."

"The roads leading in were all plowed."

"Yeah." Impatience shimmered around him. "So?"

"It would have been handier if I could have been stuck in a snow-drift. But a breakdown's good enough."

"What are you talking about?"

"I'm talking about working together." She opened her eyes, pinned him with them. "You don't like the way I work, I don't like the way you work. So we're going to have to find a middle ground. I'm calling this in, arranging to have the local police back us up, and I'm going to have them get word to Boyd. See if he can get some paperwork started."

"I told you—"

"I don't care what you told me," she said calmly. "This is how it's going down. We can't go bursting in there. Number one, we might be wrong about the cabin. Number two," she said, cutting him off again, "it puts Liz in increased jeopardy if they're holding her there. And number three, without probable cause, without proper procedure, these bastards might wiggle out, and I want them put away. Now, you listen..."

He didn't like it. It didn't matter how much sense it made or how good a plan she'd devised. But during the long trek to the cabin she defused whatever arguments he voiced with calm, simple logic.

She was going in.

"What makes you think they'll let you inside just because you ask?"

She tilted her head, slanted a look up from under her lashes. "I haven't wasted any on you, Nightshade, but I have a tremendous amount of charm at my disposal." She lengthened her stride to match his. "What do you think most men will do when a helpless woman comes knocking, begging for help because she's lost, her car's broken down and—" she gave a delicate shiver and turned her voice into a purr "—and it's so awfully cold outside."

He swore and watched his breath puff away in smoke. "What if they offer to drive you back to your car and fix it?"

"Well, I'll be terribly grateful. And I'll stall them long enough to do what needs to be done."

"And if they get rough?"

"Then you and I will have to kick butt, won't we?"

He couldn't help but look forward to that. And yet… "I still think I should go in with you."

"They're not going to be sympathetic if the little woman has a big strong man with her." Sarcasm dripped in the chilly air. "With any luck, the local boys will be here before things get nasty." She paused, judging the distance. "We're close enough. One of them might be out for a morning stroll. We don't want to be spotted together."

Colt shoved his fists into his pockets, then made them relax. She was right—more, she was good. He pulled his hands out, grabbed her shoulders and hauled her close. "Watch your step, Lieutenant."

She kissed him, hard. "Same goes."

She turned, walked away with long, ground-eating strides. He wanted to tell her to stop, to tell her he loved her. Instead, he headed over the rough ground toward the rear of the cabin. This wasn't the time to throw her any emotional curves. He'd save them for later.

Blocking everything from his mind, he sprinted through the hard-crusted snow, keeping low.

Althea moved fast. She wanted to be out of breath and a little teary-eyed when she reached the cabin. Once she came into view of the windows, she switched to a stumbling run, pantomiming relief. She all but fell against the door, calling and banging.

She recognized Kline when he opened it. He wore baggy gray sweats, and his bleary eyes were squinting against the smoke from the cigarette tucked into the corner of his mouth. He smelled of tobacco and stale whiskey.

"Oh, thank God!" Althea slumped against the doorjamb. "Thank God! I was afraid I'd never find anyone. I feel like I've been walking forever."

Kline sized her up. She was one sweet-looking babe, he decided, but he wasn't big on surprises. "What do you want?"

"My car…" She pressed a fluttering hand to her heart. "It broke down—it must be a mile from here, at least. I was coming to visit some friends. I don't know, maybe I made a wrong turn." She shuddered, wrapped her parka closer around her. "Is it all right if I come in? I'm so cold."

"There ain't nobody up around here. No other cabins near here."

She closed her eyes. "I knew I must have turned wrong somewhere. Everything starts to look the same. I left Englewood before sunup—wanted to start my vacation first thing." Staring up at him, wide-eyed, she managed a weak smile. "Some vacation so far. Look, can I just use the phone, call my friends so they can come get me?"

"I guess." The broad was harmless, Kline decided. And a pleasure to look at.

"Oh, a fire..." With a moan of relief, Althea dashed toward it. "I didn't know I could be so cold." While she rubbed her hands together, she beamed over her shoulder at Kline. "I can't thank you enough for helping me out."

"No problem." He pulled the dangling cigarette from his mouth. "We don't get much traffic up here."

"I can see why." She shifted her gaze to the windows. "Still, it is lovely. And this place!" She circled, looking dazzled. "It's just fabulous. I guess if you were all cozied up by the fire with a bottle of wine, you wouldn't mind sitting out a blizzard or two."

His lips curled. "I like to cozy up with something other than a bottle."

Althea fluttered her lashes, lowered them modestly. "It certainly is romantic, Mr—?"

"Kline. You can call me Harry."

"All right, Harry. I'm Rose," she said, giving him her middle name in case he'd recognized the name of Wild Bill's cop. She offered her hand. "It's a real pleasure. I think you've saved my life."

"What the hell's going on down there?"

Althea glanced up to the loft and saw a tall, wiry man with an untended shock of blond hair. She tagged him as the second male actor in the video.

"Got us an unexpected guest, Donner," Kline called up. "Car broke down."

"Well, hell..." Donner blinked his eyes clear and took a good look. "You're out early, sweetie."

"I'm on vacation," she said, and flashed him a smile.

"Isn't that nice?" Donner started downstairs, preening, Althea noticed, like a rooster in a henhouse. "Why don't you fix the lady a cup of coffee, Kline?"

"Tidal Wave's already in the kitchen. It's his turn."

"Fine." Donner sent what was meant to be an intimate smile toward Althea. "Tell him to pour another cup for the lady."

"Why don't you—"

"Oh, I would *love* a cup of coffee," Althea said, turning her big brown eyes on Kline. "I'm just frozen."

"Sure." He shrugged, shot Donner a look that made Althea think of one male dog warning off a competitor, then strode off.

How many more of the organization were in the cabin? she wondered. Or was it just the three of them?

"I was just telling Harry how beautiful your house is." She wandered the living room, dropping her purse onto a table. "Do you live here year-round?"

"No, we just use it now and again."

"It's so much bigger than it looks from outside."

"It does the job." He moved closer as Althea sat on the arm of a chair. "Maybe you'd like to hang out here for your vacation."

She laughed, making no objection when he brushed a finger through her hair. "Oh, but my friends are expecting me. Still, I do have two weeks…" She laughed again, low and throaty. "Tell me, what do you guys do around here for fun?"

"You'd be surprised." Donner laid a hand on her thigh.

"I don't surprise easily."

"Back off." Kline came back in with a mug of black coffee. "Here you are, Rose."

"Thanks." She sniffed deeply, curling her shoulders in for effect. "I feel warm and toasty already."

"Why don't you take off your coat?" Donner put a hand to her collar, but she shifted, smiling.

"As soon as my insides defrost a little more." She'd taken the precaution of removing her shoulder rig, but she preferred more camouflage, as her weapon was snug at the small of her back. "Are the two of you brothers?" she asked conversationally.

Kline snorted. "Not hardly. You could say we're partners."

"Oh, really? What kind of business are you in?"

"Communications," Donner stated, flashing white teeth.

"That's fascinating. You sure have a lot of equipment." She glanced toward the big-screen TV, the state-of-the-art VCR and stereo. "I love watching movies on long winter nights. Maybe we can get together sometime and…" She let her words trail off, alerted by a movement at the back of the loft. Glancing up, she saw the girl.

Her hair was tousled, and her eyes were unbearably tired. She'd lost weight, Althea thought, but she recognized Liz from the snapshot Colt had shown her.

"Why, hello there," she said, and smiled.

"Get back in your room," Kline snapped. "Now."

Liz moistened her lips. She was wearing tattered jeans and a bright blue sweater that was tattered at the cuffs. "I wanted some breakfast." Her voice was quiet, Althea noted, but not cowed.

"You'll get it." He glanced back at Althea, satisfied that she was smiling with friendly disinterest. "Now get on back to your room until I call you."

Liz hesitated, long enough to aim one cold glare at him. That warmed Althea's heart. The kid wasn't beaten yet, Althea noted as Liz turned and walked to the door behind her. It shut with a slam.

"Kids," Kline muttered, and lit another cigarette.

"Yeah." Althea smiled sympathetically. "Is she your sister?"

Kline choked on the smoke, but then he grinned. "Right. Yeah, she's my sister. So, you wanted to use the phone?"

"Oh, yes." Setting the mug of coffee aside, Althea rose. "I appreciate it. My friends'll be getting worried about me soon."

"There it is." He gestured. "Help yourself."

"Thanks." But when she picked up the receiver, there was no dial tone. "Gee, I think it's dead."

Kline swore and strode over, pulling a thin L-shaped tool from his pocket. "Forgot. I, ah, lock it up at night, so the kid can't use it. She was making all these long-distance calls and running up the bill. You know how girls are."

"Yes." Althea smiled. "I do." When she heard the dial tone, she punched in the number for the local police. "Fran," she said merrily, addressing the dispatcher as they had arranged. "You won't believe what happened. I got lost, my car broke down. If it hadn't been for these terrific guys, I don't know what I'd have done." She laughed, hoping Colt was making his move. "I do *not* always get lost. I hope Bob's up to coming for me."

\* \* \*

While Althea chatted with the police dispatcher, Colt shinnied up a pole to the second floor. With his binoculars, he'd seen everything he needed to see through the expansive glass of the cabin. Althea was holding her own, and Liz was on the second floor.

They'd agreed that if the opportunity presented itself, he would get her out of the house. Out of harm's way. He might have preferred a direct route—straight through Kline and the other jerk in the living room, and on into the big guy doing kitchen duty.

But Liz's safety came first. Once he got her out, he'd be coming back.

With a grunt, he swung himself onto the narrow overhang and clutched at the window ledge. He saw Liz lying on a rumpled bed, her body turned away and curled up protectively. His first urge was to throw up the window and leap inside. Afraid he might frighten her into crying out, he tapped gently on the glass.

She shifted. When he tapped again, she turned wearily over, unfocused eyes gazing into the sunlight. Then she blinked and cautiously pushed herself up from the bed. Hurriedly Colt put a finger to his lips, signaling silence. But it didn't stop the tears. They poured out of her eyes as she rushed to the window.

"Colt!" She shook the window, then laid her cheek against the glass and wept. "I want to go home! Please, please, I want to go home!"

He could barely hear her through the glass. Afraid their voices would carry, he tapped again, waiting until she turned her head to look at him.

"Open the window, baby." He mouthed it carefully, but she only shook her head.

"Nailed shut." Her breath hitched, and she rubbed her fists against her eyes. "They nailed it shut."

"Okay, okay. Look at me. Look." He used hand signals to focus her attention. "A pillow. Get a pillow."

A dim spark glowed in her eyes. He'd seen it before, that cautious return of hope. She moved fast, doing as he instructed.

"Hold it against the glass. Hold it steady, and turn your head. Turn your head away, baby."

He used his elbow to smash the glass, satisfied that the pillow muffled most of the noise. When he'd broken enough to ease his body through, he nudged the pillow aside and swung inside.

She was immediately in his arms, clinging, sobbing. He picked her up, cradled her like a baby. "Shh...Liz. It's going to be all right now. I'm going to take you home."

"I'm sorry. I'm so sorry."

"Don't worry about it. Don't worry about anything." He drew back to look into her eyes. She looked so thin, he thought, so pale. And he had a lot more to ask of her. "Honey, you're going to have to be tough for a little while longer. We're going to get you out, and we have to move fast. Do you have a coat? Shoes?"

She shook her head. "They took them. They took everything so I couldn't run away. I tried, Colt, I swear I did, but—"

"It's all right." He pressed her face to his shoulder again, recognizing bubbling hysteria. "You're not going to think about it now. You're just going to do exactly what I tell you. Okay?"

"Okay. Can we go now? Right now?"

"Right now. Let's wrap you in this blanket." He dragged it off the bed with one hand and did his best to bundle it around her. "Now we're going to have to take a little fall. But if you hang on to me, and stay real loose, real relaxed, it's going to be fine." He carried her to the window, careful to cover her face against the cold and the jagged teeth of broken glass. "If you want to scream, you scream in your head, but not out loud. That's important."

"I won't scream." With her heart hammering, she pressed hard against his chest. "Please, just take me home. I want Mom."

"She wants you, too. So does your old man." He kept talking in the same low, soothing tone as he inched toward the edge. "We're going to call them as soon as we get out of here." He said a quick prayer and jumped.

He knew how to fall, off a building, down stairs, out of a plane. Without the child, he would simply have tucked and rolled. With her, he swiveled his body to take the brunt of the impact, so that he would land on his back and cushion her.

The impact stole his breath, wrenched his shoulder, but he was up almost as soon as he landed, with Liz still cradled against his chest. He sprinted toward the road and was halfway there when he heard the first shot.

## Chapter 10

Althea drew out her conversation with the police dispatcher, pausing in her own chatter to take in the information that her backup's E.T.A. was ten minutes. She sincerely hoped Colt had managed to get Liz away from the cabin, but either way, it looked like it was going to go down as smooth as silk.

"Thanks, Fran. I'm looking forward to seeing you and Bob, too. Just let me get some idea of where I am from Harry. I don't have a clue." Beaming a new smile in Harry's direction, Althea cupped a hand over the phone. "Do you have, like, an address or something? Bob's going to come pick me up and take a look at my car."

"No problem." He glanced over as Tidal Wave came in from the kitchen. "Hope you made enough breakfast for our guest," Harry told him. "She's had a rough morning."

"Yeah, there's enough." Tidal Wave turned his hard brown eyes on Althea, narrowed them. "Hey! What the hell is this?"

"Try for some manners," Donner suggested. "There's a lady present."

"Lady, hell! That's a cop. That's Wild Bill's cop."

He made his lunge, but Althea was ready. She'd seen the recognition in his eyes and had already reached for her weapon. There wasn't time to think or to worry about the other two men, as two hundred and sixty pounds of muscle and bulk rammed her.

Her first shot veered wide as she went flying, slamming against an antique table. A collection of snuff bottles crashed, spewing shards of amethyst and aquamarine. She saw stars. Through them, she saw her opponent bearing down on her like a freight train.

Pure instinct had her rolling to the left to avoid a blow. Tidal Wave was big, but she was quick. Althea scrambled to her knees and gripped her weapon in both hands.

This time her shot was true. She had only an instant to note the spread of blood on his white T-shirt before she leapt to her feet.

Donner was heading for the door, and Kline was swearing as he dragged open a drawer. She saw the glint of chrome.

"Freeze!"

Her order had Donner throwing up his hands and turning into a statue, but Kline whipped out the gun.

"Do it and die," she told him, stepping back so that she could keep both Kline and Donner in sight. "Drop it, Harry, or you're going to be staining the carpet like your friend there."

"Son of a bitch." Teeth set, he tossed the weapon down.

"Good choice. Now, on the floor, facedown, hands behind your head. You, too, Romeo," she told Donner. While they obeyed, she picked up Kline's gun. "You two should know better than to invite a stranger into the house."

Lord, she hurt, Althea realized now that her adrenaline was leveling off. From the top of her head to the soles of her feet, she was one huge ache. She hoped Tidal Wave's flying tackle hadn't dislodged anything vital.

She caught the thin wail of a siren in the distance. "Looks like old Fran told the troops to come in. Now, in case you don't get the picture, I'm the law, and you're under arrest."

Althea was calmly reading her prisoners their rights when Colt burst in, a gun in one hand, a knife in the other. By her calculations, it had been roughly three minutes since she'd fired the first shot. The man moved fast.

She spared him a glance, then finished the procedure. "Cover these idiots, will you, Nightshade?" she asked as she picked up the dangling receiver. "Officer Mooney? Yes, this is Lieutenant Grayson. We'll need an ambulance out here. I have a suspect down with a chest wound. No, the situation's under control. Thank you. You were a big help.''

She hung up and looked back at Colt. ''Liz?''

''She's okay. I told her to wait by the road for the cops. I heard the shots.'' His hands were steady. He could be grateful for that. But his insides were jelly. ''I figured they'd made you.''

''You figured right. That one.'' She jerked her head toward Tidal Wave. ''He must have seen me with Wild Bill. Why don't you go find us a towel? We'd better try to stop that bleeding.''

''The hell with that!'' The fury came so suddenly, and so violently, that the two men on the floor quaked. ''Your head's cut.''

''Yeah?'' She touched her fingers to the throbbing ache at her right temple, then studied her·blood-smeared fingers in disgust. ''Hell. That better not need stitches. I really hate stitches.''

''Which one of them hit you?'' Colt scanned the three men with icy eyes. ''Which one?''

''The one I shot. The one who's currently bleeding to death. Now get me a towel, and we'll see if we can have him live long enough to go to trial.'' When he didn't respond, she stepped between him and the wounded man. Colt's intentions were clear as crystal. ''Don't pull this crap on me, Nightshade. I'm not a damsel in distress, and white knights annoy the hell out of me. Got it?''

''Yeah.'' He sucked·in his breath. There were too many emotions ripping through him. None of them could change the situation. ''Yeah, I got it, Lieutenant.''

He turned away to do as she'd asked. After all, he thought, she could handle the situation. She could handle anything.

It wasn't until they were in the plane again that he began to calm. He had to at least pretend to be calm for Liz's sake. She'd clung to him, begging him not to send her back with the police, to stay with her. So he'd agreed to fly back with Liz in the copilot's seat and Althea in the jump seat behind.

Looking lost in his coat, Liz stared through the windscreen. No matter how Colt had tried to bundle her up, she continued to shiver. When they leveled off, heading east, the tears began to flow. They fell fast, hot, down her cheeks. Her shoulders shook violently, but she made no sound. No sound at all.

"Come on, baby." Helpless, Colt reached out to take her hand. "Everything's all right now. Nobody's going to hurt you now."

But the silent tears continued.

Saying nothing, Althea rose. She came forward, calmly unstrapped Liz. Communicating by touch, Althea urged Liz to shift, then took her place in the chair. Then she gathered the girl on her lap, cradled her head on her shoulder. Enfolded her grief.

"Don't hold back," she murmured.

Almost at once, Liz's sobs echoed through the cabin. The pain in them cut at Althea's heart as she rocked the girl and held her close. Devastated by the weeping, Colt lifted a hand to brush it down Liz's tangled hair. But she only curled closer to Althea at the touch.

He dropped his hand and concentrated on the sky.

It was Althea's gentle insistence that convinced Liz it would be wise to go to the hospital first. She wanted to go home, she said over and over again. And over and over again, Althea patiently reminded Liz that her parents were already on their way to Denver.

"I know it's hard." Althea kept her arm tight around Liz's shoulders. "And I know it's scary, but the doctor needs to check you out."

"I don't want him to touch me."

"I know." How well she knew. "But he's a she." Althea smiled, rubbing her hand down Liz's arm. "She won't hurt you."

"It'll be over real quick," Colt assured her. He fought to keep his easy smile in place. What he wanted to do was scream. Kick something. Kill someone.

"Okay." Liz glanced warily toward the examining room again. "Please..." She pressed her lips together and looked pleadingly at Althea.

"Would you like me to go in with you? Stay with you?" At Liz's nod, she drew the girl closer. "Sure, no problem. Colt, why don't you go find a soft-drink machine, maybe a candy bar?" She smiled down at Liz. "I could sure use some chocolate. How about you?"

"Yeah." Liz drew in a shaky breath. "I guess."

"We'll be back in a few minutes," Althea told Colt. He could read nothing in her eyes. Feeling useless, he strode down the corridor.

Inside the examining room, Althea helped Liz exchange her tattered clothes for a hospital gown. She noted the bruises on the girl's flesh, but made no comment. They would need an official statement from Liz, but it could wait a little longer.

"This is Dr. Mailer," she explained as the young doctor with the soft eyes approached the table.

"Hello, Liz." Dr. Mailer didn't offer her hand, or touch her patient in any way. She specialized in trauma patients, and she understood the terrors of rape victims. "I'm going to need to ask you some questions, and to run some tests. If there's anything you want to ask me, you go ahead. And if you want me to stop, to wait a while, you just say so. Okay?"

"All right." Liz lay back and focused on the ceiling. But her hand remained tight around Althea's.

Althea had requested Dr. Mailer because she knew the woman's reputation. As the examination progressed, she was more than satisfied that it was well deserved. The doctor was gentle, kind and efficient. It seemed she instinctively knew when to stop, to give Liz a chance to regroup, and when to continue.

"We're all done." Dr. Mailer stripped off her gloves and smiled. "I just want you to rest in here for a little while, and I'm going to have a prescription for you before you leave."

"I don't have to stay here, do I?"

"No." Dr. Mailer closed a hand over Liz's. "You did fine. When your parents get here, we'll talk again. Why don't I see about getting you something to eat?"

As she left, Dr. Mailer sent Althea a look that clearly stated that they, too, would talk later.

"You did do fine," Althea said, helping Liz to sit up. "Do you want me to go see if Colt found that candy bar? I don't imagine that's the sort of food Dr. Mailer had in mind, so we'll have to sneak it while we can."

"I don't want to be alone here."

"Okay." Althea took her brush from her purse and began to untangle Liz's hair. "Let me know if I'm pulling."

"When I saw you downstairs—at the cabin—I thought you were another of the women they brought up. That it was going to happen again." Liz squeezed her eyes shut. Tears spilled through her lashes. "That they were going to make me do those things again."

"I'm sorry. There wasn't any way to let you know I was there to help you."

"And when I saw Colt at the window, I thought it was a dream. I kept dreaming somebody would come, but no one did. I was afraid Mom and Dad just didn't care."

"Honey, your parents have been trying to find you all along." She tipped Liz's chin upward. "They've been so worried. That's why they sent Colt. And I can tell you he loves you, too. You can't imagine the stuff he's bullied me into doing so he could find you."

Liz tried to smile, but it quivered and fell. "But they don't know about— Maybe they won't love me after they find out…everything."

"No." Althea's fingers firmed on Liz's chin. "It'll upset them, and it will hurt them, and it'll be hard, really hard, for them. That's because they do love you. Nothing that happened is going to change that."

"I—I can't do anything but cry."

"Then that's all you have to do, for now."

Liz swiped a shaky hand across her cheeks. "It was my fault I ran away."

"It was your fault you ran away," Althea agreed. "That's all that was your fault."

Liz jerked her head away. The tears gushed out again as she stared at the tiles on the floor. "You don't understand how it feels. You don't know what it's like. How awful it is. How humiliating."

"You're wrong." Gently, firmly, Althea cupped Liz's face again, lifting it until their eyes met. "I do understand. I understand exactly."

"You?" Air shuddered out between Liz's lips. "It happened to you?"

"When I was just about your age. And I felt as though someone had carved something out of me that I'd never get back again. I thought I'd never get clean again, be whole again. Be me again. And I cried for a long, long time, because there didn't seem to be anything else I could do."

Liz accepted the tissue Althea pressed into her hand. "I kept telling myself it wasn't me. It wasn't really me. But I was so scared. It's over. Colt keeps saying it's over now, but it hurts."

"I know." Althea cradled Liz in her arms again. "It hurts more than anything else can, and it's going to hurt for a while. But you're not alone. You have to keep remembering you're not alone. You have your family, your friends. You have Colt. And you can talk to me whenever you need to."

Liz sniffled, rested her cheek against Althea's heart. "What did you do? After. What did you do?"

"I survived," Althea murmured, staring blankly over Liz's head. "And so will you."

Colt stood in the doorway of the examining room, his arms piled high with cans of soda and candy bars. If he'd felt useless before, he now felt unbearably helpless.

There was no place for him here, no way for him to intrude on this woman's pain. His first and only reaction was rage. But where to channel it? He turned away to dump the cans and candy onto a table in the waiting room. If he couldn't comfort either of them, couldn't stop what had already happened, then what could he do?

He scrubbed his hands over his face and tried to clear his mind. Even as he dropped them, he saw Liz's parents dashing from the elevator.

This, at least, he could do. He strode to meet them.

Inside the examining room, Althea finished tidying Liz's hair. "Do you want to get dressed?"

Liz managed what passed for a smile. "I don't ever want to put those clothes on again."

"Good point. Well, maybe I can scrounge up—" She turned at a flurry of movement in the doorway. She saw a pale woman and a haggard man, both with red-rimmed eyes.

"Oh, baby! Oh, Liz!" The woman raced forward first, with the man right on her heels.

"Mom!" Liz was sobbing again even as she threw open her arms. "Mom!"

Althea stepped aside as parents and child were reunited, with tears and desperate embraces. When she spotted Colt in the doorway, she moved to him. "You'd better stay with them. I'll tell Dr. Mailer they're here before I go."

"Where are you going?"

She slid her purse back on her shoulder. "To file my report."

She did just that before she went home to indulge in that long, steamy bath. She soaked until her body was numb. Giving in to exhaustion, both physical and emotional, she fell into bed naked and slept dreamlessly until the battering on her door awoke her.

Groggy, she fumbled for her robe, belting it as she walked to the door. She scowled at Colt through the peephole, then yanked the door open.

"Give me one good reason why I shouldn't book you for disturbing the peace. My peace."

He held out a flat, square box. "I brought you pizza."

She blew out a breath, then drew one in—as well as the rich scent of cheese and spice. "That might get you off. I guess you want to come in with it."

"That was the idea."

"Well, come on, then." With that dubious invitation, she walked away to fetch plates and napkins. "How's Liz holding up?"

"Surprisingly well. Marleen and Frank are as solid as they come."

"They'll have to be." She came back to set the plates on the table. "I hope they understand they're all going to need counseling."

"They've already talked to Dr. Mailer about it. She's going to help them find a good therapist back home." Trying to choose his words properly, he took his time sliding pizza onto the plates. "The first thing I want to do is thank you. And don't brush me off, Thea. I'd really like to get this out."

"All right, then." She sat, picked up a slice. "Get it out."

"I'm not just talking about the official cooperation, the way you helped me find her and get her out. I owe you big for that, but that's professional. You got anything to drink with this?"

"There's some burgundy in the kitchen."

"I'll get it," he said as she started to rise.

Althea shrugged and went back to eating. "Suit yourself." She was working on her second slice when Colt came back with a bottle and two glasses. "I guess I was too tired to realize I was starving."

"Then I don't have to apologize for waking you up." He filled both glasses, but didn't drink. "The other thing I have to thank you for is the way you were with Liz. I figured getting her out was enough—playing that white knight you said irritates you so much." He looked up, met her eyes. There was a new understanding in them, and a weariness she hadn't seen before. "It wasn't. Telling her it was all right, that it was over—that wasn't enough, either. She needed you."

"She needed a woman."

"You are that. I know it's a lot to expect—over and above, so to speak—but she asked about you a couple of times after you left." He toyed with the stem of his glass. "They're going to be staying in town at least for another day, until Dr. Mailer has some of the results in. I was hoping you could talk to Liz again."

"You don't have to ask me that, Colt." She reached out for his hand. "I got involved, too."

"So did I, Thea." He turned their joined hands over, brought them to his lips. "I'm in love with you. Big-time. No, don't pull away from me." He tightened his grip before she could. "I've never said that to another woman. I used alternate terms." He smiled a little. "I'm crazy about you, you're special to me, that kind of thing. But I never used *love,* not until you."

She believed him. What was more frightening, she wanted to believe him. Tread carefully, she reminded herself. One step at a time. "Listen, Colt, the two of us have been on a roller coaster since we met—and that's only been a short while. Things, emotions, get blown out of proportion on roller coasters. Why don't we slow this down some?"

He could feel her nerves jittering, but he couldn't be amused by them this time. "I had to accept that I couldn't change what had happened to Liz. That was hard. I can't change what I feel for you. Accepting that's easy."

"I'm not sure what you want from me, Colt, and I don't think I can give it to you."

"Because of what happened to you before. Because of what I heard you telling Liz in the examining room."

She withdrew instantly and completely. "That was between Liz and me," she said coldly. "And it's none of your business."

It was exactly the reaction he'd expected, the one he'd prepared for. "We both know that's not true. But we'll talk about it when you're ready." Knowing the value of keeping an opponent off balance, he picked up his wine. "You know they're giving Scott a fifty-fifty chance of making it."

"I know." She watched him warily. "I called the hospital before I went to bed. Boyd's handling the interrogation of Kline and Donner for now."

"Can't wait to get at them, can you?"

"No." She smiled again. "I can't."

"You know, I heard those shots, and it stopped my heart." Feeling more relaxed, he bit into his pizza. "I come tearing back, ready to kick butt, crash through the door like the cavalry, and what do I see?" He shook his head and tapped her glass with his. "There you are, blood running down your face…" He paused to touch a gentle finger to the bandage at her temple. "A gun in each hand. There's a three-hundred-pound hulk bleeding at your feet, and two others facedown with their hands behind their heads. You're just standing there, looking like Diana after the hunt, and reciting Miranda. I have to say, I felt pretty superfluous."

"You did okay, Nightshade." She let out a small, defeated breath. "And I guess you deserve to know that I was awfully glad to see you. You looked like Jim Bowie at the Alamo."

"He lost."

She gave in and leaned forward to kiss him. "You didn't."

"We didn't," he corrected, pleased that her mouth had been soft, relaxed and friendly. "I brought you a present."

"Oh, yeah?" Because the dangerous moment seemed to have passed, her lips curved and she kissed him again. "Gimme."

He reached behind himself for his coat, dug into the pocket. Taking out a small paper bag, he tossed it into her lap.

"Aw, and you wrapped it so nice." Chuckling, she dipped into the bag. And pulled out a lacy bra and panties, in sheer midnight blue. Her chuckle turned into a rich appreciative laugh.

"I pay my debts," he informed her. "Since I figured you probably had a supply of the white kind, I picked out something a little different." He reached over to feel the silk and lace. "Maybe you'll try them on."

"Eventually." But she knew what she wanted now. What she needed now. And she rose to take it. She combed her fingers through his hair, tugging so that his face lifted and his mouth met hers. "Maybe you'll come to bed with me."

"Absolutely." He skimmed his hands up her hips, keeping his mouth joined to hers as he stood to gather her close. "I thought you'd never ask."

"I didn't want the pizza to get cold."

He slipped a finger down the center of her body to toy with the belt of her robe. "Still hungry?"

She tugged his shirt out of his jeans. "Now that you mention it." Then she laughed as he swung her up into his arms. "What's this for?"

"I decided to sweep you off your feet. For now." He started toward the bedroom, deciding she was in for another surprise.

The spread was turned back, but the plain white sheets were barely disturbed from her nap. Colt laid her down, following her onto the bed as he skimmed light, teasing kisses over her face.

Her fingers were busy undoing his buttons. She knew what it would be like, and was prepared—eager—for the storm and the fire and the fast flood of sensations. When her hands pushed away cotton and encountered warm, firm flesh, she gave a low, satisfied moan.

He continued to kiss her, nibbling, nuzzling, as she hastily stripped off his clothes. There was a frantic energy burning in her that promised the wild, the frenzied. Each time desire stabbed through him, he absorbed the shock and kept his pace easy.

Eager, edgy, Althea turned her mouth to his and arched against him. "I want you."

He hadn't realized that three breathy words could make the blood swim in his head. But it would be too easy to take what she offered, too easy to lose what she held back. "I know. I can taste it."

He dipped his mouth to hers again, drawing out the kiss with such trembling tenderness that she groaned again. The hand that had been fisted tight against his bare shoulder went lax.

"And I want you," he murmured, levering back to stare down at her. "All of you." Fascinated, he drew his fingers through her hair, spreading it out until it lay flaming against the white sheet. Then he lowered his head again, gently, so gently, to kiss the bandage at her temple.

Emotion curled inside her like a spiked fist. "Colt—"

"Shh...I just want to look."

And look he did, while he traced her face with a fingertip, rubbed her lower lip with his thumb, then trailed it down to her jawline, skimmed over the pulse that fluttered in her throat.

"The sun's going down," he said quietly. "The light does incredible things to your face, your eyes. Just now they're gold, with darker, brandy-colored specks sprinkled through them. I've never seen eyes like yours. You look like a painting." He brushed his thumb over her collarbone. "But I can touch you, feel you tremble, know you're real."

She lifted a hand, wanting to drag him back to her, to make the ache go away. "I don't need words."

"Sure you do." He smiled a little, turning his face into her palm. "Maybe I haven't found the right ones, but you need them." He started to press his lips to her wrist, and then he noticed the faint smudge of bruises. And remembered.

His brows drew together when he straddled her and took both of her hands. He examined her wrists carefully before looking down at her again. "I did this."

Sweet God, she thought, there had to be a way to stop this terrible trembling. "It doesn't matter. You were upset. Make love with me."

"I don't like knowing I hurt you in anger, or that I'm liable to do it again eventually." Very carefully, he touched his lips to each of her wrists, and felt her pulse scramble. "You make it too easy to forget how soft you are, Althea." The sleeves of her robe slithered down her arms as he skimmed his lips to her elbow. "How small. How incredibly perfect you are. I'll have to show you."

He cupped a hand under her head, lifting her so that her hair tumbled back, her face tilted up. Then his mouth was on hers again, savoring a deep, dreamy kiss that left her weak. He felt her give, felt yet another layer dissolve. Her arms linked around his neck; her muscles quivered.

What was he doing to her? She only knew she couldn't think, couldn't resist. She'd been prepared for need, and he'd given her tenderness. What defense could there be against passion wrapped so softly in sweetness? His mouth was gentle, enchanting her even as it seduced.

She wanted to tell him that seduction was unnecessary, but, oh, it felt glorious to surrender to the secrets he unearthed with that quietly devastating mouth and those slow, easy hands.

The last rays of the sun slanted across her eyes as he eased her back so that he could trail his lips down her throat. She heard the whisper of her robe as he slipped it down to bare her shoulder, to free it for lazy, openmouthed kisses and the moist trail of his tongue.

He could feel it the instant she let herself go. The warmth of triumph surged through him as her hands, as gentle as his, began to caress. He resisted the urge to quicken his pace, and let his hands explore her, over the robe, under it, then over again, as her body melted like warm wax.

All the while, he watched her face, aroused by each flicker of emotion, lured by the way her breath would catch, then rush through her lips at his touch. He could have sworn he felt her float as he slipped the robe away.

Then her eyes opened, dark and heavy. He understood that, though she had surrendered, she would not be passive. Her hands were as thorough as his, seeking, touching, possessing, with that unbearable tenderness.

Until he was as seduced as she.

Soft, breathy moans. Quiet secrets told in murmurs. Long, lingering caresses. The sunlight faded to dusk, and dusk to that deepening of night. There was need, but no frantic rush to sate it. There was pleasure, and the dreamy desire to prolong it.

Indulgence. Tonight there was only indulgence.

He touched, she trembled. She tasted, he shuddered.

When at last he slipped into her, she smiled and gathered him close. The rhythm they set was patient, loving, and as true as music. They climbed together, steadily, beautifully, until his gasp echoed hers. And then they floated back to earth.

She lay a long time in silence, dazed by what had happened. He had given her something, and she had given freely in return. It couldn't be taken back. She wondered what steps could be taken to protect herself now that she had fallen in love.

For the first time. For the only time.

Perhaps it would pass. A part of her cringed at the thought of losing what she'd just found. No matter how firmly she reminded herself that her life was precisely the way she wanted it, she couldn't bring herself to think too deeply about what it would be like without him.

And yet she had no choice. He would leave. And she would survive.

"You're thinking again." He rolled onto his back, hooking an arm around her to gather her close. "I can almost hear your brain humming." Outrageously content, he kissed her hair, closed his eyes. "Tell me the first thing that pops into your mind."

"What? I don't—"

"No, no, don't analyze. This is a test. The first thing, Thea. Now."

"I was wondering when you were going back," she heard herself say. "To Wyoming."

"Ah." He smiled—smugly. "I like knowing I'm the first thing on your mind."

"Don't get cocky, Nightshade."

"Okay. I haven't made any firm plans. I have some loose ends to tie up first."

"Such as?"

"You, for starters. We haven't set the date."

"Colt..."

He grinned again. Maybe it was wishful thinking, but he thought he'd heard exasperation in her tone instead of annoyance. "I'm still shooting for New Year's Eve—I guess I've gotten sentimental—but we've got time to hash that out. Then there's the fact that I haven't finished what I came here to do."

That brought her head up. "What do you mean? You found Liz."

"It's not enough." His eyes glowed in the shadows. "We don't have the head man. It's not finished until we do."

"That's for me and the department to worry about. Personal vendettas have no place here."

"I didn't say it was a vendetta." Though it was. "I intend to finish this, Althea. I'd like to keep working with you on this."

"And if I say no?"

He twirled her hair around his finger. "I'll do my best to change your mind. Maybe you haven't noticed, but I can be tenacious."

"I've noticed," she muttered. But there was a part of her that glowed at the idea that their partnership wasn't at an end. "I suppose I can give you a few more days."

"Good." He shifted her so that he could run a hand down her side to her hips. "Does the deal include a few more nights?"

"I suppose it could." Her smile flashed wickedly. "If you make it worth my while."

"Oh, I will." He lowered his head. "That's a promise."

# Chapter 11

With the scream still tearing at her throat, Althea shot up in bed. Blind with terror and rage, she fought the arms that wound around her, struggling wildly against the hold while she sucked in the air to scream again. She could feel his hands on her, feel them groping at her, hot, hurtful. But this time...God, please, this time...

"Althea." Colt shook her, hard, forcing his voice to remain calm and firm, though his heart was hammering against his ribs in fast, hard blows. "Althea, wake up. You're dreaming. Pull out of it."

She clawed her way through the slippery edges of the dream, still fighting him, still dragging in air. Reality was a dim light through the murky depths of the nightmare. With a final burst of effort, she grasped at it, and at Colt.

"Okay, okay..." Still shaken by the sound of the scream that had awakened him, he rocked her, holding her close to warm her body, which was chill with clammy sweat. "Okay, baby. Just hold on to me."

"Oh, God..." Her breath came out in a long, shaky sob as she buried her face against his shoulder. Her hands fisted impotently at his back. "Oh, God... Oh, God..."

"It's okay now." He continued to stroke and soothe, growing concerned when her hold on him increased. "I'm right here. You were dreaming, that's all. You were only dreaming."

She'd fought her way out of the dream, but the fear had come back with her, and it was too huge to allow for shame. So she clung, shivering, trying to absorb some portion of the strength she felt in him.

"Just give me a minute. I'll be all right in a minute." The shaking would stop, she told herself. The tears would dry. The fear would ebb. "I'm sorry." But it wasn't stopping. Instinctively she turned her face into his throat for comfort. "God, I'm sorry."

"Just relax." She was quivering like a bird, he thought, and she felt as frail as one. "Do you want me to turn on the light?"

"No." She pressed her lips together, hoping to stop the trembling in her voice. She didn't want the light. Didn't want him to see her until she'd managed to compose herself. "No. Let me get some water. I'll be fine."

"I'll get it." He brushed the hair from her face, and was shaken all over again to find it wet with tears. "I'll be right back."

She brought her knees up close to her chest when he left her. Control, she ordered herself, but dropped her head onto her knees. While she listened to water striking glass, watched the splinter of light spill through the crack around the bathroom door, she took long, even breaths.

"Sorry, Nightshade," she said when he came back with the water. "I guess I woke you up."

"I guess you did." Her voice was steadier, he noted. But her hands weren't. He cupped his around hers and lifted the glass to her lips. "Must have been a bad one."

The water eased her dry throat. "Must have been. Thanks." She pushed the glass back into his hands, embarrassed that she couldn't hold it herself.

Colt set the glass on the night table before easing down on the bed beside her. "Tell me."

She moved her shoulders dismissively. "Chalk it up to a rough day and pizza."

Very firmly, very gently, he took her face in his hands. The light he'd left on in the bathroom sent out a dim glow. In it he could see how pale she was.

"No. I'm not going to brush this off, Thea. You're not going to brush me off. You were screaming." She tried to turn her head away, but he wouldn't permit it. "You're still shaking. I can be every bit as stubborn as you, and right now I think I have the advantage."

"I had a nightmare." She wanted to snap at him, but couldn't find the strength. "People have nightmares."

"How often do you have this one?"

"Never." She lifted a weary hand and dragged it through her hair. "Not in years. I don't know what brought it on."

He thought he did. And unless he was very much mistaken, he thought she did, as well. "Do you have a shirt, a nightgown or something? You're cold."

"I'll get one."

"Just tell me where." Her quick, annoyed sigh did quite a bit toward easing his mind.

"Top drawer of the dresser. Left-hand side."

He rose, and opening the drawer grabbed the first thing that came to hand. Before he tugged it over her head, he examined the oversize man's undershirt. "Nice lingerie you have, Lieutenant."

"It does the job."

He smoothed it down over her, tucked pillows behind her, as fussy as a mother with a colicky infant.

She scowled at him. "I don't like being pampered."

"You'll live through it."

When he was satisfied he'd made her as comfortable as possible, he tugged on his jeans. They were going to talk, he decided, and sat beside her again. Whether she wanted to or not. He took her hand, waited until they were eye-to-eye.

"The nightmare. It was about when you were raped, wasn't it?" Her fingers went rigid in his. "I told you I heard you talking to Liz."

She ordered her fingers to relax, willed them to, but they remained stiff and cold. "It was a long time ago. It doesn't apply now."

"It does when it wakes you up screaming. It brought it all back," he continued quietly. "What happened to Liz, seeing her through it."

"All right. So what?"

"Trust me, Althea." He said it quietly, his eyes on hers. "Let me help."

"It hurts," she heard herself say. Then she shut her eyes. It was the first time she had admitted that to anyone. "Not all the time. Not even most of the time. It just sneaks up now and then and slices at you.''

"I want to understand.'' He brought her hand to his lips. When she didn't pull away, he left it there. "Talk, talk to me.''

She didn't know where to begin. It seemed safest to start at the beginning. Letting her head rest against the pillows, she closed her eyes again.

"My father drank, and when he drank, he got drunk, and when he got drunk, he got mean. He had big hands.'' She curled hers into fists, then relaxed them. "He used them on my mother, on me. My earliest memory is of those hands, the anger in them that I couldn't understand, and couldn't fight. I don't remember him very well. He tangled with somebody meaner one night and ended up dead. I was six.''

She opened her eyes again, realizing that keeping them closed was just another way of hiding. "Once he was gone, my mother decided to take up where he'd left off—in the bottle. She didn't hit it as hard as he did, but she was more consistent.''

He could only wonder how the people she'd described could have created anything as beautiful or as true as the woman beside him. "Did you have anyone else?''

"I had grandparents, on my mother's side. I don't know where they lived. I never met them. They hadn't had anything to do with her since she'd run off with my father.''

"But did they know about you?''

"If they did, they didn't care.''

He said nothing, trying to comprehend it. But he couldn't, simply couldn't understand family not caring. "Okay. What did you do?''

"When you're a child, you do nothing,'' she said flatly. "You're at the mercy of adults, and the reality is, a great many adults have no mercy.'' She paused a moment to pick up the threads of the story. "When I was about eight, she went out—she went out a lot—but this time she didn't come home. A couple of days later, a neighbor called Social Services. They scooped me up into the system.''

She reached for the water again. This time her hands didn't shake. "It's a long, typical story.''

"I want to hear it.''

"They placed me in a foster home." She sipped her water. There wasn't any point in telling him how frightened, how lost, she'd been. The facts were enough. "It was okay. Decent. Then they found her, slapped her wrists a couple of times, told her to clean up her act, and gave me back."

"Why in the hell did they do that?"

"Things were different back then. The court believed the best place for a kid was with her mother. Anyway, she didn't stay dry for long, and the cycle started all over again. I ran away a few times, they dragged me back. More foster homes. They don't leave you in any one too long, especially when you're recalcitrant. And I'd developed my own mean streak by that time."

"Small wonder."

"I bounced around in the system. Social workers, court hearings, school counselors. All overburdened. My mother hooked up with another guy and finally took off for good. Mexico, I think. In any case, she didn't come back. I was twelve, thirteen. I hated not being able to say where I wanted to go, where I wanted to be. I took off every chance I got. So they labeled me a j.d.—juvenile delinquent— and they put me in a girls' home, which was one step up from reform school." Her lips twisted into a dry smile. "That put the fear of God into me. It was rough, as close to prison as I ever want to be. So I straightened up, put on my best behavior. Eventually they placed me in foster care again."

She drained the glass and set it aside. She knew her hands wouldn't be steady for long. "I was scared that if I didn't make it work this time, they'd put me back until I was eighteen. So I took a real shot at it. They were a nice couple, naive, maybe, but nice, good intentions. They wanted to do something to right society's ills. She was PTA president, and they went to protest rallies against nuclear power plants. They talked about adopting a Vietnamese orphan. I guess I smirked at them behind their backs sometimes, but I really liked them. They were kind to me."

She took a moment, and he said nothing, waiting for her to build to the next stage. "They gave me boundaries, good ones, and they treated me fairly. There was one drawback. They had a son. He was seventeen, captain of the football team, homecoming king, A student. The apple of their eye. A real company man."

"Company man?"

"You know, the kind who's all slick and polished on the outside, he's got a terrific rap, lots of charm, lots of angles. And underneath, he's slime. You can't get to the slime because you keep slipping on all that polish, but it's there." Her eyes glinted at the memory. "I could see it. I hated the way he looked at me when they weren't watching." Her breath was coming quicker now, but her voice was still controlled. "Like I was a piece of meat he was sizing up, getting ready to grill. They couldn't see it. All they saw was this perfect child who never gave them a moment's grief. And one night, when they were out, he came home from a date. God."

When she covered her face with her hands, Colt gathered her close. "It's all right, Thea. That's enough."

"No." She shook her head violently, pushed back. She'd gone this far. She'd finish it. "He was angry. I suppose his girl hadn't surrendered to his many charms. He came into my room. When I told him to get out, he just laughed and reminded me it was his house, and that I was only there because his parents felt sorry for me. Of course, he was right."

"No. No, he wasn't."

"He was right about that," Althea said. "Not about the rest, but about that. And he unzipped his pants. I ran for the door, but he threw me back on the bed. I hit my head pretty hard on the wall. I remember being dizzy for a minute, and hearing him telling me that he knew girls like me usually charged for it, but that I should be flattered that he was going to give me a thrill. He got on the bed. I slapped him, I swore at him. He backhanded me, and pinned me. And I started to scream. I kept screaming and screaming while he raped me. When he was finished, I wasn't screaming anymore. I was just crying. He got off the bed, and zipped up his pants. He warned me that if I told anyone he'd deny it. And who were they going to believe, someone like him, or someone like me? He was blood, so there was no contest. And he could always get five of his buddies to say that I'd been willing with all of them. Then they'd just put me back in the home.

"So I didn't say anything, because there was nothing to say and no one to say it to. He raped me twice more over the next month, before I got the nerve to run away again. Of course, they caught me. Maybe I'd wanted them to that time. I stayed in the home until I was eighteen. And when I got out, I knew no one was ever going to have that kind of control over me again. No one was ever going to make me feel like I was nothing ever again."

Unsure what to do, Colt reached up tentatively to brush a tear from her cheek. "You made your life into something, Althea."

"I made it into mine." She let out a breath, then briskly rubbed the tears from her cheeks. "I don't like to dwell on before, Colt."

"But it's there."

"It's there," she agreed. "Trying to make it go away only brings it closer to the surface. I learned that, too. Once you accept it's simply a part of what makes you what you are, it doesn't become as vital. It didn't make me hate men, it didn't make me hate myself. It did make me understand what it is to be a victim."

He wanted to gather her close, but was afraid she might not want to be touched. "I wish I could make the hurt go away."

"Old scars," she murmured. "They only ache at odd moments." She sensed his withdrawal, and felt the ache spread. "I'm the same person I was before I told you. The trouble is, after people hear a story like that, they change."

"I haven't changed." He started to touch her, drew back. "Damn it, Thea, I don't know what to say to you. What to do for you." Rising, he paced away from the bed. "I could make you some tea."

She nearly laughed. "Nightshade's cure-all? No thanks."

"What do you want?" he demanded. "Just tell me."

"Why don't you tell me what you want?"

"What I want." He strode to the window, whirled back. "I want to go back to when you were fifteen and kick that bastard's face in. I want to hurt him a hundred times worse than he hurt you. Then I want to go back further and break your father's legs, and I want to kick your mother's butt while I'm at it."

"Well, you can't," she said coolly. "Pick something else."

"I want to hold you!" he shouted, jamming his fists into his pockets. "And I'm afraid to touch you!"

"I don't want your tea, and I don't want your sympathy. So if that's all you have to offer, you might as well leave."

"Is that what you want?"

"What I want is to be accepted for who and what I am. Not to be tiptoed around like an invalid because I survived rape and abuse."

He started to snap back at her, then stopped himself. He wasn't thinking of her, he realized, but of his own rage, his own impotence, his own pain. Slowly he walked back to the bed and sat beside her. Her eyes were still wet; he could see them gleaming against the shadows. He slipped his arms around her, gently drew her close until her head rested on his shoulder.

"I'm not going anywhere," he murmured. "Okay?"

She sighed, settled. "Okay."

Althea awakened at sunrise with a dull headache. She knew instantly that Colt was no longer beside her. Wearily she rolled onto her back and rubbed her swollen eyes.

What had she expected? she asked herself. No man would be comfortable around a woman after hearing a story like the one she'd told him. And why in God's name had she dumped out her past that way? How could she have trusted him with pieces of herself that she'd never given anyone before?

Even Boyd, the person she considered her closest friend, knew only about the foster homes. As for the rest, she'd buried it—until last night.

She didn't doubt that her tie to Liz had unlocked the door and let the nightmare back in. But she should have been able to handle it, to hold back, to safeguard her privacy. The fact that she hadn't could mean only one thing.

Indulging in a sigh, Althea pushed herself up and rested her brow on her knees.

She was in love with Colt. Ridiculous as it was, she had to face the truth. And, just as she'd always suspected, love made you stupid, vulnerable and unhappy.

There ought to be a pill, she mused. A serum she could take. Like an antidote for snakebite.

The sound of footsteps had her whipping her head up. Her eyes widened when Colt came to the doorway carrying a tray.

He had a split second to read her reaction before she closed it off. She'd thought he'd taken a hike, he realized grimly. He was going to have to show the lady that he was sticking, no matter how hard she tried to shake him off.

"Morning, Lieutenant. I figured you'd planned on a full day."

"You figured right." Cautious, she watched as he crossed to the bed, waited until he'd set the tray at her feet. "What's the occasion?" she asked, gesturing toward the plates of French toast.

"I owe you a breakfast. Remember?"

"Yeah." Her gaze shifted from the plates to his face. Love still made her feel stupid, it still made her feel vulnerable, but it no longer made her unhappy. "You're a regular whiz in the kitchen."

"We all have our talents." He sat cross-legged on the other side of the tray and dug in. "I figure—" he chewed, swallowed "—after we're married, I can handle the meals, you can handle the laundry."

She ignored the quick sprint of panic and sampled her first bite. "You ought to see someone about this obsessive fantasy life of yours, Nightshade."

"My mother's dying to meet you." He grinned when Althea's fork clattered against her plate. "She and Dad send their best."

"You—" Words failed her.

"She and my father know Liz. I called to relieve their minds, and I told them about you." Smiling, he brushed her hair back from her shoulders. He hadn't known a woman could look so sexy in a man's undershirt. "She's for a spring wedding—you know, all that June-bride stuff. But I told her I wasn't waiting that long."

"You're out of your mind."

"Maybe." His grin faded. "But I'm in yours, Thea. I'm in there real good, and I'm not getting out."

He was right about that, but it didn't change the bottom line. She was not walking down the aisle and saying 'I do.' That was that.

"Listen, Colt." Try reason, she thought. "I'm very fond of you, but—"

"You're what?" His mouth quirked again. "You're what of me?"

"Fond," she spit out, infuriated by the gleam of good humor in his eyes.

"Euphemisms." Affectionately he patted her hand, shook his head. "You disappoint me. I had you pegged as a straight shooter."

Forget reason. "Just shut up and let me eat."

He obliged her, because it gave him time to think, and to study her. She was still a bit pale, he mused. And her eyes were swollen from the bout of tears during the night. But she wouldn't let herself be fragile. He had to admire her unceasing supply of strength. She didn't want sympathy, he remembered, she wanted understanding. She would just have to learn to accept both from him.

She'd accepted his comfort the night before. Whether she knew it or not, she'd already come to rely on him. He wasn't about to let her down.

"How's the coffee?"

"Good." And because it was, because the meal he'd prepared had already conquered her headache, she relented. "Thanks."

"My pleasure." He leaned forward, touched his mouth to hers. "I don't suppose I could interest you in an after-breakfast tussle."

She smiled now, fully, easily. "I'll have to take a rain check." But she spread a hand over his chest and kissed him again. Her fingers closed over his medal. "Why do you wear this?"

"My grandmother gave it to me. She said that when a man was determined not to settle down in one place, he should have someone looking out for him. It's worked pretty well so far." He set the tray on the floor, then scooped Althea into his arms.

"Nightshade, I said—"

"I know, I know." He hitched her up more comfortably. "But I had this idea that if we had that tussle in the shower, we could stay pretty much on schedule."

She laughed, nipped at his shoulder. "I'm a firm believer in time management."

She had more than a full day to fit into twenty-four hours. There was a mountain of paperwork waiting for her, and she needed to talk to Boyd about his interrogation of Donner and Kline before she met with them herself. She wanted, for personal, as well as professional, reasons, to interview Liz again.

She sat down and began efficiently chipping away at the mountain.

Cilla knocked on the open door. "Excuse me, Lieutenant. Got a minute?"

"For the captain's wife," she said, smiling and gesturing Cilla inside, "I've got a minute and a half. What are you doing down here?"

"Boyd filled me in." Cilla leaned down, peered close and, as a woman would, saw through the meticulously applied cosmetics to the signs of a difficult night. "Are you all right?"

"I'm fine. I have decided that anyone who camps out on purpose needs immediate psychiatric help, but it was an experience."

"You should try it with three kids."

"No," Althea said definitely. "No, I shouldn't."

With a laugh, Cilla rested a hip against the edge of the desk. "I'm so glad you and Colt found the girl. How's she doing?"

"It'll be rough for a while, but she'll come through."

"Those creeps should be—" Cilla's eyes flashed, but she cut herself off. "I didn't come here to talk cop, I came to talk turkey."

"Oh?"

"As in Thanksgiving. Don't give me that look." Cilla angled her chin, readying for battle. "Every year you've got some excuse for not coming to Thanksgiving dinner, and this time I'm not buying it."

"Cilla, you know I appreciate the offer."

"The hell with that. You're family. We want you." Even as Althea was shaking her head, Cilla was plowing on. "Deb and Gage are coming. You haven't seen them in a year."

Althea thought of Cilla's younger sister, Deborah, and her husband. She would like to see Deb again. They'd gotten close while Deborah was in Denver finishing up college. And Gage Guthrie. Althea pursed her lips as she thought of him. She genuinely liked Deborah's husband, and a blind man could have seen that he adored his wife. But there was something about him—something Althea couldn't put her finger on. Not a bad thing, she thought now, not a worrying thing. But something.

"Taking a side trip?" Cilla asked.

"Sorry." Althea snapped back and fiddled with the papers on her desk. "You know I'd love to see them again, Cilla, but—"

"They're bringing Adrianna." Cilla's secret weapon was her sister's baby girl, whom Althea had seen only in snapshots and videotapes. "You and I both know what a sucker you are for babies."

"You want to keep that down?" Althea stated with an uneasy glance toward the bull pen. "I've got a reputation to uphold around here." She sighed and leaned back in her chair. "You know I want to see them, all of them. And since I'm sure they'll be here through the holiday weekend, I will. We'll shoot for Saturday."

"Thanksgiving dinner." Cilla dusted her hands together as she straightened. "You're coming this year, if I have to tell Boyd to make it an order. I'm having my family. My whole family."

"Cilla—"

"That's it." Cilla folded her arms. "I'm taking this to the captain."

"You're in luck," Boyd said as he came to the door. "The captain happens to be available. And he's brought you a present." He stepped aside.

"Natalie!" With a whoop of pleasure, Cilla threw her arms around her sister-in-law and squeezed. "I thought you were in New York."

"I was." Natalie's dark green eyes sparkled with laughter as she drew Cilla back to kiss her. "I had to fly in for a few days, and I figured I'd make this my first stop. I didn't know I'd hit the jackpot. You look great."

"You look phenomenal, as always." It was perfectly true. The tall, willow-slim woman with the sleek blond hair and the conservatively cut suit would always turn heads. "The kids are going to be thrilled."

"I can't wait to get my hands on them." She turned, held out both hands. "Thea. I can't believe I'm lucky enough to get all three of you at once."

"It's really good to see you." With their hands still linked, Althea pressed her cheek to Natalie's. In the years Althea had been Boyd's partner, she and his younger sister had become fast friends. "How are your parents?"

"Terrific. They send love to everyone." In an old habit, she glanced around Althea's office, let out a sigh. "Thea, can't you at least get a space with a window?"

"I like this one. Less distractions."

"I'm calling Maria as soon as I get to the station," Cilla announced. "She'll whip up something special for tonight. You're coming, Thea."

"Wouldn't miss it."

"What is this?" Colt demanded as he tried to squeeze into the room. "A conference? Thea, you're going to have to get a bigger—" He broke off, stared. "Nat?"

Her stunned expression mirrored his. "Colt?"

His grin split his face. "Son of a gun." He elbowed past Boyd to grab Natalie in a hug that lifted her feet from the floor. "I'll be damned. Pretty Natalie. What's it been? Six years?"

"Seven." She kissed him full on the mouth. "We ran into each other in San Francisco."

"At the Giants game, right. You look better than ever."

"I am better than ever. Why don't we have a drink later, and catch up?"

"Now, that's…" He fumbled to a halt when he glanced at Althea. She was sitting on the edge of her desk, watching their reunion with an expression of mild curiosity and polite interest. When he realized his arm was still around Natalie's waist, he dropped it quickly to his side. "Actually, I, ah…"

How was a man supposed to talk to an old female friend when the woman he loved was studying him as if he were something smeared on a glass slide?

Natalie caught the look that passed between Althea and Colt. Surprise came first, then a chuckle she disguised by clearing her throat. Well, well, she thought, what an interesting stew she'd dropped into. She couldn't resist stirring the pot.

"Colt and I go way back," she said to Althea. "I had a terrible crush on him when I was a teenager." She smiled wickedly up at Colt. "I've been waiting for years for him to take advantage of it."

"Really?" Althea tapped a finger to her lips. "He doesn't strike me as being slow off the mark. A little dense, maybe, but not slow."

"You're right about that. Cute, too, isn't he?" She winked at Althea.

"In an overt sort of way," Althea agreed, enjoying Colt's discomfort. "Why don't you and I have that drink later, Natalie? It sounds as though you and I have quite a bit to chat about."

"It certainly does."

"I don't think this is the place to set up social engagements." Well aware that he was outnumbered and outgunned, Colt stuck his hands into his pockets. "Althea looks busy."

"Oh, I've got a minute or two. What are you doing in town, Natalie?"

"Business. Always nice when you can mix it with pleasure. I have an emergency meeting in an hour with the board of directors on one of Boyd's and my downtown units. Owning real estate is a full-time job. Without proper management, it can be a huge headache," she explained.

"You don't happen to own one on Second Avenue, do you?" Althea asked.

"Mmm, no. Is one up for sale?" A gleam came into her eyes, and then she laughed. "It's a weakness," she explained. "There's something about owning property, even with all the problems that come with it."

"What's the trouble now?" Boyd asked, trying to work up some interest.

"The manager decided to up all the rents and keep the difference." Natalie said, her eyes hardening in startling contrast to her soft, lovely face. "I hate being duped."

"Pride," Boyd said, and tapped a finger on her nose. "You hate making a mistake."

"I didn't make a mistake." Her chin angled upward. "The man's résumé was outstanding." When Boyd continued to grin, she wrinkled her nose at him. "The problem is, you have to give a manager autonomy. You can't be everywhere at once. I remember one manager we had who was running a floating crap game in an empty apartment. He kept it rented under a fake name," she continued, nearly amused now. "He'd even filled out an application, complete with faked references. He made enough profit off the games to afford the overhead, so the rent came in like clockwork. I'd never have found out if someone hadn't tipped the cops and they raided the place. It turned out he'd done the same thing twice before.''

"Good Lord," Althea said, looking stunned.

"Oh, it wasn't that bad," Natalie went on. "Actually, it was pretty exciting stuff. I just— What is it?" she demanded when Althea sprang to her feet.

"Let's move." Colt was already headed out the door.

Althea grabbed her coat and sprinted after him. "Boyd, run a make on—"

"Nieman," he called out. "I got it. You want backup?"

"I'll let you know."

When the room emptied, Natalie threw up her hands and stared at Cilla. "What brought that on?"

"Cops." Cilla shrugged. That said it all.

# Chapter 12

"I can't believe we let that slip by us." Colt slammed the door to the Jeep and peeled away from the curb. This time he didn't bother to remove the parking ticket under the windshield wiper.

"We're going on a hunch," Althea reminded him. "We could very well get slapped down."

"You don't think so."

She shut her eyes a moment, letting the pieces fall into place. "It fits," she said grimly. "Not one single tenant could swear they'd ever seen this Mr. Davis. He was the man who wasn't there—maybe because he never was."

"And who would have had access to the penthouse? Who could have faked references—references that didn't have to exist? Who could have slipped through the building virtually unnoticed, because he was always there?"

"Nieman."

"I told you he was a weasel," Colt said between his teeth.

She was forced to agree, but cautiously. "Don't get ahead of yourself, Nightshade. We're doing some follow-up questioning. That's all."

"I'm getting answers," he shot back. "That's all."

"Don't make me pull rank on you, Colt." She said it quietly, calming him. "We're going in there to ask questions. We may be able to shake him into slipping up. We may very well have to walk out without him. But now we have a place to start digging.''

They'd dig, all right, Colt thought. Deep enough to bury Nieman. ''I'll follow your lead,'' he said. For now. He pulled up at a red light, drumming his fingers impatiently on the wheel. ''I'd like to, ah…explain about Nat.''

''Explain what?''

''That we aren't—weren't. Ever,'' he said savagely. ''Got it?''

''Really?'' She'd laugh about this later, she was sure. Once there weren't so many other things on her mind. Still, she wasn't so preoccupied that she'd blow a chance to bait him. ''Why not? She's beautiful, she's fun, she's smart. Looks like you fell down on that one, Nightshade.''

''It wasn't that I didn't… I mean, I thought about it. Started to—'' He swore, revved the engine when the light turned. ''She was Boyd's sister, all right? Before I knew it, she was like my sister, too, so I couldn't…think about her that way.''

She sent him a long, curious look. ''Why are you apologizing?''

''I'm not.'' His voice took on a vicious edge, because he realized he was doing just that. ''I'm explaining. Though God knows why I'd bother. You think what you want.''

''All right. I think you're overreacting to a situation in typical, and predictable, male fashion.'' The look he speared at her should have sliced to the bone. She merely smiled. ''I don't hold it against you. Any more than I would hold it against you if you and Natalie *had* been involved. The past is just that. I know that better than anyone.''

''I guess you do.'' He jammed the gearshift into fourth, then reached out to cover her hand with his. ''But we weren't involved.''

''I'd have to say that was your loss, pal. She's terrific.''

''So are you.''

She smiled at him. ''Yeah, I am.''

Colt steered to the curb, parking carelessly in a loading zone. He waited while Althea called in their location. ''Ready?''

''I'm always ready.'' She stepped out of the car. ''I want to play this light,'' she told Colt. ''Just follow-up questions. We've got nothing on him. Nothing. If we push too hard, we'll lose our chance. If we're right about this—''

"We are right. I can feel it."

So could she. She nodded. "Then I want him. For Liz. For Wild Bill." And for herself, she realized. To help her close the door this ordeal had opened again.

They walked in together and approached Nieman's apartment. Althea sent Colt one last warning look, then knocked.

"Yes, yes…" Nieman's voice came through the door. "What is it?"

"Lieutenant Grayson, Mr. Nieman." She held her shield up to the peephole. "Denver PD. We need a few minutes of your time."

He pulled open the door to the width of the security chain. His eyes darted from Althea's face to Colt's and back again. "Can't this wait? I'm busy."

"I'm afraid not. It shouldn't take long, Mr. Nieman. Just routine."

"Oh, very well." With a definite lack of grace, he yanked off the chain. "Come in, then."

When she did, Althea noted the packing boxes set on the carpet. Many were filled with shredded paper. For Althea, they were as damning as a smoking gun.

"As you can see, you've caught me at a bad time."

"Yes, I can see that. Are you moving, Mr. Nieman?"

"Do you think I would stay here, work here, after this—this scandal?" Obviously insulted, he tugged on his tightly knotted tie. "I think not. Police, reporters, badgering tenants. I haven't had a moment's peace since this began."

"I'm sure it's been a trial for you," Colt stated. He wanted to get his hands on that tie. Nieman would hang nicely from it.

"It certainly has. Well, I suppose you must sit." Nieman waved a hand toward chairs. "But I really can't spare much time. I've a great deal of packing left to do. I don't trust the movers to do it," he added. "Clumsy, always breaking things."

"You've had a lot of experience with moving?" This from Althea as she sat and took out her pad and pencil.

"Naturally. As I've explained before, I travel. I enjoy my work." He smiled by tightening his lips over his teeth. "But I find it tedious to remain in one place for too long. Landlords are always looking for a responsible, experienced manager."

"I'm sure they are." She tapped her pencil against the pad. "The owners of this building..." She began to flip pages.

"Johnston and Croy, Inc."

"Yes." She nodded when she found the notation. "They were quite upset when they were told about the activities in the penthouse."

"I should say." Nieman hitched up the knees of his trousers and sat. "They're a respectable company. Quite successful in the West and Southwest. Of course, they blame me. That's to be expected."

"Because you didn't do a personal interview with the tenant?" Althea prompted.

"The bottom line in real estate, Lieutenant, is regular monthly rentals and low turnover. I provided that."

"You also provided the scene of the crime."

"I can hardly be held responsible for the conduct of my tenants."

It was time, Althea decided, to take a risk. A calculated one. "And you never entered the premises? Never checked on it?"

"Why would I? I had no reason to bother Mr. Davis or go into the penthouse."

"You never went in while Mr. Davis was in residence?" Althea asked.

"I've just said I didn't."

She frowned, flipped more pages. "How would you explain your fingerprints?"

Something flickered in Nieman's eyes, then was gone. "I don't know what you mean."

She was reaching, but she pressed a bit further. "I wondered how you would explain it if I told you that your fingerprints were found inside the penthouse—since you claim never to have entered the premises."

"I don't see..." He was scrambling now. "Oh, yes, I remember now. A few days before...before the incident...the smoke alarm in the penthouse went off. Naturally, I used my passkey to investigate when no one answered my knock."

"You had a fire?" Colt asked.

"No, no, simply a defective smoke detector. It was so minor an incident, I quite forgot it."

"Perhaps you've forgotten something else," Althea said politely. "Perhaps you forgot to tell us about a cabin, west of Boulder. Do you manage that property, as well?"

"I don't know what you're talking about. I don't manage any property but this."

"Then you just use it for recreation," Althea continued. "With Mr. Donner, Mr. Kline and Mr. Scott."

"I have no knowledge of a cabin," Nieman said stiffly, but a line of sweat had popped out above his top lip. "Nor do I know any people by those names. Now you'll have to excuse me."

"Mr. Scott isn't quite up to visitors," Althea told him, and remained seated. "But we can go downtown and see Kline and Donner. That might refresh your memory."

"I'm not going anywhere with you." Nieman rose then. "I've answered all your questions in a reasonable and patient manner. If you persist in this harassment, I'll have to call my attorney."

"Feel free." Althea gestured toward the phone. "He can meet us at the station. In the meantime, I'd like you to think back to where you were on the night of October 25. You could use an alibi."

"Whatever for?"

"Murder."

"That's preposterous." He drew a handkerchief out of his breast pocket to wipe his face. "You can't come in here and accuse me this way."

"I'm not accusing you, Mr. Nieman. I'm asking for your whereabouts on October 25, between the hours of 9:00 and 11:00 p.m. You might also tell your lawyer that we'll be questioning you about a missing woman known as Lacy, and about the abduction of Elizabeth Cook, who is currently in protective custody. Liz is a very bright and observant girl, isn't she, Nightshade?"

"Yeah." She was amazing, Colt thought. Absolutely amazing. She was cracking Nieman into pieces with nothing but innuendo. "Between Liz and the sketches, the D.A. has plenty to work with."

"I don't believe we mentioned the sketches to Mr. Nieman." Althea closed her notebook. "Or the fact that both Kline and Donner were thoroughly interrogated yesterday. Of course, Scott is still critical, so we'll have to wait for his corroboration."

Nieman's face went pasty. "They're lying. I'm a respectable man. I have credentials." His voice cracked. "You can't prove anything on the word of some two-bit actors."

"I don't believe we mentioned Kline and Donner were actors, did we, Nightshade?"

"No." He could have kissed her. "No, we didn't."

"You must be psychic, Nieman," Althea stated. "Why don't we go to the station and see what else you can come up with?"

"I know my rights." Nieman's eyes glittered with rage as he felt the trap creaking shut. "I'm not going anywhere with you."

"I'll have to insist." Althea rose. "Go ahead and call your lawyer, Nieman, but you're coming in for questioning. Now."

"No woman's going to tell me what to do." Nieman lunged, and though Althea was braced, even eager, Colt stepped between them and merely used one hand to shove Nieman back onto the couch.

"Assaulting an officer," he said mildly. "I guess we'll take him in on that. It should give you enough time to get a search warrant."

"More than enough," she agreed. She took out her cuffs.

"Ah, Lieutenant…" Colt watched as she competently secured Nieman's skinny wrists. "They didn't find prints upstairs, did they?"

"I never said they did." She tossed her hair back. "I simply asked what he'd say *if* I said they were found."

"I was wrong," he decided. "I do like your style."

"Thanks." Satisfied, she smiled. "I wonder what we might find in all these neatly packed boxes."

They found more than enough. Tapes, snapshots, even a detailed journal in Nieman's own hand. It painstakingly recorded all his activities, all his thoughts, all his hatred for women. It described how the woman named Lacy had been murdered, and how her body had been buried behind the cabin.

By that afternoon, he had been booked on enough charges to keep him away from society for a lifetime.

"A little anticlimactic," Colt commented as he followed Althea into her office, where she would type up her report. "He was so revolting, I couldn't even drum up the energy to kill him."

"Lucky for you." She sat, booted up her machine. "Listen, if it's any consolation, I believe he was telling the truth about not touching Liz himself. I'm betting the psychiatric profile bears it out. Impotence, accompanied by rage against women and voyeuristic tendencies.''

"Yeah, he just likes to watch.'' His fury came and went. Althea had been right about not being able to change what had been.

"And to make piles of money from his hobby,'' she added. "Once he rounded up his cameraman and a couple of sleazy actors, he went into the business of pandering to others with his peculiar tastes. Got to give him credit. He kept a very precise set of books on his porn business. Kept him in antiques and silk ties.''

"He won't need either one in a cell.'' He rested his hands on her shoulders. "You did good, Thea. Real good.''

"I usually do.'' She glanced over her shoulder to study him. Now all she had to do was figure out what to do about Colt. "Listen, Nightshade, I really want to get this paperwork moving, and then I need some downtime. Okay?''

"Sure. I hear there's going to be some spread at the Fletchers' tonight. Are you up for it?''

"You bet. Why don't I meet you there?''

"All right.'' He leaned down to press his lips to her hair. "I love you, Thea.''

She waited until he left, shutting her door behind him. *I know,* she thought, *I love you, too.*


She went to see Liz. It helped to be able to give the girl and her family some sort of resolution. Colt had beaten her to it, had already come and gone. But Althea sensed that Liz needed to hear it from her, as well.

"We'll never be able to repay you.'' Marleen stood with her arm around Liz as if she couldn't bear not to touch her daughter. "I don't have the words to tell you how grateful we are.''

"I—'' She'd almost said she'd just been doing her job. It was the truth, but it wasn't all of it. "Just take care of each other,'' she said instead.

"We're going to spend a lot more time doing just that.'' Marleen pressed her cheek against Liz's. "We're going home tomorrow.''

"We're going into family counseling," Liz told Althea. "And I—I'm going to join a rape victims' support group. I'm a little scared."

"It's all right to be scared."

Nodding, Liz looked at her mother. "Mom, can I—I just want to talk to Lieutenant Grayson for a minute."

"Sure." Marleen clung for a final moment. "I'll just go down to the lobby, help your father when he gets back with that ice cream."

"Thanks." Liz waited until her mother left the room. "Dad doesn't know how to talk about what happened to me yet. It's awful hard on him."

"He loves you. Give him time."

"He cried." Liz's own eyes filled with tears. "I never saw him cry before. I thought he was too busy with work and stuff to care. I was stupid to run away." Once she'd blurted it out, she exhaled deeply. "I didn't think they understood me, or what I wanted. Now I see how bad I hurt them. It won't ever be exactly the same again, will it?"

"No, Liz, it won't. But if you help each other through it, it can be better."

"I hope so. I still feel so empty inside. Like a part of me's not there anymore."

"You'll fill it with something else. You can't let this block off your feelings for other people. It can make you strong, Liz, but you don't want it to make you hard."

"Colt said—" She sniffled and reached for the box of tissues her mother had left on the coffee table. "He said whenever I felt like I couldn't make it, I should think of you."

Althea stared. "Of me?"

"Because you'd had something horrible happen to you, and you'd used it to make yourself beautiful. Inside and out. That you hadn't just survived, you'd triumphed." She gave a watery smile. "And I could, too. It was funny to hear him talk that way. I guess he must like you a lot."

"I like him, too." And she did, Althea realized. It wasn't a weakness to love someone, not when you could admire and respect him at the same time. Not when he saw exactly what you were, and loved you back.

"Colt's the best," Liz stated. "He never lets you down, you know? No matter what."

"I think I do."

"I was wondering... I know the counseling's important, and everything, but I wonder if I could just call you sometimes. When I— when I don't think I can get through it."

"I hope you will." Althea rose to go over and sit beside Liz. She opened her arms. "You call when you're feeling bad. And when you're feeling good. We all need somebody who understands us."

Fifteen minutes later, Althea left the Cooks to their ice cream and their privacy. She decided she had a lot of thinking to do. She'd always known where her life was going. Now that it had taken this sudden and dramatic detour, she needed to get her bearings again.

But Colt was waiting for her in the lobby.

"Hey, Lieutenant." He tipped her head back and kissed her lightly.

"What are you doing here? Marleen said you'd been by already."

"I went with Frank. He needed to talk."

She touched a hand to his cheek. "You're a good friend, Nightshade."

"It's the only kind of friend there is." She smiled, because she knew he meant it. "Want a lift?"

"I've got my car." But when they walked outside together, she discovered she didn't want that downtime alone after all. "Look, do you want to take a walk or something? I'm wired."

"Sure." He draped an arm casually over her shoulder. "You can help me scope out some of the shop windows. My mother has a birthday next week."

Resistance surged instantly—a knee-jerk response. "I'm no good at picking out presents for people I don't know."

"You'll get to know her." He strolled to the corner and turned left, heading toward a row of downtown shops. He glanced in one window at an elegant display of fine china and crystal. "Hey, you're not the type who, like, registers a pattern and that stuff, are you? You know, for wedding presents?"

"Get a grip." She moved past him so that he had to lengthen his stride to catch up.

"What about a trousseau? Do women still do that?"

"I haven't any idea, or any interest."

"It's not that I mind the T-shirt you wore in bed last night. I was just thinking that something a little more…no, a little less, would be nice for the honeymoon. Where do you want to go?"

"Are you going to cut this out?"

"No."

With an impatient breath, she turned and stared at the next window. "That's a nice sweater." She pointed to a rich blue cowl-neck on a mannequin. "Maybe she'd go for cashmere."

"Maybe." He nodded. "Fine. Let's go get it."

"See, that's your problem." Althea whirled around, hands on hips. "You don't give anything enough thought. You look at one thing, and boom—that's it."

"When it's the right thing, why look around?" He smiled and tugged on her hair. "I know what works for me when I see it. Come on." He took her hand and pulled her into the shop. "The blue sweater in the window?" he said to the clerk. "Have you got it in a size…" He measured in the air with his hands.

"Ten?" the clerk guessed. "Certainly, sir. Just one moment."

"You didn't ask how much it cost," Althea pointed out.

"When something's right, cost is irrelevant." He turned to smile at her. "You're going to keep me in line. I appreciate that. I tend to let details slip."

"There's news." She stepped away to poke through a rack of silk blouses.

He was careless, Althea reminded herself. He was impulsive and rash and quick on the draw. All the things she was not. She preferred order, routine, meticulous calculation. She had to be crazy to think they could mesh.

She turned her head, watching him as he waited for the clerk to ring up the sweater and gift-wrap it.

But they did mesh, she realized. Everything about him fitted her like a glove. The hair wasn't really blond or brown and was never quite disciplined. The eyes, caught somewhere between blue and green, that could stop her heart with one look. His recklessness. His dependability.

His total and unconditional understanding.

"Problem?" he asked when he caught her staring.

"No."

"Would you like a pink bow, sir, or blue?"

"Pink," he said, without glancing back. "Do you have any wedding dresses in here?"

"Not formal ones, no, sir." But the clerk's eyes lit up at the prospect of another sale. "We do have some very elegant tea gowns and cocktail suits that would be perfect for a wedding."

"It should be something festive," he decided, and the humor was back in his eyes. "For New Year's Eve."

Althea straightened her shoulders, turned on her heel to face him. "Get this, Nightshade. I am not marrying you on New Year's Eve."

"Okay, okay. Pick another date."

"Thanksgiving," she told him, and had the pleasure of watching his mouth fall open as he dropped the box the clerk had handed him.

"What?"

"I said Thanksgiving. Take it or leave it." She tossed her hair back and strode out the door.

"Wait! Damn!" He started after her, kicked the gift box halfway across the room. The clerk called after him as he scooped it up on the run.

"Sir, the dresses?"

"Later." He swung through the door and caught up with Althea halfway down the block. "Did you say you'd marry me on Thanksgiving?"

"I hate repeating myself, Nightshade. If you can't keep up, that's your problem. Now, if you've finished your shopping, I'm going back to work."

"Just one damn minute." Exasperated, he stuffed the box under his arm, crushing the bow. It freed his hands to snag her by the shoulders. "What made you change your mind?"

"It must have been your smooth, subtle approach," she said dryly. Lord, she was enjoying this, she realized. Deep-down enjoying it. "Keep manhandling me, pal, and I'll haul you in."

He shook his head, as if to realign his thoughts. "You're going to marry me?"

She arched a brow. "Ain't no flies on you."

"On Thanksgiving. *This* Thanksgiving. The one that's coming up in a few weeks?"

"Getting cold feet already?" she began, then found her mouth much too occupied for words. It was a heady kiss, filled with promises and joy. "Do you know the penalty for kissing a police officer on a public street?" she asked when she could speak again.

"I'll risk it."

"Good." She dragged his mouth back to hers. Pedestrians wound around them as they clung. "You're going to get life for this, Nightshade."

"I'm counting on it." Carefully he drew her back so that he could see her face. "Why Thanksgiving?"

"Because I'd like to have a family to celebrate it with. Cilla's always bugging me to join them, but I...I couldn't."

"Why?"

"Is this an interrogation or an engagement?" she demanded.

"Both, but this is the last one. Why are you going to marry me?"

"Because you nagged me until I broke down. And I felt sorry for you, because you seemed so set on it. Besides, I love you, and I've kind of gotten used to you, so—"

"Hold on. Say that again."

"I said I've kind of gotten used to you."

Grinning, he kissed the tip of her nose. "Not that part. The part right before that."

"Where I felt sorry for you?"

"Uh-uh. After that."

"Oh, the I-love-you part."

"That's the one. Say it again."

"Okay." She took a deep breath. "I love you." And let it out. "It's tougher to say it all by itself that way."

"You'll get used to it."

"I think you're right."

He laughed and crushed her against him. "I'm betting on it."

# Epilogue

"I think I need to consider this again."

Althea stood in front of the full-length mirror in Cilla's bedroom, staring at her own reflection. There was a woman inside the mirror, she noted dispassionately. A pale woman with a tumble of red hair. She looked elegant in a slim ivory suit trimmed with lace and accented with tiny pearl buttons that ran the length of the snugly fitted jacket.

But her eyes were too big, too wide, and too fearful.

"I really don't think this is going to work."

"You look fabulous," Deborah assured her. "Perfect."

"I wasn't talking about the dress." She pressed a hand to her queasy stomach. "I meant the wedding."

"Don't start." Cilla tugged at the line of Althea's ivory silk jacket. "You're fidgeting again."

"Of course I'm fidgeting." For lack of anything better to do, Althea reached up to make sure the pearl drops at her ears were secure. Colt's mother had given them to her, she remembered, and felt a trickle of warmth at the memory. Something to be handed down, his mother had said, as they had been from Colt's grandmother to her.

Then she'd cried a little, and kissed Althea's cheek and welcomed her to the family.

Family, Althea thought on a fresh wave of panic. What did she know about family?

"I'm about to commit myself for life to a man I've known a matter of weeks," she muttered to the woman in the mirror. "I should *be* committed."

"You love him, don't you?" Deborah asked.

"What does that have to do with it?"

Laughing, Deborah took Althea's restless hand in hers. "Only everything. I didn't know Gage very long, either." And had known the depths of his secrets for an even shorter time. "But I loved him, and I knew. I've seen the way you look at Colt, Thea. You know, too."

"Lawyers," Althea complained to Cilla. "They always turn things around on you."

"She's great, isn't she?" Pride burst through as Cilla gave her sister a hard squeeze. "The best prosecutor east of the Mississippi."

"When you're right, you're right," Deborah returned with a grin. "Now, let's take a look at the matron of honor." She tilted her head to examine her sister. "You look wonderful, Cilla."

"So do you." Cilla brushed a hand through her sister's dark hair. "Marriage and motherhood agree with you."

"If you two will finish up your admiration hour, I'm having a nervous breakdown over here." Althea sat down on the bed, squeezed her eyes shut. "I could make a run for it out the back."

"He'd catch you," Cilla decided.

"Not if I had a really good head start. Maybe if I—" A knock on the door interrupted her. "If that's Nightshade, I am not going to talk to him."

"Of course not," Deborah agreed. "Bad luck." She opened the door to her husband and daughter. That was good luck, she thought as she smiled at Gage. The very best luck of all.

"Sorry to break in on the prep work, but we've got some restless people downstairs."

"If those kids have touched that wedding cake…" Cilla began.

"Boyd saved it," Gage assured her. Barely. With the baby tucked in one arm, he slipped the other around his wife. "Colt's wearing a path in the den carpet."

"So he's nervous," Althea shot back. "He should be. Look what he's gotten us into. Boy, would I like to be a fly on the wall down there."

Gage grinned, winked at Deborah. "It has its advantages." He nuzzled his infant daughter when she began to fuss.

"I'll take her, Gage." Deborah gathered Adrianna into her arms. "You go help Boyd calm down the groom. We're nearly ready."

"Who said?" Althea twisted her hands together.

Cilla brushed Gage out of the room, closed the door. It was time for the big guns. "Coward," she said softly.

"Now, just a minute..."

"You're afraid to walk downstairs and make a public commitment to the man you love. That's pathetic."

Catching on, Deborah soothed the baby, and played the game. "Now, Cilla, don't be so harsh. If she's changed her mind—"

"She hasn't. She just can't make it up. And Colt's doing everything to make her happy. He's selling his ranch, buying land out here."

Althea got to her feet. "That's unfair."

"It certainly is." Deborah ranged herself beside Althea, and bit the inside of her lip to keep from grinning. "I'd think you'd be a little more understanding, Cilla. This is an important decision."

"Then she should make it instead of hiding up here like some vestal virgin about to be sacrificed."

Althea's chin jutted out. "I'm not hiding. Deb, go out and tell them to start the damn music. I'm coming down."

"All right, Thea. If you're sure." Deborah patted her arm, winked at her sister, and hurried out.

"Well, come on." Althea stormed to the door. "Let's get going."

"Fine." Cilla sauntered past her, then started down the steps.

Althea was nearly to the bottom before she realized she'd been conned. The two sisters had pulled off the good cop–bad cop routine like pros.

Now her stomach jumped. There were flowers everywhere, banks of color and scent. There was music, soft, romantic. She saw Colt's mother leaning heavily against his father and smiling bravely through a mist of tears. She saw Natalie beaming and dabbing at her eyes. Deborah, her lashes wet, cradling Adrianna.

There was Boyd, reaching out to take Cilla's hand, kissing her damp cheek before looking back at Althea to give her an encouraging wink.

Althea came to a dead stop. If people cried at weddings, she deduced, there had to be a good reason.

Then she looked toward the fireplace, and saw nothing but Colt.

And he saw nothing but her.

Her legs stopped wobbling. She crossed to him, carrying a single white rose, and her heart.

"Good to see you, Lieutenant," he murmured as he took her hand.

"Good to see you, too, Nightshade." She felt the warmth from the fire that glowed beside them, the warmth from him. She smiled as he brought her hand to his lips, and her fingers were steady.

"Happy Thanksgiving."

"Same goes." She brought their joined hands to her lips in turn. Maybe she didn't know about family, but she'd learn. They'd learn. "I love you, very much."

"Same goes. Ready for this?"

"I am now."

As the fire crackled, they faced each other and the life they'd make together.

# Night Smoke

For opposites who attract

# *Prologue*

Fire. It cleansed. It destroyed. With its heat, lives could be saved. Or lives could be taken. It was one of the greatest discoveries of man, and one of his chief fears.

And one of his fascinations.

Mothers warned their children not to play with matches, not to touch the red glow of the stove. For no matter how pretty the flame, how seductive the warmth, fire against flesh burned.

In the hearth, it was romantic, cozy, cheerful, dancing and crackling, wafting scented smoke and flickering soft golden light. Old men dreamed by it. Lovers wooed by it.

In the campfire, it shot its sparks toward a starry sky, tempting wide-eyed children to roast their marshmallows into black goo while shivering over ghost stories.

There were dark, hopeless corners of the city where the homeless cupped their frozen hands over trash-can fires, their faces drawn and weary in the shadowy light, their minds too numb for dreams.

In the city of Urbana, there were many fires.

A carelessly dropped cigarette smoldering in a mattress. Faulty wiring, overlooked, or ignored by a corrupt inspector. A kerosene heater set too close to the drapes, oily rags tossed in a stuffy closet. A flash of lightning. An unattended candle.

All could cause destruction of property, loss of life. Ignorance, an accident, an act of God.

But there were other ways, more devious ways.

Once inside the building he took several short, shallow breaths. It was so simple, really. And so exciting. The power was in his hands now. He knew exactly what to do, and there was a thrill in doing it. Alone. In the dark.

It wouldn't be dark for long. The thought made him giggle as he climbed to the second floor. He would soon make the light.

Two cans of gasoline would be enough. With the first he splashed the old wooden floor, soaking it, leaving a trail as he moved from wall to wall, from room to room. Now and again he stopped, pulling stock from the racks, scattering matchbooks over the stream of flammables, adding fuel that would feed the flames and spread them.

The smell of the accelerant was sweet, an exotic perfume that heightened his senses. He wasn't panicked, he wasn't hurried as he climbed the winding metal stairs to the next floor. He was quiet, of course, for he wasn't a stupid man. But he knew the night watchman was bent over his magazines in another part of the building.

As he worked, he glanced up at the spider-like sprinklers in the ceiling. He'd already seen to those. There would be no hiss of water from the pipes as the flames rose, no warning buzz from smoke alarms.

This fire would burn, and burn, and burn, until the window glass exploded from the angry fists of heat. Paint would blister, metal would melt, rafters would fall, charred and flaming.

He wished...for a moment he wished he could stay, stand in the center of it all and watch the sleeping fire awaken, grumbling. He wanted to be there, to admire and absorb as it stirred, snapped, then stretched its hot, bright body. He wanted to hear its triumphant roar as it hungrily devoured everything in its path.

But he would be far away by then. Too far to see, to hear, to smell. He would have to imagine it.

With a sigh, he lit the first match, held the flame at eye level, admiring the infant spark, mesmerized by it. He was smiling, as proud as any expectant father, as he tossed the tiny fire into a dark pool of gas. He watched for a moment, only a moment, as the animal erupted into life, streaking along the trail he'd left for it.

He left quietly, hurrying now, into the frigid night. Soon his feet had picked up the rhythm of his racing heart.

# *Chapter 1*

Annoyed, exhausted, Natalie stepped into her penthouse apartment. The dinner meeting with her marketing executives had run beyond midnight. She could have come home then, she reminded herself as she stepped out of her shoes. But no. Her office was en route from the restaurant to her apartment. She simply hadn't been able to resist stopping in for one more look at the new designs, one last check on the ads heralding the grand opening.

Both had needed work. And really, she'd only intended to make a few notes. Draft one or two memos.

So why was she stumbling toward the bedroom at 2:00 a.m.? she asked herself. The answer was easy. She was compulsive, obsessive. She was, Natalie thought, an idiot. Particularly since she had an eight-o'clock breakfast meeting with several of her East Coast sales reps.

No problem, she assured herself. No problem at all. Who needed sleep? Certainly not Natalie Fletcher, the thirty-two-year-old dynamo who was currently expanding Fletcher Industries into one more avenue of profit.

And there *would* be profit. She'd put all her skill and experience and creativity into building Lady's Choice from the ground up. Before profit, there would be the excitement of conception, birth, growth, those first pangs and pleasures of an infant company finding its own way.

Her infant company, she thought with tired satisfaction. Her baby. She would tend and teach and nurture—and, yes, when necessary, walk the floor at 2:00 a.m.

A glance in the mirror over the bureau told her that even a dynamo needed rest. Her cheeks had lost both their natural color as well as their cosmetic blush and her face looked entirely too fragile and pale. The simple twist that scooped her hair back and had started the evening looking sophisticated and chic now only seemed to emphasize the shadows that smudged her dark green eyes.

Because she was a woman who prided herself on her energy and stamina, she turned away from the reflection, blowing her honey-toned bangs out of her eyes and rotating her shoulders to ease the stiffness. In any case, sharks didn't sleep, she reminded herself. Even business sharks. But this one was very tempted to fall on the bed fully dressed.

That wouldn't do, she thought, and shrugged out of her coat. Organization and control were every bit as important in business as a good head for figures. Ingrained habit had her walking to the closet, and she was draping the velvet wrap on a padded hanger when the phone rang.

Let the machine get it, she ordered herself, but by the second ring she was snatching up the receiver.

"Hello?"

"Ms. Fletcher?"

"Yes?" The receiver clanged against the emeralds at her ear. She was reaching up to remove the earring when the panic in the voice stopped her.

"It's Jim Banks, Ms. Fletcher. The night watchman over at the south side warehouse. We've got trouble here."

"Trouble? Did someone break in?"

"It's fire. Holy God, Ms. Fletcher, the whole place is going up."

"Fire?" She brought her other hand to the receiver, as if it might leap from her ear. "At the warehouse? Was anyone in the building? Is anyone in there?"

"No, ma'am, there was just me." His voice shook, cracked. "I was downstairs in the coffee room when I heard an explosion.

Must've been a bomb or something, I don't know. I called the fire department.''

She could hear other sounds now, sirens, shouts. ''Are you hurt?''

''No, I got out. I got out. Mother of God, Ms. Fletcher, it's terrible. It's just terrible.''

''I'm on my way.''

It took Natalie fifteen minutes to make the trip from her plush west-side neighborhood to the dingy south side, with its warehouses and factories. But she saw the fire, heard it before she pulled up behind the string of engines. Men with their faces smeared with soot manned hoses, wielded axes. Smoke and flame belched from shattered windows and spewed through gaps in the ruined roof. The heat was enormous. Even at this distance it shot out, slapping her face while the icy February wind swirled at her back.

Everything. She knew everything inside the building was lost.

''Ms. Fletcher?''

Struggling against horror and fascination, she turned and looked at a round middle-aged man in a gray uniform.

''I'm Jim Banks.''

''Oh, yes.'' She reached out automatically to take his hand. It was freezing, and as shaky as his voice. ''You're all right? Are you sure?''

''Yes, ma'am. It's an awful thing.''

They watched the fire and those who fought it for a moment, in silence. ''The smoke alarms?''

''I didn't hear anything. Not until the explosion. I started to head upstairs, and I saw the fire. It was everywhere.'' He rubbed a hand over his mouth. Never in his life had he seen anything like it. Never in his life did he want to see its like again. ''Just everywhere. I got out and called the fire department from my truck.''

''You did the right thing. Do you know who's in charge here?''

''No, Ms. Fletcher, I don't. These guys work fast, and they don't spend a lot of time talking.''

''All right. Why don't you go home now, Jim? I'll deal with this.

If they need to talk to you, I have your beeper number, and they can call."

"Nothing much to do." He looked down at the ground and shook his head. "I'm mighty sorry, Ms. Fletcher."

"So am I. I appreciate you calling me."

"Thought I should." He gave one last glance at the building, seemed to shudder, then trudged off to his truck.

Natalie stood where she was, and waited.

A crowd had gathered by the time Ry got to the scene. A fire drew crowds, he knew, like a good fistfight or a flashy juggler. People even took sides—and a great many of them rooted for the fire.

He stepped out of his car, a lean, broad-shouldered man with tired eyes the color of the smoke stinging the winter sky. His narrow, bony face was set, impassive. The lights flashing around him shadowed, then highlighted, the hollows and planes, the shallow cleft in his chin that women loved and he found a small nuisance.

He set his boots on the sodden ground and stepped into them with a grace and economy of motion that came from years of training. Though flames still licked and sparked, his experienced eye told him that the men had contained and nearly suppressed it.

Soon it would be time for him to go to work.

Automatically he put on the black protective jacket, covering his flannel shirt and his jeans down past the hips. He combed one hand through his unruly hair, hair that was a deep, dark brown and showed hints of fire in sunlight. He set his dented, smoke-stained hat on his head, lit a cigarette, then tugged on protective gloves.

And while he performed these habitual acts, he scanned the scene. A man in his position needed to keep an open mind about fire. He would take an overview of the scene, the weather, note the wind direction, talk to the fire fighters. There would be all manner of routine and scientific tests to run.

But first, he would trust his eyes, and his nose.

The warehouse was most probably a loss, but it was no longer his job to save it. His job was to find the whys and the hows.

He exhaled smoke and studied the crowd.

He knew the night watchman had called in the alarm. The man would have to be interviewed. Ry looked over the faces, one by one. Excitement was normal. He saw it in the eyes of the young man who watched the destruction, dazzled. And shock, in the slack-jawed woman who huddled against him. Horror, admiration, relief that the fire hadn't touched them or theirs. He saw that, as well.

Then his gaze fell on the blonde.

She stood apart from the rest, staring straight ahead while the light wind teased her honey blond hair out of its fancy twist. Expensive shoes, Ry noted, of supple midnight leather, as out of place in this part of town as her velvet coat and her fancy face.

A hell of a face, he thought idly, lifting the cigarette to his lips again. A pale oval that belonged on a cameo. Eyes... He couldn't make out their color, but they were dark. No excitement there, he mused. No horror, no shock. Anger, maybe. Just a touch of it. She was either a woman of little emotion, or one who knew how to control it.

A hothouse rose, he decided. And just what was she doing so far out of her milieu at nearly four o'clock in the morning?

"Hey, Inspector." Grimy and wet, Lieutenant Holden trudged over to bum a cigarette. "Chalk up another one for the Fighting Twenty-second." .

Ry knew Holden, and was already holding the pack out. "Looks like you killed another one."

"This was a bitch." Cupping his hands against the wind, Holden lit up. "Fully involved by the time we got here. Call came in from the night watchman at 1:40. Second and third floors took most of it, but the equipment on one's pretty well gone, too. You'll probably find your point of origin on the second."

"Yeah?" Though the fire was winding down, Ry knew Holden wasn't just shooting the breeze.

"Found some streamers going up the steps at the east end. Probably started the fire with them, but not all the material went up. Ladies' lingerie."

"Hmmm?" .

"Ladies' lingerie," Holden said with a grin. "That's what they were warehousing. Lots of nighties and undies. You've got a nice stream of underwear and matchbooks that didn't go up.'' He slapped Ry on the shoulder. ''Have fun. Hey, probie!'' he shouted to one of the probationary fire fighters. ''You going to hold that hose or play with it? Got to watch 'em every minute, Ry.''

''Don't I know it...''

Out of the corner of his eye, Ry watched his hothouse flower pick her way toward a fire engine. He and Holden separated.

''Isn't there anything you can tell me?'' Natalie asked an exhausted fire fighter. ''How did it start?''

''Lady, I just put them out.'' He sat on a running board, no longer interested in the smoldering wreck of the warehouse. ''You want answers?'' He jerked his thumb in Ry's direction. ''Ask the inspector.''

''Civilians don't belong at fire scenes,'' Ry said from behind her. When she turned to look at him, he saw that her eyes were green, a deep jade green.

''It's my fire scene.'' Her voice was cool, like the wind that eased her hair, with a faint drawl that made him think of cowboys and schoolmarms. ''My warehouse,'' she continued. ''My problem.''

''Is that so?'' Ry took another survey. She was cold. He knew from experience that there was no place colder than a fire scene in winter. But her spine was straight, and that delicate chin lifted. ''And that would make you?''

''Natalie Fletcher. I own the building, and everything in it. And I'd like some answers.'' She cocked one elegantly arched brow. ''And that would make you—?''

''Piasecki. Arson investigator.''

''Arson?'' Shock had her gaping before she snapped back into control. ''You think this was arson.''

''It's my job to find out.'' He glanced down, nearly sneered. ''You're going to ruin those shoes, Miz Fletcher.''

''My shoes are the least of my—'' She broke off when he took her arm and started to steer her away. ''What are you doing?''

''You're in the way. That would be your car, wouldn't it?'' He nodded toward a shiny new Mercedes convertible.

"Yes, but—"

"Get in it."

"I will not get in it." She tried to shake him off and discovered she would have needed a crowbar. "Will you let go of me?"

She smelled a hell of a lot better than smoke and sodden debris. Ry took a deep gulp of her, then tried for diplomacy. It was something, he was proud to admit, that had never been his strong suit.

"Look, you're cold. What's the point in standing out in the wind?"

She stiffened, against both him and the wind. "The point is, that's my building. What's left of it."

"Fine." They'd do it her way, since it suited him. But he placed her between the car and his body to shelter her from the worst of the cold. "It's kind of late at night to be checking your inventory, isn't it?"

"It is." She stuck her hands in her pockets, trying fruitlessly to warm them. "I drove out after the night watchman called me."

"And that would have been…"

"I don't know. Around two."

"Around two," he repeated, and let his gaze skim over her again. There was a snazzy dinner suit under the velvet, he noted. The material looked soft, expensive, and it was the same color as her eyes. "Pretty fancy outfit for a fire."

"I had a late meeting and didn't think to change into more appropriate clothes before I came." Idiot, she thought, and looked back grimly at what was left of her property. "Is there a point to this?"

"Your meeting ran until two?"

"No, it broke up about midnight."

"How come you're still dressed?"

"What?"

"How come you're still dressed?" He took out another cigarette, lit it. "Late date?"

"No, I went by my office to do some paperwork. I'd barely gotten home when Jim Banks, the night watchman, called me."

"Then you were alone from midnight until two?"

"Yes, I—" Her eyes cut back to his, narrowed. "Do you think

I'm responsible for this? Is that what you're getting at here—? What the hell was your name?''

"Piasecki," he said, and smiled. "Ryan Piasecki. And I don't think anything yet, Miz Fletcher. I'm just separating the details.''

Her eyes were no longer cool, controlled. They had flared to flash point. "Then I'll give you some more. The building and its contents are fully insured. I'm with United Security.''

"What kind of business are you in?''

"I'm Fletcher Industries, Inspector Piasecki. You may have heard of it.''

He had, most certainly. Real estate, mining, shipping. The conglomerate owned considerable property, including several holdings in Urbana. But there were reasons that big companies, as well as small ones, resorted to arson.

"You run Fletcher Industries?''

"I oversee several of its interests. Including this one." Most particularly this one, she thought. This one was her baby. "We're opening several speciality boutiques countrywide in the spring, in addition to a catalog service. A large portion of my inventory was in that building.''

"What sort of inventory?''

Now she smiled. "Lingerie, inspector. Bras, panties, negligees. Silks, satins, lace. You might be familiar with the concept.''

"Enough to appreciate it." She was shivering now, obviously struggling to keep her teeth from chattering. He imagined her feet would be blocks of ice in those thin, pricey shoes. "Look, you're freezing out here. Get in the car. Go home. We'll be in touch.''

"I want to know what happened to my building. What's left of my stock.''

"Your building burned down, Miz Fletcher. And it's unlikely there's anything left of your stock that would raise a man's blood pressure." He opened the car door. "I've got a job to do. And I'd advise you to call your insurance agent.''

"You've got a real knack for soothing the victims, don't you, Piasecki?''

"No, can't say that I do." He took a notebook and pencil stub from his shirt pocket. "Give me your address and phone number. Home and office."

Natalie took a deep breath, then let it out slowly, before she gave him the information he wanted. "You know," she added. "I've always had a soft spot for public servants. My brother's a cop in Denver."

"That so?"

"Yes, that's so." She slid into the car. "You've managed, in one short meeting, to change my mind." She slammed the door, sorry she didn't do it quickly enough to catch his fingers. With one last glance at the ruined building, she drove away.

Ry watched her taillights disappear and added another note to his book. Great legs. Not that he'd forget, he mused as he turned away. But a good inspector wrote everything down.

Natalie forced herself to sleep for two hours, then rose and took a stinging-cold shower. Wrapped in her robe, she called her assistant and arranged to have her morning appointments canceled or shifted. With her first cup of coffee, she phoned her parents in Colorado. She was on cup number two by the time she had given them all the details she knew, soothed their concern and listened to their advice.

With cup number three, she contacted her insurance agent and arranged to meet him at the site. After downing aspirin with the remains of that cup, she dressed for what promised to be a very long day.

She was nearly out of the door when the phone stopped her.

"You have a machine," she reminded herself, even as she darted back to answer it. "Hello?"

"Nat, it's Deborah. I just heard."

"Oh." Rubbing the back of her neck, Natalie sat on the arm of a chair. Deborah O'Roarke Guthrie was a double pleasure, both friend and family. "I guess it's hit the news already."

There was a slight hesitation. "I'm sorry, Natalie, really sorry. How bad is it?"

"I'm not sure. Last night it looked about as bad as it gets. But I'm going out now, meeting my insurance agent. Who knows, we may salvage something."

"Would you like me to come with you? I can reschedule my morning."

Natalie smiled. Deborah would do just that. As if she didn't have enough on her plate with her husband, her baby, her job as assistant district attorney.

"No, but thanks for asking. I'll let you know something when I know something."

"Come to dinner tonight. You can relax, soak up some sympathy."

"I'd like that."

"If there's anything else I can do, just tell me."

"Actually, you could call Denver. Keep your sister and my brother from riding east to the rescue."

"I'll do that."

"Oh, one more thing." Natalie rose, checked the contents of her briefcase as she spoke. "What do you know about an Inspector Piasecki? Ryan Piasecki?"

"Piasecki?" There was a slight pause as Deborah flipped through her mental files. Natalie could all but see the process. "Arson squad. He's the best in the city."

"He would be," Natalie muttered.

"Is arson suspected?" Deborah said carefully.

"I don't know. I just know he was there, he was rude, and he wouldn't tell me anything."

"It takes time to determine the cause of a fire, Natalie. I can put some pressure on, if you want me to."

It was tempting, just for the imagined pleasure of seeing Piasecki scramble. "No thanks. Not yet, anyway. I'll see you later."

"Seven o'clock," Deborah insisted.

"I'll be there. Thanks." Natalie hung up and grabbed her coat. With luck, she'd beat the insurance agent to the site by a good thirty minutes.

Luck was with her—in that area, anyway. When Natalie pulled up behind the fire-department barricade, she discovered she was going to need a great deal more than luck to win this battle.

It looked worse, incredibly worse, than it had the night before.

It was a small building, only three floors. The cinder-block outer walls had held, and now stood blackened and streaked with soot, still dripping with water from the hoses. The ground was littered with charred and sodden wood, broken glass, twisted metal. The air stank of smoke.

Miserable, she ducked under the yellow tape for a closer look.

''What the hell do you think you're doing?''

She jolted, then shaded her eyes from the sun to see more clearly. She should have known, Natalie thought, when she saw Ry making his way toward her through the wreckage.

''Didn't you see the sign?'' he demanded.

''Of course I saw it. This is my property, Inspector. The insurance adjuster is meeting me here shortly. I believe I'm within my rights in inspecting the damage.''

He gave her one disgusted look. ''Don't you have any other kind of shoes?''

''I beg your pardon?''

''Stay here.'' Muttering to himself, he stalked to his car, came back with a pair of oversize fireman's boots. ''Put these on.''

''But—''

He took her arm, throwing her off balance. ''Put those ridiculous shoes into the boots. Otherwise you're going to hurt yourself.''

''Fine.'' She stepped into them, feeling absurd.

The tops of the boots covered her legs almost to the knee. The navy suit and matching wool coat she wore were runway-model smart. A trio of gold chains draped around her neck added flash.

''Nice look,'' he commented. ''Now, let's get something straight. I need to preserve this scene, and that means you don't touch anything.'' He said it even though his authority to keep her out was debatable, and he'd already found a great deal of what he'd been looking for.

''I have no intention of—''

''That's what they all say.''

She drew herself up. "Tell me, Inspector, do you work alone because you prefer it, or because no one can stand to be around you for longer than five minutes?"

"Both." He smiled then. The change of expression was dazzling, charming—and suspicious. She wasn't sure, but she thought the faintest of dimples winked beside his mouth. "What are you doing clunking around a fire scene in a five-hundred-dollar suit?"

"I..." Wary of the smile, she tugged her coat closed. "I have meetings all afternoon. I won't have time to change."

"Executives." He kept his hand on her arm as he turned. "Come on, then. Be careful where you go—the site's not totally safe, but you can take a look at what she left you. I've still got work to do."

He led her in through the mangled doorway. The ceiling was a yawning pit between floors. What had fallen, or had been knocked through, lay in filthy layers of sodden ash and alligatored wood. She shivered once at the sight of the twisted mass of burned mannequins that lay sprawled and broken.

"They didn't suffer," Ry assured her, and her eyes flashed back to his.

"I'm sure you can view this as a joke, but—"

"Fire's never a joke. Watch your step."

She saw where he'd been working, near the base of a broken inner wall. There was a small wire screen in a wooden frame, a shovel that looked like a child's toy, a few mason jars, a crowbar, a yardstick. While she watched, Ry pried off a scored section of baseboard.

"What are you doing?"

"My job."

She set her teeth. "Are we on the same side here?"

He glanced up. "Maybe." With a putty knife, he began to scrape at residue. He sniffed, he grunted and, when he was satisfied, placed it in a jar. "Do you know what oxidation is, Ms. Fletcher?"

She frowned, shifted. "More or less."

"The chemical union of a substance with oxygen. It can be slow, like paint drying, or fast. Heat and light. A fire's fast. And some things help it move faster." He continued to scrape, then looked up again, held out the knife. "Take a whiff."

Dubious, she stepped forward and sniffed.

"What do you smell?"

"Smoke, wet...I don't know."

He placed the residue in the jar. "Gasoline," he said, watching her face. "See, a liquid seeks its level, goes into cracks in the floor, into dead-air corners, flows under baseboard. If it gets caught under there, it doesn't burn. You see the place I cleared out here?"

She moistened her lips, studied the floor he had shoveled or swept clear of debris. There was a black stain, like a shadow burned into the wood. "Yes?"

"The charred-blob pattern. It's like a map. I keep at this, layer by layer, and I'll be able to tell what happened, before, during."

"You're telling me someone poured gas in here and lit a match?"

He said nothing, only scooted forward a bit to pick up a scrap of burned cloth. "Silk," he said with a rub of his fingertips. "Too bad." He placed the scrap in what looked like a flour tin. "Sometimes a torch will lay out streamers, give the fire more of an appetite. They don't always burn." He picked up an almost perfectly preserved cup from a lacy bra. Amused, his eyes met Natalie's over it. "Funny what resists, isn't it?"

She was cold again, but not from the wind. It was from within, and it was rage. "If this fire was deliberately set, I want to know."

Interested in the change in her eyes, he sat back on his haunches. His black fireman's coat was unhooked, revealing jeans, worn white at the knees, and a flannel shirt. He hadn't left the scene since his arrival.

"You'll get my report." He rose then. "Draw me a picture. What did this place look like twenty-four hours ago?"

She closed her eyes for a moment, but it didn't help. She could still smell the destruction.

"It was three stories, about two thousand square feet. Iron balconies and interior steps. Seamstresses worked on the third floor. All of our merchandise is handmade."

"Classy."

"Yes, that's the idea. We have another plant in this district where most of the sewing is done. The twelve machines upstairs were just for finish work. There was a small coffee room to the left, rest rooms... On the second, the floor was made of linoleum, rather than wood. We stored the stock there. I kept a small office up there, as well, though I do most of my work uptown. The area down here was for inspecting, packaging and shipping. We were to begin fulfilling our spring orders in three weeks."

She turned, not quite sure where she intended to go, and stumbled over debris. Ry's quick grab saved her from a nasty spill.

"Hold on," he murmured.

Shaken, she leaned back against him for a moment. There was strength there, if not sympathy. At the moment, she preferred it that way. "We employed over seventy people in this plant alone. People who are out of work until I can sort this out." She whirled back. He gripped her arms to keep her steady. "And it was deliberate."

Control, he thought. Well, she didn't have it now. She was as volatile as a lit match. "I haven't finished my investigation."

"It was deliberate," she repeated. "And you're thinking I could have done it. That I came in here in the middle of the night with a can of gasoline."

Her face was close to his. Funny, he thought, he hadn't noticed how tall she was in those fancy ankle-breaking shoes. "It's a little hard to picture."

"Hired someone, then?" she tossed out. "Hired someone to burn down the building, even though there was a man in it? But what's one security guard against a nice fat insurance check?"

He was silent for a moment, his eyes locked on hers. "You tell me."

Infuriated, she wrenched away from him. "No, Inspector, you're going to have to tell me. And whether you like it or not, I'm going to be on you like a shadow through every step of the investigation. Every step," she repeated. "Until I have all the answers."

She strode out of the building, dignified despite the awkward boots. Her temper was barely under control when she saw the car pull up beside hers. Recognizing it, she sighed, made her way to the tape barrier and under it.

"Donald." She held out her hands. "Oh, Donald, what a mess..."

Gripping her hands, he looked beyond her to the building. For a moment he just stood there, holding her hands, shaking his head. "How could this have happened? The wiring? We had the wiring checked two months ago."

"I know. I'm so sorry. All your work." Two years of his life, she thought, and hers. Up in smoke.

"Everything?" There was a faint tremor in his voice, in his hand as it gripped hers. "Is it all gone?"

"I'm afraid it is. We have other inventory, Donald. This isn't going to whip us."

"You're tougher than me, Nat." After a last quick squeeze he released her hands. "This was my biggest shot. You're the CEO, but I feel like I was captain. And my ship just sank."

Natalie's heart went out to him. It wasn't simply business with Donald Hawthorne, she thought, any more than it was simply business with her. This new company was a dream, a fresh excitement, and a chance for both of them to try something completely different.

No, not just to try, she reminded herself. To succeed.

"We're going to have to work our butts off for the next three weeks."

He turned back, a small smile curving his lips. "Do you really think we can pull it off, after this, on schedule?"

"Yes, I do." Determination hardened her lips. "It's a delay, that's all. So we shuffle things around. We'll certainly have to postpone the audit."

"I can't even think of that now." He stopped, blinked. "Jesus, Nat, the files, the records."

"I don't think we're going to salvage any of the paperwork that was in the warehouse." She looked back toward her building. "It's going to make things more complicated, add some work hours, but we'll put it back together."

"But how can we manage the audit when—"

"It goes on the back burner until we're up and running. We'll talk about it back at the office. As soon as I meet the insurance agent, get the ball rolling, I'm heading back in." Already her mind was working out the details, the steps and stages. "We'll put on some double shifts, order new material, pull in some inventory from Chicago and Atlanta. We'll make it work, Donald. Lady's Choice is going to open in March, come hell or high water.''

His smile flashed into a grin. ''If anybody can make it work, you can.''

''*We* can,'' she told him. ''Now I need you to get back uptown, start making calls.'' PR, she knew, was his strong suit. He was overly impulsive perhaps, but she needed the action-oriented with her now. ''You get Melvin and Deirdre hopping, Donald. Bribe or threaten distributors, plead with the union, soothe the clients. That's what you do best.''

''I'm on it. You can count on me.''

''I know I can. I'll be in the office soon to crack the whip.''

Boyfriend? Ry wondered as he watched the two embrace. The tall, polished executive with the pretty face and shiny shoes looked to be her type.

As a matter of course, he noted down the license number of the Lincoln beside Natalie's car, then went back to work.

# Chapter 2

"She's going to be here any minute." Assistant District Attorney Deborah O'Roarke Guthrie put fisted hands on her hips. "I want the whole story, Gage, before Natalie gets here."

Gage added another log to the fire before he turned to his wife. She'd changed out of her business suit into soft wool slacks and a cashmere sweater of midnight blue. Her ebony hair fell loose, nearly to her shoulders.

"You're beautiful, Deborah. I don't tell you that often enough."

She lifted a brow. Oh, he was a smooth operator, and charming. And clever. But so was she. "No evasions, Gage. You've managed to avoid telling me everything you know so far, but—"

"You were in court all day," he reminded her. "I was in meetings."

"That's beside the point. I'm here now."

"You certainly are." He walked to her, slipped his arms through hers and circled her waist. His lips curved as they lowered to hers. "Hello."

More than two years of marriage hadn't diluted her response to him. Her mouth softened, parted, but then she remembered herself and stepped back. "No, you don't. Consider yourself under oath and in the witness chair, Guthrie. Spill it. I know you were there."

"I was there." Annoyance flickered in his eyes before he crossed over to pour mineral water for Deborah. Yes, he'd been there, he thought. Too late.

He had his own way of combating the dark side of Urbana. The gift—or the curse—he'd been left with after surviving what should have been a fatal shooting gave him an edge. He'd been a cop too long to close his eyes to injustice. Now, with the odd twist fate had dealt him, he fought crime his own way, with his own special talent.

Deborah watched him stare down at his hand, flex it. It was an old habit, one that told her he was thinking of how he could make it, make himself fade to nothing.

And when he did, he was Nemesis, a shadow that haunted the streets of Urbana, a shadow that had slipped into her life, and her heart as real and as dear to her as the man who stood before her.

"I was there," he repeated, and poured a glass of wine for himself. "But too late to do anything. I didn't beat the first engine company by more than five minutes."

"You can't always be first on the scene, Gage," Deborah murmured. "Even Nemesis isn't omnipotent."

"No." He handed her the glass. "The point is, I didn't see who started the fire. If indeed it was arson."

"Which you believe it was."

He smiled again. "I have a suspicious mind."

"So do I." She tapped her glass against his. "I wish there was something I could do for Natalie. She's worked so hard to get this new company off the ground."

"You're doing something," Gage told her. "You're here. And she'll fight back."

"That's one thing you can count on." She tilted her head. "I don't suppose anyone saw you around the warehouse last night."

Now he grinned. "What do you think?"

She blew out a breath. "I think I'll never quite get used to it." When the doorbell sounded, Deborah set her glass aside. "I'll get it." She hurried to the door, then opened her arms to Natalie. "I'm so glad you could come."

"I wouldn't miss one of Frank's meals for anything." Determined to be cheerful, Natalie kissed Deborah, then linked arms with her as they walked back into the sitting room. She offered her host a brilliant smile. "Hello, gorgeous."

She kissed Gage, as well, accepted the drink he offered and a seat by the fire. She sighed once. A beautiful house, a beautiful couple, so incredibly in love. Natalie told herself if she were inclined toward domesticity, she might be envious.

"How are you coping?" Deborah asked her.

"Well, I love a challenge, and this is a big one. The bottom line is, Lady's Choice will have its grand opening, nationwide, in three weeks."

"I was under the impression that you lost quite a bit of merchandise," Gage commented. Cloaked by the shadow of his gift, he'd watched her arrive at the scene the night before. "As well as the building."

"There are other buildings."

In fact, she had already arranged to purchase another warehouse. It would, even after the insurance payoff, put a dent in the estimated profits for the year. But they would make it up, Natalie thought. She would see to that.

"We're going to be working overtime for a while to make up some of the losses. And I can pull some stock in from other locations. Urbana's our flagship store. I intend for it to go off with a bang."

She sipped her wine, running the stages through her mind. "I've got Donald with a phone glued to his ear. With his background in public relations, he's the best qualified to beg and borrow. Melvin's already flown out on a four-city jaunt to swing through the other plants and stores. He'll work some of his wizardry in figuring who can spare what merchandise. And Deirdre's working on the figures. I've talked to the union leaders, and some of the laborers. I intend to be back in full production within forty-eight hours."

Gage toasted her. "If anyone can do it..." He was a businessman himself. Among other things. And knew exactly how much work, how much risk and how much sweat Natalie would face. "Is there anything new on the fire itself?"

"Not specifically." Frowning, Natalie glanced into the cheerful flames in the hearth. So harmless, she thought, so attractive. "I've talked with the investigator a couple of times. He implies, he interrogates, and, by God, he irritates. But he doesn't commit."

"Ryan Piasecki," Deborah stated, and it was her turn to smile. "I stole a few minutes today to do some checking on him. I thought you'd be interested."

"Bless you." Natalie leaned forward. "So, what's the story?"

"He's been with the department for fifteen years. Fought fires for ten, and worked his way up to lieutenant. A couple of smears in his file."

Natalie's lips curved smugly. "Oh, really?"

"Apparently he belted a city councilman at a fire scene. Broke his jaw."

"Violent tendencies," Natalie muttered. "I knew it."

"It was what they call a class C fire," Deborah continued. "In a chemical plant. Piasecki was with engine company 18, and they were the first to respond. There was no backup. Economic cutbacks," she added as Natalie's brows knit. "Number 18 lost three men in that fire, and two more were critically injured. The councilman showed up with the press in tow and began to pontificate on our system at work. He'd spearheaded the cutbacks."

Damn it. Natalie blew out a breath. "I guess I'd have belted him, too."

"There was another disciplinary action when he stormed into the mayor's office with a bagful of fire-site salvage and dumped it on the desk. It was from a low-rent apartment building on the east side, that had just passed inspection—even though the wiring was bad, the furnace faulty. No smoke alarms. Broken fire escapes. Twenty people died."

"I wanted you to tell me that my instincts were on target," Natalie muttered. "That I had a good reason for detesting him."

"Sorry." Deborah had developed a soft spot for men who fought crime and corruption in untraditional manners. She shot Gage a look that warmed them both.

"Well." Natalie sighed. "What else do you have on him?"

"He moved to the arson squad about five years ago. He has a reputation for being abrasive, aggressive and annoying."

"That's better."

"And for having the nose of a bloodhound, the eyes of a hawk, and the tenacity of a pit bull. He keeps digging and digging until he finds the answers. I've never had to use him in court, but I asked around. You can't shake him on the stand. He's smart. He writes everything down. Everything. And he remembers it. He's thirty-six, divorced. He's a team player who prefers to work alone."

"I suppose it should make me feel better, knowing I'm in competent hands." Natalie moved her shoulders restlessly. "But it doesn't. I appreciate the profile."

"No problem," Deborah began, then broke off when the sound of crying came through the baby monitor beside her. "Sounds like the boss is awake. No, I'll go," she said when Gage got to his feet. "She just wants company."

"Am I going to get a peek?" Natalie asked.

"Sure, come on."

"I'll tell Frank to hold dinner until you're done." With a frown in his eyes, Gage watched Natalie head upstairs with his wife.

"You know," Natalie said as they started up to the nursery, "you look fabulous. I don't see how you manage it all. A demanding career, a dynamic husband and all the social obligations that go with him, and the adorable Adrianna."

"I could tell you it's all a matter of time management and prioritizing." With a grin, Deborah opened the door of the nursery. "But what it really comes down to is passion. For the job, for Gage, for our Addy. There's nothing you can't have, if you're passionate about it."

The nursery was a symphony of color. Murals on the ceiling told stories of princesses and magic horses. Primary tones brightened the walls and bled into rainbows. With her hands gripped on the rail of her Jenny Lind crib, legs wobbling, ten-month-old Addy pouted, oblivious of the ambiance.

"Oh, sweetie." Deborah reached down, picked her up to nuzzle. "Here you are, all wet and lonely."

The pout transformed into a beaming, satisfied smile. "Mama."

Natalie watched while Deborah laid Addy on the changing table.

"She's prettier every time I see her." Gently she brushed at the dark thatch of hair on the baby's head. Pleased with the attention, Addy kicked her feet and began to babble.

"We're thinking about having another."

"Another?" Natalie blinked into Deborah's glowing face. "Already?"

"Well, it's still in the what-if stage. But we'd really like to have three." She pressed a kiss to the soft curve of Addy's neck, chuckling when she tugged on her hair. "I just love being a mother."

"It shows. Can I?" Once the fresh diaper was in place, Natalie lifted the baby.

There was envy, she discovered, for this small miracle who curved so perfectly into her arms.

Two days later, Natalie was at her desk, a headache drumming behind her eyes. She didn't mind it. The incessant throbbing pushed her forward.

"If the mechanic can't repair the machines, get new ones. I want every seamstress on-line. No, tomorrow afternoon won't do." She tapped a pen on the edge of her desk, shifted the phone from ear to ear. "Today. I'll be in myself by one to check on the new stock. I know it's a madhouse. Let's keep it that way."

She hung up and looked at her three associates. "Donald?"

He skimmed a hand over his burnished hair. "The first ad runs in the *Times* on Saturday. Full-page, three-color. The ad, with necessary variations, will be running in the other cities simultaneously."

"The changes I wanted?"

"Implemented. Catalogs shipped today. They look fabulous."

"Yes, they do." Pleased, Natalie glanced down at the glossy catalog on her desk. "Melvin?"

As was his habit, Melvin Glasky slipped off his rimless glasses, polishing them as he spoke. He was in his mid-fifties, addicted to bow ties and golf. He was thin of frame and pink of cheek, and sported a salt-and-pepper toupee that he naively believed was his little secret.

"Atlanta looks the best, though Chicago and L.A. are gearing up."

He gestured to the report on her desk. "I worked out deals with each location for inventory transfers. Not everybody was happy about it." His lenses glinted like diamonds when he set them back on his nose. "The store manager in Chicago defended her stock like a mama bear. She didn't want to give up one brassiere."

Natalie's lips twitched at his drawling pronunciation. "So?"

"So I blamed it on you."

Natalie leaned back in her chair and chuckled. "Of course you did."

"I told her that you wanted twice what you'd told me you needed. Which gave me negotiating room. She figured you should filch from catalog. I agreed." His eyes twinkled. "Then I told her how you considered catalog sacred. Wouldn't touch one pair of panties, because you wanted all catalog orders fulfilled within ten days of order. You're inflexible."

Her lips twitched again. In the eighteen months they'd worked together on this project, she'd come to adore Melvin. "I certainly am."

"So I told her how I'd take the heat, and half of what you ordered."

"You'd have made a hell of a politician, Melvin."

"What do you think I am? In any case, you've got about fifty percent of your inventory back for the flagship store."

"I owe you. Deirdre?"

"I've run the projected increases in payroll and material expenses." Deirdre Marks tossed her flyaway ginger braid behind her shoulder. Her slightly flattened tones were pure Midwest, and her mind was as quick and controlled as a high-tech computer. "Also the outlay for the new site and equipment. With the incentive bonuses you authorized, we'll be in the red. I've done graphs—"

"I've seen them." Mulling over her options, Natalie rubbed the back of her neck. "The insurance money, when it comes through, will offset that somewhat. I'm willing to risk my investment, and add to it, to see that this works."

"From a straight financial standpoint," Deirdre continued, "any return looks dim. At least in the foreseeable future. First-year sales alone would have to be in excess of..." She shrugged her narrow shoulders at Natalie's stubborn expression. "You have the figures."

"Yes, and I appreciate the extra work. The files at the south side warehouse were destroyed. Fortunately, I'd had Maureen make copies of the bulk of them." She rubbed her eyes, caught herself and folded her hands. "I'm very aware that the majority of new business ventures fold within the first year. This isn't going to be one of them. I'm not looking for short-term profits, but for long-term success. I intend for Lady's Choice to be at the top on retail and direct sales within ten years. So I'm certainly not going to take a step back at the first real obstacle."

She flicked a finger over a button when her buzzer sounded. "Yes, Maureen?"

"Inspector Piasecki would like to see you, Ms. Fletcher. He doesn't have an appointment."

Automatically Natalie scanned her desk calendar. She could spare Piasecki fifteen minutes and still make it to the new warehouse. "We'll have to finish this later," she said with a glance at her associates. "Show him in, Maureen."

Ry preferred meeting friends or foes on their own turf. He hadn't yet decided which category Natalie Fletcher fell into. He had, however, decided to swing by her office to get a firsthand look at that part of her operation.

He couldn't say he was disappointed. Fancy digs for a fancy lady, he thought. Thick carpet, lots of glass, soft-colored, cushy chairs in the waiting area. Original paintings on the walls, live, thriving plants.

And her secretary, or assistant, or whatever title the pretty little thing at the lobby desk carried, worked with top-grade equipment.

The boss's office was no surprise, either. Ry's quick scan showed him more thick carpet, in slate blue, rosy walls decorated with the splashy modern art he'd never cared for. Antique furniture—probably the real thing.

Her desk was some old European piece, he supposed. They went in for all that gingerbread work and curves. Natalie sat behind it, in one of her tidy suits, a wide, tinted window at her back.

Three other people stood like soldiers ready to snap to attention at her command. He recognized the younger man as the one she'd embraced at the fire site. Tailored suit, shiny leather shoes, ruthlessly knotted tie. Pretty face, blow-dried hair, soft hands.

The second man was older, and looked to be on the edge of a smile. He wore a polka-dot bow tie and a mediocre toupee.

The woman made a fine foil for her boss. Boxy jacket—slightly wrinkled—flat-heeled shoes, messy hair that couldn't decide if it wanted to be red or brown. Closing in on forty, Ry judged, and not much interested in fighting it.

"Inspector," Natalie waited a full ten seconds before rising and holding out a hand.

"Ms. Fletcher." He gave her long, narrow fingers a perfunctory squeeze.

"Inspector Piasecki is investigating the warehouse fire." And in his usual uniform of jeans and a flannel shirt, she noted. Didn't the city issue official attire? "Inspector, these are three of my top-level executives—Donald Hawthorne, Melvin Glasky and Deirdre Marks."

Ry nodded at the introductions, then turned his attention to Natalie again. "I'd have thought a smart woman like you would know better than to put her office on the forty-second floor."

"I beg your pardon?"

"It makes rescue hell—not only for you, but for the department. No way to get a ladder up here. That window's for looks, not for ventilation or escape. You've got forty-two floors to get down, in a stairway that's liable to be filled with smoke."

Natalie sat again, without asking him to join her. "This building is equipped with all necessary safety devices. Sprinklers, smoke detectors, extinguishers."

He only smiled. "So was your warehouse, Ms. Fletcher."

Her headache was coming back, double-time. "Inspector, did you come here to update me on your investigation, or to criticize my work space?"

"I can do both."

"If you'll excuse us." Natalie glanced toward her three associates. Once the door had closed behind them, Natalie gestured to a chair. "Let's clear the air here. You don't like me, I don't like you. But we both have a common goal. Very often I have to work with people I don't care for on a personal level. It doesn't stop me from doing my job.'' She tilted her head, aimed what he considered a very cool, very regal stare at him. "Does it stop you?"

He crossed his scuffed hightops at the ankles. "Nope."

"Good. Now what do you have to tell me?"

"I've just filed my report. You no longer have a suspicious fire. You've got arson."

Despite the fact that she'd been expecting it, her stomach clutched once. "There's no question?" She shook her head before he could speak. "No, there wouldn't be. I've been told you're very thorough."

"Have you? You ought to try aspirin, before you rub a hole in your head."

Annoyed, Natalie dropped the hand she'd been using to massage her temple. "What's the next step?"

"I've got cause, method, point of origin. I want motive."

"Aren't there people who set fires simply because they enjoy it? Because they're compelled to?"

"Sure." He started to reach for a cigarette, then noticed there wasn't an ashtray in sight. "Maybe you've got a garden-variety spark. Or maybe you've got a hired torch. You were carrying a lot of insurance, Ms. Fletcher."

"That's right. I had a reason for it. I lost over a million and a half in merchandise and equipment alone."

"You were covered for a hell of a lot more."

"If you know anything at all about real estate, Inspector, you're aware that the building was quite valuable. If you're looking for insurance fraud, you're wasting your time."

"I've got time." He rose. "I'm going to need a statement, Ms. Fletcher. Official. Tomorrow, my office, two o'clock."

She rose, as well. "I can give you a statement here and now."

"My office, Ms. Fletcher." He took a card out of his pocket, set it on her desk. "Look at it this way. If you're in the clear, the sooner we get this done, the sooner you collect your insurance."

"Very well." She picked up the card and slipped it into the pocket of her suit. "The sooner the better. Is that all for the moment, Inspector?"

"Yeah." His eyes skimmed down to the cover of the catalog lying on the desk. An ivory-skinned model was curled over a velvet settee, showing off a backless red gown with a froth of tantalizing lace at the bodice.

"Nice." His gaze shot back to Natalie's. "A classy way to sell sex."

"Romance, Inspector. Some people still enjoy it."

"Do you?"

"I don't think that applies."

"I just wondered if you believe in what you're selling, or if you just go for the bucks." Just as he'd wondered if she wore her own products under those neatly tailored suits.

"Then I'll satisfy your curiosity. I always believe in what I'm selling. And I enjoy making money. I'm very good at it." She picked up the catalog and held it out to him. "Why don't you take this along? All our merchandise is unconditionally guaranteed. The toll-free number will be in full operation on Monday."

If she'd expected him to refuse or fumble, she was disappointed. Ry rolled the catalog into a tube and tucked it into his hip pocket. "Thanks."

"Now, if you'll excuse me, I have an outside appointment."

She stepped out from behind the desk. He'd been hoping for that. Whatever he thought about her, he enjoyed her legs. "Need a lift?"

Surprised, she turned away from the small closet at the end of the room. "No. I have a car." It more than surprised her when he came up behind her to help her on with her coat. His hands lingered lightly, briefly, on her shoulders.

"You're stressed out, Ms. Fletcher."

"I'm busy, Inspector." She turned, off balance, and was annoyed when she had to jerk back or bump up against him.

"And jumpy," he added, with a quick, satisfied curve of his lips. He'd wondered if she was as elementally aware of him as he was of her. "A suspicious man might say those were signs of guilt. It so happens I'm a suspicious man. But you know what I think?"

"I'm fascinated by what you think."

Sarcasm apparently had no effect on him. He just continued to smile at her. "I think you're just made up that way. Tense and jumpy. You've got plenty of control, and you know just how to keep the fires banked. But now and again it slips. It's interesting when it does."

It was slipping now. She could feel it sliding greasily out of her hands. "Do you know what I think, Inspector?"

The dimple that should have been out of place on his strong face winked. "I'm fascinated by what you think, Ms. Fletcher."

"I think you're an arrogant, narrow-minded, irritating man who thinks entirely too much of himself."

"I'd say we're both right."

"And you're in my way."

"You're right about that, too." But he didn't move, wasn't quite ready to. "Damned if you don't have the fanciest face."

She blinked. "I beg your pardon?"

"An observation. You're one classy number." His fingers itched to touch, so he dipped them into his pockets. He'd thrown her off. That was obvious from the way she was staring at him, half horrified, half intrigued. Ry saw no reason not to take advantage of it. "A man's hard-pressed not to do a little fantasizing, once he's had a good look at you. I've had a couple of good looks now."

"I don't think..." Only sheer pride prevented her stepping back. Or forward. "I don't think this is appropriate."

"If we ever get to know each other better, you'll find out that propriety isn't at the top of my list. Tell me, do you and Hawthorne have a personal thing going?"

His eyes, dark, intense, close, dazzled her for a moment. "Donald? Of course not." Appalled, she caught herself. "That's none of your business."

Her answer pleased him, on professional and personal levels. "Everything about you is my business."

She tossed up her chin, eyes smoldering. "So, this pitiful excuse for a flirtation is just a way to get me to incriminate myself?"

"I didn't think it was that pitiful. Obvious," he admitted, "but not pitiful. On a professional level, it worked."

"I could have lied."

"You have to think before you lie. And you weren't thinking." He liked the idea of being able to frazzle her, and pushed a little further. "It so happens that, on a strictly personal level, I like the way you look. But don't worry, it won't get in the way of the job."

"I don't like you, Inspector Piasecki."

"You said that already." For his own pleasure, he reached out, tugged her coat closed. "Button up. It's cold out there. My office," he added as he turned for the door. "Tomorrow, two o'clock."

He strolled out, thinking of her.

Natalie Fletcher, he mused, punching the elevator button for the lobby. High-class brains in a first-class package. Maybe she'd torched her own building for a quick profit. She wouldn't be the first or the last.

But his instincts told him no.

She didn't strike him as a woman who looked for shortcuts.

He stepped into the elevator car, which tossed his own image back to him in smoked glass.

Everything about her was top-of-the-line. And her background just didn't equal fraud. Fletcher Industries generated enough profit annually to buy a couple of small Third World countries. This new arm of it was Natalie's baby, and even if it folded in the first year, it wouldn't shake the corporate foundations.

Of course, there was emotional attachment to be considered. Those same instincts told him she had a great deal of emotional attachment to this new endeavor. That was enough for some to try to eke out a quick profit to save a shaky investment.

But it didn't jibe. Not with her.

Someone else in the company, maybe. A competitor, hoping to sabotage her business before it got off the ground. Or a classic pyro, looking for a thrill.

Whatever it was, he'd find it.

And, he thought, he was going to enjoy rattling Natalie Fletcher's cage while he was going about it.

One classy lady, he mused. He imagined she'd look good—damn good—modeling her own merchandise.

The beeper hooked to his belt sounded as he stepped from the elevator. Another fire, he thought, and moved quickly to the nearest phone.

There was always another fire.

## Chapter 3

Ry kept her cooling her heels for fifteen minutes. It was a standard ploy, one she'd often used herself to psych out an opponent. She was determined not to fall for it.

There wasn't even enough room in the damn closet he called an office to pace.

He worked in one of the oldest fire stations in the city, two floors above the engines and trucks, in a small glassed-in box that offered an uninspiring view of a cracked parking lot and sagging tenements.

In the adjoining room, Natalie could see a woman pecking listlessly at a typewriter that sat on a desk overflowing with files and forms. The walls throughout were a dingy yellow that might, decades ago, have been white. They were checkerboarded with photos of fire scenes—some of which were grim enough to have had her turning away—bulletins, flyers, and a number of Polish jokes in dubious taste.

Obviously Ry had no problem shrugging off the clichéd humor about his heritage.

Metal shelves were piled with books, binders, pamphlets, and a couple of trophies, each topped with a statuette of a basketball player. And, she noted with a sniff, dust. His desk, slightly larger than a card table and badly scarred, was propped up under one shortened leg by a tattered paperback copy of *The Red Pony*.

The man didn't even have respect for Steinbeck.

When her curiosity got the better of her, Natalie rose from the folding chair, with its torn plastic seat, and poked around his desk.

No photographs, she noted. No personal mementos. Bent paper clips, broken pencils, a claw hammer, a ridiculous mess of disorganized paperwork. She pushed at some of that, then jumped back in horror when she revealed the decapitated head of a doll.

She might have laughed at herself, if it wasn't so hideous. The remnant of a child's toy, the frizzy blond hair nearly burned away, the once rosy face melted into mush on one side. One bright blue eye remained staring.

"Souvenirs," Ry said from the doorway. He'd been watching her for a couple of minutes. "From a class A fire up in the east sixties. The kid made it." He glanced down at the head on his desk. "She was in a little better shape than her doll."

Her shudder was quick and uncontrollable. "That's horrible."

"Yeah, it was. The kid's father started it with a can of kerosene in the living room. The wife wanted a divorce. When he was finished, she didn't need one."

He was so cold about it, she thought. Maybe he had to be. "You have a miserable job, Inspector."

"That's why I love it." He glanced around as the outer door opened. "Have a seat. I'll be right with you." Ry pulled the office door closed before he turned to the uniformed fire fighter who'd come in behind him.

Through the glass, Natalie could hear the mutter of voices. She didn't need to hear Ry raise his voice—as he soon did—to know that the young fireman was receiving a first-class dressing-down.

"Who told you to ventilate that wall, probie?"

"Sir, I thought—"

"Probies don't think. You're not smart enough to think. If you were, you'd know what fresh air does for a fire. You'd know what happens when you let it in and there's a damn puddle of fuel oil sloshing under your boots."

"Yes, sir. I know, sir. I didn't see it. The smoke—"

"You'd better learn to see through smoke. You'd better learn to see through everything. And when the fire goes into the frigging wall, you don't take it on yourself to give it a way out while you're standing in accelerant. You're lucky to be alive, probie, and so's the team who were unlucky enough to be with you.''

''Yes, sir. I know, sir.''

''You don't know diddly. That's the first thing you remember the next time you go in to eat smoke. Now get out of here.''

Natalie crossed her legs when Ry came into the room. ''You're a real diplomat. That kid couldn't have been more than twenty.''

''Be nice if he lived to a ripe old age, wouldn't it?'' With a flick of his wrist, Ry tugged down the blinds, closing them in.

''Your technique makes me regret I didn't bring a lawyer with me.''

''Relax.'' He moved to his desk, pushed some files out of his way. ''I don't have the authority to arrest, just to investigate.''

''Well, I'll sleep easy now.'' Deliberately she took a long look at her watch. ''How long do you think this is going to take? I've already wasted twenty minutes.''

''I got held up.'' He sat, opened the bag he'd brought in with him. ''Have you had lunch?''

''No.'' Her eyes narrowed as he took out a wrapped package that smelled tantalizingly of deli. ''Are you telling me that you've kept me waiting in here while you picked up a sandwich?''

''It was on my way.'' He offered her half of a corned beef on rye. ''I've got a couple of coffees, too.''

''I'll take the coffee. Keep the sandwich.''

''Suit yourself.'' He handed her a small insulated cup. ''Mind if we record this?''

''I'd prefer it.''

Eating with one hand, he opened a desk drawer, took out a tape recorder. ''You must have a closet full of those suits.'' This one was the color of crushed raspberries, and fastened at the left hip with gold buttons. ''Do you ever wear anything else?''

''I beg your pardon?''

''Small talk, Ms. Fletcher.''

"I'm not here for small talk," she snapped back. "And stop calling me *Ms.* Fletcher in that irritating way."

"No problem, Natalie. Just call me Ry." He switched on the recorder and began by reciting the time, date and location of the interview. Despite the tape, he took out a notebook and pencil. "This interview is being conducted by Inspector Ryan Piasecki with Natalie Fletcher, re the fire at the Fletcher Industries warehouse, 21 South Harbor Avenue, on February 12 of this year."

He took a sip of his coffee. "Ms. Fletcher, you are the owner of the aforesaid building, and its contents."

"The building and its contents are—were—the property of Fletcher Industries, of which I am an executive officer."

"How long has the building belonged to your company?"

"For eight years. It was previously used to warehouse inventory for Fletcher Shipping."

The heater beside him began to whine and gurgle. Ry kicked it carelessly. It went back to a subdued hum.

"And now?"

"Fletcher Shipping moved to a new location." She relaxed a little. It was going to be routine now. Business. "The warehouse was converted nearly two years ago to accommodate a new company. We used the building for manufacturing and warehousing merchandise for Lady's Choice. We make ladies' lingerie."

"And what were the hours of operation?"

"Normally eight to six, Monday through Friday. In the last six months, we expanded that to include Saturdays from eight to noon."

He continued to eat, asking standard questions about business practices, security, vandalism. Her answers were quick, cool and concise.

"You have a number of suppliers."

"Yes. We use American companies only. That's a firm policy."

"Ups the overhead."

"In the short term. I believe, in the long term, the company will generate profits to merit it."

"You've put a lot of personal time into this company. Incurred a lot of expenses, invested your own money."

"That's right."

"What happens if the business doesn't live up to your expectations?"

"It will."

He leaned back now, enjoying what was left of his cooling coffee. "If it doesn't."

"Then I would lose my time, and my money."

"When was the last time you were in the building, before the fire?"

The sudden change of topic surprised but didn't throw her. "I went by for a routine check three days before the fire. That would have been the ninth of February."

He noted it down. "Did you notice any inventory missing?"

"No."

"Damaged equipment?"

"No."

"Any holes in security?"

"No. I would have dealt with any of those things immediately." Did he think she was an idiot? "Work was progressing on schedule, and the inventory I looked over was fine."

His eyes cut back to hers, lingered. "You didn't look over everything?"

"I did a spot check, Inspector." The stare was designed to make her uncomfortable, she knew. She refused to allow it. "It isn't a productive use of time for me or my staff to examine every negligee or garter belt."

"The building was inspected in November. You were up to code on all fire regulations."

"That's right."

"Can you explain how it was that, on the night of the fire, the sprinkler and smoke alarm systems were inoperative?"

"Inoperative?" Her heart picked up a beat. "I'm not sure what you mean."

"They were tampered with, Ms. Fletcher. So was your security system."

She kept her eyes level with his. "No, I can't explain it. Can you?"

He took out a cigarette, flicked a wooden match into flame with his thumbnail. "Do you have any enemies?"

Her face went blank. "Enemies?"

"Anyone who'd like to see you fail, personally or professionally?"

"I— No, I can't think of anyone, personally." The idea left her shaken. She pulled a hand through her hair, from the crown to the tips that swung at chin level. "Naturally, I have competitors...."

"Anyone who's given you trouble?"

"No."

"Disgruntled employees? Fire anyone lately?"

"No. I can't speak for every level of the organization. I have managers who have autonomy in their own departments, but nothing's come back to me."

He continued to smoke as he asked questions, took notes. He wound the interview down, closing it by logging the time.

"I spoke to your insurance adjuster this morning," he told her. "And your security guard. I have interviews set up with the foremen at the warehouse." When she didn't respond, he crushed out his cigarette. "Want some water?"

"No." She let out a breath. "Thank you. Do you think I'm responsible?"

"What I know goes into the report, not what I think."

"I want to know." She stood then. "I'm asking you to tell me what you think."

She didn't belong here. That was the first thought that crossed his mind. Not here, in the cramped little room that smelled of whatever the men were cooking downstairs. Boardrooms and bedrooms. He was certain she'd be equally adept in both venues.

"I don't know, Natalie, maybe it's your pretty face affecting my judgment, but no—I don't think you're responsible. Feel better?"

"Not much. I suppose my only choice now is to depend on you to find out the who and why." She let out a little sigh. "As much as it galls me, I have a feeling you're just the man for the job."

"A compliment, and so early in our relationship."

"With any luck, it'll be the first and the last." She shifted, reached down for her briefcase. He moved quickly and quietly. Before she could lift it, his hand closed over hers on the strap.

"Take a break."

She flexed her hand under his once, felt the hard, callused palm, then went still. "Excuse me?"

"You're revved, Natalie, but you're running on empty. You need to relax."

It was unlikely she would, or could, with him holding on to her. "What I need to do is get back to work. So, if that's all, Inspector..."

"I thought we were on a first-name basis now. Come on, I want to show you something."

"I don't have time," she began as he pulled her out of the room. "I have an appointment."

"You always seem to. Aren't you ever late?"

"No."

"Every man's fantasy woman. Beautiful, smart, and prompt." He led her down a staircase. "How tall are you without the stilts?"

She lifted a brow at his description of her elegant Italian pumps. "Tall enough."

He stopped, one step below her, and turned. They were lined up, eye to eye, mouth to mouth. "Yeah, I'd say you are, just tall enough."

He tugged her, as he might have a disinterested mule, until they reached the ground floor.

There were scents wafting out from the kitchen. Chili was on the menu for tonight. A couple of men were checking equipment on one of the engines. Another was rolling a hose on the chilly concrete floor.

Ry was greeted with salutes and quick grins, Natalie with pursed lips and groans.

"They can't help it," Ry told her. "We don't get legs like yours walking through here every day. I'll give you a boost."

"What?"

"I'll give you a boost," he repeated as he opened the door on an engine. "Not that the guys wouldn't appreciate the way that skirt would ride up if you climbed in on your own. But—'' Before she could protest, Ry had gripped her by the waist and lifted her.

She had a moment to think the strength in his arms was uncannily effortless before he joined her.

''Move over,'' he ordered. ''Unless you'd rather sit on my lap.''

She scooted across the seat. ''Why am I sitting in a fire engine?''

''Everybody wants to at least once.'' Very much at home, he stretched his arm over the seat. ''So, what do you think?''

She scanned the gauges and dials, the oversize gearshift, the photo of Miss January taped to the dash. ''It's interesting.''

''That's it?''

She caught her bottom lip between her teeth. She wondered which control operated the siren, which the lights. ''Okay, it's fun.'' She leaned forward for a better view through the windshield. ''We're really up here, aren't we? Is this the—''

He caught her hand just before she could yank the cord over her head. ''Horn,'' he finished. ''The men are used to it, but believe me, with the acoustics in here and the outside doors shut, you'd be sorry if you sounded it.''

''Too bad.'' She skimmed back her hair as she turned her face toward him. ''Are you showing me your toy to relax me, or just to show off?''

''Both. How'm I doing?''

''Maybe you're not quite the jerk you appear to be.''

''You keep being so nice to me, I'm going to fall in love.''

She laughed and realized she was almost relaxed. ''I think we're both safe on that count. What made you decide to sit in a fire engine for ten years?''

''You've been checking up on me.'' Idly he lifted his fingers, just enough to reach the tips of her hair. Soft, he thought, like sunny silk.

''That's right.'' She shot him a look. ''So?''

''So, I guess we're even. I'm a third-generation smoke eater. It's in the blood.''

''Mmm…'' That she understood. ''But you gave it up.''

''No, I shifted gears. That's different.''

She supposed it was, but it wasn't a real answer. ''Why do you keep that souvenir on your desk?'' She watched his eyes closely as she asked. "The doll's head."

"It's from my last fire. The last one I fought." He could still remember it—the heat, the smoke, the screaming. "I carried the kid out. The bedroom door was locked. My guess is he'd herded his wife and kid in—you know, you can't live with me, you won't live without me. He had a gun. It wasn't loaded, but she wouldn't have known that."

"That's horrible." She wondered if she would have risked the gun, and thought she would have. Better a bullet, fast and final, than the terrors of smoke and flame. "His own family."

"Some guys don't take kindly to divorce." He shrugged. His own had been painless enough, almost anticlimactic. "The way it came out, he made them sit there while the fire got bigger, and the smoke snuck under the door. It was a frame house, old. Went up like a matchstick. The woman had tried to protect the kid, had curled over her in a corner. I couldn't get them both at once, so I took the kid."

His eyes changed now, darkened, focused on something only he could see. "The woman was gone, anyway. I knew she was gone, but there's always a chance. I was headed down the steps with the kid when the floor gave way."

"You saved the child," Natalie said gently.

"The mother saved the child." He could never forget that, could never forget that selfless and hopeless devotion. "The son of a bitch who torched the house jumped out the second-story window. Oh, he was burned, smoke inhalation, broken leg. But he lived through it."

He cared, she realized. She hadn't seen that before. Or hadn't wanted to. It changed him. Changed her perception of him. "And you decided to go after the men who start them, instead of the fires themselves."

"More or less." He snapped his head up, like a wolf scenting prey, when the alarm shrilled. The station sprang to life with running feet, shouted orders. Ry pitched his voice over the din. "Let's get out of the way."

He pushed open the door, caught Natalie in one arm and swung out.

"Chemical plant," someone said as they hurried by, pulling on protective gear.

In seconds, it seemed, the engines were manned and screaming out the arched double doors.

"It's so fast," Natalie said, ears still ringing, pulse still jumping. "They move so fast."

"Yeah."

"It's exciting." She pressed a hand to her speeding heart. "I didn't realize. Do you miss it?" She looked up at him then, and her hand went limp.

He was still holding her against him, and his eyes were dark and focused on hers. "Now and again."

"Well, it's— I should go."

"Yeah. You should go." But he shifted her until she was wrapped in both his arms. Maybe it was a knee-jerk reaction to the sirens, maybe it was the exotic and irresistible scent of her, but his blood was pumping.

And he wanted to see, just once, if she tasted as good as she looked.

"This is insane," she managed to say. She knew what he intended to do. What she wanted him to do. "This has got to be wrong."

His lips curved, just a little. "What's your point?" Then his mouth closed over hers.

She didn't push back. For nearly one heartbeat, she didn't respond. In that instant she thought she'd been paralyzed, struck deaf, dumb and blind. Then, in a tidal wave, every sense flooded back, every nerve snapped, every pulse jolted.

His mouth was hard, as his hands were, as his body was. She felt terrifyingly, gloriously, feminine pressed against him. A need she hadn't been aware of exploded into bloom. Her briefcase hit the floor with a thud as she wrapped herself around him.

He was no longer thinking "just once." A man would starve to death after only one taste. A man would certainly beg for more. She was soft and strong and sinfully sweet, with a flavor that both tempted and tormented.

Heat radiated between them as the wind whipped in through the open doors at their back. The clatter of street noises, horns and tires, sounded around them, along with her dazed, throaty moan.

He pulled back once to look at her face, saw himself in the cloudy green of her eyes, and then his mouth crushed hers again.

No, this wasn't going to happen just once.

She couldn't breathe. No longer wanted to. His lips were moving against hers, forming words she could neither hear nor understand. For the first time in her memory, she could do nothing but feel. And the feelings came so fast, so sharp and strong, they left her in tatters.

He pulled back again, staggered by what had ripped through him in so short a time. He was winded, weak, and the sensation infuriated as much as it baffled him. She only stood there, staring at him with a mixture of shock and hunger in her eyes.

"Sorry," he muttered, and hooked his thumbs in his pockets.

"Sorry?" she repeated. She sucked in a deep breath, wondered if her head would ever stop spinning. *"Sorry?"*

"That's right." He couldn't decide whether to curse her or himself. Damn it, his knees were weak. "That was out of line."

"Out of line."

She brushed her hair back from her face, furious to find her skin heated. He'd torn aside every defense, every line of control, and now he dared to apologize? Her chin snapped up, her shoulders straightened.

"You've certainly got a way with words. Tell me, Inspector, do you paw all your suspects?"

His eyes narrowed, kindled. "It was mutual pawing, and no, you're the first."

"Lucky me." Amazed, appalled, that she was very near tears, Natalie snatched up her briefcase. "I believe this concludes our meeting."

"Hold it." Ryan played fair and cursed them both when she continued striding toward the doors. "I said, hold it." He headed after her, and with one hand on her arm he spun her around.

Her breath hissed out between clenched teeth. "I refuse to give in to the typical cliché of slapping you, but it's costing me."

"I apologized."

"Stuff it."

Be reasonable, he cautioned himself. It was either that or kiss her again. "Look, Ms. Fletcher, you didn't exactly fight me off."

"A mistake, I assure you, that will not be repeated." She made it to the sidewalk this time before he caught her.

"I don't want you," he said definitely.

Insulted, provoked beyond her control, she jabbed a finger into his chest. "Oh, really? Then perhaps you'd care to explain that ham-handed maneuver in there?"

"There was nothing ham-handed about it. I hardly touched you, and you went off like a rocket. It's not my fault if you were ripe."

Her eyes went huge, ballistic. "Ripe? *Ripe?* Why you—you over-bearing, arrogant self-absorbed idiot!"

"Tell him, honey" was the advice of a toothy bag lady who shoved past with her teetering cart. "Don't let him get away with it."

"That was a bad choice of words," Ry responded, goaded into adding more fuel to the fire. "I should have said *repressed.*"

"I am going to hit you."

"And," he continued, ignoring her, "I should have said I don't like wanting you."

Natalie concentrated for one moment on simply breathing. She would not, absolutely would not, lower herself to having a public brawl on the sidewalk. "That, Inspector Piasecki, may be the first and last time we ever have the same sentiment about anything. I don't like it, either."

"Don't like me wanting you, or don't like you wanting me?"

"Either."

He nodded, and they eyed each other like boxers between rounds. "So, we'll talk it out tonight."

"We will not."

He would, he promised himself, be patient if it killed him. Or her. "Natalie, just how complicated do you want to make this?"

"I don't want to make it complicated, *Ry.* I want to make it im-possible."

"Why?"

She speared him with a look, skimming her gaze from the toes of his shoes to the top of his head. "I should think that would be obvious, even to you."

He rocked back on his heels. "I don't know what it is about that snotty attitude of yours—it just does something for me. You want to play this traditional, with me asking you out to dinner, that routine?"

She closed her eyes and prayed for patience. "I don't seem to be getting through." She opened them again. "No, I don't want you asking me out to dinner, or any routine. What happened inside there was—"

"Wild. Incredible."

"An aberration," she said between her teeth.

"It wouldn't be a hardship to prove you wrong. But if we started that again out here, we'd probably be arrested before we were finished." Ryan was enjoying himself now, immersed in the simple challenge of her. And he intended to win. "But I see what it is. I've spooked you. Now you're afraid to be alone with me, afraid you'll lose control."

Heat stung her cheeks. "That's very lame."

He shrugged. "Works for me."

She studied him. He wanted to prove something? He was about to be disappointed. "All right. Eight o'clock. Chez Robert, on Third. I'll meet you there."

"Fine."

"Fine." She turned away. "Oh, Piasecki," she called over her shoulder. "They frown on eating with your fingers."

"I'll keep it in mind."


Natalie was sure she had lost her mind. She dashed into her apartment at 7:15. Facts, figures, projections, graphs, were all running through her head. And her phone was ringing.

She caught the cordless on the fly and dashed into the bedroom to change. "Yes? What?"

"Is that how Mom taught you to answer the phone?"

"Boyd." Some of the tension of the day drained away at the sound of her brother's voice. "I'm sorry. I've just come in from the last of several mind-numbing meetings."

"Don't look for sympathy here. You're the one who opted to carry on the family tradition."

"Right you are." She stepped out of her shoes. "So how's the fight against crime and corruption in Denver, Captain Fletcher?"

"We're holding our own. Cilla and the kids send love, kisses and so forth."

"And send mine back at them. Aren't they going to talk to me?"

"I'm at the station. I'm a little concerned about crime out there in Urbana."

She searched through her closet, the phone caught in the curve of her shoulder. "How did you find out the fire was arson already? I barely found out myself."

"We have ways. Actually, I just got off the phone with the investigator in charge."

"Piasecki?" Natalie tossed a black dinner dress on her bed. "You talked to him?"

"Ten minutes ago. It sounds like you're in good hands, Nat."

"Not if I can help it," she muttered.

"What?"

"He appears to know his job," she said calmly. "Though his methods lack a certain style."

"Arson's a dirty business. And a dangerous one. I'm worried about you, pal."

"Don't be. You're the cop, remember." She struggled out of her jacket, promising herself she'd hang it up before she left. "I'm the CEO in the ivory tower."

"I've never known you to stay there. I want you to keep me up-to-date on the investigation."

"I can do that." She wiggled out of her skirt, and guiltily left it pooled on the floor. "And tell Mom and Dad, if you talk to them before I do, that things are under control. I won't bore you with all the business data—"

"I appreciate that."

She grinned. Boyd had no patience with ledgers or bar graphs.

"But I'm about to put another very colorful feather in the Fletcher Industries cap."

"With underwear."

"Lingerie, darling." A little breathless, she fastened on a strapless black bra. "You can buy underwear at a drugstore."

"Right. Well, I can tell you on a personal level, Cilla and I have both thoroughly enjoyed the samples you sent out. I particularly liked the little red thing with the tiny hearts."

"I thought you would." She stepped into the dress, tugged it up to her hips. "With Valentine's Day coming up, you should think about ordering her the matching peignoir."

"Put it on my tab. Take care of yourself, Nat."

"I intend to. With any luck, I'll be seeing you next month. I'm going to scout out locations in Denver."

"Your room's ready for you anytime. And so are we. I love you."

"I love you, too. Bye."

She hung up by dropping the phone on the bed, freeing herself to zip the dress into place. Not exactly a sedate number, she mused, turning toward the mirror. Not with the way it draped off the shoulders and veed down over the curve of the breasts.

Repressed? She shook back her hair. This ought to show him.

The phone rang again, making her swear in disgust. She ignored the first ring and picked up her brush. By the third, she'd given up and pounced on the phone.

"Hello?"

Just breathing, quick, and a faint chuckle.

"Hello? Is someone there?"

"Midnight."

"What?" Distracted, she carried the phone to the dresser to select the right jewelry. "I'm sorry, I didn't catch that."

"Midnight. Witching hour. Wait and see."

When the phone clicked, she disconnected, set it down with a shake of her head. Cranks.

"Use the answering machine, Natalie," she ordered herself. "That's what it's there for."

A glance at her watch had her swearing again. She forgot the call as she went into grooming overdrive. She absolutely refused to be late.

# Chapter 4

Natalie arrived at Chez Robert precisely at eight. The four-star French restaurant, with its floral walls and candlelit corners, had been a favorite of hers since she relocated to Urbana. Just stepping inside put her at ease. She had no more than checked her coat when she was greeted enthusiastically by the maître d'.

He kissed her hand with a flourish and beamed. "Ah, Mademoiselle Fletcher...a pleasure, as always. I didn't know you were dining with us this evening."

"I'm meeting a companion, André. A Mr. Piasecki."

"Pi..." Brows knit, André scanned his reservation book while he mentally sounded out the name. "Ah, yes, two for eight o'clock. Pizekee."

"Close enough," Natalie murmured.

"Your companion has not yet arrived, *mademoiselle*. Let me escort you to your table." With a few quick and ruthless adjustments, André shifted Ryan's reservation to suit his favorite customer, moving the seating from a small central table in the main traffic pattern to Natalie's favorite quiet corner booth.

"Thank you, André." Already at home, Natalie settled into the booth with a little sigh. Beneath the table, her feet slipped out of her shoes.

"My pleasure, as always. Would you care for a drink while you wait?"

"A glass of champagne, thank you. My usual."

"Of course. Right away. And, *mademoiselle,* if I may be so presumptuous, the lobster Robert, tonight it is…" He kissed his fingers.

"I'll keep that in mind."

While she waited, Natalie took out her date book and began to make notations on her schedule for the next day. She had nearly finished her champagne when Ry walked up to the table.

She didn't bother to glance up. "It's a good thing I'm not a fire."

"I'm never late for a fire." He took his seat, and they spent a moment measuring each other.

So, he owned a suit, Natalie thought. And he looked good in it. Dark jacket, crisp white shirt, subtle gray tie. Even though his hair wasn't quite tamed, it was definitely a more classic look than she'd expected from him.

"I use it for funerals," Ry said, reading her perfectly.

She only lifted a brow. "Well, that certainly sets the tone for the evening, doesn't it?"

"You picked the spot," he reminded her. He glanced around the restaurant. Quiet class, he mused. Just a tad ornate and stuffy—exactly what he'd expected. "So, how's the food here?"

"It's excellent."

"Mademoiselle Fletcher." Robert himself, small, plump, and tuxedoed, stopped by the table to kiss Natalie's hand. *"Bienvenue…"* he began.

Ry sat back, took out a cigarette and watched as they rattled away in French. She spoke it like a native. That, too, he'd expected.

*"Du champagne pour mademoiselle,"* Robert told the waiter. *"Et pour vous, monsieur?"*

"Beer," Ry said. "American, if you've got it."

*"Bien sûr."* Robert strutted back to the kitchen to harass his chef.

"Well, Legs, that should have made your point," Ry commented.

"Excuse me?"

"Just how out of place will he be in a fancy French restaurant where the owner kisses your knuckles and asks after your family?"

"I don't know what you're—" Natalie frowned as she picked up her glass. "How do you know he asked after my family?"

"I have a French-Canadian grandmother. I probably speak the lingo nearly as well as you do, even if the accent isn't as classy." He blew out a stream of smoke and smiled at her through it. "I didn't peg you as a snob, Natalie."

"I certainly am not a snob." Insulted, she set her glass down again, her shoulders stiffening. But when he only continued to smile, a little frisson of guilt worked its way through her conscience. "Maybe I wanted to make you a little uncomfortable." She sighed, gave up. "A lot uncomfortable. You annoyed me."

"I did better than that." Angling his head, he gave her a long, slow study. She looked like something a man might beg for. Creamy skin flowing out of a black dress, just a few sparkles here and there, sleek golden hair curving around her face. Big, sulky green eyes, red mouth.

Oh, yes, he decided. A man would surely beg.

Her nerves began to jangle as he continued to stare. "Is there a problem?"

"No, no problem. Did you wear that dress to make me uncomfortable?"

"Yes."

He picked up his menu. "It's working. How's the steak here?"

Relax, she ordered herself. Obviously he was trying to make her crazy. "You won't get better in the city. Though I generally prefer the seafood."

She pouted a bit as she studied her menu. The evening was not going as she'd planned. Not only had he seen through her, but he'd already turned the tables so that she looked and felt foolish. Try again, she told herself, and make the best of a bad deal.

After they'd given their orders, Natalie took a deep breath. "I suppose, since we're here, we might as well have a truce."

"Were we fighting?"

"Let's just try for a pleasant evening." She picked up her champagne flute again, sipped. She was, after all, an expert in negotiations and diplomacy. "Let's start with the obvious. Your name. Irish first, Eastern European last."

"Irish mother, Polish father."

"And a French-Canadian grandmother."

"On my mother's side. My other grandmother's a Scot."

"Which makes you—"

"An all-American boy. You've got high-tea hands." He picked up her hand, startling her by running his fingers down hers. "They go with your name. Upper-crust. Classy."

"Well." After she'd tugged her hand free, she cleared her throat, giving undue attention to buttering a roll. "You said you were third-generation in the department."

"Do I make you nervous when I touch you?"

"Yes. Let's try to keep this simple."

"Why?"

Since she had no ready answer for that, she let out a little huff of relief when their appetizers were served. "You must have always wanted to be a fire fighter."

All right, he decided, they could cruise along at her speed for now. "Sure I did. I practically grew up at engine company 19, where my pop worked."

"I imagine there was some family pressure."

"No. How about you?"

"Me?"

"The Fletcher tradition. Big business, corporate towers." He lifted a brow. "Family pressure?"

"Plenty of it," she said, and smiled. "Ruthless, unbending, determined. And all from my corner." Her eyes glinted with amusement. "It had always been assumed that my brother Boyd would take over the reins. Both he and I had different ideas about that. So he strapped on a badge and a gun, and I harassed my parents into accepting me as heir apparent."

"They objected?"

"No, not really. It didn't take them long to realize I was serious. And capable." She took a last bite of her coquilles Saint-Jacques and offered Ry the rest. "I love business. The wheeling, the dealing, the paperwork, the meetings. And this new company. It's all mine."

"Your catalog's a big hit down at the station."

The amusement settled in, and felt comfortable. "Oh, really?"

"A lot of the men have wives, or ladies. I'm just helping you pick up a few orders."

"That's generous of you." She studied him over the rim of her glass. "What about you? Are you going to make any orders?"

"I don't have a wife, or a lady." Those smoky eyes flicked over her face again. "At the moment."

"But you did have. A wife."

"Briefly."

"Sorry. I'm prying."

"No problem." He shrugged and finished off his beer. "It's old news. Nearly ten years old. I guess you could say she fell for the uniform, then decided she didn't like the hours I had to be in it."

"Children?"

"No." He regretted that, sometimes wondered if he always would. "We were only together a couple of years. She hooked up with a plumber and moved to the suburbs." He reached out, skimmed a fingertip down the side of her neck, along the curve of her shoulder. "I'm beginning to think I like your shoulders as much as your legs." His eyes locked on hers. "Maybe it's the whole package."

"That's a fascinating compliment." She didn't give in to the urge to shift away, but she did switch from champagne to water. Suddenly her mouth was dry as dust. "But don't you think the current circumstances require a certain professional detachment?"

"No. If I thought you had anything to do with setting that fire, maybe." He liked the way her eyes lit and narrowed when he pushed the right button. "But, as it stands, I can do my job just fine, and still wonder what it would be like to make love with you."

Her pulse jolted, scrambled. She used the time while their entrées were served to steady it. "I'd prefer if you'd concentrate on the first. In fact, if you could bring me up-to-date—"

"Seems a waste to talk shop in a joint like this." But he shrugged his shoulders. "The bottom line is arson, an incendiary fire. The motive could be revenge, money, straight vandalism or malicious destruction. Or kicks.''

"A pyromaniac.'' She preferred that one, only because it was less personal. "How do you handle that?''

"First, you don't go in biased. A lot of times people, and the media, start shouting 'pyro' whenever there's a series of fires. Even if they seem related, it's not always the case.''

"But it often is.''

"And it's often simple. Somebody burns a dozen cars because he's ticked he bought a lemon.''

"So don't jump to conclusions.''

"Exactly.''

"But if it *is* someone who's disturbed?''

"Head doctors are always working on the whys. Are you going to let me taste that?''

"Hmmm? Oh, all right.'' She nudged her plate closer to his so that he could sample her lobster. "Do you work with psychiatrists?''

"Mostly the shrinks don't come into it until you've got the firebug in custody. That's good stuff,'' he added, nodding toward her plate. "Anyway, that could be after any number of fires, months of investigation. Maybe they blame his mother. She paid too much attention to him. Or his father, because he didn't pay enough. You know how it goes.''

Amused, interested, she cut off a piece of lobster and slipped it onto his plate. "You don't think much of psychiatry?''

"I didn't say that. I just don't go in for blaming somebody else when you did the crime.''

"Now you sound like my brother.''

"He's probably a good cop. Want some of this steak?''

"No, thanks.'' Like a bulldog, she kept her teeth in the topic. "Wouldn't you, as an investigator, have to know something about the psychology of the fire starter?''

Ry chewed his steak, signaled for another beer. "You really want to get into this?''

"It's interesting. Particularly now.''

"Okay. Short lesson. You can divide pathological fire starters into four groups. The mentally ill, the psychotic, the neurotic, and the sociopath. You're going to have some overlap most of the time, but that sorts them. The neurotic, or psychoneurotic, is the pyromaniac.''

''Aren't they all?''

''No. The true pyro's a lot rarer than most people think. It's an uncontrollable compulsion. He *has* to set the fire. When the urge hits him, he goes with it, wherever, whenever. He's not really thinking about covering up or getting away, so he's usually easy to catch.''

''I thought *pyro* was more of a general term.'' She started to tuck her hair behind her ear. Ry beat her to it, letting his fingers linger for a moment.

''I like to see your face when I talk to you.'' He kept his hand on hers, bringing them both back to the table. ''I like to touch you when I talk to you.''

Silence hung for a full ten seconds.

''You're not talking,'' Natalie pointed out.

''Sometimes I just like to look. Come here a minute.''

She recognized the light in his eyes, recognized her own helpless response to it. And to him. Deliberately she eased away. ''I don't think so. You're a dangerous man, Inspector.''

''Thanks. Why don't you come home with me, Natalie?''

She let out a long, quiet breath. ''You're also a very blunt one.''

''A woman like you could get poetry and fancy moves any time she wanted.'' Ry neither had them nor believed in them. ''You might want to try something more basic.''

''This is certainly basic,'' she agreed. ''I think we could use some coffee.''

He signaled the waiter. ''You didn't answer my question.''

''No, I didn't. And no.'' She waited until the table was cleared, the coffee order given. ''Despite a certain elemental attraction, I think it would be unwise to pursue this any further. We're both committed to our careers, diametrically opposed in personality and life-style. Even though our relationship has been brief and abrasive, I think it's clear we have nothing in common. We are, as we might say in my business, a bad risk.''

He said nothing for a minute, only studied her, as if considering. "That makes sense."

Her stomach muscles relaxed. She even smiled at him as she picked up her coffee. "Good, then we're agreed—"

"I didn't say I agreed," he pointed out. "I said it made sense." He lit a cigarette, his eyes on hers over the flame. "I've been thinking about you, Natalie. And I've got to tell you, I don't much like the way you make me feel. It's distracting, annoying and inconvenient."

Her chin angled. "I'm so glad we cleared this up," she said coolly.

"God knows it gets me right in the gut when you talk to me like that. Duchess to serf." He shook his head, drew in smoke. "I must be perverse. Anyway, I don't like it. I'm not altogether sure I like you." His eyes narrowed, the light in them stopping the pithy comment before it could slip through her lips. "But I've never wanted anyone so damn much in my whole life. That's a problem."

"*Your* problem," she managed.

"Our problem. I've got a rep for being tenacious."

She set her cup down, carefully, before it could slip from her limp fingers. "I'd think a simple no would do, Ry."

"So would I." He shrugged. "Go figure. I haven't been able to clear you out of my head since I saw you standing there freezing at the fire scene. I made a mistake when I kissed you this afternoon. I figured once I had, that would be it. Case closed."

He moved quickly, and so smoothly she barely had time to blink before his mouth was hot and hard on hers. Dazed, she lifted a hand to his shoulder, but her fingers only dug in, held on, as she was buffeted with fresh excitement.

"I was wrong." He drew back. "Case isn't closed, and that's *our* problem."

"Yeah." She let out a shaky breath. No amount of common sense could outweigh her instant and primitive response to him. He touched, she wanted. It was as simple and as terrifying as that. But common sense was her only defense. "This isn't going to work. It's ridiculous to think that it could. I'm not prepared to jump into an affair simply because of some basic animal lust."

"See? We do have something in common." Despite the fact that the kiss had stirred him to aching, he smiled at her. "The lust part."

Laughing, she dragged her hair back from her face. "Oh, I need to get away from you for a while and consider the options."

"This isn't a business deal, Ms. Fletcher."

She looked at him again and wished she could have some distance, just a little distance, so that she could think clearly. "I never make a decision without considering the bottom line."

"Profit and loss?"

Wary, she inclined her head. "In a manner of speaking. You could call it risk and reward. Intimate relationships haven't been my strong suit. That's been my choice. If I'm going to have one with you, however brief, that will be my choice, as well."

"That's fair. Do you want me to work up a prospectus?"

"Don't be snide, Ry." Then, because it soothed some of the tension to realize she'd annoyed him, she smiled. "But I'd certainly give it my full attention." Playing it up, she cupped her chin on her hands, leaning closer, skimming her gaze over his face. "You are very attractive, in a rough-edged, not-quite-tamed sort of way."

He shifted, drew hard on his cigarette. "Thanks a lot."

"No, really." So, she thought, he could be embarrassed. "The faint cleft in the chin, the sharp cheekbones, the lean face, the dark, sexy eyes." Her lips curved as he narrowed those eyes. "And all that hair, just a little unruly. The tough body, the tough attitude."

Impatient, he crushed out his cigarette. "What are you pulling here, Natalie?"

"Just giving you back a little of your own. Yes, you're a very attractive package. Wasn't that your word? Dangerous, dynamic. Like Nemesis."

Now he winced. "Give me a break."

Her chuckle was warm and deep. "No, really. There's a lot of similarity between you and Urbana's mysterious upholder of justice. You both appear to have your own agenda, and your own rough-edged style. He fights crime, appearing and disappearing like smoke. An interesting connection between the two of you.

"I might even wonder if you could be him—except that he's a very romantic figure. And there, Inspector, you part company."

She tossed back her hair and laughed. "I believe you're speechless. Who would have thought it would be that easy to score a point off you?"

She might have scored one, but the game wasn't over. He caught her chin in his hand, held it steady and close, even as her eyes continued to dance. "I guess I could handle it if you wanted to treat me like an object. Just promise to respect me in the morning."

"Nope."

"You're a hard woman, Ms. Fletcher. Okay, scratch respect. How about awe?"

"I'll consider it. If and when it becomes applicable. Now, why don't we get the check? It's late."

When the check was served, as it always was in such establishments, with a faint air of apology, Natalie reached for it automatically. Ry pushed her hand aside and picked it up himself.

"Ry, I didn't mean for you to pay the tab." Flustered, she watched him pull out a credit card. She knew exactly what a meal cost at Chez Robert, and had a good idea what salary a city employee pulled down. "Really. It was my idea to come here."

"Shut up, Natalie." He figured the tip, signed the stub.

"Now I feel guilty. Damn it, we both know I picked this place to rub your nose in it. At least let me split it."

He pocketed his wallet. "No." He slid out of the booth, offered his hand. "Don't worry," he said dryly. "I can still make the rent this month. Probably."

"You're just being stubborn," she muttered.

"Where's the ticket for your coat?"

Male ego, she thought on a disgusted sigh as she took the ticket from her purse. She exchanged good-nights with André and Robert before Ry helped her into her coat.

"Do you need a lift?" Ry asked her.

"No, I have my car."

"Good. I don't have mine. You can give me a ride home."

She shot a suspicious look over her shoulder as they stepped outside. "If this is some sort of maneuver, I'll tell you right now, I'm not falling for it."

"Fine. I can take a cab." He scanned the street. "If I can find one. It's a cold night," he added. "Feels like snow on the way."

Her breath streamed out. "My car's in the lot around the corner. Where am I taking you?"

"Twenty-second, between Seventh and Eighth."

"Terrific." It was about as far out of her way as possible. "I have to make a stop first, at the store."

"What store?" He slipped an arm around her waist, as much for pleasure as to protect her from the cold.

"My store. We had the carpets laid today, and I didn't have time to check it before dinner. Since it's halfway between your place and mine, I might as well do it now."

"I didn't think business execs checked on carpet at nearly midnight."

"This one does." She smiled sweetly. "But if it's inconvenient for you, I'd be happy to drop you off at the bus stop."

"Thanks anyway." He waited while she unlocked her car. "Do you have any stock in that place yet?"

"About twenty percent of what we want for the grand opening. You're welcome to browse."

He slid into the car. "I was hoping you'd say that."

She drove well. That was no surprise. From what Ry had observed, Natalie Fletcher did everything with seamless competence. The fact that she could be shaken, the fact that the right word, the right look, at the right time, could bring a faint bloom to her cheeks, made her human. And outrageously appealing.

"Have you always lived in Urbana?" As she asked, she automatically turned down the radio.

"Yeah. I like it."

"So do I." She liked the movement of the city, the noise, the crowds. "We've had holdings here for years, of course, but I never lived in Urbana."

"Where?"

"Colorado Springs, mostly. That's where we're based, home and business. I like the East.'' The streets were dark now, and the wind was whipping through the canyons formed by the spearing buildings. ''I like eastern cities, the way people live on top of each other and rush to get everywhere.''

''No western comments about overcrowding and crime rates?''

''Fletcher Industries was founded on real estate, remember? The more people, the more housing required. And, as to crime...'' She shrugged. ''We have a hardworking police force. And Nemesis.''

''You're interested in him.''

''Who wouldn't be? Of course, as the sister of a police captain, I should add that I don't approve of private citizens doing police work.''

''Why not? He seems to get the job done. I wouldn't mind having him on my side.'' He frowned as she stopped at a light. The streets were nearly empty here, with dark pockets and narrow alleys. ''Do you do many runs like this alone?''

''When necessary.''

''Why don't you have a driver?''

''Because I like to drive myself.'' She shot him a look just as the light turned green. ''You're *not* going to be typical and give me a lecture about the dangers facing a woman alone in the city....''

''It's not all museums and French restaurants.''

''Ry, I'm a big girl. I've spent time alone in Paris, Bangkok, London and Bonn, among other cities. I think I can handle Urbana.''

''The cops, and your pal Nemesis, can't be everywhere,'' he pointed out.

''Any woman who has a big brother knows just how to drop a man to his knees,'' she said blithely. ''And I've taken a self-defense course.''

''That should make every mugger in the city tremble.''

Ignoring the sarcasm, she pulled up to the curb and turned off the engine. ''This is it.''

The quick surge of pride rose the moment she was out of the car and facing the building. Her building. ''So, what do you think?''

It was sleek and feminine, like its owner. All marble and glass, and its wide display window was scrolled with the Lady's Choice

logo in gold leaf. The entrance door was beveled glass etched with
rosettes that glinted in the backwash from the streetlights.

Pretty, he thought. Impractical. Expensive.

"Nice look."

"As our flagship store, I wanted it to be impressive, classic,
and..." she ran her fingertip over the etching "subtly erotic."

She dealt with the locks. Sturdy, Ry noted with some approval.
Solid. Just inside the door, she paused to enter her code on the com-
puterized security system. Natalie turned on the lights, relocked the
front door.

"Perfect." She nodded with approval at the mauve carpet. The
walls were teal, freshly painted. A curvy love seat and gleaming tea
table were set in a corner to invite customers to relax and decide
over merchandise.

Racks were recessed. Natalie could already envision them full,
dripping with silks and laces in pastels, bold, vibrant colors and
creamy whites.

"Most of the stock hasn't been put out yet. My manager and her
staff will see to that this week. And the window treatment. We have
the most incredible brocade peignoir. That'll be the focus."

Ry moved over to a faceless mannequin, fingered the lace at the
leg of a jade teddy. The same color as Natalie's eyes, he thought.
"So, what do you charge for something like this?"

"Mmm..." She examined the piece herself. Silk, seed pearls at
the bodice. "Probably about one-fifty."

"One hundred and fifty? Dollars?" He shook his head in disgust.
"One good tug and it's a rag."

Instantly she bristled. "Our merchandise is top-quality. It will certainly hold up to normal wear."

"Honey, a little number like this isn't designed for normal." He
cocked a brow. "Looks about your size."

"You keep dreaming, Piasecki." She tossed her coat over the love
seat. "The point of good lingerie is style, texture. The sheen of silk,
the foam of lace. Ours is designed to make a woman feel attractive
and good about herself—pampered."

"I thought the idea was to make a man beg."

"That couldn't hurt," she tossed back. "Look around, if you like. I'm going to run upstairs and check a couple of invoices while I'm here. It won't take me more than five minutes."

"I'll come with you. Offices upstairs?" he asked as they started toward a white floating staircase.

"Just the manager's. We'll have more merchandise up there, and changing rooms. We've also set up a separate area for brides. Specialized wedding-dress undergarments, honeymoon lingerie. Once we're fully operational—"

She broke off when he grabbed her arm. "Quiet."

"What—?"

"Quiet," he said again. He didn't hear it. Not yet. But he could smell it. Just the faintest sting in the air. "Do you have extinguishers in here?"

"Of course. In the storeroom, up in the office." She tugged at his hand. "What is this? Are you going to try to cite me for fire-code violations?"

"Get outside."

With her gaping after him, he darted toward the back of the store.

She was organized, he had to admit. He found the fire extinguisher, up to code, in full view in the crowded storeroom.

"What are you doing with that?" she demanded when he came back.

"I said get outside. You've got a fire."

"A—" He was halfway up the steps before she unfroze and raced after him. "That's impossible. How do you know? There's nothing—"

"Gas," he snapped out. "Smoke."

She started to tell him he was imagining things. But she smelled it now. "Ry..."

He cursed and kicked aside a streamer of papers and matches. It hadn't caught yet, but he saw where they were leading. The glossy white door was closed, and smoke was creeping sulkily under it.

He felt the door, and the heat pushing against it. His head whipped toward hers, the eyes cold. "Get out," he said again. "Call it in."

A scream strangled in her throat as he kicked the door open. Fire leapt out. Ry walked into it.

# Chapter 5

It was like a dream. A nightmare. Standing there, frozen, while flame licked at the door frame and Ry stepped in to meet it. In the instant he disappeared into smoke and fire, her heart seemed to stop, its beat simply ceasing. Then the panic that had halted it whipped it to racing. Her head buzzed with the echo of a hundred pulses as she dashed to the door after him.

She could see him, smothering the fire that sprinted across the floor and ate merrily at the base of the walls. Smoke billowed around him, seared her eyes, burned her lungs. Like some warrior, he challenged it, fought it down. In horror, she saw it strike back and lick slyly at his arm.

Now she did scream, leaping in to pound at the smoke that puffed from his back. He whirled to face her, furious to find her there.

"You're on fire." She barely choked the words out. "For God's sake, Ry! Let it go."

"Stay back."

With an arching movement, he smothered the flames that had begun to lap at the central desk. The paperwork left on its top, he knew, would feed the fire. Focused, he turned to attack the smoldering baseboard, the intricately carved trim that was flaming.

"Take this." He shoved the extinguisher into her hands. The main fire was out, and the smaller ones were all but smothered. He nearly had it. From the terror in her eyes, he could see that she didn't realize the beast was nearly beaten. "Use it," he ordered, and in one stride he had reached the flaming curtains and torn them down. There would be pain later—he knew that, as well. But now he fought the fire hand to hand.

Once the smoldering, smoke-stained lace was nothing more than harmless rags, he snatched the extinguisher out of her numbed hands and killed what was left.

"It didn't have much of a start." But his jacket was still smoking. He yanked it off, tossed it aside. "Wouldn't have gotten this far this fast, if there weren't so many flammables in here." He set the nearly empty extinguisher aside. "It's out."

Still he checked the room, kicking through the ruined drapes, searching for any cagey spark that waited to burn clean again.

"It's out," he repeated, and shoved her toward the door. "Get downstairs."

She stumbled, almost falling to her knees. A violent fit of coughing nearly paralyzed her. Her stomach heaved, her head spun. Near fainting, she braced a hand against the wall and fought to breathe.

"Damn it, Natalie." In one sweep, he had her up in his arms. He carried her through the blinding smoke, down the elegant staircase. "I told you to get out. Don't you ever listen?"

She tried to speak, and only coughed weakly. It felt as though she were floating. Even when he laid her against the cool cushions of the love seat, her head continued to reel.

He was cursing her. But his voice seemed far away, and harmless. If she could just get one breath, she thought, one full breath to soothe her burning throat.

He watched her eyes roll back. Jerking her ruthlessly, he pushed her head between her knees.

"Don't you faint on me." His voice was curt, his hand on the back of her head firm. "Stay here, breathe slow. You hear me?"

She nodded weakly. He left her, and when cold, fresh air slapped her cheeks, she shivered. After propping the outside door open, Ry came back, rubbing his hands up and down her spine.

She'd scared him, badly. So he did what came naturally to combat the fear—he yelled at her.

"That was stupid and thoughtless! You're lucky to get out of there with a sick stomach and some smoke inhalation. I *told* you to get out."

"You went in." She winced as the words tormented her abused throat. "You went right in."

"I'm trained. You're not." He hauled her back into a sitting position to check her over.

Her face was dead white under sooty smears, but her eyes were clear again. "Nausea?" he asked in clipped tones.

"No." She pressed the heels of her hands to her stinging eyes. "Not now."

"Dizzy?"

"No."

Her voice was hoarse, strained. He imagined her throat felt as though it had been scored with a hot poker. "Is there any water around here? I'll get you some."

"I'm all right." She dropped her hands, let her head fall back against the cushion. Now that the sickness was passing, fear was creeping in. "It seemed so fast, so horribly fast. Are you sure it's out?"

"It's my job to be sure." Frowning, he caught her chin, his eyes narrowing as he studied her face. "I'm taking you to the hospital."

"I don't need a damn hospital." In a bad-tempered movement, she shoved at him. Then gasped when she saw his hands. "Ry, your hands!" She grabbed his wrists. "You're burned!"

He glanced down. There were a few welts, some reddening. "Nothing major."

Reaction set in with shudders. "You were on fire, I saw your jacket catch fire."

"It was an old jacket. Stop," he ordered when tears swam in her eyes, overflowed. "Don't." If he hated one thing more than fire, it was a woman's tears. He swore and crushed his mouth to hers, hoping that would stop the flood.

Her arms came hard around him, surprising him with their strength and urgency. But her mouth trembled beneath his, moving him to gentle the kiss. To soothe.

"Better?" he murmured, and stroked her hair.

"I'm all right," she said again, willing herself to believe it. "There should be a first-aid kit in the storeroom. You need to put something on your hands."

"It's no big deal...." he began, but she shoved away from him and rose.

"I have to do something. Damn it, I have to do something."

She dashed off. Baffled by her, Ry stood and moved to relock the door. He needed to go up again and ventilate the office, but he wanted her out of the way before he made a preliminary investigation. He tugged off his tie, loosened his collar.

"There's some salve in here." Steadier now, Natalie came back in with a small first-aid kit.

"Fine." Deciding tending to him would do her some good, he sat back and let her play nurse. He had to admit the cool balm and her gentle fingers didn't do him any harm, either.

"You're lucky it isn't worse. It was insane, just walking into that room."

He cocked a brow. "You're welcome."

She looked up at him then. His face was smeared from the smoke, his eyes were reddened from it. "I am grateful," she said quietly. "Very grateful. But it was just things, Ry. Just things." She looked away again, busying herself replacing the tube of salve. "I guess I owe you a new suit."

"I hate suits." He shifted uncomfortably when he heard her quick, unsteady sob. "Don't cry again. If you really want to thank me, don't cry."

"All right." She sniffed inelegantly and rubbed her hands over her face. "I was so scared."

"It's over." He gave her hand an awkward pat. "Will you be all right for a minute? I want to go up and open the window. The smoke needs a way to escape."

"I'll come—"

"No, you won't. Sit here." He rose again, put a firm hand on her shoulder. "Please stay here."

He turned and left her. Natalie used the time he was gone to compose herself. And to think. When he came back down, she was sitting with her hands folded in her lap.

"It was the same as the warehouse, wasn't it?" She lifted her gaze to his. "The way it was set. We can't pretend it was a coincidence."

"Yes," he said. "It was the same. And no, we can't. We'll talk about this later. I'll drive you home."

"I'm—"

The words slid back down her throat when he dragged her roughly to her feet. "If you tell me one more time that you're all right, I'm going to punch you. You're sick, you're scared, and you sucked in smoke. Now this is the way we're going to work this. I'm driving you home. We'll report this on the phone in that snazzy car of yours. You're going to go to bed, and tomorrow you're going to see a doctor. Once you check out, we'll go from there."

"Stop yelling at me."

"I wouldn't have to yell if you'd listen." He grabbed her coat. "Put this on."

"This is my property. I have a right to be here."

"Well, I'm taking you out." He shoved her arm into the sleeve of her coat. "If you don't like it, call your fancy lawyers and sue me."

"There's no reason for you to take this attitude."

He started to swear, stopped himself. As a precaution, he took one slow breath. "Natalie, I'm tired." His voice was quiet now, nearly reasonable. "I've got a job to do here, and I can't do it if you're in my way. So cooperate. Please."

He was right, she knew he was right. She turned away, picked up her purse. "Keep my car. I'll arrange to have it picked up tomorrow."

"I appreciate it."

She gave him the car keys and the keys to the shop. "I'll be here tomorrow, Ry."

"I figured you would." He lifted a hand and rubbed his knuckles along her jawline. "Hey—try not to worry. I'm the best."

She nearly smiled. "So I've been told."

It was nearly eight the following morning when the cab dropped Natalie off in front of Lady's Choice. She noted, without surprise, that her car was out front, a fire-department sign visible through the windshield.

Instead of bothering with the buzzer, she used the spare set of keys she'd picked up that morning at the office and let herself in.

She couldn't smell the smoke. That was a relief. She'd spent a great deal of time during the night worrying and calculating the possible losses if the stock already in place had been damaged by smoke.

The first floor looked as pristine and elegant as it had the night before. If Ry gave her the go-ahead, she'd contact her manager and reestablish business as usual.

She took off her coat and gloves and started upstairs.

For Ry, it had been a long and productive night. He'd stopped in at the station after he dropped Natalie off, to change and to pick up his tools. He'd worked alone through the night—the way he preferred it. He was just sealing an evidence jar when she walked in.

"Good morning, Legs." Crouched on the floor amid the rubble, he didn't bother to look past them.

She scanned the room, sighed. The carpet was a blackened mess. Charred pieces of wood trim had been pried from the sooty walls and lay scattered. The elegant Queen Anne desk was blackened and scored, and the Irish-lace drapes were a heap of useless rags.

Despite the open window where the light wind shook in thin snow, the air stank with stale smoke.

"Why does it always look worse the next day?"

"It's not so bad. A little paint, new trim."

She ran a fingertip over the wallpaper, the violet-and-rosebud pattern she'd chosen personally. Ruined now, she thought.

"Easy for you to say."

"Yeah," he agreed, labeling the evidence jar. "I guess it is."

He glanced up then. Today she'd scooped her hair up. The style appealed to him, the way it showed off the line of her neck and jaw. This morning's suit was royal purple, military in style. It looked, he thought, as though the lady were ready for a fight.

"How'd you sleep?"

"Surprisingly well, all in all." Except for one bone-chilling nightmare she didn't want to mention. "You?"

He hadn't been to bed at all, and merely shrugged. "Have you called your adjuster?"

"I will, as soon as his office opens." Her voice cooled automatically. "Are you going to interview me again, Inspector?"

Annoyance flared briefly in his eyes. "I don't think that's necessary, do you?" He began to replace his tools in their box. "I'll have a report by tomorrow."

She closed her eyes a moment. "I'm sorry. I'm not angry with you, Ry. I'm just angry."

"Fair enough."

"Can you—?" She broke off, turning quickly at the sound of footsteps on the stairs. "Gage." She forced a smile, held out her hands when he walked in.

"I heard." With one quick glance, he took in the damage. "I thought I'd come by and see if there was anything I could do."

"Thanks." She kissed him lightly on the cheek before she turned back to Ry. He was still crouched—very much, she thought, intrigued, like an animal about to spring. "Gage Guthrie, Inspector Ryan Piasecki."

"I've heard you do good work."

After a moment, Ry straightened and accepted the hand Gage offered. "I've heard the same about you." Feeling territorial, Ry measured the man as he spoke to Natalie. "Are you two pals?"

"That's right. And a bit more." She watched, fascinated, as Ry's eyes kindled. "If you can follow the connections, Gage is married to my brother's wife's sister."

The fire banked; Ry's shoulders relaxed. "Extended family."

"In a manner of speaking." Judging the situation quickly and accurately, Gage decided to do a little checking on the inspector himself. "Are you looking at the same fire starter here?"

"We're not ready to release that information."

"He's got his official hat on," Natalie said dryly. "Unofficially," she continued, ignoring Ry's scowl, "it looks the same. When we came in last night—"

"You were here?" Gage interrupted her, gripping Natalie's arm. "You?"

"I had a few things I wanted to check on. Fortunately." Blowing out a breath, she took another scan of the room. "It could have been a lot worse. I happened to have a veteran fire fighter along."

Gage relaxed fractionally. "You've got no business going around the city alone, at night."

"Yeah." Ry took out a cigarette. "You try to tell her."

Natalie merely lifted a brow. "Do you go around the city, Gage, alone? At night?"

He tucked his tongue in his cheek. If she only knew. "It's entirely different. And don't give me a lecture on equality," he went on, before she could speak. "I'm all for it. In the home, in the workplace. But on the street it comes down to basic common sense. A woman's more of a target."

"Mmm, hmmm..." Natalie smiled pleasantly. "And does Deborah buy that line from you?"

Now his lips did curve. "No. She's every bit as hardheaded as you." Frustrated that he'd been on the other side of town when Nat needed him, Gage tucked his hands in his pockets. "If I can't do anything else, I can offer you any of the facilities or staff of Guthrie International."

"I'll take you up on that if it becomes necessary." She sent him a quick, hopeful look. "I don't suppose you could use your influence to keep your wife from calling my brother and Cilla and relating all of this?"

He patted her cheek. "Not a chance. Maybe I should mention that she talked to Althea last week and filled her in on what happened at the warehouse."

Giving in to fatigue, Natalie rubbed her temples. Althea Grayson, her brother's former partner on the force, was very pregnant. "I'm surrounded by cops," she muttered. "There's no reason to get Althea upset in her condition. She and Colt should be concentrating on each other."

"It's a problem when you have so many people who care about you. Stay out of empty buildings," Gage added, and kissed her. "Nice to meet you, Inspector."

"Yeah. See you."

"Give Deborah and Addy my love," Natalie said as she walked Gage to the doorway. "And stop worrying about me."

"I'll do the first, but not the second."

"Who's Addy?" Ry asked before he heard the downstairs door close behind Gage.

"Hmmm? Oh, their baby." Distracted, she circled around a charred hole in the carpet to examine her antique filing cabinets. It was some consolation to see that they were undamaged. "I really need to clear this up, Ry. Too many people are losing sleep."

"You've got a lot of close ties." He walked to the open window and put out his cigarette. "I can't make this work any faster to please them. Just take your friend's advice. Stay off the streets at night and out of empty buildings."

"I don't want advice. I want answers. Someone broke in here last night and tried to burn me out. How and why?"

"Okay, Ms. Fletcher, I can give you the how." Ry leaned a hip against the partially burned desk. "On the night of February twenty-sixth, a fire was discovered by Inspector Piasecki, and Natalie Fletcher, owner of the building."

"Ry…"

He held up a hand to stop her. "After entering the building, Piasecki and Fletcher started up to the second floor when Piasecki detected the odor of an accelerant, and smoke. Piasecki then ordered Fletcher to flee the building. An order, I might add, that she stupidly ignored. Finding an extinguisher in the storeroom, Piasecki proceeded to the fire, which had involved an office on the second floor. Streamers of paper, clothing and matchbooks were observed. The fire was extinguished without extensive damage."

"I'm very aware of that particular sequence of events."

"You wanted a report, you're getting one. An examination of the debris led the investigator to believe that the fire had been started approximately two feet inside the door, with the use of gasoline as an accelerant. No forced entry into the building could be determined by the inspector, or the police department. Arson is indicated."

She took a careful breath. "You're angry with me."

"Yeah, I'm angry with you. You're pushing me, Natalie, and yourself. You want this all tidied up, because people are worried about you, and you're concerned with selling your pantyhose on time. And you're missing one small, very important detail."

"No, I'm not." She was pale again, and rigid. "I'm trying not to be frightened by it. It isn't difficult to add the elements and come up with the fact that someone is doing this to me deliberately. Two of my buildings within two weeks. I'm not a fool, Ry."

"You're a fool if you're not frightened by it. You've got an enemy. Who?"

"I don't know," she shot back. "If I did, don't you think I'd tell you? You've just told me there was no forced entry. That means someone I know, someone who works for me, could have gotten in here and started the fire."

"It's a torch."

"Excuse me?"

"A pro," Ry explained. "Not a very good one, but a pro. Somebody hired a torch to set the fires. It could be that somebody let him in, or he found a way to bypass your security. But he didn't finish the job here, so it's likely he'll hit you again."

She forced back a shudder. "That's comforting. That's very comforting."

"I don't want you to be comforted. I want you to be alert. How many people work for you?"

"At Lady's Choice?" Frazzled, she pushed at her hair. "Around six hundred, I think, in Urbana."

"You got a personnel list?"

"I can get one."

"I want it. Look, I'm going to run the data through the computer.

See how many known pros we have in the area who use this technique. It's a start.''

"You'll keep me up-to-date? I'll be in the office most of the day. My assistant will know how to reach me if I'm out."

He straightened, walked to her and cupped her face. "Why don't you take the day off? Go shopping, go see a movie."

"Are you joking?"

He dropped his hands, shoved them in his pockets. "Listen, Natalie, you've got one more person worried about you. Okay?"

"I think it's okay," she said slowly. "I'll stay available, Ry. But I have a lot of work to do." She smiled in an attempt to lighten the mood. "Starting with getting a cleaning crew and decorators in here."

"Not until I tell you."

"How did I know you'd say that?" Resigned, she glanced toward the wooden cabinets against the left wall. "Is it all right if I get some files out? I only moved them out of the main office a few days ago so I could work on them here." She lifted a shoulder. "Or I'd hoped to work on them here. More delays," she said under her breath.

"Yeah, go ahead. Watch your step."

He watched it, as well, and shook his head. He didn't see how she could walk so smoothly on those skyscraper heels she seemed addicted to. But he had to admit, they did fascinating things to her legs.

"How are your hands?" she asked as she flipped through the files.

"What?"

"Your hands." She glanced back, saw where his gaze was focused, and laughed. "God, Piasecki, you're obsessed."

"I bet they go all the way up to your shoulders." He skimmed his eyes up to hers. "The hands aren't too bad, thanks. When's your doctor's appointment?"

She turned away to give unmerited attention to the files. "I don't need a doctor. I don't like doctors."

"Chicken."

"Maybe. My throat's a little sore, that's all. I can deal with that without a doctor poking at me. And if you're going to lecture me on that, I'll lecture you on deliberately sucking smoke into your lungs."

With a wince, he tucked away the cigarette he'd just pulled out. "I didn't say anything. Are you about done? I want to get this evidence to the lab."

"Yes. The fact that the files didn't go up saves me a lot of time and trouble. I need Deirdre to run an audit after we've dealt with this other mess. I'm hoping things look solid enough for me to scout around and open a branch in Denver."

The little flutter under his heart wasn't easily ignored. "Denver? Are you going to be moving back to Colorado?"

"Hmmm…" Satisfied, she tucked the paperwork in her briefcase. "It depends. I'm not thinking that far ahead yet. First we have to get the stores we have off the ground. That isn't going to happen overnight." She swung the strap of her briefcase over her shoulder. "That should do it."

"I want to see you." It cost him to say it. Even more to admit it to himself. "I need to see you, Natalie. Away from all this."

Her suddenly nervous fingers tugged at the strap of her briefcase. "We're both pretty swamped at the moment, Ry. It might be smarter for us to concentrate on what needs to be done and keep a little personal distance."

"It would be smarter."

"Well, then." She took one step toward the door before he blocked her path.

"I want to see you," he repeated. "And I want to touch you. And I want to take you to bed."

Heat curled inside her, threatening to flash. It didn't seem to matter that his words were rough, blunt, and without finesse. Poetry and rose petals would have left her much less vulnerable.

"I know what you want. I need to be sure what *I* want. What I can handle. I've always been a logical person. You've got a way of clouding that."

"Tonight."

"I have to work late." She felt herself weakening, yearning. "A dinner meeting."

"I'll wait."

"I don't know when I'll be finished. Probably not much before midnight."

He backed her toward the wall. "Midnight, then."

She began to wonder why she was resisting. Her eyes started to cloud and close. "Midnight," she repeated, waiting for his mouth to cover hers. Wanting to taste it, to surge under it.

Her eyes sprang open. She jerked back. "Oh, God. Midnight."

Her cheeks had gone white again. Ry lifted his hands to support her. "What is it?"

"Midnight," she repeated, pressing a hand to her brow. "I didn't put it together. Never thought of it. It was just past twelve when we got here last night."

He nodded, watching her. "So?"

"I got a call when I was dressing for dinner. I never seem to be able to ignore the ring and let the machine pick up, so I answered. He said midnight."

Eyes narrowed, Ry braced her against the wall. "Who?"

"I don't know. I didn't recognize the voice. He said— Let me think." She pushed away to pace out into the hall. "Midnight. He said midnight. The witching hour. Watch for it, or wait for it—something like that." She gestured toward the charred and ruined carpet. "This must be what he meant."

"Why the hell didn't you tell me this before?"

"Because I just remembered." Every bit as angry as he, she whirled on Ry. "I thought it was a crank call, so I ignored it, forgot it. Then, when this happened, I had a little more on my mind than a nuisance call. How was I supposed to know it was a warning? Or a threat?"

He ignored that and took his notebook out of his pocket to write down the words she'd related. "What time did you get the call?"

"It must have been around seven-thirty. I was looking for earrings, and rushing because I'd gotten held up and was running late."

"Did you hear any background noises on the line?"

Unsure, she fought to remember. She hadn't been paying attention. She'd been thinking of Ry. "I didn't notice any. His voice was high-pitched. It was a man, I'm sure of that, but it was a girlish kind of voice. He giggled," she remembered.

Ry's gaze shot to her face, then back to his book. "Did it sound mechanical, or genuine?"

She went blank for a moment. "Oh, you mean like a tape. No, it didn't sound like a tape."

"Is your number listed?"

"No." Then she understood the significance of the question. "No," she repeated slowly. "It's not."

"I want a list of everyone who has your home number. Everyone."

She straightened, forcing herself to keep calm. "I can give you a list of everyone I know who has it. I can't tell you who might have gotten it by other means." She cleared her aching throat. "Ry, do professionals usually call their victims before a fire?"

He tucked his notebook away and looked into her eyes. "Even pros can be crazy. I'll drive you to your office."

"It's not necessary."

Patience. He reminded himself he'd worked overtime so that he could be patient with her. Then he thought, the hell with it. "You listen to this, real careful." He curled his fingers around the lapel of her jacket. "I'm driving you to your office. Got that?"

"I don't see—"

He tugged. "Got it?"

She bit back an oath. It would be petty to argue. "Fine. I'm going to need my car later today, so you'll have to get yourself wherever you're going after you drop me off."

"Keep listening," he said evenly. "Until I get back to you, you're not to go anywhere alone."

"That's ridiculous. I've got a business to run."

"Nowhere alone," he repeated. "Otherwise, I'm going to call some of my pals in Urbana P.D. and have them sit on you." When she opened her mouth to protest, he overrode her. "And I can sure as hell keep your little shop here off-limits to everyone but official fire- and police-department personnel until further notice."

"That sounds like a threat," she said stiffly.

"You're a real sharp lady. You get one of your minions to drive you today, Natalie, or I'll slap a fire-department restriction on the front door of this place for the next couple of weeks.''

He could, she realized, reading the determination on his face. And he would. From experience, she knew it was smarter, and more practical, to give up a small point in a negotiation in order to salvage the bottom line.

''All right. I'll assign a driver for any out-of-the-office meetings today. But I'd like to point out that this man is burning my buildings, Ry, not threatening me personally.''

''He called you personally. That's enough.''

She hated the fact that he'd frightened her. Stringent control kept her dealing with office details coolly, efficiently. By noon, she had a cleanup crew on standby, waiting for Ry's okay. She'd ordered her assistant to contact the decorator about new carpet, wallpaper, draperies and paint. She'd dealt with a frantic call from her Atlanta branch and an irate one from Chicago, and managed to play down the problem with her family back in Colorado.

Impatient, she buzzed her assistant. ''Maureen, I needed those printouts thirty minutes ago.''

''Yes, Ms. Fletcher. The system's down in Accounting. They're working on it.''

''Tell them—'' She bit back the searing words, and forced her voice to level. ''Tell them it's a priority. Thank you, Maureen.''

Deliberately she leaned back in her chair and closed her eyes. Having an edge was an advantage in business, she reminded herself. Being edgy was a liability. If she was going to handle the meetings set for the rest of the day, she had to pull herself together. Slowly she unfisted her hands and ordered her muscles to relax.

She'd nearly accomplished it when a quick knock came at her door. She straightened in her chair as Melvin poked his head in.

''Safe?''

''Nearly,'' she told him. ''Come in.''

''I come bearing gifts.'' He carried a tray into the room.

''If that's coffee, I may find the energy to get up and kiss your whole face.''

He flushed brightly and chuckled. "Not only is it coffee, but there's chicken salad to go with it. Even *you* have to eat, Natalie."

"Tell me about it." She pressed a hand to her stomach as she rose to join him at the sofa. "I'm empty. This is very sweet of you, Melvin."

"And self-serving. You've been burning up the interoffice lines, so I had my secretary put this together. You take a break—" he fiddled with his bright red bow tie "—we take a break."

"I guess I have been playing Simon Legree today." With a little sigh, Natalie inhaled the scent of coffee as she poured.

"You're entitled." He sat beside her. "Have you got time over lunch to tell me how bad things are over at the flagship?"

"Not as bad as they could have been." She indulged herself by slipping out of her shoes and tucking her legs up as she ate. "Minor, really. From what I could tell, it looked like mostly cosmetic damage to the manager's office. It didn't get to the stock."

"Thank God," he said heartily. "I don't know how much my charm would have worked a second time in persuading the branches to part with inventory."

"Unnecessary," she said between bites. "We got lucky this time, Melvin, but—"

"But?"

"There's a pattern here that concerns me. Someone doesn't want Lady's Choice to fly."

Frowning, he picked up the roll on her plate, broke it in half. "Unforgettable Woman's our top competitor. Or we'll be theirs."

"I've thought of that. It just doesn't fit. That company's been around nearly fifty years. It's solid. Respectable." She sighed, hating what she needed to say. "But I am worried about corporate espionage, Melvin. Within Lady's Choice."

"One of our people?" He'd lost the taste for the roll.

"It isn't a possibility I like—or one I can overlook." Thoughtful, she switched from food to coffee. "I could call a meeting of department heads, get input and opinions about their people." And she would, she thought. She would have to. "But that doesn't deal with the department heads themselves."

"A lot of your top people have been with Fletcher for years, Natalie."

"I'm aware of that." Restless, she rose, drinking coffee as she paced. "I can't think of any reason why someone in the organization would want to delay the opening. But I have to look for that reason."

"That puts us all under the gun."

She turned back. "I'm sorry, Melvin. It does."

"No need to be sorry. It's business." He waved it aside, but his smile was a little strained as he rose. "What's the next step?"

"I'm going to meet the adjuster at the shop at one." She glanced at her watch and swore. "I'd better get started."

"Let me do it." Anticipating her, Melvin held up a hand. "You have more than you can handle right here. Delegate, Natalie, remember? I'll meet the agent, give you a full report when I get back."

"All right. It would save me a very frenzied hour." Frowning, she stepped back into her shoes. "If the arson inspector is on-site, you might ask him to contact me with any progress."

"Will do. There's a shipment due in to the shop late this afternoon. Do you want to put a hold on it?"

"No." She'd already thought it through. "Business as usual. I've put a security guard on the building. It won't be easy for anyone to get in again."

"We'll stay on schedule," Melvin assured her.

"Damn right we will."

## Chapter 6

Ry preferred good solid human reasoning to computer analysis, but he'd learned to use all available tools. The Arson Pattern Recognition System was one of the best. Over the past few years, he'd become adept enough at the keyboard. Now, with his secretary long gone for the day and the men downstairs settled into sleep, he worked alone.

The APRS, used intelligently, was an effective tool for identifying and classifying trends in data. It was possible, with a series of fires suspected to be related, to use the tool to predict where and when future arsons in the series were most likely to occur.

The computer told him what he'd already deduced. Natalie's production plant was a prime target. He'd already assigned a team to patrol and survey the area.

But he was more concerned about Natalie herself. The phone call she'd received made it personal. And it had given him a very specific clue.

Reaching for coffee with one hand, Ry tapped on keys and linked up with the National Fire Data System. He plugged in his pattern—incident information, geographical locations and fire data. The process would not only help him, but serve to aid future investigators.

Then he worked on suspects. Again he input the fire data, the method. To these he was able to add the phone call, Natalie's impression of the voice and the wording.

He sat back and watched the computer reinforce his own conclusions.

Clarence Robert Jacoby, a.k.a. Jacoby, a.k.a. Clarence Roberts. Last known address 23 South Street, Urbana. White male. D.O.B. 6/25/52.

It went on to list half a dozen arrests for arson and incendiary fires, all urban. One conviction had put him away for five years. Another arrest, two years ago was still pending, as he'd skipped out on bail.

And the pattern was there.

Jacoby was a part-time pro who liked to burn things. He habitually preferred gasoline as an accelerant, used streamers of convenient, on-site flammables, along with matchbooks from his own collection. He often called his victims. His psychiatric evaluation classified him as a neurotic with sociopathic tendencies.

"You like fire, don't you, you little bastard?" Ry muttered, tapping his finger against the keyboard. "You don't even mind when it burns you. Isn't that what you told me? It's like a kiss."

Ry flipped a switch and had the data printing out. Wearily he rubbed the heels of his hands over his eyes as the machine clattered. He'd caught about two hours' sleep on the sofa in the outer office that evening. Fatigue was catching up with him.

But he had his quarry now. He was sure of it. And, he thought, he had a trail.

More out of habit than desire, Ry lit a cigarette before punching in numbers on the phone. "Piasecki. I'm swinging by the Fletcher plant on my way home. You can reach me…" He trailed off, checking his watch. Midnight, he noted. On the dot. Maybe he should take that as a sign. "You can reach me at this number until I check in again." He recited Natalie's home number from memory, then hung up.

He shut down the computer, grabbed the printout and his jacket, then hit the lights.

Natalie pulled on a robe, one of her favorites from the Lady's Choice line, and debated whether to crawl into bed or sink into a hot bath. She decided to soothe her nerves with a glass of wine before she did either. She'd tried to reach Ry three times that afternoon, only to be told he was unavailable.

*She* was supposed to be available, she thought nastily. But he could come and go as he pleased. Not a word all day. Well, he was going to get a surprise first thing in the morning when she walked right into his office and demanded a progress report.

As if she didn't have enough to worry about, with department meetings, production meetings, meeting meetings. And she was tracking the early catalog orders by region. At least that looked promising, she thought, and walked over to enjoy her view of the city.

She wasn't going to let anything stand in her way. Not fires, and certainly not a fire inspector. If there was someone on her staff—in any position—who was responsible for the arson, she would find out who it was. And she would deal with it.

Within a year, she would have pushed Lady's Choice over the top. Within five, she would double the number of branches.

Fletcher Industries would have a new success, one she would have nurtured from inception. She could be proud, and satisfied.

So why was she suddenly so lonely?

His fault, she decided, sipping her wine, for making her restless with her life. For making her question her priorities at a time when she needed all her concentration and effort focused.

Physical attraction, even with this kind of intensity, wasn't enough, shouldn't be enough, to distract her from her goals. She'd been attracted before, and certainly knew how to play the game safely. After all, she was thirty-two, hardly a novice in the relationship arena. Skilled and cautious, she'd always come through unscathed. No man had ever involved her heart quite enough to cause scarring.

Why did that suddenly seem so sad?

Annoyed with the thought, she shook it off.

She was wasting her time brooding about Ryan Piasecki. God knew, he wasn't even her type. He was rough and rude and undeniably abrasive. She preferred a smoother sort. A safer sort.

Why did that suddenly seem so shallow?

She set her half-full glass aside and shook back her hair. What she needed was sleep, not self-analysis. The phone rang just as she reached out to switch off the lights.

"Oh, I hate you," she muttered, and picked up the receiver. "Hello."

"Ms. Fletcher, this is Mark, at the desk downstairs?"

"Yes, Mark, what is it?"

"There's an Inspector Piasecki here to see you."

"Oh, really?" She checked her watch, toying with the idea of sending him away. "Mark, would you ask him if it's official business?"

"Yes, ma'am. Is this official business, Inspector?"

She heard Ry's voice clearly through the earpiece, asking Mark whether he would like him to get a team down there in the next twenty minutes to look for code violations.

When Mark sputtered, Natalie took pity on him. "Just send him up, Mark."

"Yes, Ms. Fletcher. Thank you."

She disconnected, then paced to the door and back. She certainly wasn't going to check her appearance in the mirror.

Of course, she did.

By the time Ry pounded on her door, she'd managed to dash into the bedroom, brush her hair and dab on some perfume.

"Don't you think it's unfair to threaten people in order to get your way?" she demanded when she yanked open the door.

"Not when it works." He took his time looking at her. The floor-length robe was unadorned, the color of heavy cream. The silk crossed over her breasts, nipped in at the belted waist, then fell, thin and close, down her hips.

"Don't you think it's a waste to wear something like that when you're alone?"

"No, I don't."

"Are we going to talk in the hall?"

"I suppose not." She closed the door behind him. "I won't bother to point out that it's late."

He said nothing, only wandered around the living area of the apartment. Soft colors, offset by those vibrant abstract paintings she apparently liked. Lots of trinkets, he noted, but tidy. There were fresh flowers, a fireplace piped for gas, and a wide window through which the lights of the city gleamed.

"Nice place."

"I like it."

"You like heights." He moved to the window and looked down. She was a good twenty floors above any possible ladder rescue. "Maybe I will have this place checked to see if it's up to code." He glanced back at her. "Got a beer?"

"No." Then she sighed. Manners would always rise above annoyance. "I was having a glass of wine. Would you like one?"

He shrugged. He wasn't much of a wine drinker, but his system couldn't handle any more coffee.

Taking that as an indication of assent, Natalie went into the kitchen to pour another glass.

"Got anything to go with it?" he asked from the doorway. "Like food?"

She started to snap at him about mistaking her apartment for an all-night diner, but then she got a good look at his face in the strong kitchen light. If she'd ever seen exhaustion, she was seeing it now.

"I don't do a lot of cooking, but I have some Brie, crackers, some fruit."

Nearly amused, he rubbed his hands over his face. "Brie." He gave a short laugh as he dropped his hands. "Great. Fine."

"Go sit down." She handed him the wine. "I'll bring it out."

"Thanks."

A few minutes later, she found him on her sofa, his legs stretched out, his eyes half-closed. "Why aren't you home in bed?"

"I had some stuff to do." With one hand, he reached for the tray she'd set on the table. With the other, he reached for her. Content with her beside him, he piled soft cheese on a cracker. "It's not half-bad," he said with his mouth full. "I missed dinner."

"I suppose I could send out for something."

"This is fine. I figured you'd want an update."

"I do, but I thought I'd hear from you several hours ago." He mumbled something over a new cracker. "What?"

"Court," he said, and swallowed. "I had to be in court most of the afternoon."

"I see."

"Got your messages, though." The refueling helped, and he grinned. "Did you miss me?"

"The update," she said dryly. "It's the least you can do while you're cleaning out my pantry."

He helped himself to a handful of glossy green grapes. "I've ordered surveillance for your plant on Winesap."

Her fingers tightened on the stem of her glass. "Do you think it's a target?"

"Fits the pattern. Have you noticed a man around any of your properties? White guy, about five-four, a hundred and thirty. Thinning sandy hair. Forty-something, but with this round, moony face that makes him look like a kid." He broke off to wash crackers down with wine. "Pale, mousy-looking eyes, lots of teeth."

"No, I can't think of anyone like that. Why?"

"He's a torch. Nasty little guy, about half-crazy." The wine wasn't half-bad, either, Ry was discovering, and sipped again. "All-the-way crazy would be easier. He likes to make things burn, and he doesn't mind getting paid for it."

"You think he's the one," Natalie said quietly. "And you know him, personally, don't you?"

"We've met, Clarence and me. Last time I saw him was, oh, about ten years ago. He'd hung around too long on one of his jobs. He was on fire when I got to him. We were both smoking by the time I got him out."

Natalie struggled for calm. "Why do you think it's him?"

Briefly Ry gave her a rundown on his work that evening. "So, it's his kind of job," he added. "Plus, the phone call. He likes the phone, too. And the voice you described—that's pure Clarence."

"You could have told me that this morning."

"Could've." He shrugged. "Didn't see the point."

"The point," she said between her teeth, "is that we're talking about my building, my property."

He studied her a moment. It wasn't such a bad idea, he supposed, to use anger to cover fear. He couldn't blame her for it. "Tell me, Ms. Fletcher, in your position as CEO, or whatever it is you are, do you make reports before, during, or after you've checked your data?"

It irritated, as he'd meant it to. And it deflated. As he'd meant it to. "All right." She expelled a rush of air. "Tell me the rest."

Ry set his glass aside. "He moves around, city to city. I'm betting he's back in Urbana. And I'll find him. Is there an ashtray around here?"

In silence, Natalie rose and took a small mosaic dish from another table. She was being unfair, she realized, and it wasn't like her. Obviously he was dead tired because he'd put in dozens of extra hours—for her.

"You've been working on this all night."

He struck a match. "That's the job."

"Is it?" she asked quietly.

"Yeah." His eyes met hers. "And it's you."

Her pulse began to drum. She couldn't stop it. "You're making it very hard for me, Ry."

"That's the idea." Lazily he skimmed a finger along the lapel of her robe, barely brushing the skin. Her scent rose up from it, subtly, tantalizingly. "You want me to ask you how your day went?"

"No." With a tired laugh, she shook her head. "No."

"I guess you don't want to talk about the weather, politics, sports?"

Natalie paused before she spoke again. She didn't want her voice to sound breathy. "Not particularly."

He grunted, leaned over to crush out his cigarette. "I should go, let you get some sleep."

Her emotions tangled, she rose as he did. "That's probably best. Sensible." It wasn't what she wanted, just what was best. And it wasn't, she'd begun to realize, what she needed. Just what was sensible.

"But I'm not going to." His eyes locked on hers. "Unless you tell me."

Her heartbeat thickened. She could feel the shudder start all the way down in the soles of her feet and work its way up. "Tell you what?"

He smiled, moved closer, stopping just before their bodies brushed. The first answer, whether she wanted him to go or stay, was already easily read in her eyes.

"Where's the bedroom, Natalie?"

A little dazed, she looked over his shoulder, gesturing vaguely. "There. Back there."

With that quick, surprising grace of his, he scooped her up. "I think I can make it that far."

"This is a mistake." She was already raining kisses over his face, his throat. "I know it's a mistake."

"Everybody makes one now and again."

"I'm smart." While her breath hitched, her fingers hurried to unbutton his shirt. "And I'm level-headed. I have to be, because…" She let out a groan as her fingers found flesh. "God, I love your body."

"Yeah?" He nearly staggered as she tugged his shirt out of his jeans. "Consider it all yours. I should have known."

"Mmm…" She was busy biting at his shoulder. "What?"

"That you'd have a first-class bed." He tumbled with her onto the satin covers.

Already half-mad for him, she dragged at his shirt. "Hurry," she demanded. "I've wanted you to hurry since the first time you touched me."

"Let me catch up." Equally frantic, he crushed his mouth to hers, sinking in.

Breathless, she yanked at the snap of his jeans. "This is insane." She struggled to find him, drinking hungrily from his mouth as they rolled across the bed.

He couldn't catch his breath, or even a slippery hold on control. "It's about to be," he muttered. Tugging her robe open, he found the thin swatch of matching silk beneath. A moan ripped through him as he closed his mouth over her cream-covered breast.

Silk and heat and fragrant flesh. Everything she was filled him, taunted him, tormented him. Woman, all woman. Beauty and grace and passion. Temptation and torment and triumph. All of it, all of her, obsessed him.

. They thrashed over the slick satin spread, groping for more.

Here was fire, the bright, dangerous flash of it. It seared through him, burned, scarred, while her hands and mouth raced over him, igniting hundreds of new flames. He didn't fight it back. For once he wanted to be consumed. With an oath, he tore at the silk and dined greedily on her flesh.

His hands were rough and hard. And wonderful. She'd never felt more alive, or more desperate. She craved him, knew that she had, on some deep level, right from the beginning.

But now she had him, could feel the press of that hard, muscled body against her, could taste the violent urgency of his need whenever their mouths met, could hear his response to her touch, to her taste, in every hurried breath.

If it was elemental, so be it. She felt lusty and wanton and absolutely free. Her teeth dug into his shoulder as he whipped her ruthlessly over the first crest. She cried out his name, all but screamed it, arching upward, taut as a bow.

He arrowed into her, hard, deep.

She was blind and deaf from the pleasure of it, oblivious of her own sobbing breaths as they mated in a frenzied rhythm. Her body plunged against his, tireless, driven by a need that seemed insatiable.

Then body and need erupted.

The light was on. Funny he hadn't even noticed that, when normally he was accustomed to picking up every small detail. The lamp's glow was soft, picking up the cool sherbet tones of her bedroom.

Ryan lay still, his head on her breast, and waited for his system to level. Beneath his ear, her heart continued to thunder. Her flesh was damp, her body limp. Every few moments a tremor shook her.

He didn't smile in triumph, as he might have done, but simply stared in wonder.

He'd wanted to conquer her. He couldn't—wouldn't—deny it.

He'd craved the sensation of having her body buck and shudder under his from the first moment he saw her.

But he hadn't expected the tornado of need that had swept through them both, that had them clawing at each other like animals.

He knew he'd been rough. He wasn't a particularly gentle man, so that didn't bother him. But he'd never lost control so completely with any woman. Nor had he ever wanted one so intensely only moments after he'd had her.

"That should have done it," he muttered.

"Hmmm?" She felt weak as water. Achy and sweet.

"It should have gotten it out of my system. Gotten *you* out. At least started getting you out."

"Oh." She found the energy to open her eyes. The light, dim as it was, had her wincing. Slowly, her mind began to clear; quickly, her skin began to heat. She remembered the way she'd torn at his clothes, wrestled him into bed without a single coherent thought except having him.

She let out a breath, drew another in.

"You're right," she decided. "It should have. What's wrong with us?"

With a laugh, he lifted his head, looking at her flushed face, her tousled hair. "Damned if I know. Are you okay?"

Now she smiled. The hell with logic. "Damned if I know. What just happened here's a bit out of the usual realm for me."

"Good." He lowered his head, skimmed his tongue lightly over her breast. "I want you again, Natalie."

She quivered once. "Good."

When the alarm went off, Natalie groaned, rolled over to shut it off, and bumped solidly into Ry. He grunted, slapped at the buzzer with one hand and brought her to rest on top of him with the other.

"What's the noise for?" he asked, and ran an interested hand down her spine to the hip.

"To wake me up."

He opened one eye. Yeah, he thought, he should have known it.

She looked just as good in the morning as she did every other time of the day. "Why?"

"It goes like this." Still groggy, she pushed her hair out of her face. "The alarm goes off, I get up, shower, dress, drink copious cups of coffee, and go to work."

"I've had some experience with the process. Anybody tell you today's Saturday?"

"I know what day it is," she said. At least she did now. "I have work."

"No, you don't, you just think you do." He cradled her head against his shoulder, casting one bleary eye at the clock. It was 7:00 a.m. He calculated they'd had three hours' sleep, at the outside. "Go back to sleep."

"I can't."

He let out a long-suffering sigh. "All right, all right. But you should have warned me you were insatiable." More than willing to oblige, he rolled her over again and began to nibble on her shoulder.

"I didn't mean that." She laughed, trying to wiggle free. "I have paperwork, calls to make." His hand was sneaking up to stroke her breast. Fire kindled instantly in the pit of her stomach. "Cut it out."

"Uh-uh. You woke me up, now you pay."

She couldn't help it, simply couldn't, and she began to stretch under his hands. "We're lucky we didn't kill each other last night. Are you sure you want to take another chance?"

"Men like me face danger every day." He covered her grinning mouth with his.

She was more than three hours behind schedule when she stepped out of the shower. So, she'd work late, Natalie decided, and after wrapping a towel around her hair she began to cream her legs. A good executive understood the merits of flextime.

Yawning, she wiped steam from the bathroom mirror and took a good look at her face. She should be exhausted, she realized. She certainly should look exhausted after the wild night she and Ry had shared.

But she wasn't. And she didn't. She looked…soft, she thought. Satisfied.

And why not? she thought, dragging the towel from her hair. When a woman took thirty-two years to experience just what a bout of hot, sweaty sex could do for the mind and body, she ought to look satisfied.

Nothing, absolutely nothing, she'd ever experienced, came close to what she'd felt, what she'd done, what she'd discovered, during the night with Ry.

So if she smiled like a fool while she combed out her wet hair, why not? If she felt like singing as she wrapped her tingling body in her robe, it was understandable.

And if she had to rearrange her schedule for the day because she'd spent most of the night and all of the morning wrestling in bed with a man who made her blood bubble, more power to her.

She stepped back into the bedroom and grinned at the tangled sheets. Lips pursed, she picked up the remains of her chemise. The strap was torn, and a froth of lace hung limp. Apparently, she decided, her merchandise didn't quite live up to Ry Piasecki's idea of wear and tear.

And wasn't it fabulous?

Laughing out loud, she tossed the chemise aside and followed her nose into the kitchen.

"I smell coffee," she began, then paused in the doorway.

He was breaking eggs into a bowl with those big, hard hands of his. His hair was damp, as hers was, because he'd beaten her to the shower. He was barefoot, jeans snug at his hips, flannel shirt rolled up to the elbows.

Incredibly, she wanted him all over again.

"You have next to nothing in this place to eat."

"I eat out a lot." With an order to control herself, she moved to the coffeepot. "What are you making?"

"Omelets. You had four eggs, some cheddar and some very limp broccoli."

"I was going to steam it." She cocked her head as she sampled the coffee. "So you cook."

"Every self-respecting fire fighter cooks. You take shifts at the station." He located a whisk, then turned to her. Wet hair, glowing face, sleepy eyes. "Hello, Legs. You look good."

"Thanks." She smiled over the rim of her cup. If he continued to look at her in just that way, she realized, she would drag him right down onto the floor. It might be wise, she decided, to tend to some practical matters. "Am I supposed to help?"

"Can you handle toast?"

"Barely." She set her cup aside and opened the cupboard. They worked in silence for a moment, he beating eggs, she popping bread in the toaster. "I..." She wasn't sure how to put it, delicately. "I suppose when you were fighting fires, you faced a lot of dangerous situations."

"Yeah. So?"

"The scars on your shoulder, your back." She'd discovered them in her explorations in the night, the raised welts and scarred ridges over that taut, really beautiful body. "Line of duty?"

"That's right." He glanced up. In truth, he didn't think about them. But it occurred to him in the harsh light of day that a woman like her might find them offensive. "Do they bother you?"

"No. I just wondered how you got burned."

He set the bowl aside and placed a pan on the stove to heat. Maybe they bothered her, he thought, maybe they didn't. But it seemed best to get the matter out of the way.

"Our friend Clarence. While I was pulling him out of the fire he started, the ceiling collapsed." Ry could remember it still, the rain of flame, the animal roar of it, the staggering nightmare of pain. "It fell down on us like judgment. He was screaming, laughing. I got him outside. I don't remember much after that, until I woke up in the burn ward."

"I'm sorry."

"It could have been a lot worse. My gear went a long way toward protecting me. I got off lucky." Deliberately focused, he poured the beaten eggs into the pan. "My father went down like that. Fire went into the walls. When they ventilated the ceiling, it went. It all went."

He cursed under his breath. Where the hell had that come from?

he wondered. He hadn't meant to say it. The death of his father certainly wasn't typical morning-after conversation.

"You should butter that toast before it gets cold."

She said nothing, could think of nothing, only went to him, wrapping her arms around his waist, pressing her cheek to his back.

"I didn't know you'd lost your father." There was so much, she thought, that she didn't know.

"Twelve years ago. It was in a high school. Some kid who wasn't happy with his chemistry grade torched the lab. It got away from him. Pop knew the risks," he muttered, uncomfortable with the sensation her quiet sympathy was stirring. "We all know them."

She held on. "I didn't mean to open old wounds, Ry."

"It's all right. He was a hell of a smoke eater."

Natalie stayed where she was another moment, baffled by what she was feeling. This need to comfort, to share, this terrible urge to be part of what he was. Cautious, she stepped back. It wouldn't do, she reminded herself. It wouldn't do at all to look for more between them than what there was.

"And this Clarence—how will you find him?"

"I could get lucky and track him down through contacts." With a quick, competent touch, Ry folded the egg mixture. "Or we'll pick him up when he scouts out his next target."

"My plant."

"Probably." More relaxed now that there was a little distance between them, he shot her a look over his shoulder. "Cheer up, Natalie. You've got the best in the city working to protect your nighties."

"You know very well it's not just—" She broke off when her doorbell rang. "Never mind."

"Hold on. Doesn't your doorman call up when someone's coming to see you?"

"Not if it's a neighbor."

"Use the judas hole," he ordered, and reached for plates.

"Yes, Daddy." Amused by him, Natalie went to the door. One look through the peephole had her stifling a shout and dragging back the locks. "Boyd, for heaven's sake!" She threw her arms around her brother. "Cilla!"

"The whole crew," Cilla warned her, laughing as they hugged. "The cop wouldn't let me call ahead and alert you to the invasion."

"I'm just so glad to see you." She bent down to hug her niece and nephews. "But what are you doing here?"

"Checking up on you." Boyd shifted the bag of take-out he carried to his other hip.

"You know the captain," Cilla said. "Bryant, touch nothing under penalty of death." She aimed a cautious look at her oldest son. At eight, he couldn't be trusted. "The minute Deborah called us about the second fire, he herded us up and moved us out. Allison, this isn't a basketball court. Why don't you put that down now?"

Territorial, Allison hugged the basketball to her chest. "I'm not going to throw it or anything."

"She's fine," Natalie assured Cilla, stroking a distracted hand down Allison's golden hair. "Boyd, I can't believe you'd drag everyone across the country for something like this."

"The kids have Monday off at school." Boyd crouched down to pick up the jacket their youngest had already tossed on the floor. "So we're taking a quick weekend, that's all."

"We're staying with Deborah and Gage," Cilla added. "So don't panic."

"It's not that..."

"And we brought supplies." Boyd held out the bag filled with take-out burgers and fries. "How about lunch?"

"Well, I..." She cleared her throat and looked toward the kitchen. How, she wondered, was she going to explain Ry?

Keenan, with the curiosity of an active five-year-old, had already discovered him. From the kitchen doorway, he grinned up at Ry. "Hi."

"Hi yourself." Curious to see just how Natalie handled things, Ry strolled out of the kitchen.

"Want to see what I can do?" Keenan asked him before anyone else could speak.

"Sure."

Always ready to show off a new skill, Keenan shinnied up Ry's leg, scooting up and around until he was riding piggy-back.

"Not bad." Ry gave the boy a little boost to settle him in place.

"That's Keenan," Cilla explained, running her tongue over her teeth as she considered. "Our youngest monkey."

"I'm sorry. Ah…" Natalie dragged a hand through her damp hair. She didn't have to look at Boyd to know he'd have that speculative big-brother look in his eyes. "Boyd and Cilla Fletcher, Ry Piasecki." She cleared her throat. "And this is Allison, and Bryant." Now she sighed. "You've already met Keenan."

"Piasecki," Boyd repeated. "Arson?" Just the man he wanted to see, Boyd thought. But he hadn't expected to find him barefoot in his sister's kitchen.

"That's right." Brother and sister shared strong good looks, Ry mused. And, he thought, an innate suspicion of strangers. "You're the cop from Denver."

Bryant piped up. "He's a police captain. He wears a gun to work. Can I have a drink, Aunt Nat?"

"Sure. I—" But Bryant was already darting into the kitchen. "Well, this is…" Awkward, she thought. "Maybe I should get some plates before the food gets cold."

"Good idea. All she has is eggs." Ry eyed the bag Boyd still carried, recognizing the package. "Maybe we can work a deal for some of your french fries."

"You're the one investigating the fires, right?" Boyd began.

"Slick," Cilla said, glaring at her husband. "No interrogations on an empty stomach. You can grill him after we eat. We've been on a plane for hours," she explained when Bryant came back in and tried to wrestle the ball away from Allison. "We're a little edgy."

"No problem." An instant before Boyd, Ry snatched the ball that squirted out of flailing hands. "Like to shoot hoop?" he asked Allison.

"Uh-huh." She gave him a quick, winning smile. "I made the team. Bryant didn't."

"Basketball's stupid." Sulking, Bryant slouched in a chair. "I'd rather play Nintendo."

Ry juggled Keenan on his back as he turned the ball in his hands. "It so happens I've got a game in a couple of hours. Maybe you'd like to come."

"Really?" Allison's eyes lit as she turned to Cilla. "Mom?"

"It sounds like fun." Intrigued, Cilla strolled toward the kitchen. "I'll just give Natalie a hand."

And, she thought, pump her sister-in-law for details.

# Chapter 7

The last place Natalie expected to spend her Saturday afternoon was courtside, watching cops and fire fighters play round ball. She sulked through most of the first quarter, her elbow on her knee, her chin on her fist.

After all, Ry hadn't mentioned the game to her, hadn't directly invited her. She was there to witness what was obviously an important annual rivalry only because of her niece.

Not that it mattered to her, she assured herself. Ry was certainly under no obligation to include her in his personal entertainment.

The pig.

Beside her, Allison was in basketball heaven, cheering on the red jerseys with a rabid fan's passionate enthusiasm. Her brandy-colored eyes glinted as she followed the action up and down the court of the old west-side gym.

"It's not such a bad way to spend the afternoon," Cilla commented over the shrill sound of the ref's whistle. "Watching a bunch of half-naked guys sweat." Her eyes, the same warm shade as her daughter's, danced. "By the way, your guy's very cute."

"I told you, he's not my guy. We're just..."

"Yeah, you told me." Chuckling, Cilla wrapped an arm around Natalie's shoulders. "Cheer up, Nat. If you'd gone along with Boyd and the boys to unload at Deborah's, your big bro would be grilling you right now.''

''You've got a point.'' She let out a sigh. Despite herself, she was following the action. The cops were double-teaming Ry consistently, she noted. Not a bad strategy, as he played like a steamroller, and had already scored seven points in the first quarter.

Not that she was counting.

''He didn't mention this game to me,'' she muttered.

''Oh?'' Fighting back a grin, Cilla ran her tongue over her teeth. ''He must have had something else on his mind. Hey!'' She surged to her feet, along with most of the crowd, as one of the blue jerseys rammed an elbow sharply in Ry's ribs. ''Foul!'' Cilla shouted between her cupped hands.

''He can take it,'' Natalie mumbled, and tried not to care as Ry approached the foul line. ''He's got an iron stomach.'' She struggled between pride and resentment when he sank his shot.

''Ry's the best.'' Allison beamed, well into a deep case of hero worship. ''Did you see how he moves up-court? And he's got a terrific vertical leap. He's already blocked three shots under the hoop.''

So, maybe he looked good, Natalie conceded. Those long, muscled legs pumping, those broad shoulders slick with sweat, all that wonderful hair flying as he pivoted or leapt. Then there was that look that came into his eyes, wolfish and arrogant.

So, maybe she wanted him to win. That didn't mean she was going to stand up and cheer.

By the third quarter, she was on her feet, like the rest of the crowd, when Ry sank a three-pointer that put the Smoke Eaters over the Bloodhounds by two.

''Nothing but net,'' she shouted, jostling Cilla. ''Did you see that?''

''He's got some great moves,'' Cilla agreed. ''Fast hands.''

''Yeah.'' Natalie felt the foolish grin spread over her face. ''Tell me about it.''

Heart thumping, she dropped back on the bench. She was leaning forward now, her gaze glued to the ball. The sound of running feet echoed as the men pounded up-court. The cops took a shot; the Smoke Eaters blocked it. The ensuing scuffle left two men on the ground, others snarling in each other's faces as the ref blew his whistle.

Now, Natalie thought grimly, they were playing dirty. With a grunt, she dipped her hand into the bag of salted nuts Cilla offered.

Fast break. Flying elbows, a tangle of bodies under the net as the ball shot up, careened, was pursued.

"Going to put out your fire, Piasecki," one of the cops taunted.

Natalie saw Ry flick the sweaty hair out of his eyes and grin. "Not with that equipment."

Trash talk. Natalie sneered at the cop as she chomped a peanut. No round ball game was complete without it. She hooted down the referee as he stepped between two over-enthusiastic competitors, barely preventing an informal boxing match.

"Boys, boys," Cilla said with a sigh. "They always take their games so seriously."

"Games are serious," Natalie muttered.

It was too close to call. Natalie continued to munch on peanuts as a sensible alternative to her fingernails. When a time-out was called, she glanced at the clock. There was less than six minutes to go, and the Bloodhounds were up, 108 to 105.

On the sidelines, the Smoke Eaters' coach was surrounded by his team. The lanky, silver-haired man was punching his fist into his palm to accentuate whatever instructions he was giving his men. Most were bent at the waist, hands on knees, as they caught their breath for the final battle. As they headed back onto the court, Ry turned. His gaze shot unerringly to Natalie. And he grinned. Quick, cocky, arrogant.

"Wow," Cilla murmured. "Now *that's* serious. Very powerful stuff."

"You're telling me." Natalie blew out a breath. When that did nothing to level her system, she used the excess energy to cheer on her team.

It was a fight to the finish, the lead tipping back to the Smoke

Eaters, then sliding away. As time dripped away, second by second, the crowd stayed on its feet, building a wall of sound.

With seconds to go, the Smoke Eaters a point behind, Natalie was chewing on her knuckles. Then she saw Ry make his move. "Oh, yes..." She whispered it first, almost like a prayer. Then she began to shout it as he burst through the line of defense, controlling the ball as if it were attached to the palm of his hand by an invisible string.

They blocked, he pivoted. He had one chance, and he was surrounded. Natalie's heart tripped as he feinted, faked, then sprang off the floor with a turnaround jump shot that found the sweet spot.

The crowd went wild. Natalie knew *she* did, spinning around to hug Allison, then Cilla. What was left of the peanuts flew through the air like rain. The instant the clock ran out, the stands emptied in a surge of bodies onto the court.

She caught a glimpse of Ry a moment before he was swallowed up. She sank back onto the bench with a hand over her heart.

"I'm exhausted." She laughed and rubbed her damp hands on the knees of her jeans. "I've got to sit."

"What a game!" Allison was bouncing up and down in her sneakers. "Wasn't he great? Did you see, Mom? He scored thirty-three points! Wasn't he great?"

"You bet."

"Can we tell him? Can we go down and tell him?"

Cilla studied the jostling crowd, then looked into her daughter's shining eyes. "Sure. Coming, Natalie?"

"I'll stay here. If you manage to get to him, tell him I'll hang around and wait."

"Okay. You'll bring him to dinner at Deb's tonight?"

Cautious, Natalie drummed her fingers on her knee. "I'll run it by him."

"Bring him," Cilla ordered, then leaned over and kissed Natalie's cheek. "See you later."

Gradually the gym emptied, the fans swarming out to celebrate, the players heading off to shower. Content, Natalie sat in the quiet.

It had been her first full day off in six months, and she'd decided it wasn't such a bad way to spend it after all.

And since Ry hadn't actually asked her to come, he was under no real obligation. Neither of them was. Sensibly, neither of them was looking for restrictions, for commitments, for romance. It was simply a primal urge on both parts, fiercely intense now, and very likely to fade.

It was fortunate that they both understood that, right from the beginning. There was some affection between them, naturally. And respect. But this wasn't a relationship, in the true sense of the word. Neither of them wanted that. It was simply an affair—enjoyable while it lasted, no harm done when it ended.

Then he walked out on court, his hair dark and damp from his shower. His gaze swept up and locked on hers.

Oh, boy, was all she could think while her heart turned a long, slow somersault. She was in trouble.

"Good game," she managed, and forced herself to stand and walk down to him.

"It had its moments." He cocked his head. "You know, it's the first time I've seen you dressed in anything but one of those high-class suits."

To cover the sudden rash of nerves, Natalie reached down and picked up one of the game balls. "Jeans and sweaters aren't usually office attire."

"They look good on you, Legs."

"Thanks." She turned the ball in her hand, studying it rather than him. "Allison had the time of her life. It was nice of you to invite her."

"She's a cute kid. They all are. She's got your mouth, you know. And the jawline. She's going to be a real heartbreaker."

"Right now she's more interested in scoring points on court than scoring them with boys." More relaxed, Natalie looked up again, smiling at him. "You scored a few yourself today, Inspector."

"Thirty-three," he said. "But who's counting?"

"Allison." And she had been, too. Carrying the ball, she wandered out on the court. "I take it this was your annual battle against the Bloodhounds."

"Yeah, we take them on once a year. The proceeds go to charity and all that. But mostly we come to beat the hell out of each other."

Head down, she bounced the ball once, caught it. "You never mentioned it. I mean, not until Allison showed up."

"No." He was watching her, intrigued. If he wasn't mistaken, there was a touch of annoyance in her voice. "I guess I didn't."

She turned her head. "Why didn't you?"

Definitely annoyed, he decided, and scratched his cheek. "I didn't figure it would be your kind of thing."

Now her chin angled. "Oh, really?"

"Hey, it's not the opera, or the ballet." He shrugged and tucked his thumbs in his front pockets. "Or a fancy French restaurant."

She let out a slow breath, drew another in. "Are you calling me a snob again?"

Careful, Piasecki, he warned himself. There was definitely a trap-door here somewhere. "Not exactly. Let's just say I couldn't see someone like you getting worked up over a basketball game."

"Someone like me," she repeated. Stung, she pivoted, planted her feet, and sent the ball sailing toward the hoop. It swished through, bounced on the court. When she looked back at Ry, she had the satisfaction of seeing his mouth hanging open. "Someone like me," she said again, and went to retrieve the ball. "Just what does that mean, Piasecki?"

He got his hands out of his pockets just in time to catch the ball she heaved at him before it thudded into his chest. He passed it back to her, hard, lifting a brow when she caught it.

"Do that again," he demanded.

"All right." Deliberately she stepped behind the three-point line, gauged her shot and let it rip. The whisper of the ball dropping through the hoop made her smile.

"Well, well, well..." This time Ry retrieved the ball himself. He was rapidly reassessing his opponent. "I'm impressed, Legs. Definitely impressed. How about a little one-on-one?"

"Fine." She crouched, circling him as he dribbled.

"You know, I can't—"

Quick as a snake, she darted in, snatched the ball. She executed a perfect lay-up, tapping the ball on the backboard and into the hoop. "I believe that's my point," she said, and passed the ball back to him.

"You're good."

"Oh, I'm better than good." Flicking her hair back, she moved in to block him. "I was all-state in college, pal. Team captain my junior and senior years. Where do you think Allison gets it?"

"Okay, Aunt Nat, let's play ball."

He pivoted away. She was on him like glue. Good moves, he noted. Smooth, aggressive. Maybe he held back. After all, he wasn't about to send a woman to the boards, no matter how much male ego was on the line.

She didn't have the same sensitivity, and turned into his block hard enough to take his breath away.

Frowning, he rubbed the point under his heart where her shoulder had rammed. Her eyes were glittering now, bold as the Emerald City.

"That's a foul."

She stole the ball, made the point with an impressive over-the-shoulder hook. "I don't see a ref."

She had the advantage, and they both knew it. Not only had he played full-out for an entire game, but she'd had that time to assess his technique, study his moves.

And she was better, he had to admit, a hell of a lot better, than half the cops who had gone up against him that afternoon.

And, worse, she knew it.

He scored off her, but it was no easy thing. She was sneaky, he discovered, using speed and grace and old-fashioned guts to make up for the difference in height.

They juggled the lead. She'd shoved the sleeves of her sweater up. She leapt with him, blocking his shot by a fingertip. And, having no compunctions about using whatever talent she had, let her body bump, linger, then slide against his.

His blood heated, as she'd meant it to. Panting, he picked up the ball and stared at her. Her lips were curved smugly, her face was flushed, her hair was tumbled. He realized he could eat her alive. .

He moved in quickly, startling her. She let out a squeal when he snatched her around the waist and hauled her over his shoulder. She was laughing when he sent the ball home with his free hand.

"Now that's definitely a foul."

"I don't see any ref." He shifted her, letting gravity take her down until they were face-to-face, her legs clamped at his waist. He reached out, gathered her hair in one hand and pulled her mouth to his.

Whatever breath she had left clogged. Opening to him, she dived into the greedy kiss and demanded more.

The blood drained so quickly, so completely, out of his head, he nearly staggered. With a sudden, voracious appetite, he tore his mouth from hers and devoured the flesh of her throat.

Smooth, salty, with the lingering undertone of that haunting scent she used. His mouth watered.

"There's a storeroom in the back that locks."

Her hands were already tugging at his shirt. Her breathing was ragged. "Then why are we out here?"

"Good question."

With her locked around him, her teeth doing incredible things to his ear, he pushed through the swinging doors and turned into a narrow corridor. Desperate for her, he fumbled at the knob of the storeroom door, swore, then shoved it open. When he slammed it and locked it at their backs, they were closed in a tiny room crammed with sports equipment and smelling of sweat.

Impatient, Natalie tugged at his hair, dragging his mouth back to hers. He nearly tripped over a medicine ball as he looked around frantically for something, anything, that could double as a bed.

He settled on a weight bench with Natalie on his lap.

"I feel like a damn teenager," he muttered, pulling at the snap of her jeans. Beneath the denim, her skin was hot, damp, trembling.

"Me too." Her heart was beating against her ribs like a hammer. "Oh God, I want you. Hurry."

Frantic hands tore at clothes, scattered them. There was no time, no need, for finesse. Only for heat. It was building inside her so fast, so hot, she felt she might implode and there would be nothing left of her but a shell.

His hands were at her throat, her breasts, her hips, thrilling her. Tormenting her. Nothing and no one mattered but him and this wild, incendiary fire they set together.

She wanted it hotter, higher, faster.

With a low, feline sound that shuddered through his blood, she straddled him. His heart seemed to stop in the instant she imprisoned him, as her body arched back, her eyes closing. She filled his vision, his mind, left him helpless. Then her eyes opened again and locked on his.

She began to move, fast and agile. Already it was flash point. He let the power take him, and her.

"I've never done anything like this before." Staggered and spent, Natalie struggled back into her clothes. "I mean *never.*"

"It wasn't exactly the way I'd planned it." Baffled, Ry dragged a hand through his hair.

"We're worse than a couple of kids." Natalie smoothed down her sweater, sighing lavishly. "It was fabulous."

His lips twitched. "Yeah." Then he sobered. "So are you."

She smiled and tried finger-combing her hair into place. "We'd better stop pushing our luck and get out of here. And I've got to get home and change." She discovered that one of her earrings had fallen out, and located it on the floor. "There's dinner at the Guthries' tonight."

He watched her fasten the earring, foolishly charmed by the simple female act. "I'll give you a lift home."

"I'd appreciate it." Feeling awkward, she turned to unlock the door. "You're welcome to come to dinner. I know Boyd wants a chance to talk with you. About the fires."

He closed a hand over hers on the knob. "How's the food?"

She smiled again, looking back at him. "Fabulous."

She was right about the food, Ry discovered. Rack of lamb, fresh asparagus, glossy candied yams, all accompanied by some golden

French wine.

He knew, of course, that Gage Guthrie was dripping with money. But nothing had prepared him for the Gothic mansion of a house, with its towers and turrets and terraces. The next thing to a castle, Ry had thought when he viewed it from the outside.

Inside, it was home, rich and elaborate, certainly, but warm. Deborah had given him a partial tour down winding corridors, up curving steps, before they all settled into the enormous dining room with its ox-roasting stone fireplace and winking crystal chandeliers.

It might, Ry thought, have had the flavor of a museum, if not for the people in it.

He'd clicked with Deborah instantly. He'd heard she was a tough and tenacious prosecutor. She had a softer, more vulnerable look than her sister, but she had a reputation for being formidable in court.

It was obvious her husband adored her. There were little signs— the quick, shared looks, the touch of a hand.

It was very much the same between Boyd and Cilla. Ry calculated that they'd been together for a decade or so, but the spark was still very much in evidence.

And the kids were great. He'd always had a soft spot for children. He recognized and was touched by Allison's preadolescent crush, and obliged her by going over the highlights of the game.

Since Cilla had wisely seen to it that her oldest son was across the table and two chairs down from his sister, Bryant was free to badger Deborah about how many bad guys she'd locked up since last he'd seen her.

And dinner was a relatively peaceful affair.

"Do you ride in a fire truck?" Keenan wanted to know.

"I used to," Ry told him.

"How come you stopped?"

"I told you," Bryant said, rolling his eyes with the disdain only a sibling knows and understands. "He goes after bad guys now, like Dad. Only just bad guys who burn things down. Don't you?"

"That's right."

"I'd rather ride in a fire truck." In a canny move to avoid the asparagus on his plate, Keenan slipped out of his chair and into Ry's lap.

"Keenan," Cilla said. "Ry's trying to eat."

"He's okay." Enjoying himself, Ry shifted the boy onto his knee. "Did you ever ride in one?"

"Nuh-uh." He smiled winningly, using his big, soft eyes. "Can I?"

"If your mom and dad say it's okay, you could come down to the station tomorrow. Take a look around."

"Cool." Bryant had immediately picked up on the invitation. "Can we, Dad?"

"I don't see why not."

"Aunt Nat knows where it is," Ry added as Keenan bounced gleefully on his knee. "Make it around ten, and I'll give you a tour."

"Pretty exciting stuff." Cilla rose. "And if we're going to pull it off, I'd say you three better get washed up and bedded down." The knee-jerk protest might have been stronger if not for the long day the children had put in. Cilla merely shook her head, looking at Boyd. "Slick?"

"Okay." He rose and tossed Bryant up and over his shoulder, turning whines into giggles. "Let's move out."

"I'll give you a hand." Natalie plucked Keenan from Ry's lap. "Say good-night, pal."

"Good night, pal," he echoed, and nuzzled into her neck. "You smell as good as Thea, Aunt Nat."

"Thanks, honey."

"Am I going to get a story?"

"Swindler," she laughed and carried him out.

"Nice family," Ry commented.

"We like them." Deborah smiled at him. "You've certainly given them something to look forward to tomorrow."

"No big deal. The guys love to show off for kids. Great meal."

"Frank's one in a million," she agreed. "A former pickpocket." She closed her hand over Gage's. "Who now uses those nimble fingers to create gastronomic miracles. Why don't we have coffee in the small salon? I'll go help Frank with it."

"This is some house," Ry said as he and Gage left the dining room and wound their way toward the salon. "Ever get lost?"

"I've got a good sense of direction."

There was a fire burning in the salon, and the lights were low and welcoming. Again Ry got the impression of home, settled, content.

"You used to be a cop, didn't you?"

Gage stretched out in a chair. "That's right. My partner and I were working on a sting that went wrong. All the way wrong." It still hurt, but the wounds were scarred over now. "He ended up dead, and I was the next thing to it. When I came out of it, I didn't want to pick up a badge again."

"Rough." Ry knew it was a great deal more than that. If he had the story right in his head, Gage had lingered in a coma for months before facing life again. "So you picked up the family business instead."

"So to speak. We have something in common there. You're running the family business, too."

Ry gave Gage a level look. "So to speak."

"I checked you out. Natalie's important to Deborah, and to me. I can tell you in advance, Boyd's going to ask if she's important to you." He glanced up as Boyd walked in. "That was fast."

"I saw my chance and went over the wall." He dropped into a chair, crossed his feet at the ankles. "So, Piasecki, what's going on between you and my sister?"

Ry decided he'd been polite long enough, and took out a cigarette. He lit it, flipped the match into a spotless crystal ashtray. "I'd say anybody who makes captain on the force should be able to figure that out for himself."

Gage smothered a laugh with a cough as Boyd's eyes narrowed. "Natalie's not a tossaway," Boyd said carefully.

"I know what she is," Ry returned. "And I know what she isn't. If you want to grill someone on what's going on between us, Captain, you'd better start with her."

Boyd considered, nodded. "Fair enough. Give me a rundown on the arson investigation."

That he could, and would, do. Ry related the sequence, the facts, his own steps and conclusions, answering Boyd's terse questions with equal brevity.

"I'm betting on Clarence," he finished. "I know his pattern, and how his warped mind works. And I'll get him," he said, and blew out a last stream of smoke. "That's a promise."

"In the meantime, Natalie needs to beef up security." Boyd's mouth thinned. "I'll see to that."

Ry tapped out his cigarette. "I already have."

"I was talking about personal security, not business."

"So was I. I'm not going to let anything happen to her," he continued as Boyd studied him. "That's another promise."

Boyd let out a snort. "Do you really think she'll listen to you?"

"Yeah. She's not going to get a choice."

Boyd paused, reevaluated. "Maybe I'm going to like you after all, Inspector."

"Okay, break it up," Deborah ordered as she wheeled in a cart laden with a huge silver coffee urn and Meissen china. "I know you're talking shop."

Gage rose to take the cart from her and kiss her. "You're just mad because you might have missed something."

"Exactly."

"Jacoby," Boyd tossed at her. "Clarence Robert. Ring any bells?"

Her brow furrowed as she poured coffee. "Jacoby. Also known as Jack Jacoby?" She served Boyd, took another cup to Ry. "Skipped bail a couple of years ago on an arson charge."

"I like your wife," Ry said to Gage. "There's nothing quite like a sharp mind in a first-class package."

"Thanks." Gage poured a cup for himself. "I often think the same."

"Jacoby," Deborah repeated, focusing on Ry. "You think he's the one?"

"That's right."

"We'd have a file on him." She glanced at her husband. The computers in Gage's hidden room could access everything about Jacoby, right down to his shoe size. "I'm not sure who had the case, but I can find out on Monday, see that you get whatever we have."

"I'd appreciate it."

"How'd he manage bail?" Boyd wanted to know.

"I can't tell you until I see the file," Deborah began.

"I can tell you about him." Ry drank his coffee, keeping one ear out for Natalie's return. He wasn't sure she'd appreciate having her business discussed while she was out of the room. "His pattern's empty buildings, warehouses, condemned apartments. Sometimes the owners hire him for the insurance, sometimes he does it for kicks. We only tried him twice, convicted him once. There wasn't any loss of life either time. Clarence doesn't burn people, just things."

"So now he's loose," Boyd said in disgust.

"For the time being," Ry returned. "We're ready for him." He picked up his cup again when he heard Natalie and Cilla laughing in the hallway.

"You're a softie, Nat."

"It's my duty, and my privilege, to spoil them."

They entered together. Cilla immediately headed for Boyd and dropped into his lap. "They had her jumping through hoops."

"They did not." Natalie poured her coffee, then laughed again. "Not exactly." She smiled at Ry before settling beside him. "So," she began, "have you finished discussing my personal and business life?"

"A sharp mind," Ry commented. "In a first-class package."

Later, as they drove away from the Guthrie mansion, Natalie studied Ry's profile. "Should I apologize for Boyd?"

"He didn't pull out the rubber hoses." Ry shrugged. "He's okay. I've got a couple of sisters, I know how it is."

"Oh." Frowning, she looked out the window. "I didn't realize you had siblings."

"I'm Polish and Irish, and you figured me for an only child?" He grinned at her. "Two older sisters, one in Columbus, the other down in Baltimore. And a brother, a year younger than me, living in Phoenix."

"Four of you," she murmured.

"Until you count the nieces and nephews. There were eight of them, last time I checked, and my brother has another on the way."

Which probably explained why he was so easy around children. "You're the only one who stayed in Urbana."

"Yeah, they all wanted out. I didn't." He turned down her street, slowed. "Am I staying tonight, Natalie?" ·

She looked at him again. How could he be so much of a stranger, she wondered, and so much of a need? "I want you to," she said. "I want you."

# Chapter 8

"Can I slide down the pole, Mr. Pisessy? Please, can I slide down it?"

Ry grinned at the way Keenan massacred his name and flipped the brim of the boy's baseball cap to the back of his curly head. "Ry."

"'Cause," Keenan said, big eyes sober and hopeful. "I never, ever did it before."

"No, not why, Ry. You call me Ry. And sure you can slide down it. Hold it." Laughing, he caught Keenan at the waist before the boy could make the leap from floor to pole. "No flies on you, huh?"

Keenan looked around, grinned. "Nuh-uh."

"Let's do it this way." With Keenan firmly at his hip, Ry reached out to grip the pole. "Ready?"

"Let's go!"

In a smooth, practiced move, Ry stepped into air. Keenan laughed all the way down.

"Again!" Keenan squealed. "Let's do it again!"

"Your brother wants a turn." Ry looked up, saw Bryant's anxious, eager face in the opening. "Come on, Bryant, go for it."

"Definitely daddy material," Cilla murmured, watching her son zip down the pole.

"Shut up, Cilla." Natalie slipped her hands into the pockets of her blazer. She was itching to try the ride herself.

"Just an observation. Attagirl, Allison," she added, cheering her daughter on when Allison dropped lightly to the floor. "He's giving the kids the time of their lives here."

"I know. It's very sweet of him." She smiled as Ry obliged Keenan with another trip down the pole. "I didn't know he could be sweet."

"Ah, hidden qualities." Cilla glanced over to where Boyd was holding a conversation with two uniformed fire fighters. "Often the most attractive kind in a man. Especially when he's crazy about you."

"He's not." It amazed Natalie to feel heat rising to her cheeks. "We're just...enjoying each other."

"Yeah, sure." With a mother's honed reflexes, Cilla crouched and caught her youngest as he flew at her.

"Look, Mom. It's a real, actual fireman's hat." The helmet Ry had given Keenan to wear slipped down over the boy's face. Inside, it smelled mysteriously, fascinatingly, of smoke. "And Ry says we can go sit in the fire engine now." After wriggling down and dancing in place, he shouted at his brother and sister. "Let's go!"

Accompanied by two fire fighters, the children dashed off to check out the engine. With a signal to Cilla to wait, Boyd disappeared up the steps with Ry.

"Well." Cilla sniffed and shrugged. "The womenfolk have been dismissed. They'll go upstairs to grunt significantly over official business."

"I wish Boyd wouldn't worry so much. There's really nothing he can do."

"Older siblings are programmed to worry." Cilla slung an arm around Natalie's shoulder. "But, if it helps, he's feeling a lot less worried since he's met Ry."

"That's something, I suppose." Relaxed again, she walked with Cilla toward the back of the engine. "So, how's Althea doing?" Around the front, the children were barraging the fire fighters with questions. "The last time I talked to her, she claimed she was as big as two houses and miserably bored with desk duty."

"She's the sexiest expectant mother I've ever seen. Since Colt and

Boyd ganged up on her, she's at home on full maternity leave. I dropped over to see her one day a couple of weeks ago and caught her knitting.''

"Knitting?'' Natalie let out a full-throated laugh. "Althea?''

"Funny what marriage and family can do to you.''

"Yeah.'' Natalie's smile faded a bit. "I suppose that's true.''

Upstairs, Boyd was frowning over Ry's reports. "Why upstairs, in the office?'' he asked. "Why didn't he start the fire in the showroom? It seems to me there would have been more damage more quickly.''

"The showroom window could have put him off. I figure the storeroom would have made more sense if he was just looking to burn the place down. It's private, full of stock and boxes.'' Ry set aside his coffee. He really had to start cutting down. "I figure he was following instructions. Clarence is real good at following instructions.''

"Whose?''

"That's the ticket.'' Ry kicked back in his chair and propped his feet on his desk. "I've got two incendiary fires that are obviously related. The target in both cases is a single business, and both, I believe, were started by a single perpetrator.''

"So he's on somebody's payroll.'' Boyd set the reports aside. "A competitor?''

"We're checking it out.''

"But it's unlikely a competitor would be able to give your pal Clarence access to either building. You didn't find any sign of forced entry.''

"That's right.'' Ry lit a cigarette. A man couldn't cut down on two vices at once. "Which leads us to Natalie's organization.''

Boyd got up to pace. "I can't claim to know her staff, certainly not in this new project of hers. I don't deal with the business end of Fletcher unless I'm backed into a corner.'' He regretted that now, only because he would have been more help if he'd been familiar with her procedures and personnel. "But I can get a lot of information from my parents, particularly on her top people.''

"It couldn't hurt. The fact that there was only cosmetic damage at the last fire leads to the conclusion that there'll be another. If Clarence follows his pattern, he'll hit her again within the next ten days.'' He tossed papers aside. ''We'll be waiting for him.''

Boyd looked back and measured the man. Tough, smart. But, as he knew from personal experience, the job could get sticky when a man found himself involved with a target.

''And while you're waiting for him, you'll keep Natalie out of it.''

''That's the idea.''

''And while you're doing that, you're going to be able to separate the woman you're involved with from the case you're trying to close.''

Ry lifted a brow. That was going to be a challenge, and the difficulty of meeting that challenge had crossed his mind more than once. The trouble was, he wasn't willing to give up either the woman or the case.

''I know what needs to be done, Captain.''

With a nod, Boyd placed his palms on the desk and leaned forward. ''I'm trusting you with her, Piasecki, on every level. If she gets hurt—on any level—I'm coming after you.''

''Fair enough.''

An hour later, Natalie stood on the curb outside the station, waving goodbye. ''You were a big hit, Inspector.''

''Hey, a shiny red fire truck, a long brass pole—how could I miss?''

Laughing, she turned to link her arms around his neck. ''Thanks.'' She kissed him lightly.

''For?''

''For being so nice to my family.''

''It wasn't a hardship. I like kids.''

''It shows. And—'' she kissed him again ''—that's for putting Boyd's mind at ease.''

''I don't know if I'd go quite that far. He's still thinking about punching me out if I make the wrong move with his baby sister.''

''Well, then...'' Her eyes danced up at his. ''You'd better be careful, because my big brother is plenty tough.''

"You don't have to draw me a picture." He swung her toward the doors. "Come on back up with me. I need to get a couple of things."

"All right." They'd barely started up the stairs when the bells sounded. "Oh." The sound of clattering feet echoed below them. "I'm sorry the kids missed this." Then she stopped, wincing. "That's terrible, acting like a fire's a form of entertainment."

"It's a natural reaction. Bells, whistles, men in funny uniforms. It's a hell of a show."

They crossed over to his office. She waited while he sorted through papers. "Do you ever get cats out of trees?"

"Yep. And kids' heads out of the pickets on railings. I got someone's pet iguana out of a sewer pipe once."

"You're joking."

"Hey, we don't joke about rescue."

He looked up and grinned. She looked so tidy, he thought, in her navy blazer and slacks, with the cashmere sweater, red as one of his engines, softly draped at the neck. Her hair was loose, honey gold. When she tucked it behind her ear in that fluid, unconscious movement, he could see the wink of rich blue stones. Sapphires, he assumed. Only the genuine article would suit Natalie Fletcher.

"What is it?" A little self-conscious under his stare, she shifted. "Did Keenan leave something edible smeared on my face?"

"No. You look good, Legs. Want to go somewhere?"

"Go somewhere?" The idea put her off balance. Apart from the challenge of that first meal, they hadn't actually *gone* anywhere.

"Like a movie. Or..." He supposed he could handle it. "A museum or something."

"I... Yes, that'd be nice." It shouldn't be so awkward, she thought, to plan a simple date with someone you'd been sleeping with.

"Which?"

"Either."

"Okay." He stuffed some papers in a battered briefcase. "The guys should have a newspaper downstairs. We'll check it out."

"Fine." When they started out, Natalie glanced first toward the stairs and then back toward the poles. She took a deep breath and gave up. "Ry?"

"Yeah."

"Can I slide down the pole?"

He stopped dead and stared down at her. "You want to slide down the pole?"

Amused at herself, Natalie shrugged her shoulders. "Ry, I've *got* to slide down the pole. It's driving me crazy."

"No kidding?" His grin broke out as he put a hand on her shoulder and turned her around. "Okay, Aunt Nat. I'll go down first, in case you lose your nerve."

"I'm not going to lose my nerve," she said huffily. "I'll have you know I've been rock-climbing dozens of times."

"There's that height thing again. You get a good grip," he continued, demonstrating. "Swing yourself forward. You can wrap your legs around it as you go down."

He flowed down, smooth and fast. Frowning, she leaned over, peering at him through the opening.

"You didn't wrap your legs around it."

"I don't have to," he said dryly. "I'm a professional. Come on, and don't worry—I'll catch you."

"I don't need you to catch me." Insulted, she tossed back her hair. She reached out, took a good grip on the brass pole, then swung agilely into space.

It took a matter of seconds. Her heart had barely had time to settle before her feet hit the floor. Laughing, she looked longingly up again. "See? I didn't need—" Her boast ended on a squeal of surprise as he scooped her up into his arms. "What?"

"You're a natural." He was grinning as he lowered his mouth to hers. And a constant surprise to him, he thought.

She angled her head, settling her arms comfortably around his neck. "I could do it again."

"If you'd do it in red suspenders, a pair of those really little shorts and let me take a picture, the guys would be very grateful."

She lifted a brow. "I think I'll just make a cash donation to the department."

"It's not the same."

"Inspector?" The dispatcher poked his head out of a doorway. His smile spread slowly at the sight of the woman bundled in Ry's arms. "Suspicious fire over at 12 East Newberry. They want you."

"Tell them I'm on my way." He set Natalie back on her feet. "Sorry."

"It's all right. I know how it is." Her disappointment was completely out of proportion, she lectured herself. "I've got some work I should be catching up on, anyway. I'll grab a cab."

"I'll take you home," Ry told her. "On my way." He steered her toward the bench where she'd left her coat. "Are you just going to be hanging around at the apartment?"

"Yes. There are some spreadsheets I should have looked at yesterday."

"So I'll call you."

As Ry helped her on with her coat, she glanced over her shoulder. "All right."

He turned her completely around and indulged himself with one long, hard kiss. "Tell you what, I'll just come by when I'm done."

Natalie worked on getting her breath back. "Better," she managed. "That's even better."

By the middle of the week, Natalie had discovered that for the first time in memory she was behind on her own personal schedule. Not only had she blown the previous weekend, but she hadn't put in a decent night's work all week.

How could she, when she and Ry were spending every free moment together? Every evening they settled into her apartment, ordered dinner—which more often than not had to be reheated after they'd feasted on each other.

She didn't think of work from the time he arrived on her doorstep until she rushed into her office the next morning.

She didn't think of anything but him.

Besotted was what she was, Natalie admitted as she stared out her office window. Fascinated by the man, and by what happened every time they got within arm's reach of each other.

It was crazy, of course. She knew it. But it was so wonderful at the moment, it didn't seem to matter.

And she could justify it, since she hadn't yet missed any meetings or business deadlines. Now that Ry had given her the go-ahead, she'd authorized the cleanup and redecorating at the flagship store. The stock there was nearly all in place, and the window-dressing was complete.

It was only a matter of days before the grand opening, nationwide, and there'd been no more incidents. That was how she liked to think of the fires now. As incidents.

She should, of course, be making plans to visit all the branches within the next ten days. But the thought of traveling just then seemed so annoying, so depressing. So lonely.

She could delegate Melvin or Donald to make the tour. It wouldn't even be outside of proper business procedure to do so. But it wasn't her style to delegate what should be done by her.

Maybe, if things got settled somehow, Ry could get a few days off, go with her. It would be wonderful to have company—his company—on a quick business trip. She could put it off until after the grand opening, instead of before, and then—

Turning away from the window, she answered the buzzer on her desk. "Yes, Maureen."

"Ms. Marks to see you, Ms. Fletcher."

"Thanks. Send her in." With an effort, Natalie shifted her personal thoughts to the back of her mind and welcomed her accounting executive. "Deirdre, have a seat."

"I'm sorry I'm so behind." Deirdre blew her choppy bangs out of her eyes before she dropped a thick stack of files on Natalie's desk. "Every time we turn around, the system's down."

Natalie frowned as she picked up the first file. "Have you called in the engineer?"

"He's practically living in my lap." Deirdre plopped into a chair and set one practical flat-heeled shoe on her knee. "He fixes it, we forge ahead, and it goes down again. Believe me, running figures has become a challenge."

"We've still got some time before the end of the quarter. I'll call .

the computer people myself this afternoon. If their equipment's unstable, they'll have to replace it. Immediately.''

"Good luck," Deirdre said dryly. "The good news is, I was able to run a chart on the early catalog sales. I think you'll be pleased with the results.''

"Mmm, hmm…" Natalie was already flipping through the files. "Fortunately, the fires didn't destroy records. You'd have a real accounting nightmare on your hands if it had gotten to the files at the flagship.''

"You're telling me." Deirdre rubbed her fingers over her eyes. "The way the system's been hiccuping, I'd sweat bullets without those hard copies.''

"Well, relax. I've got copies of the copies, as well as the backup disks, tucked away. I was hoping to run a full audit by the middle of March." She saw the wince before Deirdre could mask it. "But," she added, leaning back, "if we keep running into these glitches, we'll have to put it off until after the tax-season rush.''

"My life for you." Solemnly, Deirdre thumped a fist on her breast. "Now to the nitty-gritty. Your outlay is still within the projected parameters. Barely. With the insurance payments, we'll offset some of that.''

Natalie nodded, and made herself focus on budgets and percentages.

A few hours later, in a seedy downtown motel, Clarence Jacoby sat on his sagging bed, lighting matches. His hands were pudgy, smooth as a girl's. Each time he would strike the match and watch the magic flare, waiting, waiting until the heat just kissed the tips of his fingers, before blowing it out.

The ashtray beside him was overflowing with the matches that had already flared and burned. Clarence could entertain himself for hours with nothing more.

He thought nearly every night about burning down the hotel. It would be exciting to start the blaze right in his own room, watch it grow and spread. But he wouldn't be alone, and that stopped him.

Clarence didn't care overmuch about people, or the risk to their lives. He simply preferred to be alone with his fires.

He'd learned not to stay overlong after he'd ignited them. The rippling scars over his neck and chest were daily reminders of how quickly, how fiercely, the dragon could turn, even on one who loved it.

So he contented himself with merely conceiving the fire, basking for a regrettably short time in its heat, before fleeing.

Six months before, in Detroit, he'd torched an abandoned warehouse that the owner had no longer needed or wanted. It was the kind of favor, a profitable one on all sides, that Clarence enjoyed. He had stayed to watch that fire burn. Oh, he'd been out of the building and deep in the shadows. But they'd nearly caught him. Those cops and arson people scanned the crowds at the scene just for a face like his.

A worshipful face. A happy face.

With a giggle, Clarence struck another match. But he'd gotten away. And he'd learned another lesson. It wasn't smart to stay and watch. He didn't need to stay and watch. There were so many fires, so many fierce and beautiful blazes living in his mind and heart, he didn't need to stay.

He had only to close his eyes and see them. Feel them. Smell them.

He was humming to himself when the phone rang. His round, childlike face beamed happily when he heard the sound. Only one person had his number here. And that person would have only one reason to call.

It was time, he knew, to free the dragon again.


At his desk, Ry pored over lab reports. It was nearly seven, and already dark outside. He'd given up on cutting down on coffee, and drank it hot and black from a chipped mug.

He needed to quit for the day. He recognized the slow process of shutting down in his mind and body. Somehow or other, in the past couple of weeks, he'd gotten into a routine he was now beginning to depend on.

No, not somehow or other, Ry reminded himself, scrubbing his hands over his face. Someone.

He was getting much too used to knocking off for the day and heading for her apartment. He even had a key to her front door in his pocket now. Something that had been given and taken without ceremony. As if neither of them wanted to acknowledge what that simple piece of metal stood for.

They'd have a meal, he thought. They'd talk, maybe watch one of the old movies on television—something they'd discovered by accident they both loved.

Most of what they'd discovered about each other, he mused, had been by accident. Or by observation.

He knew she liked long bubble baths in the evening, with the water too hot and a glass of chilled wine sitting on the rim of the tub. She stepped out of those ankle-breakers she wore the minute she walked in the door. And she put everything away in its place.

She slept in silk and hogged the blankets. Her alarm went off at seven on the dot every morning, and if he wasn't quick enough to delay her, she was out of the bed seconds later.

She had a weakness for strawberry ice cream and big-band music.

She was loyal and smart and strong.

And he was in love with her.

Sitting back, Ry rested his eyes. A problem, he thought. His problem. They'd had an unspoken agreement going in, and he knew it. No ties, no tangles.

He didn't want them.

God knew he couldn't afford them with her.

They were opposites on every level but one. The physical needs that had brought them together, no matter how intense, couldn't override everything else. Not in the long term.

So there couldn't be a long term.

He would do what was smart, what was right, and see her through the arson investigation. And that would be that. Would have to be that.

And to save them both an unpleasant scene, he'd start backing away a little. Starting now.

He rose and grabbed his jacket. He wouldn't go to her place to-night. He looked guiltily at the phone, thinking of calling her, making some excuse.

With an oath, he turned out the lights. He wasn't her damn husband, he reminded himself.

He never would be.


Compelled by a nagging sense of unrest, like an itch between his shoulder blades, Ry drove out to Natalie's plant. He'd done a great deal of driving around since he left the station.

It was after ten o'clock now, moonless, windless.

He sat in his car, slumped behind the wheel, and tried not to think of her.

Of course, he thought of her.

She was probably wondering where he was, he figured. She'd assume he'd gotten a call. She'd wait up. Guilt worked at him again. It was his least favorite emotion. It wasn't right to be inconsiderate, to worry her just because he'd had a scare.

And maybe he wasn't in love with her. Maybe he was just hung up. A man could get hung up on a woman without wanting to slit his throat when she walked away. Couldn't he?

Disgusted, Ry reached for his car phone. The least he could do was call and tell her he was busy. It wasn't like checking in, he assured himself. It was just being polite.

And since when had he worried about manners?

Cursing, he began to dial.

But the itch came back. Slowly, his eyes scanning the dark, he replaced the phone. Had he heard something? A check of his watch told him the patrol he'd assigned would make their run by in another ten minutes.

No harm, he decided, in taking a look around himself on foot in the meantime.

He eased his door open and slipped out. He could hear nothing now but the faint swish of traffic two blocks away. Cautious, he reached back in the car for his flashlight, but he didn't turn it on.

Not yet, he thought. His eyes were accustomed enough to the dark for him to see where he was going.

Instinct had him heading silently around the back.

He'd already cased the plant himself, noting where the exits were located, the security, the fire doors. He'd make a circle, check each door and window on the main level himself.

He heard it again, the scrape of a foot over gravel. Ry shifted the flashlight in his hand, holding it like a weapon now as he moved closer. Tensed, ready, he slipped through the shadows. If it was the security guard, Ry knew, he was about to give the man the fright of his life. Otherwise…

A giggle. Faint and delighted. The slow, moaning whine of a metal door moving on its hinges.

Ry flashed on his light, and spotlighted Clarence Jacoby.

"How's it going, Clarence?" Ry grinned as the man blinked against the glare. "I've been waiting for you."

"Who's that?" Clarence's voice raced up a register. "Who's that?"

"Hey, I'm hurt." Ry lowered the light out of Clarence's eyes and stepped closer. "Don't you recognize your old pal?"

Squinting, Clarence separated the man from the shadows. In a moment, his baffled face exploded in a wide grin. "Piasecki. Hey, Ry Piasecki. How's it going? You're Inspector now, right? I hear you're an inspector now."

"That's right. I've been looking for you, Clarence."

"Oh, yeah?" Shyly, Clarence dipped his head. "How come?"

"I put out that little campfire you started the other night. You must be losing your touch, Clarence."

"Oh, hey…" Still grinning, Clarence spread his arms out. "I don't know nothing about that. You remember when we got burned, Piasecki? Hell of a night, wasn't it? That dragon was really big. Almost ate us up."

"I remember."

Clarence moistened his lips. "Scared you bad, too. I heard the nurses talking in the burn ward about the nightmares."

"I had a few of them."

"And you don't fight fire no more, do you? Don't want to slay the dragon now, do you?"

"I like squashing little bugs like you better." Ry swung his light down, shone it on the gas cans at Clarence's feet. "What do you know, Clarence? You still use premium grade, too."

"I didn't do nothing." Clarence whirled to make a dash into the dark. Even as Ry leapt forward, the man jerked back, as if on a string.

Staggered, Ry stared at the dark-clad arms that seemed to shoot straight out from the building's wall and wrap around Clarence's neck.

Then it was a shadow flowing out of nothing. Then it was a man flowing out of the shadow.

"I don't believe the inspector was finished talking to you, Clarence." Nemesis kept one arm hooked around Clarence's neck as he faced Ry. "Were you, Inspector?"

"No, I wasn't." Ry let out a long breath. "Thanks."

"My pleasure."

"It's a ghost. A ghost's got me." Clarence's eyes turned up, white, and he fainted dead away.

"I imagine you could have handled him on your own." Nemesis passed the limp body to Ry, waiting until Ry had hefted Clarence over his shoulder.

"I appreciate it, anyway."

There was a quick flash of teeth as Nemesis smiled. "I like your style, Inspector."

"Same goes. You want to explain that little trick when you came out of the wall?" Ry began, but he was talking to air before the sentence was finished. "Not bad," he muttered, and was shaking his head as he carted Clarence to the car. "Not bad at all."

The phone awakened Natalie from where she'd dozed off on the couch. Groggy, she stumbled toward it, trying to read the time on her watch.

"Yes, hello?"

"It's Ry."

"Oh." She rubbed the sleep from her eyes. "It's after one. I was—"

"Sorry to wake you."

"No, it's not that. I just—"

"We've got him."

"What?" Her irritation that he had yet to let her finish a sentence sharpened the word.

"Clarence. I picked him up tonight. I thought you'd want to know."

Now her head was reeling. "Yes, of course. That's wonderful. But when—?"

"I'm tied up here, Natalie. I'll get back to you when I can."

"All right, but—" She took the receiver away from her ear and glared at the dial tone. "Congratulations, Inspector," she muttered, and hung up.

With her hands on her hips, she took several deep breaths to calm herself, and to clear her head.

She'd been worried sick. Her own fault, she admitted. Ry was certainly under no obligation to come to her after work, or to call. Even if he had been doing just that for days. And even if she had waited by the phone for hours until simple fatigue spared her the continued humiliation.

Put that aside, she ordered herself. The important matter here was that Clarence Jacoby was in custody. There would be no more fires— no more incidents.

And in the morning, she promised herself as she stomped bad-temperedly off to the bedroom, she'd track Ry down and get the whole story.

In the meantime, she thought as she slipped out of her robe, all she had to do was teach herself to sleep alone again.

Even as she settled onto the pillow, she knew it was going to be a very long night.

# Chapter 9

Since there seemed little point in going home after he'd finished at the police station, Ry dropped down on the sagging sofa in his office and caught three hours' sleep before the sirens awakened him.

Following old habit, his feet hit the floor before he remembered he didn't have to answer the bell any longer. Years of training would have allowed him to simply roll over and go back to sleep. Instead, he staggered, bleary-eyed, toward the coffeepot, measuring, flipping switches. His only goal at the moment was to take a giant mug of coffee to the showers with him, and to stay there for an hour.

He lit a cigarette, scowling at the pot as it filled, drop by stingy drop.

The brisk knock on his door only made his scowl deepen. Turning, he aimed his bad temper at Natalie.

"Your secretary isn't in."

"Too early," he mumbled, and rubbed a hand over his face. Why in hell did she always have to look so perfect? "Go away, Natalie. I'm not awake yet."

"I won't go away." Struggling not to be hurt, she set her briefcase down, put her hands on her hips. Obviously, she told herself, he'd had little or no sleep. She'd be patient. "Ry, I need to know what happened last night, so I can plan what steps need to be taken."

"I told you what happened."

"You weren't very generous with details."

Muttering, he snatched up a mug and poured the miserly half cup that had brewed. "We got your torch. He's in custody. He won't be lighting any fires for a while."

Patience, Natalie reminded herself and took a seat. "Clarence Jacoby?"

"Yeah." He looked at her. What choice did he have? She was there, stunning and polished and perfect. "Why don't you go to work, let me pull it together here? I'll have a report for you."

Nerves jittered up her spine, and down again. "Is something wrong?"

"I'm tired," he snapped. "I can't get a decent cup of coffee, and I need a shower. And I want you to stop breathing down my neck."

Surprise registered first, then retreated behind hurt. "I'm sorry," she said, voice cool and stiff, as she rose. "I was concerned about what happened last night. And I wanted to make sure you were all right. Since I can see that you are fine…" She picked up her briefcase. "And since you haven't had time to put your report together, I'll get out of your way."

He swore, dragging a hand through his hair. "Natalie, sit down. Please," he added, when she just stood aloofly in the doorway. "I'm sorry. I'm feeling a little raw this morning, and you made the mistake of being the first person in the line of fire."

"I was worried about you." She said it quietly, but didn't step back into the room.

"I'm fine." Turning away, he topped off his coffee. "Want some of this?"

"No. I should have waited for you to contact me. I realize that." It was, she thought, like suddenly walking on eggshells. One night apart shouldn't make them so awkward with each other.

"If you had, I'd have been worried about you." He managed a smile. It was low, he decided, real low, to lash out at her because all at once he was deathly afraid of where they were heading. "Sit down. I'll give you the highlights."

"All right."

While she did, he walked around his desk and kicked back in his chair. "I had an itch, a hunch. Whatever. I decided to take a run by your plant—take a look around, check the security myself." He blew out a stream of smoke, smiled through it. "Somebody else had the same idea."

"Clarence."

"Yeah, he was there. It was a real party. He'd knocked out the alarm. Had himself a full set of keys to the rear door."

"Keys." Eyes sharpening, Natalie leaned forward.

"That's right. Shiny new copies. The cops have them now. There wouldn't have been any sign of break-in. He also had a couple of gallons of high-test gas, a few dozen matchbooks. So we started to have a little conversation. I guess Clarence didn't like the way it was going, and he made a break for it."

Ry paused, drawing in smoke, shaking his head. "I've never seen anything like it," he murmured. "I'm still not sure I *did* see it."

"What?" Impatient, Natalie rapped a hand on his desk. "Did you chase him?"

"Didn't have to. Your pal took care of it."

"My pal?" Baffled she sat back again. "What pal?"

"Nemesis."

Her eyes went wide and stunned. "You saw him? He was there?"

"Yes and no. Or no and yes. I'm not sure which. He came out of the wall," Ry said, half to himself. "He came out of the damn wall, like smoke. He wasn't there, then he was. Then he wasn't."

Natalie cocked a brow. "Ry, I really think you need some sleep."

"No question about that." Rubbing the back of his stiff neck, he blew out a breath. "But that's how it went. He came out of the wall. First his arms. I was standing a foot away, and I saw arms come out of the wall and grab Clarence. Then he was just there—Nemesis. Clarence took one look at him and fainted." Enjoying the memory, Ry grinned. "Folded up like a deck chair. So Nemesis hands him over to me and I haul him over my shoulder. Then he's gone."

"Clarence?"

"Nemesis. Keep up."

She blinked, trying to. "He—Nemesis—just left?"

"He just went. Back into the wall, into the air." He flicked his fingers to demonstrate. "I don't know. I probably stood there for five minutes with my mouth hanging open before I carried Clarence to the truck."

Brow knit, Natalie spoke slowly, carefully. "You're telling me the man disappeared. In front of your eyes. Just vanished?"

"That's exactly what I'm telling you."

"Ry," she said, still patient. "That's not possible."

"I was there," he reminded her. "You weren't. Clarence came to and started babbling about ghosts. He was so spooked he tried to jump out of the car while I was driving." Ry sipped at his coffee. "I had to knock him out."

"You...you knocked him out."

It was another memory he couldn't help but relish. One short punch to that moon-shaped jaw. "He was better off. Anyway, he's in custody now. He's not talking, but I'm going to interview him in a couple hours and see if we can change that."

She sat silently for a moment, trying to absorb it all, and sort it out. The business with Nemesis was fascinating, and not so difficult to explain. It had been dark. Ry was a trained observer, but even he could make a mistake in the dark. People didn't just vanish.

Rather than argue with him about it, she focused on Clarence Jacoby. "He hasn't said why, then? If he was hired, or by whom?"

"Right now he's claiming he was just out for a walk."

"With several gallons of gasoline?"

"Oh, he says I must have brought the gas with me. I'm framing him because I got burned saving his worthless life."

Insulted, Natalie lunged to her feet. "No one believes that."

Her instant defense amused and touched him. "No, Legs, nobody's buying it. We've got him cold on this one, and it shouldn't take long for the cops to tie him in with the other fires. Once Clarence realizes he's looking at a long stretch, he's likely to sing a different tune. Nobody likes to go down alone."

Natalie nodded. She didn't believe in honor among thieves. "If and when he does name someone, I'll need to know right away. I'm limited as to the steps I can take in the meantime."

Ry rapped his fingers on the desk. He didn't like the possibility that someone in her organization, someone who might be close to her, could be behind the fires. "If Clarence points the finger at one of your people, the cops take the steps. And they're going to be a lot tougher on them than just firing them or taking away their dental plan."

"I'm aware of that. I'm also aware that even though the man who held the match had been caught and my property is safe, it's not over." But the tension that had knotted her shoulders was smoothing away. "I appreciate you looking out for what's mine, Inspector."

"That's what your tax dollars are for." He studied her over the rim of his cup. "I missed being with you last night," he said, before he could stop himself.

Her lips curved slowly. "Good. Because I missed being with you. We could make up for it tonight. Celebrate seeing my tax dollars at work."

"Yeah." If he was sinking, Ry thought, he just didn't have the energy to fight going under for the third time. "Why don't we do that?"

"I'll let you get that shower." She bent down for her briefcase. "Will you let me know what happens when you talk to Clarence?"

"Sure. I'll be in touch."

"I'm going to plan on getting home early," she said as she headed for the door.

"Good plan," he murmured when the door shut behind her. Third time, hell, he thought. He'd drowned days ago, and hadn't even noticed.

Natalie arrived at work with a spring in her step, and called a staff meeting. By ten she was seated at the head of the table in the boardroom, her department heads lining both sides of the polished mahogany.

"I'm pleased to announce that the national grand opening of Lady's Choice will remain, as scheduled, for this coming Saturday."

As expected, there were polite applause and congratulatory murmurs.

"I'd like to take this opportunity," she continued, "to thank you all for your hard work and dedication. Launching a new company of this size takes teamwork, long hours, and constant innovation. I'm grateful to all of you for giving me your best. I particularly appreciate all of your help in the past couple of weeks, when the company faced such unexpected difficulties.''

She waited until the murmurs about the fires had died down.

''I'm aware that our budget is stretched, but I'm also aware that we wouldn't be on schedule without the extra effort each one of you, and your staff, have given. Therefore, Lady's Choice is pleased to present bonuses to each and every employee on the first of next month.''

This announcement was greeted with a great deal of enthusiasm. Only Deirdre winced and rolled her eyes. Natalie flashed a grin at her that held more pleasure than apology.

''We still have a great deal of work ahead of us,'' Natalie went on. ''I'm sure Deirdre will tell you that I've given her an enormous headache, rather than a bonus.'' Natalie waited for the laughter to subside. ''I have faith in her, and in Lady's Choice warranting it. In addition...'' She paused, the smile still in place, her gaze sweeping from face to face. ''I want to ease everyone's mind. Last night the arsonist was apprehended. He's now in police custody.''

There was applause, a barrage of questions. Natalie sat with her hands folded on the table, watching for, waiting for, some sign that would tell her if one of the people sitting with her had begun to sweat.

''I don't have all the details,'' she said, holding up a hand for quiet. ''Only that Inspector Piasecki apprehended the man outside our plant. I expect a full report within forty-eight hours. In the meantime, we can all thank the diligence of the fire and police departments, and get on with our jobs.''

''Was there a fire at the plant?'' Donald wanted to know. ''Was anything damaged?''

''No. I do know that the suspect was caught before he entered the building.''

''Are they sure it's the same one who started the fires at the warehouse and the flagship?'' Brow furrowed, Melvin tugged at his bow tie.

Natalie smiled. ''As a sister of a police captain, I'm certain the authorities won't make a statement like that until they have absolute proof. But that's the way it looks.''

''Who is he?'' Donald demanded. ''Why did he do it?''

''Again, I don't have all the details. He's a known arsonist. A professional, I believe. I'm sure the motive will come to light before too long.''

Ry wasn't nearly as certain. By noon, he'd been with Jacoby for an hour, covering the same ground. The interrogation room was typically dull. Beige walls, beige linoleum, the wide mirror that everyone knew was two-way glass. He sat on a rock-hard chair, leaning against the single table, smoking lazily, while Clarence grinned and toyed with his own fingers.

''You know they're going to lock the door on you, Clarence,'' Ry said. ''By the time you get out this round, you'll be so old, you won't be able to light a match by yourself.''

Clarence grinned and shrugged his shoulders. ''I didn't hurt nobody. I never hurt nobody.'' He looked up then, his small, pale eyes friendly. ''You know, some people like to burn other people. You know that, don't you, Ry?''

''Yeah, Clarence, I know that.''

''Not me, Ry. I never burned nobody.'' The eyes lit up happily. ''Just you. But that was an accident. You got scars?''

''Yeah, I got scars.''

''Me too.'' Clarence giggled, pleased that they shared something. ''Wanna see?''

''Maybe later. I remember when we got burned, Clarence.''

''Sure. Sure you do. Like a dragon's kiss, right?''

Like being in the bowels of hell, Ry thought. ''The landlord paid you to light the dragon that time, remember?''

''I remember. Nobody lived there. It was just an old building. I like old, empty buildings. The fire just eats along, sniffs up the walls, hides in the ceiling. It talks to you. You've heard it talk, haven't you?''

"Yeah, I've heard it. Who paid you this time, Clarence?''

Playfully Clarence put the tips of his fingers together, making a bridge. "I never said anybody paid me. I never said I did anything. You could've brought the gas, Ry. You're mad at me for burning you.'' Suddenly his smile was crafty. "You had nightmares in the burn ward. I heard about them. Nightmares about the dragon. And now you don't slay the dragon anymore.''

The throb behind his eyes had Ry reaching for another cigarette. Clarence was fascinated by the nightmares, had probed time and again during the interview for details. Even if he'd wanted to, Ry couldn't have given many. It was all a blur of fire and smoke, blessedly misted with time.

"I had nightmares for a while. I got over it. I got over being mad at you, too, Clarence. We were both just doing our job, right?''

Ry caught the glint in Clarence's eyes when the match was lit. Experimentally, Ry held the small flame between them. "It's powerful, isn't it?'' he murmured. "Just a little flame. But you and me, we know what it can do—to wood, paper. Flesh. It's powerful. And when you feed it, it gets stronger and stronger.''

He touched the match to the tip of his cigarette. Still watching Clarence, Ry licked his forefinger and snuffed out the flame. "Douse it with water, cut off its air, and *poof*.'' He tossed the broken match into the overburdened ashtray. "We both like to control it, right?''

"Yeah.'' Clarence licked his lips, hoping Ry would light another match.

"You get paid for starting them. I get paid for putting them out. Who paid you, Clarence?''

"They're going to send me up anyway.''

"Yeah. So what have you got to lose?''

"Nothing.'' Sly again, Clarence looked up at Ry through thin, pale lashes. "I'm not saying I started any fire. But if we was to suppose *maybe* I did, I couldn't say who asked me to.''

"Why not?''

"Because if we was to suppose I did, I never saw who asked me to."

"Did you talk to him?"

Clarence began to play with his fingers again, his face so cheerful Ry had to grit his teeth to keep himself from reaching out and squeezing the pudgy neck. "Maybe I talked to somebody. Maybe I didn't. But maybe if I did, the voice on the phone was all screwed up, like a machine."

"Man or woman?"

"Like a machine," Clarence repeated, gesturing toward Ry's tape recorder. "Maybe it could have been either. Maybe they just sent me money to a post-office box before, and after."

"How'd they find you?"

Clarence moved his right shoulder, then his left. "Maybe I didn't ask. People find me when they want me." His grin lit his face. "Somebody always wants me."

"Why that warehouse?"

"I didn't say nothing about a warehouse," Clarence said, pokering up.

"Why that warehouse?" Ry repeated. "Maybe."

Pleased that Ry was playing the game, Clarence scooted forward in his chair. "Maybe for the insurance. Maybe because somebody didn't like who owned the place. Maybe for fun. There's lots of reasons for fire."

Ry pressed him. "And the store. The same person owned the store."

"There were pretty things in the store. Pretty girl things." Forgetting himself, Clarence smiled in reminiscence. "It smelled pretty, too. Even prettier after I poured the gas."

"Who told you to pour the gas, Clarence?"

"I didn't say I did."

"You just did."

Clarence pouted like a child. "Did not. I said maybe."

The tape would prove different, but Ry kept his probing steady. "You liked the girl things in the store."

Clarence's eyes twinkled. "What store?"

Biting back an oath, Ry leaned back. "Maybe I should call my friend back and let him talk to you."

"What friend?"

"From last night. You remember last night."

All color drained from Clarence's face. "He was a ghost. He wasn't really there."

"Sure he was there. You saw him. You felt him."

"A ghost." Clarence began to gnaw on his fingernails. "I didn't like him."

"Then you'd better talk to me, or I'm going to have to go get him."

Panicked, Clarence darted his eyes around the room. "He's not here."

"Maybe he is," Ry said, enjoying himself. "Maybe he isn't. Who paid you, Clarence?"

"I don't know." His lips began to tremble. "Just a voice. That's all. Take the money and burn. I like money, I like to burn. Started on the nice shiny desk in the store with the girl things, just like the voice said to. Coulda done better in the storeroom, but the voice said do the desk." Uneasy, he looked around. "Is he in here?"

"What about the envelopes? Where are the envelopes the money came in?"

"Burned them." Clarence grinned again. "I like to burn things."

Natalie very nearly burned the chicken.

It wasn't that she was incompetent in the kitchen. It was simply, she told herself, that she rarely found the opportunity to use the culinary skills she possessed—meager though they might be.

With a great deal of cursing and trepidation, she removed the browned chicken from the skillet and set it aside, as per Frank's meticulous directions. By the time she had the sauce simmering, she was feeling smug. Cooking wasn't really such a big deal, she decided, if you just concentrated and went step-by-step. Read the recipe as if it were a contract, she thought, carefully sliding the chicken into the sauce. Overlook no clause, study the small print. And... Humming to herself, she set the cover on the skillet, then looked around at the wreck of her kitchen.

And, she decided, blowing the hair out of her eyes, clean up after yourself—because no deal should ever look as though you'd sweat over it.

It took her longer to set the kitchen, and herself, to rights than it had to prepare the meal. After one quick glance at the time, she dashed to light the candles and create the mood.

With a long sigh, she dropped onto the arm of the sofa and scanned the room. Soft lights, quiet music, the scent of flowers and good food, the golden glow of sedate flames in the hearth. Pleased, Natalie smoothed a hand down her long silk skirt. Everything was perfect, she decided.

Now where was Ry?

He was pacing the hallway outside her door.

Making too big a deal out of it, Piasecki, he warned himself. You're just two people enjoying each other. No strings, no promises. Now that Clarence was in custody, they would start to drift apart. Naturally. No sweat, no strain.

So why in the hell was he standing outside her door, nervous as a teenager on a first date? Why was he holding a bunch of stupid daffodils in his hand?

He should never have brought her flowers in the first place, he decided. But if he'd had the urge, he should have gone for roses, at least, or orchids. Something with class. Just because the yellow blooms had caught his eye and the street vendor had been pushing them, that was no reason to dump a bunch of backyard flowers on a woman like Natalie.

He thought seriously about dropping them in front of her neighbor's door. The idea made him feel even more foolish. Muttering under his breath, he pulled out his key and unlocked the door.

Coming home. It was a ridiculous sensation, walking into an apartment that wasn't his. But it was there, as bold as a ten-foot sign, as subtle as a peck on the cheek.

She rose from her perch on the couch and smiled at him. "Hi."

"Hi."

He had the flowers behind his back, hardly realizing the move was defensive. She looked incredible, the thin-strapped, flowing dress—the color of ripe peaches—skimming down, candle and firelight flickering over her. When she moved, he swallowed. The dress sliced open from the ankle to the trio of gold buttons running down her left hip.

"Long day," she asked, and kissed him lightly on the mouth.

"Yeah. I guess." His tongue had tied itself into knots. "You?"

"Not too bad. The good news has everybody pumped up. I have some wine chilling." She tilted her head, smiling at him. "Unless you'd rather have a beer."

"Whatever," he murmured as she strolled toward the table by the window, which she had set for two. "It looks nice in here. You look nice."

"Well, I thought, since we were celebrating..." She poured two glasses. "I had planned on doing this after the grand opening on Saturday, but it seems appropriate now." With the glasses on the table behind her, she held out a hand. "I have a lot to thank you for."

"No, you don't. I did what I was paid to do...." He trailed off, seeing that her gaze had shifted, softened. With some discomfort, he realized it was riveted on the flowers he'd used to gesture her thanks away.

"You brought me flowers." The simple shock in her voice didn't help his nerves.

"This guy on the corner was selling them, and I just—"

"Daffodils," she said with a sigh. "I love daffodils."

"Yeah?" Miserably awkward, he thrust them at her. "Well, here you go."

Natalie buried her face in the bright trumpets and, for reasons she couldn't fathom, wanted to weep. "They're so pretty, so happy." She lifted her head again, eyes glowing. "So perfect. Thank you."

"It's no big—" But the rest of his words were cut off when her mouth closed over his.

Instant desire. Like a switch flicked on inside him. One touch, he thought as his arms came hard around her, and he wanted her. Her body molded to his, her arms circled. He fought back a desperate need to drag her to the floor and release the helpless passion she stirred up inside him.

"You're tense," she murmured, stroking a hand over his shoulders. "Did something happen with Clarence during the interview that you didn't tell me?"

"No." Clarence Jacoby and his moon-pie face were the last things on Ry's mind. "I'm just wired, I guess." And in need of some basic control. "Something smells good," he said as he eased back. "Besides you."

"Frank's fricassee."

"Frank's?" Taking another step back, Ry reached for his wine. "Guthrie's cook made us dinner?"

"No, it's his recipe." She tucked her hair behind her ear. "I made us dinner."

Ry snorted into his wine. "Yeah. Right. Where'd you get it? The Italian place?"

Torn between amusement and insult, Natalie took her wine. "*I* made it, Piasecki. I know how to turn on a stove."

"You know how to pick up the phone and order." More relaxed now, Ry took her hand and pulled her toward the kitchen. He walked directly to the skillet and lifted the lid. It certainly looked homemade. Frowning, he sniffed at the thick, bubbling sauce covering the golden pieces of chicken. "You cooked this? Yourself?"

Exasperated, Natalie tugged her hand away and sipped her wine. "I don't see why that should be such a shock. It's just a matter of following directions."

"You cooked this," he said again, shaking his head. "How come?"

"Well, because... I don't know." With a little snap of metal on metal, she covered the skillet again. "I felt like it."

"I just can't picture you puttering around the kitchen."

"There wasn't a lot of puttering." Then she laughed. "And it wasn't a very pretty sight. So, no matter what it tastes like, you're required to praise, lavishly. I need to put the flowers in water."

He waited while she got a vase and arranged the daffodils on the kitchen counter.

She looked softer tonight, he thought. All feminine and cozy. And she handled each individual bloom as though he'd brought her rubies. Unable to resist, he lifted his hand to stroke it gently down her hair. She looked up, with surprise, her uncertainty at the show of tenderness evident.

"Is something wrong?"

"No." Cursing himself, he dropped his hand to his side. "I like to touch you."

Her eyes cleared, danced. "I know." She turned into his arms, inviting. "The chicken needs to simmer for a while." She nipped lightly, teasingly, at his lip. "An hour, anyway. Why don't we—"

"Sit down," he finished, to keep from exploding. He was not, he absolutely was not, going to drag her down and take her on the kitchen floor.

"Okay." Left uneasy by his withdrawal, she nodded and picked up her wine again. "We should enjoy the fire."

In the living room, she curled up next to him and rested her head on his shoulder. Obviously, he had something on his mind. She could wait for him to share it with her. It was lovely just sitting here, she thought with a sigh, watching the fire together as dinner cooked and an old Cole Porter tune drifted through the speakers.

It was as if they sat like this every night. Comfortable with each other, knowing there was time, all the time in the world simply to be. After a long, busy day, what better end could there be than to sit beside someone you loved and—

Oh, God. Her thoughts had her jerking straight upright. *Loved.* She loved him.

"What's wrong?"

"Nothing." She swallowed hard, fought to keep her voice even. "Just something I...forgot. I can deal with it later."

"No shoptalk, okay?"

"No." She took a hasty sip of wine. "Fine."

She couldn't get a decent night's sleep when he wasn't beside her. She'd had an irresistible urge to cook him a meal. Her heart turned over every time he smiled at her. She'd even been rerouting a business trip with him in mind.

Oh, why hadn't she seen it before? It had been staring her in the face every time she looked in the mirror.

What was she going to do?

Closing her eyes, she ordered her body to relax. Her emotions were her problem, she reminded herself. She was a grown woman who had gone into an affair with the rules plain on both sides. She couldn't—wouldn't—change the terms in midstream.

What was needed was some clear and careful thought. Some time, she added, concentrating on breathing evenly. Then a plan. She was an excellent planner, after all.

His fingertips brushed lightly over her shoulder. Her pulse scrambled.

"I'd better check on dinner."

"It hasn't been an hour." He liked the way she was curled against him, and wanted to keep her there. Stupid to be worried about where they were heading, he decided, letting himself get drunk on the smell of her hair. Where they were now was exactly the right place to be.

"I was…going to make a salad," she said uncertainly.

"Later."

He slid his fingers under her chin and turned her face toward his. Odd, he thought, it seemed as though his nerves had drained out of him and into her. Experimentally he dipped his head, letting his lips cruise over hers.

She trembled against him.

Intrigued, he drew her lower lip into his mouth, bathing it with his tongue while his eyes watched emotions come and go in hers.

She shuddered.

"Why are we always in a hurry?" he murmured, addressing the question as much to himself as to her.

"I don't know." She had to get away, clear her head, before she made some foolish mistake. "We need more wine."

"I don't think so." Slowly he brushed the hair back from her face so that he could frame it with his hands. He held her there, his eyes on hers. "Do you know what I think, Natalie?"

"No." She moistened her lips, struggling to find her balance.

"I think we've missed a step here."

"I don't know what you mean."

He pressed his lips to her brow, drew back, and watched her eyes cloud. "Seduction," he whispered.

# Chapter 10

Seduction? She didn't need to be seduced. She wanted him, always wanted him. Before she realized she loved him, she had equated her response to him as a kind of volatile chemical reaction. But now, couldn't he see...

Her thoughts trailed off into smoke as his lips roamed lazily down her temple.

"Ry." She put her hand to his chest, told herself she would keep her voice light, joking...disentangle herself long enough to clear her mind and regain her balance. But his fingers were stroking along her collarbone, and his mouth was nipping closer, closer to hers. She only said, "Ry," again.

"We're good at moving straight ahead, you and me, aren't we, Natalie?" But now there was something smooth and easy gliding through him. Fascinated by his own reaction, he traced his tongue over her lips. "Fast, with no detours, that's us. I think it's time we took a little side trip."

"I think..." But she couldn't think. Not after his mouth fit itself to hers. He'd never kissed her like this before, never like this, so slow, so deep, with a lazy kind of possession that shot simmering heat straight to the marrow of her bones.

Her body went lax, as fluid as the wax pooling the wicks of the candles around them. Beneath her palm, his heart beat hard, and not quite steady, and the low, helpless sound that vibrated in her throat quickened it. Yet he continued that slow, deep exploration of her mouth, as if he would be content with that, only that, for hours.

Her head fell back. He cupped it, shifting her slightly to change the angle of the kiss, toying with her lips, her tongue. Her breath caught and released, caught and released, shuddering once when his fingers brushed up over her breast.

Now, she knew, now would come the speed and the power she understood. There would be control again, in the sheer lack of control as they rushed to take each other. But his fingers simply skimmed up her throat and lay with devastating tenderness on her cheek.

In defense, she reached for him, pulling him tight against her.

"Not this time." He drew back just enough to study her face. Confusion, need, and arousal made a beautiful combination. However much his own blood was pounding, he intended to confuse her more, intended to see to each and every need, and arouse her until her body was limp.

"I want you." She tore hurriedly at the buttons of his shirt. "Now, Ry. I want you now."

He pulled her down on the floor in front of the fire. The light from the flames flickered over her skin, danced in her hair. She was golden. Like some exotic treasure a man might spend his life in search of. And for now, for tonight, Ry thought, she was only his.

He stretched her arms out to the sides, linked his fingers with hers. "You'll have to wait," he told her. "Until I'm finished seducing you."

"I don't need to be seduced." She arched up to him, offering her mouth, her body, herself.

"Let's see."

He covered her mouth with his, softly, dipping in when her lips trembled open. Under his hands, hers flexed, and gripped hard. How often had he loved her? It hadn't been long since they'd met, but he couldn't count the number of times he'd let his body take control, go wild with hers.

This time, he'd make love to her with his mind.

"I love your shoulders," he murmured, taking his mouth from hers for a slow exploration of the curve. "Soft, strong, smooth."

With his teeth, he caught the thin strap of her dress, tugged it down until there was nothing between him and flesh. Warmth, her taste, her scent, were all warmth. Absorbing them, he trailed his tongue over her shoulder, along the elegant line of throat, down again until the other strap gave way.

"And this spot here." He rubbed his lips just above the silk that curved over her breast. Teasingly, devastatingly, he dampened the skin under the silk with his tongue until her body moved restlessly beneath his. "You should relax and enjoy, Natalie. I'm going to be a while."

"I can't." The gentle brush of lips, the solid weight of him, were tormenting her. "Kiss me again."

"My pleasure."

There was a flicker of heat this time, bright and hot, before he banked the fires again. She moaned, straining against him, wanting release, craving the torture. He made the choice for her, kissing her with a focused intensity until her fingers went limp and her rushed breathing slowed and thickened.

Smoke. She could all but smell it. She was rising up on clouds of it, weightless, helpless, unable to do more than float and sigh when his mouth left hers to trail down again. A gentle nip at the jaw, and then light, slow kisses down her throat, her shoulders.

His body shifted downward, his hands still covering hers. Inch by inch, he tasted her, nudging the silk down. She felt his hair brush her breast, then his mouth traveling around the curve, nuzzling at the sensitive underside. His tongue slid over her nipple, shooting an ache down to her center. Then he caught the peak between his teeth, making her moan his name, and her body began to throb to a low, primitive beat.

He wanted her to absorb him, and all the pleasure he could give her. Her eyes were closed, her lips just parted. And much too tempting. He needed to taste them again, and when he did, he let himself sink into the texture, the flavor.

Time spun out.

There was power here, in tenderness. He'd never felt it before, not in himself, and certainly not for anyone else. But for her he had a bottomless well of tenderness, of soft, sumptuous kisses, of endless sighs.

He took his hands from hers to shrug out of his shirt, to feel the thrill of his flesh against her flesh. Sliding smooth, building heat. With a murmur of approval, he slipped his hand through the slit of her skirt, lightly caressing, teasing the edge of some frilly something she wore beneath.

He flicked open a button, then two, then the third, fascinated by the way the material slid and parted under his hands. Nuzzling along her bared hip, he fought back a sudden, vicious urge to take when her hands brushed, then pressed, at his shoulders.

More, he promised himself. There was more.

For his own pleasure, he slipped the silk aside. And found more.

Beneath she wore a fancy of silk and lace, the same color as the dress that pooled beside them. Strapless, it hugged her breasts, rode high up her hips. Letting out a long breath, he sat back on his heels and toyed with one lacy garter.

"Natalie."

Weak…she was so gloriously weak she could barely open her eyes. When she did, she saw only him, the firelight teasing the red out of his dark hair, his eyes nearly black. She reached out, her arm heavy, nearly boneless. He merely took her hand, and kissed it.

"I wanted to tell you how happy I am you're in the lingerie business."

Her lips curved. She nearly managed a laugh before, with one quick flick, he detached the first garter. She could only utter a helpless moan.

"And how beautiful you look." Flick went the second garter. "Modeling your own products." With his eyes on hers, he rolled the stocking down thigh and knee and calf.

Her vision hazed. She could feel him. Oh, God, she could feel him—every brush of fingertip and mouth. Surrender had come gliding through her like a shadow, and had left her completely vulnerable.

Whatever he wanted. Anything he wanted, she would give, as long as he never stopped touching her.

There was the low, steady heat from the fire. It was nothing, nothing, compared to the slow burn he had kindled inside her. As if down a long, velvet-lined tunnel, she could hear the music still. A quiet backdrop to her own trembling breathing. The scent of flowers and candle wax, the taste of him and the wine that lingered on her tongue, all melded together into one stunning intoxication.

Then he slipped a finger under the lace-edged hem, sliding it slowly toward, and then into, the heat.

She erupted. Her body quaked and reared. His name burst from her lips, even as the staggering pleasure careened through her system. She was wrapped around him as the power of the climax built in force, then echoed away and left her drained.

She wanted to tell him she was empty, had to be empty. But he was peeling away the silk and lace, exposing her with those clever fingers, swallowing whatever words she might have spoken with that relentlessly patient mouth.

"I want to fill you, Natalie." His hands weren't as steady as they had been, but he laid her gently back on the carpet so that he could tug off his clothes. "All of you. With all of me."

While the blood pounded in his ears, he began a slow journey up her legs, stroking the fires again, waiting, watching, for that moment before she would flash again.

He felt her body tense, saw the power of what was to come flicker over her face. Even as she cried out, he was inside her.

It was almost painful to hold himself back. And it was very sweet. Seeing her heavy eyes open, seeing the glaze of pleasure cloud them as he fought to keep from racing for the finish.

Swamped by a swirl of sensations, all but suffocating in the layers of them, she groped for his hands. When their fingers locked again, her heart was ready to burst. Her eyes stayed open and looked on his as each thrust rocked them, pushed them closer.

Then she was cartwheeling off the edge, reeling, tumbling free. His mouth came to hers, his lips forming her name as he leapt with her.

* * *

Twice on the elevator ride to her office the next morning, Natalie caught herself singing. Both times, she cleared her throat, shifted her briefcase from hand to hand and pretended not to notice the speculative looks of her fellow passengers.

So what? she thought as the elevator climbed. She felt like singing. She felt like dancing. So what? She was in love.

And what was wrong with that? she asked herself as the elevator stopped to let off passengers on the thirty-first floor. Everyone was entitled to be in love, to feel as though their feet would never touch the ground again, to know the air had never smelled sweeter, the sun had never shone brighter.

It was wonderful to be in love. So wonderful, she wondered why she'd never tried it before.

Because there'd never been Ry before, she thought, and grinned.

How foolish she'd been to panic when she realized what she felt for Ry. How cowardly and ridiculous to be afraid, even for a moment, of loving.

If it made a woman vulnerable, comical, if it dazed and baffled her, what was wrong with that? Love should make you feel giddy and strong and soft-headed. She'd just never realized it before.

Humming to herself, she stepped out of the elevator on her floor and all but waltzed toward her office.

"Good morning, Ms. Fletcher." Maureen glanced surreptitiously at her clock. It wasn't up to her to point out that the boss was late. Even three minutes late was a precedent for Natalie Fletcher.

"Good morning, Maureen." She all but sang it, and thrust out a clutch of daffodils.

"Oh, thank you. They're lovely."

"Everyone should have daffodils this morning. Absolutely everyone." Natalie shook back her hair, scattering raindrops. "It's a gorgeous day, isn't it?"

Drizzling and chilly was what it was, but Maureen found herself grinning back. "Absolutely a classic spring morning. You've got a conference call scheduled for ten. Atlanta, Chicago."

"I know."

"And Ms. Marks was hoping you could fit her in afterward."

"Fine."

"Oh, and you're due at the flagship at 11:15, right after your 10:30 with Mr. Hawthorne."

"No problem."

"You have a lunch with—"

"I'll be there," Natalie called out, and swung into her office.

For the first time in recent memory, Natalie bypassed the coffeepot. She didn't need caffeine to pump through her blood. It was already swimming. She hung up her coat, set her briefcase aside, then moved to the office safe behind her favorite abstract print.

Taking out a pair of disks, she went to her desk to draft a brief memo to Deirdre.

An hour later, she was elbow-deep in work, making hasty notes as she juggled information and requests from three of her branches on the conference call.

"I'll fax authorization for that within the hour," she promised Atlanta. "Donald, see if you can squeeze out the time to go to the flagship with me—11:15. We can have our meeting on the way."

"I've got an 11:30 with Marketing," he told her. "Let me see if I can push it to after lunch."

"I'd appreciate it. I'd like tear sheets of all the ads and newspaper articles in Chicago. You can fax copies, but I'd like you to overnight the originals. I'll be checking in with L.A. and Dallas this afternoon, and we'll have a full report for all branches by end of day tomorrow."

She sat back, let out a long breath. "Gentlemen, synchronize your watches and alert the troops. Ten a.m., Saturday. Coast to coast."

After she closed the conference, Natalie pressed her buzzer. "Maureen, let Deirdre know I'm free for about twenty minutes. Oh, and buzz Melvin for me."

"He's in the field, Ms. Fletcher."

"Oh, right." Annoyed with her lapse, Natalie glanced at her watch, calculated time. "I'll see if I can catch him at the plant later this afternoon. Leave a memo on his voice mail that I should be by around three."

"Yes, ma'am."

"After you buzz Deirdre, get me the head of shipping at the new warehouse."

"Right away."

By the time Deirdre knocked on the door and stepped in, Natalie was tapping at the keys on her desk computer. "Yes, I see that." Phone tucked at her ear, she gestured Deirdre to a seat. "Put a trace on that shipment. I want it in Atlanta no later than 9:00 a.m. tomorrow." She nodded, tapped. "Let me know as soon as it's located. Thanks."

She hung up, brushed a stray hair from her cheek. "There's always a glitch near zero hour."

Deirdre's brow wrinkled. "Bad?"

"No, just a slight delay on a shipment. Even without it, Atlanta's well stocked for the opening. But I don't want them to run low. Coffee?"

"No, I've already burned a hole in my stomach lining, thanks. Or you have." She aimed a steely look at her boss. "Bonuses."

"Bonuses," Natalie agreed. "I have the percentages I want you to work with right here. Salary ratios, and so forth." She smiled a little. "I figured you wouldn't be wondering about how best to murder me if I did the preliminaries."

"Wrong."

Now Natalie laughed. "Deirdre, do you know why I value you so highly?"

"Nope."

"You have a mind like a calculator. The bonuses were earned, and I also consider them a good investment. Incentive to keep up the pace during the weeks ahead. There's usually a dip after the initial sales in a new business, both in profit and in labor. I think this will keep that dip from becoming a dive."

"That's all very well in theory," Deirdre began.

"Let's make it reality. And since it's basically a standard ratio across the board, I'd like you to hand the problem over to your assistant. That way you can concentrate on running the audit."

Still smiling, she handed over the disks, and her memo. "A great deal of what you'll need to run will be parallel with tax preparation.

Take whatever time, and however many bodies in Accounting, you feel you'll need.''

With a grimace, Deirdre accepted the disk. ''You know why I value you so highly, Natalie?''

''Nope.''

''Because there's no budging you, and you give impossible orders with such reasonableness.''

''It's a gift,'' Natalie agreed. ''You might want these hard copies.''

Deirdre rose, hefting the file. ''Thanks a lot.''

''Anytime.'' She glanced up with a smile as Donald poked his head in the door.

''I'm clear until 12:30,'' he told her.

''Great. We'll head out now. Take your time,'' Natalie repeated to Deirdre as she crossed to the closet for her coat. ''As long as I have the first figures on this quarter's profit and loss, and the totals from each department, by the end of next week.''

Deirdre rolled her eyes at Donald. ''Reasonably impossible.'' She set the disks on top of the file. ''You're next,'' she warned him.

''Don't let her scare you, Donald. She's just gearing up to pit black ink against red.'' Natalie sailed through the door. ''Just make sure the black wins.''

''Quite a mood she's in,'' Donald murmured to Deirdre.

''She's flying, all right.'' Deirdre stared down at the files. ''Let's hope we can keep it that way.''


''Perfect, isn't it?'' Content after their visit to the store, Natalie stretched out her legs in the back of the car, while her driver threaded through the lunch-hour traffic. ''You'd never know there was a fire.''

''A hell of a job,'' Donald agreed. ''And the window treatment's spectacular. The salesclerks are going to be run ragged come Saturday.''

''I'm counting on it.'' She touched a hand to his arm. ''A lot of it's your doing, Donald. We never would have gotten off the ground like this without you, especially after the warehouse.''

''Damage control.'' He brushed off her thanks with a shrug. ''In six months we'll barely remember we had damage to control. And the profits will bring a smile even to Deirdre's face." He was counting on it.

"That would be a real coup."

"Just drop me off at the next corner," he told the driver. "The restaurant's only a couple of doors down."

"I appreciate you making time to go with me."

"No problem. Seeing the flagship back in shape made my day. It wasn't pleasant visualizing the office torn up like that. That wonderful antique desk ruined. The replacement's stunning, by the way."

"I had it shipped out from Colorado," Natalie said absently, as something niggled at her brain. "I had it in storage."

"Well, it's perfect." He patted her hand as the car swung to the curb.

She waved him off, then settled back, dissatisfied, when the car merged back into traffic. Then, with a shrug, she gauged the traffic, the distance to her lunch meeting, and decided she had time for one quick phone call.

Ry answered himself on the third ring. "Arson. Piasecki."

"Hi." The pleasure of hearing his voice wiped out everything else. "Your secretary's out?"

"Lunch."

"And you're having yours at your desk."

He glanced down at the sandwich he had yet to touch. "Yeah. More or less." He shifted, making his chair squeak. "Where are you?"

"Looks like Twelfth and Hyatt, heading east, toward the Menagerie."

"Ah." The Menagerie, he thought. High-class. No tuna on wheat for lunch there. He could see her, ordering designer water and a salad with every leaf called a different name. "Look, Legs, about tonight—"

"I was thinking about that. Maybe you could meet me at the Goose Neck." She rolled her shoulders. "I have a feeling I'm going to want to unwind."

He rubbed a hand over his chin. "I, ah... Come by my place instead. Okay?"

"Your place?" This was new. She'd stopped wondering why he'd never taken her there.

"Yeah. About seven, seven-thirty."

"All right. Do you want me to pick up something for dinner?"

"No, I'll take care of it. See you." He hung up and sat back in his chair. He was going to have to take care of a lot of things.

He picked up Chinese. It was nearly seven when Ry carried the little white cartons up the two flights to his apartment. He took a good look around while he did.

It wasn't a dump. Unless, of course, you compared it with Natalie's glossy building. There was no graffiti on the walls, but the walls were thin. As he climbed the steps, Ry could hear the muted sounds of televisions playing, children squabbling. The steps themselves were worn down in the centers from the passage of countless feet.

As he turned onto the second floor, he heard a door slam beneath him.

"All right, all right. I'll go get the damn beer myself."

Lip curled, Ry unlocked his door. Yeah, he thought. It was a real class joint. There was a definite scent of garlic in the hall. Courtesy of his neighbor, he assumed. The woman was always cooking up pots of pasta.

He let himself in, flicked on the lights and studied the room.

It was clean. A little dusty, maybe. He barely spent enough time in it to mess it up. It had been nearly three weeks since he'd spent a night there. The sofa that folded out into a bed needed recovering. It wasn't something he'd noticed before, or would have bothered with. But now the faded blue upholstery annoyed him.

He walked past it, taking about half a dozen steps into the alcove that served as his kitchen. He got out a beer and popped the top. The walls needed painting, too, he decided, chugging the beer as he looked around. And the bare floors could have used a carpet.

But it served him well enough, didn't it? he thought grimly. He didn't need fancy digs. Just a couple of rooms a short hop from the office. He'd been content here for nearly a decade. That was enough for anyone.

But it wasn't enough, couldn't be enough, for Natalie.

She didn't belong here. He knew it. And he'd asked her to come to prove it to both of them.

The night before had been a revelation to him. That she could make him feel the way she'd made him feel. That she could make him forget, as he'd forgotten, that there was anything or anyone on the planet except the two of them.

It wasn't fair to either of them to go on this way. The longer he let it drift, the more he needed her. And the more he needed, the more difficult it would be to let her walk away.

His divorce hadn't hurt him. Oh, a couple of twinges, he thought now. Plenty of regrets. But no real pain. Not the deep-rooted, searing kind of pain he was already feeling at the thought of living without Natalie.

He could keep her. There was a good chance he could keep her. The physical thing between them was outrageously intense. Even if it faded by half, it would still be stronger than anything he'd ever experienced before.

And he was well aware of his effect on her.

He could hold her with sex alone. It might be enough for her. But he'd understood when he awakened beside her this morning that it wasn't enough for him.

No, it wasn't enough, not when he'd started to imagine white picket fences, kids in the yard—the kind of things that went with marriage, permanence, a lifetime.

That hadn't been the deal, he reminded himself. And he had no right to change the rules, to expect her to settle. He'd already proven he wasn't any good at marriage, and that had been with someone from his own neighborhood, his own life-style. No way was he going to fit in with Natalie, and the fact that he wanted to, needed to, scared the hell out of him.

Worse than that, even worse, was the idea that she would turn him down cold if he asked her to try.

He wanted all of her. Or nothing. So it made sense, didn't it, to push her out before he got in any deeper? And he would do it here, right here, where the differences between them would slap her between the eyes.

At the knock of his door, he carried his beer over to answer it.

It was just as he'd thought. She stood in the hallway, slim, golden, an exotic fish completely out of water. She smiled at him, leaning up to kiss him.

"Hi."

"Hi. Come on in. No trouble finding the place?"

"No." She skimmed her sweep of hair back, looking around. "I took a cab."

"Good thinking. If you left that fancy car on the street around here, there'd be nothing left but the door handles when you went back out. Want a beer?"

"No." Interested, she wandered over to the window.

"Not much of a view," he said, knowing she was looking out at the face of the next building.

"Not much," she agreed. "It's still raining," she added and slipped out of her coat. She smiled when she spotted another of his basketball trophies. "MVP," she murmured, reading the plaque. "Impressive. I say I can outscore you nine times out of ten."

"I wasn't fresh." He turned into the kitchen. "I don't have any wine."

"That's okay. Mmm...Chinese." She opened one of the cartons he'd set on the counter, and sniffed. "I'm starved. All I had was a stingy salad for lunch. I've been all over the city today, nailing down details for Saturday. Where are the plates?" Very much at home, she opened a cabinet herself. "I'm really going to have to make a sweep of the branches next week. I was thinking—" She broke off when she turned back and found him staring at her. "What?"

"Nothing," he muttered, and took the plates out of her hands.

She wasn't supposed to stride right in and start chattering, he thought, and dumped food on a plate. She was supposed to see how wrong it was, right from the start. She was supposed to make it easy on him.

"Damn it, do you see where you are?" He whirled on her, taking her back a step.

She blinked. ''Ah…in the kitchen?''

''Look around you.'' Incensed, he took her by the arm and dragged her into the next room. ''Look around. This is it. This is the way I live. This is the way I am.''

''All right.'' She pushed his hand away, because his fingers hurt. Trying to oblige, she took another survey of the room. It was spartan, masculine in its very simplicity. Small, she noted, but not crowded. A table across the room held framed snapshots of a family she hoped to get a closer look at.

''It could use some color,'' she decided after a moment.

''I'm not asking for decorating advice,'' he snapped out.

There was something under the anger in his tone, something final, that had her heart stuttering. Very slowly, she turned back to him. ''What are you asking for?''

Cursing, he spun into the kitchen for his beer. If she was going to look at him with that confused, wounded look in her eyes, he was a dead man. So, he would have to be cruel, and he would have to be quick. He sat on the arm of the couch, and tipped back his beer.

''Let's get real here, Natalie. You and I started this thing because we were hot for each other.''

She could feel the warmth drain out of her cheeks, leaving them cold and stiff. But she kept her eyes level, and her voice steady. ''Yes, that's right.''

''Things happened fast. The sex, the investigation. Things got tangled up.''

''Did they?''

His mouth was dry, and the beer wasn't helping. ''You're a beautiful woman. I wanted you. You had a problem. It was my job to fix it for you.''

''Which you did,'' she said carefully.

''For the most part. The cops'll track down whoever was paying Clarence. Until they do, you've got to be careful. But things are pretty much under control. On that level.''

''And on the personal level?''

He frowned down into the bottle. ''I figure it's time to step back, take a clearer look.''

Natalie's legs were trembling. She locked her knees to stop it. "Are you dumping me, Ry?"

"I'm saying we've got to look behind the way things are in bed. The way you are." He lifted his gaze. "The way I'm not. We've got plenty of heat, Natalie. The problem with that is, you get blinded by the smoke. Time to clear the air, that's all."

"I see." She wouldn't beg. Nor would she cry, not in front of him. Not when he was looking at her so coolly, his voice so casual as he cut out her heart. She wondered if he'd been so gentle, so loving and sweet, the night before because he'd already decided to break things off.

"Well, I suppose you've cleared it." Despite her resolve, her vision blurred, the lamplight refracting in the tears that trembled much too close to the surface.

The minute her eyes filled, he was on his feet. "Don't."

"I won't. Believe me, I won't." But the first tear spilled over as she turned toward the door. "I appreciate you not doing this in a public place." She clamped a hand over the doorknob. Her fingers were numb, she realized. She couldn't even feel them.

"Natalie."

"I'm all right." To prove it to both of them, she turned to face him, her head up. "I'm not a child, and this isn't the first relationship I've had that hasn't worked. It is the first time for something, though, and you're entitled to know it. You jerk." She sniffed, and wiped a tear away. "I've never been in love with anyone before, but I fell in love with you. I hate you for it."

She yanked open the door and dashed out without her coat.

## Chapter 11

For ten minutes, Ry paced the room, convincing himself he'd done the right thing for both of them. Sure, she'd be a little hurt. Her pride was bruised. He hadn't exactly been a diplomat.

For the next ten, he worked on convincing himself that she hadn't meant what she'd said. That parting shot had been just that. A weapon hurled to hurt as she'd been hurt.

She wasn't in love with him. She couldn't be. Because if she was, then he was the world's biggest idiot.

Oh, God. He was the world's biggest idiot.

He snatched up her coat, forgot his own, and raced downstairs and out into the rain.

He'd left his car at the station, and cursed himself for it. Praying for a cab, he loped to the corner, then to the next, working his way across town.

His impatience cost him more time than a simple wait would have. By the time he hailed an empty cab, he was twelve blocks from his home and soaking wet.

The cab fought its way through rain and traffic, creeping along, then sprinting, creeping, then sprinting, until Ry tossed a fistful of money at the driver and leapt out.

He'd have made better time on foot.

Nearly an hour had passed by the time he arrived at Natalie's door.

He didn't bother to knock, but used the key she hadn't thought to demand back from him.

There was no welcome this time, no cozy sense of coming home. He knew the minute he stepped inside that she wasn't there. Denying it, he called out for her and began a dripping search through the apartment.

So he'd wait, he told himself. She'd come home sooner or later, and he'd be there. Make things right again somehow. He'd grovel if he had to, he decided, pacing from the living room to the bedroom.

She'd probably gone to her office. Maybe he should go there. He could call. He could send a telegram. He could do something.

Good God, the woman was in love with him, and he'd used both hands to shove her out the door.

He dropped to the side of the bed and snatched up the phone. It was then that he saw the note, hastily scrawled, on the nightstand.

Atlanta—National—8:25

National, he thought. National Airlines. The airport.

Ry was out of the apartment and harassing the doorman for a cab in three minutes flat.

He missed her plane by less than five.

"No, Inspector Piasecki, I don't know precisely when Ms. Fletcher expects to return." Cautiously, Maureen smiled. The man looked wild, as though he'd spent a very rough night in his clothes. Things were upended enough, with the boss's sudden trip, without her having to face down a madman at 9:00 a.m.

"Where is she?" Ry demanded. He'd very nearly caught the next flight out to Atlanta the night before, but then it had occurred to him that he didn't have a clue where to find her.

"I'm sorry, Inspector. I'm not allowed to give you that information. I will be happy to relay any message you might have when Ms. Fletcher calls in."

"I want to know where she is," Ry said between his teeth.

Maureen gave serious thought to calling Security. "It's company policy—"

He gave a one-word assessment of company policy and pulled out his ID. "Do you see this? I'm in charge of the arson investigation. I've got information Ms. Fletcher requires immediately. Now, if you don't let me know where to reach her, I'll have to go to my superiors."

He let that hang, and hoped.

Torn, Maureen bit her lip. It was true Ms. Fletcher had ordered her specifically not to divulge her itinerary. It was also true that during the harried phone call the night before, nothing had been mentioned specifically about information from Inspector Piasecki. And if it was something to do with the fires...

"She's staying at the Ritz-Carlton, Atlanta."

Before she'd finished the sentence, Ry was out the door. It was best, he decided, if a man was going to whimper, to do it in private.

Fifteen minutes later, he burst into his office, startling his secretary, and slammed the door behind him. "Ritz-Carlton, Atlanta. Get them on the phone."

"Yes, sir."

He paced his office, muttering to himself, until she signaled him. "Natalie Fletcher," he barked into the phone. "Connect me."

"Yes, sir. One moment, please."

One endless moment, while the line whispered, then began to ring. Ry let out a long, relieved breath when he heard Natalie's voice at the other end.

"Natalie—what the hell are you doing in Atlanta? I need to—" Then he could only swear as the phone clicked loudly in his ear. "Damn it all to hell and back, get that number for me again."

Wide-eyed, his secretary hurriedly placed the call.

Calm, Ry ordered himself. He knew how to be calm in the face of fire and death and misery. Surely he could be calm now. But when the phone continued to ring and he pictured her coolly looking out the window of her hotel room and ignoring it, he nearly ripped the receiver out of the wall.

"Call the airport," Ry ordered while his secretary goggled at him. "Book me on the next available flight to Atlanta."

She was gone when he got there.

He couldn't believe it. More than ten hours after his rushed departure, Ry was back in Urbana. Alone. He hadn't even managed to see her. He'd spent hours on planes, more time chasing her around Atlanta, from her hotel to the downtown branch of Lady's Choice, back to her hotel, to the airport. Each time he'd missed her by inches.

It was, he thought as he trudged up the stairs to his apartment, as if she'd known he was behind her. He dropped down on the couch, rubbing his hands over his face.

He had no choice but to wait.

"I'm so glad to see you." Althea Grayson Nightshade smiled as she rubbed a hand over her mountain of a belly.

"That goes double." Natalie laughed. "Literally. How are you feeling?"

"Oh, like a cross between the Goodyear blimp and Moby Dick."

"Neither of them ever looked so good." It was true, Natalie mused. Pregnancy had only enhanced Althea's considerable beauty. Her eyes were gold, her skin was dewy, her hair was a fiery cascade to her shoulders.

"I'm fat, but I'm healthy." Althea's lips twitched. "Colt's been a demon about seeing that I eat right, sleep enough, exercise, rest. He even typed up a daily schedule. Mr. Play-It-By-Ear went into a tailspin when he found out we were expecting."

"The nursery's wonderful." Natalie wandered the sunny mint-and-white room, running her fingers over the antique crib, the fussy dotted-swiss curtains.

"I'll be glad when it's filled. Any time now," Althea said with a sigh. "I feel great, really, but I swear, this has been the longest pregnancy in recorded history. I want to see my baby, damn it." She stopped and laughed at herself. "Listen to me. I never thought I'd want children, much less be itching to change the first diaper."

Intrigued, Natalie looked over her shoulder. Althea sat in a rocking chair, a small, poorly knit blanket in her hands. "No? You never wanted to be a mom?"

"Not with the job and my background." She shrugged. "Didn't figure I was cut out for it. Then along comes Nightshade, and then this." She patted her belly. "Maybe gestating isn't my natural milieu, but I've loved every minute of it. Now I'm antsy to get on to the nurturing. Can you see me," she said with a laugh, "sitting here, rocking a baby?"

"Yes, I can." Natalie came back, crouched, and took Althea's hands. "I envy you, Thea. So much. To have someone who loves you, to make a baby between you. Nothing else is as important." Defenses crumbled. Her eyes filled.

"Oh, honey, what is it?"

"What else?" Disgusted with herself, Natalie straightened.

"A man."

"A jerk." She fought back the tears and stuffed her hands in her pockets.

"Would this jerk be an arson investigator?" Althea smiled a little when Natalie scowled at her. "News travels, even to Denver. The fact is, your family and Colt and I have been biting our tongues, trying not to ask what you're doing out here."

"I explained. I'm siting. I want to open another branch here. I was traveling, anyway."

"Instead of being in Urbana for your opening."

She resented that, laid the blame for it right at Ry's doorstep. "I was in Dallas for the opening there. Each of my branches is of equal importance to me."

"Yeah, and word is it was a smash."

"The tallies for the first week's sales look promising."

"So why aren't you back home, basking in it?" Althea inclined her head. "The jerk?"

"I'm entitled to a little time before I... Well, yes," she admitted. "The jerk. He dumped me."

"Oh, come on. Cilla said the guy was crazy about you."

"We were good in bed," Natalie said flatly, then pressed her lips together. "I made the mistake of falling in love with him. A real first for me. And he broke my heart."

"I'm sorry." Concerned, Althea pushed herself out of the chair.

"I'll get over it." Natalie squeezed Althea's offered hands. "It's just that I've never felt this way about anyone. I didn't know I could. I've managed to get through my whole life without being hurt like this. Then, *pow.* It's like being cut into very small pieces," she murmured. "I just haven't been able to put them all back together yet."

"Well, he's not worth it," Althea said loyally.

"I wish that were true. It'd be easier. He's a wonderful man, tough, sweet, dedicated." She moved her shoulders restlessly. "He didn't mean to hurt me. He's called several times while I've been on the road."

"He must want to apologize, to make things up with you."

"Do you think I'd give him the chance?" Natalie's chin angled. "I'm not taking his calls. I'm not taking anything from him. He can send me flowers all over the country, for all the difference it would make."

"He sends you flowers." A smile was beginning to lurk around the corners of Althea's mouth.

"Daffodils. Every time I turn around, I'm getting a bunch of idiotic daffodils." She set her teeth. "Does he think I'm going to fall for that again?"

"Probably."

"Well, I'm not. One broken heart's enough for me. More than enough."

"Maybe you should go back, let him beg. Then kick him in the teeth." Althea winced at the twinge. The third one, she noted with a glance at her watch, in the past half hour.

"I'm thinking about it. But until I'm ready, I'm not—" Natalie broke off. "What is it? Are you all right?"

"Yeah." Althea let out a long breath. This twinge was lasting longer. "You know, I think I could be going into labor."

"What?" The blood drained out of Natalie's face. "Now? Sit. Sit down, for God's sake. I'll get Colt."

"Maybe I will." Gingerly Althea lowered herself back into the chair. "Maybe you'd better."

Deirdre was glad she'd decided to take the work home with her. The miserable cold she'd picked up from somewhere was hanging on like a leech. At least she could take her mind off her stuffy head and scratchy throat with work.

She sniffed disinterestedly at the cup of instant chicken soup she'd zapped in the microwave and indulged herself with the hot toddy instead. Nothing like a good shot of whiskey to make a cup of tea sit up and sing.

If she was lucky, very lucky, she'd have the cold on the run and the preliminary figures in before Natalie got back from Denver.

She took another hefty slug of the spiked tea and tapped keys. She stopped, frowned, and adjusted her glasses.

That couldn't be right, she thought, and tapped more keys. No way in hell could that be right. Her mouth became drier, and a thin line of sweat rolled down her back that had nothing to do with the slight fever she was fighting.

She sat back and took a couple of easy breaths. It was simply a mistake, she assured herself. She'd find the discrepancy and fix it. That was all.

But it didn't take much longer for her to realize it wasn't a mistake. Or an accident.

It was a quarter of a million dollars. And it was gone.

She snatched up the phone, and rapidly dialed. "Maureen. Deirdre Marks."

"Ms. Marks, you sound dreadful."

"I know. Listen, I need to talk to Natalie, right away."

"Who doesn't?"

"It's urgent, Maureen. She's with her brother, right? Let me have the number."

"I can't do that, Ms. Marks."

"It's urgent, I tell you."

"I understand, but she's not there. Her plane left Denver an hour ago. She's on her way home."

* * *

A son. Althea and Colt had a son, a tiny and beautiful boy. It had taken Althea twelve hard hours to push him into the world, and he'd come out howling.

Natalie remembered it now as her plane traveled east. It had been a thrill to be allowed in the birthing room, to support Colt when he was ready to climb the walls, to watch him and Althea work together to welcome that new life.

She hadn't wept until it was over, until she'd left Colt and Althea nuzzling their new son. Boyd had left the hospital with her. He'd either been too deep in the memories of his own children's births or had sensed her mood. Either way, he hadn't badgered her.

Now she was going home, because there was work to do. And because it was cowardly to keep jumping from city to city because she was hurt.

It had been a good trip. Professionally successful. Personally sooth-·ing. She was going to give some thought to moving back to Colorado. She'd found an excellent site. And a new branch in Denver would benefit from her personal touch.

If the move would have the added benefit of escape, whose business was it but hers?

She would have to wait, of course, until they had unearthed whoever had paid Clarence Jacoby. If it was indeed one of her people in Urbana, that person had to be weeded out. Once that was done, Donald could take over that office.

It would be a simple matter. Donald had the talent. From a business standpoint, the change would be little more than having him move from his office to hers, his desk to hers.

Desk, she thought, frowning. There was something odd about the desk. Not her desk, she realized all at once. The desk that had been damaged at the flagship.

He'd known about that. Her heart began to thud uncomfortably. How had Donald known the desk in the manager's office was an antique? How had he known specifically that it had been damaged?

Cautiously she began to think over the details, recalling her movements from the time of the second fire to the day she and Donald had visited the flagship. He hadn't been in the office there since it had been decorated. At least not to her knowledge. So how could he have known the desks had been switched?

Because he'd been there. That was all, she tried to assure herself. He'd swung by at some point and hadn't mentioned it. It made sense, more sense than believing he had had something to do with the fires.

Yet he'd been at the warehouse the morning after it had burned. Early, she remembered. Had she called him? She couldn't be sure, didn't recall. He could have heard about it on the news. Had there been reports that early? Detailed reports? She wasn't sure about that, either, and it worried her.

Why should he do something so drastic to harm a business he was an integral part of? she wondered. What possible motive could there be for him to want to see stock and equipment destroyed?

Stock, equipment, and, she thought on a jolt of alarm, records. There'd been records at the warehouse, and at the flagship—at the point of the fire's origin.

Determined to keep calm, she thought of the files she'd given Deirdre, of the copies still in the safe at her office. She'd check them herself the minute she landed, just to ease her mind.

She was wrong about Donald, of course. She had to be wrong.

She was late. It was a hell of a thing, Ry thought as he paced the gate area at the airport, for a woman who was so fixated on being on time. Now, when he was all but jumping out of his skin, she had to be late.

It didn't matter that the plane was late, and she just happened to be on it. He took it as a personal affront.

If Maureen hadn't taken pity on him, he wouldn't have known she was coming back tonight. It grated a bit, to know that Natalie's secretary felt sorry for him. That she must have seen that he looked like a lovesick mongrel.

Even the men at the station were starting to talk about him behind his back.

Oh, he knew it, all right. The mutters, the snickers, the pitying looks. Anybody with eyes in his head could see that the past ten days had been torment for him.

He'd made a mistake, damn it. One little mistake, and she'd paid him back. Big-time.

They were just going to have to put that behind them.

He clutched the daffodils, paced, and felt like a fool. His heart took one frantic leap when her flight was announced.

He saw her, and his palms began to sweat.

She saw him, turned sharply left, and kept walking.

"Natalie." He caught up with her in two strides. "Welcome home."

"Go to hell."

"I've been there for the past ten days. I don't like it." It wasn't hard to keep up with her, since she was wearing heels. "Here."

She glanced down at the daffodils, cutting a scathing look up to his face. "You don't want me to tell you what you can do with those stupid flowers, do you?"

"You could have talked to me when I called."

"I didn't want to talk to you." Deliberately she swung into the closest ladies' room.

Ry gritted his teeth and waited.

She told herself she wasn't pleased that he was still there when she came out. Saying nothing, she quickened her pace toward the baggage-claim area.

"How was your trip?"

She snarled at him.

"Look, I'm trying to apologize here."

"Is that what you're doing?" With a toss of her head, she stepped onto the escalator heading down. "Save it."

"I screwed up. I'm sorry. I've been trying to tell you for days, but you won't take my calls."

"That should indicate something, Piasecki, even to someone of your limited intelligence."

"So," he continued, biting back hot words, "I'm here to pick you up, so we can talk."

"I've ordered a car."

"We canceled it. That is…" He had to choose his words carefully, with that icy look in her eyes freezing him. "I canceled it, when I found out you were coming in." No need to make Maureen fry with him, he decided. "So I'll give you a lift."

"I'll take a cab."

"Don't be so damn stubborn. I'll get tough if I have to," he muttered as they joined the throng at Baggage Claim. "I can have you up in a fireman's carry in two seconds. Embarrass the hell out of you. Either way, I'm driving you home."

She debated. He would embarrass her. There was no point in giving him the satisfaction. Nor was she going to tell him of her suspicions, not until she had something solid. Not until she had no choice but to deal with him on a professional level.

"I'm not going home. I need to go to the office."

"The office is closed. It's almost nine o'clock."

"I'm going to the office," she said flatly, and turned away from him.

"Fine. We'll talk at the office."

"That one." She pointed to a gray tweed Pullman. "And that one." A matching garment bag. "And that." Another Pullman.

"You didn't have time to pack all this before I got to your apartment that night."

Interested despite herself, she watched him heft cases. "I picked up luggage and clothes along the way."

"Enough for a damn modeling troupe," he muttered.

"I beg your pardon?" Her tone lowered the temperature in the terminal by ten degrees.

"Nothing. Your opening made a real splash," he continued as they walked out of the terminal.

"It met our expectations."

"You're getting write-ups in *Newsday* and *Business Week.*" He shrugged when she looked at him. "I heard."

"And *Women's Wear Daily,*" she added. "But who's counting?"

"I've been. It's great, Natalie, really. I'm happy for you. Proud of you." He set her luggage beside his car, and his limbs went weak. "God, I've missed you."

She stepped back, evading him, when he reached for her. He was not going to hurt her again, she promised herself. She would not allow it.

"Okay." Slowly, stunned by the ache that one quick rejection caused, he lifted his hands, palms out. "I had that coming. I've got plenty coming. I'll give you the chance to take all the shots you want."

"I'm not interested in fighting with you," she said wearily. "I've had a long trip. I'm too tired to fight with you."

"Let me take you home, Natalie."

"I'm going to the office." She stepped back and waited for him to unlock the car. Once inside, she sat back and shut her eyes. She just sighed when Ry laid the bright yellow flowers in her lap.

"They, ah, haven't gotten any more out of Clarence," he said, hoping to chip at the wall she'd erected between them.

"I know." She couldn't think about her suspicions yet. "I've kept in touch."

"You moved around fast."

"I had a lot of ground to cover."

"Yeah." He dug out money for the parking attendant. "I got the picture, after I chased you around Atlanta."

She opened her eyes then. "Excuse me?"

"I couldn't get a damn cab," he muttered. "You must have hooked one the minute you walked out of my apartment."

"Yes, I did."

"Figures. I'm running the marathon to your apartment, then you're gone when I get there. I see the note, figure the airport, and get there in time to see your plane take off."

She felt herself softening, and stiffened. "Is that supposed to be my fault, Piasecki?"

"No, it's not your fault, damn it. It's my fault. But if you could have sat still in Atlanta for five minutes, we'd have settled this."

"We *have* settled it."

"Not by a long shot." Turning his head, he aimed a deadly look at her. "I hate it when people hang up on me."

"It was," she said with relish, "my pleasure."

"I might have strangled you for it when I got down there. If I could have caught you. 'No, Ms. Fletcher's at her shop.' Then I get to the shop, and it's 'Sorry, Ms. Fletcher's gone back to her hotel.' I get back to the hotel, and you've checked out. I get to the airport and you're in the sky. I spent hours chasing my tail, trying to catch up with you.''

She shrugged. She didn't want to be pleased, but she couldn't prevent a little frisson of pleasure at the frustration in his voice. ''Don't expect an apology.'' Still, she gathered up the flowers to keep them from sliding from her lap when he braked.

''I'm trying to give *you* one.''

''There's no need. I've had time to think about it, and I've decided you were absolutely right. I don't like the style you used, but the bottom line rings true. We had some interesting chemistry. That's all.''

''We had a lot more than that. We've got more than that. Natalie—''

''This is my stop.'' Forgetting her luggage, she bolted out of the car. By the time Ry had parked, illegally, she was waiting for the security guard to open the front door of her building.

''Damn it, Natalie, would you hold still?''

''I have work. Good evening, Ben.''

''Ms. Fletcher. Working late?''

''That's right.'' She breezed past the guard, with Ry at her heels. ''There's no need for you to come up with me, Ry.''

''You said you loved me.''

Ignoring the guard's speculative look, Natalie pressed the elevator button. ''I got over it.''

Panic spurted through him, freezing him in place. He barely made it into the elevator before the doors shut in his face. ''You did not.''

''I know what I did, I know what I didn't.'' She jabbed the button for her floor. ''It's all ego with you. You're causing a scene because I didn't come back when you called.'' She tossed her hair back. Her eyes were bright. Not with tears, he saw with some relief. But with anger. ''Because I don't need you.''

''It has nothing to do with ego. I was—'' He couldn't admit he'd been scared, down-to-the-bone scared. ''I was wrong,'' he said. That was hard enough, but at least it wasn't humiliating. "It was you—there in my place. I asked you to come because it was so obvious."

"What was obvious?"

"That it couldn't be real. I didn't see how it could be real. Who you are, the way you are. And me."

Her eyes sharpened, narrowed. "Am I following you here, Inspector? You dumped me because I didn't fit in with your apartment."

It didn't have to sound that stupid. His voice rose in defense. "With everything. With me. I can't give you...the things. The first time I remembered I should give you flowers once in a while, you looked at me like I'd clipped you on the jaw. I never take you anywhere. I don't think of it. You've got friends who live in mansions. And look, damn it, you've got diamonds in your ears right now." He tossed up his hands, as if that should explain everything. "Diamonds, for God's sake."

Her cheeks were hot now. She was all but radiating heat as she stepped toward him. "Is this about money? Is that it? You broke my heart over money?"

"No, it's about...things." How could he explain what made no sense at all anymore? "Natalie, let me touch you."

"The hell with you." She shoved him back, bounding through the elevator the minute the doors open. "You tossed me aside because you thought I wanted you to get me diamonds, or a mansion, or flowers?" Furious, she tossed the daffodils on the floor. "I can get my own diamonds, or anything else I want. What I wanted was you."

"Don't walk away. Don't." Swearing, he rushed after her. Somewhere down the long corridor, a phone rang. "Natalie." He grabbed her by the shoulders, spun her around. "I didn't think that, exactly."

She rammed her briefcase hard into his gut. "And you had the nerve to call me a snob."

Out of patience, he rammed her back against the wall. "It was wrong. It was stupid. *I* was stupid. What more do you want me to say? I wasn't thinking. I was just feeling."

"You hurt me."

"I know." He rested his brow on hers, tried to get his bearings. He could smell her, feel her, and the thought of losing her made him weak in the knees. "I'm sorry. I didn't know I could hurt you. I thought it was just me. I thought you'd walk."

"So you walked first."

He drew back a little. "Something like that."

"Coward." She jerked away. "Go away, Ry. Leave me alone. I have to think about this."

"You're still in love with me. I'm not going anywhere until you tell me."

"Then you'll have to wait, because I'm not ready to tell you anything." Phones were ringing. Wearily rubbing her temple, Natalie wondered who would be calling so long after hours. "I'm raw, don't you understand? I realized I loved you and had you break it off almost simultaneously. I'm not going to serve you my emotions on a platter."

"Then I'll give you mine," he said quietly. "I love you, Natalie."

Her heart swam into her eyes. "Damn you. *Damn* you! That's not fair."

"I can't be worried about fair." He stepped closer, and reached out to touch her hair. His hand froze when he saw the flicker of light at the end of the hall. It danced through the glass in a pattern he recognized too well. "Take the fire stairs down, now. Call Dispatch."

"What? What are you talking about?"

"Go," he repeated, and dashed down the hall. He could smell smoke now, and cursed it. Cursed himself for being so intent on his own needs that he'd missed it. He saw it, the crafty plume under the door that flowed out, sucked in.

"Oh, God. Ry."

She was right behind him. He had time to see the flames writhing behind the glass, time to judge. Then he turned, leapt and knocked Natalie to the ground as the window exploded. Lethal shards of glass rained over them.

# Chapter 12

She felt pain, sharp and shocking, as her head thudded against the floor, and pinpricks of heat from the glass and flame. For a terrifying moment, she thought Ry was unconscious, or dead. His body was fully spread over hers, a shield protecting her from the worst of the blast.

Before she could even sob in the breath to scream his name, he was up and dragging her to her feet.

"Are you burned?"

She shook her head, aware only of the throbbing, and the smoke that was beginning to sting her eyes, her throat. She could barely see his face through it, but she saw the blood.

"Your face, your arm—you're bleeding."

But he wasn't listening. He had her hand vised in his, and was dragging her away from the flame. Even as they dashed down the hall, another window exploded. Fire roared out.

It surrounded them, golden and greedy, unbelievably hot. She screamed once as she saw it race along the floor, eating its way toward them, spitting like a hundred hungry snakes.

Panic gripped her, icy fingers clutching at her stomach, squeezing her throat, in taunting contrast to the heat pulsing around them. They were trapped, fire writhing on either side of them. Terrified, she fought him when he pushed her to the floor.

"Stay low." However grim his thoughts, his voice was calm. He gripped her hair in one hand to keep her face turned to his. He needed her to hold on to control.

"I can't breathe." The smoke was choking her, making her gasp for air and expel what little she had in gritty coughs.

"There's more air down here. We don't have much time." He was aware—too well aware—of how quickly the fire would reach them, how well it blocked their exit to the stairs. He had nothing with which to fight it.

If the fire didn't kill them, the smoke would, long before rescue could reach them.

"Get out of your coat."

"What?"

Her movements were already sluggish. He fought back panic and yanked her coat from her shoulders. "We're going through it."

"We can't." She couldn't even scream at the next explosion of glass, could only huddle, racked by coughing. Her mind was dull, stunned by smoke. She wanted only to lie down and draw in the precious air that still hovered just above the floor. "We'll burn. I don't want to die that way."

"You're not going to die." Tossing the coat over her head, he dragged her to her feet. When she staggered, he lifted her over his shoulder. He stood, fire lapping on both sides, a flaming sea around him. In seconds, the tidal wave would reach them, and they'd drown in it.

He gauged the distance and sprinted into the wave.

For an instant, they were in hell. Fire, heat, the roaring of its anger, the quick, ravenous licking of its tongues. For no more than two heartbeats—an eternity—flames engulfed them. He felt the hair on his hands singe, knew from the intense heat on his back and arms that his jacket would catch. He knew exactly what fire did to human flesh. He wouldn't allow it to have Natalie.

Then they were through it, and into a wall of smoke. Blinded, lungs straining, he groped for the fire door.

Instinctively he checked it for heat, thanked God, then shoved it open. Smoke was billowing up the stairwell, rising as if in a chimney that meant fire below, as well, but they didn't have a choice. Moving fast, he ripped the smoldering coat away from her and leaned her against the wall while he stripped off his own jacket.

The leather was burning, sluggishly.

Dazed by the smoke and teetering into shock, Natalie slid bonelessly to the floor.

"You're not giving up," he snapped at her as he hauled her back over his shoulder. "Hang on, damn it. Just hang on."

He streaked down the steps, one flight, then two, then a third. She was dead weight now, her head lolling, her arms limp. His eyes were watering from the smoke, the tears joining the river of sweat rolling down his face. The coughing that seized him felt as if it would shatter his ribs. All he knew was that he had to get her to safety.

He counted each level, keeping his mind focused. The smoke began to thin, and he began to hope.

She never stirred, not even when he tested the door at the lobby level, found it cool, and staggered through.

He heard the shouts, the sirens. His vision grayed as two fire fighters rushed toward him.

"God almighty, Inspector."

"She needs oxygen." Still holding her, Ry shoved the offer of assistance aside and carried her outside, into clean air.

Lights were swirling. All the familiar sounds and scents and sights of a fire scene. Like a drunk, he weaved toward the closest engine.

"Oxygen," he ordered. "Now." Another coughing fit battered him as he laid her down.

Her face was black with soot, and her eyes were closed. He couldn't see if she was breathing, couldn't hear. Someone was shouting, raging, but he had no idea it was him. Hands pushed his own fumbling ones aside and fit an oxygen mask over Natalie's face.

"You need attention, Inspector."

"Keep away from me." He bent over her, searching for a pulse. Blood dripped down his arm and onto her throat. "Natalie. Please."

"Is she all right?" With tears streaming down her face, Deirdre dropped down beside him. "Is she going to be all right?"

"She's breathing," was all Ry could say. "She's breathing," he repeated, stroking her hair.

Mercifully, most of the next hour was a blur. He remembered climbing into the ambulance with her, holding her hand. Someone pressed oxygen on him, bound up his arm. They took her away the minute they hit the E.R. His panicked raging came out in hacking coughs.

Then the world turned upside down.

He found himself flat on his back on an examining table. When he tried to push himself upright, he was restrained.

"Just lie still." A small, gray-haired woman was scowling at him. "I like my stitches ncat and tidy. You lost a fair amount of blood, Inspector Piasecki."

"Natalie…"

"Ms. Fletcher's being tended to. Now let me do my job, will you?" She stopped what she was doing and eyed him again. "If you keep shoving at me, mister, I'm going to sedate you. My job was a lot easier when you were out cold."

"How long?" he managed to croak.

"Not long enough." She knotted the suture, and snipped. "We picked the glass out of your shoulder. Not much damage there, but this arm's nasty. Fifteen stitches." She granted him a smile. "Some of my best work."

"I want to see Natalie." His voice was raspy, but there was no mistaking the threat underneath. "Now."

"Well, you can't. You're going to stay where I put you until I'm done. Then, if you're a very good boy, I'll have someone check on Ms. Fletcher for you."

Ry used his good arm and grabbed the doctor by the coat. "Now."

She only sighed. In his condition, she was well aware, she could knock him back with a shrug. But agitation wasn't going to help him. "Stay," she ordered, and went to the curtain. Pushing it aside, she called for a nurse. After a few brisk instructions, she turned back to Ry. "Your update's on the way. I'm Dr. Milano, and I'll be saving your life this evening."

"She was breathing," he said, as if daring Milano to disagree.

"Yes." She moved back to take his hand. "You took in a lot of smoke, Inspector. I'm going to treat you, and you're going to cooperate. After we've cleaned you out, I'll arrange for you to see Ms. Fletcher."

The nurse came back to the curtained opening, and Milano moved off again to hold a murmured consultation with her.

"Smoke inhalation," she announced. "And she's in shock. A few minor burns and lacerations. I imagine we'll keep her in our fine establishment for a day or two." Her face softened when she saw Ry's eyes close in relief. "Come on, big guy, let's work together here."

He might be weak as a baby, but he wasn't going to let them shove him into a hospital room. Over Milano's disgusted protests, he walked out into the waiting area. Deirdre sprang up from a chair the moment she saw him.

"Natalie?"

"They're working on her. They told me she's going to be all right."

"Thank God." With a muffled sob, Deirdre covered her face.

"Now, Ms. Marks, why don't you tell me what the hell you were doing outside the office tonight?"

Taking a deep breath, Deirdre levered herself into a chair. "I'd be glad to. I called Natalie's brother," she added. "I suppose he's already on his way out. I told him she was hurt, but I tried to play it down."

Ry merely nodded. Though he hated the weakness, he had to sit. Nausea was threatening again. "That was probably wise."

"I also gave him the bare bones of what I found out earlier today." She took a long breath. "I haven't been in the office the last couple of days—I've been nursing a cold. But I took work home. Including files and a couple of computer disks Natalie gave me before she went on the road. I was running figures, and I found some discrepancies. Some very large discrepancies. The kind that equals embezzlement."

Money, Ry thought. It almost always came around to money. "Who?"

"I can't say for sure—"

He interrupted her, in a tone that made her shiver. "Who?"

"I'm telling you, I can't be sure. I can only narrow it down, considering how and where the money was siphoned off. And I'm not giving you a name so you can go off and beat somebody to a pulp."

Which was exactly what he had in mind, she was certain. Despite the fact that he looked like a survivor of a quick trip to hell, there was murder in his eyes.

"I could be wrong. I need to talk to Natalie," she said, half to herself. "As soon as I was sure of what I'd found, I tried to contact her in Colorado, but she'd already left. I knew she'd go by the office before heading home. It's the way she works. So I decided I'd meet her there. Tell her what I'd found out." She tapped the briefcase at her feet. "Show her. When I parked outside, I glanced up. I saw—"

She shut her eyes, knew she would relive it over and over again. "I saw these crazy lights in some of the windows. At first I didn't know, then I realized what it was. I called 911 on the car phone." Unnerved by the memory, she pressed a hand to her mouth. "I ran inside, told the security guard. And we heard, like, an explosion."

She was crying now, quietly. "I knew she was up there. I just knew it. But I didn't know what to do."

"Yes, you did. And you did it." Ry patted her awkwardly on the shoulder.

"Inspector?" Milano strode out, the usual scowl on her face. "I got you a pass to see your lady, not that you'll bother to thank me for it."

He was on his feet. "She's okay?"

"She's stabilized, and sedated. But you can look at her, since that seems to be your goal in life."

He glanced back at Deirdre. "Are you going to wait?"

"Yes. If you'd just let me know how she is."

"I'll be back." He headed off after the quick-stepping doctor.

Natalie's room was private, and dimly lit. She lay very still, very pale. But her hand, when he took it in his, was warm.

"Are you planning on spending the night here?" Milano asked from the doorway.

"Are you going to give me a hard time about it?" Ry returned without looking around.

"Who, me? I aim to serve. It's not likely she'll wake up, but that's not going to stop you. Neither is trying to sleep in that hideously uncomfortable chair."

"I'm a fireman, Doc. I can sleep anywhere."

"Well, fireman, make yourself at home. I'll go tell your friend in the waiting room that all's well."

"Yeah." He never took his eyes from Natalie's face. "That'd be good."

"Oh, you're more than welcome," Milano said sourly, and closed the door behind her.

Ry pulled the chair up to the side of the bed and sat with Natalie's hand in his.

He dozed once or twice. Occasionally a nurse came into the room and scooted him out. It was during one of those short, restless breaks that he saw Boyd rushing down the corridor.

"Piasecki."

"Captain. She's sleeping." Ry gestured toward the door. "There."

Without another word, Boyd moved past him and inside.

Ry walked into the waiting lounge, poured a cup of muddy coffee, and stared out the window. He couldn't think. It seemed better that way, just to let the night drift. If he focused, he would see it again, the terror on her face, the fire around her. And he would remember how he'd felt, carrying her down flight after flight, not knowing if she was alive or dead.

The burning on his hand made him look down. He saw he'd crushed the paper cup into a ball and spilled the hot coffee over his bandaged hands.

"Want another?" Boyd said from behind him.

"No." Ry tossed the cup away, and wiped his hand on his jeans. "You want to go outside and pound on me awhile?"

With a short laugh, Boyd poured coffee for himself. "Have you taken a look in a mirror?"

"Why?"

"You look like hell." Experimentally, Boyd sipped. It was even more pathetic than precinct coffee. "Worse than hell. It wouldn't look good for me to start swinging at a guy in your condition."

"I heal quick." When Boyd said nothing, Ry shoved his hands in his pockets. "I told you I wouldn't let her get hurt. I damn near killed her."

"You did?"

"I lost it. I knew it wasn't just Clarence. I knew there was some-body behind it. But I was so…wrapped up in her. I never thought about him getting another torch, or trying something himself. The phones, damn it. I heard the phones ringing."

Intrigued, Boyd sat back. "Which means?"

"A delaying device," Ry shot back, whirling around. "It's a clas-sic. Matchsticks, soaked in accelerant. Tape them to the phone, call the number. The phone rings, the ringer sparks the match."

"Clever. But you know, you can't think of everything all the time."

"It's my job to think of everything."

"And to have a crystal ball."

His voice was raw from the abuse his throat had taken, tight with the emotion he couldn't afford to let loose. "I was supposed to take care of her."

"Yeah." Acknowledging that, Boyd sipped again. "I made a lot of calls on the flight from Denver. One of the perks of Fletcher Industries is having a private plane at your disposal. I talked to the fire marshal, to the doctor who treated Natalie, to Deirdre Marks. You got her out, carried her down every damn step in that building. How many stitches have you got in that arm?"

"That's hardly the point."

"The point is, the fire marshal gave me some idea of what you were facing up there on the forty-second floor, and what kind of shape you were in when you got her outside. Her doctor told me that if she'd been in there another ten minutes, it isn't likely she'd be sleeping right now. So, do I want to punch you? I don't think so. I owe you my sister's life.''

Ry remembered how she had looked when he laid her on the ground next to the engine. How she looked now, pale and still, in a hospital bed. ''You don't owe me anything.''

''Natalie's as important to me as she is to you.'' Boyd set his coffee aside and rose. ''What did you do to tick her off?''

Ry grimaced. ''We're working it out.''

''Well, good luck.'' Boyd held out a hand.

After a moment, Ry clasped it with his. ''Thanks.''

''I figure you're going to be here awhile. I've got a little job to do.''

Ry tightened his grip, and narrowed his eyes. ''Deirdre told you who's responsible.''

''That's right. I also spoke with my counterpart here in Urbana while I was in the air. It's being taken care of.'' He saw the look in Ry's eyes, understood it. ''This part's up to my team, Ry. You and yours just make damn sure you hang him for the arson.''

''Who?'' Ry said between his teeth.

''Donald Hawthorne. I got it down to four likely suspects two days ago.'' He smiled a little. ''Some background checks, bank and phone records. Sometimes it pays to be a cop.''

''And you didn't pass the information along to me.''

''I intended to, when I narrowed it down a bit further. Now I have, and I am.''

Boyd knew what it was to love, to need to protect, and to live with the terror of seeing your woman fight for her life.

''Listen,'' he said briskly, ''if you kill him—however much it might appeal to both of us right now—I'd have to arrest you. I'd hate to throw my brother-in-law in a cell.''

Ry unfisted his hands long enough to stick them in his pockets. ''I'm not your brother-in-law.''

''Not yet. Go on in with her, get some sleep.''

''You'd better put Hawthorne somewhere where I can't find him.''

''I intend to,'' Boyd said as he walked away.

\* \* \*

Natalie stirred at dawn. Ry was watching the way the slats of light through the blinds bloomed over her when her lashes fluttered.

He bent over her, talking softly, quickly, so that her first clear thoughts wouldn't be fearful ones. "Natalie, you're okay. We got out okay. You just swallowed some smoke. Everything's all right now. You've been sleeping. I'm right here. I don't want you to talk. Your throat's going to be miserable for a while."

"You're talking," she whispered, her eyes still closed.

"Yeah." And it felt as though he'd swallowed a flaming sword. "That's why I don't recommend it."

She swallowed and winced. "We didn't die."

"Doesn't look like it." Gently he cupped her head and held a cup of water so that she could sip through the straw. "Just take it easy."

There was a fear lurking deep inside her. But she had to know. "Are we burned badly?"

"We're not burned. A couple of singes, maybe."

Relief made her shiver. "I can't feel anything, except—" She reached up to touch the bruise on her forehead.

"Sorry." He pressed his lips to the lump, felt himself begin to tremble, and drew back again. "You got that when I tackled you."

She opened her eyes then. They felt weighted. Her whole body felt weighted. "Hospital?" she asked. Then her breath caught as she focused on him. Scratches on his face, a bandage at his temple, and a larger one that started just below his shoulder and nearly reached the elbow. His hands, his beautiful hands, were wrapped in gauze.

"Oh, God, Ry. You're hurt."

"Cuts and bruises." He smiled at her. "Singed my hair a little."

"You need a doctor."

"I've had one, thanks. I don't think she likes me. Now shut up and rest."

"What happened?"

"You're going to have to move your office." When she started to speak again, he held up a hand. "I'll tell you what I know if you keep quiet. Otherwise, I'll just leave you to stew. Deal?" Satisfied, he sat on the edge of the bed. "Deirdre tried to call you in Colorado," he began.

When he finished, her head was throbbing. Impotent fury ate away at the remnant of the sedative until she was wide awake and aching. Anticipating her, Ry laid his hand over her mouth.

"There's nothing you can do until you're on your feet. Not much you can do then. It's up to the departments—fire and police. And it's being handled. Now I'm going to ring for the nurse so they can take a look at you."

"I don't—" Her protest turned into a spasm of coughing. By the time she'd regained control, a nurse was gesturing Ry out of the room.

She didn't see him again for more than twenty-four hours.

"You could use another day here, Nat." Boyd crossed his feet at the ankles as he watched Natalie pack the small overnight case he'd brought her.

"I hate hospitals."

"You've made that clear. I need your word you're taking a full week off, at home, or I'm calling in the troops. And not just Cilla, but Mom and Dad."

"There's no need for them to fly all the way out here."

"That's up to you, pal."

She pouted. "Three days off."

"A full week. Anything less is a deal-breaker. I can be just as tough a negotiator as you," he said with a grin. "It's in the blood."

"Fine, fine, a week. What difference does it make?" She snatched up the water glass and drank. It seemed she could never get enough to drink these days. "Everything's in shambles. Half my building's destroyed, one of my most trusted executives is responsible. I don't even have an office to go to."

"You'll take care of that. Next week. Hawthorne has a lot to answer for. The fact that he didn't know you and Ry were in the building isn't going to save him."

"All for greed." Too angry to pack the few things Boyd had brought her, she paced. Her body still felt weak, but there was too much energy boiling within to allow her to keep still. "Draining a little here, a little there, losing it on speculative stocks. Then draining more and more, until he was so desperate he risked burning down entire buildings just to destroy records and delay the audit records.''

She whirled back. ''How frustrated he must have been when I told him I had duplicates of everything that was lost in the warehouse fire.''

''And he wasn't sure where you kept them. Fire destroys everything,'' Boyd pointed out. ''So, he'd take one of the buildings, and hope. If he didn't hit, the confusion in the aftermath would keep everyone so busy, you wouldn't get around to the audit until, he hoped, he'd managed to replace the siphoned funds.''

''So he thought.''

''He doesn't know you like I do. You always get things done on time. The office was his last shot, and the most desperate, since he had to do it himself. When we picked him up and he found out you and Ry had been in there and that he was facing attempted murder charges, he gave us everything.''

''I trusted him,'' Natalie murmured. ''I can't stand knowing I could be so wrong about anyone I thought I knew.'' She glanced up as the door opened.

''Good to see you, Ry,'' Boyd said, and rose. This looked like his cue to make a quick and discreet exit.

Ry nodded at Boyd, then focused on Natalie. ''Why aren't you in bed?''

''I've been discharged.''

''You're not ready to leave the hospital.''

''Excuse me.'' Boyd slipped toward the door. ''I have a sudden urge for a cup of bad coffee.''

Neither Natalie nor Ry bothered to say goodbye. They only continued to argue in raspy croaks.

''Do you have a medical degree now, Inspector?''

''I know what shape you were in when you got here.''

''Well, if you'd bothered to check in since, you'd have seen that I'm recovered.''

''I had a lot of details to tie up,'' he told her. ''And you needed to rest.''

''I'd rather have had you.''

He held out the flowers. "I'm here now."

She sighed. Should she let him off the hook so easily when she'd been pining for him for so long? And why shouldn't she make him pay a bit for dumping her for the most ridiculous reason?

"Why don't you go take those daffodils to someone who needs them."

He tossed them on the bed. "I'm going to go talk to the doctor."

"You certainly will not talk to *my* doctor. I don't need your permission to leave the hospital. You didn't ask me for mine. And I did not need rest. I needed to see you. I was worried about you."

"Were you?" Encouraged, he lifted a hand to her face.

"I wanted you here, Ry. Dozens of other people came, but obviously you didn't see the need—"

"I had work," he shot back. "I wanted to get the evidence on that sonofabitch as soon as possible. It's all I can do. I'd kill him if I could get to him."

She started to snap back, then felt an icy chill at the look on his face. "Stop that." Unnerved, she turned her back on him, away from the murder in his eyes, and tossed a robe in her case. "I don't want to hear you talk that way."

"I didn't know if you were alive." He spun her around, his fingers digging into her shoulders. "I didn't know. You weren't moving. I didn't know if you were breathing." Suddenly he dragged her against him and buried his face in her hair. "God, Natalie, I've never been so scared."

"All right." She brought her arms around him, to soothe. "Don't think about it."

"I didn't let myself, until you woke up yesterday. Since then I haven't been able to think about anything else." Struggling for composure, he eased away. "I'm sorry."

"Sorry for saving my life? For risking your own to keep me from being hurt? You shielded me from the explosion. You carried me through fire." She shook her head quickly, before he could speak. "Don't tell me you were doing your job. I don't give a damn whether you want to be a hero or not. You're mine."

"I love you, Natalie."

Her heart softened and swelled. Carefully she turned and picked up the daffodils. It was foolish to waste their emotions on anger. They were alive. "You mentioned that, before we were interrupted."

"There's something else I should have mentioned. Why I pushed you away."

Staring down, she flicked a finger over a bright yellow trumpet. "You listed the reasons."

"I listed the excuses. Not the reason. Maybe you could look at me while I grovel?"

She turned back, trying to smile. "It's not necessary, Ry."

"Yeah, it is. You haven't decided whether you're going to give me another chance yet." He reached out, tucked her hair behind her ear. "I could wear you down eventually, because you're crazy about me. But you deserve to know what was going on in my head."

She stiffened automatically. "I don't think arrogance is very appropriate, so why don't you—"

"I was scared," he said quietly, and watched the heat fade from her eyes. "Of you, of me. Of us." He let out a long breath when she said nothing. "I didn't think I could say it. Admit it. Not until I realized what it was to be *really* scared. Down-to-the-bone scared. It makes being afraid of being in love pretty stupid."

"Then it looks like we were both stupid, because I was scared, too." Her mouth curved a little. "You were more stupid, of course."

"My whole life," he said quietly, "I've never felt anything like what I feel for you. Not for anyone."

"I know." Her breath trembled out. "I know. It's the same with me."

"And it just keeps getting bigger, and scarier. Are you going to give me another chance?"

She looked at him—the bony face, the dark eyes, the unruly hair. "I probably owe you that much, seeing as you've saved my life and come clean, groveled and apologized." Her smile spread. "I suppose I could give us both another chance."

"Want to marry me?"

The flowers drifted to the floor as her fingers went numb. "Excuse me?"

"With you feeling generous, it seemed like a good time to push my luck." Feeling foolish, he bent down and gathered up the daffodils. "But it can wait."

She cleared her aching throat, accepting the flowers again. "Would you mind repeating the question?"

His eyes shot back to hers. It took him a moment to find his voice again. It was a risk, he realized. One of the biggest risks he'd ever faced. And he had to leave his fate in her hands.

"Will you marry me?"

"I could do that," she said, and let out the breath she'd been holding, even as Ry let out his own. "Yes, I could do that." Laughing, she launched herself into his arms.

"I've got you." Dazzled, Ry buried his face in her hair. "I've got you, Legs, from now on." And kissed her.

"I want babies," she told him the minute her mouth was free.

"No kidding?" With a grin, he pushed her hair back so that he could read her face. What he saw made his heart leap. "Me, too."

"That makes it handy."

He scooped his arms under her legs and lifted her. "What do you say we get out of here and get started?"

She managed to snag her overnight case before he headed to the door. "That'll make it nine months from today." She kissed his cheek as he carried her from the room. "And I'm always on time."

In this case, she managed to be eight days early.

*#1* New York Times *bestselling author*

*NORA*
*ROBERTS*

*and Silhouette Books present*
*the brand-new sequel to NIGHT TALES:*

*NIGHT*
*SHIELD*

*Available from Silhouette Intimate Moments (#1027)*
*this month!*

*Here's a preview....*

Last call was enough to make Ally all but weep with gratitude. She'd been on her feet since eight that morning, having worked at the precinct all day before going undercover at the club that night. Her fondest wish was to go home, fall into bed and sleep for the precious five hours she had before starting it all over again.

Ally stepped out of the lounge and bumped solidly into Jonah.

"Where'd you park?" he asked her.

"I didn't. I walked." Ran, she remembered, but it came to the same thing.

"I'll drive you home."

"I can walk. It's not far."

"It's two in the morning. A block is too far."

"For heaven's sake, Blackhawk, I'm a cop."

"So, naturally, bullets bounce off you."

Before she could argue, he caught her chin in his hand. The gesture, the firm grip of his fingers shocked her to silence. "You're not a cop at the moment," he murmured. "You're a female employee and the daughter of a friend. I'll drive you home."

"Fine. Dandy. My feet hurt anyway."

She started to shove his hand away, but he beat her to it and shifted his grip to her arm.

"'Night, boss," Beth called out, grinning at them as they passed the bar. "Get that girl off her feet."

"That's my plan. Later, Will. 'Night, Frannie."

Suspicion was buzzing in Ally's brain as Will lifted his brandy snifter and Frannie watched her with quiet and serious eyes.

"What was that?" Ally demanded when they stepped out in the cool air. "What exactly was that?"

"That was me saying good-night to friends and employees. I'm parked across the street."

"Excuse me, my feet have gone numb, not my brain. You gave those people the very distinct impression that we have a thing here."

"That's right. I didn't consider it either until Beth made some remark earlier. It simplifies things."

She stopped beside a sleek black Jaguar. "Just how do you figure that having people think there's a personal thing between us simplifies anything?"

"And you call yourself a detective." He unlocked the passenger door, opened it. "You're a beautiful blonde with legs up to your ears. I hire you, out of the blue, when you have basically no experience. The first assumption from people who know me is I'm attracted to you. The second would be you're attracted to me. Add all those together and you end up with romance. Or at least sex. Are you going to get in?"

"You haven't explained how those deductions equal simple."

"If people think we're involved they won't think twice if I give you a little leeway, if you come up to my office. They'll be friendlier."

Ally said nothing while she let it run through her head. Then she nodded. "All right. There's an advantage to it."

Going with impulse he shifted, boxed her in between his body and the car door. There was a light breeze, just enough to stir her scent. There was a three-quarter moon, bright enough to sprinkle silver into her eyes. The moment, he decided, seemed to call for it.

"Could be more than one advantage to it."

The thrill that sprinted straight up her spine irritated her. "Oh, you're going to want to step back, Blackhawk."

"Beth's at the window of the bar, and she's got a romantic heart despite everything that's happened to her. She's hoping for a moment here. A long, slow kiss, the kind that slides over melting sighs and heats the blood."

His hands came to her hips as he spoke, rode up to just under her breasts. Her mouth went dry and the ache in her belly was a wide stretch of longing.

"You're going to have to disappoint her."

Jonah skimmed his gaze down to her mouth. "She's not the only one." But he released her, stepped back. "Don't worry, Detective. I never hit on cops, or daughters of friends."

"Then I guess I've got a double shield against your wild and irresistible charms."

"Good thing for both of us, because I sure as hell like the look of you. You getting in?"

"Yeah, I'm getting in." She got into the car and waited until the door shut before letting out the long, painful breath she'd been holding.

Wherever that spurt of lust inside her had come from, it would just have to go away again. Cool off and focus on the job, she ordered herself, but her heart was bumping madly against her rib cage....

# MONTANA MAVERICKS

# WED IN WHITEHORN

*The legend lives on...as bold as before!*

## M·M

Coming in October...

# BIG SKY LAWMAN

by

# MARILYN PAPPANO

Finding a murderer was the only thing that deputy
Sloan Ravencrest could think about. Until his investigation
led him straight into Crystal Cobbs's welcoming arms.
But would the secret Crystal was keeping drive the
lovers apart...or bind their hearts together?

**MONTANA MAVERICKS:**
**WED IN WHITEHORN** continues with
**THE BABY QUEST** by **Pat Warren**,
available in November from Silhouette Books.

*Available at your favorite retail outlet.*

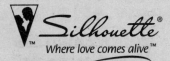

*Where love comes alive*™

USA Today Bestselling Author

# SHARON SALA

has won readers' hearts with thrilling tales
of romantic suspense. Now Silhouette Books
is proud to present five passionate stories from
this beloved author.

Available in August 2000:
## ALWAYS A LADY
A beauty queen whose dreams have been dashed in a
tragic twist of fate seeks shelter for her wounded spirit
in the arms of a rough-edged cowboy....

Available in September 2000:
## GENTLE PERSUASION
A brooding detective risks everything to protect the
woman he once let walk away from him....

Available in October 2000:
## SARA'S ANGEL
A woman on the run searches desperately for a reclusive
Native American secret agent—the only man who can
save her from the danger that stalks her!

Available in November 2000:
## HONOR'S PROMISE
A struggling waitress discovers she is really a rich heiress—
and must enter a powerful new world of wealth and
privilege on the arm of a handsome stranger....

Available in December 2000:
## KING'S RANSOM
A lone woman returns home to the ranch where she was
raised, and discovers danger—as well as the man she once
loved with all her heart....

**Don't miss
an exciting opportunity
to save on the purchase of
Harlequin and Silhouette books!**

Buy any two Harlequin or
Silhouette books and save
**$10.00 off** future Harlequin
and Silhouette purchases

OR

buy any three
Harlequin or Silhouette books
and save **$20.00 off** future
Harlequin and Silhouette purchases.

**Watch for details
coming in October 2000!**

PHQ400TR

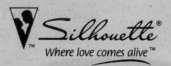